THE BEST of the WEST

THE

BEST of the WEST

A TREASURY OF WESTERN ADVENTURE

SELECTED
AND CONDENSED BY
THE EDITORS OF
THE READER'S DIGEST

VOLUME 2

THE READER'S DIGEST ASSOCIATION
Pleasantville, New York
Montreal, Sydney, Cape Town, Hong Kong

The condensations in this volume have been
created by The Reader's Digest Association, Inc.

The Ox-Bow Incident, copyright 1940, © renewed 1968
by Walter Van Tilburg Clark, is condensed by permission
of Random House, Inc.

Shane, copyright 1949 by Jack Schaefer, copyright 1954
by John McCormack, is used by permission of
Houghton Mifflin Company.

Bugles in the Afternoon, copyright 1943 by The
Curtis Publishing Company, copyright 1944, © renewed
1972 by Ernest Haycox, is published by permission
of Mrs. Ernest Haycox and her agents, Scott Meredith
Literary Agency, Inc., 580 Fifth Avenue,
New York, New York 10036.

Cheyenne Autumn, copyright 1953 by Mari Sandoz, is used by
permission of the publishers, Hastings House, Publishers, Inc.

© 1976 by The Reader's Digest Association, Inc.
Copyright © 1976 by The Reader's Digest Association
(Canada) Ltd.
© 1976 by Reader's Digest Services Pty. Ltd.,
Sydney, Australia
Copyright © 1976 by The Reader's Digest Association
South Africa (Pty.) Limited
Copyright © 1976 by Reader's Digest Association
Far East Limited

First Edition

All rights reserved, including the right to reproduce
this book or parts thereof in any form.

Library of Congress Catalog Card Number: 75-10496

Printed in the United States of America

CONTENTS

The Violent Years   7

THE OX-BOW INCIDENT Walter Van Tilburg Clark   27

The Cowboys   161

SHANE Jack Schaefer   181

The Soldiers   259

BUGLES IN THE AFTERNOON Ernest Haycox   279

The Indians   409

CHEYENNE AUTUMN Mari Sandoz   429

THE VIOLENT YEARS

Law, for a time, is left behind,
and miner's gold and the hard-won savings
of honest men are prey to outlaws,
unchecked save by vigilante justice

Vigilante Ways by O. C. Seltzer

His eyes glinting savagely, Jesse James and his men prepare for action in *The James Gang* by N. C. Wyeth.

Missouri "wanted" circular of the 1880s

On April 3, 1882, Jesse James was shot dead by one of his own men. His operations had been limited to the border states, but his style quickly spread westward. And outrage echoed across the land. "For fifteen years Missouri has been under the bloody sway of cutthroats, outlaws and assassins," thundered the New York *Illustrated Times*. "The emigrant hastened through it; and no man ventured within its borders unless business compelled him. When a traveler got into a Missouri train he did so with little expectation of getting through alive."

The elusive Jameses rarely allowed themselves to be photogr

this picture was taken at a secure hideout in Iowa. Jesse stands in back, at right, Frank James at left.

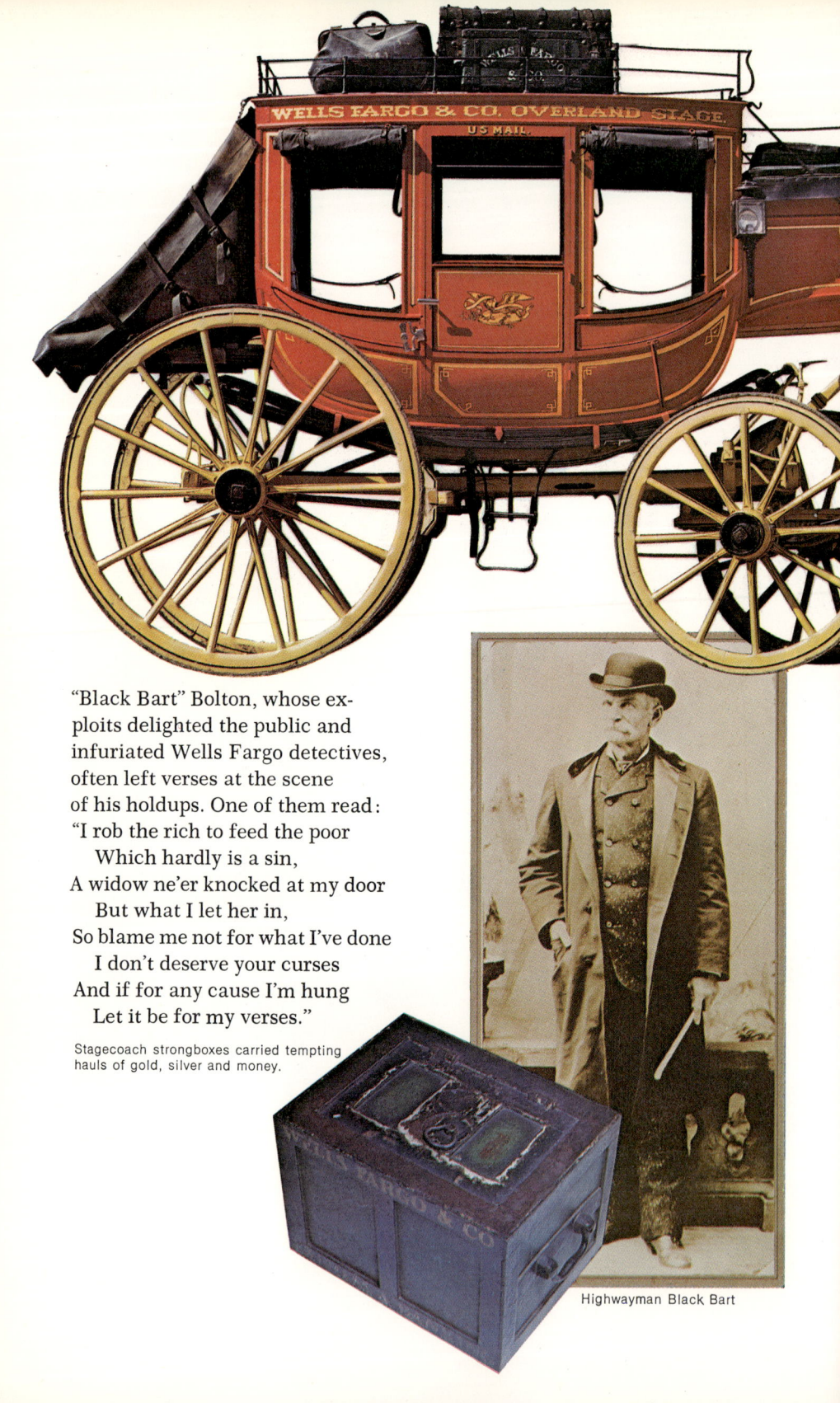

"Black Bart" Bolton, whose exploits delighted the public and infuriated Wells Fargo detectives, often left verses at the scene of his holdups. One of them read:
"I rob the rich to feed the poor
   Which hardly is a sin,
A widow ne'er knocked at my door
   But what I let her in,
So blame me not for what I've done
   I don't deserve your curses
And if for any cause I'm hung
   Let it be for my verses."

Stagecoach strongboxes carried tempting hauls of gold, silver and money.

Highwayman Black Bart

A tense night brings a shotgun to the ready in Frederic Remington's *The Old Stage Coach of the Plains*.

Kid Curry Holdup by O. C. Seltzer is based on an actual event—the robbery of a Great Northern train near Malta, Mo

The more daring gangs, like Butch Cassidy's Wild Bunch— train-robbery specialists and freebooters—were often popularly portrayed as heroes, but the Denver *Daily News* recalled in 1903 that Cassidy's operations were at one time so bold as to lead Governor Wells of Utah to suggest that the governors of Colorado, Wyoming, and Utah unite in concentrated action to wipe them out.

belonged to Butch Cassidy's Wild Bunch (below left). Cassidy sits at right, the Sundance Kid at left.

In his first train stickup Cassidy used too much dynamite on the safe.

15

The famous shoot-out at the O.K. Corral took place in Tombstone, Arizona, on the street next to the one above.

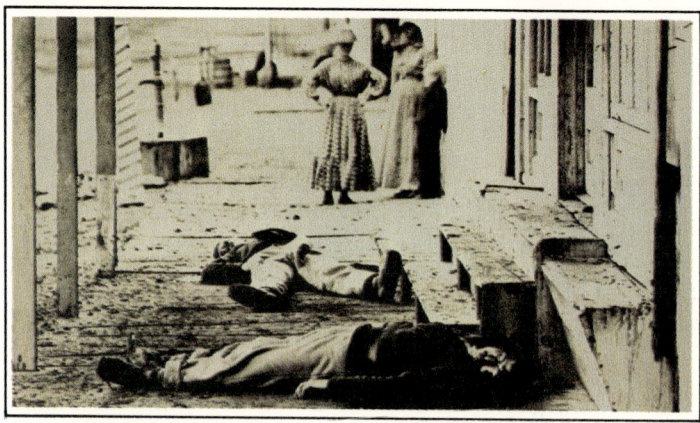
The morning after a brawl in Hays, Kansas, two lie dead outside a saloon.

It wasn't just the lure of money, outlaw Henry Starr once said, but "the thrill of dashing into a town, guns blazing. From every window rifles and shotguns are spitting lead at you. The boys who had gone into the bank come running out with a grain sack bulging with loot. One of your boys is down. You vault into the saddle and roar out of town. You think of the boy lying back there in the dust. It may be you the next time."

A Western town's warning to outlaws

Gunfight by N. C. Wyeth. For such shoot-outs the Colt .45 Peacemaker (above) was the favorite weapon.

An old-timer named McNulta, who was wise in the ways of Dodge City, gave this fatherly counsel to a group of young cowboys going there for the first time: "Don't ride your horses into a saloon, or shoot out lights in Dodge. And when you leave town, don't ride out shooting. Most cowboys think it's an infringement on their rights to give up shooting in town, [but] your six-shooters are no match for Winchesters and buckshot; and Dodge's officers are as game a set of men as ever faced danger."

Dodge City Peace Commission, 1883, included Bat Masterson (standing, right) and Wyatt Earp (seated, second from left).

In 1878 one of the more elegant of Dodge City's sixteen saloons was the Varieties. Presiding over the bar at right is Bat Masterson's brother, George.

Sidewalk justice: Gus Mentzer was hanged without trial after a dispute in Raton, New Mexico, in 1882.

Of the vigilante groups formed by desperate citizens, Professor Thomas J. Dimsdale wrote in the 1860s: "Swift and terrible retribution is the only preventive of crime, while society is organizing in the far West. Gladly would the Vigilantes cease from their labor, and joyfully would they hail the advent of power, civil or military, to take their place; but till this is furnished by Government, society must be preserved from anarchy; murder, arson and robbery must be prevented, and road agents must die." The awesomely armed United States marshals at right typify the men who eventually replaced vigilante action with a system of legal justice.

Deputy U.S. marshals in Indian Territory in the early 1890s

In his Texas saloon Judge Roy Bean held court and sold beer between poker hands.

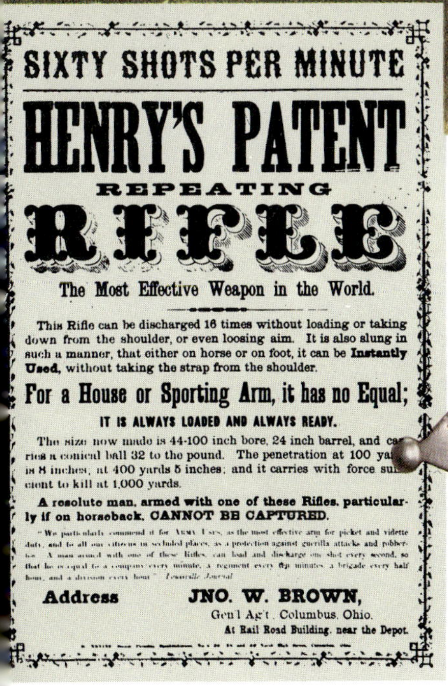

SIXTY SHOTS PER MINUTE
HENRY'S PATENT
REPEATING
RIFLE
The Most Effective Weapon in the World.

This Rifle can be discharged 16 times without loading or taking down from the shoulder, or even loosing aim. It is also slung in such a manner, that either on horse or on foot, it can be **Instantly Used**, without taking the strap from the shoulder.

For a House or Sporting Arm, it has no Equal;
IT IS ALWAYS LOADED AND ALWAYS READY.

The size now made is 44-100 inch bore, 24 inch barrel, and carries a conical ball 32 to the pound. The penetration at 100 yards is 8 inches, at 400 yards 5 inches; and it carries with force sufficient to kill at 1,000 yards.

A resolute man, armed with one of these Rifles, particularly if on horseback, CANNOT BE CAPTURED.

"We particularly commend it for Army Uses, as the most effective arm for picket and vidette duty, and to all our citizens in secluded places, as a protection against guerilla attacks and robbers. A man armed with one of these Rifles, can load and discharge one shot every second, so that he is equal to a company every minute, a regiment every ten minutes, a brigade every half hour, and a division every hour." *Louisville Journal.*

Address   **JNO. W. BROWN,**
Gen'l Ag't. Columbus, Ohio.
At Rail Road Building, near the Depot.

©Time Inc. from the Time-Life series The Old West.

An advertising pitch to the outlaw trade

This crude oath bound Montana vigilantes to secrecy when they took the law into their own hands: "We the undersigned uniting ourselves in a party for the Laudible purpos of arresting thievs & murderers & recovering stollen propperty do pledge ourselves upon our sacred honor each to all others & solemnly swear that we will reveal no secrets, violate no laws of right & never desert each other or our standerd of justice so help us God as witness our hand & seal this 23 of December A D 1863."

A rope, a prayer, and an oak tree near.
And a score of hands to swing him clear.

A grim black thing for the setting sun
And the moon and the stars to look upon.

Madison Cawein

THE OX-BOW INCIDENT

A CONDENSATION OF THE
NOVEL BY

**Walter
Van Tilburg Clark**

TITLE-PAGE PAINTING BY
W. H. D. Koerner

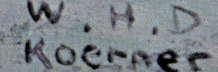

In *The Ox-Bow Incident* the familiar ingredients of countless Western sagas have been transmuted into something far more compelling—an unsparing drama of real people faced with terrible choices.

The time is 1885, the place Bridger's Wells, a small Nevada cow town. Into the ramshackle settlement ride two cowboys, eager for a bit of fun after long months on the lonely winter range. In the one saloon they hear that a well-liked fellow cowboy has been ambushed and murdered by rustlers, and indignation explodes into action. The sheriff is away, but a posse forms on the spot, and at once a struggle begins between the hotheads, who would ride in pursuit immediately, and the few voices insisting on the forms of law.

Thus is launched a novel that has been called a masterpiece of Western literature, in which a dramatic narrative is combined with a searching study of men under stress.

Chapter 1

GIL AND I CROSSED the eastern divide about two by the sun. We pulled up for a look at the little town in the big valley and the mountains on the other side, with the crest of the sierra showing faintly beyond like the rim of a day moon. We didn't look as long as we do sometimes; after winter range, we were excited about getting back to town. When the horses had stopped trembling from the last climb, Gil took off his sombrero, pushed his sweaty hair back with the same hand, and returned the sombrero, the way he did when something was going to happen. He reined to the right and went slowly down the steep stage road. It was a switchback road, gutted by the runoff of the winter storms. In the pockets under the red earth banks, where the wind was cut off, the spring sun was hot as summer, and the air was full of a hot, melting pine smell. Rivulets of water trickled down, shining on the sides of the cuts. The jays screeched in the trees and flashed through the sunlight in the clearings in swift, long dips. Squirrels and chipmunks chittered in the brush and along the tops of snow-sodden logs. On the outside turns, though, the wind got to us and dried the sweat under our shirts and brought up, instead of the hot resin, the smell of the marshy green valley. In the west the heads of a few clouds showed, the kind that come up with the early heat, but they were lying still, and over us the sky was clear and deep.

It was good to be on the loose again, but winter range stores up a lot of things in a man, and spring roundup hadn't worked them all out. Gil Carter and I had been riding together for five years, but just the two of us in that shack in the snow had made us cautious. We didn't dare talk much, and we wanted to feel easy together again. When we came onto the last gentle slope into the valley, we let the horses out and loped across the flat. Out in the big meadows on both sides the long grass was bending under the wind and shining. We could hear the cows lowing in the north, a mellow sound at that distance, like little horns.

It was about three when we rode into Bridger's Wells, past the boarded-up church on the right and the houses back under the cottonwoods. Most of the yards were just let run to long grass, and the buildings were log or unpainted board, but there were a few brick houses and a few painted clapboards. Around them the grass was cut, and lilac bushes were planted in the shade. There were big purple cones of blossom on them at this time of year.

Since the stagecoach ran less than it used to, Bridger's Wells was losing its stage-stop look and beginning to settle into being a half-empty village of the kind that hangs on sometimes where all the real work is spread out on the land around it, and most of the places take care of themselves. Besides the houses on the main street and the cross street, there wasn't much to the town: Arthur Davies' general store, the land and mining claims office, Canby's saloon, the long, sagging Bridger Inn with its double-decker porch, and the Union Church, square as a New England meetinghouse, set out on the west edge of town.

The street was nearly dried, though with hardened wagon ruts, so you could see how the teams had slithered and plowed in it. It drummed hard when we touched up our horses to come in right. After all the thinking we'd done about it, the place looked dead as a Paiute graveyard. There were a few horses switching at the tie rails in front of the inn and Canby's, but not one man in sight.

At Canby's we swung down, tied up, crossed the boardwalk, our boots knocking loudly, and went up the three steps to the high double door with the frosted-glass panels.

It was dark and cool inside, and smelled of stale beer and tobacco. The bar ran along one side, and opposite it there were four green-covered tables. The same old pictures were on the walls too. Up back of the bar there was a big, grimy oil painting in a gilded frame showing a woman stretched on a couch and draped with a blue cloth. She was pretending to play with an ugly bird on her wrist, but really encouraging a man who was sneaking up on her from a background so dark you could see only his little white face. The picture had a brass plate which said dryly, *Woman with Parrot.*

On the other wall was a huge yellowish print of a reception at the Crystal in Virginia City. In it President Grant and a lot of senators, generals, and other celebrities were posed around so you could get a full-length view of each. The figures were numbered, and underneath was a list telling you who they were. Then there was a bright-colored print of an Indian princess in front of a waterfall, a big painting of a stagecoach coming in, and an oval black-and-white picture of the heads of three white horses, all wild-eyed and their manes flying.

Four men were playing poker at a back table, with a lamp over them. I didn't know any of the men. Canby was behind his bar, a tall, thin, take-your-time kind of man with seedy gray hair combed over his bald spot. All of Canby's bones were big and heavy, and those in his wrists were knobby and red. His arms were so long that he could sit on the back counter, where his glasses and bottles were arranged, and mop the bar. It was clean and dry now, but he mopped it while he waited for us. He looked at us, first one, then the other.

"Well?" he said, when we just stood looking at the painting of the woman.

Gil pushed his hat back so his red curly hair showed, and folded his arms on the bar. Gil has a big, pale, freckled face that won't darken and never shows any expression except in the eyes, and then only temper. His nose has been broken three times, and his mouth is thick and straight. He's a quick but not a grudgy kind of fighter, and always talks as if he had a little edge, which is his kind of humor.

"That guy," said Gil, still looking at the man in the picture, "is awful slow getting there."

Canby didn't look at the picture. "I feel sorry for him," he said. "Always in reach and never able to make it." They said something like this every time we came in. It was a ritual.

"I got a feeling she could do better," Gil said.

"You're boasting," Canby told him, and then said again, "Well?"
"Don't rush me," Gil said.
"Take your time," Canby said.
"It don't look to me," Gil said, "like you was so rushed you couldn't wait!"
"It's not that. I hate to see a man who can't make up his mind. What'll you have? Whiskey?"
"What have you got?"
"Whiskey."
"Did you ever know such a guy?" Gil said to me. "All this time I'm thinkin', and all he's got's whiskey. And that's rotten, ain't it?" he asked, looking at Canby.
"Rotten," Canby agreed.
"Two glasses and a bottle," Gil said.

Canby set them out in front of us and uncorked the bottle. Gil poured us one apiece, and we took them down. It was raw and made the eyes water after we'd been dry so long. We hadn't had a drop since Christmas.

Canby looked at me. "Do you always have this much trouble with him?"

"More, mostly," I said, and told him about the fight we'd had, which Gil had finished by knocking me across the red-hot stove. We drank slowly while we talked, and Gil listened politely, as if I were telling a dull story about somebody else. "It was just being cooped up together so long," I said, remembering all those fights, the one-room shack with the snow piled up to the window ledge, blowing against the glass like sand; the lonely sound of the wind, and Gil and I at opposite ends of the room, with two lamps burning, except for a truce at mealtimes.

"He's naturally mean," Canby said. "You can tell that."

"A man needs exercise," Gil said. "He's not much of a fighter, but there wasn't anything else handy." He poured us another. "Besides, he started them all."

"Like hell I did," I said. "Do I look like I'd start them?" I asked Canby. I'm as tall as Gil is, but flat and thin, while Gil is built like a bull; his hands are twice as big as mine. Gil looks like a fighter too, with a long, heavy chin and those angular eyes with a challenging stare in them. I could see myself in the mirror under the *Woman with Parrot.* My face was burned dark as old leather, but it's thin, with big eyes.

"You should have heard the things he said," Gil told Canby.

"By January," I put in, "he'd only talk about one thing, women. And then he kept telling the same stories about himself and the same women."

"Well, he wouldn't talk," Gil said, "and somebody had to. He'd sit there reading. Then I'd try to sing, and he'd get nasty."

"Gil has a fine voice," I said, "but he only knows three songs, all with the same tune."

We kept on talking off our edge, Canby putting in a word now and then to keep us going.

Finally Canby said, "Now that you two are peaceable again, what's on your mind?" He was talking to Gil.

"Does something have to be on my mind?" Gil asked.

"What's he so bashful about?" Canby asked me.

"He wants to know if his girl is still in town," I told him.

"*His* girl?" said Canby, mopping a wet place on the bar. "If you mean Rose Mapen," he said, straightening up, "no. She went to Frisco the first stage out this spring."

Gil stood looking at him.

"It's a fact," Canby said.

"Hell," Gil said furiously. He finished his drink in a toss.

"Have a drink," Canby said, opening another bottle, "but don't get drunk while you're feeling like that. The only unmarried woman I know of in town is eighty-two, blind, and a Paiute."

He poured another for each of us and took one himself. You could see it tickled him that Gil had given himself away like that. But Gil was really feeling bad. All winter he'd talked about Rose, until I'd been sick of her. I thought she was a tart anyway. But Gil had dreamed out loud about buying a ranch and settling.

"It's my guess the married women ran her out," Canby said.

"Yeh?" Gil said.

"Oh, no tar and feathers; no rails. They just righteously made her uncomfortable. Not that she ever did anything; but they couldn't get over being afraid she would. Most of the men were afraid to be seen talking to her, even the unmarried ones. The place is too small."

Gil kept looking at him, but didn't say anything. It's queer how deeply a careless guy like Gil can be cut when he does take anything seriously.

"Anything come of this gold they were talking about last fall?" I asked Canby.

"Do I look it?" he asked. "No," he went on. "A couple of young fellows from Sacramento found loose gold in Belcher's Creek, up at the north end, and traced it down to a pocket. They got several thousand, I guess, but there was no lode. A lot of claims were staked, but nobody found anything, and it was too near winter for a real boom to get started. Not even enough to get more than two or three women in, and they left before the pass was closed."

"It's nothing to me," I lied.

"What is there to do in this town anyway?" Gil demanded.

"Nothing. Unless you aim to get in line to woo Drew's daughter."

Drew was the biggest rancher in the valley. "We don't," I informed Canby.

"No," he agreed. "Well, then, you have five choices: eat, sleep, drink, play poker or fight. Or you can shoot some pool. There's a new table in the back room."

"Great," Gil said.

The door opened and Moore, the foreman from Drew's ranch, came in. Moore was past forty and getting fat so his belt hung under his belly. His face was heavily lined and sallow and his hair streaked with gray. He had a lot of pain, I guess; his insides were all shot from staying at bronco busting too long. But he'd been a great rider once, one of the best, and he was still worth his salt. He knew horses and cattle and country as he knew his own mind, which was thoroughly; and his eyes were still quiet and sure.

He came over, said hello to us, and threw a silver dollar onto the bar, nodding at Canby. Canby poured him a glass and he downed it. Then he filled him another, which Moore let sit while he rolled a cigarette and licked it into shape.

"I see Risley's still around," Canby said. Moore nodded.

Risley was the sheriff for this territory, but he wasn't often closer than Reno, except on special call. I could see Moore didn't want to talk about it, hadn't liked Canby's mentioning Risley in front of us. But I was curious.

"There was talk about rustling last fall, wasn't there?" I asked Moore.

"Some," he said. He didn't look at me but at the rows of dark bottles behind Canby. Canby wiped the dry bar again. He was ashamed. It was all right for Moore, but I didn't like Canby acting as if we were outsiders. Neither did Gil.

"Is that why Risley's out here?" Gil asked Moore. "Because of rustling?"

Moore finished his whiskey and nodded at the glass, which Canby filled a third time. "Yes, that's why he's here," he said. He put his change in his pocket and took his glass and the bottle over to the table by the front window. He sat down with his back to us.

"It's getting touchy, huh?" Gil said to Canby.

"They don't like to talk about it," Canby said, "except with fellows they sleep with."

"It's a long way from any border," he said after a minute, "and everybody in the valley would know if there was a stranger around."

"And there isn't?" I asked.

"There hasn't been—at least any that know cattle," said Canby, sitting back up on the counter, "except you two."

"That's not funny," Gil told him, and set his glass down very quietly.

"Now who's touchy?" Canby asked him. He was grinning.

"You're talking about my business," Gil said. "Just stick to my pleasures."

"Sure," Canby said. "I thought I'd let you know how you stand, that's all."

"Listen," Gil said, taking his hands down from the bar.

"Take a drink of water, Gil," I said. And to Canby, "He's had five whiskeys, and he's sore about Rose." I didn't really believe Gil would fight Canby, but I wasn't sure after his disappointment. Whenever Gil gets low in spirit or confused in his mind, he doesn't feel right again until he's had a fight. It doesn't matter whether he wins or not; if it's a good fight, he feels fine again afterward. But he usually wins.

"And you keep your mouth shut about Rose, see?" Gil told me. He had turned around so he was facing right at me, and I could tell by his eyes he was a little drunk already.

"All right, Gil," I reassured him. "All right."

"No offense meant, Carter," Canby said, and he filled Gil's glass again, pouring slowly, as if he were doing it very carefully for somebody he thought a lot of.

"It's all right, it's all right," Gil said. "Forget it."

Canby put two plates on the bar, and then got some hard bread and dried beef and put them on the plates. I ate some of the food. It tasted good, now that I was wet down. We'd had a long ride and nothing to eat since before daybreak. Finally Gil began to eat too, at first as though he weren't thinking about it, but just picking at it absentmindedly, then without pretense.

"Are they sure about this rustling?" I asked Canby.

"Sure enough," he said. "They thought they'd lost some stock last fall, but with this range shut in the way it is by the mountains, they'd been kind of careless in the tally and couldn't be too sure. Only Bartlett was sure. He doesn't run so many cattle anyway, and his count was over a hundred short. He started some talk that might have made trouble, but Drew got that straightened out and had them take another tally, a close one. During the winter they even checked by the head on the cows that were expected to calve this spring.

"Then Kinkaid, who was doing the snow riding for Drew, got suspicious. He thought one of the bunches that had wintered mostly at the south end was thinning out more than the thaw explained. He and Farnley kept an eye out. They even rode nights. Just before roundup they found a small herd trail and signs of shod horses in the south draw. They lost them over in the Antelope, where there'd been a new fall of snow. But in the Antelope, in a ravine west of the draw, they found a branding camp—a kind of lean-to shelter, and the ashes of several fires that had been built under a ledge to keep the smoke down. They figured about thirty head of cattle and four riders."

"And the count came short this spring?"

"Way short," Canby said. "Nearly six hundred head, counting calves."

"Six hundred?" I said, only half believing it.

"That's right," Canby said. "They tallied twice, and with everybody there."

"God," Gil said.

"So they're touchy," said Canby.

"Did everybody lose?" I asked after a minute.

"Drew was heaviest, but everybody lost."

We could see how it was, now, and we didn't feel too good being off our range. Not when they'd been thinking about it all year.

"What's Risley doing here? Have they got a lead?" Gil asked.

"You want to know a lot," said Canby. "He's down just in case of trouble. It's Judge Tyler's idea, not the cattlemen."

I was going to ask more questions. I didn't want to and yet I did. But Moore got up and came back to the bar with the partly emptied bottle. He pushed it across to Canby, with another dollar beside it.

"Three out of that," he said. Then he asked us, "Lost any over your way?"

"No," I admitted. "No more than winter and the coyotes could account for."

"Got any ideas?" Gil asked him. Canby paused, holding Moore's change in his hand.

"No ideas, except not to have any ideas," Moore said. He reached for his change and put it in his pocket. "Game?" he asked, to show we were all right.

Canby fished a deck of cards out of a drawer for us, and the three of us sat down at the front table. We played a twenty-five-cent limit, which was steep enough. Canby sat in until others began coming. Then he went back to the bar. Most of the men who came in were riders and men we knew. I thought they looked at Gil and me curiously and longer than usual, but probably that wasn't so. Each of them nodded, or raised a hand, or said "Hi," in the usual manner. They all went to the bar first, and had a drink or two. Then some of them got up a game at the table next to ours, and the rest settled into a row at the bar, elbows up and hats back.

The place was full of the gentle vibration of deep voices talking mostly in short sentences, with a lot of give and take. Things didn't seem any different than usual, and yet there was a difference underneath. For one thing, nobody, no matter how genially, was calling his neighbor an old horse thief, or a card sharp, or a liar, or anything that had moral implications.

Some of the village men came in too: old Bartlett, who was a rancher, but had his house in the village; Davies, the store owner; and Davies' clerk, Joyce, a tall, thin, sallow boy with pimples, a loose lower lip and big hands. Even Osgood, the minister from the one working church, came in, though he ostentatiously didn't take a drink. He was a Baptist, bald-headed, with a small nose and close-set eyes, but built like a wrestler. His voice was too enthusiastic and his manner too intimate to be true. I noticed that none of the men would be caught alone with him, and that they all became stiff or too much at ease when he approached, though they kept on drinking and playing, and spoke with him, but called him Mr. Osgood.

Bartlett came over to the table and watched us play. He was a tall man, looking very old and tired and cross. The flesh of his face was pasty and hung in loose folds. He had on a flat Spanish sombrero and a long black frock coat, such as only the old men were wearing then. When Jeff Farnley, Kinkaid's riding partner, came over too, Moore invited them to sit in. Farnley had a thin face, burned brick red, stiff yellow hair and pale hostile eyes, but with a quick grin on a hard mouth. He wiped his hands on his red-and-white cowhide vest, and sat. Bartlett sat down slowly, letting himself go the last few inches, and fumbled for a cigar in his vest. When he got to playing he would chew the cigar and forget to draw on it, so that after every hand he had to relight it.

Gil was tight enough by now so I could see him squinting to make out what he had in his hand. He was having a big run of luck. I knew he wasn't cheating; Gil didn't cheat. Even if he'd wanted to he couldn't, with hands like his, not even sober. But with his gripe on he wasn't taking his winning right, and that worried me. He wasn't showing any signs of being pleased, not boasting, or bulling the others along about how thin they'd have to live, the way you would in an ordinary game with a bunch of friends. He was just sitting there with a sullen deadpan and raking in the pots slow and contemptuous, like he expected it. He'd signal Canby to fill his glass again when he'd made a good haul. Then he'd toss the drink off in one gulp and set the glass down and flick it halfway to the middle of the table with his finger. If there hadn't been anything else in the air, you couldn't play long with a man acting like that without getting your chin out, especially when he was winning three hands out of four. I was getting riled myself.

It didn't seem to be bothering Moore. Once when Gil took in the chips three times running on straight poker, Moore looked at him and then at me, and shook his head a little, but that was all. A couple of other riders, who'd sat in after Bartlett and Farnley, started prodding Gil about it, but they stayed good-natured and Gil just looked at them and went on playing cold. But that made their jokes sound pretty hollow, and after a little they didn't joke anymore. Old Bartlett, though, was beginning to mutter at his cards, and he was throwing his hands in early and exasperated. But it was Farnley I was really worried about. He had a flaring kind of face, and he wasn't letting off steam in any way, not by a look or a word or a move, but staring a long time at his bad hands and then laying the cards down quietly, sliding them onto the table and keeping his fingers on them for a moment, as if he had half a mind to do something else with them.

I hoped Gil's luck would change enough to look reasonable, but it didn't, so I dropped out of the game, saying he'd had enough off me. I thought maybe he'd follow suit, but even if he didn't, it would look better without his buddy in there. He didn't, and he kept winning. I didn't want to get too far from him, so I did the best I could and stood right behind him, where I could see his hand but nobody else's.

After two more rounds Farnley said, "How about draw?" He said it quietly and watching Gil, as if changing the game would make a real difference.

Gil was dealing and Farnley had no business asking for the change, but Gil said, "Sure. Why not?" and he began to deal out the cards. "Look 'em over careful, boys," he said, when they were all out. "Maybe somebody has two aces of spades."

Farnley let it go. He picked up his cards, and his face didn't change from its set look, but I could tell from the way he looked them all over again that he thought he had something this time. He drew two cards out and slid them onto the table face down, and this time didn't keep his fingers on them.

I looked at Gil's hand. He had the queen, jack and ten of spades, the ten of clubs and the four of hearts. He looked at it for a moment, then threw off the club and the heart.

"How many?" he asked.

They drew around, Gil dropping Farnley's cards where he had to reach for them. Gil drew the nine of spades and the king of spades.

"Place your bets," he said, sharp.

Moore, on his left, tossed his hand in. So did the next man. Farnley bet the limit. Bartlett and the other puncher, a fellow with curly black sideburns like wire hair, stayed.

Gil threw a half-dollar out on top of his quarter so it clinked.

"Double," he said.

"There's a limit," Moore said.

"How about it?" Gil asked Farnley, as if the other two weren't in the game.

Farnley put in the quarter, then threw a silver dollar after it.

Bartlett balked, but I guess he had something too. When they didn't pay any attention to him he stayed. So did the other man, but sheepishly.

Gil matched the dollar.

Moore pushed his chair back from the table. The change in the game had got to the men at the bar. Five or six of them came over to watch, and the others turned around, leaning on the bar with their elbows, and were quiet too. Canby stood with his towel over his shoulder and that dry look on his face, but watching Gil and Farnley just the same.

"Your bet," Gil told Farnley.

Farnley tossed out another silver dollar. Bartlett snorted violently and slapped his hand down. So did the sheepish man. Gil threw out two dollars. Farnley raised it another. Men stirred uneasily, but were careful to be quiet.

Only when Farnley made it five Canby said, "Enough's enough. See him, Carter, or I'll close up the game."

Gil put out the dollar to see, and we started to relax, when he counted five more off the top of his pile and shoved them out.

"And five," he said.

That still didn't make it any sky-limit game, but it was mean for the kind of a game this had started out to be. There was plenty left in Gil's stack, but when Farnley had counted out the five there was only one dollar left on the green by his hand.

"Make it six," Gil said, and put in the extra one.

"Pick it up, Gil," I said. "You were seen at five."

There was some muttering from others too. Gil didn't pay any attention. He sat looking at Farnley. Farnley was breathing hard, and his eyes were narrowed, but he looked at his hand, not Gil. Then he threw in the sixth dollar.

"I'm seeing you," he said, and laid out his hand carefully in front of him. It was a full house, kings and jacks.

Gil tossed his cards into the center and reached for the pot.

"Hold it," Moore said. Moore spread Gil's cards out so everybody could see them, a king-high straight flush, pretty near the highest hand you can get. One of the watchers whistled.

"Suit you?" Gil asked Moore.

Moore nodded, and Gil reached the money in and began to put it in neat stacks.

Farnley sat staring at Gil's cards for a moment. "God," he finally said, "that's damned long luck," and he banged the table with his fist so hard that Gil's stacks of chips slid down into a loose pile. Gil had the canvas sack out of his jeans and was just ready to scoop the silver into it. He stopped and held the sack in the air. But Farnley wasn't going to start anything. He got up and turned toward the bar. He was doing well, I thought; you could tell by his face he was crazy mad. Gil was the fool.

"Wouldn't suggest it was anything but luck, would you?" he asked, letting his sack drop.

At first Farnley stood there with his back turned. Then he came back to the table, but slow enough so Moore had time to get to his feet before he spoke.

"I wasn't going to," Farnley said, "but now you mention it."

Gil stood up too. "Make it clear," he said, his voice thick and happy.

"There's a lot of things around here aren't clear," Farnley said.

And then Gil had to say, "You're talking about cows now, maybe?"

I got set to hit him. There wasn't any use grabbing.

"You're saying it this time too," Farnley told him.

"Come on, boys, the game's over," Canby put in. "The drinks are on you, Carter. You're heavy winner."

I swung. But Gil was already partway around the table. In spite of his weight and all he'd had to drink, he was quick, clumsy quick, like a bear. Canby reached but missed. Gil shoved Moore nearly off his feet and was on Farnley in three jumps, letting go a right that would have broken Farnley's neck. Farnley got under that one, but ducked right into a wild left that caught him on the corner of the mouth. He spun partway around, crashed across two chairs, and folded up under the front window, banging his head against the sill. Gil stood swaying and laughing as if he loved it. Then his face straightened and got that deadly pleased look again.

"Called me a rustler, did he?" he said thickly, as if somebody had just reminded him of it again.

I knew the look; he was going to pile Farnley and hammer him. Nobody seemed to move. They were standing back, leaving Gil alone by the table. I yelled something and started around, bumping into Moore, who was just getting set on his feet again. But I was too far behind. Canby turned the trick. Without even looking excited, he reached back to the bar, got hold of a bottle, and rapped Gil, not too hard either, right under the base of the skull. He must have done it a thousand times to be that careful about it. For a moment Gil's tension held him up. Then his knees bellied like cloth, and he came down in a heap and rolled over onto his back, where he lay with a silly, surprised grin on his face, and his eyes rolled up so only the whites showed.

"Looks happy, don't he?" Canby said, standing over Gil with the bottle in his hand. "He'll be all right," he told me. "I just gave him a touch of it."

"It was neat," I said, and laughed. Others laughed too, and the talk began.

I got Gil's sack and scooped his winnings into it. Then I helped Canby with Gil, who was heavy and limp and hard to prop in a chair. When we had him there I got some whiskey to throw in his face. Farnley was slow coming back, without any chatter or struggle. Finally he sat up and leaned forward, his arms on his knees. Gil started to talk before he was out of it, muttering and sort of joking and protesting. When he really woke up he pushed us off, but gently, not wanting to jar himself. He got up, testing his legs. Then he got a queer, strangled look on his face. He put a hand up to his mouth and turned and hurried out through the back room. I followed him with his sack in my hand. He was staggering some, and bumped against the outside kitchen door, but he got out quickly. I could hear the men laughing behind us. They liked the way Gil took it; he made it all right for them to laugh, and he did look funny.

When I got to him he was standing in a little cleared black space, leaning over, with his hands on his knees. He was pretty well emptied out already, and just getting hold of himself again. He stood up with his eyes watering and his face red.

"Holy cow," he gulped. "It must have been Canby. Now I've got to start all over again."

"Take your time," I advised. "You've got head enough."

From somewhere down the side street we caught the sound of a running horse on the hardpan. By the clatter, he was being pushed.

"Somebody's in a hell of a hurry," Gil said.

We got a glimpse of the rider as he rounded onto the main street. The horse banked around at a considerable angle, and was running hard and heavily. There was white dropping away from his bit. The rider had been bent over, with his hat pulled down hard, but even in the little space we could see him, he straightened back and began to rein in strong. Then they were out of sight behind Canby's.

"I'm not in any hurry, though," Gil said.

I liked it out there too. It was good after the stale darkness inside. A roundup makes you restless inside houses for a while. Now and then in the freshening wind we could hear a meadowlark, *chink-chink-a-link*, and then another, way off and higher, *tink-tink-a-link*. I could see how they'd be leaping up out of the grass, fluttering, and then dropping back again.

Gil, though, was thinking about something else.

"He didn't knock me out with his fist, did he?"

"No, a bottle."

"That's all right, then. I thought it must have been that." And after breathing in a couple of times, he said, "He shouldn't have stopped me, though. I don't feel any better."

"It takes a lot to please you," I told him. "Anyway, lay off Farnley. You were pretty low on that."

"Yeh, I guess I was at that," he said. "Maybe I ought to give him back his money. Say, the money . . ."

"I've got it," I told him, and gave him the sack.

"You think I ought to give it back?" he asked unhappily.

"Not all of it. Most of it was won fair. But not the last pot; that was no poker."

That cheered him up. "Yeh, the last pot," he agreed. "How much was it?"

"Ten dollars is near enough," I said.

"Is that all?" he said, feeling better.

We went back in through the kitchen. But when we got to the bar door I could see right away something was wrong. Farnley was standing at the other end, by the front door, looking like he hadn't come out of his daze yet, and Moore, Drew's foreman, had hold of him by the arm and was talking to him. Davies, the store owner, was trying to say something too. Just when we stopped, Farnley shook Moore off, though still standing there.

"The lousy sons of bitches," he said, and then repeated it slowly, each word by itself.

At first I was going to try to get Gil out the back way again. Then I saw how the men were, all gathered together along the bar there, looking quiet and angry, and not paying any attention to us. When they heard our boots a few glanced at us, but didn't even seem to see us.

They'd been watching Farnley at first, and now they were looking at a new rider who was talking excitedly, so I couldn't get what he said. He was a young fellow, still in his teens, I thought, and he was out of breath. He was feeling important, but wild too, talking fast and waving his right hand, and then slapping the gun on his thigh, which was tied down like a draw fighter's. His black sombrero was pushed onto the back of his head, and his open vest was flapping. There was a movement and mutter beginning among the men, but at the end the kid's voice came up so we could hear what he was saying.

"Shot right through the head, I tell you," he cried, like somebody was arguing with him, though nobody was.

Farnley reached out, grabbed the kid by his vest, yanked him close, and spoke right in his face. The kid looked scared and said something low. Farnley still held him for a moment, staring at him. Then he let him go, turned, and pushed through the front door and out onto the walk. Some of the men followed him, but most of them milled around the kid, whose name was Greene. They were trying to get something more out of him, but not being noisy now either.

"Come on," I told Gil, "it's not us."

"It better not be," Gil said, starting slow to come with me.

"It's the kid that was riding so fast," I explained.

They were all beginning to crowd outside now. Canby went and stood in the door behind the others, looking out.

"What's up?" I asked Canby, trying to see past him.

He didn't turn his head. "Lynching, I'd judge," he said, like it didn't interest him.

"Those rustlers?" I asked.

"Maybe," he said, looking at me kind of funny. "They don't know who yet. But somebody's been in down on Drew's range and killed Kinkaid, and they think there's cattle gone too."

"Killed Kinkaid?" I echoed, and thought that over quick.

Kinkaid had been Farnley's buddy. They'd been riding together from the Panhandle to Jackson Hole ever since they were kids. Kinkaid was a little dark Irishman who liked to be by himself, and never offered to say anything, but only made short answers when he had to. He always seemed halfway sad, and though he had a fine, deep singing voice, he wouldn't often sing when he knew anybody could hear. He was only an ordinary rider, with no flair to give him a reputation, but there was something about him which made men cotton to him, nothing he did or said, but a gentle, permanent reality that was in him like his bones or his heart, that made him seem like an everlasting part of things. You didn't notice when he was there, but you noticed it a lot when he wasn't. You could no more believe that Kinkaid was dead than you could that a mountain had moved and left a gap in the sky. The men would go a long way, and all together, to get the guy that had killed Kinkaid. And I was remembering Canby's joke about Gil and me.

"When?" Gil asked.

Then Canby looked at him too. "They don't know," he said. "About noon, maybe. They didn't find him till a lot later." And he looked at me again.

I wanted to feel the way the others did about this, but you can feel awful guilty about nothing when the men you're with don't trust you. I knew Gil was feeling the same way when he started to say something, and Canby looked back at him, and he didn't say it. But we couldn't afford to stand in there behind Canby either. I pushed past him and went down onto the walk, and Gil came right behind me.

Chapter 2

FARNLEY WAS CLIMBING onto his horse. He moved slowly and deliberately, like a man with his mind made up. A rider yelled, "Hey, Jeff. Wait up; we'll form a posse."

"I can get the sons of bitches," Farnley said, and reined around.

Moore said, "He's crazy," and started out into the street. But Davies, the store owner, was ahead of him. He came alongside Farnley and took hold of his bridle. The horse, checked, wheeled and switched its tail, and Farnley looked down. Davies was an old man, short, narrow, and so round-shouldered he was nearly a hunchback, and with very white silky hair. His hollow, high-cheeked face had deep forehead lines and two deep, clear lines each side of a wide, thin mouth. His eyes were strangely young, bright and shining blue. Farnley looked at those eyes and held himself.

"There's no rush, Jeff," Davies said, coaxing him. "You don't know how many of them there are. There might be twenty. It won't help Larry to get yourself killed too." Davies let go of the bridle. "We aren't even certain which way they went, Jeff, or how long they've had. You just wait till we know what we're doing. We're all with you about Kinkaid. You know that, son."

Farnley must have begun to think a little. He waited. Moore went out to them. Osgood was standing beside me on the walk. "They mustn't do this; they mustn't," he said, waving his hands and looking as if he were going to cry. Then he suddenly went out to the two men by the horse. His bald head was pale in the sun. The wind fluttered his coat and the legs of his trousers. He looked helpless and timid. I knew he was trying to do what he thought was right, but he had no heart in his effort.

"Farnley," he said, in a voice which was too high from being forced. "Farnley, if such an awful thing has actually occurred, it is the more reason that we should retain our self-possession. In such a position, Farnley, we are likely to lose our reason and our sense of justice. . . . Men," he orated to us, "let us not act hastily. We must act, certainly, but we must act in a reasoned and legitimate manner, not as a lawless mob. We are not savages to be content with revenge. We desire justice, and justice has never been obtained in haste and strong feeling." He stopped there, pathetically.

Farnley paid no attention but just sat his saddle rigidly. The men at the edge of the walk stirred and spat. It was not Osgood, really, who was delaying them, but uncertainty, and perhaps the fear that they were going to hunt somebody they knew. They had been careful a long time.

"We'll organize a posse right here, Jeff," Moore promised. "If we go right, we'll get what we're after."

For Moore, that was begging. He waited, looking up at Farnley.

Then Farnley pulled his horse around so he sat facing us. "Well, make your posse," he said. He sat watching us as if he hated us all. His cheeks were twitching.

Canby was still leaning in the door behind us, his towel in his hand. "Somebody had better get the sheriff, first thing," he advised. He didn't sound as if it mattered to him whether we got the sheriff or not.

"And Judge Tyler," Osgood said.

"To hell with that," somebody told him. That started others. "We know what that'll mean," yelled another. "We don't need no trial for this business. We've heard enough of Tyler and his trials." The disturbance spread. Men began to get on their horses. "This ain't just rustling," someone yelled.

"Rustling is enough," Bartlett, the old rancher, told him. Then he pulled off his flat sombrero and waved it above his head. He curled his upper lip when he talked angrily, showing his yellow gappy teeth and making his mustache jerk.

"I don't know about the rest of you," he cried. He had a big, hollow voice when he was angry enough to lift it. "But I've had enough rustling. Do we have rights as men and cattlemen, or don't we? We know what Tyler is. If we wait for Tyler, or any man like Tyler," he added, glaring at Osgood, "if we wait, I tell you, there won't be one head of anybody's cattle left in the meadows by the time we get justice." He ridiculed the word justice by his tone. "For that matter," he called, raising his voice still higher, "what is justice? Is it justice that we sweat ourselves sick and old every damned day in the year to make a handful of honest dollars, and then lose it all in one night to some miserable thief because Judge Tyler, whatever God made him, says we have to fold our hands and wait for his eternal justice? Waiting for Tyler's kind of justice, we'd all be beggars in a year!

"What led rustlers into this valley in the first place?" Bartlett bellowed on. "I'll tell you what did it! Judge Tyler's kind of justice, that's what did it. They don't wait for that kind of justice in Texas anymore, do they? No, they don't. They get the man and they string him up. They don't wait in San Francisco anymore, do they? No, they don't. The Vigilance Committee does something—and it doesn't take them six months to get started either, the way it does justice in some places.

"By the Lord God, men, I ask you," he exhorted, "are we going to slink on our own range like a pack of sniveling boys, and wait till we can't buy the boots for our own feet, before we do anything? Well I, for one, am not," he informed us. "Maybe if we do one job with our own hands, the law will get a move on. Maybe. But one thing is sure. If we do this job ourselves, and now, it will be one job that won't have to be done again.

"But, by God," he begged, "if we stand here yapping and whining and wagging our tails till Judge Tyler pats us on the head, we'll have every thieving Mex and Indian and runaway reb in the whole territory eating off our own plates. I say, stretch the bastards," he yelped. "Stretch them."

He was sweating, and he stared around at us, rolling his bloodshot eyes. He had us all excited. Gil and I were quiet, because men had moved away from us, but I was excited too. I wanted to say something that would square me, but I couldn't think what. Bartlett wasn't done, though. He wiped his face on his sleeve, and when he spoke again his voice went up so high it cracked, but we could understand him. Faces around me were hard and angry, with narrow, shining eyes.

"And that's not all. Like the boy here says, it's not just a rustler we're after, it's a murderer. Kinkaid's lying out there now, with a hole in his head, a damned rustler's bullet hole. Let that go, and I'm telling you, men, there won't be anything safe—not our cattle, not our homes, not our lives, not even our women. I say we've got to get them. I have two sons, and we all know how to shoot; yes, and how to tie a knot in a rope, if that's what's worrying you, a knot that won't slip.

"I'm for you, Jeff," he shouted at Farnley, waving his hat in a big arc in front of him. "I'm going to get a gun and a rope, and I'll be back. If nobody else will do it, you and I and the boys will do it. We'll do it alone." He turned around and pushed through us in a hurry, not even putting his hat on. I could hear him wheezing when he shoved past me.

Farnley raised one hand, carelessly, in a kind of salute, but his face was still tight, expressionless and twitching. At his salute the men all shouted. They told him loudly that they were with him too. Bartlett stirred us, but Farnley, sitting there in the sun, saying nothing, stirred us even more. If we couldn't do anything for Kinkaid now, we could for Farnley. He became a hero, just sitting there, the figure which concentrated our purpose.

Thinking about it afterward, I was surprised that Bartlett succeeded so easily. None of the men he was talking to owned any cattle or any land. None of them had any property but their horses and their outfits. None of them were even married, and the kind of women they got a chance to know weren't likely to be changed by what a rustler would do to them. Some out of that many were bound to have done a little rustling on their own, and maybe one or two had even killed a man. But they weren't thinking of those things then, any more than I was. Old Bartlett was amazing. It seemed incredible that so much ferocity hadn't killed him, weak and shaky as he appeared. Instead, it had made him seem straighter and stronger.

"Listen, men," Osgood called. "Listen! This violence is insane! Think, won't you; think. If you were mistaken, if . . ."

But most of the men were already on their horses. Osgood ran to

Davies. "They won't listen to me, Mr. Davies," he babbled. "They won't listen. They never would. Perhaps I'm weak. Any man is weak when nobody cares for the things that mean something to him. But they'll listen to you. You know how to talk to them, Davies. You tell them."

Davies, without moving away from Farnley, said clearly, "Mr. Osgood is right, men. We should wait until—"

Canby interrupted. "You're wasting a lot of time. Whoever you're after has made five miles while you argued."

"You gotta get guns," piped Greene, the kid who had brought the news. "They shot Kinkaid. They got guns."

Only two or three of the men had guns. Gil and I had ours, because we were on the loose and felt better with them. The others told Farnley they'd be back and went off after guns, some of them riding, some running on the walks. A few called to each other, reminding that it might be a long ride, or to bring a rope, or advising where a gun might be borrowed, since most of them were from ranches outside the village. The sun was still bright in the street, but it was a late-in-the-afternoon light. And the wind had changed. The spring feeling was gone. Even right out in the sun it was pretty cold now. I took a look west; the clouds over the mountains were dark under their bellies.

"I'm going to have a drink," Gil said. "I want one hell of a long drink." I followed him inside, and Davies came too. There were already half a dozen men at the bar. Canby had left the door open, and through it I could see Farnley still sitting in his saddle. Nobody was going to change his mind with Farnley sitting there.

"What makes you so hot for a drink?" I asked Gil.

"Nothing; I'm thirsty," he said, drinking one and pouring another. Then he admitted, "Yes, there is a reason. I'd forgot all about it until now. I was layin' up in Montana that winter, stayin' with an old woman. Sittin' right on her front porch, I saw them hang three men on one limb."

He took his other drink down. That didn't worry me now. Feeling this way, he could drink twenty and not know it. He poured another. He talked low and quick, as if he didn't mind my hearing it, but didn't want anyone else to.

"They kicked a barrel out from under each one of them, and the poor bastards kept trying to reach them with their toes." He looked down at his drink. "They didn't tie their legs," he said, "just their arms." After a minute he said, "That was an official posse, sheriff and all. All the same . . ." He started his third drink, but slowly, like he didn't want it much.

"Rustlers?" I asked him.

"Held up a stagecoach," he told me. "The driver was shot."

"Well, they had it coming," I said.

"One of them was a boy," he said. "Just a kid. He was scared to death and kept crying and telling them he hadn't done it. When they put the rope around his neck his knees gave out. He fell off the barrel and nearly choked."

I could see how Gil felt. It wasn't a nice thing to remember, with a job of this kind in front of you. But I could tell Davies was listening to Gil. He wasn't looking at us, but he was just sipping his drink and being too quiet.

"We got to watch ourselves, Gil," I told him, very low, and looking up at the painting of the woman with the parrot.

"To hell with them," he said. But he didn't say it loudly.

"Greene was all mixed up," I said, still muttering over my chin. "He wasn't sure of anything except Kinkaid was shot in the head. But he thought it was about noon."

"I know," Gil said.

Then he said, "They're gettin' back already. Hot for it, ain't they?" It sounded like remembering that Montana job had changed his whole way of looking at things.

I could tell without turning who was coming. There wasn't a big, flat-footed *clop-clop* like horses make on hardpan, but a kind of edgy *clip-clip-clip*. There was only one man around here would ride a mule, at least on this kind of business. That was Bill Winder, who drove the stage between Reno and Bridger's Wells. A mule is tough all right; a good mule can work two horses into the ground and not know it. But there's something about a mule a man can't get fond of; it's like he had no insides, no soul. Winder didn't like mules either, but that's why he rode them. It was against his religion to get on a horse; horses were for driving.

We saw him stop beside Farnley and say something and, when he got his answer, shake his head angrily and spit, then pull his mule into the tie rail with a jerk. Waiting wasn't part of Winder's plan of life either. He believed in action first and make your explanation to fit.

Gabe Hart was with him, on another mule. Gabe was his hostler, a big, ape-built man, stronger than was natural, but weak-minded; not crazy, but childish, like his mind had never grown up. He had a huge face and little, empty eyes. He slept in the stables with his horses, and his knees and elbows were always out of his clothes, and his long hair and beard always had bits of hay and grain chaff in them. Gabe was gentle, though; not a mean streak in him, like there generally is in stupid, very strong men. Gabe was the only man I ever knew who could really love a mule, and with horses he was one of them. That's why Winder kept him. Gabe was no use for anything else, but he could do everything with horses. Outside of horses there were only two things in Gabe's life, Winder and sitting. Winder was his god, and sitting was his way of worshipping. Gabe could sit for hours if there wasn't something to do to a horse.

Winder had a Winchester with him, but he left it against the tie rail and came in, Gabe behind him, then looked at Davies like a stranger, and ordered a whiskey. He drank one down and put his glass out to be filled again. He was a short, stringy blond man, with a freckled face with no beard or mustache but always a short reddish stubble. He had pale blue eyes with a constant hostile stare.

"They're takin' their time, ain't they?" he said.

"They might as well," Davies said. "They haven't much to go on yet."

"They got enough, from what I heard."

"Maybe, but not enough to know what to do."

"How do you mean?"

"Well, for one thing they don't know who did it."

"That's what we aim to find out, ain't it?"

"You can't tell who it might be."

"What the hell does that matter?" Winder said. "I'd string any son-of-a-bitchin' rustler like that." He slapped the bar. "If he was my own brother, I would," he said furiously. "This sorta thing's gotta stop, no matter who's doin' it."

"It has," Davies agreed. "But we don't know how many of them there are, or which way they went, either. There's no use going off half-cocked."

"What the hell way would they go?" Winder asked him. "Out the south end by the draw, wouldn't they? There ain't no other way. They wouldn't head right back up this way, would they, with the whole place layin' for them? You're damn shootin' they wouldn't."

"No," Davies said. He hadn't finished his drink; was just sipping it, but he filled his glass again and asked Winder, "Have one with me?"

"I don't mind," Winder said.

Canby filled Winder's glass.

"No particular hurry, though," Davies went on. "If they're from around here, they aren't going far. If they aren't, they're going a long ways, too long for a few hours to matter when they've already got a big start."

"And how do you know they've got a start?" Winder asked.

"That's what young Greene said."

"Oh, him."

"He was tangled, but if he had anything straight it was the time. He figured Kinkaid must have been killed about noon."

"Well?"

"It's four thirty now. Say they have a four-hour start. You aren't going to ride your head off to pick that up, are you?"

"Maybe not," Winder admitted.

"No," Davies said. "It's a long job at best. It's more than five hundred miles to the first border that will do them any good. Part of that will be a tracking job too. The same way if they're heading for a hideout to let things cool. It'll be dark in a couple of hours. We can take our time and form this posse right."

"Who the hell said anything about a posse?" Winder flared.

"Risley's here," Davies said.

"Risley's been here all summer," Winder said. "It didn't stop Kinkaid gettin' killed, did it?"

"One man can't be every place," I had to chip in. "This is a big valley."

"He could be a hell of a lot more places than Risley is," Winder told me, staring across at me so I wanted to get up and let him have one.

"Risley's a good man," Davies said, "and a good sheriff."

"You 'mind me of Tyler and the preacher," Winder went on. "What have they got us, your good men? A thousand head of cattle gone and a man killed, that's what they got us. We gotta do this ourselves. One good fast job, without no fiddlin' with legal papers, and that's all there'll be to it. You and your posses and waitin'. That kind of law, it gives a murderer plenty of time to get away and cover up, and then helps him find his excuses by the book. I say get goin' before we're cooled off and the lily liver that's in half these dudes gets time to pisen 'em again, so we gotta just set back and listen to Judge Tyler spout his law-and-order junk. God, it makes me sick." He spit on the floor and then glared at Davies.

Davies let him cool. Then he said, without looking up, "Legal action's not always just, that's true."

"You're damn shootin' it ain't," Winder said.

"What would you say real justice was, Bill?"

Winder got cautious. "Whadya mean?" he asked.

"I mean, if you had to say what justice was, how would you put it?"

That wouldn't have been easy for anyone. It made Winder wild. He couldn't stand getting reined down logical.

"It sure as hell ain't lettin' things go till any sneakin' cattle thief can shoot a man down and only get a laugh out of it. It ain't that, anyway," Winder defended.

"No, it certainly isn't that," Davies agreed.

"It's seein' that everybody gets what's comin' to him, that's what it is," Winder said.

Davies thought that over. "Yes," he said, "that's about it."

"You're damn shootin' it is."

"But according to whom?" Davies asked him.

"Whadya mean, 'according to whom'?"

"I mean who decides what everybody's got coming to him?"

Winder looked at us, daring us to grin. "We do," he said belligerently.

"Who are we?"

"Who the hell would we be? The rest of us. The straight ones."

"But how do we decide?" Davies asked, as if it were troubling him.

"Decide what?"

"Who's got what coming to him?"

"How does anybody? You just know, don't you? You know murder's not right and you know rustlin's not right, don't you?"

"Yes, but what makes us feel so sure they aren't?"

"God, what a fool question," Winder said. "They're against the law. Anybody . . ." Then he saw where he was, and his neck began to get red.

But Davies wasn't just being smart. He let his clincher go and made his point that it took a bigger "we" than the valley to justify a hanging, and that the only way to get it was to let the law decide. "If we go out and hang two or three men," he finished, "without doing what the law says, forming a posse and bringing the men in for trial, then, by the same law, we're not officers of justice, but due to be hanged ourselves. Our crime's worse than a murderer's. His act puts him outside the law, but keeps the law intact. Ours would weaken the law."

"But what if the law don't work at all?" Gil said; and Winder grinned.

"Then we have to make it work," Davies said.

"God," Winder said patiently, "that's what we're tryin' to do." And when Davies repeated they would only be doing that if they formed a posse and brought the men in for trial, Winder said, "Yeah; but then if your law lets them go?"

"They probably ought to be let go. At least there'll be a bigger chance that they ought to be let go than that a lynch gang can decide whether they ought to hang."

Then Davies said a lynch gang always acts in a panic, and has to get angry enough to overcome its panic before it can kill, so it doesn't ever really judge, but just acts on what it's already decided to do, each man afraid to disagree with the rest. He tried to prove to us that lynchers knew they were wrong; that their secrecy proved it, and their sense of guilt afterward.

"Did you ever know a lyncher who wasn't afraid to talk about it afterward?" he asked us.

He got warmed up like a preacher on his favorite sermon, and at the end he was pleading with us again, not to go as a lynching party, not to weaken the conscience of the nation, not to commit this sin against society.

"Sin against society," Winder said, imitating a woman with a lisp.

"Yes," Davies repeated, "a sin against society. Law is more than words. True law is the conscience of society. It has taken thousands of years to develop, and it is the greatest quality which has evolved with mankind. It is the spirit of the moral nature of man; it is an existence apart, like God, and as worthy of worship as God."

He stopped, not as if he had finished, but as if he suddenly saw he was wasting something precious.

"Sin against society," Winder repeated the same way, and got up.

Gil got up too. "That may all be true," he said, "but it don't make any difference now. Why didn't you tell them all this out there?"

"I tried to," Davies said, "and Osgood tried. They wouldn't listen. You know that."

"No," Gil said. "Then why tell us?" He included me. "We're just a couple of the boys. We don't count."

Davies said, "Sometimes two or three men will listen."

"Well," Gil said, "we've listened. What can we do?"

Winder grinned like he'd won the argument by a neat point, and he and Gil went to the door.

Outside we could hear the men beginning to come back, the hoofs and harness and low talk. Finally Davies turned his head slowly and looked at me. His mouth had a crooked smile that made me sorry for him.

"Why take it so hard?" I asked him. "You did all you could."

He shook his head. "I failed," he said. "I got talking my ideas. It's my greatest failing."

"They had sense," I said. But I wasn't sure of this myself. I'm slow with a new idea and want to think it over alone.

Davies looked at me. "Will you do me a favor?" he asked all of a sudden.

"That depends," I said.

"I have to stay here," he said. "I have to stop them if I can, till they know what they're doing. If I can make this regular, that's all I ask."

"Yes?"

"I'm going to send Joyce, the clerk from my store, to fetch Risley and Judge Tyler. I want you to go with him. Will you?"

"You know how Gil and I stand here. We came in at a bad time," I said. I didn't like being put over the fence into the open.

"I know," he said, and waited.

"All right," I said unwillingly. "But why do two have to go?"

"Do you know Mapes?" he asked.

"The one they call Butch?"

"That's the one. Risley's made him deputy for times he's out of town, and we don't want Mapes."

"No," I said. I could see why, and I could see why he didn't want Joyce to have to go alone if there was a question of keeping Mapes out of it, though I still thought that was chiefly sucking me in. Mapes was a powerful man and a crack shot with a six-gun, but he was a bully, and like most bullies he was a play-the-crowd man. He wouldn't be any leader.

"Tyler may not help much," Davies said, as if to himself, "but he ought to be here. Risley's the man we want," he told me.

When he saw Joyce he went over and talked to him for a minute. The boy looked scared, and kept nodding his head in little jerks, as if he had the palsy.

"Where you off to?" Gil was asking me, standing beside me.

I rolled a cigarette and took my time to answer. When I'd had a drag I told him. He didn't take it the way I'd thought he would, but looked at me with a lot of questions in his eyes that he didn't ask.

"Davies is right," I said. "Want to come along?"

"Thanks," he said, "but somebody's got to keep this company in good ree-pute." He said it quiet.

The sky was really changing now, fast; it was coming on to storm, or I didn't know signs. Before, it had been mostly sunlight, with only a few cloud shadows. Now it was mostly shadow, with just gleams of sunlight breaking through and shining for a moment on the men and horses in the street, making the guns and metal parts of the harnesses wink and lighting up the big sign on Davies' store.

The wind was flapping the men's garments and blowing out the horses' tails like plumes. The smoke from houses where supper had been started was lining straight out to the east. It was a heavy wind with a damp, chill feel to it, the kind that comes before snow, and it wuthered under the arcade and sometimes whistled, the kind of wind that even now makes me think of Nevada. Out at the end of the street, where it merged into the road to the pass, the look of the mountains had changed too. Before, they had been big and shining, so you didn't notice the clouds much. Now they were dark and crouched down, looking heavier, and it was the clouds coming up so thick and shifting so rapidly that you had to look at instead of the mountains.

Probably partly because of this sky change and partly because a lot of them were newcomers who hadn't heard that there were any doubts about this lynching, the temper of the men in the street had changed too. They weren't fired up the way some of them had been after Bartlett's harangue, but they weren't talking much or joking, and they were all staying on their horses except those that had been in Canby's. Most of them had on stiff cowhide coats, and some even had scarves tied down around their heads under their hats, like you wear on winter range. They all had gun belts, and had ropes tied to their saddles, and a good many had carbines, generally carried across the saddle, but a few in long holsters by their legs, the shoulder curved, metal-heeled, slender stocks showing out at the top. Their roughened faces were set, and their eyes were narrowed, partly against the wind, but partly not.

Every new rider that came in, they'd just glance at Davies out of those narrow eyes, like they hated his guts and figured things were getting too public. And there were new men coming in all the time; about twenty there already. It just seemed funny now to think I'd been listening to an argument about what the soul of the law was. Right here and now was all that was going to count. I felt less than ever like going on any missions for Davies. But then Joyce came over for me, Davies made a motion at us, and I started.

"Take it easy, law-and-order," Gil said to me. "This ain't our picnic."

I was getting touchy, and for a second I thought he was trying to talk me out of lining up with the party that wasn't going to be any too popular, win or lose. I looked around at him a bit hot, I guess, but he just grinned at me and shook his head once, not to say no, but to say it was a tough spot.

Then I knew he wasn't thinking of sides right then, but just of me, me and him, the way it was when we were best. I shook my head at him the same way, and had to grin the same way too. I felt a lot better.

Joyce and I crossed the street, picking our way among the riders, which made us step a bit because the horses were restless. I knew the men were watching us, and I felt queer myself, walking instead of riding, but Joyce had said it wasn't far, and he didn't have a horse. I passed in front of Farnley's horse, but he held him, and didn't say anything. Just when we got to the other side of the street I heard Winder calling me by my last name, but I just kept going.

"Croft," he yelled again, and when I still kept going he yelled louder and angrily, "Croft, tell the Judge he'll have to step pronto if he wants to see us start."

Joyce was breathing in little short whistles, and I knew how he felt. That yell had marked us all right. I thought quickly, in the middle of what I was really thinking, that now I didn't know any of those men; they were strangers and enemies, except Gil. And yet I did know most of them, at least by their faces and outfits, and to talk to, and liked them: quiet, gentle men, and the most independent in the world too, you'd have said, not likely, man for man, to be talked into anything. But now, stirred up or feeling they ought to be, one little yelp about Judge Tyler and I might as well have raped all their sisters, or even their mothers. And the queerest part of it was that there weren't more than two or three, those from Drew's outfit, who really knew Kinkaid; he wasn't easy to know. And the chances were ten to one that a lot more than that among them had, one time or another, done a little quiet brand changing themselves. It wasn't near as uncommon as you'd think; the range was all still pretty well open then, and those riders came from all ends of cow country from the Rio to the Tetons. It wouldn't have been held too much against them either, as long as it wasn't done on a big scale so somebody took a real loss. More than one going outfit had started that way, with a little easy picking up here and there.

"Don't mind that bigmouth," I told Joyce.

I'd underrated the kid. He was scared, all right, but that wasn't what he was going to think about.

"Do you think Mr. Davies can hold them?" he asked.

"Sure he can," I said. Then I asked him, "Does Risley hang out at the Judge's too?"

"When he's here," Joyce said. "We've got to get him, though. We've got to get him anyway."

"Sure," I pacified. "We'll get him."

He led me onto the cross street and we walked faster. There was no boardwalk here, and the street wasn't used much, so my boot-heels sank into the mud. There were a few people standing in front of their houses or on the edge of the street, looking toward the crossing, men in their shirt sleeves, hunched against the wind, but more women, wearing aprons and holding shawls over their hair. They looked at us, not knowing whether to be frightened or to ask us their questions. To try us, one man joked, "Roundup going on?"

"That's it," I gave him back. "Yessir, a roundup."

Joyce thought he ought to say something. "Mr. Davies didn't think they'd go. Not if somebody stood up against them."

I wasn't so sure of that. Most men are more afraid of being thought cowards than of anything else, and a lot more afraid of being thought physical cowards than moral ones. There are a lot of loud arguments to cover moral cowardice, but even an animal will know if you're scared. Davies was resisting something that had immediacy and a strong animal grip, with something remote and mistrusted. He'd have to make his argument look common sense and hardy, or else humorous, and I wasn't sure he could do either.

"Maybe," I said.

"He says they have to get a leader; somebody they can blame."

"Scapegoat," I said.

"That's what he calls it too," Joyce said. "He says that's what anyone has to have, good or bad, before they can get started, somebody they can blame."

"Sometimes it's just that they can't get anywhere without a boss."

"It's the same thing," he argued.

We kept moving. Joyce had to trot a little to catch up with me. Finally I said, "Mr. Davies doesn't think we've got a leader, then?"

"No," Joyce said. "That's why he thought they'd wait."

I gave that a turn and knew he was right. That was half what ailed us; we were waiting for somebody, but didn't know who. Bartlett had done the talking, but talk won't hold. Moore was the only man who could take us, and Moore wouldn't.

"He's not far wrong," I said.

"If we can get Risley," Joyce said, "before they pick somebody . . ."

He really looked at me then, and I saw why Davies might talk to him. He was pimply and narrow and gawky, but his eyes weren't boy's eyes.

We passed a house with a white picket fence, and then another with four purple lilac trees in the yard. Their sweetness was kind of strange, as if we should have been thinking about something else.

"That's the place," Joyce said, pointing across the street.

Judge Tyler's house was one of the brick ones, with a mansard roof, patterns in the shingles, and dormer windows. It was three stories high, with a double-decker veranda, and there were a lot of steps up to the front door. There was a lawn, and lilac bushes, and out back a long carriage house and stable. It was a new place, and the brick looked very pink and the veranda and stonework very white.

"Scrape your boots, put your hat on your arm, and straighten your wig," I told Joyce as we went up onto the porch. He grinned like it hurt.

I gave the doorbell knob a yank. Way inside the house there was a little, jingly tinkle that kept on after I let go of the knob. There were slow, heavy steps inside. Then the door opened. In front of us stood a tall, big-boned woman with a long, mistrustful face and gold-rimmed glasses. She blocked the opening with her hands on her hips, so nobody could have squeezed by, and took a hard look at my gun belt and chaps.

"Well?" she wanted to know.

I figured a soft beginning wasn't going to hurt, and took off my hat.

"The Judge in, ma'am?"

"Yes, he is."

I waited for the rest, but it didn't come.

"Could we see him?" I asked.

"You got business?"

I was getting a little sore. "No," I said, "we just dropped over for tea."

"Humph," she said, and didn't crack a bit.

"Mr. Davies sent us, ma'am," Joyce explained. "It's important, ma'am. The Judge would want to know."

"Mr. Davies, eh?" she said. "That's different. But it's not regular office hours," she added.

I started to follow her in, and she stopped.

"You wait here," she told us. "I'll ask the Judge if he'll see you. What's your name?"

I told her. She grunted again and went about five steps in the dark, red-carpeted hall, and gave a couple of sharp raps on a door, half turning around at the same time to keep an eye on us. A big voice boomed out like it had been looking forward for hours to that knock. "Come in, come in."

She gave us another look, and went in and closed the door firmly behind her.

"That the Judge's wife?" I asked.

Joyce shook his head. "She died before I came here. That's his housekeeper, Mrs. Larch."

"Well," I said, "you can see why the Judge has times when he don't seem able to make up his mind."

The office door opened again, and Mrs. Larch came out. She closed the door and advanced on us, but this time, when she halted, she left us room to squeeze by.

"Go on in," she ordered.

"Is the sheriff here too?" I asked her.

"No, he isn't," she said as she closed the outside door behind us.

"Do you know where he is, Mrs. Larch? The sheriff, I mean?" Joyce asked.

"No, I don't," she said, and went toward the back of the house.

After that I knocked at the office door too. The same big voice called, "Come in, come in." When we got inside the big voice kept booming. "Well, well, Croft; how are things out in your neck of the woods?"

"All right, I guess," I said.

The Judge looked the same as I'd always seen him outside—wide and round, in a black frock coat, a white big-collared shirt, and a black string tie. He had a large pasty face, with folds of fat over the collar, bulging brown eyes, and a mouth with a shape like a woman's mouth, but with a big, pendulous lower lip. He got up from his rolltop desk in the corner and came to meet me with his hand out, as if he were conferring a special favor. The Judge never missed a chance on that sort of thing. But not only was Risley not there, Mapes was. He was sitting with his chair tilted back, right next to the door. His gun belt and sombrero and coat were hanging on the hooks above him.

"Well, well," said the Judge, smoothing back his thick black mane of hair. "What can I do for you gentlemen?"

"We're here for Mr. Davies," I said. "Could we see you alone for a minute, Judge?"

Mapes let his chair down, but it wasn't to go. He sat there looking at us.

"Mr. Davies said particularly, just you and Mr. Risley, sir," I said.

"Well . . ." said the Judge, and looked at Mapes.

"Risley ain't here," Mapes said. "I'm actin' sheriff. Anything you can tell Risley, you can tell me." He thumbed the badge on his vest.

"That's right, quite right," the Judge assured us. "The sheriff deputized Mr. Mapes before me last night."

I tried to pick up the ground we'd lost. "Where'd he go?" I asked Mapes.

"Down to Drew's, early this mornin'."

It was more than ten miles down to Drew's. "When'll he be back?" I asked.

"He didn't say. Maybe not for a couple of days." He grinned like he wanted to see me try to get out of that one. Then he stood up. "I saw that kid Greene, from down to Drew's, come by here hell-for-leather half an hour ago. I thought it didn't look like no pleasure jaunt. What's up?"

"Butch," I said, "it's not us. We're here for Mr. Davies. Now if you'd let us have a minute alone, we'll give the Judge our story, and then if he thinks it's your job, he'll tell you."

"Certainly, certainly," the Judge said. "If the matter touches your official capacity, I shall let you know at once, Mapes."

Mapes stood with his feet apart and stared at us. He had a huge chest and shoulders, and a small head with a red fleshy face and small black eyes. Like Winder, he always looked angry. "All right," he said finally, as if he'd decided that whatever we had to say couldn't matter much anyway.

With Mapes out of the way, Joyce spoke rapidly. I went over to the front window, but listened while the Judge, all business, asked Joyce questions about who was there and just what Greene had said. He asked him other things too, most of which Joyce couldn't answer very well. But I figured my job, which was bodyguard, was done, and didn't horn in. From the window I could see Mapes standing at the top of the porch steps with his thumbs in his belt. Joyce was getting excited.

"It's not that Mr. Davies doesn't want them to go," he explained for the third time. "He just doesn't want it to be a lynching."

"No. Can't let that sort of thing start, of course," the Judge agreed.

Joyce explained again how he wanted a posse sworn in.

"Assuredly," the Judge said. "Only proper procedure. Anything else inevitably leads to worse lawlessness, violence. I've been telling them that for years."

"So Mr. Davies asks will you come at once, sir," Joyce said. "The men are already gathering, and they wouldn't listen to him or Mr. Osgood."

I saw a rider coming down the street at a lope. He was one of the men who had been at Canby's when Greene came. He saw Mapes and yelled something to him. Mapes called out to him, and the rider pulled around, yelling something more.

"Mr. Davies wanted you and Mr. Risley to come, sir," Joyce was pleading.

"Eh? Oh, yes, yes. But Risley isn't here."

"If you would come, sir. You could talk to them."

"It's not my position—" the Judge began. Then he said, angrily, "No, no. It's not the place of either a judge or a lawyer. It lies in the sheriff's office. I have no police authority."

The rider had wheeled his horse toward the main street and pushed him up to a lope again. Mapes was coming in. I turned around.

"Risley's at Drew's?" I asked.

"Yes, yes. Thought there might be something—" the Judge began.

I cut in. "If you could get the men to promise they'd take orders from Risley . . . They'll have to go that way anyhow."

Mapes came in, leaving the door open again. He didn't look at us, or say anything, but took his gun down and buckled it on.

"Where are you going, Mapes?" the Judge fumed.

"Rustlers got Kinkaid this morning," Mapes said. "There's a

posse forming, just in case you hadn't heard. That's sheriff's work, ain't it, Judge?" He reached his coat down.

"That's no posse, Mapes," the Judge roared. "It's a lawless mob, a lynching mob, Mapes."

"It'll be a posse when I get there, Judge. I'll deppitize 'em all proper," Mapes said. His coat was on, and he put his sombrero on the back of his head.

"You can't do it," the Judge told him. "Risley's the only one empowered to deputize."

Mapes started to answer back. He put one foot upon his chair, and spit over on the corner stove first. He liked it when he had the Judge this way, and didn't want to hurry it too much. There was going to be a wrangle, but I could only see one end of it. I saw Joyce look from one to the other of them. Then he slipped out the door. I started out after Joyce. We'd give Davies warning anyhow, though I didn't see what he could do with it.

I stopped in the door and said, loud enough so the Judge could hear over what Mapes was saying, "I'll tell Davies you're coming then, Judge."

"Yes, yes, of course," he said, just glancing away from Mapes for an instant and giving me a big, fixed smile. I figured that had him hooked the best I could manage, and ducked out quick, not stopping when I heard him call out in a different voice, showing he knew now what I'd said. "Wait, wait a moment. . . ." I passed Mrs. Larch in the hall, gave her a wink, and went on out without bothering to close the front door.

Joyce, running ahead, was nearly at the crossing already. He could tell Davies all there was to tell. I eased off when I'd got beyond fair cry of the Judge's house. There's better things to run in than high-heeled boots, and it looked like the word had really got around now. I didn't want to make a fool of myself. People in front of every house were craning down toward the corner, and I passed women in the street who were trying to call back their children. One of them looked at me with a scared face. She looked at my gun belt and twisted her apron. But it wasn't me that scared her.

"The horses," she said, like I knew everything she was thinking. "Send Tommy home if you see him, please," she begged. She didn't even know she didn't know me.

At the next house a man in chaps was getting on his horse. There was a Winchester on his saddle. A woman, his wife I suppose, was standing right beside the horse and holding on to the man's leg with both hands. She was looking up at him and trying to say something and trying not to cry.

The man wasn't answering, but just shaking his head. His face was set and angry, like so many faces I'd been seeing, and he was trying to get her to let go of him before the horse, which was nervy, stepped on her. He was trying to do it without being rough, but she kept hanging on. A little kid, maybe two or three years old, was standing out in front of the house and crying hard, with her hands right down at her sides.

More people than before were out in the middle of the street watching the crossing, where they could see one of the riders who had let his horse go that far. The excitement had gone through the whole village. And there were people along all the walks now too, a few old men and a good many women and excited small boys, some of the women holding smaller children by the hands to keep them from getting out where the horses were.

In the edge of the street opposite Canby's, where things were thickest, I saw a little fellow no bigger than the one that had been crying because her mother and father were arguing. He was barefoot and had on patched overalls, and had a big head of curls bleached nearly white. He was all eyes for what was going on, and stood there squirming his toes on the hard mud without a notion where he was. I didn't see any other kid as small who wasn't attached, so I figgered he must be Tommy.

"Young fellow, your mother's looking for you," I told him.

He said for me to look at the horsies. It was too bad to spoil his big time, but he was in a bad place. I put on a hard face and put it right down close to him and said, "Tommy, you git for home," and switched him around and patted him on the pants. I guess I overdid it, because he backed as far as the boardwalk and then burst out bawling. I started toward him to ease it off a little, but when he saw me coming he let out a still louder wail and lit out for the corner at a jog that I figured was going to take him all the way. Well, I probably wouldn't have to see that woman again anyway.

When I got across the street to Davies he was done talking to

Joyce, and was standing there staring blankly at the men, his face tired as it had been after the talk in the bar, but the jaw muscles still bulging.

"Bartlett not back yet?" I asked him.

He shook his head.

"Wonder what's holding him?" I said.

He shook his head again.

"I'm sorry about Risley," I said, "but I think the Judge will come."

He nodded. Then he brought his eyes back to see me, and smiled a little. "There wasn't anything else you could do," he said. "Maybe there isn't anything any of us can do. They've made a show out of it now."

"Yeh," I said, looking at the riders in the street. There was a change in them. What with the wait, and the women standing on the walk watching them, they looked as grim as ever, but not quite honest. There was a lot of playacting in it now, and they were having more trouble with the horses than they had to.

I told Davies what I'd told the Judge about their having to go by Drew's anyway. "You could get them to promise to pick Risley up, and he'd take care of it."

He considered that and nodded more vigorously. He thought it was a clincher too. "It's queer what simple things you don't think of when you're excited," he said. "There's a simple little thing, and it's the whole answer."

Then he added, "We'll have to let the Judge tell them, though. They wouldn't listen to me." He went on as if he were thinking it over to himself. "Yes, that will do it." Then he said to me, "Thank you. I know it was a hard place for you."

"That's all right," I said.

It was just about then that one of the crowd, a man called Smith, being tight and bored, picked this time to play the clown. "Coming along, Sparks?" he called out.

All the men grinned, finding that old joke funny about a darky always being easy to scare. I hadn't noticed Sparks, but I saw him now, standing on the other side of the street with that constant look of his of pleasant but not very happy astonishment.

Sparks was a queer, slow, careful fellow, who got his living as a sort of general handyman to the village, splitting wood, shoveling snow, things like that. He was a tall, stooped, thin, chocolate-colored man with kinky hair, gray as if powdered, and big, limp hands and feet. When he talked his deep, easy voice always sounded anxious to please, slow and cheerful, but when he sang, which he did about most any work which had a regular rhythm, like sweeping or raking, he sang only slow, unhappy hymn tunes. He was anything but a fast worker, but he did things up thorough and neat, and he was honest to the bone. It was said that he'd been a minister back in Ohio before he came west, but he didn't talk about himself, outside of what he was doing right at the time, so nobody really knew anything about him, yet they all liked him, and there wasn't anything they wouldn't trust him with. They made jokes about him and to him, but friendly ones, the sort they might make to any town character who could take joking right.

When the men grinned they all looked across at Sparks. He was embarrassed.

"No, suh, I don't guess so," he said, shaking his head but smiling to show he wasn't offended.

"You better come, Sparks," Smith yelled again. "That is unless Mr. Osgood here is going along. He has first call, of course, being in practice." The men laughed.

"I'm not going, if it interests you," Osgood said, with surprising sharpness for him. "If you men choose to act in violence, I wash my hands. Willful murderers are not company for a Christian."

That stung, but not effectively. A bawling out from a man like Osgood doesn't sit well. Some of the men still grinned a little, but the sour way.

"I was afraid the shepherd would feel his flock was a bit too far astray for him to risk herding them this time," Smith lamented. Osgood was hit, and looked it. He knew the men tolerated him at best, and the knowledge, even when he could delude himself into believing it private, made it doubly difficult for him to keep trying to win them. Sometimes, as now, he was even pitiable. But he had an incurable gift of robbing himself even of their pity. After a moment he answered, "I am sorry for you, all of you."

"Don't cry, Parson," Smith warned him. "We'll do the best we can without you. I guess it's up to you, Sparks," he yelled.

Sparks surprised us. "Maybe it is, Mistah Smith," he said seriously.

"Somebody ought to go along that feels the way Mistah Osgood and I do; beggin' yoh pardon, Mistah Osgood. If he don' feel it's right foh him to go, it looks like I'm the only one left."

This unassuming conviction of duty, and its implication of distinct right and wrong, was not funny.

Sparks came across the street in his slow, dragging gait. "But I'm a slow walkah," he said, smiling especially at Winder. "You wouldn't have another mule I could borrow, would you, Mistah Windah?"

Winder didn't know what to say, knowing it was still a joke except to Sparks.

"They're kidding you, Sparks," Canby said from the door. He liked the fellow.

"I know that, Mistah Canby," Sparks said, grinning again. "But I think maybe Mistah Smith was accidentally right when he said I should go."

"You really want to go?" Winder asked him.

"Yessuh, Mistah Windah, I do."

Winder studied him, then shrugged and said, "There's a horse in the shed you can use. There's no saddle, but he's got a headstall on, and there's a rope in the back stall you can use for a bridle. But move along, or you'll get left. We're only waiting for Mr. Bartlett and his boys."

Sparks went on down the street toward the stage depot, walking quickly for him. You could tell by his carriage that he was pleased in the way of a man doing what he ought to do.

Sparks had given a kind of body, which the men could recognize, to an ideal which Davies' argument hadn't made clear and Osgood's self-doubt had even clouded. I thought it would be a good time for Davies to tackle them again, and looked at him. He saw the chance too, but found it hard to get started, and then waited too long. A rider called out, "Here comes Ma," and there was a cheering sound to greet her. Here was a person could head them up.

Ma was up the street quite a ways when they hailed her, but she waved at them, a big, cheerful, unworried gesture. It made me feel good, too, just to see Ma and the way she waved. She was riding, and was dressed like a man, in jeans and a shirt and vest, with a blue bandanna around her neck and an old sombrero on her head. She had a Winchester across her saddle, and after she waved she held it up, and then held up a coil of rope she had hitched to her saddle. There was another cheer, stronger than the first, that showed how much better the men were feeling. She changed the whole attitude in two moves, and from a quarter mile off.

Jenny Grier was the name of the woman we called Ma. She was middle-aged and massive, with huge, cushiony breasts and rump, great thighs and shoulders, and long, always unkempt gray hair. Her wide face had fine, big gray eyes in it, but was fat and folded, and she always appeared soiled and greasy. There were lively, and some pretty terrible, stories about her past, but now she kept a kind of boardinghouse on the cross street, and it was always in surprisingly good order, considering how dirty she was about herself. She was a lot more than ordinarily set against what she thought was wrongdoing.

In ways, I think she was crazy, and that all her hates and loves came out of thinking too much about her own past. Most of the time, though, she was big and easy, and she had the authority of a person who knew her own mind and was past caring what anybody else thought about anything. She had a way of talking to us in our own language so we'd laugh and still listen—the style Judge Tyler would like to have had. I knew that, at least until she had seen the victims in the flesh, she'd be as much for lynching a rustler as Winder or Bartlett. The only thing that made me wonder how she'd turn was that she liked Davies quite a lot.

She was greeted right and left when she joined us, and she spoke to Gil and me with the others, calling me boy, as she had when I'd stayed at her place, so we stood a lot better with the rest just on that. Then she started asking questions, and they told her what they knew, which she saw right off, from the different versions, wasn't straight. She set out to straighten it. It wasn't that she was trying to be boss. She simply wanted things in order in her mind when she had anything to do, and in putting them in order she just naturally took over.

When they told her about Davies she just looked down at him standing on the walk and grinned and asked him if he wasn't going. Davies said he was if they went right, if anybody really needed to go. He explained that Risley was already down at Drew's, and that Drew had a dozen men down there, and that he thought it would be just good sense not to go unless we were sent for by Risley, who would really know what was going on. There was muttering around him at that. I was surprised myself. So that was why he'd thought that little fact could do a lot; he believed he could use it to stop them from going at all.

Ma said to him, "Art, you read too many books," and began to dig into young Greene, calling him son, and acting as if what he thought was just as important as what he knew. At that she boiled it down better than anybody else had. Kinkaid had been killed way down in the southwest corner of the valley, eight miles below the ranch. They didn't know just when, but it must have been noon or earlier, because a couple of the riders had picked up his horse clear over by the ranch road, and at about two o'clock had found Kinkaid lying on his back in the sun in a dry wash under the mountains. Greene didn't know if there were any more cattle gone; they hadn't been able to distinguish the rustlers' tracks. Too many cattle had been working over the range there.

Ma kept him toned down except on that one thing, that Kinkaid had been shot through the head. That was the one thing he seemed to have clear without question. He had kept on saying that to the men too. It impressed him that Kinkaid had been shot through the head, as if he could feel it more, as if he would have felt better if Kinkaid had been shot in the belly or in the back, or anywhere but in the head. When Ma asked him, he admitted that he hadn't seen Kinkaid, but that the man who told him had. No, he hadn't seen the sheriff down there; it must have been three o'clock before they sent him to Bridger's, and he hadn't seen the sheriff all day.

Ma said to Davies, "I guess we're goin', Art; as quick as Bartlett gets here."

Somebody said, "He's comin' now."

The men who weren't mounted climbed up, Gil and I with them. Only Davies and Osgood and Joyce were left standing on the walk, and Canby on the steps. Sparks was back too, on an old and sick-looking horse, with a wheat sack for a saddle.

Davies said, "At least wait for Judge Tyler," but no one listened.

Bartlett came up at a lope, followed by his son Carl, the blond one. The other son, Nate, wasn't with him.

"Carl was riding," Bartlett explained. "We had to get him in. Tetley not here?" he asked, looking around. And then, "We'll have to wait for Tetley. Nate's gone for him."

"What do we need with God-almighty Tetley?" Winder said. But he didn't say it loudly; if I hadn't been right next to him, I wouldn't have heard it. All the men were uneasy, but not loud. They were irritated at the further delay, but they were quiet about it, nearly sullen. It was news if Tetley was coming. It would make a difference; even Ma was afraid of Tetley.

Excepting Drew, Tetley was the biggest man in the valley, and he'd been there a lot longer than Drew. He'd been the first big rancher in the valley, coming there the year after the Civil War. On the west edge of town he'd built a white wooden mansion with pillars, like a southern plantation home, and bordered the big grounds around it with a white picket fence. The lawns were always cut, and there were shrubbery and flower beds, a stone fountain where birds drank, and benches set about under the trees. Tetley was like his house, quiet and fenced away; something we never felt natural with, but didn't deride either. Except for the servants, he had only his son, Gerald, living with him now, and they didn't get on. Tetley had been a Confederate cavalry officer and was the son of a slave owner, and he had that kind of a code, and a sharp, quiet head for management. Gerald was always half sick, kept to himself, stayed in the big library as much as his father would let him, and hated the ranching life.

Things had been better between them before Mrs. Tetley had died; she had acted as a go-between, and even as a shield for Gerald. She'd been such a charming little thing herself that nothing could be very unpleasant around her. But when she died each of them had become only more what he was. People who had been there said the house was like it never had the dust covers off the furniture now, and Tetley, though he wouldn't tolerate a word about the boy from anyone else, was himself ashamed of him, and a hard master.

I knew that if Tetley came he'd take over. Wherever he came things always quieted down, and nothing sounded important except what Tetley had to say. That was because nothing else seemed important to Tetley either. A man so sure of himself can always sound important if he isn't a windbag, and Tetley was no windbag.

The word that Tetley was coming gave Davies a little more time, if that could do him any good now. Tetley wouldn't be coming to do Bartlett a favor, and if he objected to the lynching on principle, which wasn't likely, he still wouldn't be coming down himself to stop it. There was only one reason that I could see that Tetley might be coming; it would be because he wanted the lynching to take place.

Davies must have figured the same way, but he was still going to make a try. I saw him talking hard and quickly to Joyce again, and then Joyce, looking more frightened than ever, went off down the street at a run, and Davies went out to talk to Bartlett. Bartlett wasn't so wild anymore, just touchy; he answered a bit short, but didn't blow off. Davies knew better than to argue the soul of society with Bartlett; he just stuck to trying to get a promise Bartlett wouldn't act without Risley. He stayed friendly while he made his points, always seeming to be making just suggestions, and asking Bartlett's opinion, and Ma's, and even Winder's. The men let him talk because they had to wait anyhow. But Davies hadn't got anywhere when the Judge and Mapes appeared.

When they pulled up, just on the edge of the crowd of riders, everything was silent, even the people on the walks waiting to see what the Judge would say. They didn't have much respect for the Judge, but he was the law, and they waited to see what line he would take. The Judge felt the hostility and was nervous about the quiet; he made a bad start, taking off his hat by habit, like he was starting an oration, and raising his voice more than he had to.

"I understand how it is, men," he began, and went on about their long tolerance, and their losses, and the death of a dear friend—a long apology for what he was working up to.

One of the men called, "Cut the stumping, Judge," and when the Judge hesitated, "It's all been said for you, Tyler. All we want's your blessing."

Davies came over beside the Judge's horse before the Judge could start again, and said something; he didn't want Tyler to get into an oration any more than the rest did.

"Certainly, certainly, Mr. Davies," the Judge said. "Just the point I was coming to. Men," he addressed us, "you cannot flinch from what you believe to be your duty, of course, but I'm sure you would not wish to act in the very spirit which begot the deed you would punish."

"By the time you got us ready to act, Tyler," the man named Smith shouted, "the rustlers could be over the Rio." There was agreement; others called ribald advice. Some jeered, and the joking rose to shouting. Ma leaned on her saddle directly in front of the Judge and grinned at him. The Judge's neck and jowls began to swell slowly and turn red.

In the general roar you could hear Farnley's voice, so furious it was high and breaking. "For God's sake, Butch, let's get out of this."

Horses began to mill and yank, and the riders chose to let them. A woman, holding on to a post of the arcade with one hand, leaned out and shrieked at us. She was a tall, sallow, sooty-looking woman, with black hair streaming down and her sunbonnet fallen back off her head so she looked wild. She kept screaming something about Kinkaid. Smith called out to know what Kinkaid was to her.

"More than he was to any of you, it looks like," she screamed back at him.

Some of the women, too, called out at us then, laughing angrily and jibing. Still others, who had men in the street, were quiet and scared-looking. One small boy, being yanked about by his mother, began to cry. This scared the other children.

Davies hadn't paid any attention to the uproar, but talked up earnestly to the Judge. He got the Judge calmed a little. He nodded and said something.

"Where's Greene?" Ma Grier called back. Things quieted down. "Greene," she called to him, "come on up here. The Judge wants to talk to you."

The rest of us wanted to hear, and tried to bunch around the talkers, but the horses kept sidling out, and were blowing and hammering and making leather squeal. We couldn't hear much, but only catch glimpses of young Greene on his horse, facing the Judge and making answers. They didn't appear to be getting anywhere; the kid grinned sardonically a couple of times.

Then, apparently, Davies took over again. The kid began giving answers and not looking so sure. The men right around them had quieted down a lot. Though we couldn't hear anything, we could feel that the drift was changing. Men close in began to look at each other. The temper was out of them. When, after four or five minutes, the woman with the black hair wanted to know if they were holding a prayer meeting, one of the men angrily called to her to shut up.

It became quiet enough to hear the voices, the kid's choked and stubborn, Davies' easy in short, even questions, and then the Judge's, his voice being so heavy we could catch a word here and there. Then the kid was let out of the ring. His face was red, and he wouldn't look at any of us, or answer. When Winder asked him a question he only shrugged his shoulders.

Next Davies came through the crowd. At the edge of the arcade he climbed up onto the tie rail and stood there, holding on to a post to steady himself. He didn't call out, but just waited until it was quiet. Most of us reined around to listen to him; only Farnley and young Greene stayed clear out, Farnley cursing us for listening to more such lily-livered talk.

"We don't know anything about those rustlers," Davies told us, "or whether they were rustlers, or who shot Kinkaid. Young Greene there wasn't trying to make trouble; he was doing what he thought he ought to do, what he was told to do. But he got excited; he was sent to fetch the sheriff, but on the way up he got to thinking about it, and forgot what he should do, and did what seemed to him like the quickest thing. Really, he doesn't know anything about it. He didn't see any rustlers or any killer. He didn't even see Kinkaid. He only heard what Olsen told him, and Olsen was in a hurry. All that Olsen told him, when we get down to the facts, was that Kinkaid had been shot, that they'd found him in the draw, and that the boy was to come to town for the sheriff. That's not much to go on.

"Then there's another thing. It's late now. If it was a gang that Kinkaid ran into, they must have gone out by the south pass, as they did before." Davies went on to show us that it was twenty miles to that pass; it would be dark before we got there, and the rustlers had at least a five- or six-hour start of us. He showed us that the sheriff had been down there since early morning, that there were a dozen men there if he wanted them, and pointed out that it wasn't the sheriff who had sent for us, that nobody had sent for us, that Greene had been sent only for the sheriff, and that if the sheriff had wanted more men, we'd have heard from him by now.

"It's my advice, men, for what it's worth," Davies concluded, "that you all come in and have a drink on me. . . ."

"Drinks," said Canby from the door, "on the house. But only one round, by God. I'm not filling any bucket bellies."

"Our friend Canby offers the drinks," Davies said, "and I'll make it two. I guess I owe it. Then, I'd say, we'd all better go home and have supper, and get a good night's sleep. If we're wanted, we'll hear. I sent Joyce to the ranch to find out what the sheriff has to say. If any of you want to stay in town, Mrs. Grier can put you up, or Canby, or the inn, if they can still get the doors open. And I can bed two myself."

"I can take six," Canby said, "if they don't mind sleeping double. And no charge either."

Ma, feeling defeated, was a bit surly, but she had to offer rooms too. "Only," she told them belligerently, "any lazy puncher that holes up with me is going to pay for his grub. I'm no charity organization."

They jeered her cheerfully, and she seemed to feel better. Still they didn't break up, though, or get off their horses. Neither did I; I didn't want to look like I was anxious to quit; not any more than anybody else.

"It's not like you were giving up, boys," Davies told us. "It's just good sense. If it's a short chase, it's over by now. If it's a long one, the sheriff will let you know, and you'll have time to get ready."

"I'm settin' 'em up, boys," Canby called.

The riders closest in began to dismount. They felt foolish, didn't look at each other much, and made bad jokes about how old they were getting. But I guess they felt chiefly the way I did. I hadn't had much stomach for the business from the beginning. I got down too. Gil tied up beside me.

"Well, the little bastard pulled it," he said. "Jees, and just when I thought for once there'd be something doin'." But he wasn't sore.

We heard the Judge calling, "Going home, Jeff?" We looked. Farnley was riding off down the street. Winder was with him, and of course Winder's half-wit servant, Gabe. He didn't pay any attention, and the Judge called again, bellowing this time, ordering Jeff to come back.

Jeff came back. When the Judge saw his face he explained, "You might as well have a shot with us, Jeff. It'll be cold riding. You don't need to worry. This business will be taken care of."

Farnley rode his horse straight in until it was shouldering the Judge's. In the Judge's face, as if spitting on him, Farnley told him, "Yeh, but I know now who's going to take care of it. The bastard that shot Larry Kinkaid ain't comin' in here for you to fuddle with your damned lawyer's tricks for six months. Kinkaid didn't have six months to decide if he wanted to die, did he?"

"Now look here, Jeff . . ." the Judge began.

Davies went out and stood by Jeff's horse. "Jeff," he said, "Jeff, you know nobody in this country is going to let a thing like this go. Risley is a good man, Jeff; he'll get him. And there aren't twelve men in the West that wouldn't hang him."

The rest of us were keeping out of it, except Gil. He was unhitching again. "By God," he told me, with pleasure, "if he goes, I'm going. That won't be no hanging; that'll be a fight."

We'd all been watching this business so close that we didn't see Tetley coming until Winder pointed, and Farnley pulled around to look. With military rigidity, Tetley was riding toward us on his tall palomino. He wore a Confederate field coat with the epaulets and collar braid removed, and a Confederate officer's hat, but his gray trousers were tucked into an ordinary pair of cowboy boots. There was a gun belt strapped around his waist, over the coat. It had a flap holster, like a cowboy would never wear, which let show just the butt of a pearl-handled Colt.

Behind him, like aides-de-camp, almost abreast, were three riders: his son, Gerald, his Mex hand called Amigo, and Nate Bartlett.

When he had drawn up, his three riders stopping behind him, he looked us over, his small, lean, gray-looking face impassive; he reviewed us. Irony was the constant expression of Tetley's eyes, dark and maliciously ardent under his thick black eyebrows. His hair, an even gray, was heavy, cut off straight at his coat collar, and curling up a little. There were neat, thin sideburns to the lower lobes of his ears, and a still thinner gray mustache went clear to the corners of his mouth without covering the upper lip, which was long, thin, inflexibly controlled, but as sensitive as a woman's. He was a small, slender man who appeared frail and as if dusted all over, except his eyes and brows, with a fine gray powder. Yet, as he sat quietly, rigidly, his double-reined bridle drawn up snugly in his left hand in a fringed buckskin glove, his right arm hanging straight down, we all sat or stood quietly too. He addressed Tyler as the man who should be in authority.

"Disbanding?"

Tyler avoided the condemnation. "Davies convinced us, Major Tetley."

"So?" Tetley said. "Of what, Mr. Davies?" he asked him.

Even Davies was confused. He began an explanation that sounded more like an excuse than a plea. Nate Bartlett cut him short, speaking to Tetley.

"I guess they don't know about their having gone by the pass, sir."

Tetley nodded. Davies looked from one to the other of them uncertainly.

"You were acting on the supposition that the raiders left by the south draw, I take it, Mr. Davies?" said Tetley.

"Yes," Davies said doubtfully.

"They didn't." Tetley smiled. "They left by the pass."

We knew what he meant. He meant Bridger's Pass, which went through the mountains to the west; it was part of the stage road to Pike's Hole, the next grazing range over, which had a little town in it like Bridger's Wells. It was a high pass, going up to about eight thousand. Snow closed it in the winter, and with the first thaws the creek came down beside it like a steep river, roaring and splashing in the narrows; then it bent south in the meadows and went brimming down toward Drew's and through the draw at the south. The west road from Drew's came up along the foothills and joined the stage road right at the foot of the pass. It was only a little off this west road that Greene thought Kinkaid had been found. If the rustlers had gone by the pass, it changed the whole picture. Then it was the sheriff who was off the track. If he'd gone to the draw, toward that branding camp Kinkaid had found, he'd be twenty miles off. We began to really listen.

"By the pass, from the south end?" Davies said. "That would be crazy." He didn't sound convinced.

Tetley still smiled. "Not so crazy, perhaps," he said, "knowing how crazy it would look; or if you lived in Pike's Hole."

"You seem pretty sure," Ma said.

"Amigo saw them," Tetley said.

Half a dozen of us echoed that—"Saw them?" Farnley came back in, Winder and Gabe with him.

"He was coming back from Pike's and had trouble getting by them in the pass."

"Trouble?" Mapes asked importantly.

The Judge was just sitting in his saddle and staring at Tetley. Osgood, I thought, was going to cry. It was hard, when it had all been won. And Davies was standing there as if somebody had hit him but not quite dropped him.

"*Si*," Amigo said for himself. He was grinning, and had very white teeth in a face darker than Sparks'. He liked the attention he was getting. Tetley didn't look around, but let him talk.

"He not see me, I think," Amigo explained. "It was low down, where I can still get out from the road. I take my horse into the hollow place so they can get by. At first I think I say hello when they come; I have no to smoke left by me. Then I think it funny to drive the cattle then."

"Cattle," Moore said sharply.

"But sure," Amigo said. He grinned at Moore. "Why you think I have to get out of the road?"

"Go on," Moore said.

"Well," Amigo said, "when I think that, I be quiet. Then, when I see what marks those cattle have, I be very quiet; very slow I take my horse behind the bush, and we be still." He explained his conduct. "See, I have not the gun with me." He slapped his hip.

"What were the marks?" Mapes asked.

"What you think? On the throat, swinging nice, three little what-you-call-hims—" He didn't need to say any more. We all knew Drew's dewlap mark.

"Why, the dirty rats," Gil said. "To kill a man, and still risk a drive!"

"I told you, didn't I?" old Bartlett cried. "Let them get away with it a few times, I said, and there's no limit to what they'll try."

Davies was looking at Amigo. "Were they all Drew's?" he asked.

"You can't get around it that way," Bartlett yelped. "With roundup just over they'd still be bunched. Ain't that right, Moore?"

"That's right," Moore said.

"How many of them?" Farnley asked Tetley.

"About forty head," Tetley answered. "That's what you said, isn't it, Amigo?"

"*Si,*" said Amigo, grinning.

"No; I mean rustlers," Farnley said.

"Three, eh, Amigo?"

"*Si,* they was three."

"Did you know any of them?" Ma asked Amigo.

Amigo shook his head. "I not ever see these men before," he said, "not any of them."

"Well, you can't find a way out of this one, can you?" Farnley asked. But he didn't look at Davies. He seemed to be asking us all. Davies was looking at the Judge, but the Judge couldn't think of anything to say.

Davies looked whipped. Until then I hadn't known how hard he was taking this; I'd felt it was just a kind of contest between his ideas and our feelings. Now I saw he was feeling it too. But I knew that I, for one, wasn't with him. I untied and mounted. Others were doing the same. Some slipped in to claim their drink from Canby, but came right out again.

Davies, without much conviction, tried Tetley. "Major Tetley," he said, "it's late. You can't get them tonight."

"If we can't," Tetley told him, "we can't get them at all. It's going to storm; snow, I think. We have time. They will move slowly with those cattle, and in the pass there is no place for them to branch off."

"Yes," admitted Davies, "yes, that's true." He ran a hand through his hair as if he were puzzled.

"What time did Amigo see them?" Ma asked.

"About four o'clock, I believe. Wasn't it, Amigo?"

"*Si.*"

"In the lower pass at four," said Farnley. "Sure we can get 'em."

"You were a long time bringing the word, Major," the Judge said. I was surprised to hear him still sounding like a friend of Davies'.

Tetley looked at him with that same smile. It had a different meaning every time he used it.

"I wanted my son to go along," he said. "He was out on the range."

Young Tetley was sitting tensely in his saddle. His face got red, but he gave no other signs of having heard. We all had the same notion, I guess, that young Tetley hadn't been on the range at all. But nobody would have said so, and it didn't matter.

Davies made one more try. "The sheriff should be here," he protested.

"Isn't he?" Tetley asked. "We must do what we can, then," he said.

"Major Tetley," Davies pleaded, "you mustn't let this be a lynching...."

"It's scarcely what I choose, Davies," Tetley said. His voice was dry and disgusted.

"You'll bring them in for trial, then?"

"I mean that I am only one of those affected. I will abide by the majority will."

Davies looked around, but he didn't find friends. I didn't look at him myself. We knew what we were after now, and where, and it encouraged us to know there were only three rustlers. We'd thought, perhaps, if they were bold enough to work right in daylight on a small range, there might be twenty of them.

The Judge expanded and said, "Tetley, you know what's legal in a case like this as well as I do. Davies is only asking what any law-abiding man should choose to do without the asking. He wants the posse to act under a properly constituted officer of the law."

"Risley made me deputy," Mapes said loudly.

The Judge went on. "This action is illegal, Major." Tetley stared at him without any smile. "In a measure I sympathize with it," the Judge admitted. "Sympathize. The circumstances make action imperative. But a lynching I cannot and will not condone."

"No?" Tetley inquired.

"No, by God. I insist, and that's all Davies asks too; that's all any of us ask, that you bring these men in for a fair trial!"

"The Judge ain't had anything bigger to deal with than a drunk and disorderly Indian since he got here, Major," Ma said, with a sympathetic face. "You can see how he'd feel about it."

"That attitude," shouted the Judge, waving a hand at Ma, "that's what I must protest, Major. Levity, levity and prejudice in a matter of life and law."

"Regrettable," said Tetley, smiling at Ma. "We shall observe order and true justice, Judge," he told him.

"Are we going, or aren't we?" Farnley wanted to know.

Tetley looked at him. "In time. Mapes," he said, turning to Butch, "you said Risley made you deputy?"

"Yes, sir," said Mapes.

"Then suppose you deputize the rest of us."

"It's not legal," Tyler told him. He appeared infuriated by Tetley's smiling, elusive talk. "No deputy has the right to deputize."

"It'll do for me, Butch; go ahead and pray," Smith yelled.

Mapes looked at Tetley. Tetley said nothing; he just smiled, that thin little smile that barely moved the corners of his mouth.

"How about it, boys?" Mapes asked us.

"Mapes," Tyler bellowed at him, "it's ineffective. You're violating the law yourself in such an act."

Men called out to Mapes: "Go ahead, Butch"; "I guess it will take as well with you as any, Butch"; "Fire away, Sheriff."

"Raise your right hands," Mapes told us. We did. He recited an oath, which he seemed to have not quite straight. "Say 'I do,'" he told us. We said it together.

Farnley had already ridden out of the press. We began to swing into loose order after him. Davies was standing in the road with a stricken face. When the Judge bellowed after us in a sudden access of fury, "Tetley, you bring those men in alive, or, by God, as I'm justice of this county, you'll pay for it, you and every damned man jack of your gang," Davies didn't even seem to hear him. Suddenly he ran down the road, and then was running beside Tetley's horse, talking to the major. Then he dropped back and let them go. I called to ask him if he wasn't coming. He looked up at me, and God, I felt sorry for the man. He'd looked funny, an old man running stiffly in the road after armed men, on horses, who wouldn't pay any attention to him. But now he wasn't funny. He didn't say anything, but nodded after a moment. When I was going to pull up to wait for him, he made a gesture for me to go on.

Looking back I saw him standing with Osgood in the street. The Judge was talking to them, waving his hands rapidly. Canby hadn't come down, but was watching them and us from the door. I could see the white towel he still had in his hand.

Chapter 3

DAVIES CAUGHT UP with us after we had passed Tetley's big house behind its picket fence and were out in the grassy road between the meadows. He was riding a neat little sorrel with white socks and small feet. His saddle was of old, dark leather which had turned cherry color and shiny. He'd put on a plaid blanket coat to keep warm, but he had no gun. He still looked hard-bitten, but not the way he had in the street.

I asked him, "Still aiming to cure us?" and he shook his head and smiled.

"I guess not," he said.

Davies and I were riding last, and up ahead we could see the whole cavalcade strung out by ones and twos. We counted twenty-eight of us in all, with a little bunch riding separately at the front—Tetley, Mapes, Farnley, Winder, Bartlett and Ma.

Right ahead of us was Sparks, slowly singing something about Jordan to himself. We could hear sad bits of it now and then in the wind. He looked queer, elongated and hunched, saddleless astride that tall old mare with joints that projected like a cow's. Ahead of him young Tetley and the Mex were riding together, young Tetley silent and not looking around, Amigo pleased with himself, talking a lot and illustrating with his bridle hand while he rolled a cigarette against his chaps with the other. When he had lit the cigarette he talked with the hand that held it. His horse, a red-and-white pinto, like Gil's but smaller and neater, had to take two steps to every one of young Tetley's horse, a long-legged, stable-bred black that picked each foot up with a flick, as if it wanted to dance.

An old, empty board shack with one window was the last place west of town. Beyond it we opened out into a lope. The horses, after so much standing and fidgeting, were too willing and kept straining to gallop, moving up on each other until the riders had to pull them to escape the clods of soggy turf they were throwing. We pulled to the jog again and held it, all the hoofs trampling *squilch-squelch, squilch-squelch,* and little clods popping gently out to the side.

    The blackbirds, usually noisy this time of day, were just taking short flights among the reeds, and out farther, in the meadows, the cattle weren't feeding, but moving restlessly in small bunches. I looked for a meadowlark. Usually about sunset you can see them playing, leaping up and fluttering for a moment and then dropping again, suddenly, as if they'd been hit; then, after they're down again, that singing will come to you, thin and sweet, *chink-chink-a-link*. But there was too much wind. Probably all over the big meadow they were down flat in the grass and ruffled. They could feel the storm coming too. Ahead of us the shadowy mountains, stippled all over by their sparse pelt of trees and spotted with lingering snow, loomed up high, right against the moving sky.

    "It'll be dark before we're out of the pass," I said to Davies.

    He looked up at the mountains and at the clouds and nodded. "Snow too," he said.

    We didn't say anything more. He was full of the same feeling of mortality I had, I guess. I think we were all feeling it some, out in the great spread of the valley, under the big mountains, under the storm coming. Even Amigo wasn't talking anymore, and had quit trying to smoke in that wind. Somehow I understood for the first time what we were really going to do, and my breath and blood came quicker.

    We rode that way across half the valley until, right under a steep foothill, we came to the fork where the road bent right to go into the draw, and the west lane from Drew's came into it.

    There, while the rest of us jockeyed in a half circle, waiting and watching, Tetley rode a ways into the lane and pulled up. He sat there like he was carefully looking over a field to be fought. Mapes got off his horse and, drawing it on the bridle after him, went slowly along one side of the lane, looking down. This lane was even less of a track than the one across the valley.

    On the valley side of it, perhaps fifty yards down, was the creek winding south, with willows, aspens and alders forming a screen along it; here and there a big, half-leafed cottonwood rose above this brush. On the other side began the pine forest of the mountain. Through the trees, black in the shadow, showed patches of snow which hadn't melted yet. The forest rose steeply from there, and when you could no longer see the shape of the mountain leaning away from you, you could feel it rolling on up much higher. On the east side of the valley the tops of the mountains had disappeared above the plane of cloud.

The lane was churned with sharp tracks, fresh, the grass beside it crushed down into the mud. Mapes went about thirty or forty yards, then crossed the lane and came back up the other side in the same way. When he got back to Tetley he said something, and mounted. Tetley nodded. I could guess he was smiling his I-knew-it-all-the-time smile. They rode back to us and Tetley said, "They're fresh tracks, the first made this spring. We can't tell how many head, of course...."

"Forty," Amigo said, looking around at us.

"Possibly," Tetley said. "There were three riders. They left tracks going both ways." We nodded like that settled it.

Tetley rode around us to get ahead again. Mapes and Ma Grier, with Bartlett and Winder, followed him. Farnley had ridden farther up the main road and waited alone, watching Tetley and Mapes playing field officers, but he let them pass him, and turned in with the rest of us. I was nearer the middle of the bunch now, and when we strung out I was riding with young Tetley. I looked back; Sparks was behind us, and behind him were Davies, the Bartlett boys, and Moore and Gil riding together.

In the shadow under the mountain we felt hurried because of the lateness. We stepped up to the jog again until we came around the bend where the pass opened above us. There the road began climbing stiffly from the start and we had to walk. The soft lane of the meadow turned into a mountain track, hard and bouldery, with loose gravel and deep ruts made by the water, but already dry. The horses clicked and stumbled, climbing with a clear, slow, choppy rhythm. Sparks began another one of his hymns; it came in lonely fragments through the sounds of the horses and the rushing of the creek below us on the right.

Young Tetley was riding easily, but too slumped for a cowboy. He was a thin, very young-looking fellow. In this light his face was a pale daub, with big shadows for eyes. His black hair came out over his shirt collar in the back. He looked lonely and unhappy. I knew he didn't know me.

"Cold wind," I began.

He looked at me as if I'd said something important. Then he said, "It's more than wind," and stared ahead of him again.

"Maybe," I said. I didn't get his drift, but if he wanted to talk, "maybe" shouldn't stop him.

"It's a lot more," he said, as if I'd contradicted him. "You can't go hunting men like coyotes after rabbits and not feel anything about it. Not without being like any other animal. The worst kind of animal."

"There's a difference; we have reasons."

"Names for the same thing," he said sharply. "Does that make us any better? Worse, I'd say. At least coyotes don't make excuses. We think we can see something better, but we go on doing the same things, hunt in packs like wolves, hole up in warrens like rabbits."

"There's still a difference," I said.

"Oh, we're smart," he said bitterly. "But all we use it for is power. Yes, we've got them scared all right, all of them, except the tame things we've taken the souls out of. We're the bullies of the globe, all right."

"We're not hunting rabbits tonight," I reminded him.

"No; our own kind. A wolf wouldn't do that; nor even a mangy coyote. That's the hunting we like now, our own kind. The rest can't excite us anymore."

"We don't hunt men often," I told him. "Most people never do it at all. They get along pretty well together."

"Oh, we love each other," he said. "We labor for each other, suffer for each other, admire each other. We have all the pack instincts, all right, and nice names for them."

"All right," I said. "What's the harm in their being pack instincts, if you want to put it that way? They're real."

"They're not. They're just to keep the pack with us. We don't dare hunt each other alone, that's all. There's more ways of hunting than with a gun."

He'd jumped too far for me on that one. I didn't say anything.

"Think I'm stretching it, do you?" he asked. "Well, I'm not. All any of us really want anymore is power. We'd buck the pack if we dared. Instead, we trick it to help us in our own little killings."

"Most of life's pretty simple and quiet," I said. "You talk like we all had knives out."

"Your simple life," he said. "Your quiet life? All right. Take women visiting together, neighbors, old friends. What do they talk about? Each other, all the time, don't they? And what are the parts they like? Gossip, scandal—that's what wakes them up, makes them talk faster, as if they were stalking enemies in their minds. Something about a woman they know—that's what wakes them up. And do you know why?"

I didn't like the way the talk was getting to sound like a quarrel. I tried to ease it off.

"No," I said. "Why?" as if I were really curious.

"Because it makes them feel superior; makes them feel they're the wolves, not the rabbits. . . . If each of them had it the way she wants it," he said after a moment, "she'd be the only woman left in the world."

"People can be pretty mean sometimes," I admitted, "picking on the weak ones." It was no good.

"It's not always the weak ones," he said angrily. "They're worse than wolves, I tell you. They don't weed out the unfit, they weed out the best. They band together to keep the best down, the ones who won't share their dirty gossip, the ones who have more beauty or charm or independence, more anything, than they have. They did it right there in Bridger's Wells this spring," he blazed.

"How was that?" I asked, remembering what Canby had said about Rose Mapen.

"They drove a girl out. Made a whore of her with talk."

"Why? What did she do?"

"Nothing. That's what I'm telling you. You know what they had against her? You know what was her intolerable sin against the female pack?"

"How would I know?"

"She was better-looking than any of them, and men liked her."

"That can make a whore sometimes," I said.

"She wasn't, and they knew it."

"There must have been something."

"There was when they got done," he said. "Everything. But not before. They were scared of her, that's all."

I had to grin; this kid talking about women like he'd had the testing of the whole breed. And he the kind that would fall over himself to do anything for any of them if they asked it, or just looked it.

He didn't say anything more for a moment, and I heard the creek far down, and the horses clicking and heaving on the grade.

"You don't think much of women, do you?" I said.

"Men are no better," he said. "Men are worse. They're not so sly about their murder, because they're stronger. They're bullies instead of sneaks, and that's worse. And they all lie about what they think, hide what they feel, to keep from looking queer to the pack."

"Is there anything so fine about being different?" I asked.

I'm not sure he heard me.

"Even in dreams," he went on after a bit, as if he were talking to himself, "even in dreams it's the pack that's worst; it's the pack that we can never quite see but always feel coming, like a cloud, like a fog with death in it. It's the spies of the pack who are always hidden behind the pillars of the temples and palaces we dream we're in. They're behind the trees in the black woods we dream about; they're behind the boulders on the mountains we dream we're climbing, behind the windows on the square of every empty dream city we wander in. We've all heard them breathing; we've all run from them, screaming with fear; we've all waked up in the night and lain there trembling, staring at the dark for fear they'll come again." Suddenly he turned toward me.

"But we don't tell about it, do we?" he dared me. And said quickly, "No, no, we don't even want to hear anybody else tell. That's what makes you sick now, to hear me. That's what makes you so damned superior and quiet." His voice choked. "You're just hiding the truth, even from yourself," he babbled.

My hands were twitching, but I didn't say anything. Then he said more quietly, "You think I'm crazy, don't you? It always seems crazy to tell the truth. We don't like it; we won't admit what we are. So I'm crazy."

I was thinking that. I don't like to hear a man pouring out his insides without shame. And taking it for granted everyone else must be like him. Still, he was a kid, weak and unhappy, and his own father, they said, was his enemy.

"Every man's got a right to his own opinion," I told him.

After a moment he said, "Yes," low and to his saddle horn.

Having heard myself speak I realized that queer, weak and bad-tempered as it was, there had been something in the kid's raving. To me his idea appeared just the opposite of Davies'. To the kid, what everybody thought was low and wicked, and their hanging together was a mere disguise of their evil. To Davies, what everybody thought became just and fine, and to act up to it was to elevate oneself. And yet both of them gave you that feeling of thinking outside yourself, in a big place; the kid gave me that feeling even more, if anything, though he was disgusting.

I heard him talking again. "Why are we riding up here, twenty-eight of us," he demanded, "when every one of us would rather be doing something else?"

"I thought you said we liked killing?"

"Not so directly as this," he said. "Not so openly. We're doing it because we're in the pack, because we're afraid not to be in the pack."

"What do you want us to do," I asked, "sit and play a harp and worry about how bad we are while some damned rustler kills a man?"

"It isn't that," he said. "How many of us do you think are really here because cattle have been stolen, or because Kinkaid was shot?"

"I'm not wrong about your being here, am I?" I asked him.

Then he was quiet. I felt mean. I knew he didn't want to quarrel; he was just scared.

"No," he said finally. "I'm here, all right." He had dug himself up by the roots to say that.

"Well?" I said, easier.

"I'm here because I'm weak," he said, "and my father's not."

There wasn't anything a guy could say to that.

"I'm not claiming to be superior to anyone else," he said. "I'm not. I'm not fit to be alive. I know better than to do what I do. I've always known better, and not done it. And that's hell; can you understand that that's hell?"

"You kind of take it for granted nobody else is as smart as you are, don't you, kid?" I asked him.

He hunched over the saddle. "I didn't mean it that way," he said after a while. He sounded far away now and tired; ashamed he'd said so much.

"You take it too hard, son," I told him. "You didn't start this."

"Well, one thing is sure," he said. "If we get those men and hang them, I'll kill myself. I'll hang myself." Louder he said, "I tell you I won't go on living and remembering. I couldn't. I'd go really crazy." Then he said, quietly again, "It's better to kill yourself than to kill somebody else. That settles the mess anyway; really settles it."

I'd had enough. I'd heard drunks talk like this and it was half funny, but the kid was sober.

"You seem to think you matter a lot," I said.

I could see the pale patch of his face turned toward me in the dusk, then away again.

"It does sound that way, doesn't it?" he asked.

I began humming the "Buffalo Gals" to myself. He didn't say anything more, but after a bit dropped back and rode behind Sparks.

At the first level stretch in the road we stopped to breathe the horses. It was dark now, and really cold, not just chilly. There was frost on my blanket roll when I went to get my sheepskin out. The sheepskin was good, cutting the wind right away, and I swung my arms across my chest to get warm inside it. Others were warming themselves too. I could see them spreading and closing like dark ghosts, and hear the thump of their fists.

Gil came up alongside and peered to make sure who it was. Then he said, "Doing this in the middle of the night is crazy. Moore don't like it much either," he added. We sat there, listening to the horses breathe, and to some of the other men talking in low voices. "If it hadn't clouded up," he said, "there would have been a full moon tonight, bright as day."

When the horses were breathing quietly again, and beginning to stamp, we started on, Gil and I riding together, which felt more natural. Except right in front of us and right behind us we couldn't see the riders. We could only hear small sounds of foot and saddle and voice from along the line. Gil was quiet, for him. He didn't talk or hum; he didn't change position in his saddle or play with the quirt end of his bridle. If I knew him, he was thinking about something he didn't like. I should have let him alone, but I didn't.

"Still seeing those three guys reaching for the barrels, Gil?"

"No," he said, coming out of it. "I'd forgot all about them until you mentioned it. Why should I worry about that now?"

"What's eating you, then?"

He didn't say anything.

"I thought you liked excitement," I said. "I thought you'd be honing for something to do."

"I've got nothing against hanging a rustler," he said, "but I don't like it in the dark. There's always some fool will get wild and plug anything that moves; like young Greene there, or maybe young Tetley."

"He won't do any shooting," I said.

"Maybe not; but he scares easy; he's scared now. And he's got a gun." He went on. "That ain't what bothers me most, though. I like to pick my bosses. We didn't pick any bosses here, but we got 'em just the same. We was just herded in. So, and who herded us in? That kid Greene, if I remember, with a wild-eyed story he couldn't get straight, and Bartlett blowing off, and Osgood because he got us sore. That's a sweet outfit to tell you what you're going to do, ain't it?"

"They didn't really get us in," I said.

"They started us, them and Farnley. Not that Farnley's like them; Farnley's got plenty of sand. But when he's mad he's crazy. He's no kind of a guy to have in this business. When he's mad he can't think at all.

"I remember once," he began narrating, "I saw Farnley get mad. We was together in Hazey's outfit over on the Humboldt Range. It was beef roundup. Some wise guy trying to improve his stock had got a lot of longhorns in with his reds that spring. They was big as a chuck wagon and wild.

"Well, in the thick of it, all dust and flurry, one of these long-horns got under Farnley's pony and ripped him open like splitting a fish; the guts sagged right out in a belch of black blood. The pony went over all at once. Farnley got clear; he's quick as a cat and smooth. But then you know what he done? He took one look at the pony, it was his best one, and then he went wild-eyed for that steer. Yes he did, on his feet, no gun or anything; like he thought he could break its neck with his hands. Lucky I saw him, and there was another fellow, Corny we called him, not too far off. We got the steer turned off before he'd more than punched one hole under Farnley's ribs; not too deep, a sort of rip. But even that wasn't enough for Farnley. He fought us like a wildcat to get at the critter again. I was sore enough to let him go ahead and be mashed, but Corny'd known him a long time. He just stood there cool and knocked Farnley out with one punch.

"Now you'd think that was enough, wouldn't you? Corny'd risked his own neck plenty, gettin' down in the middle of all that. The steer was near as wild as Farnley was, dodging around us, trying to get in another poke. But do you think Farnley even said thanks? He did not. It was pretty near the end of roundup before Farnley'd even see us when he went by. And he never did mention the thing, not to this day. That's how long he can stay that way."

I thought Gil was off the track, but he wasn't.

"And that's the guy that's going to do something when it comes to doing something," he said.

"He's had time to think it over. It's not the same. Tetley can stop him."

"Not Tetley or anybody else," Gil said. "And that's another thing. Who picked Tetley? He's not our man, the damn reb dude."

"We can quit," I reminded him. "There's no law makes us be part of this posse."

Gil said quickly, "Hell, no. I'll see this thing out as far as any man will. I'm just warnin' you that we got to keep an eye on some of these guys. Farnley and Bartlett and Winder and Ma; yes, and Tetley too. No slick-smiling bastard's going to suck me into a job I don't like, that's all."

"Have your own way, whatever way that is."

"Shut up," he ordered.

We rode along saying nothing then, Gil angry because he couldn't make his feelings agree, and me laughing at him, though not out loud. He'd have ridden right over me if I'd even peeped.

We came to a steeper pitch, where I could feel the shoulders of my horse, Blue Boy, pump under the saddle and hear his breath coming in jerks. Then we came into a narrows and I knew we were nearly at the top of the pass. The road there just hung on the face of a cliff, and the other wall across the creek wasn't more than twenty feet away. On a night as dark as that you wouldn't think it could get any darker, but it did in that narrows. The wall went straight up beside us, probably forty or fifty feet. The clambering of the horses echoed a little against it even with the wind, and with the creek roaring as if we were on the edge of it. The wind was strong in the slot and smelled like snow again.

We all hugged the cliff side of the road, not being able to see the drop-off side clearly. I was on the inside, and sometimes my foot scraped the wall, and sometimes Gil and I clicked stirrups, he had pulled over so far. His horse sensed the edge and didn't like it, and kept twisting around trying to face it.

"A nice place for a holdup," Gil said, showing he was willing to talk again.

"In here three men could do in a hundred," I agreed.

"But they won't."

"I wouldn't think so."

After a minute I said, "It's going to snow."

He must have been testing the wind himself; then he said, "Hell. Won't that be just lovely! Still, it can't be much of a storm this time of year."

"I don't know. I remember trying to get through Eagle Pass the first week in June one year. I had to go back; the horse was up to his belly and we weren't halfway to the summit."

"Yeh, but that wasn't all new snow."

"Every inch of it. The trail had been clear two days before."

"Eagle Pass is higher, though."

"Some. But this is nearly eight thousand feet."

"Maybe they'll have to call it off," Gil suggested.

"Depends on how much of a lead they thought the rustlers had."

"Well, it won't be any picnic," Gil said, "but we'll be making a lot better time than they can. This was a fool way to come with cattle. And they'd have to stop when it got dark too. You can't drive cattle on this road in the dark."

"By the same sign," I said, "we could go right by them and never know it."

Gil thought. Then he said, "Not unless they stopped in the Ox-

Bow. There's no place else from here to the Hole where they could get forty head of cattle off the road."

The Ox-Bow was a little valley up in the heart of the range, about a mile beyond the top of the pass. Gil and I had stayed there a couple of days once, on the loose. It was maybe two or three miles long and half or three-quarters of a mile wide. The peaks were stacked up on all sides of it, showing snow most of the summer. The creek in the middle of it wound back on itself like a snake trying to get started on loose sand, and that shape had named the valley. There was sloping meadow on both sides of the creek, and in the late spring millions of purple and gold violets grew there, violets with blossoms as big as the ball of a man's thumb. Beyond the meadow, on each side, there was timber to the tops of the hills.

It was a lovely, chill, pine-smelling valley, as lonely as you could want. Scarcely anybody came there unless there was a dry season. Just once in a while, if you passed in the late summer, you'd see a sheepherder small out in the middle, with his burro and dogs and flock. The rest of the time the place belonged to squirrels, chipmunks and mountain jays. They would all be lively in the edge of the wood, scolding and flirting.

Someone had lived there once, though, and tried to ranch the place. Toward the west side, he'd built a log cabin, and a corral too, and a regular barn. But whoever he was, he'd given up years before. The door and windows were out of the cabin, and the floor was rotten, seedling pines and sagebrush coming up through it. There were only a few posts of the corral left, and the snow had flattened the barn, splitting the sides out and settling the roof right over them. Small circles of blackened stone showed where short stoppers, like Gil and me, had burned pieces of the barn and fences.

We discussed the chances of the rustlers' using the Ox-Bow. The road ran right along the edge of it at the south end; there was good grazing and water and wood to be picked up. For men driving cattle, there was no other place on the trail where they could have stopped. There was a clearing right at the summit, but the road ran through the middle of it, and there was no grass or water. And the road down the other side was like this one, steep and narrow all the way. There was only that one way in or out for cattle, so we couldn't see anything but the Ox-Bow or keep going.

THE OX-BOW INCIDENT

On the summit the wind hit full force, as if you'd stepped out from behind a wall. It was bitter cold and damp. I thought I felt a few flakes of snow on my face, but my face was already too numb to be sure. Even the horses ducked their heads into the wind.

In the clearing at the summit Tetley and Mapes stopped us to breathe the horses again. Also they began arguing what Gil and I had thought about the trail and the Ox-Bow, and some were for turning back. With snow beginning to come, and that wind blowing, they felt sure of a blizzard. Tetley maintained that was all the more reason for pressing the chase. With their trail covered with snow, and a day or two's start, time to switch brands, what would we have to go on?

Davies, with Moore backing him up, was for sending a couple of riders on across to Pike's Hole, and getting the men there to pick the rustlers up. I could see what he wanted. Kinkaid was nothing to most of the Pike's Hole men, and it wasn't their cattle that had been rustled. They'd pick the men up on principle, but they'd be willing to hold them for the sheriff and a trial.

Winder accused Davies, and even Moore, of being so scared of the job they'd rather let a murderer slip away than do it. Davies admitted he'd rather let ten murderers go than have it on his soul that he'd hanged an honest man. Tetley said he wasn't going to hang an innocent man; he'd make sure enough of that to suit even Davies. To Farnley, even Tetley's manner smacked of delay. He told them he'd rather see a murderer hanged than shot, it was a dirtier death, but that he'd bushwhack all three of those men before he'd let one of them get out of the mountains free. I tried to shut Gil up when he started, but he went ahead and told Farnley that nobody who wasn't a horse thief himself would bushwhack any man, let alone three men for one, and that one a man he hadn't seen do it. Farnley was going to climb Gil, but others held him back. I tried to talk Gil quiet, but he said, "Aw, hell," in disgust. He spit as if it were on the whole bunch of us, and rode farther out by himself. It looked as if it might be another long squabble, but it wasn't. Winder and Ma and most of the others sided with Tetley, and that about settled it.

Then all at once something happened. Somebody in the middle of the clearing sang out, "Scatter, boys, there's horses coming."

Tetley didn't seem to like the order, for I heard him giving his own orders quickly, but not loud enough so I could understand. In the dark the group was already scattering to both sides of the clearing. I could see the shadowy huddle in the middle fanning out toward the edges. In the wind I couldn't hear them, any more than I'd heard anything coming. They were so many shadows floating off slowly, like a cloud breaking up in front of the moon. The middle of the clearing became just a gray open space waiting for something to come into it. I could see why Tetley hadn't liked that order, besides its being yelled that way. There wasn't a man among us, in the edge of the woods, that could risk a shot into the clearing in the dark and with others right across from him.

I listened hard, but still couldn't hear the running horses I expected from that shout. All I could hear was the wind, roaring on and off in the pines, and higher up booming at intervals, as if clapping in space; and faintly, like a lesser wind, the falling of the creek. One shadow, on foot and leading his horse, came toward me and disappeared under the trees very near. Then I was listening for him too. A man hates to have somebody near him in the dark when he doesn't know who it is.

A voice from the other side of me, Mapes I thought, called out, "Stay where you are till I give you the hail. Then circle out slow if it's anything we want. Don't do any shooting."

It struck me that in that darkness and wind a rider could be across the clearing and into the narrows before we were sure he was there. And on that downgrade, riding alone, he'd have a big advantage on us. That thought kept me tense.

I found the canteen on my saddle and had two long swallows. It was rotten stuff of Canby's, all right, but it was hot in the mouth and warming in the belly. It gave me a good shiver, then settled broadly in my middle and began to spread through my body like a fire creeping in short grass. I stood there and let her spread for a minute; then I had another, corked the canteen, tied it back on the saddle, and rolled a cigarette. I turned my back to the clearing to cover the flare I'd make; two or three voices called at me, though, low and angry. Having started, I held the flame until my cigarette was going. The smoke was good, drawn in that cold air, and after the whiskey in my mouth.

I could hear somebody loading his horse, and stopping close on my right.

"You damn fool," he said in a low, hostile voice. "Want to give us away?" I thought it was Winder. I knew I was in the wrong, which made me even sorer.

"Who to?" I asked him out loud. "You guys have been hearing things. Let's get moving before we freeze stiff and can't. Or are we giving this up?"

I heard his hammer click; the sound brought me awake, quick and clear. I kept the cigarette in my mouth, but didn't draw on it, and got hold of my own gun.

"You chuck that butt," he ordered, "or I'll plug you."

"Start something," I told him. "For every hole you make, I'll make two."

I was scared though. I knew Winder's temper, and he wasn't more than five steps off. When I'd talked the cigarette had bobbed in my mouth too, in spite of my trying to talk stiff-lipped; he'd know where it was. I made a swell target; he could judge every inch of me. When he didn't say anything, my back began to crawl. I wouldn't have thought I could feel any colder, but I did, all under the back of my shirt. Still, after the way he'd put it, I couldn't let that cigarette go either. I drew my own gun slowly, and kept staring hard to see what he was doing, but couldn't.

I jumped when Sparks spoke behind me, but felt better at once. My mind was beginning to freeze on the situation, and his voice brought me to my senses.

"It looks like you'll have a lot of shootin' to do, Mistah Bahtlett," Sparks said. So he thought it was Bartlett. That idea made me feel a lot happier. I looked along the edge of the woods and saw what Sparks meant. Half a dozen men were lighting up. They felt the same way I did, I guess, foolish about waiting so long. The closest man was Tetley's Amigo. He had his hands cupped around the match, and I could see his brown, grease-shining face before he flipped the match out.

"Damned fools," the man said, whoever he was. Then I heard him let the hammer down again, and his horse following him off.

"Let's go," I said to Sparks. Other shadows were moving out into the clearing again.

It was a thick dark; you couldn't even have told it was snowing except by the feel. I didn't get used to the feel; it kept on being a surprise. I could see shapes moving when they crossed against a snowbank, but that was about all.

Then somebody else, I don't know who, said, "Reckon we must have been hearing our own ears, boys."

"We heard it, and it warn't no ears," a voice told him. That was Winder, I was sure, under the trees.

"To hell with it," the somebody said. "This is no kind of a night for the job." His voice was nervous from waiting blind.

"You're right there," another agreed.

"This snow will be three feet deep by morning," the first man said.

"Hey," a man in back of us yelled. "Look out!"

Then I saw it. It was the stagecoach. It wasn't coming fast, but it was already close. The trees and bank had hidden it till it was nearly on us. We scattered out to the sides, some of the horses wheeling and acting up.

"Stop him," Mapes yelled.

"He can tell us," Ma called.

Others were shouting too, and some of them rode back toward the coach, calling at the driver to stop.

Caught by surprise, the driver started to pull up; his lead horse reared and the brakes squealed. Then he changed his mind. There was a lantern swinging off the seat on the road side. It made a long, narrowing shadow of the coach and driver up a snowbank on the far side. By its light I saw the driver stand straight up and let his whip go out over the horses. The tip exploded like a pistol shot. The horses yanked from side to side, then scrambled and dug and got under way. Checked and then yanked forward again like that, the coach rocked on its straps like a cradle, and the lantern banged back and forth.

The driver was huddled down as much as he dared, with that hill coming. When the lantern swung up I could see over him that there was another man. He was trying to stick with the bucking seat and get himself laid over the top to shoot. There were four horses, and by the middle of the clearing that whip had them stretching together. We all yelled at the driver then, but there were too many yelling. There were passengers too. A woman screamed, and behind the flapping curtain a light went out. The guard shouted from the roof.

"Keep down," he yelled at the people inside. "It's a stickup. Keep down, I tell you, they'll shoot."

Several riders had started out to come alongside, but seeing the guard, they had pulled away. Winder, though, didn't seem to see him. That was his coach heading for the narrows and the creek below. He kept calling, "Hey, Alec, hey, Alec; hey Alec, you damned fool," but his mule couldn't keep beside the coach. We were all yelling at the driver and at Bill now. I saw it wasn't doing any good, and touched Blue Boy up, intending to turn Winder anyhow, before he was drilled. It was all serious enough, God knows, and yet so crazy, all that commotion suddenly, and the driver and the guard playing hero, that I was nearly laughing too, while I yelled.

I was hit in the shoulder, so unexpectedly it nearly drove me out of the saddle. At once I heard the bang of the guard's carbine, and then somebody screamed and kept moaning for a moment while I pulled straight in the saddle. The report was a flat sound in the clearing, but distinct above all the others. The yelling stopped, and then, even in the wind, the explosion echoed faintly in the narrows.

Distantly, with the sounds of the coach, I heard Ma Grier's big voice calling her name at the driver; then saw the horses dip suddenly onto the steep downgrade and the coach yank over after them. One instant the lantern was there, flying like a comet gone loco, and the next it had winked out. There was a long screeching and wailing of brakes which echoed so I couldn't tell which was brakes and which echo.

Blue Boy was still trying to bolt with the others following the coach, but for some reason I was pulling him. On the edge of the pitchover I got him stopped. Then I just sat there. I was hanging on to the saddle horn, and my stomach was sick, and I was trembling all over. It wasn't until I reached up and felt of my shoulder, because it was hot and tickling, and found my shirt wet, that it got through to me that I'd been shot.

I wondered how bad it was, and started to get down, but couldn't. After trying, I started making a silly little chattering, whining noise, which I couldn't stop. I thought, by God, if he's killed me, what a fool way to die; what a damned fool way to die!

The driver had got the coach stopped at the foot of the first pitch; I don't know how. It was standing on the level just before the first turn, which would have put it into the creek. The lantern made a big shadow of the coach on the wall of the gorge. Most of the riders passed me and went down to the coach. One rider passed me, but turned in the saddle and peered at me, then pulled around and came back. It was Gil.

"That you, Art?" he asked, still peering.

"I guess so," I said.

"What's the matter?"

I told him.

"Where?" he asked.

"In the shoulder, I think; in the left shoulder."

"Lemme see," he said.

"Hell," he said after a moment. "Can't tell a thing here. How do you feel?"

"All right."

"Can you make it to the coach? We can see something there."

When we started down he steadied me in the saddle, but I was already a lot clearer. The shoulder was beginning to hurt, so the dizziness was gone and I didn't feel so much like throwing up. I told him I could make it.

There was a lot of talk around the coach. The driver, who was pale and still trembling in the knees from his close call, was repeating, "I thought it was a stickup. God, there was a lot of you. I thought it was a stickup."

He was Alec Small, a little, thin blond man with a droopy mustache, a nice fellow, but not tough, and not the driver Winder was. Winder was bawling him out and looking at the horses' ankles between curses. The horses were trembling and restless; Gabe was getting down to quiet them. Small didn't seem to hear Winder. He was drunk, and the mob dazed him.

I knew the guard too, Jimmy Carnes, a big, black-bearded man with a slouch hat and a leather coat. He'd been a government hunter for the army. It had been a good thing for Winder, if not for me, that it was dark and the coach rocking.

Carnes was saying, "I hope I didn't get him too bad."

"Get who?" Ma asked him.

"I got somebody," he said. "I heard him yell. You know," he went on, "you hadn't ought to have come barging out like that, in the dark, especially. I was pretty near asleep when Alec yelled at me, and I couldn't see who you was."

Now Winder was wanting to know what the hell the stage was doing on the pass at night anyway. For a minute Gil and I couldn't get through the press; I didn't care if we got through; I felt far away, like I was watching a picture. The passengers were getting out while everybody watched them. They were two women and a man, and, by their looks, they'd been thrown around. Their stylish clothes were askew, and the ladies were trying to straighten themselves without being too obvious about it.

Finally Gil managed to guide his horse through to the lantern, and he said, "Art's shot. Carnes got him in the shoulder."

Davies understood right away and helped me down, telling Gil to get a trunk from the coach for me to sit on. I sat down on the trunk, and Sparks brought the lantern over and held it while Davies began to take my shirt off. It was beginning to stick.

"It's nothing," I told him. "But do the women have to watch?" I was going to feel sick again.

Davies began picking at the wound. I'd spilled quite a lot of blood. But the wound itself wasn't so much. The bullet had just gone through the flesh and ripped on out at the back, Davies told me. He was careful, but too slow. I had to go out to the edge of the road and throw up, with Gil holding on to me. Then Moore gave me a stiff drink, and another when Davies was done picking the threads of shirt out of the hole, and I felt strong enough, just light-headed. All that bothered me was that I continued to tremble all over, as if I had a chill, but Davies said that was probably just from the impact; that it would take time for the shock to wear off. He washed the wound clean with whiskey, but told me they'd have to fire it to prevent infection. They took the lantern and heated a pistol barrel red-hot in the flame. Then Gil and Moore held me down while the wound was burned. I got through the front side well enough, just holding my breath and sweating, but on the back I passed out.

When I next knew where I was, Davies had me bandaged up tightly with strips of somebody's shirt, my sheepskin was on me again, and Moore was trying to pour another drink into me. I felt shaky and empty, but angry too, because so many people had watched me pass out.

The men pretended they hadn't seen any weakness; they were going about their business, remounting and forming above the coach. Gil lit me a cigarette, and when I looked at the men and then at him, he nodded. I felt weak, all washed out, and it was snowing harder than before. And when Davies told me that "the fools still meant to go on," but there was room for me in the coach, and I'd better go back and rest at Canby's, I told him hell no, there was nothing the matter with me. He argued a little, and Ma came and joked but helped him argue, and I got to feeling stubborn and just sat there smoking my cigarette and saying no.

Finally I had to stand up so they could put the trunk back on the coach. Then Winder came and told me not to be a damned fool, to get in the coach and go on home, where I wouldn't be in the way. Gil told Winder to mind his own business, that he'd look after me himself if I needed any looking after. And Mapes told Winder to let the idiot, meaning me, go ahead and act like an idiot if he wanted to, it was none of their funeral. That made Gil grin, and he helped me get up on Blue Boy.

The stagecoach left. I learned later that the people on it hadn't seen a sign of any rustlers, coming up to the pass; but that didn't mean much, what with the dark and the snow. As our group lined up to get moving, Gil said, "If you get to feelin' it, fellow, sound off. This still ain't any of our picnic."

"I will."

"I should have made you go down in the coach," he apologized, "but with all of them raggin' you, I didn't think."

I told him I was all right. In a way I was too. The whiskey was working good, like I had all the blood back, and somehow being hit like that, now that I was patched up, made me feel like I had a stake in the business.

So we set out again. In the dark we rode across the clearing and under the trees on the other side. The snow was right in our faces, and we couldn't see farther than the rumps of the horses ahead. We went slowly, but even so the procession kept stopping while Tetley and Mapes made sure we were still on the road.

We rode some distance then without any halt, the trees being even on the two sides so the road was plain. In all that darkness, with nothing to think about, I began to feel unreal, like we were all crazy and just wandering around in the mountains. I started dozing a little and remembered a story I'd heard once about the Flying Dutchman and wondered vaguely if that's the way we were getting. It made a fine picture, twenty-eight riders you could see through, riding around forever in mountain snowstorms, looking for three dead rustlers they had to find before their souls could be at peace.

Then came another halt, and I knew I'd nearly fallen asleep. Up ahead, men were exclaiming about something in low voices. I saw what they were talking about. To the right, far through the trees and through the snow, a fire was burning. It looked very small in the big darkness, and sometimes disappeared when the trees moved in the wind.

Then I realized we were at the end of the Ox-Bow valley, and that the fire must be way out toward the center, and partially concealed by the old abandoned cabin. But it must have been a big fire at that, because even when it was out of sight I thought I could see a kind of halo of light from around it. It was easy, though, to see how the men on the stage had missed it.

And then, with a turn of the wind, we heard a steer bellowing. Nobody said anything, or moved, and we heard it a second time.

Word came back along the line that we were turning down into the valley, and then to bunch up for last orders. We had passed the turnoff into the valley, and had to slide and scramble down a bank. Even in the wind you could hear the horses snort, and the slap of leather and the jangle of jerked bits. They didn't like it in the dark. By the time I got to the slide it was a long black streak torn down through the snow. Blue Boy smelled the rim, tossed his head two or three times, and pitched over. He descended, scraping and stiff-legged, like a dog sitting down.

When we were grouped among the cottonwoods in the hollow, Tetley gave us our marching orders. He cautioned us about playing safe, and against any shooting or rough work until we were sure.

"They must have an opportunity to tell it their way," he said. "Mapes and I will do the talking, and if there's any shooting to do, I'll tell you. The rest of you hold your fire unless they try to break through you. We'll divide to close in on them. . . . Where is Croft?" he asked.

"Here," I said.

"How do you feel?"

"I'm all right."

"Good. But you stay with my group. We'll go the most direct way."

Farnley said, "The son of a bitch that got Kinkaid is mine, Tetley. Don't forget that."

"He's yours when we're sure," Tetley told him.

Then, like an officer enjoying mapping out a battle plan that pleases him because the surprise element is with him, he directed our attack. He picked Bartlett and Winder and Ma Grier to lead on the other three sides, and divided the rest among the four parties. Gil and I both wound up with Tetley's group. He put Farnley in his own group, and his son, Gerald, too.

Winder's party was to work around through the woods and come down back of the cabin; Bartlett's was to circle clear around and come in by the far side; Ma Grier's was to come up from the valley side. They were to fan out so they'd contact by the time they got close to the firelight, then make a closed circle.

"They're least likely to break for the valley or the side away from this," he continued. "So the unarmed men, unless they'd rather wait here, had best go, one with Mr. Bartlett and one with Mrs. Grier."

"Give them guns," Winder said. "Lots of us have a couple."

"Will you take a gun, Davies?" Tetley asked.

Davies answered from the other side of him, "No, thanks. I'll go with the Bartletts."

"Just as you choose," Tetley said. His voice was even, but the scorn was there. "Sparks?" he asked.

"No, suh, Cun'l Tetley, thank you jus' the same."

"With Mrs. Grier, then."

"Yessuh."

"Keep your eyes and ears open," Tetley warned us. "They may

have pickets out. And if you come on the cattle, ride easy; don't disturb them. If any party does spring a picket, shoot into the air once. All of you, if you hear the shot, close in as quickly as you can, but keep spread."

"This is no battle, you know," Farnley said. "We're after three rustlers, not an army."

"We don't know what we're after until we see. Unnecessary risk is simply foolish," Tetley told him, still evenly.

"And don't fire," he told the rest of us, "unless they fire first, except if they should break through. Then stop them any way you have to. But surprise is what we want, and no shooting if we can help it. All clear?"

We said it was.

"All right," Tetley said. "My group will wait until we judge the rest of you have had time to move into position. Good luck, boys."

Chapter 4

WINDER AND HIS OUTFIT started off, working single file into the woods. Ma Grier and Bartlett led off at an angle toward the valley. In a moment you couldn't tell which were riders and which trees. The snow blurred everything, and blotted up sound too, into a thick, velvety quiet.

Gil came alongside me on his pinto.

"How you feeling now, fellow?" he asked.

"Good," I said.

"Take care of yourself," he said. "This still don't have to be our picnic."

"It looks like it is," I said.

"Yeah," he agreed. "But it ain't."

There was nothing to do but wait. Through the trees we watched the fire out by the cabin. Once it began to die down, and then a shadow went across it, and back across, and the fire darkened and flattened completely. At first we thought they had wind of us, but the fire gradually grew up, brighter than ever. It was just somebody throwing more wood on. The snowing relaxed for a spell, and then started again, steady and slanting. The branches rattled around us when the wind blew. Being in the marshy end of the valley they weren't pines, but aspens, and willow grown up as big as trees. When the horses stirred, the ground squelched under them, and you could see the dark shadow of water soaking up around their hoofs through the snow. In places, though, the slush was already getting icy, and split when it was stepped on.

Several times we heard the steers bellowing as before, hollow in the wind, and sounding more distant than they could have been.

After a time Tetley led us out to the edge of the trees to where the wind was directly on us. We waited there, peering into the snow and the dark gulf of the valley itself, but unable to see the other riders, of course, or anything but the fire. It felt to me as if it must be one o'clock at least. Finally Tetley said, as if he had been holding a watch before him all the time and had predetermined the exact moment to start, "All right, let's go. We'll ride in on them in a bunch, unless there's shooting."

We went out in a group, plowing a wide track through the half-frozen sponginess. Tetley, Farnley and Mapes rode in front, abreast. Mapes reached under his armpit and got his gun. Farnley's carbine was across his saddle, and I thought I heard the hammer click. Tetley just rode right ahead. I reached my gun out too.

As we came closer there was nothing to see but the fire, beginning to die again, and the little its light revealed of the cabin wall. I got to wondering if they had built the fire up as a blind and had already run out on us, or even were lying up somewhere, ready to pick us off. My head came clear again and I didn't even notice my shoulder. We were really into the edge of the firelight before Tetley stopped us. I had my mind made up they were laying for us, so what I saw surprised me.

Between Tetley and Mapes I could see a man asleep on the ground in a blanket with a big pattern on it. His head was on his saddle and toward the fire, his face in shadow. As we looked at him he drew an arm up out of his blanket and laid it across his eyes. He had on an orange shirt, and the hand and wrist lifted into the light were as dark as an old saddle. We were so close that I could see on his middle finger a heavy silver ring with an egg-shaped turquoise, a big one, in it; a Navaho ring. By the bulk of him he was a big, heavy man. There were two other men asleep in blankets—one with his side to the fire and his head away from me, the other on the far side with his feet to the fire. I couldn't make out anything but their shapes.

Tetley waited long enough to be sure they were not playing possum, and then rode into the light and right up to the feet of the man with the ring. We followed him, spreading around that edge of the fire as he motioned us to. After looking down at the man for a moment, he said sharply and loudly, "Get up."

The other two stirred in their blankets and began to settle again, but the man with the ring woke immediately. When he saw us he said something short to himself and twisted up out of his blanket in one continuous, smooth movement, trailing one hand into the blanket as he came up.

"Drop it," Farnley ordered. He was holding the carbine at his thigh, the muzzle pointing at the man. The man had heavy black hair and a small black mustache. He looked like a Mex, though his hair was done up in a club at his neck, like an Indian's, and his face was wide, with high, flat cheeks. He looked to me like a Mex playing Navaho.

He looked quickly but not nervously around at all of us, sizing us up, but didn't move the hand which had come up behind him.

"I said drop it," Farnley told him again, and nudged the carbine out toward him, so he wouldn't make any mistake about what was meant.

The Mex suddenly smiled, as if he had just understood, and dropped a long-barreled, nickel-plated revolver behind him onto the blanket. He was an old hand, and still thinking.

"Now put 'em up," Farnley told him.

The smile died off the Mex's face, and he just stared at Farnley and shrugged his shoulders. "No sabby," he said.

Farnley grinned. "I said reach." He jerked the muzzle of the carbine upward two or three times. The Mex got that, and put his hands up slowly. He was studying Farnley's face all the time.

"That's better," Farnley said, still grinning, "though some ways I'd just as soon you hadn't, you son of a bitch." He was talking as quietly as Tetley usually did, only not so easily. He seemed to be enjoying calling the man a name he couldn't understand, and doing it in a voice like he was making an ordinary remark.

"No sabby," the Mex said again.

"That's all right, brother," Farnley told him. "You will."

The other two were coming out of their sleep. I was covering one, and Mapes the other. Mapes' man just sat up, still in his blanket. He was a thick, wide-faced old-timer with long, tangled gray hair and a long, droopy gray mustache. He had eyebrows so thick they made peaked shadows on his forehead. The way he was staring now, he didn't appear to be all there. My man rose quickly enough, though tangling a little with his blanket. He started to come toward us, and I saw he'd been sleeping with his gun on and his boots off. He was a tall, thin, dark young fellow, with thick black hair, but no Indian or Mex.

"Take it easy, friend," I told him. "Stay where you are and put your hands up."

He didn't understand but stared at me, and then at Tetley, and then back at me. He didn't reach for his gun, didn't even twitch for it, and his face looked scared. "Put your hands up," I told him again. He did, looking as if he wanted to cry.

"What are you trying to do? What do you want? We haven't got anything," he babbled, half out of breath.

"Shut up," Mapes instructed him. "We'll tell you when we want you to talk."

"This is no stickup, brother," I explained to him. "This is a posse, if that means anything to you."

"But we haven't done anything," he protested. "What have we done?" He wasn't over his first fright yet.

"Shut up," Mapes said, with more emphasis.

The old man was out of his blanket now too, and standing with his hands raised.

"Gerald, collect their guns," Tetley said.

Young Tetley was sitting in his saddle, staring at the three men. He dismounted dreamily and picked up the Mex's gun from the blanket. Then, like a sleepwalker, he came over to the young fellow

"Behind him," said Tetley sharply.

The boy looked around. "What?" he asked.

"Wake up," Tetley ordered. "I said go behind him. Don't get between him and Croft."

"Yes," Gerald said, and did what he was told. He fumbled around a long time before he found the old man's gun, which was under his saddle.

"Give the guns to Mark," Tetley ordered, jerking his head at one of the two riders I didn't know. Gerald did that, handing them up in a bunch—belts, holsters and all.

It made me ashamed the way Tetley was bossing the kid's every move, like a mother making a three-year-old do something over because he'd messed up the first try.

"Now," he said, "go over them all, from the rear. Then shake out the blankets."

Gerald seemed to be waking a little now. His jaw was tight. He found another gun on the Mex, a little pistol like gamblers carry. It was in an arm sling under his vest. There was a carbine under the young fellow's blanket. He shrank from patting the men over, the way he was told to, and when he passed me to give Mark the carbine and pistol I could hear him breathing hard.

Tetley spoke to my prisoner. "Are there any more of you?"

The young fellow was steadier. He looked angry now, and started to let his arms down, asking, "May I inquire what business—"

"Shut up," Mapes said, "and keep them up."

"It's all right, Mapes," Tetley said. "You can put your hands down now," he said to the young man. "I asked you, are there any others with you?"

"No," the kid said.

I didn't think the kid was lying. Tetley looked at him hard, but I guess he thought it was all right too. He turned his head toward Mark and the other rider I didn't know.

"Tie their hands," he ordered.

The young fellow started to come forward again.

"Stay where you are," Tetley told him quietly, and he stopped. He had a wide, thick-lipped mouth that was nonetheless sensitive, and now it was tight down in the corners. His eyes were big and dark in his thin face, like a girl's. His hands were long and bony and nervous, but hung on big, square wrists.

He spoke in a husky voice. "I trust that at least you'll tell us what we're being held for."

Mapes was still busy being an authority. "Save your talk till it's asked for," he advised.

Tetley studied the young man all during the time the two punchers were tying the prisoners on one lass-rope and pushing them over to the side of the fire away from the cabin. He still looked at him and the others when they were standing there, shoulder to shoulder, the Mex in the middle, their faces to the fire and their backs to the woods. It was as if he believed he could solve the whole question of their guilt or innocence by just looking at them and thinking his own thoughts; the occupation pleased him. The Mex was stolid now, the old man remained blank, but the kid was humiliated and angry at being tied. He repeated his question in a manner that didn't go well with the spot he was in.

Then Tetley told him, "I'd rather you told us," and smiled that way.

After that he signaled to the other parties still in the woods. Then he dismounted, giving the bridle to his son, and walked over to the fire, where he stood with his legs apart and held out his hands to warm them, rubbing them together. He might have been in front of his own fireplace. Without looking around he ordered more wood put on the fire. All the time he continued to look across the fire at the three men in a row, and continued to smile.

We were all on foot now, walking stiff-legged from sitting the saddle so long in the cold. I got myself a place to sit near the fire, and watched the Mex. He had his chin down on his chest, like he was both guilty and licked, but he was watching everything from under his eyebrows. He looked smart and hard. I'd have guessed he was about thirty, though it was difficult to tell, the way it is with an Indian. The lines around his mouth and at the corners of his eyes and across his forehead were deep and exact, as if they were cut in dark wood with a knife. His skin shone in the firelight. There was no expression on his face, but I knew he was still thinking how to get out.

Then all at once his face changed, though you couldn't have

said what the change was in any part of it. I guess in spite of his watchfulness he'd missed Tetley's signal, and now he saw Ma and her gang coming up behind us. He looked around quickly, and when he saw the other gangs coming in too, he turned back and stared at the ground in front of him. He was changed all over then, the fire gone out of him; he was empty, all done.

The old man stood and stared, as he had from his first awakening. He didn't seem to have an idea, or even a distinct emotion, merely a vague dread. He'd look at one of us and then another with the same expression, pop-eyed and stupid, his mouth never quite closed, and the gray stubble sticking out all over his jaws.

When the young fellow saw the crowd he said to Tetley, "It appears we're either very important or very dangerous. What is this, a vigilance committee?" He shivered before he spoke, though. I thought the Mex elbowed him gently.

Tetley kept looking at him and smiling, but didn't reply. It was hard on their nerve. Ma Grier had ridden up right behind us and said, before she got down, "No, it ain't that you're so dangerous, son. It's just that most of the boys has never seen a real triple hangin'."

There wasn't much laughter.

Everybody was in now except the Bartlett boys, who had stayed out to mind the cattle. Some remained on their horses, not expecting the business to take much time, and maybe just as glad there were others willing to be more active. Some dismounted and came over to the fire with coils of rope; there was enough rope to hang twenty men with a liberal allowance for each.

As if it had taken all that time for the idea to get through, the young fellow said, "Hanging?"

"That's right," Farnley said.

"But why?" asked the kid, beginning to chatter. "What have we done? We haven't done anything. I told you already we haven't done anything."

Then he got hold of himself and said to Tetley, more slowly, "Aren't you even going to tell us what we're accused of?"

"Of course," Tetley said. "This isn't a mob. We'll make sure first."

He half turned his head toward Mapes. "Sheriff," he said, "tell him."

"Rustling," said Mapes.

"Rustling?" the kid echoed.

"Yup. Ever heard of it?"

"And murder," said Farnley. "Maybe he'll have heard of that."

"Murder?" the kid repeated foolishly. I thought he was going to fold, but he didn't. He took a brace and just ran his tongue back and forth along his lips a couple of times, as if his throat and mouth were all dried out. He looked around, and it wasn't encouraging. There was a solid ring of faces, and they were serious.

The old man made a long, low moan, like a dog that's going to howl but changes its mind. Then he said, his voice trembling badly, "You wouldn't kill us. No, no, you wouldn't do that, would you?"

Nobody replied. The old man's speech was thick, and he spoke very slowly, as if the words were heavy and he was considering them with great concentration. They didn't mean anything, but you couldn't get them out of your head once he'd said them. He looked at us so I thought he was going to cry. "Mr. Martin," he said, "what do we do?" He was begging, and seemed to believe he would get a real answer.

The young man tried to make his voice cheerful, but it was hollow. "It's all right, Dad. There's some mistake."

"No mistake, I guess." It was old Bartlett speaking. He was standing beside Tetley, looking at the Mex and idly dusting the snow off his flat sombrero. The wind was blowing his wispy hair up like smoke. When he spoke the Mex looked up for a second. He looked down again quickly, but Bartlett grinned. He had a good many teeth out, and his grin wasn't pretty.

"Know me, eh?" he asked the Mex. The Mex didn't answer.

Farnley stepped up to him and slapped him across the belly with the back of his hand. "He's talking to you, mister," he said.

The Mex looked wonderfully bewildered. "No sabby," he repeated.

"He don't speak English," Mapes told Bartlett.

"I got a different notion," Bartlett said.

"I'll make him talk," Farnley offered. He was eager for it; he was so eager for it he disgusted me. It made me feel sorry for the Mex.

The young fellow appeared bewildered. He was looking at them and listening, but he didn't seem to make anything of it. He kept closing his eyes more tightly than was natural, and then opening them again quickly, as if he expected to find the whole scene changed.

Even without being in the spot he was in, I could understand how he felt. It didn't look real to me either—the firelight on all the red faces watching in a ring, and the big, long heads of horses peering from behind, and up in the air, detached from it, the quiet men still sitting in the saddles.

When Farnley started to prod the Mex again, Tetley said sharply, "That will do, Farnley."

"Listen, you," Farnley said, turning on him, "I've had enough of your playing God Almighty. Who in hell picked you for this job anyway? Next thing you'll be kissing them, or taking them back for Tyler to reform them. We've got the bastards; well, what are we waiting for? Let them swing, I say."

"Control yourself, and we'll get along better," Tetley told him.

Farnley's face blanched and stiffened, as it had in the saloon when he'd heard the news about Kinkaid. I thought he was going to jump Tetley, but Tetley didn't even look at him again. He leaned the other way to listen to something Bartlett was saying privately. When he had heard it he nodded and looked at the young fellow across the fire.

"Who's boss of this outfit?" he asked.

"I am," the young fellow said.

"And your name's Martin?"

"Donald Martin."

"What outfit?"

"My own."

"Where from?"

"Pike's Hole."

The men didn't believe it. The man called Mark said, "He's not from Pike's, or anyplace in the Hole. I'll swear to that."

For the first time there was real antagonism in the crowd, instead of just doubt and waiting.

"Mark there lives in Pike's," Tetley told the kid, smiling. "Want to change your story?"

"I just moved in three days ago," the kid said.

"We're wasting time, Willard," Bartlett said to Tetley.

"We'll get there." Tetley smiled. "I want this kept regular for the Judge."

Not many appreciated his joking. He was being too slow for a job like this, acting like he took pleasure in it. Most of us would have had to do it in a hurry. If you have to hang a man, you have to, but it's not my kind of fun to stand around and watch him keep hoping he may get out of it.

Tetley may have noticed the silence, but he didn't show it. He went on asking Martin questions.

"Where did you come from before that?"

"Ohio," he said angrily, "Sinking Spring, Ohio. But not just before. I was in Los Angeles. I suppose that proves something."

"What way did you come up?"

"By Mono Lake. Look, mister, this isn't getting us anywhere, is it? We're accused of murder and rustling, you say. Well, we haven't done any rustling, and we haven't killed anybody. You've got the wrong men."

"We'll decide as to that. And I'm asking the questions."

"God," the kid broke out. He stared around wildly at the whole bunch of us. "God, don't anybody here know I came into Pike's Hole? I drove right through the town; I drove a Conestoga wagon with six horses right through the middle of the town. I'm on what they call the Phil Baker place, up at the north end."

Tetley turned to Mark.

"Phil Baker moved out four years ago," Mark said. "The place is a wreck—barns down, sagebrush sticking up through the porch."

Tetley looked back at Martin.

"I met him in Los Angeles," Martin explained. "I bought the place from him there. I paid him four thousand dollars for it."

"Mister, you got robbed," Mark told him. "Even if Baker'd owned the place you'da been robbed, but he didn't. He didn't even stay on it long enough to have squatter's rights." We couldn't help grinning at that one. Mark said to Tetley, "Baker's place is part of Peter Wilde's ranch now."

Martin was nearly crying. "You can't hang me for being a sucker," he said.

"That depends on the kind of sucker you are."

"You haven't got any proof. Just because Baker robbed me doesn't make me a murderer. You can't hang me without any proof."

"We're getting it," Tetley said.

"Is it so far to Pike's that you can't go over there and look?" Martin cried. "Maybe I don't even own the Baker place; maybe I've been sold out. But I'm living there now. My wife's there now; my wife and two kids." His jaw tightened. "This is murder, as you're going at it," he told Tetley. "Even in this godforsaken country I've got a right to be brought to trial, and you know it. I have, and these men have. We have a right to trial before a regular judge."

"You're getting the trial," Tetley said, "with twenty-eight of the only kind of judges a murderer and a rustler gets in what you call this godforsaken country."

"And so far," Winder put in, "the jury don't much like your story."

The kid looked around slowly at as many of us as he could see, the way he was tied. It was as if he hadn't noticed before that we were there, and wanted to see what we were like. He must have judged Winder was right.

"I won't talk further without a proper hearing," he said slowly.

"Suit yourself, son," Ma said. "This is all the hearing you're likely to get short of the last judgment."

"Have you any cattle up here with you?" Tetley asked him.

The kid looked around at us again. He was breathing hard. One of the men from Bartlett's gang couldn't help grinning a little. The kid started to say something, then shut his mouth hard. We all waited, Tetley holding up a hand when the man who had grinned started to speak. Then he asked the question again in the same quiet way.

The kid looked down at the ground

"I'm not going to ask you again," Tetley said. The man named Smith stepped out with a rope in his hands. He was making a hangman's noose. The place was so quiet the tiny crackling of the burned-down wood sounded loud. Martin looked at the rope, sucked in his breath, and looked down again.

After a moment he said, so low we could hardly hear him, "Yes, I have."

"How many?"

"Fifty head."

"You miscounted, Amigo," Tetley remarked. Amigo grinned and spread his hands, palms up, and shrugged his shoulders.

"Where did you get them, Mr. Martin?"

"From Harley Drew, in Bridger's Valley."

When he looked up, there were tears in his eyes. Most of the watchers looked down at their boots for a moment, some of them making wry faces.

"I'm no rustler, though. I didn't steal them. I bought them and paid for them." Then suddenly he wanted to talk a lot. "I bought them this morning; paid cash for them. My own were so bad I didn't dare try to risk bringing them up. I didn't know what the Mono Lake country was like. I sold them off in Salinas. I had to stock up again."

He could see nobody believed him.

"You can wait, can't you?" he pleaded. "I'm not likely to escape from an army like this, am I? You can wait till you see Drew, till you ask about me in Pike's. It's not too much to ask a wait like that, is it, before you hang men?"

Everybody was still just looking at him or at the ground.

"My God," he yelled out suddenly, "you aren't going to hang innocent men without a shred of proof, are you?"

Tetley shook his head very slightly.

"Then why don't you take us in, and stop this damned farce?"

"It would be a waste of time," Farnley said. "The law is almighty slow and careless around here."

The kid appeared to be trying to think fast now.

"Where do you come from?" he asked.

"Bridger's Valley," Farnley told him. There were grins again. Martin said to Tetley, "You know Drew, then?"

"I know him," Tetley said. You wouldn't have gathered it was a pleasure from the way he spoke.

"Well, didn't you even see him? Who sent you up here?"

"Drew," Tetley said.

"That's not true," Davies said. He came out from the ring and closer to the fire. He looked odd among the riders, little and hunched in an old, loose jacket, and bareheaded. "That statement is not true," he repeated. "Drew didn't send us up here. Drew didn't even know we were coming."

Tetley was watching him closely. There was only a remnant of his smile.

"As I've told you a hundred times," Davies went on, "I'm not trying to obstruct justice. But I do want to see real justice. This is a farce. As Mr. Martin has said, this is murder if you carry it through. He's perfectly within his rights when he demands trial. And that's all I've asked since we started; that's all I'm asking now, a trial." He sounded truculent, for him, and he was breathing heavily as he spoke. "This young man," he said, pointing to Martin and looking around at us, "has said repeatedly that he is innocent. I, for one, believe him."

"Then I guess you're the only one that does, Arthur," Ma told him quietly.

Tetley made a sign to Mapes with his hand. Mapes stepped out and took Davies by the arm and began to shove him back toward the ring of watchers.

Davies did not struggle much; even the little he did looked silly in Mapes' big hands. But while he went he called out angrily, "If there's any justice in your proceedings, Tetley, it would be only with the greatest certainty, it would be only after a confession. And they haven't confessed, Tetley. They say they're innocent, and you haven't proved they aren't."

"Keep him there," Mapes told the men around Davies after he'd been pushed back.

"Indirectly, Drew sent us here," Tetley said, as if Davies had not spoken. "And now, if you're done," he went on, "I'd like to ask another question or two."

Martin seemed to have taken some hope from Davies' outburst. Now he was looking down again. It was clear enough what most of the men thought.

"First," Tetley said, "perhaps you have a bill of sale for those cattle?"

Martin swallowed hard. "No," he said finally. "No, I haven't."

"No?"

"Drew said it was all right. I couldn't find him at the ranch house. He was out on the range when I found him. He didn't have a bill of sale with him. He just said it was all right, not to wait, that he'd mail it to me. He told me it would be all right."

"Moore," Tetley said, without looking away from Martin.
"Yes?" Moore said. He didn't want to talk.
"You ride for Drew, don't you?"
"You know I do."
"In fact you're his foreman, aren't you?"
"Yes. What of it?"
"How long have you been riding for Drew?"
"Six years," Moore said.
"Did you ever know Drew to sell any cattle without a bill of sale?"
"No, I can't say as I ever did. But I can't remember every head he's sold in six years."
"It's customary for Drew to give a bill of sale, though?"
"Yes."
"And Moore, did you ever know Drew to sell any cattle after spring roundup, this year, or any other year?"
"No," Moore admitted, "I don't know that he's ever done that."
"Was there any reason why he should make a change in his regular practice this spring?"

Moore shook his head slowly. Young Greene shouted from over in front of Davies, "I heard him myself say, just a couple of days ago, that he wouldn't sell a head to God Himself this spring."

"Well?" Tetley asked Martin.

"I know it looks bad," the kid said, in a slow, tired voice. He didn't expect to be believed anymore. "I can't tell you anything else, I guess, except to ask Drew. It was hard to get them from him, all right. We talked a long time, and I had to show him how I was stuck, and how nobody wanted to sell this spring because there were so few calves. He really let me have them just as a favor, I think. That's all I have to tell you; I can't say anything else, I guess, not that would make any difference to you."

"No," Tetley agreed, "I don't believe you can."

"You don't believe me?"

"Would you, in my place?"

"I'd ask," Martin said more boldly. "I'd do a lot of asking before I'd risk hanging three men who might be innocent."

"If it were only rustling," Tetley said, "maybe. With murder, no. I'd rather risk a lot of hanging before too much asking. Law, as the books have it, is slow and full of holes."

In the silence the fire crackled, and hissed when the snow fell into it. The light of it flagged up and down on the men's serious faces. The mouths were hard and the eyes bright and nervous. Finally Ma said mildly, "I guess it would be enough even for Tyler, wouldn't it, Willard?"

"For Martin, perhaps," Tetley said.

"The others are his men, ain't they?" Farnley inquired.

Others quietly said it had been enough for them. Even Moore said, "It's no kindness to keep them waiting."

Still Tetley didn't say anything, and Ma burst out, "What you tryin' to do, play cat and mouse with them, Willard? You act like you liked it."

"I would prefer a confession," Tetley said. He was talking to Martin, not to us.

Martin swallowed and wet his lips with his tongue, but couldn't speak. Finally he groaned something we couldn't understand, and abandoned his struggle with himself. The sweat broke out on his face and began to trickle down; his jaw was shaking. The old man was talking to himself, now and then shaking his head, as if pursuing an earnest and weighty debate. The Mex was standing firmly, with his feet a little apart, like a boxer anticipating his opponent's lunge or jab, saying nothing and showing nothing. It got to Gil even.

"I don't see your game, Tetley," he said. "If you got any doubts, let's call off this party and take them in to the Judge, like Davies wants."

This was the first remark that had made any impression on Tetley's cool disregard. He looked directly at Gil and told him, "This is only very slightly any of your business, my friend. Remember that."

Gil got hot. "Hanging is any man's business that's around, I'd say."

"Have you a brief for the innocence of these men?" Tetley asked him. "Or is it merely that your stomach for justice is cooling?"

"Mister, take it easy with that talk," Gil said, swinging out of line and hitching a thumb over his gun belt. A couple of men tried to catch hold of him, but he shook them off short and sharp, without looking at them or using a hand. He was staring at Tetley in a way I knew enough to be scared of. I got up, but I didn't know what I'd do.

"No man," Gil said, standing just across the corner of the fire from Tetley, "no man is going to call me yellow. If that's what you mean, make it plainer."

Tetley was smooth. "Not at all," he said. "But we seem to have a number of men here only too willing to foist the burden of a none too pleasant task on others, even when those others, as we all know, may well never perform it. I was just wondering how many such men. It would be a kindness, in my estimation, to let them leave before we proceed further. Their interruptions are becoming tiresome."

Gil stood where he was. "Well, I'm not one of them, get it?" he said.

"Good," Tetley said, nodding as if he were pleased. "We have no quarrel, then, I guess."

"No," Gil admitted. "But I still say I don't see your game. Hanging is one thing. To keep men standing and sweating for it while you talk is another. I don't like it."

Tetley examined him as if to remember him for another time. "Hurry is scarcely to be recommended at a time like this," he said finally. "I am taking, it seems to me, the chief responsibility in this matter, and I do not propose to act prematurely, that's all."

I could see Gil didn't believe this any more than I did, but there wasn't anything to say to it, no clear reason that you could put a finger on, for doubt. Gil stood there, but said nothing more. It was a hard spot for him to retreat from. Martin was watching him, hoping to God something would break. He sagged again, though, and closed his eyes and worked his mouth, when Gil just stood balanced and Tetley said, "But since these three men will not ease our task directly, we'll get on."

"We've had enough questions," Winder said. "They aren't talking."

Tetley said to Martin, "You called the old man Dad. Is he your father?"

"No," Martin said, and again added something too low to hear.

"Speak up, man," Tetley said. "You're taking it like a woman."

"Everybody's gotta die once, son. Keep your chin up," Ma said. That was bare comfort for him, but I knew Ma wasn't thinking of him so much as of us. His weakness was making us feel as if we were mistreating a dog instead of trying a man.

The kid brought his head up and faced us, but that was worse. The tears were running down his cheeks and his mouth was working harder than ever.

"God Almighty, he's bawlin'," said Winder, and spit as if it made him sick.

"No," said Martin, thick and blubbery. "He works for me."

"What's your name?" Tetley asked, turning to the old man. The old man didn't hear him; he continued to talk to himself. Mapes went and stood in front of him and said loudly in his face, "What's your name?"

"I didn't do it," argued the old man. "No, how could I have done it? You can see I didn't do it, can't you?" He paused, thinking how to make it clear. "I didn't have anything in my gun," he explained. "Mr. Martin won't let me have any bullets for my gun, so how could I do it? I wasn't afraid to, but I didn't have any bullets."

"You didn't do what?" Tetley asked him gently.

"No, I didn't, I tell you. I didn't." Then his wet wreck of a face seemed to light up with an idea. "He done it," he asserted. "He done it."

"Who did it?" said Tetley, still quietly, but slowly and distinctly.

"He did," burbled the old man. "Juan did. He told me so. No, he didn't; I saw him do it. If I saw him do it," he inquired cutely, "I know, don't I? I couldn't have done it if I saw him do it, could I?"

The Mex didn't stir. Farnley was watching the Mex, and even his hard grin was gone. He was holding his breath, and then breathing by snorts.

Martin spoke, "Juan couldn't have done anything. I was with him all the time."

"Yes, he did too do it, Mr. Martin. He was asleep; he didn't mean to tell me, but I was awake and I heard him talking about it. He told me when he was asleep."

"The old man is feebleminded," Martin said, slowly and quietly, trying to speak so the old man wouldn't hear him. "He doesn't know what he's talking about. He's dreamed something." He looked down; either it hurt him to say this or he was doing a better job of acting than his condition made probable. "You can't trust anything he says. He dreams constantly; when he's awake he invents things. After a little while he really believes they have happened. He's a good old man; you've scared him, and he's inventing things he thinks will save him."

Then he flared, "If you've got to go on with your filthy joke, you can let him alone, can't you?"

"You keep out of this," Mapes shouted, stepping quickly past the Mexican and standing in front of Martin. "You've had your say. Now shut up."

Martin stared at him. "Then let the old man alone," he said.

Mapes suddenly struck him across the face so hard it would have knocked him over if he hadn't been tied to the others. As it was, one knee buckled under him, and he ducked his head down to shake off the sting or block another slap if it was coming.

"Lay off, Mapes," somebody shouted, and Moore said, "You've got no call for that sort of thing, Mapes."

"First he wouldn't talk, and now he talks too damned much," Mapes said, but let Martin alone.

We had closed the circle as much as the fire would let us. Tetley moved closer to Martin, and Mapes made room for him, though strutting because of the yelling at him.

"You mean the old man's actually feebleminded?" Tetley asked.

"Yes."

"What's his name?"

"Alva Hardwick."

"And the other speaks no English?"

Martin didn't reply.

"What's his name?"

"Juan Martinez."

"No, it isn't," old Bartlett said.

Tetley turned and looked at Bartlett. "You know something about this man?" he asked.

"I've been trying to tell you ever since this fool questioning started," Bartlett told him, "but you've got to be so damned regular."

"All right, all right," Tetley said impatiently. "What is it?"

Bartlett suddenly became cautious. "I don't want to say until I'm sure," he said. He went up to the Mex.

"Remember me?" he asked. "At Driver's last September?"

The Mex acted like he didn't know he was being talked to. Bartlett got angry; when he got angry his loose jowls trembled.

"I'm talking to you, greaser," he said.

The Mex looked at him, too quick and narrow for not understanding, but then all he did was shake his head and say, "No sabby," again.

"The devil you don't," Bartlett told him. "Your name's Francisco Morez, and the vigilantes would still like to get hold of you."

The Mex still didn't seem to understand.

"He talks English better than I do," Bartlett told Tetley. "He was a gambler, and claimed to be a rancher from down Sonora way somewhere. They wanted him for murder."

"What about that?" Tetley asked Martin.

"I don't know," the kid said hopelessly.

"Does he speak English?"

The kid looked at the Mex and said, "Yes." The Mex didn't bat an eye.

"How long's he been with you?"

"He joined us in Carson." Martin looked at Tetley again. "I don't know anything about him," he said. "He told me that he was a rider, and that he knew this country, and that he'd like to tie up with me. That's all I know."

"You picked him up on nothing more than that?" Tetley asked Martin.

"Why don't you come to the point?" Martin asked. "Why ask me all these questions if you don't believe anything I tell you?"

"There's as much truth to be sifted out of lies as anything else," Tetley said, "if you get enough lies. Is his name Morez?" he went on.

"I tell you I don't know. He told me his name was Martinez. That's all I know."

Without warning Tetley shifted his questioning to the old man. "What did he do?" he asked sharply.

"He did," mumbled the old man. "Yes, he did too; I saw him."

"What did he do?"

"He said that . . . he said . . ." The old man lost what he was trying to tell.

"He said . . ." encouraged Tetley.

"I don't know. I didn't do it. You wouldn't kill an old man, mister. I'm a very old man, mister." He assumed his expression of cunning again. "I wouldn't live very long anyway," he said argumentatively.

"What do you know about the old man?" Tetley asked Martin patiently.

"He's all right; he wouldn't hurt anything if he could help it."

"And he's been with you how long?"

"Three years."

"As a rider?"

"I'd rather not talk about this here," Martin said. "Can't you take me in the cabin or somewhere?"

"It's a better check on the stories if they don't hear each other, at that," Winder put in.

"What stories?" Farnley asked. "One of them don't talk and the other don't make sense. There's only one story."

"We'll do well enough here," Tetley said. "Does the old man here ride for you?"

"Only ordinary driving. He's not a cowboy. He's a good worker if he understands, but you have to tell him just what to do."

"Not much use in this business, then, is he?" Tetley spoke absentmindedly, as if just settling the point for himself, but he was watching Martin. Martin didn't slip.

"He's a good worker."

"Why did you take him on, if he's what you say?"

Martin was embarrassed. Finally he said, "You would have too."

Tetley smiled. "What did he do before he came to you?"

"He was in the army. I don't know which army; he doesn't seem to be clear about it himself. Maybe he was in both armies at different times; I've thought so sometimes, from things he's said. Or that might be just his way of imagining. You can't always tell what's been real with him."

"I know," said Tetley, still smiling. "You've made a point of that. But you're sure he was in the army?"

"He was in one of them. Something started him thinking that way."

"A half-wit in the army?" Tetley asked, tilting his head to one side.

Martin swallowed and wet his lips again. "He must have been," he insisted.

"Still, you say he wouldn't hurt anything?"

"No," Martin said, "he wouldn't. He's foolish, but he's gentle."

Tetley just stood and smiled at him and shook his head.

"I believe," Martin persisted, "some experience in the war must have injured his mind. There's one he always talks about, and never finishes. He must have been all right before, and something in the war did it to him."

Tetley considered the old man. Then suddenly he drew himself up stiffly and clicked his heels together, and barked out, "Attention," with all the emphasis on the last syllable.

Old Hardwick just looked around at all of us with a scared face, more nervous and vacant than ever because he knew we were all watching him.

Tetley relaxed. "I don't think so," he said to Martin.

"He's forgotten. He forgets everything."

Tetley shook his head, still smiling. "Not that," he said.

"You still don't talk English?" he asked the Mex. The Mex was silent.

Soon after, Tetley sent two riders to help the Bartlett boys shag in the cattle they'd been holding. At the edge of the clearing, seeing the fire, and the men and horses, and being wild with this unusual night hazing, they milled. But they didn't have to come any closer. As they turned, with the firelight on them, we could see Drew's brand, and his notches on the dewlaps.

"Anything you haven't said that you want to say?" Tetley asked Martin.

Martin drew a deep breath to steady himself. He could feel the set against him that one look at those cattle had brought on if all the talk hadn't.

"I've told you how I got them," he said.

"We heard that," Tetley agreed.

"You have the steers, haven't you?" Martin asked. He was short of breath. "Well, you haven't lost anything, then, have you? You could wait to hang us until you talk to Drew, couldn't you?"

"It's not the first time," Tetley said. "We waited before." He studied Martin for a moment. "I'll make you a deal, though," he offered. "Tell us which of you shot Kinkaid, and the other two can wait."

Martin halfway glanced at the Mex, but if he was going to say anything, he changed his mind. He shook his head before he spoke, as if at some thought of his own. "None of us killed anybody," he said in that tired voice again. "We were all three together all the time."

"That's all, I guess," Tetley said regretfully. He motioned toward the biggest tree on the edge of the clearing.

"My God," Martin said huskily, "you aren't going to, really! You wouldn't, really! You can't do it," he wailed, and started fighting his bond, jerking the other two prisoners about. The old man stumbled and fell to his knees and got up again, as if it were a desperate necessity to be on his feet, but as clumsily as a cow because of his bound wrists.

"Tie them separately, Mapes," Tetley ordered.

Winder helped Mapes. Only Martin was hard to tie. He'd lost his head, and it took two men to hold him while he was bound. Then the three were standing there separately, each with his arms held flat to his sides by half a dozen turns of rope. Their feet were left free to walk them into position. Each of them had a noose around his neck too, and a man holding it.

In spite of Mapes' trying to hold him up, Martin slumped down to his knees. We couldn't understand what he was babbling. When Mapes pulled him up again he managed to stand, but waving like a tree in a shifting wind. Then we could understand part of what he was saying. "One of them's just a baby," he was saying, "just a baby. They haven't got anything to go on, not a thing. They're alone; they haven't got anything to go on, and they're alone."

"Take them over," Tetley ordered, indicating the tree again. It was a big pine with its top shot away by lightning. It had a long branch that stuck out straight on the clearing side, about fifteen feet from the ground. We'd all spotted that branch.

"The Mex is mine," Farnley said. Tetley nodded and told some others to get the rustlers' horses.

Martin kept hanging back, and when he was shoved along kept begging, "Give us some time, it's not even decent; give us some time."

Old Hardwick stumbled and buckled, but didn't fall. He was silent, but his mouth hung open, and his eyes were protruding enormously. The Mex, however, walked steadily, showing only a wry grin, as if he had expected nothing else from the first.

THE OX-BOW INCIDENT

When the three of them were lined up in a row under the limb, waiting for their horses, Martin said, "I've got to write a letter. If you're at least human you'll give me time for that anyway." His breath whistled when he talked, but he seemed to know what he was saying again.

"We can't wait all night," Mapes told him, getting ready to throw up the end of the rope, which had a heavy knot tied in it to carry it over.

"He's not asking much, Tetley," Davies said.

Old Hardwick seemed to have caught the idea. He burbled about being afraid of the dark, that he didn't want to die in the dark, that in the dark he saw things.

"He's really afraid of the dark," Martin said. "Can't this wait till sunrise? It's customary anyway, isn't it?"

Men were holding the three horses just off to the side now. Farnley was holding the hang rope on the Mex. He spoke to Tetley angrily.

"Now what are you dreaming about, Tetley? They're trying to put it off, that's all; they're scared, and they're trying to put it off. Do you want Tyler and the sheriff to get here, and the job not done?" As if he had settled it himself, he threw the end of the Mex's rope over the limb.

"They won't come in this snow," Davies said.

"I believe you're right," Tetley told Davies. "Though I doubt if you want to be." He asked Bartlett, "What time is it?"

Bartlett drew a thick silver watch from his waistcoat pocket and looked at it. "Five minutes after two," he said.

"All right," Tetley said after a moment, "we'll wait till daylight."

Farnley stood holding the end of the rope and glaring at Tetley. Then slowly he grinned up one side of his face and tossed down the rope, like he was all done. "Why not?" he said. "It will give the bastard time to think about it." Then he walked down to the fire and stood there by himself. He was wild inside; you could tell that just by looking at his back.

In a way, none of us liked the wait, when we'd have to go through the whole thing over again anyway. But you couldn't refuse to give three or four hours to men in a spot like that if they thought they wanted them.

"Reverend," Tetley said to Sparks, "you can settle your business at leisure."

The fire was fed up again, and the three men were put on different sides of it. It was hard to tell where to go yourself. You wanted to stay near the fire, and still not right around those men.

Martin asked to have his hands untied. "I can't write like this," he explained. The Mex said something too, in Spanish.

"He wants to eat," Amigo told us, grinning. "He say he is much hungry from so much ride and so much talk." The Mex grinned at us while Amigo was talking.

"Let him ask for it himself, then," Bartlett said.

"Untie them all," Tetley said, and appointed Winder and two other men to keep them covered.

When he was freed, Martin moved to sit on a log on his side of the fire. He sat there rubbing his wrists. Then he asked for paper and a pencil. Davies had a little leather account book and a pencil in his vest. He gave them to Martin, showing him the blank pages in the back of the book. But Martin's hands were shaking so he couldn't write. Davies offered to write for him, but he said no, he'd be better in a few minutes; he'd rather write this letter for himself.

"Will the others want to write?" Davies asked him.

"You can ask Juan," Martin said, looking at the Mex. Whenever he looked at the Mex he had that perplexed expression of wanting to say something and deciding not to. "It's no use with the old man, though," he said, looking up at Davies and remembering to smile to show he was grateful. "He wouldn't know what to say, or how to say it. I don't believe he has anybody to write to, for that matter. He forgets people if they're not right around him."

When Amigo asked him, Juan said no, he didn't care to write. For some reason he seemed to think the idea of his writing to anyone was humorous.

Ma was examining the rustlers' packs. She was going to get a meal for the Mex. She drew articles out, naming them for everybody to hear as she removed them. There was a lot more than three men could want for a meal or two. There was a whole potato sack of very fresh beef, which had been rolled up in paper and then put in the sack, and the sack half buried in an old snowdrift. There was coffee too.

When Ma had called off part of her list, one of the men yelled to her to fix a spread for everybody. If they had to freeze and lose sleep because somebody was afraid of the dark, he said, they didn't have to starve too, and it wasn't exactly robbery because by the time all of it was eaten, the food wouldn't belong to anybody anyway. A few men looked around hard at that, but most pretended they were thinking about something and hadn't heard it. Moore spoke up, though, and told Ma he didn't want anything; then others of us told her the same thing. You can't eat a man's food before him and then hang him.

But when Ma set to cooking it, with Sparks helping her, many changed their minds. There was a belly-searching odor from that meat propped on forked sticks and dripping and scorching over the coals. None of us had had a real meal since midday, and some not then, and the air was cold and snowy, with a piny edge. It carried the meat smell very richly.

I drank some of the coffee because my teeth were chattering. I wasn't really so cold as thinned out by the loss of blood. Coffee was better than the whiskey had been, and after it I sneaked a bit of the meat too, being careful that Martin didn't see me eat it. I only chewed a little, though, and knew I didn't want it. I took more coffee.

Sparks took meat and bread and coffee on their own plates and in their own cups to the three prisoners. The Mex ate with big mouthfuls, taking his time and enjoying it. The strong muscles in his jaws worked in and out so the firelight shone on them when he chewed. He washed it down with long draughts of coffee too hot for me to have touched, and nodded his head at Ma to show it was all good. When he was done eating he took a pull of whiskey from Gil, rolled and lit a cigarette, and sat cross-legged, drawing the smoke in and blowing it out between his lips in strong jets that bellied out into clouds at the end. He watched the fire and the smoke from his cigarette, and sometimes smiled to himself reminiscently.

Old Hardwick ate his meat and bread too, but didn't know he was doing it. He chewed with the food showing out of his mouth, and didn't stop staring. Sometimes he continued to chew when he had already swallowed. Some of the bread he pulled into little pieces and dropped while he was chewing the meat.

Martin drank some coffee, but refused food. He was holding the notebook and pencil and thinking. It was a hard letter to write. He would stare at the fire with glazed eyes, wake up with a shiver and look around him, put the pencil to the paper, then relapse into that staring again. It was a long time before he really began to write, and then he twice tore out a page on which there were only a few words, and began again. Finally, he seemed to forget where he was, and what was going to happen to him, and wrote slowly and steadily, occasionally crossing out a line.

Gil made me lie down with a couple of blankets around me and my back against the cabin, but between Ma and Tetley sitting and smoking and not talking much, I could see Martin's face and his hand busy writing.

The young Bartletts were relieved and came in. They wouldn't eat either, but drank coffee and smoked. It was very quiet, all the men sitting around except the guards. Tetley insisted that the guards stand up. Some of the men talked in low voices, and now and then one of them would laugh, but stop quickly. Tetley kept looking over at his son. Gerald hadn't eaten or even taken any coffee, and he wasn't smoking, but was sitting there picking up little sticks and digging hard at the ground with them; then, realizing he had them, tossing them away. When another squall of wind brought the snow down in waves again, the men looked up at the sky, where there wasn't anything to see. The wind wasn't steady, however, and shortly the snow thinned out again. Most of it had shaken from its loose lodging on the branches of the pines. I became drowsy, and felt that I was observing a distant picture. All the others were trying to stay awake, though some of them would nod and then jerk up and stare around, as if something had happened or they felt a long time had passed.

Only young Tetley kept the scene from going entirely dreamlike. Betweentimes of playing with his sticks he would rise abruptly and walk out to the edge of the dark and stand there with his back turned, and then suddenly turn and come back to the fire and stand there for a long time before he sat down again. After the third or fourth time his father leaned toward him when he sat down, and spoke to him. The boy remained seated then, but always with those busy hands.

Then I slept myself, after short broken dozes. I woke suddenly, with my hurt shoulder aching and with Gil's hand on my other shoulder.

"What's eating you?" he asked. "You were jabbering and flopping around like a fish out of water. I thought maybe you was out of your head."

"No, I'm all right," I told him.

"You must have been dreaming," Gil said. "You was scared to death when I took hold of you."

I said I couldn't remember.

"I wouldn'ta woke you up," he apologized, "only I was afraid you'd start that shoulder bleeding again."

"I'm glad you did," I told him. I didn't like the idea of lying there talking in my sleep. "Have I been asleep long?"

"An hour or two, I guess."

"An hour or two?" I felt like a traitor, as if I'd wasted the little time those three men had by sleeping myself.

Martin had finished his letter and was sitting hunched over, with his forehead in his hands. I saw him stare around once, and then bend his head again, locking his hands behind it and pulling down hard, like he was stretching his neck and shoulders. Then he relaxed again, and put his arms across his knees and his head down on them. He was having a hard time of it, I judged.

Sparks was busy with old Hardwick, squatting in front of him, exhorting, and every now and then taking hold of him gently to make him pay attention. But the old man was scared out of what little wits he had and wasn't listening; instead, he was staring and talking to himself. Davies was trying to get Tetley to talk to him, it seemed, but failing. The Mex was sitting there drowsily, with his elbows on his knees and his forearms hanging loosely between his legs.

Only two men were standing—one on guard with a carbine across his arm, and Farnley, who had moved around to put his back against the big tree.

There was no wind, and no snow falling, and no stars showing; just thick, dark cold.

I heard Tetley making a retort to Davies. It was the first time either of them had raised his voice, and Davies nervously motioned him to be quiet, but he finished what he was saying clearly enough so I could hear it. "It may be a fine letter; apparently, from what you say, it's a very fine letter. But if it's an honest letter, it's none of my business to read it; and if it isn't, I don't want to."

Martin had heard. He lifted his head and looked across at them.

"Is that my letter you're showing?" he asked.

"It's yours," Tetley told him. He was smiling when he said it.

"What are you doing, showing my letter?" Martin asked Davies. His voice had aroused the whole circle to watch them now. Martin stood up. "If I remember rightly, all I asked was that you keep that letter and make sure it was delivered."

"I'm sorry," Davies said, "I was just trying to prove—"

Martin began to move across toward Davies. The veins were standing out in his neck. Several men scrambled to their feet. Davies rose too, defensively. The guard didn't know what to do. He took a step or two after Martin, but then stood there holding his carbine like it was a live rattler. Farnley came down from his stand against the tree. He had his gun out when he got to the fire.

"Sit down, you, and pipe down," he ordered.

Martin stood still, but he didn't show any signs of retreating or of sitting down. He didn't even look around at Farnley. Mapes ordered Martin to sit down also, and drew his gun when Martin didn't move or even glance at him.

"It's enough," Martin said in a smothered voice to Davies, "to be hanged by a pack of bullying outlaws, without having your private thoughts handed around to them for a joke."

"I've said I'm sorry," Davies reminded him, sharply for him. "I was merely doing—"

"I don't give a damn what you were doing. I didn't write that letter to be passed around. I wrote that letter to— Well, it's none of your business, and it's none of the business of any of these other murdering bastards."

"Take it easy on that talk," Farnley said behind him.

"I made no promise," Davies told Martin.

"All right, you made no promise. I should have known I'd need a promise. Or would that have done any good? I thought there was one decent man among you. Well, I was wrong."

Then he became general in his reference. He waved an arm

around to take us all in. "But what good would an oath do, in a pack like this, an oath to do what any decent man would do by instinct? You eat our food in front of us, in front of men about to die, and sleep while we wait. What good would an oath do where there's not so much conscience in the lot as a good dog has?

"Give me that letter," he ordered, taking another step toward Davies.

"I'll see that she gets it," Davies said stiffly.

"I wouldn't have her touch it," Martin said.

Tetley stood up. "That's enough," he said. "You've been told to go back and sit down. If I were you, I'd do that. Give him the letter, Davies."

Still holding the letter, Davies said quietly, "Your wife ought to hear from you, son. None of us could be so kind as that letter; and she'd want it to keep."

Martin stared at him. His face changed, the wrath dying out of it. "Thanks," he said. "I'm sorry. Yes, keep it, please, and see that she gets it."

"Hey, the Mex," Ma yelled. She was pointing up to the edge of the woods, where the horses were tied. There was the Mex, working at the rope on one of the bays, the horse nearest the woods on the road side. There was a general yell and scramble. Somebody yelled to spread, he might have a gun. Several yelled to shoot. They circled out fast, snapping hammers as they ran. They were mad and ashamed at having been caught napping. Tetley was as angry as anyone, but he kept his head.

"Mapes, Winder," he called out, "keep an eye on the other two. You," he said to Davies, "if you're part of this trick . . ." but didn't finish it. Instead, he went around the fire quickly to where he could see better.

Martin stood where he was, and old Hardwick, when he saw the men take their guns out, put his hands up over his eyes, like a little, scared kid.

The Mex did have a gun. At the first shout he just worked harder on the tie, but when Farnley shot and then two more shots came from off at the side, he yanked the horse around in front of him and shot back. In the shadow you could see the red jet of the gun. I heard the bullet whack into the cabin. Everybody broke farther to the sides to get out of the light, and nobody was crowding in very fast. Farnley, creeping up at the edge of the woods, tried another shot and nicked the horse, which squealed and reared so the Mex lost him. The other horses were scared, and wheeled and yanked hard at their tie ropes.

Nobody could see the Mex to shoot again. He must have given up trying to get the horse, though, and made a break for it on foot, because Farnley quit creeping and stood up and shot again. Then he came back running and took the carbine away from the guard and plunged back into the woods, yelling something as he went. Others fanned out into the woods too.

Then it was quiet for a few minutes. Finally it began, somewhere up on the mountain and over toward the road—not too far, from the loudness of the reports. There were three short, flat shots in quick succession, then a deeper one that got an echo from some canyon up among the trees. Then it was quiet again, and we thought it was all over, when there were two more of the flat explosions and after a moment the deeper one again. Then it stayed quiet.

We were all nervous, waiting, and nobody talked, just watched around the edge of the woods to see where they'd come out. The wait seemed so long that some of the men who weren't on guard began edging cautiously into the woods to see what had happened.

Then we saw the others coming down again. Two of them had the Mex between them, but he wasn't dead; he wasn't even out. They carried him down into the light and set him on the log Martin had been sitting on. He was sweating, but not saying anything, and not moaning.

"Tie the others up again," Tetley ordered.

"That must have been some fine shooting," he said to Farnley. "Where's he hit?"

Farnley flushed. "It was good enough," he retorted. "It was dark in there; you couldn't even see the barrel sometimes, let alone the sights." Then he answered, "I hit him in the leg."

"Saving him for the rope, eh?"

"No, I wasn't. I wanted to kill the bastard bad enough. It was the slope that done it; it's hard to tell, shooting uphill."

They were talking like it had been a target shoot, and the Mex right there.

One of the men who had gone in after Farnley came up to Tetley and handed him something. "That's the gun he had," he said, nodding at the Mex. It was a long, blue-barreled Colt six-shooter with an ivory grip. "It's empty," the man said. "He shot 'em all out, I guess."

Farnley was looking at the gun in Tetley's hand. He was staring at it. After a moment, without asking, he reached out and took it away from Tetley.

"Well," he said, after turning it over in his own hands, "I guess we know now, don't we? If there was ever anything to wonder about, there ain't now."

Tetley watched him and waited for his explanation.

"It's Larry's gun," Farnley said. "Look," he said to the rest of us, and pointed to the butt and gave it to us to look at. Kinkaid's name, all of it, Laurence Liam Kinkaid, was inlaid in tiny letters of gold in the ivory of the butt.

Tetley recovered the gun and took it over and held it for the Mex to see.

"Where did you get this?" he asked. His tone proved he would take only one answer. Sweating from his wound, the Mex grinned at him savagely.

"If somebody will take this bullet out of my leg, I will tell you," he said.

"God, he talks American," Ma said.

"And ten other languages," said the Mex, "but I don't tell anything I don't want to in any of them. My leg, please. I desire I may stand upright when you come to your pleasure."

"What's a slug or two to you now?" Farnley asked.

"If he wants it out, let him have it out," Moore said. "There's time."

The Mex looked around at us all with that angry grin. "If somebody will lend me the knife, I will take it out myself."

"Don't give him no knife," Bartlett said. "He can throw a knife better than most men can shoot."

"Better than these men, it is true," said the Mex. "But if you are afraid, then I solemnly give my promise I will not throw the knife. When I am done, then quietly I will give the knife back to its owner, with the handle first."

Surprisingly, young Tetley volunteered to remove the slug. His face was white, his voice smothered when he said it, but his eyes were bright. In his own mind he was championing his cause still, in the only way left. He felt that doing this, which would be difficult for him, must somehow count in the good score. He crossed to the Mex and knelt beside him, but when he took the knife one of the men offered him, his hand was shaking so he couldn't even start. He put up a hand, as if to clear his eyes, and the Mex took the knife away from him.

Farnley quickly turned the carbine on the Mex, but he didn't pay any attention. He made a quick slash through his chaps from the thigh to the boot top. His leg was muscular and thick, and hairless as an Indian's. Just over the knee there was the bullet hole, ragged and dark, but small; dark tendrils of blood had dried down from it, not a great deal of blood. Young Tetley saw it close to his face, and got up drunkenly and moved away, his face bloodless. The Mex grinned after him.

"The little man is polite," he commented, "but without the stomach for the blood, eh?"

Then he said, while he was feeling from the wound along his leg up to the thigh, "Will someone please to make the fire better? The light is not enough."

Tetley ordered them to throw on more wood. He didn't look to see them do it. He was watching Gerald stagger out toward the dark in the edge of the woods to be sick.

When the fire had blazed up, the Mex turned his thigh to the light and went to work. Everybody watched him; it's hard not to watch a thing like that, though you don't want to. The Mex opened the mouth of the wound so it began to bleed again, freely, but then again he traced with his fingers up his thigh. He set his jaw, and high on the thigh made a new incision. His grin froze so it looked more like showing his teeth, and the sweat beads popped out on his forehead. He rested a moment when the first cut had been made and was bleeding worse than the other.

"That is very bad shooting," he said. He panted from the pain.

Nonetheless, when he began to work again he hummed a Mexican dance tune through his teeth. He halted the song only once, when something he did with the point of the knife made his leg straighten involuntarily. It made him grunt in spite of himself. After that his own hand trembled badly, but he took a breath and began to dig and sweat and hum again. It got so I couldn't watch it either. I turned and looked for young Tetley instead, and saw him standing by a tree, leaning on it with one hand, his back to the fire. His father was watching him too.

There was a murmur, and I looked back, and the Mex had the bloody slug out and was holding it up for us to look at. When we had seen it he tossed it to Farnley.

"You should try again with that one," he said.

Sparks brought some hot water, and after propping the knife so the blade was in the coals, the Mex began washing out the two wounds with a purple silk handkerchief he'd had around his neck. He took care of himself as carefully as if he still had a lifetime to go. Then, when the knife blade was hot enough, he drew it out of the fire and clapped it right against the wounds, one after the other. Each time his body stiffened, the muscles of his jaw and the veins of his neck protruded, and the sweat broke out over his face, but still he drew the knife away from the thigh wound slowly, as if it pleased him to take his time. He asked for some of the fat from the steaks, rubbed the grease over the burned cuts, and bound them with the purple kerchief and another from his pocket. Then he lit a cigarette and took it easy.

After inhaling twice, long and slow, he picked up the knife he'd used and tossed it over in front of the man who had lent it. He tossed it so it spun in the air and struck the ground, point first, with a *chuck* sound, and dug in halfway to the hilt. It struck within an inch of where the man's boot had been, but he'd drawn off quickly when he saw it coming. The Mex grinned at him.

Martin and old Hardwick were bound again. Tetley told them they needn't tie the Mex; he wouldn't go far for a while. The Mex thanked him, grinning through the smoke of his cigarette.

But when Tetley began to question him about the gun, all he'd say was that he'd found it; that it was lying right beside the road, and he'd brought it along, thinking to meet somebody he could send it back with. When Tetley called him a liar and repeated the questions, the Mex at first just said the same thing, and then suddenly became angry and stubborn-looking, called Tetley a blind fool, lit another cigarette, and said no sabby, as he had at first. Martin told the same story about the gun—that they'd found it lying by the west lane when they came out from Drew's place, that all the cartridges had been in it, that he'd told the Mex to leave it because it was too far back to the ranch to take it, but that the Mex had thought they might meet somebody who could return it. There wasn't anything else to be had out of either of them.

The Mexican's courage, and even, in a way, young Martin's pride in the matter of the letter, had won them much sympathy, and I think we all believed now that the old man was really a pitiful fool; but whatever we thought, there was an almost universal determination to finish the job now. The gun was a clincher with us.

All but Davies. Davies was trying to get other men to read the letter. He maintained stronger than ever that young Martin was innocent, that Martin was not the kind of a man who could either steal or kill. He worked on those of us who had shown some sympathy with his ideas before. He tried hard not to let Tetley notice what he was doing, to stand naturally when he talked, and not to appear too earnest to a person who couldn't hear him. But he didn't make much headway. Most of the men had made up their minds, or felt that the rest had and that their own sympathy was reprehensible and should be concealed. That was the way I felt. None of us would look at the letter. When he came to us, telling us to read the letter, Gil said, "I don't want to read the letter. It's none of my business. You heard the kid; you ought to remember if anybody does."

"Do you suppose it matters to his wife who sees this letter?" Davies said. "In her place which would you rather have, a live husband with some of his secrets with you revealed, or a dead husband and all your secrets still?

"I don't like to pry any more than you do," he insisted, "but you can't put a life against a scruple. I tell you, if you'll read this letter, you'll know he couldn't have done it; not any of it. And if the letter's a fake, we have only to wait to know, don't we?"

It wasn't long until daylight, and the men hadn't really settled down again, but were moving around in groups, talking and smoking. I thought Tetley was watching us.

"That must be some letter," Gil was saying.

Davies held it out to him. "Read it," he pleaded.

"You get Martin to ask me to read it and I will," Gil told him, grinning.

"Then you read it," Davies said, turning to me. Gil was watching me, still grinning.

"No," I said. "I'd rather not." I was curious to read that letter, but I couldn't, there, like that.

Davies stood and looked from one to the other of us, despairingly. "Do you want that kid to hang?" he asked finally.

"You can't change rustlin' and murder," Gil said.

"Never mind that," Davies said. "Don't think about anything but the way you really feel about it. Do you feel that you'd like to have that kid hanged; any of them, for that matter?"

"My feelings haven't got anything to do with it," Gil said.

Davies began to argue to show us that feelings had everything to do with it; that they were the real guide in a thing like this, when Tetley called out to him by name. Everyone looked at Tetley and Davies, and stopped moving around or talking.

"Don't you know a trick when you see one, Davies?" Tetley asked him, for all of us to hear. "Or are you in on this?"

Davies retorted that he knew a trick as well as the next man, and that Tetley himself knew that this wasn't any trick; yes, and that Tetley knew he'd had no part in any such games himself. He was defiant, and stated again, defiantly, his faith in the innocence of the three men. But he talked hurriedly, defensively, and finally stopped of his own accord at a point that was not a conclusion. Whatever else was weakening him, I believe he felt all the time that it was ugly to talk so before the men themselves, that his own defense sounded no prettier there than Tetley's side. Then too, he had little support, and he knew it. He knew it so well that, when he had faltered to silence, and Tetley asked him, "Are you alone in this, Davies?" he said nothing.

"I think we'd better get this settled," Tetley said. "We must act as a unit in a job like this. Then we need fear no mistaken reprisal. Are you content to abide by a majority decision, Davies?"

Davies looked him in the face, but even that seemed to be an effort. He wouldn't say anything.

"How about the rest of you men?" Tetley asked. "Majority rule?"

There were sounds of assent. Nobody spoke out against it.

"It has to be," Ma said. "Among a bunch of pigheads like this you'd never get everybody to agree to anything."

"We'll vote," Tetley said. "Everybody who is with Mr. Davies, who favors putting this thing off and turning it over to the courts, step out here." He pointed to a space among us on the south side of the fire.

Davies walked out there and stood. Nobody else came for a moment, and he flushed when Tetley smiled at him. Then Sparks shambled out too, but smiling apologetically. Then Gerald Tetley joined them. His fists were clenched as he felt the watching, and saw his father's sardonic smile disappear slowly until his face was a stern mask. There was further movement, and some muttering, as Carl Bartlett and Moore stood out with them also. No more came.

"Five," said Tetley. "Not a majority, I believe, Mr. Davies."

He was disappointed that anyone had ventured to support Davies; I'm sure he hadn't expected as many as four others. I know I hadn't. And he was furious that Gerald had been among them. But he spoke quietly and ironically, as if his triumph had been complete.

Davies nodded, and slowly put Martin's letter away in his shirt pocket, under his waistcoat.

It was already getting light; the cabin and the trees could be seen clearly. There was no sunrise, but a slow leaking in of light from all quarters. The firelight no longer colored objects or faces near it. The faces were gray and tired and stern. We knew it was going to happen now, and yet, I believe, most of us still had a feeling it couldn't. It had been delayed so long; we had argued so much. Only Tetley seemed entirely self-possessed; his face showed no signs of weariness or excitement.

He asked Martin if there was any other message he wished to leave. Martin shook his head. In this light his face looked hollow, pale, and without individuality. His mouth was trembling constantly, and he was careful not to talk. I hoped, for our sake as much as his, that he'd make the decent end he now had his will set on.

Sparks was talking to the old fool again, but he, seeing the actual preparations begin, was frightened sick once more, and babbled continually in a hoarse, worn-out voice about his innocence, his age, and his not wanting to die. Again and again he begged Martin to do something. This, more than anything else, seemed to shake Martin. He wouldn't look at old Hardwick, and pretended not to hear him.

We were surprised that the Mex wanted to make a confession, but he did. There wasn't any priest, so Amigo was to hear the confession, and carry it to a priest the first time he could go himself. There couldn't be any forgiveness, but it was the best they could do. They walked away a little, the Mex limping badly, and Amigo half carrying him along. Bartlett was stationed at a respectful distance as sentinel.

We saw the Mex try to kneel, but he couldn't, so he stood there confessing, with his back to us. Occasionally his hands moved in gestures of apology, which seemed strange from him. Amigo was facing us; but, when he wants, Amigo has a face like a wooden Indian. If the Mex was saying anything we ought to know now, which was what we were all thinking, we couldn't tell it from watching Amigo. He appeared merely to be intent upon remembering everything he was hearing, in order that all the Mex's sins might be reported and forgiven.

Tetley was directing in his field-officer manner. Farnley knotted and threw up three ropes so they hung over the long branch of the big pine, with the three nooses in a row. Then others staked down the ends of the ropes. The three horses were brought up again, and held under the ropes.

Tetley appointed Farnley, Gabe Hart and Gerald to whip the horses out. It was all right with Farnley, but Gabe refused. He gave no excuse, but stood there immovable, shaking his head. I was surprised Tetley had picked him.

"Gabe's not agin us, Mr. Tetley," Winder apologized. "He can't stand to hurt anything. It would work on his mind."

Tetley asked for a volunteer, and when no one else came forward Ma took the job. She was furious about it, though. When it seemed all settled, young Tetley, nearly choking, refused also.

"You'll do it," was all Tetley told him.

"I can't, I tell you."

"We'll see to it you can."

The boy stood there, very white, still shaking his head.

"It's a necessary task," Tetley told him evenly. "Someone else must perform it if you fail. I think you owe it to the others, and to yourself, on several scores."

The boy still shook his head stubbornly.

Moore, although he had refused on his own account, came over to Tetley and offered to relieve Gerald. "The boy's seen too much already. You shouldn't press him, man."

Tetley's face abruptly became bloodless; his mouth stretched downward, long, thin and hard, and his eyes glimmered with the fury he restrained. It was the first time I'd ever seen him let that nature show through, though I had felt always that it was there. He still spoke quietly, though, and evenly.

"This is not your affair, Moore. Thank you just the same."

Moore shrugged and turned his back on him. He was angry himself.

Tetley said to Gerald, "I'll have no female boys bearing my name. You'll do your part, and say nothing more." He turned away, giving the boy no opportunity to reply.

"That must have been a very busy life," he remarked, looking down where the Mex was still confessing to Amigo.

When at last the Mex was done and they came back up, and the three prisoners were stood in a row with their hands tied down, Martin said, "I suppose it's no use telling you again that we're innocent?"

"No good," Tetley assured him.

"It's not for myself I'm asking," Martin said.

"Other men have had families and have had to go for this sort of thing," Tetley told him. "It's too bad, but it's not our fault."

"You don't care for justice," Martin flared. "You don't even care whether you've got the right men or not. You want your way, that's all. You've lost something and somebody's got to be punished; that's all you know."

When Tetley just smiled, Martin's control broke again. "There's nobody to take care of them; they're in a strange place, they have nothing, and there's nobody to take care of them. Can't you understand that, you butcher? You've got to let me go; if there's a spot of humanity in you, you've got to let me go. Send men with me if you want to; I'm not asking you to trust me; you wouldn't trust anybody; your kind never will. Send men with me, then, but let me see them, let me arrange for them to go somewhere, for somebody to help them."

Old Hardwick began to whimper and jabber aloud again, and finally buckled in the knees and fell forward on his face. The Mex looked straight ahead of him and spit with contempt. "This is fine company for a man to die with," he said.

Martin started to yell something at the Mex, who was right beside him, but Mapes walked up to him and slapped him in the face. He slapped him hard, four times, so you could hear it like the crack of a lash. He paid no attention to protests or to Davies, trying to hold his arm. After the fourth blow he waited to see if Martin would say anything more. He didn't, but stood there, crying weakly and freely, great sobs heaving his chest.

Others put the old man back on his feet, and gave a couple of shots of whiskey to each of the three. Then they walked them over to the horses. The old man went flabby, and they had nearly to carry him.

I saw Davies keeping Amigo behind, holding him by the arm and talking. Amigo's face was angry and stubborn, and he kept shaking his head. Tetley saw it too, and guessed what I had. Smiling, he told Davies that a confession was a confession, and not evidence, even in a court.

"He doesn't have to tell us," Davies said. "All he has to do is say whether we'd better wait; then we could find out."

Amigo looked worried.

Tetley said, "Men have been known to lie, even in confession, under pressure less than this."

Amigo looked at him as if for the first time he questioned his divinity, and then he said, "But I'm not a priest; I don't know."

"Even if you had been," Tetley said, eyeing the Mex. "I'll give you two minutes to pray," he told the three. They were standing by the horses now, under the branch with the knotted ropes hanging down from it.

Martin was chewing his mouth to stop crying. He looked around at us quickly. We were in a fairly close circle; nobody would face him; man after man looked down. Finally, like he was choking, he ducked his head, then, awkwardly because of the rope, got to his knees. The Mex was still standing, but had his head bent and was moving his lips rapidly. The old man was down in a groveling heap, with Sparks beside him; Sparks was doing the praying for him. Moore took off his hat, and then the rest of us did the same. After a moment Davies and some of the others knelt also. Most of us couldn't bring ourselves to do that, but we all bowed and kept quiet. In the silence, in the gray light slowly increasing, the moaning of the old man, Sparks' praying, and the Mex's going again and again through his rapid patter sounded very loud. Still, you could hear every movement of the horses, leather creaking, the little clinks of metal.

"Time's up," Tetley said, and the old man wailed once, as if he'd been hit.

The Mex lifted his head and glanced around quickly. His face had a new expression, a tranquil one, the first we'd seen of such a feeling in him.

Martin rose to his feet and looked around slowly. The moments of silence and the crisis had had the reverse effect on him. He no longer appeared desperate or incoherent, but neither did he look peaceful or resigned. I have never seen another face so bitter as his was then, or one that showed its hatred more clearly. He spoke to Davies, but even his voice proved the effort against his pride and detestation.

"Will you find someone you can trust to look out for my wife and children?" he asked. "In time she will repay anything it puts you out."

Davies' eyes were full of tears. "I'll find someone," he promised.

"You'd better take some older woman along," Martin said. "It's not going to be easy."

"Don't worry," Davies said, "your family will be all right."

"Thanks," Martin said. Then he said, "My people are dead, but Miriam's are living. They live in Ohio. And Drew didn't want to sell his cattle; he'll buy them back for enough to cover their travel."

Davies nodded.

"Better not give her my things," Martin said. "Just this ring, if you'll get it."

Davies fumbled at the task. He had trouble with the rope, and his hands were shaking, but he got the ring and held it up for Martin to see. Martin nodded. "Just give her that and my letter first. Don't talk to her until she's read my letter." He didn't seem to want to say any more.

"That all?" Tetley asked.

"That's all, thanks," Martin said.

Tetley asked the Mex, who suddenly started speaking very rapidly. He was staring around, as if he couldn't quite see us. It had got to him finally. Then he stopped speaking just as suddenly and kept shaking his head. He'd been talking in Spanish. Tetley didn't ask the old man.

The three of them were lifted onto the horses and made to stand on them. Two men had to support old Hardwick.

"Tie their ankles," Mapes ordered.

"God," Gil whispered, "I was afraid they weren't going to." He felt it a great relief that their ankles were going to be tied.

Farnley got up on a horse and fixed the noose around each man's neck. Then he and Ma got behind two of the horses, with quirts in their hands. Young Tetley had to be told twice to get behind his. Then he moved to his place like a sleepwalker, and didn't even know he had taken the quirt somebody put in his hand.

The old man, on the inside, was silent, staring like a fish, and already hanging on the rope a little in spite of the men holding him up. The Mex had gone to pieces too, buckling nearly as badly as Hardwick, and jabbering, rapid and panicky, in Spanish. When the horse sidled under him once, tightening the rope, he screamed. In the pinch, Martin was taking it the best of the three. He kept his head up, not looking at any of us, and even the bitterness was gone from his face. He had a melancholy expression, such as goes with thinking of an old sorrow.

Tetley moved around behind the horses and directed Mapes to give the signal. We all moved out of the circle to give the horses room. In the last second even the Mex was quiet. There was no sound save the shifting of the three horses, restless at having been held so long. A feathery, wide-apart snow was beginning to sift down again; the end of a storm, not the beginning of another, though. The sky was becoming transparent; it was full daylight.

Mapes fired the shot, and we heard it echo in the mountain as Ma and Farnley cut their horses sharply across the haunches and the holders let go and jumped away. The horses jumped away too, and the branch creaked under the jerk. The old man and the Mex were dead at the fall, and swung and spun slowly. But young Tetley didn't cut. His horse just walked out from under, letting Martin slide off and dangle, choking to death, squirming up and down like an impaled worm, his face bursting with compressed blood. Gerald didn't move even then, but stood there shaking all over and looking up at Martin fighting the rope.

After a second, Tetley struck his boy with the butt of his pistol, a backhanded blow that dropped him where he stood.

"Shoot him," he ordered Farnley, pointing at Martin. Farnley shot. Martin's body gave a little leap in the air, then hung slack, spinning around and back, and finally settling into the slowing pendulum swing of the others.

Gil went with Davies to help young Tetley up. Nobody talked much, or looked at anybody else, but scattered and mounted. Winder and Moore caught up the rustlers' ponies. The Bartlett boys and Amigo remained to drive the cattle, and to do the burying before they started. All except Mapes shied clear of Tetley, but he didn't seem to notice. He untied his big palomino, mounted, swung him about, and led off toward the road. His face was set and white; he didn't look back.

Most of the rest of us did, though, turn once or twice to look. I was glad when the last real fall of the snow started, soft and straight and thick. It lasted only a few minutes, but it shut things out.

Chapter 5

Gil caught up and rode with me after he and Davies had helped Gerald. I'd thought, seeing him drop, that the kid had been killed, but Gil said no, it had been a glancing blow, that snow on his face and a drink had fixed him up enough to ride.

We rode slowly because of my shoulder, letting the others disappear ahead, with Gerald and Davies behind us. It was difficult for me to turn in my saddle, but I did, to get a look at Gerald.

His face had a knife-edge, marble-white look, and the circles under his eyes were big and dark, so that he appeared to have enormous eyes, or none at all, but empty sockets, like a skull. He wasn't looking where he was going, but the trouble wasn't his injury. I don't think he knew now that he had it. He was gnawing himself inside again. Passionate and womanish, but with a man's conscience and pride, that boy kept himself thin and bleached just thinking and feeling.

Davies, riding beside him, kept passing his hand over his face in a nerveless way unusual to him, rubbing his nose or fingering his mouth or drawing the hand slowly across his eyes and forehead, as if there were cobwebs on his skin.

We were all tired, even Gil was half asleep in his saddle, and we nearly rode into the horses standing in the clearing before we saw them. They were quietly bunched under the falling snow.

"It's the sheriff," Gil said. "It's Risley."

Then he said, "My God, it's Kinkaid."

It was too, with a bandage on his head, and a bit peaked, but otherwise as usual, quiet, friendly, and ashamed to be there. The other three men, besides the sheriff, were Tyler, Drew, and Davies' pimply clerk, Joyce. The Judge was red in the face and talking violently, but through the snow his voice came short and flat.

"It's murder, murder and nothing less. I warned you, Tetley, I warned you repeatedly, and Davies warned you, and Osgood. You all heard us; you were all warned. You wanted justice, did you? Well, by God, you shall have it now, real justice. Every man of you is under arrest for murder. We'll give you a chance to see how slow regular justice is when you're in the other chair."

Nobody replied to him that I could hear.

"My God," Gil said, "I knew it didn't feel right. I knew we should wait. That bastard Tetley."

Everybody would hang it on Tetley now. I didn't feel like saying anything.

The sheriff was stern, but he wasn't the kind to gabble easily, like Tyler. He was a small, stocky man with a gray walrus mustache and black bushy eyebrows. He had a heavy sheepskin on, with the collar turned up around his ears. His deep-set, hard blue eyes looked at each of us in turn. Nobody but Tetley tried to hold up against his look, and even Tetley failed.

When he'd made us all look down he said something we couldn't hear to the Judge. The Judge began to sputter, but when Risley looked level at him too the sputter died, and the Judge just stared around at us belligerently again, thrusting his lower lip out and sucking it in and making a hoarse, blowing noise.

Risley sat silent for a moment, as if considering carefully, looking us over all the time. Finally he said, "I haven't recognized anybody here. We passed in a snowstorm, and I was in a hurry."

"That's collusion, Risley," the Judge began loudly, getting redder than ever. "I'll have you understand I won't—"

"What do you want to do?" Risley cut in, looking at him.

The Judge tried to say something impressive about the good name of the valley and of the state, and the black mark against his jurisdiction and Risley's, but it was no use. Everybody just waited for him to stop; he couldn't hold out against all of us without Risley.

When he was just blowing again, Risley said, "I'm not even looking for the leaders. Nobody had to go if he didn't want to."

He went on in a changed tone, as if he had finished unimportant preliminaries and was getting down to business. "I'll want ten men for my posse."

We all volunteered. We were tired, and we'd had plenty of man hunting and judging to hold us for a long time, but we felt he was giving us a chance to square ourselves. Even Tetley volunteered, but Risley didn't notice him; he passed up Mapes also. He took Moore and a few others, and after looking at him for a long time he took Farnley.

Kinkaid looked up at that, smiled a little, and raised one hand off the horn just enough so Farnley could see it. Farnley straightened, as if he'd had half a life given back to him. Farnley was mean with a grudge, but honest. If he didn't like Risley right then, he liked himself a lot less.

When Risley had selected his ten men, he ordered the rest of us to go home. "Go on about your own business," he told us. "Don't hang around in bunches. If you have to tell anybody anything, just tell them I'm taking care of this with a picked posse. You can't stop the talk, but there'll be a lot less fuss if you keep out of it. Nobody knew these men."

He turned to the Judge. "It'll have to be that way," he apologized.

"Perhaps, perhaps," the Judge muttered. "All the same . . . " and he subsided. Actually, though, he was relieved. We didn't have to worry about him.

Risley and Drew pushed through us, the chosen men falling in behind them. The rest began to drift down toward the valley. Tetley was left to ride by himself this time. But he was iron, that man; his face didn't show anything, not even weariness.

Davies stopped Risley and Drew. Both his manner and his speech were queerly fumbling, as if he were either exhausted or a little mad. While he spoke to them he twisted his bridle, occasionally jerking a length of it between his two hands, and then halting his speech for a moment while he rubbed his forehead and eyes that feeble way. When Drew had questioned him a bit they got it straight. For some obscure reason, connected apparently only with the way Davies felt, he didn't believe he should take that letter to Martin's wife. He wanted Drew to take it. He wanted Drew to get a woman to help Martin's wife too; he was much impressed by the need of the woman, and repeated it several times, saying it should be an older woman who had had children and wouldn't gush. He insisted that Drew must be able to see why he couldn't take the letter.

You could tell by Drew's face that he couldn't see. He was a big, fleshy man with gray eyes, a yellow tan and a heavy chestnut beard. He was wearing a gray frock coat and a Spanish sombrero and was smoking a thin Mexican cigar. He talked with the cigar in the corner of his mouth. He was taking the whole thing impatiently, as business to be done. But then he hadn't seen what we had. And he wasn't totally without concern, because when Davies asked him, as if somehow the answer was very important to him personally, if he had sold the cattle to Martin, he answered only after a delay and then said, "Yes, poor kid. A lot better for him if I hadn't. It don't do to change your regular ways," he added. "Men get to banking on them."

You could see he thought there was something queer about the way Davies was acting, but he took the letter and the ring from him, assuring him that he would send somebody he could trust if he couldn't take them himself. He promised he would send a woman too, a woman who would take care of things and not be a sympathy monger.

When Davies was still fretful, like a man with a very orderly mind who is dying and can't remember if everything is arranged, Drew became short in his answers. But he also thought of the thing which seemed to relieve Davies most for the moment; he hadn't wanted to ask about it.

"I'll give his wife the money he paid me for the cattle, of course," Drew said impatiently. "I have it with me; I haven't even had a chance to get back to the house yet."

Then he got ready to go, but looked hard at Davies and decided to risk an opinion on something which wasn't strictly any of his business.

"You'd better get some rest," he told Davies. "You're taking this too hard. From what I've heard, you did all you could; there's nothing you or anybody else can do about it now."

Davies looked at him as if Drew were the crazy one. But he didn't say anything, just nodded.

Risley made a come-on motion with his hand to the posse, and they filed off slowly on the snowy road. When they had entered the aisle between the big pines they picked up to a little jog, and finally disappeared, dimming away man by man through the screen of falling snow. In the clearing there was already sunlight beginning to shine on the snow.

By the time the rest of us got to the fork at the foot of the grade it had stopped snowing and the sky was beginning to clear, not breaking up, but thinning away everywhere at once and letting pale sunlight through. It was still cold, though, and the mountains on both sides of the valley were white to their bases.

When we finally got to the edge of town Gil asked me, "How do you feel now?"

It seemed to cheer him up when I told him I was coming along all right.

"The quicker we get out of this town," he said, "the better I'll feel."

I didn't feel like two days' riding right then. I had my mind set on food and a change of bandage and a bed. I didn't say anything. But he saw what I was thinking.

"Still," he said, "I wouldn't mind getting good and drunk and staying that way for a couple of days. We'll lay up at Canby's. Canby's as good as a doctor."

"I'll be all set by tomorrow," I told him.

"Sure," he said.

When we went in at Canby's he asked us, "What'll it be?" like we'd just come from work.

"We want a room," Gil said.

"Go on up," Canby said. "The front room's empty."

I went up to the room, while Gil took the horses over to Winder's. There was a dresser with a washbowl and a pitcher of water and a glass on it, a curtain strung across one corner for a closet, one chair, and iron double bed and a small stove. Everything but the stove was painted white. There was no carpet on the floor and no curtains on the two windows, which made the room seem scrubbed and full of light. Through the eastern window I could see the mountains with the snow on them, and through the other the street, with Davies' store right across. But it was cold in there too. I built a fire in the stove and lay down on the bed.

I was half asleep when Canby came in. "Let me have a look at that shoulder," he said, starting to undo my shirt. "You didn't look right when you came in," he explained. He peeled me down to my shoulder and then yanked the rags off. He was neat and quick about it, but they stuck a little before they came away. I had to grind my teeth when he felt around it. He had brought a pitcher of hot water, some ointment and clean strips of white cloth. He washed out the wound and rubbed in the ointment, which burned. Then he bandaged it snugly and went out.

The next thing I knew it was afternoon. The room was warm, but there was no sun anymore. I forgot about the shoulder and stretched and remembered it. Downstairs I could hear the voices of a number of men. They sounded distant, and didn't interest me. But I was really hungry.

I started to get up to go downstairs and eat. I sat up, and then I saw Davies. He was sitting on the one chair, looking at the floor. Waking up from a sleep that had freshened me and put the night's business behind me some, I was surprised to see how bad he looked. His hair was tangled and he had a white stubble of beard. He looked tired too, his face slack and really old, with big, bruised pouches under the eyes, which were red-rimmed and bloodshot.

He looked up when he heard the bed creak. "You had a long sleep," he said.

"I didn't know you were here."

He wanted to say something but couldn't get started. I was afraid of it. I didn't want to get mixed up in anything more. But I had to give him a chance to unload.

"You don't look like you've slept much," I told him.

"I haven't," he said, "any."

I waited. He got up with slow labor and went to the window where he could look out into the street. Without turning around he said, "Croft, will you listen to me?"

"Sure," I said, but not encouraging him.

"I've got to talk," he protested. "I've got to talk so I can get some sleep. I thought about everybody who was up there," he explained, "and I have to talk to you, Art. You're the only one will understand."

Why in hell, I wondered, did everybody have to take me for his father confessor? "You sound like you had a confession to make," I said.

He turned around. "That's it," he said quickly. "That's it, Croft, a confession."

I still waited.

"Croft," he said, "I killed those three men."

I just stared.

"Maybe you'll think I'm crazy," he said.

Well, I did, and I didn't like a man twice my age confessing to me.

"I did it as much as if I'd pulled the ropes," he was saying.

"Why blame anybody?" I asked him. "It's done now. If we have to blame somebody, then I'd say—"

"I know," he interrupted, almost angrily, "you'd say it was Tetley. That's what you all say."

"Well, wasn't it?"

"No. Tetley couldn't help what he did."

"Oh, that way," I said. "If you take it that way, nobody can help it. We're all to blame, and nobody's to blame. It just happened."

"No," he said. "Most of you couldn't help it. Most men can't; they don't really think. They haven't any conception of basic justice. They see the sins of commission, but not of omission. They feel guilty now, when it's done, and they want somebody to blame. They've chosen Tetley."

"If it's anybody . . ." I began.

"No," he repeated, "not any more than the rest of you. He's merely the scapegoat. He saw only the sin of commission, and he couldn't feel that. Sin doesn't mean anything to Tetley."

"That doesn't mean he wasn't wrong," I said.

"No," Davies said, "but not to blame."

"If you look at it that way," I said, "only a saint could be to blame for anything."

"There's some truth in that."

I said something mean then, but I wanted to shut him up before he'd talked so much he'd be ashamed of it afterward. You can really hate a man you've talked too much to. "Meaning you're a saint?" I asked him.

He looked at me, but didn't wait even to make sure how I meant it. He was just following his own trouble.

"Something like that," he said without a smile, "by comparison. Or I was before this. Oh, God," he said suddenly. "That boy; all night."

He closed his eyes hard and turned back to the window. Holding on to the window sash, he pressed his forehead against his hand and leaned there, trembling all over, like a woman who's been told bad news too suddenly.

I waited until he wasn't shaking, and then asked him, easy as I could, "Meaning this was a sin of omission?"

He moved his head to say yes, still keeping it against his hand.

"You're thinking about it too much," I told him. "You're making it all up."

I was embarrassed that he could show so much emotion. I got up off the bed. "You get some sleep," I said. "You can sleep right here. I'm going down for some grub. I'll tell Canby not to let anybody bother you."

He shook his head, then turned around slowly, not looking at me.

"You're cutting it too fine," I told him. "This was a sin of commission if I ever saw one. We hung three men, didn't we? Or was that just a nightmare I had?"

He looked up at me, so I began to hope I was reaching him.

"And if anybody came out of it clean," I said, "you're the one. You and Sparks, and Sparks was just letting it go. Why, we're all more guilty than you are. You tried. You're the only one that did try. And Tetley's the worst of all. They're right about Tetley."

"Tetley's a beast," Davies said suddenly, with hatred in his voice. "A depraved, murderous beast."

"Now," I said, "you're talking sense. Tetley loved it."

"Yes," he agreed, "he loved it. He extracted pleasure from every morsel of their suffering. He drew it out as long as he could." Davies was quiet, and then said slowly, "But a beast is not to blame. So I keep telling myself that I couldn't have changed it; that even though Tetley can't be blamed, I couldn't have made him see."

"That's right," I said.

"And I wouldn't have killed him to try and stop him," Davies said.

"God, no," I said.

"And nothing else would have helped."

"No," I said, "nothing else. He was like a crazy animal, cold crazy."

Neither of us said anything for a minute. I heard voices downstairs again in the bar. I listened for Gil, but he wasn't there. Then Davies had said something. "What?" I asked.

"He killed the boy too," Davies repeated.

"Sure," I agreed. "All three of them."

"No," he said. "Gerald."

"Gerald?" I echoed.

"You haven't heard, then?" he asked. "I thought you'd have heard."

"I've been right here, sleeping. What would I have heard?"

"That Gerald killed himself."

"He didn't," I said.

Davies sat down slowly in the chair. Then he sat there twisting his hands.

"You didn't think he would?" he asked finally.

"No," I said. "He couldn't have. He talked too much."

"He did, though," Davies said. "He did." And suddenly he put his head down and clung to it with both hands, passing through another seizure like the one at the window. Then he was quiet again, and told me, "When he got home Tetley had locked the house against him. Gerald went out into the barn and hanged himself from a rafter. The hired man found him about noon."

"Poor kid," I said.

"Yes," he said, "poor kid. The hired man was afraid to tell Tetley. He saw Sparks and told him, and Sparks came for me."

"Did you have to see Tetley, then?"

"I didn't want to. I didn't trust myself. But I saw him. It meant nothing to him; not a flicker. Just thanked me as if I'd delivered a package from the store."

The news was like a knockout punch to me too. I should have known if anybody should, after the way the kid had opened up to me. Also I could see why that might have put Davies off on this spree of blaming himself. It could have been prevented so easily; just somebody to stay with the kid. The sins of omission.

"That's not your fault," I said. "With Tetley what he is, it would have happened sooner or later anyway. There's some things you can't butt in on."

"But you didn't think it would happen?"

"No," I said. "Well, I was wrong."

"I did," he whispered. "I knew."

"You couldn't. I should have. He talked to me all the way up."

Suddenly he switched our talk again. He couldn't sit still, tired as he was, but got up and went to the window.

"Did you believe Martin was innocent?" he asked. "I mean at the time when they put the rope up over the limb?"

I stayed careful. "I felt we were wrong," I said, looking at him. "I felt that he shouldn't hang."

"That's scarcely the same thing. Nobody wants to see a man hang."

"You couldn't *know* he was innocent," I said. "None of us would have stood there and seen him hang if we'd known."

"No," Davies said. "So you didn't know." He was very quiet saying that. "You didn't know, but I did."

"How could you know?" I asked.

"I'd read that letter," he said. "Oh, there was nothing a court would have called a proof. A court won't take the picture of a man's soul for a proof. But I knew after reading the letter, beyond any question, what he was like. From the first, I felt a boy like that couldn't have done it; not the rustling even; certainly not the murder. And when I'd read that letter I knew it."

"Is that all?" I asked.

"He talked about me in the letter," Davies mooned. "He told his wife how kind I was to him, what I risked trying to defend him. And he trusted me, you saw that. He worked so hard to ease it for his wife too," he went on, lower. "To keep her from breaking herself on grief or hating us. And he reminded her of things they had done together." He bent his head in a spasm again. "It was a beautiful letter," he whispered.

"You didn't know," I told him, "any more than the rest of us did. You knew what he was like from that letter, you say. Well, maybe. But that kind of an argument can't stand up against branded cattle, no bill of sale, a dead man's gun, and a guy that acts like that Mex did."

"It could have," he said. "You admit yourself you were ready to be stopped. You admit you thought most of them were."

"There wasn't the proof," I said angrily. "You don't get all set for a hanging and stop for some little feeling you have."

"You might," he said, "when you're hanging on a feeling too."

"You tried to stop it hard enough," I said.

"That's the point," he said. "I tried. I took the leadership, and with it I accepted the responsibility. I set myself up as the power of justice, of common pity, even. And in their hearts the men were with me; and the right was with me. Everything was with me."

"Everything," I reminded him, "except what we all took to be the facts."

"You didn't think it could be stopped?" he asked.

"It was too late for that."

"You didn't think of using your gun?"

That surprised me. "On what?" I asked.

"Tetley," he said.

"You mean . . ."

"No, just to force him to take them back for trial."

"No," I said finally. "I don't think I did. It was all settled. Maybe

I had a kind of wild idea for a moment—but I didn't really think of it. No," I said again.

"Did you have any feeling you could have turned the whole thing right then? Or that somebody could have?"

I thought. "No," I said. "I guess not."

"It should have been stopped," he said, "even with a gun."

"I can see that now," I admitted.

"I could see it then," he said.

"You didn't even *have* a gun."

"No," he said, "I didn't. But I knew Tetley could be stopped then. I knew you could all be turned by one man who would face Tetley with a gun. And you know what I felt when I thought that, Croft?"

"No," I said. "What?"

"I was glad, Croft, glad I didn't have a gun."

I didn't look up. I felt something rotten in what he was saying, or maybe just that he was saying it. It was obscure, but I didn't want to look at him.

"Now do you see?" he said triumphantly, like all he had wanted to do was make himself out the worst he could. "I knew these men were innocent. I knew it as surely as I do now. And I knew Tetley could be stopped. I knew in that moment you were all ready to be turned. And I was glad I didn't have a gun."

He was silent for a moment, breathing hard, as if he had overcome something tremendous. "I let those three men hang because I was afraid. The lowest kind of a virtue, the quality dogs have when they need it, the only thing Tetley had, guts, plain guts, and I didn't have it."

"You take it too hard," I said, still looking at the floor. "You take it too much on yourself. There was no reason—"

"Oh, I told myself I was the emissary of peace and truth," Davies broke in violently, "and that I must go as such; that I couldn't even wear the symbol of violence. I was righteous and heroic and calm and reasonable. All a great, cowardly lie. The truth was I didn't take a gun because I didn't want it to come to a showdown. The weakness that was in me all the time set up my sniveling little defense. I didn't even expect to save those men. The most I hoped was that something would do it for me.

"Something," he said bitterly.

It was impossible to make him see that nobody else could think him guilty. I tried just once to make him see that, and he stared at me till I was done. Then he laughed hard and suddenly, and stopped laughing suddenly and said, oh, yes, he was trying to play the Christ all right, but it wasn't a part for cowards, and it hadn't needed a Christ anyway; all it had needed was a man. His voice was hoarse and his words tumultuous, and then it was always self-condemnation or a blast against Tetley, but with the blasts always ending in blaming himself too. And he would end each tirade against himself with another sudden laugh about trying to play the Christ. I had to let him go; if anything would help, that would. We couldn't bridge the gap; he was all inside, I was all outside.

Finally, though, he was played out. From where I was sitting on the bed I could see through the window that it was late afternoon sun on the eastern hills, and that the snow was almost gone from them already. It was a sad light, but lovely and peaceful, glowing as if it burned within the hills themselves. Davies just sat there with his head in his hands, now and then running his fingers through his hair, then lifting his head again, as if each time he decided he wouldn't break, but stand it.

"You'd better get that sleep now," I said, as quiet as I could.

He looked at me slowly, bringing his mind back. He appeared nearly dead, the hollows of his face so sunken that his skull showed in startling relief. But his eyes were a lot calmer, and though he was shivering, it wasn't with that tightness any longer, but just as if he were exhausted and cold.

"I might as well, hadn't I?" he said. He got up. "Except—well, I've even thought," he said quietly, "that I wouldn't have needed a gun, that at the very end Tetley knew he was wrong too, and all I'd have had to do was say so."

I shook my head. "No," I said. "You were right in the first place. He was frozen onto that hanging. You'd have had to hit him over the head to bring him out of it. You'd have had to kill him."

"And I couldn't have done that," Davies said slowly.

"No," I said.

I heard the shuffle of feet coming up the stairs. The door opened, and it was Gil and Canby.

"Hello," Canby said to both of us, and then to me, "I'm fixin' some eats. Just came up to see if you wanted some."

Gil was drunk, in his steady way.

"Sorry," he said, "didn't know you had company," as if he'd found me with a girl.

"It's all right," Davies said. "I was just going."

"Where did you go to get that drunk without my hearing you?" I asked Gil.

"I took the horses over to Winder's," he said, "and he wanted to drink. He felt pretty low about the business."

"*He* did?" I said.

"Bill's not a bad guy, when you get to know him," Gil maintained, "only pigheaded. Anyway," he said cheerfully, "we won't have to have another hanging. Tetley took care of himself."

It caught me wide open, and I made a bad cover.

"Oh, Gerald, you mean?" I said, after too long a wait. "Yeah, I heard," and tried to signal him off. He didn't get it.

"No," he said, "his old man too. After he heard about the kid he locked himself in the library and jumped on a sword. They had to break the door open to get him. Saw him through the window, lying on his face in there on the rug, with that big cavalry sword of his sticking up through his back."

Canby saw me glance at Davies, and I guess I looked as funny as I felt. Canby turned quick to look at him too.

"Who would have thought the old bastard had that much feeling in him?" Gil said.

Davies just stood there for a moment, staring at Gil. Then he made a little crying noise in his throat, a sort of whimper, like a pup, and I thought he was going to cave. He didn't, though. He made that noise again, and then suddenly went out the door. We could hear him on the stairs, whimpering more and more. Once, judging by the sound he made, he fell.

"Go get him," I told Canby. "You can't leave him alone."

Canby pushed past me and went out and down the stairs three or four at a time. I went to the window, and saw Davies already out in the street. He was sagging in the knees, but trying to run like he had to get away from something. I saw Canby catch up with him, and Davies try to fight him off, but then give up. They came back together, Davies with his head down and wobbling loose on his neck. Canby was half holding him up.

"What in hell ails him?" Gil asked, watching over my shoulder.

I heard Canby getting him up the stairs, and went over and closed the door.

"He had a notion he was to blame," I told Gil.

"For what?"

"The whole business."

"*He* was?" Gil said. "That's a good one."

"Isn't it?" I said. I didn't want to talk about it. I felt sick for the old man.

Gil looked at me and then went out. I stretched out on the bed. A few minutes later he came back, carrying a bottle and glasses. He poured a drink for me and one for himself and then put the bottle on the dresser.

"I gave Winder the ten to give Farnley," he said. "You know, from the poker game."

"That's good," I said.

Downstairs I could hear more talking. Gil went over and looked out of the window into the street. It was about sunset, a clear sky again, and everything still. He opened the window, and the cool air came in, full of the smell of the meadows. Way off we could hear the meadowlarks. Gil lit a cigarette. He blew the smoke hard, and it went out the window in a long, quick stream.

"They're taking up a pot downstairs for Martin's wife," he said. "Got more than five hundred in it already. I put in twenty-five apiece for us."

I squared with him out of my money sack.

Tink-tink-a-link went the meadowlark. And then another one, even farther off, *teenk-teenk-a-leenk.*

Then Gil said, "I'll be glad to get out of here."

"Yeh," I said.

THE COWBOYS

Roper, wrassler, buckeroo,
trail cutter, broncobuster, range bum,
vaquero, cowpoke, mustangeer,
saddle stiff, fence rider—the American cowboy

Night Watch by William Gollings

Wild Horse Hunters by Charles M. Russell, a self-taught painter who started out as an itinerant ranch hand in

de to many cattle drives was a roundup of wild horses for use by the cowboys.

A dangerous moment on a cattle drive is vividly depicted in Frederic Remington's *Stampeded by Lightning*.

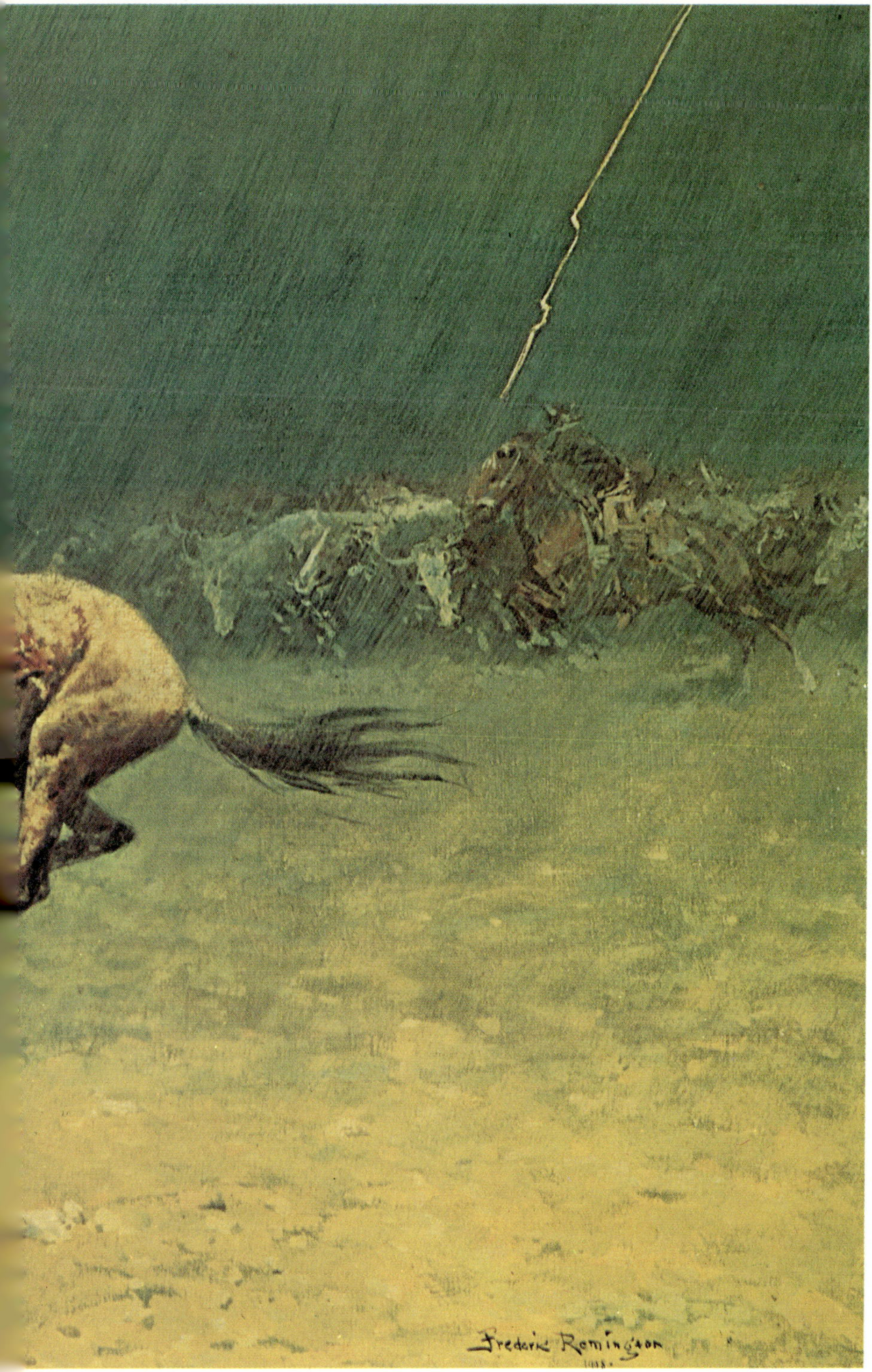

Watched over by a pipe-smoking cook, disgruntled-looking trail riders pitch into a hot dinner beside their ch

Routes of the Great Cattle Drives

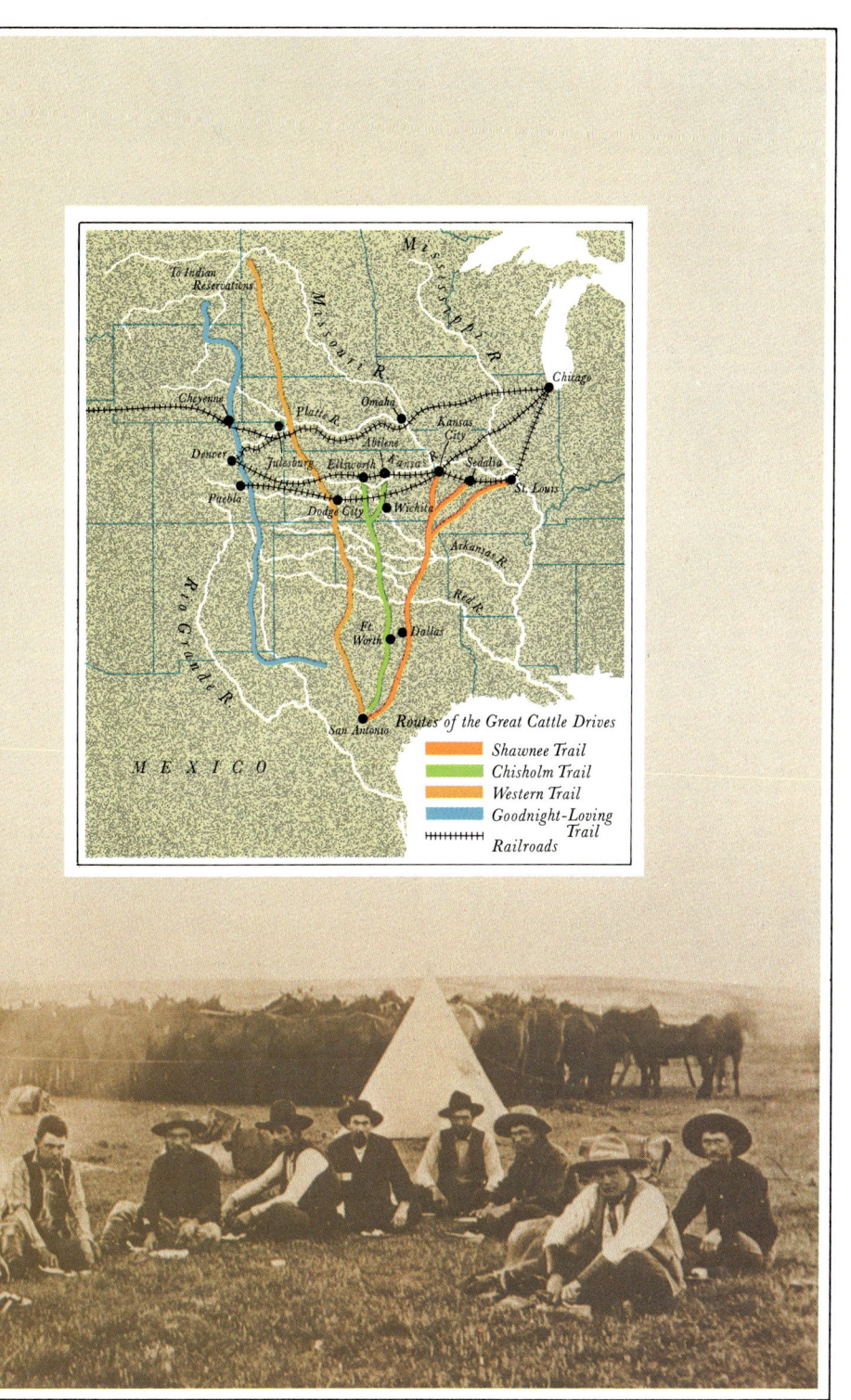

- Shawnee Trail
- Chisholm Trail
- Western Trail
- Goodnight-Loving Trail
- Railroads

fare on the great drives of the 1870s and '80s was beans, sourdough biscuits and "sonofabitch" stew.

©Time Inc. from the Time-Life series The Old West.

Watering cattle on a long drive, by Frank Reaugh

Of what stuff were good cowboys made? "We take a man and ask no questions," said one cattleman. "We know when he throws his saddle on a horse whether he understands his business or not. He may be a minister backslidin' or a train robber on his vacation—we don't care. Many of our most useful men have made their mistakes. All we care about is, will they stand the gaff? Will they sit sixty hours in the saddle, holdin' a herd that's tryin' to stampede all the time?"

Men and horses enjoy an Oklahoma wa

o cowboys pose proudly for a studio portrait.

Dust flies and shots ring out as cowboys roar into town for a hell-raising spree in Charles M. Russell's *In Without Kno*

real-life counterparts were often too tired to create so much fuss.

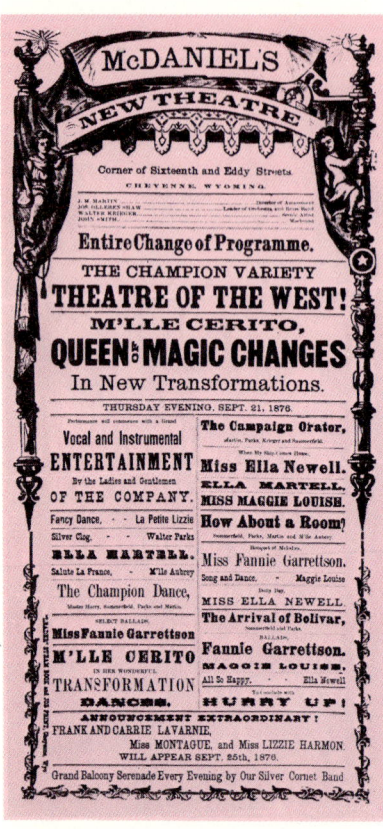

A theater poster in Cheyenne, Wyoming, 1876

A young, sprightly trio of the ladies fondly known as "soiled

Kansas pleasure spots ranged from boisterous dance halls to ramshackle bars.

er they were paid with brass tokens.

Dodge City in 1873 was a "fast" town. "Here," said one Kansas newspaper, "may be seen the 'cow boy' after his long drive, his pockets filled with silver dollars, wending his way to the dance halls to engage in merry dance with the drunken frail ones, to the music of a third-class violin and bass fiddle, until [he] finds himself without money, which is nothing remarkable, as each 'set' of ten minutes duration, costs 75 cents."

Small ranches, like this one in Johnson County, Wyoming, began to proliferate as the era of long drives ended.

This ranch crew had unusually comfortable quarters in a well-chinked bunkhouse.

"The worst hardship on the trail was loss of sleep," said one Texas cowboy. "Our day wouldn't end till nine, when we grazed the herd onto the bed ground. After that every man would have to stand two hours night guard. I would get three hours' sleep, and then ride two hours. Then I would sleep till the cook yelled 'Roll out' at half past three. Sometimes we would rub tobacco juice in our eyes to keep awake. It was rubbing them with fire. But the boss would only say: 'What the hell are you kicking about? You can sleep all winter when you get to Montana.'"

y his bunk a cowboy gathered his prized personal possessions.

A quarrel over water rights in Kansas in 1903 leaves farmer Daniel Berry and two sons dead. A third son was

Advertisement for the first patented barbed wire

Until the late 1880s cattle still roamed widely between roundups, grazing anywhere. With the spread of farm settlements, however, open grassland became scarce, as miles of wire fences were erected. Often "range cattle, drifting before a storm, came upon a fence and in utter helplessness walked back and forth along it until they fell exhausted and died by the hundred. The open-range business must soon be a matter of history or settlements be discouraged." So wrote A. S. Mercer of Wyoming, in 1894. The bitter war between cattlemen and settlers was on.

177

Frank Wolcott, who led the slayers of Nate Champion

To the cattle barons, Nate Champion was a "rustler." To his Wyoming neighbors, he was an honest, hardworking man in life— a hero in death. For he died escaping a blazing ranch house in Johnson County under the murderous fire of half a hundred cattlemen and hired gunmen who were out to get him.

The valiant Champion had little education, but he left a legacy long remembered by the homesteaders. On his body, according to A. S. Mercer, was found a "memorandum soaked with his life's blood and bearing a bullet hole through it. Under the printed date of April 9th [1892], the following entry was written in pencil:

" 'Me and Nick [Ray] was getting breakfast when the attack took place. Two men here with us. The old man went after water and did not come back. His friend went out to see what was the matter and he did not come back. Nick started out and I told him to look out. . . . Nick is shot, but not dead yet. He is awful sick. I must go and wait on him. They are still shooting and are all around the house. Boys, there is bullets coming in like hail. Nick died about 9 o'clock. I don't think they intend to let me get away this time. Boys, I feel pretty lonesome just now. It's about 3 o'clock. I heard them splitting wood. I guess they are going to fire the house to-night. I think I will make a break when night comes, if alive. Shooting again. It's not night yet. The house is all fired. Goodbye, boys, if I never see you again. Nathan D. Champion.' "

Dobe Bill, he came a-riding
   from the canyon, in the glow
Of a quiet Sunday morning
   from the town of Angelo;
Ridin' easy on the pinto
   that he dearly loved to straddle,
With a six-gun and sombrero
   that was wider than his saddle.

From "The Killer" ©

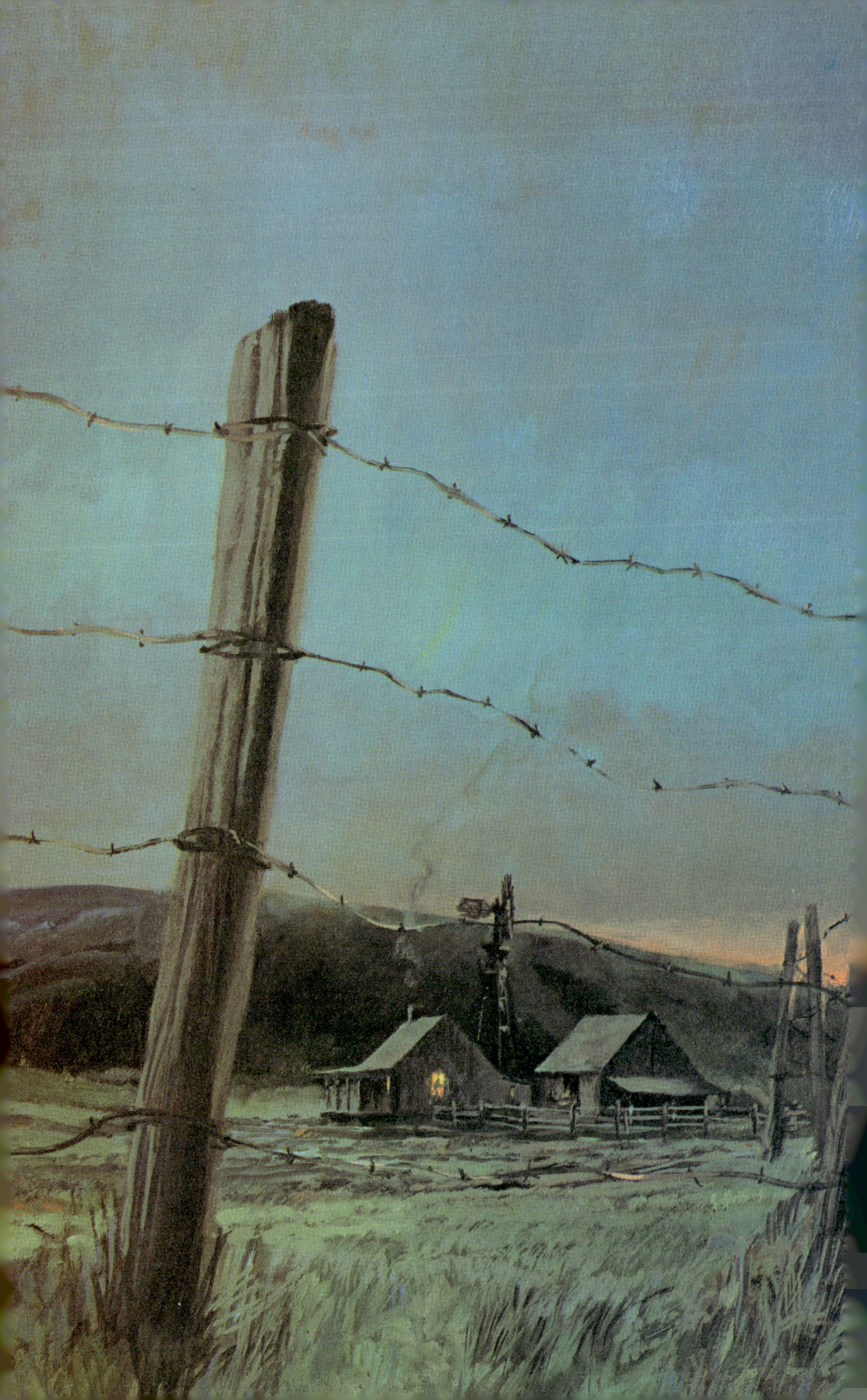

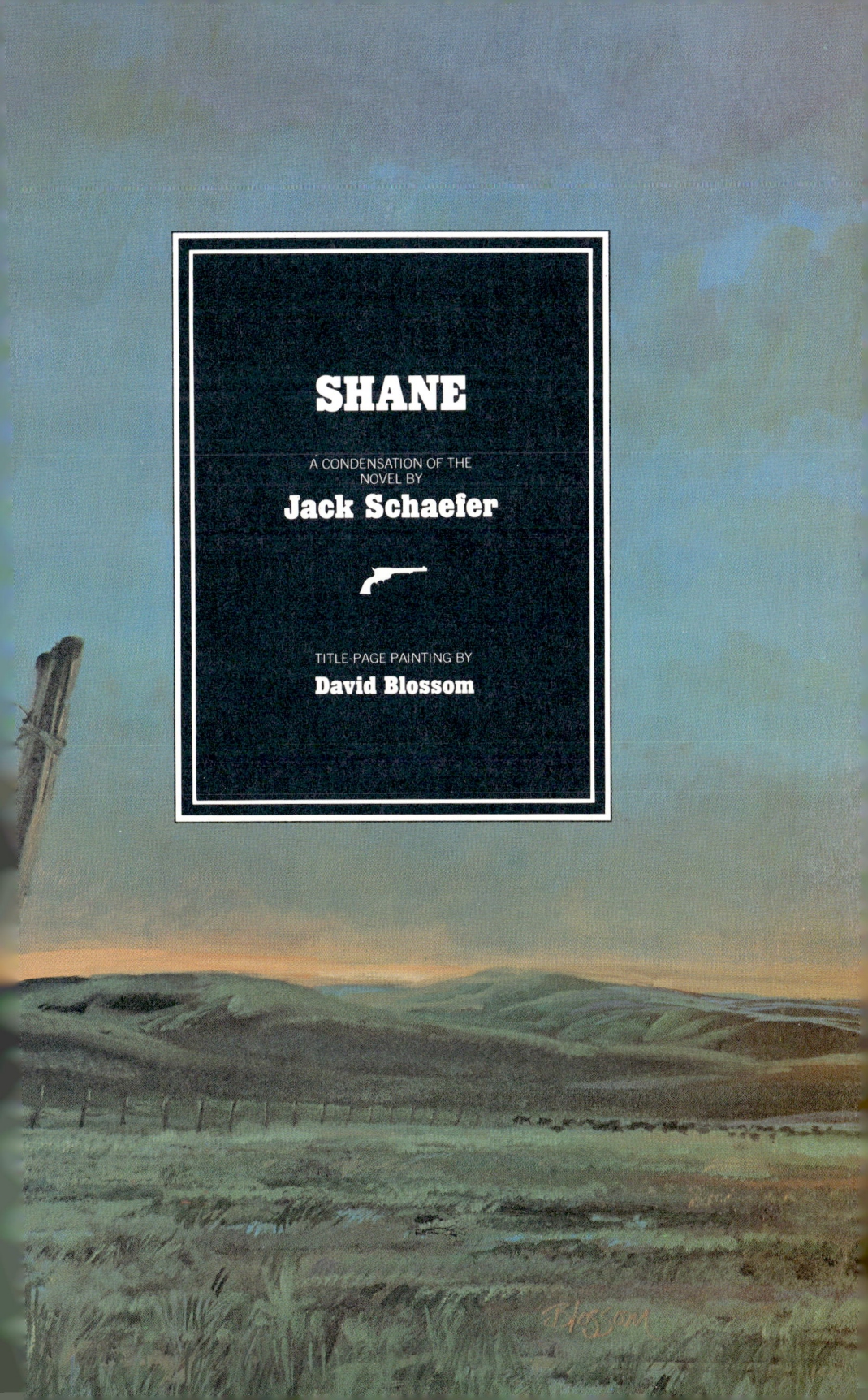

SHANE

A CONDENSATION OF THE NOVEL BY

Jack Schaefer

TITLE-PAGE PAINTING BY

David Blossom

He rode out of the open plains in the warm Wyoming sunlight and drew rein at a small homestead to ask for water. He was dusty and trail-worn, but to the boy who saw him first, there was a magnificence in him.

His name was Shane. The year was 1889, and in this lovely, once-peaceful valley the cattle kings and the settlers were already locked in a life-and-death struggle for survival. Until now Shane had been a wandering loner. But he found himself responding to the hero worship of a child, the admiration of a gentle woman and the trust of a kindly man. At the risk of his own life, he took sides with them against their powerful enemies.

Jack Schaefer's famous novel might have come straight out of the bloody Johnson County range wars, but it is not all blood and thunder. For in it the air is redolent of biscuits baking and fresh-cut petunias as well as of gunsmoke, and great matters turn on the conflict in the heart of one heroic, mysterious figure.

Chapter 1

He rode into our valley in the summer of '89. I was a kid then, barely topping the backboard of Father's old chuck wagon. I was on the upper rail of our small corral, soaking in the late afternoon sun, when I saw him far down the road where it swung into the valley from the open plain beyond.

In that clear Wyoming air I could see him plainly, though he was still several miles away. There seemed nothing remarkable about him, just another stray horseman riding toward the cluster of frame buildings that was our town. He came steadily on, straight through the town without slackening pace, until he reached the fork a half mile below our place. One branch of the road turned and crossed the river ford and went on to Luke Fletcher's big spread. The other bore ahead along the bank where we homesteaders had pegged our claims in a row up the valley. He hesitated briefly, studying the choice, and moved again steadily on our side.

As he came near, what impressed me first were his clothes. He wore dark trousers tucked into tall boots and held at the waist by a wide belt, both of a soft black leather tooled in intricate design. A coat of the same dark material as the trousers was neatly folded and strapped to his saddle roll. His shirt was finespun linen, rich brown in color. The handkerchief knotted loosely around his throat was black silk. His hat was not the familiar gray or muddy tan stetson. It was black, soft in texture, with a creased crown and a wide, curling brim swept down in front to shield the face.

All trace of newness was long since gone from these things. They were worn and dusty and several neat patches showed on the shirt. Yet a kind of magnificence remained, and with it a hint of men and manners alien to my limited boy's experience.

Then I forgot the clothes in the impact of the man himself. He was not much above medium height, almost slight in build. He would have looked frail alongside Father's square, solid bulk. But even I could read the endurance in the lines of that dark figure and the quiet power in its effortless, unthinking adjustment to every movement of the tired horse.

He was clean-shaven and his face was lean and hard and burned from high forehead to firm, tapering chin. As he came closer, I could see in the shadow of the hat's brim that his brows were drawn in a frown of fixed alertness. Beneath them the hooded eyes were endlessly searching from side to side and forward, missing nothing. As I noticed this, a sudden chill, I could not have told why, struck through me there in the warm and open sun.

He rode easily, relaxed in the saddle. Yet it was the easiness of a coiled spring, of a trap set.

HE DREW REIN not twenty feet from me. His glance hit me, dismissed me, flicked over our place. This was not much in terms of size and scope, but what there was was good. You could trust Father for that. The corral, big enough for about thirty head if you crowded them in, was railed right to true-sunk posts. The pasture behind, taking in nearly half of our claim, was fenced tight. The barn was small, but it was solid, and we were raising a loft at one end for the alfalfa growing green in the north forty. We had a fair-sized field in potatoes that year and Father was trying a new corn he had sent for all the way to Washington.

Behind the house, Mother's kitchen garden was a brave sight. The house itself was three rooms—two really, the big kitchen, where we spent most of our time indoors, and the bedroom beside it. My little lean-to room was added back of the kitchen. Father was planning, when he could get around to it, to build Mother the parlor she wanted.

We had wooden floors and a nice porch across the front. The house was painted too, white with green trim, a rare thing in all that region, to remind her, Mother said, of her native New England. Few places so spruce and well worked could be found so deep in the Territory in those days.

The stranger took it all in, sitting there easily in the saddle. I saw his eyes slow on the flowers Mother had planted by the porch steps, then come to rest on our shiny new pump and the trough beside it. They shifted back to me, and again I felt that sudden chill. But his voice was gentle and he spoke like a man schooled to patience.

"I'd appreciate a chance at the pump for myself and the horse."

I was trying to frame a reply and choking on it, when I realized that he was not speaking to me but past me. Father had come up behind me and was leaning against the gate to the corral.

"Use all the water you want, stranger."

Father and I watched him dismount and lead the horse over to the trough. He pumped it almost full and let the horse sink its nose in the cool water before he picked up the dipper for himself.

He took off his hat, slapped the dust out of it and brushed the dust from his clothes. He rolled his sleeves and dipped his arms in the trough, rubbing thoroughly and splashing water over his face. He shook his hands dry and used his handkerchief to remove the last drops from his face. Taking a comb from his shirt pocket, he smoothed back his long dark hair. Then he flipped down his sleeves and picked up his hat. Holding it in his hand, he spun about and strode directly toward the house. He bent low and snapped the stem of one of Mother's petunias and tucked this into the hatband. In another moment the hat was on his head, and he was swinging gracefully into the saddle.

I was fascinated. None of the men I knew were proud like that about their appearance. There was no longer any chill on me, and already I was imagining myself in hat and belt and boots like those.

He looked down at us, and I would have sworn the tiny wrinkles around his eyes were what with him would be a smile.

"Thank you," he said in his gentle voice, and was turning into the road before Father spoke in his slow, deliberate way.

"Don't be in such a hurry, stranger."

At the first sound of Father's voice, the man and the horse, like a single being, wheeled to face us, the man's eyes boring at Father, bright and deep in the shadow of the hat's brim. I stared in wonder as Father and the stranger looked at each other a long moment, measuring each other. Then the warm sunlight was flooding over us, for Father was smiling and he was speaking with the drawling emphasis that meant he had made up his mind.

"I said don't be in such a hurry, stranger. Food will be on the table soon and you can bed down here tonight."

The stranger nodded quietly, as if he too had made up his mind. "That's mighty thoughtful of you," he said, and swung down and came toward us, leading his horse. We all headed for the barn.

"My name's Starrett," said Father. "Joe Starrett. This here," waving at me, "is Robert MacPherson Starrett. Too much name for a boy. I make it Bob."

The stranger nodded again. "Call me Shane," he said. Then to me, "You were watching me for quite a spell coming up the road."

"Yes . . ." I stammered. "Yes. I was."

"Right," he said. "I like that. A man who watches what's going on around him will make his mark."

A man who watches . . . For all his lean, hard look, this Shane knew what would please a boy. The glow of it held me as he took care of his horse, and I fussed around, hanging up his saddle, forking over some hay, getting in his way and my own in my eagerness. Only once did he stop me. That was when I reached for his saddle roll to put it to one side. In the instant my fingers touched it he was taking it from me, and he put it on a shelf with a finality that indicated no interference.

WHEN THE THREE of us went up to the house, Mother was waiting. "I saw you through the window," she said, and came to shake our visitor's hand. She was a slender, lively woman with a fair complexion and a mass of light brown hair piled high to bring her, she used to say, closer to Father's size.

"Marian," Father said, "I'd like you to meet Mr. Shane."

"Good evening, ma'am," said our visitor. He took her hand and bowed over it. Mother stepped back and, to my surprise, dropped in a dainty curtsy.

"And a good evening to you, Mr. Shane. If Joe hadn't called you back, I would have done it myself. You'd never find a decent meal up the valley." She was proud of her cooking, was Mother. That was one thing she learned back home, she would say, that was of some use out in this raw land.

We sat down to supper and it was a good one. Mother's eyes sparkled as our visitor kept pace with Father and me. Then we all leaned back, and while I listened the talk ran on almost like old friends. But I could sense that Father was trying, with Mother helping and both of them avoiding direct questions, to get hold of facts about this Shane; yet he was dodging at every turn, aware of their purpose and not in the least annoyed by it.

He must have been riding many days, for he was full of news from towns as far as Cheyenne and even Dodge City. But he had no news about himself. All they could learn was that he was riding through, with nothing particular in mind except maybe seeing a part of the country he had not been in before.

Afterward Mother washed the dishes and I dried and the two men sat on the porch. Our visitor now had Father talking about his own plans, and Father was going strong.

"Yes, Shane, the open range can't last forever. Running cattle in big lots is good business only for the top ranchers and it's a poor business at that. Poor in terms of the resources going into it. Too much space for too little results."

"Well, now," said Shane, "I've been hearing the same a lot lately. Maybe there's something to it."

"By Godfrey, there's plenty to it. Listen to me, Shane. The thing to do is pick your spot and get your own land. Put in enough crops to carry you and get yourself a small herd, not all horns and bone, but bred for meat and fenced in and fed right. I haven't been at it long, but already I've raised stock that averages three hundred pounds more than that long-legged stuff Fletcher runs. Sure, his outfit sprawls over most of this valley and it looks big. But his way is wasteful. Too much land for what he gets out of it. He can't see that. He thinks we small fellows are nothing but nuisances."

"You are," said Shane mildly. "From his point of view."

"Yes, I guess you're right. We'd make it tough for him if he wanted to use the range behind us on this side of the river, as he used to. All together we cut some pretty good slices out of it. Worse still, we block part of the river, shut the range off from the water. He's been grumbling about that ever since we've been here."

THE BEST OF THE WEST

The dishes were done and I was edging to the door. Mother nailed me as she usually did and shunted me off to bed. After she had left me in my little back room and gone to join the men on the porch, I must have dozed, for with a start I realized that Father and Mother were again in the kitchen. By now, I gathered, our visitor was out in the barn, in the bunk Father had built there for the hired man who had been with us for a few weeks in the spring.

"Wasn't it peculiar," I heard Mother say, "how he wouldn't talk about himself? I never saw a man quite like him before."

"You wouldn't have," said Father. "Not where you come from. He's a special brand we sometimes get out here. A bad one's poison. A good one's straight grain clear through."

"How can you be so sure about him? Why, he wouldn't even tell where he was raised."

"Born back east a ways would be my guess. And pretty far south. Tennessee maybe. But he's been around plenty."

"I like him." Mother's voice was serious. "He's so nice and polite and sort of gentle. Not like most men I've met out here. But there's something about him. Something . . . " Her voice trailed away.

"Mysterious?" suggested Father.

"Yes, of course. Mysterious. But more than that. Dangerous."

"He's dangerous all right." Father said it in a musing way. Then he chuckled. "But not to us, my dear. In fact, I don't think you ever had a safer man in your house."

Chapter 2

IN THE MORNING I slept late and stumbled into the kitchen to find Father and our visitor working their way through piles of Mother's flapjacks. Our visitor nodded at me gravely.

"Good morning, Bob. You'd better dig in fast or I'll do away with your share too. Eat enough of these flannel cakes and you'll grow a bigger man than your father."

"Flannel cakes! Did you hear that, Joe?" Mother came whisking over to tousle Father's hair. "You must be right. Tennessee or some such place. I never heard them called that out here."

Our visitor looked up at her. "A good guess, ma'am. Mighty close to the mark. My folks came out of Mississippi and settled in Arkansas. Me, though—I was fiddle-footed and left home at fifteen. Haven't had anything worth being called a real flannel cake since." He leaned back and the little wrinkles at the corners of his eyes were plainer and deeper. "That is, ma'am, till now."

Mother gave what in a girl I would have called a giggle. "If I'm any judge of men," she said, "that means more." And she whisked back to the stove.

That was how it was often in our house, kind of jolly and warm with good feeling. It needed to be this morning because there was a cool grayness in the air, and while I was on my second plate of flapjacks the wind came rushing down the valley, with one of our sudden summer storms following fast.

Our visitor finished his breakfast. He started to rise, but Mother's voice held him to his chair. "You'll not be traveling in any such weather," she said. "Wait a bit. These rains don't last long. I've another pot of coffee on the stove."

Father was getting his pipe going. He kept his eyes carefully on the smoke drifting upward. "Marian's right. Only these rains sure mess up the road. Won't be fit for traveling till it drains. You better stay over till tomorrow."

You could see our visitor liked the idea. Yet he seemed somehow worried about it.

"Yes," Father went on. "That's the sensible dodge. That horse of yours was pretty beat last night. A horse doctor'd order a day's rest right off. You stick here and I'll take you around today, show you what I'm doing with the place."

Father was usually so set on working every minute that Mother would have a tussle making him ease up some once a week out of respect for the Sabbath. And here he was talking of a whole day's rest. She was puzzled. But she played right up.

"You'd be doing us a favor, Mr. Shane. We don't get many visitors from outside the valley. It'd be real nice to have you stay. And I've been waiting for an excuse to try a deep-dish apple pie I've heard tell of. It would just be wasted on these two. They eat everything in sight and don't rightly know good from poor."

He was looking straight at her. She shook a finger at him. "And another thing. I'm fair bubbling with questions about what the women are wearing back in civilization. You know, hats and such. You're the kind of man would notice them."

Shane sat back in his chair. A faint quizzical expression softened the lean ridges of his face. "Ma'am, I'm not positive I appreciate how you've pegged me. No one else ever wrote me down an expert on ladies' millinery." He pushed his cup across the table toward her. "You said something about more coffee. But I draw the line on more flannel cakes. I want to conserve space for that pie."

"You'd better!" Father sounded mighty pleased. "Only don't you go giving Marian fancy notions of new hats so she'll be throwing my money away on silly frippery. She's got a hat."

Mother knew Father was just talking. She knew that whenever she wanted anything real much, Father would bust himself trying to get it for her. She poured a fresh round of coffee, then began pestering Shane to describe the ladies he had seen in Cheyenne and the other towns. He sat there, easy and friendly, telling her how they were wearing wide, floppy-brimmed bonnets with lots of flowers in front and slits in the brims for scarves to come through and be tied in bows under their chins.

Father listened good-naturedly, as if he thought talk like that was all right, only not very interesting. He tried every so often to break in with his own talk about crops and steers and finally gave up with a smiling shake of his head at those two. Then Shane was telling about the annual stock show at Dodge City and Father was interested and excited, and it was Mother who said, "Look, the sun's shining."

It was, so clear and sweet you wanted to run out and breathe the brilliant freshness. Father jumped up and fairly shouted, "Come on, Shane. I'll show you what this hopscotch climate does to my alfalfa. You can almost see the stuff growing."

We covered the whole place pretty thoroughly, Father talking all the time, more enthusiastic about his plans than he had been for many weeks. He really hit his stride when we were behind the barn, where we could have a good view of our little herd spreading out through the pasture. Then he stopped short when he saw Shane looking at the stump.

That was the one bad spot on our place. It stuck out like an old scarred sore in the cleared space back of the barn—a big old stump, all jagged across the top, the legacy of some great tree that must have died long before we came into the valley and finally been snapped by a heavy windstorm. It was big enough, I used to think, so that if it was smooth on top you could have served supper to a good-sized family on it. But you could not have done that because you could not have got them close around it. The huge old roots humped out in every direction, some as big about as my waist, pushing out and twisting down into the ground like they would hold there to eternity.

Father had been working at it off and on, gnawing at the roots with an axe, ever since he finished poling the corral. The going was slow, even for him. The wood was so hard that he could not sink the blade much more than a quarter inch at a time. I guess it had been an old bur oak. Ironwood we called it, and he was fighting his way around, root by root.

He went over now and kicked the nearest root, a smart kick, the way he did every time he passed it. "Yes," he said. "That's the millstone around my neck. That's the one fool thing about this place I haven't licked yet. But I will." He stared at the stump like it might be a person. "You know, Shane, I've been feuding with this thing so long I've worked up a spot of affection for it. It's tough. I can admire toughness. The right kind."

He was running on again, full of words and sort of happy to be letting them out, when he noticed that Shane was not paying much attention but was listening to some sound in the distance. Sure enough, a horse was coming up the road.

Father and I turned with him to look toward town. In a moment we saw a high-necked sorrel drawing a buckboard wagon. The mud was splattering from its hoofs, but not bad, and it was stepping free and easy. Shane glanced sideways at Father.

"Road not fit for traveling," he said softly. "Starrett, you're poor shakes as a liar."

Father chuckled. "That's Jake Ledyard's outfit," he said, taking the lead toward our lane. "I thought maybe he'd get up this way this week. Hope he has the cultivator I've been wanting."

LEDYARD WAS A SMALL, thin-featured man, a peddler who came through every couple of months with things you could not get at the general store in town. He would drive a hard bargain always in his deliveries, and would pick up orders for articles to bring on the next trip. I did not like him. He smiled too much and there was no real friendliness in it.

By the time we were beside the porch, he had swung the horse into our lane and was pulling it to a stop. He jumped down, calling greetings. Father went to meet him. Shane stayed by the porch, leaning against the end post.

"It's here," said Ledyard. "The beauty I told you about." He yanked away the canvas covering from the body of the wagon and the sun gleamed brightly on a shiny new seven-pronged cultivator.

"Hm-m-m-m," said Father. "You've hit it right. That's what I've been wanting. But what's the tariff?"

"Well, now." Ledyard was slow with his reply. "It cost me more than I figured when we was talking last time, but you'll make up the difference with the work you'll save."

"Pin it down," said Father. "I've asked you a question."

Ledyard was quick now. "Tell you what, I'll take a loss to please a good customer. I'll let you have it for a hundred and ten."

I was startled to hear Shane's voice cutting in, quiet and even. "Let you have it? I reckon he will. There was one like that in a store in Cheyenne. List price sixty dollars."

Ledyard shifted partway around and looked closely at our visitor. The surface smile left his face. His voice held an ugly undertone. "Did anyone ask you to push in on this?"

"No," said Shane, quietly and evenly as before. "I reckon no one did." He was still leaning against the post, not moving.

Ledyard turned to Father, speaking rapidly. "Forget what he says, Starrett. I've spotted him now. Heard of him half a dozen times along the road up here. No one knows him. Just a stray wandering through, probably chased out of some town and hunting cover. I'm surprised you'd let him hang around."

"You might be surprised at a lot of things," said Father, biting off his words. "Now give it to me straight on the price."

"It's what I said. A hundred and ten. But I'll shave it to a hundred if that'll make you feel any better." Ledyard hesitated, watching Father. "Maybe he did see something in Cheyenne. But he's mixed up. Must have been one of those little makes—flimsy and barely half the size. That might match his price."

Ledyard waited and Father did not say anything and the climbing anger in Ledyard broke free. "Starrett! Are you going to stand there and let that—that tramp call me a liar? Look at him! He's just a cheap, tinhorn—"

Ledyard stopped short, a sudden fear showing in his face. I knew why, even as I turned my head to see Shane. That same chill I had felt the day before, intangible and terrifying, was in the air again. Shane was no longer leaning against the post. He was standing erect, his hands clenched at his sides, his eyes boring at Ledyard, his whole body alert in the leaping instant.

Then the tension passed, fading in the empty silence. Shane's eyes lost their sharp focus on Ledyard and it seemed to me that reflected in them was some pain deep within himself.

Father had pivoted so that he could see the two of them in one sweep. He swung back to Ledyard alone. "Yes, I'm taking his word. He's my guest. He's here at my invitation. But that's not the reason." Father straightened a little and his head went up. "I can figure men for myself. I'll take his word on anything he says any day of God's whole year." His voice was flat and final. "Sixty is the price. Add ten for a fair profit, even though you probably got it wholesale. Another ten for hauling it here. That tallies to eighty. Take that or leave it. Whatever you do, snap to it and get off my land."

Ledyard stared down at his hands, rubbing them together as if they were cold. "Where's your money?" he said.

Father went into the house, into the bedroom, where he kept our money in a little leather bag on the closet shelf. He came back with the crumpled bills. All this while Shane stood there, not moving, his face hard, his eyes following Father with a strange wildness in them that I could not understand.

Ledyard helped Father heave the cultivator to the ground, then drove off like he was glad to get away from our place. Then Father and I looked around for Shane, but he was not in sight. Father shook his head in wonderment. "Now where do you suppose—" he was saying, when we saw Shane coming out of the barn.

He was carrying an axe, the one Father used for heavy kindling. He went directly around the corner of the building. We stared after him and we were still staring when we heard it, the clear ringing sound of steel biting into wood.

Father started toward the barn with strides so long that I had to run to stay close behind him. We went around the far corner and there was Shane squared away at the biggest uncut root of that big old stump. He was swinging the axe in steady rhythm, chewing into that root with bites almost as deep as Father could drive.

Father halted, legs wide, hands on hips. "Now lookahere," he began, "there's no call for you—"

Shane broke his rhythm just long enough to level a straight look at us. "A man has to pay his debts," he said, and was again swinging the axe. He was really slicing into that root.

He seemed so desperate in his determination that I had to speak. "You don't owe us anything," I said. "Lots of times we have folks in for meals and—"

Father's hand was on my shoulder. "No, Bob. He doesn't mean meals." Father was smiling. He stood in silence now, not moving, watching Shane.

It was something worth seeing. When Father worked on that old stump, that was worth seeing too. He could handle an axe mighty well and what impressed you was the strength and will of him making it behave and fight for him against the tough old wood. But this was different. What impressed you as Shane found what he was up against and settled to it was the easy way the power in him poured smoothly into each stroke. The blade would sink into the parallel grooves almost as if it knew itself what to do, and the chips from between would come out in firm and thin little blocks.

Father watched him and then I watched the two of them and time passed over us, and finally the axe sliced through the last strip and the root was cut. I was sure that Shane would stop. But he stepped right around to the next root and squared away again and the blade sank in once more.

As it hit this second root, Father began to fidget. Finally he gave the nearest root a kick and hurried away. In a moment he was back with the other axe, the big double-bladed one that I could hardly heft from the ground.

He picked a root on the opposite side from Shane. He was not angry, the way he usually was when he confronted one of those roots. There was a kind of contented look on his face. He whirled that big axe as if it were only a kid's tool. The striking blade sank in maybe a whole half inch. At the sound Shane straightened on his side. Their eyes met over the top of the stump and held and neither one of them said a word. Then they swung up their axes and both of them said plenty to that old stump.

Chapter 3

IT WAS EXCITING at first, watching them. They were hitting a fast pace, making the chips dance. When Shane finished his root, he looked over at Father working steadily away, and with a grim little smile pulling at his mouth he moved on to another one. A few moments later Father smashed through his with a blow that sent the axehead into the ground beneath. Then he too tackled another root without even waiting to wipe off the dirt. This began to look like a long session, and I was starting to wander away when Mother came around the corner of the barn.

She was the freshest, prettiest thing I had ever seen. She had taken her hat and stripped the old ribbon from it and fixed some flowers in a small bouquet in front. She had cut slits in the brim, and the sash from her best dress came around the crown and through the slits and was tied in a perky bow under her chin. She was stepping along daintily, mighty proud of herself.

She went up close to the stump. Those two choppers were so busy and intent that they did not really notice her.

"Well," she said, "aren't you going to look at me?"

They both stopped then and stared at her.

"Have I got it right?" she asked Shane. "Is this the way they do it?"

"Yes, ma'am," he said. "About like that. Only their brims are wider." And he swung back to his root.

"Joe Starrett," said Mother, "aren't you at least going to tell me whether you like me in this hat?"

"Lookahere, Marian," said Father, "you know right well that whether you have a hat on or whether you don't, to me you're the nicest thing that ever happened on God's green earth. Now stop bothering us. Can't you see we're busy?"

Mother's face was a deep pink. She pulled the hat from her head and held it swinging from her hand by the sash ends. Her hair was mussed and she was really mad.

"Humph," she said. "This is a funny kind of resting you're doing today, but you'll have to quit it for a while anyhow. Dinner's hot on the stove and waiting to be served."

She flounced back to the house and we all followed her in to an uncomfortable meal. Mother always believed you should be decent and polite at mealtime, particularly with company. She was polite enough now, talking enough for the whole table of us without once saying a word about her hat lying where she had thrown it on the chair by the stove. The trouble was that she was trying too hard.

The two men listened absently to her talk, chiming in only when she asked them direct questions. But their minds were on that old stump, and they were in a hurry to get at it again.

After they had gone out and I had been helping Mother with the dishes awhile, she began humming low under her breath and I knew she was not mad anymore. She was too curious. "What went on out there, Bob?" she asked me. "What got into those two?"

I didn't rightly know. All I could do was tell her about Ledyard talking mean and the way Shane acted. She got all flushed and excited. "What did you say, Bob? You were afraid of him? He frightened you? Your father would never let him do that."

"I wasn't frightened of him," I said, struggling to make her see the difference. "I was—well, I was just frightened. I was scared of whatever it was that might happen."

She reached out and rumpled my hair. "I think I understand," she said softly. "He's made me feel a little that way too." She went to the window and stared toward the barn. The steady rhythm of double blows was faint yet clear in the kitchen. "I hope Joe knows what he's doing," she murmured to herself. Then she turned to me. "Skip along out, Bob. I'll finish myself."

It was no fun watching them now. They had eased down to a slow, dogged pace, so I slipped off. I played pretty far afield, but no matter where I went, I could hear that chopping in the distance.

Along the middle of the afternoon I wandered into the barn. There was Mother by the rear stall, up on a box peering through the little window above it. She hopped down as soon as she heard me and put a finger to her lips.

"I declare," she whispered. "In some ways those two aren't even as old as you are, Bob. Just the same—" She frowned at me in such a funny, confiding manner that I felt all warm inside. "Don't you dare tell them I said so, but there's something splendid in the battle they're giving that old monster." She went past me and toward the house with such a brisk air that I followed to see what she was going to do.

She whisked about the kitchen and in almost no time she had a pan of biscuits in the oven. While they were baking, she took her hat and carefully sewed the ribbon back into its old place. "Humph," she said, more to herself than to me. "You'd think I'd learn. This isn't Dodge City, it's Joe Starrett's farm. It's where I'm proud to be."

Out came the biscuits. She piled as many as she could on a plate, popping one of the leftovers into her mouth and giving me the rest. She picked up the plate, marched out behind the barn and set the plate on a fairly smooth spot on top of the stump. She looked at the two men. "You're a pair of fools," she said. "But there's no law against me being a fool too." Without looking at either of them again, she marched back toward the house.

The two of them stared after her, then turned to stare at the biscuits. Father gave a deep sigh, but there was nothing sad or sorrowful about it. There was just something in him too big to be held tight in comfort. He let his axe fall to the ground. He did not say a word to Shane but leaned forward and separated the biscuits into two even piles. He pitched into one pile and Shane into the other, and then the two of them faced each other over the last uncut roots, munching at those biscuits as if this were the most serious business they had ever done.

Father finished his pile and stretched his arms high and wide until he seemed a tremendous tower of strength reaching up into the late afternoon sun. He swooped suddenly to grab the plate and toss it to me. Still in the same movement he seized his axe and swung it in a great arc into the root he was working on. Quick as he was, Shane was right with him, and together they were talking again to that old stump.

I TOOK THE PLATE in to Mother. She was peeling apples in the kitchen, humming gaily to herself. "The woodbox, Bob," she said, and went on humming. I carried in stove lengths till the box would not hold any more. Then I slipped out.

I tried to keep myself busy down by the river skipping flat stones across the current all muddy still from the rain. But that steady chopping had a peculiar fascination, always pulling me toward the barn. I simply could not grasp why they should work so, hour after hour, when routing out that old stump was really not so important. I was wavering in front of the barn when I noticed that the chopping was different. Only one axe was working.

I hurried around back. Shane was still swinging, cutting into the last root. Father was using the spade, digging under one side of the stump. As I watched, he laid the spade aside and put his shoulder to it and heaved. Sweat started to pour down his face. There was a little sucking sound and the stump moved ever so slightly.

That did it. I ran to the house fast as I could. I dashed into the kitchen and took hold of Mother's hand. "Hurry!" I yelled. "You've got to see it! They're getting it out!"

She was as excited as I was and running right with me. Shane had finished the root and had come to help Father. Together they heaved against the stump. It angled up nearly a whole inch. Again and again they heaved at it. Each time it would angle up a bit farther. Each time it would fall back.

Mother watched them battling with it. "Joe," she called, "why don't you use some sense? Hitch up the horses."

Father turned his head to look at her. "Horses!" he shouted. "Great jumping Jehosaphat! No! We started this with manpower and, by Godfrey, we'll finish it with manpower."

He peered underneath the stump. "Must be a taproot," he said. Shane said nothing. He just picked up his axe and waited.

Father drew a deep breath, then he turned and backed in between two cut root ends, pressing against the stump. He pushed his feet into the ground for firm footholds and wrapped his big hands around the root ends. Slowly he began to straighten his bent knees, and slowly that huge old stump began to rise. Up it came, inch by inch.

Shane poked his axe into the opening and I heard it strike wood. But the only way he could get in position to swing the axe was to drop on his right knee and extend his left leg into the opening. Then he could bring the axe sweeping in close to the ground.

Shane flashed one quick glance at Father beside him, eyes closed, muscles locked in that great sustained effort. Then he dropped into position with the whole terrible weight of the stump poised above nearly half of his body and sent the axe sweeping under in swift powerful strokes.

Suddenly Father seemed to slip. Only he had not slipped. The stump had leaped up a few more inches. Shane jumped out and grabbed one of the root ends and helped Father ease the stump down. They both were blowing like they had run a long way.

But they would not stay more than a minute before they were heaving again at the stump. It came up more easily now, the dirt tearing loose all around it, until they had the stump way up at a high angle. They were down in the hole, one on each side of it, pushing up and forward with hands flat on the under part reared before them higher than their heads. You could fairly feel the fierce energy suddenly pouring through them in the single coordinated drive. Suddenly the whole mass tore loose from the last hold and toppled away to sprawl in ungainly defeat beyond them.

Father climbed slowly out of the hole. He walked to the stump and placed a hand on the rounded bole and patted it like it was an old friend and he was a little sorry for it. Shane was across from him, laying a hand gently on the old hardwood. Their eyes met and held as they had so long ago in the morning hours.

At last Father turned and came toward Mother. He was so tired that the weariness showed in his walk. But there was no weariness in his voice. "Marian," he said, "I'm rested now. I don't believe any man was ever more rested."

Shane too spoke only to Mother. "Ma'am, I've learned something today. Being a farmer has more to it than I ever thought. Now I'm about ready for some of that pie."

Mother had been watching them in wonder. At his last words she let out a positive wail. "Oh-h-h—you—you—men! You made me forget about it! It's probably all burned!" And she was running for the house so fast she was tripping over her skirt.

THE PIE WAS BURNED all right. We could smell it in front of the house when the men were scrubbing themselves at the pump trough. From inside came the sound of kettles banging and dishes clattering. When we went in, we saw why. Mother had the table set and was putting supper on it; she was grabbing things and putting them down on the table with solid thumps.

We sat down and waited for her to join us. She put her back to us and stood by the stove staring at her big pie tin and the burned stuff in it. Finally Father spoke kind of sharply. "Lookahere, Marian. Aren't you ever going to sit down?"

She whirled and glared at him. Her voice was sharp like Father's. "I was planning to have a deep-dish apple pie. Well, I will. None of your silly man foolishness is going to stop me."

She swept up the big tin and went outside with it. We heard the rattle of the cover of the garbage pail. Then she came in to the side bench where the dishpan was and began to scrub it. When she'd finished, she went to the apple barrel, filled her bowl, then sat by the stove and started peeling fat round ones. Father fished in a pocket and pulled out his old jackknife. He moved over to her and reached out for an apple to help her.

She did not look up. But her voice caught him like she had flicked him with a whip. "Joe Starrett, don't you dare touch a one of these apples."

He was sheepish as he returned to his chair. Then he was downright mad. He grabbed his knife and fork and dug into the food on his plate. There was nothing for our visitor and me to do but follow his example. And when we finished, there was nothing to do but wait because Mother was sitting by the stove, arms folded, staring at the wall, waiting for her pie to bake. You might have said she had forgotten we were there.

She had not forgotten because as soon as the pie was done, she cut four wide pieces, put them on plates and set them on the table. Then she sat down. Her voice was still sharp. "I'm sorry to keep you men waiting so long. Your pie is ready now."

Father inspected his portion like he was afraid of it. It was a real effort for him to take his fork and lift a piece. He chewed on it and swallowed, then flipped his eyes sideways at Mother. "That's a prime pie," he said.

Shane put a piece in his mouth and chewed on it gravely. "Yes," he said. The quizzical expression on his face was plain. "Yes. That's the best bit of stump I ever tasted."

What could a silly remark like that mean? I had no time to wonder, for Father and Mother were staring at Shane and then Father chuckled and chuckled till he was swaying in his chair.

"By Godfrey, Marian, he's right. You've done it, too."

Mother stared from one to the other of them. Her cheeks were flushed and her eyes were soft and warm and she was laughing so hard that the tears came. And all of us were pitching into that pie, and the one thing wrong in the whole world was that there was not enough of it.

Chapter 4

THE SUN WAS well up when I awakened the next morning. I had been a long time getting to sleep because my mind was full of the day's excitement and shifting moods. I could not straighten out in my mind the way the grown folks had behaved. It scarce seemed possible that our visitor out in the barn was the same man I had first seen, stern and chilling in his dark solitude, riding up our road. Something in Father, something not of words or of actions but of the human spirit, had reached out and spoken to Shane and he had replied to it and had unlocked a part of himself to us.

I had been thinking too of the effect he had on Father and Mother. They were more alive, like they wanted to show more what they were when they were with him. I felt the same way. But it puzzled me that a man so ready to respond to Father should be riding a lone trail out of a closed and guarded past.

With a jolt I realized how late it was. I was frantic that the others might have finished breakfast and that our visitor was gone. I pulled on my clothes and ran to the door.

They were still at the table, subdued and quiet. They stared at me as I burst out of my room. "My heavens," said Mother. "You came in here like something was after you. What's the matter?"

"I just thought," I blurted out, nodding at our visitor, "that maybe he had ridden off and forgotten me."

Shane shook his head. "I wouldn't forget you, Bob." He turned to Mother and his voice took on a bantering tone. "And I wouldn't forget your cooking, ma'am. If you begin having a lot of people passing by at mealtimes, that'll be because a grateful man has been boasting of your flannel cakes all along the road."

"Now there's an idea," struck in Father. "We'll turn this place into a boardinghouse. Marian'll fill folks full of her meals and I'll fill my pockets full of their money."

Mother came right back at them, threatening to take Father at his word and make him spend all his time peeling potatoes and washing dishes. But she smiled as she stirred up my breakfast. They were enjoying themselves even though I could feel a bit of constraint behind the joshing. It was remarkable how natural it was to have this Shane sitting there and joining in almost like he was a member of the family.

He stood up at last. I knew he was going to ride away and I wanted desperately to stop him. Father did it for me.

"You certainly are a man for being in a hurry. Sit down, Shane. I've a question to ask you."

Shane, standing there, was suddenly withdrawn into a distant alertness. But he dropped back into his chair.

Father looked directly at him. "Are you running away from anything?"

Shane stared at the plate in front of him for a long moment. It seemed to me that a shade of sadness passed over him. Then he raised his eyes and looked directly at Father. "No. I'm not running away from anything. Not in the way you mean."

"Good." Father stabbed at the table with a forefinger for emphasis. "Look, Shane. You've seen my place, you know I'm not a rancher. Something of a stockman, maybe. But really a farmer. I've made a fair start. But there's more work here than one man can handle. The young fellow I had ran out on me after he tangled with a couple of Fletcher's boys in town one day." Father was talking fast and he paused to draw breath.

Shane had been watching him intently. He moved his head to look out the window over the valley to the mountains marching along the horizon. He looked at Mother and then at me, and as his eyes came back to Father he seemed to have decided something. "So Fletcher's crowding you," he said gently.

Father snorted. "I don't crowd easy. But I've got a job to do here and it's too big for one man, even for me. Will you stick here awhile and help me get things in shape for the winter?"

Shane rose to his feet. "I never figured to be a farmer, Starrett. I would have laughed at the notion a few days ago. All the same, you've hired yourself a hand." Then Shane turned toward Mother. "And I'll rate your cooking, ma'am, wages enough."

Father slapped his hands on his knees. "You'll get good wages and you'll earn 'em. First off, now, why don't you drop into town and get some work clothes. Try Sam Grafton's store. Tell him to put it on my bill."

Shane was already at the door. "I'll buy my own," he said, and was gone.

Father was so pleased he could not sit still. He jumped up and whirled Mother around. "Marian, the sun's shining mighty bright at last. We've got ourselves a man. Did you notice how he took it when I told him about Fletcher's boys and young Morley? Nobody'll push him around or scare him away. He's my kind of a man."

"Why, Joe Starrett. He isn't like you at all. He's smaller and he looks different and he talks different. I know he's lived different."

"Huh?" Father was surprised. "I wasn't talking about things like that."

Shane came back with a pair of dungaree pants, a flannel shirt, stout work shoes and a good serviceable stetson. He went into the barn and emerged a few moments later in his new clothes, leading his horse. At the pasture gate he slipped off the halter, turned the horse in with a hearty slap and tossed the halter to me.

"Take care of a horse, Bob, and it will take care of you. This one has brought me better than a thousand miles in the last few weeks." And he was striding away to join Father, who was ditching the field out past the growing corn where the ground was rich but not properly drained.

It was not three days before you saw that he could stay right beside Father in any kind of work. He never shirked the meanest task. He was ever ready to take the hard end of any chore. Only he was not a farmer and never really could be. There were times when he would stop and look off at the mountains and then down at himself and any tool he happened to have in his hands as if in wry amusement at what he was doing. You had no impression that he thought himself too good for the work. He was just different—a man apart. He was shaped for other things.

I was beginning to feel my oats about then, proud of myself for being able to lick Ollie Johnson at the next place down the road. Fighting, boy style, was much in my mind.

Once, when Father and I were alone, I asked him, "Could you beat Shane? In a fight, I mean."

"If I had to, son, I might do it. But, by Godfrey, I'd hate to try it. Some men just plain have dynamite inside them, and he's one. I'll tell you, though. I've never met a man I'd rather have more on my side in any kind of trouble."

I could understand that. But there were things about Shane I could not understand. When he came in to the first meal after he agreed to stay on with us, he went to the chair that had always been Father's and stood beside it, waiting for the rest of us to take the other places. Mother started to say something, but Father quieted her with a warning glance. He walked to the chair across from Shane and sat down like this was the natural spot for him, and afterward he and Shane always used these same places.

I could not see any reason for the shift until the first time one of our homestead neighbors knocked on the door while we were eating and came straight on in as most of them usually did. Then I realized that Shane was sitting opposite the door, where he could directly confront anyone coming through it.

In the evenings after supper when he was talking lazily with us, he would never sit by a window. Out on the porch he would always face the road, with a wall behind him and not just to lean against. It was part of his fixed alertness. He always wanted to know everything happening around him.

This alertness could be noted too in the watch he kept on every approach to our place. He knew first when anyone was moving along the road and he would stop whatever he was doing to study any passing rider.

We often had company in the evenings, for the other homesteaders regarded Father as their leader and would drop in to discuss their affairs with him. They were interesting men, but Shane would share little in their talk. With us he spoke freely enough. We were, in some subtle way, his folks.

These things puzzled me and not me alone. The people in town and those who went there pretty regularly just could not make up their minds about Shane, and it seemed to worry them. More than once I heard men arguing about him in front of Mr. Grafton's store. "He's like one of these here slow-burning fuses," I heard an old mule skinner say one day. "Quiet and no sputtering. Then it sets off one mighty big blowoff of trouble when it touches powder. That's him. And there's been trouble brewing in this valley for a long spell now."

What puzzled me most, though, was that Shane carried no gun. In those days guns were as familiar all through the Territory as boots and saddles. We homesteaders went in mostly for rifles and shotguns when we had any shooting to do. A pistol slapping on the hip was a nuisance for a farmer. Still every man had his cartridge belt and holstered Colt to be worn when he was not working or loafing around the house.

But Shane never carried a gun. And that was a peculiar thing because he had a gun.

I saw it once. I was alone in the barn one day and I spotted his saddle roll lying on his bunk. I reached to sort of feel it—and I felt the gun inside. No one was near, so I unfastened the straps and unrolled the blankets. There it was, the most beautiful-looking weapon I ever saw. Beautiful and deadly-looking.

The holster and filled cartridge belt were of the same soft black leather as the boots tucked under the bunk, tooled in the same intricate design. The gun was a single-action Colt, the same model as the regular army issue that was the favorite in those days; but this was no army gun. It was black, with the darkness not in any enamel but in the metal itself. The grip was shaped to the fingers on the inner curve, and two ivory plates were set into it with exquisite skill, one on each side.

The smooth invitation of it tempted your grasp. I pulled the gun out of the holster. It came so easily that I could hardly believe it was there in my hand. You held it up to aiming level and it seemed to balance itself in your hand. It was clean and polished and oiled. The empty cylinder spun swiftly and noiselessly when I flicked it. I was surprised to see that the front sight was gone and that the hammer had been filed to a sharp point.

Why should a man do that to a gun? Why should a man with a gun like that refuse to wear it and show it off? And then, staring at that dark and deadly efficiency, I was again suddenly chilled, and I quickly put everything back exactly as before and hurried out into the sun.

The first chance I had I tried to tell Father about it. "Father," I said, all excited, "do you know what Shane has rolled up in his blankets?"

"Probably a gun."

"But—but how did you know? Have you seen it?"

"No. That's what he would have."

I was all mixed up. "Well, why doesn't he ever carry it? Do you suppose he doesn't know how to use it very well?"

Father chuckled like I had made a joke. "Son, I wouldn't be surprised if he could take that gun and shoot the buttons off your shirt with you awearing it."

"Gosh agorry! Why does he keep it hidden in the barn, then?"

"I don't know. Not exactly."

"Why don't you ask him?"

Father looked straight at me, very serious. "That's one question I'll never ask him. And don't you ever say anything to him about it. There are some things you don't ask a man. Not if you respect him. He's entitled to stake his claim to what he considers private to himself alone. But you can take my word for it, Bob, that when a man like Shane doesn't want to tote a gun, you can bet he's got a mighty good reason."

Chapter 5

The weeks went rocking past, and soon it did not seem possible that there ever had been a time when Shane was not with us. He and Father worked together more like partners than boss and hired man. The amount they could get through in a day was a marvel.

We had enough fodder to carry a few more young steers through the winter, so Father rode out of the valley and to the ranch where he worked once and came back herding a half dozen more. He was gone two days. He came back to find that, while he was gone, Shane had knocked out the end of the corral and had posted a new section, making it half again as big.

"Now we can really get going next year," Shane said, as Father sat on his horse staring at the corral like he could not quite believe what he saw. "We ought to get enough hay off that new field to help us carry forty head."

"Oho!" said Father. "So we can get going. And we ought to get enough hay." He jumped off his horse and hurried up to the house, where Mother was standing on the porch.

"Marian," he demanded right off, waving at the corral, "whose idea was that?"

"Well-l-l," she said, "Shane suggested it." Then she added slyly, "But I told him to go ahead."

"That's right." Shane had come up beside him. "She rode me like she had spurs to get it done by today. Kind of a present. It's your wedding anniversary."

"Well, I'll be blowed," said Father. "So it is." With Shane there watching, he hopped on the porch and gave Mother a kiss. I was embarrassed for him and I turned away—and hopped about a foot myself.

"Hey! Those steers are running away!"

The grown folks had forgotten about them. All six steers were wandering up the road, straggling and separating. Shane, that soft-spoken man, let out a whoop you might have heard halfway to town, then ran to Father's horse and vaulted into the saddle. He fairly lifted the horse into a gallop in one leap, and that old cow pony of Father's lit out after those steers like this was fun. By the time Father reached the corral gate, Shane had the runaways in a compact bunch and padding back at a trot. He dropped them through the gateway neat as pie, and Father closed the gate.

"It's been ten years," Shane said, "since I did anything like that."

Father grinned at him. "Shane, if I didn't know better, I'd say you were a faker. There's still a lot of kid in you."

The first real smile I had seen yet flashed across Shane's face. "Maybe. Maybe there is at that."

I THINK THAT WAS the happiest summer of my life.

The only shadow over our valley, the recurrent trouble between Fletcher and us homesteaders, seemed to have faded away. Fletcher himself was gone most of those months, trying to get a contract to supply beef to the Indian agent at the big Sioux reservation over beyond the Black Hills. Except for his foreman, Morgan, and several surly older men, his hands were young, easygoing cowboys who made a lot of noise in town once in a while but rarely did any harm. We liked them—when Fletcher was not there driving them into harassing us. Now, with him away, they kept to the other side of the river and did not bother us. Sometimes, riding in sight on the other bank, they even waved to us.

Until Shane came, they had been my heroes. Father, of course, was special all to himself. I wanted to be like him, just as he was. But first I wanted, as he had done, to ride the range, to have my own string of ponies and take part in a big cattle drive and dash into strange towns with just such a crew and with a season's pay jingling in my pockets.

Now I wanted more and more to be like Shane. I conjured up all manner of adventures for him, seeing him as a dark and dashing figure coolly passing through perils that would overcome a lesser man. I had to imagine most of it. He would never speak of his past. Even his name remained mysterious. Just Shane. We never knew whether that was his first or last name or, indeed, any name that came from his family.

It was clear that Shane was beginning to enjoy living and working with us. Little by little the tension in him was fading out. He was still alert and watchful. But the sharp edge of conscious alertness, almost of expectancy of trouble, was wearing away.

Yet why was he sometimes so strange? Like the time I was playing with a gun Mr. Grafton gave me, an old frontier model Colt with a cracked barrel someone had turned in at the store. I had rigged a holster out of a torn chunk of oilcloth and a belt of rope. I was stalking around near the barn, whirling every few steps to pick off a skulking Indian, when I saw Shane watching me from the barn door. I stopped short, afraid he would make fun of me and my old broken pistol. Instead he looked gravely at me.

"How many you knocked over so far, Bob?"

Could I ever repay the man? My hand was steady as a rock as I drew a bead on another one.

"That makes seven."

"Better leave a few Indians for the other scouts," he said gently. "It wouldn't do to make them jealous. And look here, Bob. You're not doing that quite right." He sat down on an upturned crate and beckoned me over. "Your holster's too low. Don't let it drag full arm's length. Have it just below the hip, so the grip is about halfway between your wrist and elbow when the arm's hanging limp. Take the gun as your hand's coming up and there's still room to clear the holster without having to lift the gun too high."

"Gosh agorry! Is that the way the real gunfighters do?"

A queer light flickered in his eyes and was gone. "No. Not all of them. Most have their own tricks. One likes a shoulder holster; another packs his gun in his pants belt. Some carry two guns, but that's a show-off stunt and a waste of weight. One's enough, if you know how to use it. The way I'm telling you is as good as any and better than most. And another thing—"

He reached and took the gun, and suddenly his hands seemed to have an intelligence all their own. His right hand closed around the grip and he hefted the old gun, letting it lie loosely in the hand. Then, while I gaped at him, he tossed it swiftly in the air and caught it in his left hand. He tossed it again, high this time, spinning end over end, and as it came down, his right hand flicked forward and took it. The forefinger slipped through the trigger guard and the gun spun, coming up into firing position in the one unbroken motion. That old pistol seemed alive with him, an extension of the man himself.

"If it's speed you're after, Bob, don't split the move into parts. Don't pull, cock, aim and fire. Slip back the hammer as you bring the gun up, and squeeze the trigger the second it's up level."

"How do you aim it, then? How do you get a sight on it?"

"No need to. Learn to hold it so the barrel's right in line with the fingers if they were out straight. Just point it, quick and easy, like pointing a finger."

Like pointing a finger. As the words came, he was doing it. The old gun was bearing on some target over by the corral and the hammer was clicking at the empty cylinder. Then the hand around the gun whitened and the fingers slowly opened and the gun fell to the ground. The hand sank to his side, stiff and awkward. He raised his head, and the mouth was a bitter gash in his face. His eyes were fastened on the mountains in the distance.

"Shane! Shane! What's the matter?"

He did not hear me. He was back somewhere along the dark trail of the past. Then he took a deep breath and beckoned me to pick up the gun.

"Listen, Bob," he said. "A gun is just a tool. No better and no worse than any other tool, a shovel—or an axe or a saddle or a stove or anything. It's as good—or as bad—as the man who carries it. Remember that."

He stood up and strode off into the fields and I knew he wanted to be alone. I remembered what he said all right, but in those days I remembered more the way he handled the gun and the advice he gave me about using it. I would practice with it and think of the time when I could have one that would really shoot.

And then the summer was over. School began again and the days were growing shorter and the first cutting edge of cold was creeping down from the mountains.

MORE THAN THE SUMMER was over. The season of friendship in our valley was fading with the sun's warmth. Fletcher was back and he had his contract. He was talking in town that he would need the whole range again. The homesteaders would have to go.

He was a reasonable man, he was saying in his smooth way, and he would pay a fair price for any improvements they had put in. But we knew what Luke Fletcher would call a fair price. And we had no intention of leaving. The land was ours by right of settlement, guaranteed by the government. But we knew too that the nearest marshal was a good hundred miles away. We did not even have a sheriff in our town. There never had been any reason for one. The town was growing, but it was still not much more than a roadside settlement.

The first people there were three or four miners who had come prospecting about twenty years before and had found gold traces leading to a moderate vein. You could not have called it a strike, for others that followed were soon disappointed. Those first few, however, had done fairly well and had brought in their families and a number of helpers.

Then a stage and freighting line had picked the site for a relay post where you could get drinks as well as horses, and before long the cowboys from the ranches out on the plain and Fletcher's spread in the valley were drifting in of an evening. With us homesteaders coming now, one or two more almost every season, the town was taking shape. Already there were several stores, a harness and blacksmith shop and nearly a dozen houses. Just the year before, the men had put together a one-room schoolhouse.

Sam Grafton's place was the biggest. He had a general store with several rooms for living quarters back of it in one half of his rambling building, and a saloon with a long bar and tables for cards in the other half. Upstairs he had some rooms he rented. He acted as our postmaster, and sometimes he served as a sort of magistrate in minor disputes. His wife was dead. His daughter, Jane, kept house for him and was our schoolteacher.

Fletcher was the power there in those days. He had been running cattle through the whole valley at the time the miners arrived. Then a series of bad years had cut his herds about the time the first of the homesteaders moved in and he had not objected too much. But now Fletcher was back with a contract in his pocket and wanted his full range again.

Soon as the news was around, there was hurried council in our house. Our neighbor toward town, Lew Johnson, who heard it in Grafton's store, spread the word and arrived first. He was followed by Henry Shipstead, who had the place next to him, the closest to town. These two had been the original homesteaders. They were solid, dependable men who had come west from Iowa.

You could not say quite as much for the rest. James Lewis and Ed Howells were two middle-aged cowhands who had followed Father into the valley, coming pretty much on his example. Lacking his energy and drive, they had not done too well and could be easily discouraged. Frank Torrey, from farther up the valley, was a nervous, fidgety man with a querulous wife and a string of dirty kids. He was always talking about pulling up stakes and heading for California.

Ernie Wright, who had the last stand up the valley, was a husky, likable man, so dark-complected that there were rumors he was part Indian. He was always singing and telling tall stories, and he would be off hunting when he should be working. He also had a quick temper that would trap him into doing fool things.

He was as serious as the rest of them that night. Mr. Grafton had said that this time Fletcher meant business. His contract called for all the beef he could drive in the next five years and he was determined to push the chance to the limit.

"But what can he do?" asked Frank Torrey. "The land's ours as long as we live on it, and we get title in three years. Some of you fellows have already proved up."

"I don't figure he'll start moving cattle in till spring," Father said. "My guess is he'll try putting pressure on us this fall and winter, see if he can wear us down. He doesn't like any of us. But he doesn't like me the most. So he'll probably begin by trying to convince Shane here that it isn't healthy to be working with me."

"You mean the way he—" began Ernie Wright.

"Yes." Father cut him off. "The way he did with young Morley."

I was peeping around the door of my little room. I saw Shane sitting off to one side, listening quietly. He did not seem the least bit interested in finding out what had happened to young Morley. I knew. I had seen Morley come back from town, bruised and a beaten man, and gather his things and curse Father for hiring him and ride away without once looking back.

Father was right. In some strange fashion the feeling was abroad that Shane was a marked man. Attention was on him as a sort of symbol. By taking him on, Father had accepted a challenge from the big ranch across the river. What had happened to Morley had been a warning and Father had deliberately answered it. If Shane could be driven out, there would be a break in the homestead ranks, a defeat going beyond just the loss of one man.

Chapter 6

THE PEOPLE IN TOWN were now more curious than ever about Shane. They would stop me and ask me questions when I was hurrying to and from school. I knew that Father would not want me to say anything and I pretended that I did not know what they were talking about. But I used to watch Shane closely myself and wonder how all the slow-climbing tension in our valley could be so focused on one man and he seem so indifferent to it.

Then one afternoon, when we were stowing away the second and last cutting of hay, one fork of the big tongs broke loose. "Have to get it welded in town," Father said in disgust and began to hitch up the team.

Shane stared over the river where a cowboy was riding lazily back and forth by a bunch of cattle. "I'll take it in," he said.

Father looked at Shane and then across the way and he grinned. "All right. It's as good a time as any." He started for the house. "Just a minute and I'll be ready."

"Take it easy, Joe." Shane's voice was gentle, but it stopped Father in his tracks. "I said I'll take it in."

Father whirled to face him. "Damn it all, man. Do you think I'd let you go alone? Suppose they—" He bit down on his own words. "I'm sorry," he said. "I should have known better." He stood watching silently as Shane gathered up the reins and jumped to the wagon seat.

I waited till Shane was driving out of the lane. Then I ducked behind the barn, around the end of the corral, and hopped into the wagon going past. As I did, I saw the cowboy across the river spin his horse and ride rapidly off toward the ranch house.

Shane saw it too, and it seemed to give him a grim amusement. He reached backward and hauled me over the seat and sat me beside him. "You Starretts like to mix into things." For a moment I thought he might send me back. Instead he grinned at me. "I'll buy you a jackknife when we hit town."

He did, a dandy big one with two blades and a corkscrew. After we left the tongs with the blacksmith and found the welding would take nearly an hour, I squatted on the steps on the long porch across the front of Grafton's building, busy whittling, while Shane stepped into the saloon side and ordered a drink. Will Atkey, Grafton's thin, sad-faced clerk and bartender, was behind the bar and several other men were loafing at one of the tables.

It was only a few moments before two cowboys came galloping down the road. They slowed to a walk about fifty yards off and ambled the rest of the way to Grafton's. One of them I had seen often, a young fellow everyone called Chris, who had worked with Fletcher several years and was known for a gay manner and reckless courage. The other was new to me, a sallow, pinch-cheeked man, not much older, who looked like he had crowded a lot of hard living into his years.

They stepped softly up on the porch and to the window of the saloon part of the building. As they peered through, Chris nodded

SHANE

and jerked his head toward the inside. The new man stiffened. He leaned closer for a better look. Abruptly he turned clear about and came right down past me and went over to his horse.

Chris was startled and hurried after him. "What's got into you?"

"I'm leaving."

"Huh? I don't get it."

"I'm leaving. Now. For good."

"Hey, listen. Do you know that guy?"

"I didn't say that. There ain't nobody can claim I said that. I'm leaving, that's all. You can tell Fletcher."

Chris was getting mad. "I might have known," he said. "Scared, eh. Yellow."

Color rushed into the new man's sallow face. But he climbed on his horse. "You can call it that," he said flatly and started down the road, out of town, out of the valley.

Chris stood still by the rail and shook his head in wonderment. Then he stalked up onto the porch, into the saloon.

I dashed into the store side, over to the doorway between the two big rooms. I crouched on a box just inside the store where I could hear everything and see most of the other room. It was long and fairly wide. The bar curved out from the doorway and ran all the way along the inner wall to the back wall, which closed off a room Grafton used as an office. A small stairway led up to a balcony across the back, with doors opening into several little rooms.

Shane was leaning easily with one arm on the bar, his drink in his other hand, when Chris came to perhaps six feet away and called for a whiskey bottle and a glass. Chris pretended he did not notice Shane at first and bobbed his head in greeting to the men at the table. I could have sworn that Shane, studying Chris in his effortless way, was somehow disappointed.

Chris waited until he had his whiskey and had gulped a stiff shot. Then he deliberately looked Shane over. "Hello, farmer," he said. He said it as if he did not like farmers.

Shane regarded him with grave attention. "Speaking to me?" he asked mildly, and finished his drink.

"Don't see anybody else standing there. Here, have a drink of this." Chris shoved his bottle along the bar. Shane poured himself a generous slug and raised it to his lips.

"Well, look at that," flipped Chris. "So you drink whiskey."

Shane tossed off the rest of his glass and set it down. "I've had better," he said, as friendly as could be. "But this will do."

Chris slapped his leather chaps with a loud smack. He turned to take in the other men. "Did you hear that? This farmer drinks whiskey. I didn't think these plow-pushing dirt grubbers drank anything stronger than soda pop!"

"Some of us do," said Shane, friendly as before. Then suddenly his voice was like winter frost. "You've had your fun and it's mighty young fun. Now run home and tell Fletcher to send a grown-up man next time." He turned away and sang out to Will Atkey. "Do you have any soda pop? I'd like a bottle."

Will hesitated, looked kind of funny and scuttled past me into the store room. He came back right away with a bottle of the pop Grafton kept there for us school kids. Chris was standing quiet, not so much mad, I would have said, as puzzled. He sucked on his lower lip for a while. Then he began to look elaborately around the room, sniffing loudly.

"Hey, Will!" he called. "What's been happening in here? It smells. That ain't no clean cattleman smell. That's plain dirty barnyard." He stared at Shane. "You, farmer. What are you and Starrett raising out there? Pigs?"

Shane was just taking hold of the bottle Will had fetched him. His hand closed on it and the knuckles showed white. He moved slowly, almost unwillingly, to face Chris. His eyes were blazing and every line of his body was as taut as stretched whipcord.

Chris stepped back involuntarily, one pace, two, then pulled up erect. And still nothing happened. The lean muscles along the sides of Shane's jaw were ridged like rock. Then he looked away from Chris, past him, over the tops of the swinging doors beyond, over the roof of the shed across the road, on into the distance, where the mountains loomed in their own unending loneliness. Quietly he walked, the bottle forgotten in his hand, so close by Chris as almost to brush him yet apparently not even seeing him, through the doors and was gone.

I heard a sigh of relief near me. Mr. Grafton had come up from somewhere behind me. He was watching Chris with a strange, ironic quirk at his mouth corners. Chris was trying not to look pleased with himself. But he swaggered as he went to the doors and peered over them.

"You saw it, Will," he called over his shoulder. "He walked out on me." Chris pushed up his hat, rolled back on his heels and laughed. "With a bottle of soda pop too!" He was still laughing as he went out and we heard him ride away.

"That boy's a fool," Mr. Grafton muttered.

Will Atkey came sidling over to Mr. Grafton. "I never pegged Shane for a play like that," he said.

"He was afraid, Will."

"Yeah. That's what was so funny. I would've guessed he could take Chris."

Mr. Grafton looked at Will like he was a little sorry for him. "No, Will. He wasn't afraid of Chris. He was afraid of himself." Mr. Grafton was thoughtful. "There's trouble ahead, Will. The worst trouble we've ever had." He noticed me, realizing my presence. "Better skip along, Bob, and find your friend. Do you think he got that bottle for himself?"

True enough, Shane had it waiting for me at the blacksmith shop. Cherry pop, the kind I favored most. Shane was silent and stern. He had slipped back into the dark mood that was on him when he first came riding up our road. Only once did he speak to me and I knew he did not expect me to understand or to answer.

"Why should a man be smashed because he has courage and does what he's told? Life's a dirty business, Bob. I could like that boy." And he turned inward again to his own thoughts and stayed that way until we had loaded the tongs in the wagon and were started home. By the time we swung in toward the barn, he was the way I wanted him again, crinkling his eyes at me and gravely joshing me about the Indians I would scalp with my new knife.

Father popped out the barn door, busting with curiosity. But he would not come straight out with a question to Shane. He tackled me instead. "See any of your cowboy heroes in town?"

Shane cut in ahead of me. "One of Fletcher's crew chased us in to pay his respects."

"No," I said, proud of my information. "There was two of them."

"Two?" Shane said. "What did the other one do?"

"He went up on the porch and looked in the window where you

were and came right back down and rode off. He said he was leaving for good."

Father smiled. "One down and you didn't even know it. What did you do to the other?"

"Nothing. He passed a few remarks about farmers. I went back to the blacksmith shop."

Father repeated the words like there might be meanings between them. "You—went—back—to—the—blacksmith—shop."

I was worried that he must be thinking what Will Atkey did. Then I knew nothing like that had even entered his head. He switched to me. "Who was it?"

"It was Chris."

Father was smiling again. Now he had the whole thing clear. "Fletcher was right to send two. Young ones like Chris need to hunt in pairs or they might get hurt." He chuckled. "Chris must have been considerable surprised when you walked out. It was too bad the other one didn't stick around."

"Yes," Shane said, "it was."

The way he said it sobered Father. "I hadn't thought of that. Chris is just cocky enough to take it wrong. That can make things plenty unpleasant."

"Yes," Shane said again, "it can."

Chapter 7

THE STORY CHRIS TOLD was common knowledge all through the valley the next day. Fletcher had an advantage now and he was quick to push it. He and his foreman, Morgan, a broad slab of a man with flattened face and head small in proportion to great sloping shoulders, kept their men primed to rowel us homesteaders at every chance. They took to using the upper ford, up above Ernie

Wright's stand, and riding down the road past our places every time they had an excuse for going to town. They would go by slowly, looking everything over with insolent interest and passing remarks for our benefit.

The same week, maybe three days later, a covey of them came riding by while Father was putting a new hinge on the corral gate. They acted like they were too busy staring over our land to see him there close. "Wonder where Starrett keeps the critters," said one of them. "I don't see a pig in sight."

"But I can smell 'em!" shouted another one. With that they all began to laugh and whoop and holler and went tearing off.

It was crude. It was coarse. I thought it silly for grown men to act that way. But it was effective. Shane, as self-sufficient as the mountains, could ignore it. Father, while it galled him, could keep it from getting him. The other homesteaders, though, felt insulted. It roughed their nerves and made them angry and restless.

Things became so bad they could not go into Grafton's store without someone singing out for soda pop. And wherever they went, the conversation nearby always snuck around somehow to pigs. The effect showed in the resentful attitude our neighbors now had toward Shane. They were constrained when they called to see Father and found Shane there. And as a result their opinion of Father was changing. That was what finally drove Shane. He did not mind what they thought of him. But he did care what they thought of Father. He was standing silently on the porch the night Ernie Wright and Henry Shipstead were arguing with Father in the kitchen over what they could do.

"I can't stomach much more," Ernie Wright was saying. "You know the trouble I've had with those blasted cowboys cutting my fence. Today a couple of them rode over and helped me repair a piece. Helped me, blast them! Waited till we were through, then said Fletcher didn't want any of my pigs getting loose and mixing with his cattle. My pigs! There ain't a pig in this whole valley and they know it. I'm sick of the word."

Father chuckled. Grim, maybe, yet still a chuckle. "Sounds like one of Morgan's ideas. He's smart. Mean, but—"

Henry Shipstead would not let him finish. "This is nothing to laugh at, Joe. You least of all. Man, I'm beginning to doubt your judgment. Just a while ago I was in Grafton's and Chris was there blowing high about how your Shane must be thirsty because he's so scared he hasn't been in town lately for his soda pop."

"You can't dodge it, Joe," said Wright. "Your man's responsible. Chris braced him for a fight and he ducked out."

"You know as well as I do what Fletcher's doing," growled Henry Shipstead. "He's pushing us with this and he won't let up till one of us gets enough and makes a fool play and starts something so he can move in and finish it."

"Fool play or not," said Ernie Wright, "I've had all I can take. The next time one of those—"

Father held a hand up for silence. "Listen. What's that?"

It was a horse, picking up speed and tearing down our lane into the road. Father was at the door in a single jump.

The others were close behind him. "Shane?"

Father nodded. "That's Shane," he told them. "All we can do now is wait."

They were a silent crew. Mother got up from her sewing in the bedroom where she had been listening and came into the kitchen and made up a pot of coffee. They all sat there sipping at the hot stuff and waiting. It could not have been much more than twenty minutes before we heard the horse again, coming swiftly and swinging around to make the lane without slowing. There were quick steps on the porch and Shane stood in the doorway. He was breathing strongly and his face was hard. He looked at Shipstead and Wright and he made no effort to hide the disgust in his voice.

"Your pigs are dead and buried."

As his gaze shifted to Father, his face softened. But his voice was still bitter. "There's another one down. Chris won't be bothering anybody for quite a spell." He turned and disappeared and we could hear him leading his horse into the barn.

In the quiet that followed, hoofbeats sounded in the distance like an echo. They swelled louder and then a second horse galloped into our lane and pulled to a stop. Ed Howells jumped to the porch and hurried in. "Where's Shane?"

"Out in the barn," Father said.

"Did he tell you what happened?"

"Not much," Father said mildly. "Something about burying pigs."

SHANE

Ed Howells slumped into a chair. He seemed a bit dazed. "I never saw anything like it," he said, and he told about it.

He had been in Grafton's store buying a few things, not caring about going into the saloon because Chris and Red Marlin, another of Fletcher's cowboys, had hands in the evening poker game. Then he noticed how still the place was. He went over to sneak a look and there was Shane just moving to the bar.

"Two bottles of soda pop," Shane called to Will Atkey. He leaned his back to the bar and looked the poker game over with what seemed a friendly interest while Will fetched the soda from the store. Then he took the two bottles and walked to the table and set them down, reaching over to put one in front of Chris.

"Last time I was here you bought me a drink. Now it's my turn."

You could have heard a bug crawl, I guess, while Chris carefully laid down the cards in his right hand and stretched to the bottle. He lifted it in a sudden jerk and flung it across the table at Shane.

So fast Shane moved, Ed Howells said, that the bottle was still in the air when he had dodged, lunged forward, grabbed Chris by the shirtfront and hauled him right out of his chair and over the table. As Chris struggled to get his feet under him, Shane let go the shirt and slapped him, sharp and stinging, three times, the hand flicking back and forth so quick you could hardly see it.

Shane stepped back and Chris stood swaying a little and shaking his head to clear it. He was a game one and mad down to his boots. He plunged in, fists smashing, and Shane let him come, slipping inside the flailing arms and jolting a powerful blow low into his stomach. As Chris gasped and his head came down, Shane brought his right hand up, open, and with the heel of it caught Chris full on the mouth, snapping his head back and raking up over the nose.

The force of it knocked Chris off-balance and he staggered badly. His lips were crushed. Blood was dripping over them from his battered nose. But he drove in again, swinging wildly. Shane ducked under, caught one of the flying wrists, twisted the arm to lock it and keep it from bending, then swung his shoulder into the armpit. He yanked hard on the wrist and Chris went up and over him. As the body hurtled over, Shane kept hold of the arm and wrenched it sideways and let the weight bear on it. You could hear the bone crack as Chris crashed to the floor.

A long, sobbing sigh came from Chris and died away and then there was not a sound in the room. Shane stood motionless, but his eyes shifted to Red Marlin.

"Perhaps," Shane said softly, and the very softness of his voice sent shivers through Ed Howells, "perhaps you have something to say about soda pop or pigs."

Red Marlin sat quiet like he was trying not even to breathe. Tiny drops of sweat appeared on his forehead. He was frightened, and no one blamed him at all.

Then, as they watched, the fire in Shane smoldered down and out. He turned toward Chris unconscious on the floor, then bent and scooped the sprawling figure up in his arms and carried it to one of the other tables. Gently he set it down, the legs falling limp over the edge. He crossed to the bar, took the rag Will used to wipe it and returned to the table and tenderly cleared the blood from the face. He felt carefully along the broken arm.

Shane's voice rang across the room at Red Marlin. "You'd better tote him home and get that arm fixed. Take right good care of him. He has the makings of a good man." Then he strode through the swinging doors and into the night.

That was what Ed Howells told. "The whole business," he finished, "didn't take five minutes. In my opinion that Shane is the most dangerous man I've ever seen. I'm glad he's working for Joe here and not for Fletcher."

Father leveled a triumphant look at Henry Shipstead. "So I've made a mistake, have I?"

Before anyone else could push in a word, Mother was speaking. "I think you've made a bad mistake, Joe Starrett."

Father was edging toward being peeved. "Women never do understand these things. Lookahere, Marian. Chris is young and he's healthy. Soon as that arm is mended, he'll be in good shape."

"Oh, Joe, can't you see what I'm talking about? I don't mean what you've done to Chris. I mean what you've done to Shane."

THIS TIME MOTHER was right. Shane was changed. He had lost the serenity that had seeped into him through the summer, and he was restless with some deep-hidden desperation. At times he would wander alone about our place, and this was the one thing that seemed to soothe him. Often he would disappear from the house after supper. More than once I found him far back in the pasture alone with his horse. He would be standing there, one arm on the horse's neck, the fingers gently rubbing around the ears, and he would be looking out over our land where the last light of the sun would be capping the mountains with a deep glow.

I was not sure whether Father and Mother were aware of the change in him. But one afternoon I overheard something that showed Mother knew.

I had hurried home from school, thinking of the cookies that were kept in a tin box on a shelf by the stove. Mother was firm set against eating between meals. That was a silly notion. She was settled on the porch with a batch of potatoes to peel, so I slipped up to the back of the house, through the window of my little room, and tiptoed into the kitchen. Just as I was carefully putting a chair under the shelf, I heard her call to Shane.

I peeped out the front window and saw him standing by the porch, his hat in his hand, his face tilted up slightly to look at her leaning forward in her chair.

"I've been wanting to talk to you when Joe wasn't around."

"Yes, Marian." He called her that, the same as Father did, familiar yet respectful, always regarding her with a tenderness in his eyes he had for no one else.

"You've been worrying, haven't you, about what may happen in this Fletcher business? And about what you might do if there's any more fighting?"

"You're a discerning woman, Marian."

"You've been worrying about something else too."

"You're a mighty discerning woman, Marian."

"And you've been thinking that maybe you'll be moving on."

"How did you know that?"

"Because it's what you ought to do. For your own sake. But I'm asking you not to." Mother was intense and serious, as lovely there with the light striking through her hair as I had ever seen her. "Don't go, Shane. Joe needs you. More than he would ever say."

"And you?" Shane's lips barely moved and I was not sure of the words.

Mother hesitated. "Yes. It's only fair to say it. I need you too."

"So-o-o," he said softly, the word lingering on his lips. He considered her gravely. "Do you know what you're asking, Marian?"

"I know. And I know that you're the man to stand up to it. In some ways it would be easier for me too, if you rode out of this valley and never came back. But Joe can't keep this place without you. He can't buck Fletcher alone."

Shane was silent, and it seemed to me that he was troubled. Mother was talking straight to him, slow and feeling for the words, and her voice was beginning to tremble.

"It would just about kill Joe to lose this place. He promised it to me when we were married. He had it in his mind for all the first years. He did two men's work to get the extra money for the things we would need. When Bob was big enough to walk and help some and Joe could leave us, he came out here and filed his claim and built this house with his own hands, and when he brought us here it was home. Nothing else would ever be the same."

Shane drew a deep breath and let it ease out slowly. "Joe should be proud of a wife like you. Don't fret anymore, Marian. You'll not lose this place."

Mother's face was radiant. Then, womanlike, she was talking against herself. "But that Fletcher is a mean and tricky man. Are you sure it will work out all right?"

Shane was already starting toward the barn. He stopped and turned to look at her again. "I said you won't lose this place."

Chapter 8

SINCE THE NIGHT Shane rode into town, Fletcher's cowboys had quit using the road past the homesteads. They were not annoying us at all and only once in a while was there a rider in view across the river. They had a good excuse to let us be. They were busy fixing the ranch buildings and poling a big new corral in preparation for the spring drive of new cattle Fletcher was planning.

Just the same, I noticed that Father was as watchful as Shane now. The two of them always worked together. And Father took to wearing his gun all the time, even in the fields.

Those were beautiful fall days, clear and stirring, with the coolness in the air just enough to set one atingling, not yet mounting to the bitter cold that soon would come sweeping down out of the mountains. It did not seem possible that in such a harvest season violence could flare so suddenly and swiftly.

Saturday evenings we would pile into the light work wagon, Father and Mother on the seat, Shane and I swinging legs at the rear, and go into town.

There was always a bustle in Grafton's store with people we knew coming and going. Mother would lay in her supplies for the week ahead, taking a long time about it and chatting with the womenfolk. Father would give Mr. Grafton his order for what he wanted and go direct for the mail. He was always getting catalogues of farm equipment and pamphlets from Washington. He would flip through their pages and skim through any letters, then settle on a barrel and spread out his newspaper. But like as not he would soon be bogged down in an argument with almost any man handy about the best crops for the Territory, and it would be Shane who would really work his way into the newspaper.

I used to explore the store, filling myself with crackers from the open barrel at the end of the main counter, playing hide-and-seek with Mr. Grafton's big old cat that was a whiz of a mouser. Many a time, turning up boxes, I chased out fat furry ones for her to pounce on.

This time we had a special reason for staying longer than usual, a reason I did not like. Our schoolteacher, Jane Grafton, had made me take a note home to Mother asking her to stop in for a talk. About me. Twice that week I had persuaded Ollie Johnson to sneak away with me after the lunch hour to see if the fish were still biting in our favorite pool below town. No one could expect a boy with any spirit in him to be shut up in a schoolroom in weather like we had been having.

Mother finished the last item on her list, looked around at me and sighed a little. I knew she was going to the living quarters behind the store to talk to Miss Grafton. She went over to Father. "Come along, Joe. You should hear this too. I declare, that boy is getting too big for me to handle."

Father looked at Shane, who was folding the newspaper. "This won't take long," he said. "We'll be out in a moment."

As they passed through the door at the rear of the store, Shane strolled to the saloon and stepped up to the bar, joshing Will Atkey with a grave face and saying that he didn't think he'd have soda pop tonight. I was never supposed to go in there, so I stopped at the entrance. I was letting my eyes wander about the room when I saw that one of the swinging doors was partly open and Red Marlin was peeking in. Shane saw it too.

But he could not see that more men were on the porch, for they were close by the wall on the store side. I could sense them through the window near me, hulking shapes in the darkness. I was so frightened I could scarcely move, but I went against Mother's rule anyway. I scrambled into the saloon and to Shane and I gasped, "Shane! There's a lot of them out front!"

I was too late. Red Marlin was inside and the others were hurrying in and fanning out to close off the doorway to the store. Morgan was one of them, his flat face sour and determined, his huge shoulders almost filling the front entrance as he came through. Behind him was the cowboy they called Curly because of his shock of unruly hair. He was stupid and slow-moving, but he was thick and powerful. Two others followed them, new men to me, with the tough, experienced look of old herd hands.

There was still the back office with its outside door opening on the rear alley. My knees were shaking and I tugged at Shane and tried to say something about it. He stopped me with a sharp gesture. He put one hand on my head and rocked it gently, the fingers feeling through my hair. "Bobby boy, would you have me run away?"

Love for that man raced through me, and I was ready to do as he told me when he said, "Get out of here, Bob. This isn't going to be pretty."

But I would go no farther than my perch just inside the store, where I could watch most of the big room. I was so bound in the moment that I did not even think of running for Father.

Morgan was in the lead now with his men spread out behind him. He came about half the way to Shane and stopped. The room was quiet except for the shuffling of feet as the men by the bar and the nearest tables hastened over to the far wall. Neither Shane nor Morgan gave any attention to them. They did not look aside even when Mr. Grafton stalked in from the store and pushed past Will Atkey behind the bar. He reached under the counter, his hands reappearing with a short-barreled shotgun. He laid it before him on the bar and said in a dry, disgusted voice, "There will be no gunplay, gentlemen. And all damages will be paid for."

Morgan nodded curtly, not taking his eyes from Shane, and came closer. "No one messes up one of my boys and gets away with it. We're riding you out of this valley on a rail, Shane."

"So you have it all planned," Shane said softly. Even as he was speaking, he was moving. He flowed into action so swift you could hardly believe what was happening. He scooped up his glass from the bar and whipped it and its contents into Morgan's face. Then, when Morgan's hands came up, he grasped the wrists and flung himself backward, dragging Morgan with him. His body rolled to meet the floor and his legs doubled and his feet, catching Morgan just below the belt, sent him flying on and over to fall in a grotesque spraddle amid a tangle of chairs and a table.

The other four were on Shane in a rush. As they came, he whirled behind the nearest table, tipping it in a strong heave among them. They scattered, dodging, and he stepped, fast and light, around the end and drove into one of the new men now nearest to him. He took the blows at him straight on to get in close and I saw his knee surge up and into the man's groin. A high scream tore from the man and he collapsed to the floor, dragging himself toward the doors.

Morgan was on his feet, wavering, rubbing a hand across his face, trying to focus again on the room about him. The other three were battering at Shane, seeking to box him between them. Through that blur of movement he was weaving, quick and confident. You could see the blows hit him, hear the solid chunk of knuckles on flesh. But they had no effect. They seemed only to feed that fierce energy. He would burst out of the melee and whirl and plunge back, the one man actually pressing the three.

Curly, slow and clumsy, grunting in exasperation, grabbed at Shane to grapple with him and hold down his arms. Shane dropped one shoulder and, as Curly hugged tighter, brought it up under his jaw with a jolt that knocked him loose and away.

Then Red Marlin came at him from one side, forcing him to turn that way, and at the same time the second new man did a strange thing. He jumped high in the air, like a jackrabbit in a spy hop, and lashed out viciously with one boot at Shane's head. Shane saw it coming but could not avoid it, so he rolled his head with the kick, taking it along the side. It shook him badly. But his hands shot up instantly, seizing the foot, and the man crashed down to land on the small of his back. As he hit, Shane twisted the whole leg and threw his weight on it. The man buckled on the floor, groaned sharply and hitched himself away, the leg dragging.

But the swing to bend down on the leg had put Shane's back to Curly, and now Curly's arms clamped around him, pinning his arms to his body. Red Marlin leaped to help and they had Shane caught tight between them.

"Hold him!" That was Morgan, coming forward with the hate plain in his eyes. Shane stomped one heavy work shoe, heel edged and with all the strength he could get, on Curly's near foot. As Curly winced and pulled it back and was unsteady, Shane strained with his whole body in a powerful arch and you could see their arms slipping and loosening. Morgan, circling in, saw it too. He swept a bottle off the bar and brought it smashing down from behind on Shane's head.

Shane slumped and would have fallen if they had not been holding him. Then Morgan stepped around in front of him and deliberately flung a huge fist to Shane's face. Shane tried to jerk aside and the fist missed the jaw, tearing along the cheek, the heavy ring on one finger slicing deep. Morgan pulled back for another blow. He never made it.

Nothing, I would have said, could have drawn my attention from those men. But I heard a kind of choking sob beside me.

Father was there in the entranceway!

He was big and terrible and he was looking across the overturned table and scattered chairs at Shane, at the dark, purplish bruise along the side of Shane's head and the blood running down his cheek. I had never seen Father like this. He was shaking with fury.

I never thought he could move so fast. He was on them before they even knew he was in the room. He hurtled into Morgan with ruthless force, sending that huge man reeling across the room. He reached out one broad hand and grabbed Curly by the shoulder. He took hold of Curly's belt with the other hand and ripped him loose from Shane. His shirt shredded down the back and the great muscles there knotted and bulged as he lifted Curly right up over his head and hurled the threshing body from him. Curly spun through the air and crashed on the top of a table way over by the wall. It collapsed under him in splintered pieces, and the man and the wreckage smacked against the wall. Curly tried to rise, fell back and was still.

Shane must have exploded into action the second Father yanked Curly away, for now there was another noise. It was Red Marlin, his face contorted, flung against the bar and catching at it to keep himself from falling. He staggered and caught his balance and ran for the front doorway. His flight was frantic, headlong. He tore through the swinging doors without slowing to push them. They flapped with a swishing sound and my eyes shifted quickly to Shane, for he was laughing, not in amusement at Red Marlin or any single thing, but in the joy of being alive.

Morgan was in the rear corner, his face clouded and uncertain, and Father was starting toward him.

"Wait, Joe. The man's mine." Shane was at Father's side and he put a hand on his arm. "You'd better get them out of here." He nodded in my direction, and I noticed with surprise that Mother was near and watching. She must have followed Father and have been there all this while.

Father was disappointed, but he looked over at the men by the wall. "This is Shane's play," he said. "If a one of you tries to interfere, he'll have me to reckon with." Then he came to us and looked down at Mother. "You wait out at the wagon, Marian. Morgan's had this coming to him for quite a long time now and it's not for a woman to see."

Mother shook her head without moving her eyes now from Shane. "No, Joe. He's one of us. I'll see this through." And the three of us stayed there together.

Shane advanced toward Morgan. Taller, half again as broad, Morgan had a long reputation as a bullying fighter. He rushed at Shane to overwhelm the smaller man with his weight. Shane faded from in front of him and as Morgan went past hooked a sharp blow to his stomach and another to the side of his jaw. Each time Morgan's big frame shook and halted in its rush for a fraction of a second before the momentum carried him forward. Again and again he rushed, driving his big fists ahead. Always Shane slipped away, sending in those swift, hard punches.

Breathing heavily, Morgan tried to get hold of Shane and wrestle him down. Shane let him come without dodging, disregarding the arms stretching to encircle him. He brought up his right hand, open, just as Ed Howells had told us, and the force of Morgan's own lunge as the hand met his mouth and raked upward snapped his head back and sent him staggering.

Morgan bellowed and swung up a chair. Holding it in front of him, legs forward, he rushed again at Shane, who sidestepped neatly. Morgan was expecting this and halted suddenly, swinging the chair in a swift arc to strike Shane with it full on the side. The chair shattered and Shane faltered. Then he seemed to slip and fall to the floor.

Forgetting all caution, Morgan dived at him. Shane's legs bent and he caught Morgan on his heavy work shoes and sent him flying back and against the bar with a crash. Then he was up and leaping at Morgan as if there had been springs under him. His left hand, palm out, smacked against Morgan's forehead, pushing the head back, and his right fist drove straight to Morgan's throat. Shane, using his right fist now like a club and lining his whole body behind it, struck him on the neck below and back of the ear. It made a sickening, dull sound. Morgan's eyes rolled white and he sagged slowly to the floor.

THE BIG BARROOM was so quiet that the rustle of Will Atkey straightening from below the bar level was loud and clear, and Will stopped moving, embarrassed and a little frightened.

Shane looked neither at him nor at any of the other men staring from the wall. He looked only at us, at Father and Mother and me, and it seemed to me that it hurt him to see us there.

He breathed deeply and his chest filled and he held it, held it long and achingly, and released it slowly and sighing. Now that he was still and the fire in him banked and subsided, you saw that he had taken bitter punishment.

His shirt collar was dark and sodden. Blood was soaking into it, and this came only in part from the cut on his cheek. More was oozing from the matted hair where Morgan's bottle had hit. He swayed slightly, and when he started toward us his feet dragged and he almost fell forward.

One of the townsmen, Mr. Weir, a friendly man who kept the stage post, pushed out from the wall as though to help him. Shane pulled himself erect. His eyes blazed refusal. Straight and superb, not a tremor in him, he came to us. The one man whose help he would take was there and ready.

Father stepped to meet him and put out a big arm, reaching for his shoulders. "All right, Joe," Shane said softly. His eyes closed and he leaned against Father's arm, his body relaxing and his head dropping sideways. Father bent and slipped his other arm under Shane's knees. Then he picked him up, like he did me when I stayed up too late and got all drowsy and had to be carried to bed.

Father held Shane in his arms and looked over him at Mr. Grafton. "I'd consider it a favor, Sam, if you'd figure the damage and put it on my bill."

For a man strict about bills and keen for a bargain, Mr. Grafton surprised me. "I'm marking this to Fletcher's account. I'm seeing that he pays."

Mr. Weir surprised me even more. "Listen to me, Starrett. It's about time this town worked up a little pride. Maybe it's time, too, we got to be more neighborly with you homesteaders. I'll take a collection to cover this. I've been ashamed of myself, standing here and letting five of them jump that man of yours."

Father was pleased. But he knew what he wanted to do. "That's mighty nice of you, Weir. But this ain't your fight. I wouldn't worry, was I you, about keeping out of it." He looked down at Shane. "Matter of fact, I'd say the odds tonight, without me butting in, too, was close to even." He looked again at Mr. Grafton. "Fletcher ain't getting in on this with a nickel. We're paying. Me and Shane."

He went to the swinging doors, turning sideways to push them open. Mother took my hand and we followed. She said no word while we watched Father lift Shane to the wagon seat, climb beside him, hoist him to sitting position with one arm around him and take the reins in the other hand. Mother and I perched on the back of the wagon, Father chirruped to the team and we started home.

THERE WAS NOT a sound for quite a stretch except the clop of hoofs and the little creakings of the wheels. Then I heard a chuckle up front. It was Shane. The cool air was reviving him and he was sitting straight, swaying with the wagon's motion.

"What did you do with the thick one, Joe? I was busy with the redhead."

"Oh, I just kind of tucked him out of the way." Father wanted to let it go at that. Not Mother.

"He picked him up like—like a bag of potatoes and threw him clear across the room," she said, her eyes shining in the starlight.

We turned in at our place and Father shooed us into the house while he unhitched the team. In the kitchen, Mother set some water to heat on the stove and chased me to bed. Her back was barely to me before I was peering around the doorjamb. She got several clean rags, took the water from the stove and went to work on Shane's head, tender as could be. It pained him plenty as the warm water soaked into the gash under the matted hair and as she washed the clotted blood from his cheek. But it seemed to pain her more, for her hand shook at the worst moments, and she was the one who flinched while he sat there quietly and smiled reassuringly at her.

Father came in and sat by the stove, watching them. He pulled out his pipe and made a very careful business of packing it and lighting it.

"You were magnificent, Joe," Mother said. "Tearing that man away and—"

"Shucks," said Father. "I was just peeved. Him holding Shane so Morgan could pound him."

"And you, Shane." Mother was in the middle of the kitchen, looking from one to the other. "You were magnificent too. You were so cool and quick and—"

"A woman shouldn't have to see things like that." Shane interrupted her, but she was talking right ahead.

"You think I shouldn't because it's brutal and nasty. But you didn't start it. You didn't want to do it. Not until they made you, anyway." Her voice was climbing and she was looking back and forth and losing control of herself. "Did ever a woman have two such men?" She reached out blindly for a chair, sank into it and dropped her face into her hands, and the tears came.

Shane rose and stepped over by Mother. He put a hand gently on her head and I felt again his fingers in my hair and the affection flooding through me. He walked quietly out the door and into the night.

Father rose and went to the door and out on the porch. I could see him there dimly in the darkness, gazing across the river.

Gradually Mother's sobs died down. She raised her head and wiped away the tears.

"Joe."

He turned and waited there by the door. Mother stood up. She stretched her hands toward him and he was there and had her in his arms. "Do you think I don't know, Marian?"

"But you don't. Not really. Because I don't know myself."

Father was staring over her head at the kitchen wall, not seeing anything there. "Don't fret yourself, Marian. I'm man enough to know a better when his trail meets mine. Whatever happens will be all right."

"Oh, Joe . . . Joe! Kiss me. Hold me tight and don't ever let go."

WHAT HAPPENED IN our kitchen that night was beyond me in those days. But it did not worry me because Father had said it would be all right, and how could anyone, knowing him, doubt that he would make it so?

We were not bothered by Fletcher's men anymore, and they were hardly ever seen now even in town. Fletcher himself was gone again, and nobody seemed to know why he went. Yet Father and Shane stayed even closer together and they spent no more time than they had to in the fields. There was no more talking on the porch in the evenings, though the nights were so cool and lovely they called you to be out and under the winking stars. We kept to the house, and Father polished his rifle and hung it, ready loaded, on a couple of nails by the kitchen door.

All this caution failed to make sense to me. So at dinner about a week later I asked, "Is there something new that's wrong? That stuff about Fletcher is finished, isn't it?"

"Finished?" said Shane, looking at me over his coffee cup. "Bobby boy, it's only begun."

"That's right," said Father. "Fletcher's gone too far to back out now. It's a case of now or never with him. If he can make us run, he'll be setting pretty for a long stretch. If he can't, he'll be shoved smack out of this valley."

"Why doesn't he do something, then?" I asked. "Seems to me mighty quiet around here lately."

"Seems to you, eh?" said Father. "Seems to me you're mighty young to be doing so much seemsing. Don't you worry, son. Fletcher is fixing to do something. I'd be easier in my mind if I knew what he's up to."

"You see, Bob"—Shane was speaking to me the way I liked, as if I were a man and could understand all he said—"when there's noise, you know where to look and what's happening. When things are quiet, you've got to be most careful."

Mother sighed. She was looking at Shane's cheek where the cut was healing into a scar like a thin line running back from near the mouth corner. "I suppose you two are right. But does there have to be any more fighting?"

"Like the other night?" asked Father. "No, Marian. I don't think so. Fletcher knows better now."

"He knows better," Shane said, "because he knows it won't work. He'll be watching for some way that has more finesse."

"Hm-m-m," said Father. "Some legal trick, eh?"

"Could be. If he can find one. If not—" Shane shrugged and gazed out the window. "There are other ways. Depends on how far he's willing to go."

"Hm-m-m," said Father again. "Wish I could be as patient about it as you. I don't like this waiting."

But we did not have to wait long. It was the next day, a Friday, when we were finishing supper, that Lew Johnson and Henry Shipstead brought us the news. Fletcher was back and he had not come back alone. There was another man with him.

Lew Johnson saw them as they got off the stage. He said the

stranger was tall, rather broad in the shoulders and slim in the waist. He carried himself with a sort of swagger. He had a mustache and his eyes were cold and had a glitter that bothered Johnson. When this stranger turned, his coat flapped open and Johnson could see that he was carrying two guns, big capable forty-fives, in holsters hung fairly low and forward. Those holsters were pegged down at the tips with thin straps fastened around the man's legs.

Wilson was the man's name. That was what Fletcher called him when a cowboy rode up leading a couple of horses. A funny other name. Stark. Stark Wilson. And that was not all.

Lew Johnson was worried and went into Grafton's to find Will Atkey, who always knew more about people than anyone else because he was constantly picking up information from the talk of men at the bar. Will would not believe it at first when Johnson told him the name. What would he be doing up here? Will kept saying. Then Will blurted out that this Wilson was a bad one, a killer. He was a gunfighter said to be just as good with either hand. He came to Cheyenne from Kansas, Will had heard, with a reputation for killing three men there and nobody knew how many more down in the southwest territories where he used to be.

Lew Johnson was rattling on, when Shane shut him off with a suddenness that startled the rest of us. "When did they hit town?"

"Last night."

"And you waited till now to tell it!" Shane whirled on Father. "Quick, Joe. Which one has the hottest head? Which one's the easiest to prod into being a fool? Torrey is it? Or Wright?"

"Ernie Wright," Father said slowly.

"Get moving, Johnson. Get over to Wright's on your horse and make it there in a hurry. Bring him here. Pick up Torrey too."

"He'll have to go into town for that," Henry Shipstead said heavily. "We passed them both down the road riding in."

Shane jumped to his feet and strode to the door himself, yanked it open and started out. Then he stopped suddenly, leaning forward and listening. All of us could hear it now, a horse pounding up the road at full gallop.

Shane turned back into the room. "There's your answer," he said bitterly. He swung the nearest chair to the wall and sat down, withdrawn into his own dark thoughts.

We heard the horse sliding to a stop out front. Frank Torrey burst into the doorway. His hat was gone, his hair blowing wild. His chest heaved and his voice was a hoarse whisper, though he was trying to shout. "Ernie's shot! They've killed him!"

The words jerked us to our feet and we stood staring. All but Shane. He did not move. You might have thought he was not even interested in what Torrey had said.

"Come in, Frank," Father said quietly. "Sit down and talk and don't leave anything out." He led Frank Torrey to a chair and pushed him into it, then he closed the door and returned to his own chair. He looked older and tired.

It took Frank Torrey quite a while to tell his story. He was badly frightened. He and Ernie Wright had been to the stage office asking for a parcel Ernie was expecting. They dropped into Grafton's before starting back. Since things had been so quiet lately, they were not thinking of any trouble even though Fletcher and the new man, Stark Wilson, were in the poker game at the big table. But Fletcher and Wilson chucked in their hands and came over to the bar.

Fletcher was nice and polite as could be, nodding to Torrey and singling out Ernie for talk. He said he was sorry about it, but he really needed the land Ernie had filed on. "I'll give you three hundred dollars," he said, "and that's more than the lumber in your buildings will be worth to me."

Ernie had more than that of his money in the place already. He had turned Fletcher down three or four times before. He was mad, the way he always was when Fletcher started his smooth talk.

"No," he said shortly. "I'm not selling. Not now or ever."

Fletcher shrugged like he had done all he could and slipped a quick nod at Stark Wilson. Wilson was half smiling at Ernie, but his eyes, Frank Torrey said, had nothing like a smile in them.

"I'd change my mind if I were you," Wilson said to Ernie. "That is, if you have a mind to change."

"Keep out of this," snapped Ernie. "It's none of your business."

"I see you haven't heard," Wilson said softly. "I'm Mr. Fletcher's new business agent. I'm handling his business affairs for him. His business with stubborn jackasses like you." Then he said what Fletcher had coached him to. "You're a fool, Wright. But what can you expect from a breed?"

"That's a lie!" shouted Ernie. "My mother wasn't no Indian!"

"Why, you crossbred squatter," Wilson said, quick and sharp, "are you telling me I'm wrong?"

"I'm telling you you're a low-crawling liar!"

The silence that shut down over the saloon was so complete, Frank Torrey told us, that he could hear the ticking of the old alarm clock on the shelf behind the bar.

"So-o-o-o," said Wilson, satisfied now and stretching out the word with ominous softness. He flipped back his coat on the right side and the holster there was free with the gun grip ready for his hand. "You'll take that back, Wright. Or you'll crawl out of here on your belly."

Ernie moved out a step from the bar, his arms stiff at his sides. His hand was firm on his gun and pulling up when Wilson's first bullet hit him and staggered him. The second spun him halfway around and a faint froth appeared on his lips. All expression died from his face and he sagged to the floor.

WHILE FRANK TORREY was talking, Jim Lewis and a few minutes later Ed Howells had come in. Bad news travels fast and they seemed to know something was wrong. They were all in our kitchen now, more shaken than I had ever seen them.

I pressed close to Mother, grateful for her arms around me. I noticed that she had little attention for the other men. She was watching Shane, bitter and silent across the room.

"So that's it," Father said grimly. "We'll have to face it. We sell, and at his price, or he slips the leash on his hired killer. Did Wilson make a move toward you, Frank?"

"He looked at me." Torrey shivered. "He looked at me and he said, 'Too bad, isn't it, that Wright didn't change his mind?'"

"Then what?"

"I got out of there quick as I could and came here."

Jim Lewis had been fidgeting nervously. Now he jumped up, almost shouting. "Joe! A man can't just go around shooting people!"

"Shut up, Jim," growled Henry Shipstead. "Don't you see the setup? Wilson badgered Ernie into getting himself in a spot where he had to go for his gun. Wilson can claim he shot in self-defense. He'll try the same thing on each of us."

"That's right," put in Lew Johnson. "Even if we tried to get a marshal in here, he couldn't hold Wilson. It was an even break and the faster man won is the way most people will figure it."

"Call it anything you want." Lewis was shouting now. "I call it murder."

"Yes!" Shane's word sliced through the room. He was up and his face was hard with rock ridges running along his jaw. "Yes. It's murder. Trick it out as self-defense or even break for a fair draw and it's still murder." He looked at Father and the pain was deep in his eyes. But there was only contempt in his voice as he turned to the others.

"You five can crawl back in your burrows. You don't have to worry—yet. If the time comes, you can always sell and run. Fletcher won't bother with the likes of you now. He's going the limit and he knows the game. He picked Wright to make the play plain. That's done. Now he'll head straight for the one real man in this valley. He's standing between you and Fletcher and Wilson right this minute, and you ought to be thankful that once in a while this country turns out a man like Joe Starrett."

And a man like Shane . . . Were those words only in my mind or did I hear Mother whisper them? She was looking at him and then at Father and she was both frightened and proud at once.

The others stirred uneasily. They were reassured by what Shane said and yet shamed that they should be. And they did not like the way he said it.

"You seem to know a lot about that kind of dirty business," Ed Howells said, with an edge of malice to his voice.

"I do."

Shane let the words lie there, plain and short and ugly. He stared levelly at Howells and it was the other man who dropped his eyes and turned away.

Father had his pipe going. "Maybe it's a lucky break for the rest of us," he said mildly, "that Shane here has been around a bit. He can call the cards for us plain. Ernie might still be alive, Johnson, if you had had the sense to tell us about Wilson right off. It's a good thing Ernie wasn't a family man." He turned to Shane. "How do you rate Fletcher, now he's shown his hand?"

"He'll move in on Wright's place tomorrow. He'll have a lot of men busy on this side of the river from now on to keep the pressure on all of you. How quick he'll try you, Joe, depends on how he reads you. If he thinks you might crack, he'll wait and let knowing what happened to Wright work on you. If he really knows you, he'll not wait more than a day or two before he throws Wilson at you. He'll want it, like with Wright, in a public place where there'll be plenty of witnesses. If you don't give him a chance, he'll make one."

"Hm-m-m," Father said soberly. "That rings right." He pulled on his pipe for a moment. "I reckon this will be a matter of waiting for the next few days. There's no immediate danger right off, anyway. Grafton will take care of Ernie's body tonight. We can meet in town in the morning to fix him a funeral. After that, we'd better stay out of town and stick close to home as much as possible. I'd suggest you all study on this and drop in again tomorrow night. Maybe we can figure out something."

They were ready to leave it at that. They were decent men, but not a one of them would have stood up to Fletcher. They would stay as long as Father was there. With him gone, Fletcher would have things his way. That was how they felt as they muttered their goodnights and scattered up and down the road.

Father stood in the doorway and watched them go. When he came back to his chair he seemed haggard and worn. "Somebody will have to go to Ernie's place tomorrow," he said, "and gather up his things. He's got relatives somewhere in Iowa."

"You'll not go near the place." There was finality in Shane's tone. "Fletcher might be counting on that. Grafton can do it."

"But Ernie was my friend," Father said simply.

"Ernie's past friendship. Your debt is to the living."

Father nodded assent and turned to Mother, who was hurrying to argue with him.

"Don't you see, Joe?" she said. "If you can stay away from any place where you might meet Fletcher and—and that Wilson, things will work out. He can't keep a man like Wilson in this little valley forever." She was talking rapidly and I knew why. She was not really trying to convince Father as much as she was trying to convince herself. Father knew it too.

"No, Marian. A man can't crawl into a hole somewhere and hide like a rabbit. Not if he has any pride."

"All right then. But can't you keep quiet and not let him drive you into any fight?"

"That won't work either." Father was grim. "A man can stand for a lot of pushing if he has to. Specially when he has his reasons." He glanced briefly at me. "But there are some things a man can't take. Not if he's to go on living with himself."

I was startled as Shane suddenly sucked in his breath. He was battling that old hidden desperation within him, and his eyes were dark and tormented against the paleness of his face. He strode to the door and went out. We heard his footsteps fading toward the barn.

I was startled now at Father. He was up and pacing back and forth. He swung on Mother, his voice battering at her, almost fierce in its intensity. "That's the one thing I can't stand, Marian. What we're doing to him. Shane won his fight before ever he came riding into this valley. It's been tough enough on him already. Should we let him lose just because of us? Fletcher can have his way. We'll sell out and move on."

I was not thinking. I was only feeling. I could not help what I was saying, shouting across the room. "Father! Shane wouldn't run away! He wouldn't run away from anything!"

"Bob's right, Joe," Mother said. "We can't let Shane down. He'd never forgive us if we ran away from this. If we did, there wouldn't be anything real ahead for us, any of us, even for Bob."

"Hm-m-m," said Father softly, musing to himself. "I guess you're right. The salt would be gone. There just wouldn't be any flavor. There wouldn't be much meaning left."

"Oh, Joe! Joe! That's what I've been trying to say. And I know this will work out someway if we face it and stand up to it and have faith in each other. It's got to."

"That's a woman's reason, Marian. But you're part right, anyway. We'll play this game through. Maybe we can wait Fletcher out and make him overplay his hand."

Father was more cheerful now that he was beginning to get his thoughts straightened out. He and Mother talked low in the kitchen for a long time after they sent me to bed, and I lay in my little room and saw through the window the stars wheeling distantly in the far outer darkness until I fell asleep at last.

Chapter 9

THE MORNING SUN brightened our house and everything in the world outside. We had a good breakfast, Father and Shane taking their time because they had routed out early to get the chores done and were waiting to go to town. They saddled up presently and rode off, and I moped in front of the house.

After a while Mother saw me staring down the road and called me to the porch. She got our tattered old Parcheesi board and she kept me humping to beat her. She was a grand one for games like that. She would be as excited as a kid, squealing at the big numbers and doubles and counting proudly out loud as she moved her markers ahead.

When I had won three games running, she put the board away and brought out two fat apples and my favorite book. Munching on her apple, she read to me and before I knew it the shadows were mighty short and she had to skip in to get dinner because Father and Shane were riding up to the barn.

They came in while she was putting the food on the table. We sat down and it was almost like a holiday. Father was pleased at what had happened in town.

"Yes, sir," he was saying as we were finishing dinner. "Ernie had a right good funeral. Grafton made a nice speech and, by Godfrey, I believe he meant it. That fellow Weir had his clerk put together a really fine coffin. Wouldn't take a cent for it. I was surprised at the crowd too. Not a good word for Fletcher among them. And there must have been thirty people there."

"Thirty-four," said Shane. "I counted 'em. They weren't just paying their respects to Wright, Marian. They were showing their opinion of a certain man named Starrett, who made a pretty fair speech himself. Give your husband time and he'll be mayor."

Mother caught her breath with a little sob. "Give . . . him . . .

time," she said slowly. She looked at Shane and there was panic in her eyes. The lightness was gone, and before anyone could say more we heard horses turning into our yard.

I dashed to the window to peer out. Shane pushed back his chair and spoke gently, still sitting in it. "That will be Fletcher, Joe. He's heard how the town is taking this and knows he has to move fast. You take it easy. He's playing against time now, but he won't push anything here."

Father nodded at Shane and went to the door. He had taken off his gunbelt when he came in and now passed it to lift the rifle from its nails on the wall, and, holding it in his right hand, barrel down, he opened the door and stepped out on the porch. Shane followed quietly and leaned in the doorway, relaxed and watchful. Mother was beside me at the window, staring out, crumpling her apron in her hand.

There were four of them, Fletcher and Wilson in the lead, two cowboys tagging. They pulled up about twenty feet from the porch. This was the first time I had seen Fletcher for nearly a year. He was a tall man who must once have been a handsome figure in the fine clothes he always wore. Now a heaviness was setting in about his features and a fatty softness showed in his body. His face had a shrewd cast and a kind of reckless determination was on him.

Stark Wilson seemed lean and fit. He was sitting idly in his saddle, but the pose did not fool you. He was wearing no coat and the two guns were swinging free. He was sure of himself, serene and deadly.

Fletcher was smiling and affable. He was certain he held the cards and was going to deal them as he wanted. "Sorry to bother you, Starrett, so soon after that unfortunate affair last night. I wish it could have been avoided. Shooting is so unnecessary, if only people would show sense. But Wright never should have called Mr. Wilson here a liar. That was a mistake."

"It was," Father said curtly. "But then Ernie always did believe in telling the truth." I could see Wilson stiffen and his lips tighten. Father did not look at him. "Speak your piece, Fletcher, and get off my land."

Fletcher was still smiling. "There's no call for us to quarrel, Starrett. You've worked cattle on a big ranch and you can understand my position. I'll be wanting all the range I can get from now on. Even without that, I can't let a bunch of nesters keep coming in here and choke me off from my water rights."

"We've been over that before," Father said. "You know where I stand. If you have more to say, speak up and be done with it."

"All right, Starrett. Here's my proposition. I like the way you do things. You've got some queer notions about the cattle business, but when you tackle a job, you take hold and do it thoroughly. You and that man of yours are a combination I could use. I'm getting rid of Morgan and I want you to take over as foreman. From what I hear, your man would make a top-rank driving trail boss. The spot's his. Since you've proved up on this place, I'll buy it from you. If you want to go on living here, that can be arranged. But I want you working for me."

Father was surprised. He had not expected anything quite like this. He spoke softly to Shane behind him.

"Can I call the turn for you, Shane?"

"Yes, Joe." Shane's voice was just as soft, but there was a little note of pride in it.

Father stared straight at Fletcher. "And the others," he said slowly. "Johnson, Shipstead and the rest. What about them?"

"They'll have to go."

Father did not hesitate. "No."

"I'll give you a thousand dollars for this place as it stands."

"No."

The fury in Fletcher broke over his face. Then he caught himself and forced a shrewd smile. "There's no percentage in being hasty, Starrett. I'll boost the ante to twelve hundred. I'll not take an answer now. I'll give you till tonight to think it over. I'll be waiting at Grafton's to hear you talk sense."

He swung his horse and started away. The two cowboys turned to join him by the road. Wilson did not follow at once. He leaned forward in the saddle with a sneering look at Father.

"Yes, Starrett. Think it over. You wouldn't like someone else to be enjoying this place of yours—and that woman there in the window."

He was lifting his reins with one hand to pull his horse around and suddenly he dropped them and froze to attention. It must have been what he saw in Father's face. We could not see it, Mother and I, because Father's back was to us. But we could see his hand tighten on the rifle at his side.

"Don't, Joe!"

Shane slipped past Father, down the steps and over to one side to come at Wilson on his right hand and stop not six feet from him. Wilson was puzzled and his right hand twitched and then was still as he saw that Shane carried no gun.

Shane looked up at him and his voice flicked in a whiplash of contempt. "You talk like a man because of that flashy hardware you're wearing. Strip it away and you'd shrivel down to boy size."

The very daring of it held Wilson motionless for an instant and Father's voice cut into it. "Shane! Stop it!"

Wilson smiled grimly at Shane. "You do need someone to look after you." He whirled his horse and put it to a run to join Fletcher and the others in the road.

It was only then that I realized Mother was gripping my shoulders so hard that they hurt. She dropped on a chair and held me to her. We could hear Father and Shane on the porch.

"He'd have drilled you, Joe, before you could have brought the gun up and pumped in a shell."

"But you, you crazy fool! You'd have made him plug you just so I'd have a chance to get him."

Mother jumped up. She pushed me aside. She flared at them from the doorway. "And both of you would have acted like fools just because he said that about me. I'll have you know that I can take being insulted just as much as you two can."

"But Marian," Father objected mildly, coming to her. "What better reason could a man have?"

"Yes," said Shane gently. "What better reason?" He was not looking just at Mother. He was looking at the two of them.

I DO NOT KNOW how long they would have stood there on the porch in the warmth of that moment. I shattered it by asking what seemed to me a simple question.

"Father, what are you going to tell Fletcher tonight?"

There was no need for an answer. I knew what he would tell Fletcher. The breeze blowing in from the sun-washed fields was suddenly chill and cheerless.

SHANE

Father sat down on the top porch step. He took out his pipe and drew on it as the match flamed, and fixed his eyes on the mountains far across the river. Shane took a chair, and he too looked into the distance. Mother went to Father. She sat beside him on the step, her hand on the wood between them; his covered hers and the moments merged in the slow, dwindling procession of time. I sat on the step below Father and Mother, between them, and their legs on each side of me made it seem better. I felt Father's hand on my head.

"This is tough on you, Bob." He could talk to me because I was only a kid. He was really talking to himself. "I can't see the full finish. But I can see this. Wilson down and there'll be an end to it. Fletcher'll be done. The town will see to that. I can't beat Wilson on the draw. But there's strength enough in this clumsy body of mine to keep me on my feet till I get him too. Things could be worse, though. It helps a man to know that if anything happens to him, his family will be in better hands than his own."

There was a sharp sound behind us. Shane had risen so swiftly that his chair had knocked against the wall. He strode to the steps, down past us and around the corner of the house.

Mother was up and after him, running headlong. She stopped abruptly at the house corner, clutching at the wood, panting and irresolute. Slowly she came back and sank again on the step, close against Father, and he gathered her to him with one great arm.

The silence spread and filled the whole valley and the shadows crept across the yard. Mother straightened, and as she stood up, Father rose too. Then they passed through the doorway together.

Where was Shane? I hurried toward the barn. I was almost to it when I saw him out by the pasture. He was staring over it at the great lonely mountains tipped with the gold of the sun now rushing down behind them. As I watched, he whirled and came straight back to the barn, striding with long, steady steps, his head held high. I waited, watching the barn door.

The minutes ticked past, the twilight deepened, and a patch of light sprang from the house as the lamp in the kitchen was lit. And still I waited. Then he was coming swiftly toward me. I stared, then broke and ran into the house.

"Father! Father! Shane's got his gun!"

Father and Mother barely had time to look up from the table before he was framed in the doorway. He was dressed as he was that first day when he rode into our lives, in that dark and worn magnificence, from the black hat with its wide, curling brim to the soft black boots. But what caught your eye was the single flash of white, the outer ivory plate on the grip of the gun, showing sharp and distinct against the dark material of the trousers. The tooled cartridge belt nestled around him, riding above the hip on the left, sweeping down on the right to hold the holster snug along the thigh, just as he had said, the gun handle about halfway between the wrist and elbow of his right arm hanging there relaxed and ready.

Belt and holster and gun . . . These were not things he was wearing or carrying. They were part of him. Now that he was no longer in his crude work clothes, what had for a time seemed iron was again steel. The slenderness was that of a tempered blade, and a razor edge was there. Slim and dark in the doorway, he seemed somehow to fill the whole frame.

He was in the room now, speaking to them both in that bantering tone he used to have only for Mother. "A fine pair of parents you are. Haven't even fed Bob yet. Stack him full of a good supper. Yourselves too. I have a little business to tend to in town."

Father looked fixedly at him. "No, Shane. I won't let you. It's my business."

"There's where you're wrong, Joe," Shane said gently. "This *is* my business. My kind of business. I've had fun being a farmer. You've shown me new meaning in the word, and I'm proud that for a while maybe I qualified. But there are a few things a farmer can't handle."

The strain of the long afternoon was telling on Father. He pushed up from the table. "Great Godfrey, Shane, be sensible. Don't make it any harder for me. Suppose you do put Wilson out of the way. That won't finish anything. They'd say I ducked and they'd be right. You can't do it and that's that."

"No?" Shane's voice was even more gentle, but it had a quiet, inflexible quality that had never been there before. "There's no man living can tell me what I can't do. Not even you, Joe."

As he spoke the gun was in his hand and before Father could move he swung it, swift and sharp, so the barrel lined flush along the side of Father's head, back of the temple, above the ear. Strength was in the blow; it thudded dully on the bone and Father folded over the table and slid toward the floor. Shane's arm was under him before he hit and Shane pivoted Father's loose body up and into his chair. Father's head lolled back and Shane caught it, then eased the big shoulders forward till they rested on the table, the face down and cradled in the limp arms.

Shane stood erect and looked across the table at Mother. She had not moved since he appeared in the doorway, not even when Father fell. She was watching Shane, her throat curving in a lovely proud line, her eyes wide. Darkness had shut down over the valley as they looked at each other across the table, alone now in a moment all their own. Yet, when they spoke, it was of Father.

"I was afraid," Shane murmured, "that he would take it that way. He couldn't do otherwise and be Joe Starrett."

"I know."

"He'll rest easy and come out groggy but all right. Tell him, Marian, no man need be ashamed of being beat by Shane."

The name sounded queer like that, the man speaking of himself. It was the closest he ever came to boasting. And then you understood that there was not the least hint of a boast. He was stating a fact, simple and elemental as the power that dwelt in him.

"I know," she said again. "I don't need to tell him. He knows too." She was rising, earnest and intent. "But there is something else I must know. We have battered down words that might have been spoken between us, and that is as it should be. But I have a right to know. And what I do now depends on what you tell me. Are you doing this just for me?"

Shane hesitated for a long, long moment. "No, Marian." His gaze seemed to widen and encompass us all, Mother and the still figure of Father and me huddled on a chair by the window, and somehow the room and the house and the whole place. Then he was looking only at Mother and she was all that he could see.

"No, Marian. Could I separate you in my mind and afterward be a man?"

He pulled his eyes from her and stared into the night beyond the open door. His face hardened, his thoughts leaping to what lay ahead in town. Then, so quiet and easy you were scarce aware that he was moving, he was gone into the outer darkness.

Chapter 10

NOTHING COULD HAVE kept me in the house that night. I waited until Mother turned to Father, bending over him, then I slipped out. I went softly down the steps and into the night.

Shane was nowhere in sight. I stayed in the darker shadows, looking about, and at last I saw him emerging from the barn. The moon was rising low over the mountains, a clean, bright crescent. Its light was enough for me to see him plainly in outline. He was carrying his saddle, and a sudden pain stabbed through me as I saw that with it was his saddle roll. He went toward the pasture gate, not slow, not fast, just firm and steady. I heard him give his low whistle and the horse came out of the shadows at the far end of the pasture, across the field straight to the man.

I crept along the corral fence, keeping tight to it, until I reached the road. As soon as the barn was between me and the pasture, I started to run as rapidly as I could toward town, my feet plumping softly in the thick dust of the road.

I could not let him see me. I kept looking back over my shoulder as I ran. When I saw him swing into the road, I was striking into the last open stretch to the edge of town. I scurried to the side of the road and behind a clump of bushes and waited for him to pass. The hoofbeats swelled in my ears, and when I parted the bushes and peered out, he was almost abreast of me.

He was tall and terrible there in the road, looming up gigantic in the mystic half-light. He was the man I saw that first day, a stranger, dark and forbidding, forging his lone way out of an unknown past. I could not help it. I cried out and stumbled and fell. He was off his horse and over me before I could right myself, picking me up, his grasp strong and reassuring. I looked at him, tearful and afraid, and the fear faded from me. He was no stranger. He was Shane. He was shaking me gently and smiling.

"Bobby boy, this is no time for you to be out. Skip along home. Everything will be all right."

He let go of me and turned slowly, gazing out across the far sweep of the valley silvered in the moon's glow. "Look at it, Bob. Hold it in your mind. It's a lovely land, Bob. A good place to be a boy and grow straight inside as a man should."

My gaze followed his, and I saw our valley as though for the first time. The emotion in me was more than I could stand. I choked and reached out for him and he was not there.

He was rising into the saddle and the two shapes, the man and the horse, became one and moved down the road toward the light from the windows of Grafton's building a quarter of a mile away. I wavered a moment, then started running after him.

THERE WERE SEVERAL MEN on the long porch of the building by the saloon doors when Shane rode up. As he hit the panel of light from the store window, they stiffened. Red Marlin dived quickly through the doors.

When Shane dismounted, he did not slip the reins over the horse's head as the cowboys always did. He left them looped over the pommel of the saddle and the horse seemed to know what this meant. It stood motionless, close by the steps, head up, waiting, ready for whatever swift need.

Shane went along the porch and halted briefly, fronting the two men still there. "Where's Fletcher?"

One of them jerked a hand toward the doors and then, as they moved to shift out of his way, his voice caught them.

"Get inside. Go clear to the bar before you turn."

They stared at him and stirred uneasily and swung together to push through the doors. Shane grabbed the doors as they came back, pulled them out and wide open and disappeared between them.

CLUMSY AND TRIPPING in my haste, I scrambled up the steps and into the store. Sam Grafton and Mr. Weir were the only persons there and they were both hurrying to the entrance to the saloon, so intent that they failed to notice me. They stopped in the doorway. I crept behind them to my familiar perch on my box, where I could see past them.

The big room was crowded. Men were lined up elbow to elbow nearly the entire length of the bar. The tables were full and more men were lounging along the far wall. The big round poker table at the back, between the stairway to the little balcony and the door to Grafton's office, was littered with glasses and chips. It seemed strange, for all the men standing, that there should be an empty chair at the far curve of the table. Someone must have been in that chair, because chips were at the place and a half-smoked cigar, a wisp of smoke curling up from it.

A haze of thinning smoke was by the ceiling over them all, floating in streamers around the hanging lamps. This was Grafton's saloon in the flush of a banner evening's business. But something was wrong, was missing. The hum of activity, the whir of voices that should have risen from the scene, was stilled. Instead, the attention of everyone in the room was centered on that dark figure just inside the swinging doors.

His eyes searched the room. They halted on a man sitting at a small table in the front corner with his hat on low over his forehead. It was Stark Wilson and he was studying Shane with a puzzled look on his face. Shane's eyes swept on, checking off each person. They stopped again on a figure over by the wall and the beginnings of a smile showed in them and he nodded almost imperceptibly. It was Chris, tall and lanky, his arm in a sling, and as he caught the nod a slow smile came over his face, warm and friendly, the smile of a man who knows his own mind at last.

But Shane's eyes were moving on to Will Atkey, who was trying to make himself small behind the bar.

"Where's Fletcher?"

Will fumbled with the cloth in his hands. "I—I don't know. He was here a while ago."

Shane tilted his head slightly so his eyes could clear his hat brim. He was scanning the balcony across the rear of the room. It was empty and the doors upstairs were closed. He stepped forward, disregarding the men by the bar, and walked quietly past them the long length of the room. He went through the doorway to Grafton's office and into the semidarkness beyond. Then he was in the office doorway again and his eyes bored toward Red Marlin, who was standing nearby.

"Where's Fletcher?"

The silence was taut and unendurable. It had to break. The sound was that of Stark Wilson coming to his feet in the far front corner. His voice, lazy and insolent, floated down the room.

"Where's Starrett?"

While the words yet seemed to hang in the air, Shane was moving toward the front of the room. But Wilson was moving too. He was crossing toward the swinging doors and he took his stand just to the left of them, a few feet out from the wall. The position gave him command of the wide aisle running back between the bar and the tables and Shane coming forward in it.

Shane stopped about three-quarters of the way, about five yards from Wilson. He cocked his head for one quick sideways glance again at the balcony and then he was looking only at Wilson. He did not like the setup. Wilson had the front wall and he was left in the open of the room. He assessed the fact, accepted it.

They faced each other in the aisle and then the men along the bar jostled one another in their hurry to get to the opposite side of the room. A reckless arrogance was on Wilson, certain of himself and his control of the situation.

"Where's Starrett?" he said once more, still mocking Shane.

The words went past Shane as if they had not been spoken. "I had a few things to say to Fletcher," he said gently. "That can wait. You're a pushing man, Wilson, so I reckon I had better accommodate you."

Wilson's eyes glinted coldly. "I've no quarrel with you," he said flatly, "even if you are Starrett's man. Walk out of here without any fuss and I'll let you go. It's Starrett I want."

"What you want, Wilson, and what you'll get are two different things. Your killing days are done."

Wilson had it now. You could see him grasp the meaning. This quiet man was pushing him just as he had pushed Ernie Wright. Something that was not fear but a kind of wondering and baffled reluctance showed in his face.

"I'm waiting, Wilson. Do I have to crowd you into slapping leather?"

Time stopped and there was nothing in all the world but two men looking into eternity in each other's eyes. Then the room rocked in the sudden blur of action; the roar of their guns was a single sustained blast. Shane stood, solid on his feet as a rooted oak, but Wilson swayed, his right arm hanging useless, blood beginning to show in a small stream from under the sleeve over the hand, the gun slipping from the numbing fingers.

He backed against the wall, a bitter disbelief twisting his features. His left arm hooked and the second gun was showing, and this time Shane's bullet smashed into his chest. His knees buckled, sliding him slowly to the floor.

Shane gazed across the space between them, seeming to have forgotten all else as he let his gun ease into the holster. "I gave him his chance," he murmured out of the depths of a great sadness. But the words had no meaning for me, because I noticed on the dark brown of his shirt, low and just above the belt to the side of the buckle, the darker spot gradually widening. Then others noticed too, and the room began coming to life.

Voices were starting, but no one focused on them. They were snapped short by the roar of a shot from the rear of the room. A glass of the front window shattered near the bottom.

Then I saw it. The others were turning to stare at the back of the room. My eyes were fixed on Shane and I saw it. I saw the whole man move, all of him, in the single flashing instant. I saw the head lead and the body swing. I saw the arm leap and the hand take the gun in the lightning sweep. I saw the barrel line up like—like a finger pointing—and the flame spurt even as the man himself was still in motion.

And there on the balcony Fletcher, impaled in the act of aiming for a second shot, rocked on his heels and fell back into the open doorway behind him. He clawed at the jambs and pulled himself forward. He staggered to the rail and tried to raise the gun. But the strength was draining out of him and he collapsed over the rail, jarring it loose and falling with it.

ACROSS THE STUNNED silence of the room Shane's voice seemed to come from a great distance. "I expect that finishes it," he said. Unconsciously, without looking down, he broke out the cylinder of his gun and reloaded it. The stain on his shirt was bigger now, spreading fanlike above the belt, but he did not appear to know or care.

His movements were slow, but the hands were sure and steady, and the gun dropped into the holster of its own weight.

He backed with dragging steps toward the swinging doors until his shoulders touched them. The light in his eyes was unsteady, like the flickering of a candle guttering toward darkness. And then, as he stood there, a strange thing happened.

Out of the mysterious resources of his vitality came a tide of strength that crept through him and fought and shook off the weakness. It shone in his eyes and they were alive again and alert. He faced that room full of men and read them all with the one sweeping glance and spoke to them in that gentle voice with that quiet, inflexible quality. "I'll be riding on now. And there's not a one of you that will follow."

He turned his back on them in the indifference of absolute knowledge they would do as he said. Straight and superb, he was silhouetted against the doors and the patch of night above them. The next moment they were closing with a soft swish of sound.

The room was crowded with action now. Men were clustering around the bodies of Wilson and Fletcher, pressing to the bar, talking excitedly. But there was a cleared space by the doorway, as if someone had drawn a line marking it off.

I did not care what they were doing or what they were saying. I had to get to Shane. I had to know, and he was the only one who could ever tell me.

I dashed out the store door and I was just in time. He was on his horse, already starting away from the steps.

"Shane," I whispered desperately. "Oh, Shane!"

He heard me and reined around and I hurried to him, standing by a stirrup and looking up.

"Bobby! Bobby boy! What are you doing here?"

"I've been here all along," I blurted out. "You've got to tell me. Was that Wilson—"

He knew what was troubling me. He always knew. "Wilson," he said, "was mighty fast. As fast as I've ever seen."

"I don't care," I said, the tears starting. "I don't care if he was the fastest that ever was. He'd never have been able to shoot you, would he? You'd have got him straight, wouldn't you—if you had been in practice?"

He gazed down at me and he knew. He knew what goes on in a boy's mind and what can help him stay clean inside through the muddled, dirtied years of growing up.

"Sure. Sure, Bob. He'd never even have cleared the holster."

He started to bend down toward me, his hand reaching for my head. But the pain struck him like a whiplash and the hand jumped to his shirtfront by the belt, pressing hard, and he reeled a little in the saddle.

The ache in me was more than I could bear. I stared dumbly at him, and because I was just a boy and helpless, I turned away and hid my face against the firm, warm flank of the horse.

"Bob."

"Yes, Shane."

"A man is what he is, Bob, and there's no breaking the mold. I tried that and I've lost. But I reckon it was in the cards from the moment I saw a freckled kid on a rail up the road there and a real man behind him, the kind that could back him for the chance another kid never had."

"But—but, Shane, you—"

"There's no going back from a killing, Bob. Right or wrong, the brand sticks and there's no going back. It's up to you now. Go home to your mother and father. Grow strong and straight and take care of them. Both of them."

"Yes, Shane."

"There's only one thing more I can do for them now."

I felt the horse move away from me. Shane was looking down the road and onto the open plain, the horse obeying the silent command of the reins. He was riding away and I knew that no word or thought could hold him. The big horse, patient and powerful, was already settling into the steady pace that had brought him into our valley, and the two, the man and the horse, were a single dark shape in the road as they passed beyond the reach of the light from the windows.

I strained my eyes after him, and then in the moonlight I could make out his figure receding into the distance. Lost in my loneliness, I watched him go, out of town, far down the road where it curved out to the level country beyond the valley. A cloud passed over the moon and I could not see him. The cloud passed on and the road was a plain thin ribbon to the horizon and he was gone.

I stumbled back to fall on the porch steps, my head in my arms to hide the tears. The voices around me were meaningless noises in a bleak and empty world. It was Mr. Weir who took me home.

Chapter 11

FATHER AND MOTHER were in the kitchen, almost as I had left them. Mother had hitched her chair close to Father's. He was sitting up, his face tired and haggard, the ugly red mark standing out plain along the side of his head. They did not come to meet us. They sat still and watched us move into the doorway.

They did not even scold me. Mother reached and pulled me to her and let me crawl into her lap as I had not done for three years or more. Father just stared at Mr. Weir. He could not trust himself to speak first.

"Your troubles are over, Starrett."

Father nodded. "You've come to tell me," he said wearily, "that he killed Wilson before they got him."

"Wilson," said Mr. Weir. "And Fletcher."

Father started. "Fletcher too? By Godfrey, yes. He would do it right." Father ran a finger along the bruise on his head. "He let me know this was one thing he wanted to handle by himself. I can tell you, Weir, waiting here is the hardest job I ever had."

Mr. Weir looked at the bruise. "I thought so. Listen, Starrett. There's not a man in town doesn't know you didn't stay here of your own will. And there's mighty few that aren't glad it was Shane came into the saloon tonight."

The words broke from me. "You should have seen him, Father. He was—he was—" I could not find it at first. "He was—beautiful, Father. And Wilson wouldn't even have hit him if he'd been in practice. He told me so."

"He told you!" Father drove to his feet and grabbed Mr. Weir by the coat front. "My God, man! He's alive?"

"Yes," said Mr. Weir. "He's alive all right. Wilson got to him. But no bullet can kill that man. Sometimes I wonder whether anything ever could."

Father was shaking him. "Where is he?"

"He's gone," said Mr. Weir. "He's gone, alone and unfollowed, as he wanted it."

Father slumped again into his chair. He picked up his pipe and it broke in his fingers. He let the pieces fall and stared at them on the floor. He was still staring at them when new footsteps sounded on the porch and a man pushed into our kitchen.

It was Chris. His right arm was tight in the sling, his eyes unnaturally bright. In his left hand he was carrying a bottle of red cherry soda pop. He came straight in and smacked the bottle on the table. He was embarrassed, but he spoke up firmly. "I brought that for Bob. I'm a poor substitute, Starrett. But as soon as this arm's healed, I'm asking you to let me work for you."

Father's face twisted and his lips moved, but no words came. Mother was the one who said it. "Shane would like that, Chris."

And still Father said nothing. What Chris and Mr. Weir saw as they looked at him must have shown them that nothing they could do or say would help at all. They turned and went out together.

Mother and I sat there watching Father. There was nothing we could do, either. This was something he had to wrestle alone. He was so still that he seemed even to have stopped breathing. Then a sudden restlessness hit him and he strode out the door.

I do not know how long we sat there. I know that the wick in the lamp burned low and sputtered awhile and went out and the darkness was a relief and a comfort. At last Mother rose, still holding me, the big boy bulk of me, in her arms. I was surprised at the strength in her. She carried me into my room, helped me undress, tucked me in and sat on the bed. Then, only then, she whispered to me, "Now, Bob. Tell me everything. Just as you saw it happen."

I told her, and when I was done, she murmured, "Thank you." She looked out the window and murmured the words again and they were not for me and she was still looking out over the land to the great gray mountains when finally I fell asleep.

When I woke, the first streaks of dawn were showing through the window. I crept out of bed and peeked into the kitchen. Mother was standing in the open outside doorway.

I fumbled into my clothes and tiptoed through the kitchen to her. She took my hand and I clung to hers and it was right that we should go find Father together.

We found him out by the corral, by the far end where Shane had added to it. The sun was beginning to rise through the cleft in the mountains across the river. Father's arms were folded on the top rail, his head bowed on them. When he turned to face us, he leaned back against the rail as if he needed the support.

"Marian, I'm sick of the sight of this valley, my heart isn't in it anymore. I know it's hard on you and the boy, but we'll have to pull up stakes and move on. Montana, maybe. I've heard there's good land for the claiming up that way."

Mother let go my hand and stood erect, so angry that her eyes snapped and her chin quivered. "So you'd run out on Shane just when he's really here to stay!"

"Marian, you don't understand. He's gone."

"He's not gone. He's here, in this place, in this place he gave us. He's all around us and in us, and he always will be."

She ran to the tall corner post, to the one Shane had set. She beat at it with her hands. "Here, Joe. Quick. Take hold. Pull it down."

Father stared at her, but he did as she said. No one could have denied her in that moment. He took hold of the post and pulled at it. He shook his head and braced his feet and strained at it with all his strength. Creakings ran along the rails and the ground at the base showed little cracks fanning out. But the rails held and the post stood. Father turned from it, beads of sweat breaking on his face, a light creeping up his drawn cheeks.

"See, Joe. See what I mean. We have roots here now that we can never tear loose."

And the morning was in Father's face, shining in his eyes, giving him new color and hope and understanding.

I GUESS THAT is all there is to tell. The folks in town and the kids at school liked to talk about Shane, to spin tales and speculate about him. Those nights at Grafton's became legends in the valley, and countless details were added as they grew and spread, just as the town, too, grew and spread up the riverbanks. But I never bothered, no matter how strange the tales became in the constant retelling. He belonged to me, to Father and Mother and me, and nothing could ever spoil that.

For Mother was right. He was there. He was there in our place and in us. Whenever I needed him, he was there. I could close my eyes and he would be with me and I would see him plain and hear again that gentle voice.

I would think of him in each of the moments that revealed him to me. I would think of him most vividly in that single flashing instant when he whirled to shoot Fletcher on the balcony at Grafton's saloon. I would see again the power and grace of a coordinated force beautiful beyond comprehension. I would see the man and the weapon wedded in the one indivisible deadliness. I would see the man and the tool, a good man and a good tool, doing what had to be done.

And always my mind would go back at the last to that moment when I saw him from the bushes by the roadside just on the edge of town. I would see him there in the road, tall and terrible in the moonlight, going down to kill or be killed, and stopping to help a stumbling boy and to look out over the land, the lovely land, where that boy had a chance to live out his boyhood and grow straight inside as a man should.

And when I would hear the men in town trying to pin him down to a definite past, I would smile quietly to myself. For a time they inclined to the notion, spurred by the talk of a passing stranger, that he was Shannon, a gunman and a gambler down in Arkansas and Texas who had dropped from sight without anyone knowing why or where. When that notion dwindled, others followed, pieced together in turn from scraps of information gleaned from stray travelers. But when they talked like that, I simply smiled because I knew he could have been none of these.

He was the man who rode into our little valley out of the heart of the great glowing West and when his work was done rode back whence he had come and he was Shane.

THE SOLDIERS

As towns take root and the rails stretch westward, the Indian, dispossessed, turns to fight, and now the U.S. Army takes the field against him

Returning Troops by Harold Von Schmidt

In *Custer's Demand* by Charles Schreyvogel, the flamboyant Indian fighter confronts famed Kiowa chief Satanta

the Seventh Cavalry in battle array, Satanta agreed to lead the Kiowas to a reservation in Indian Territory.

Cavalry Charge on the Southern Plains (detail) by Frederic Remington, who sketched in Arizona during Apach

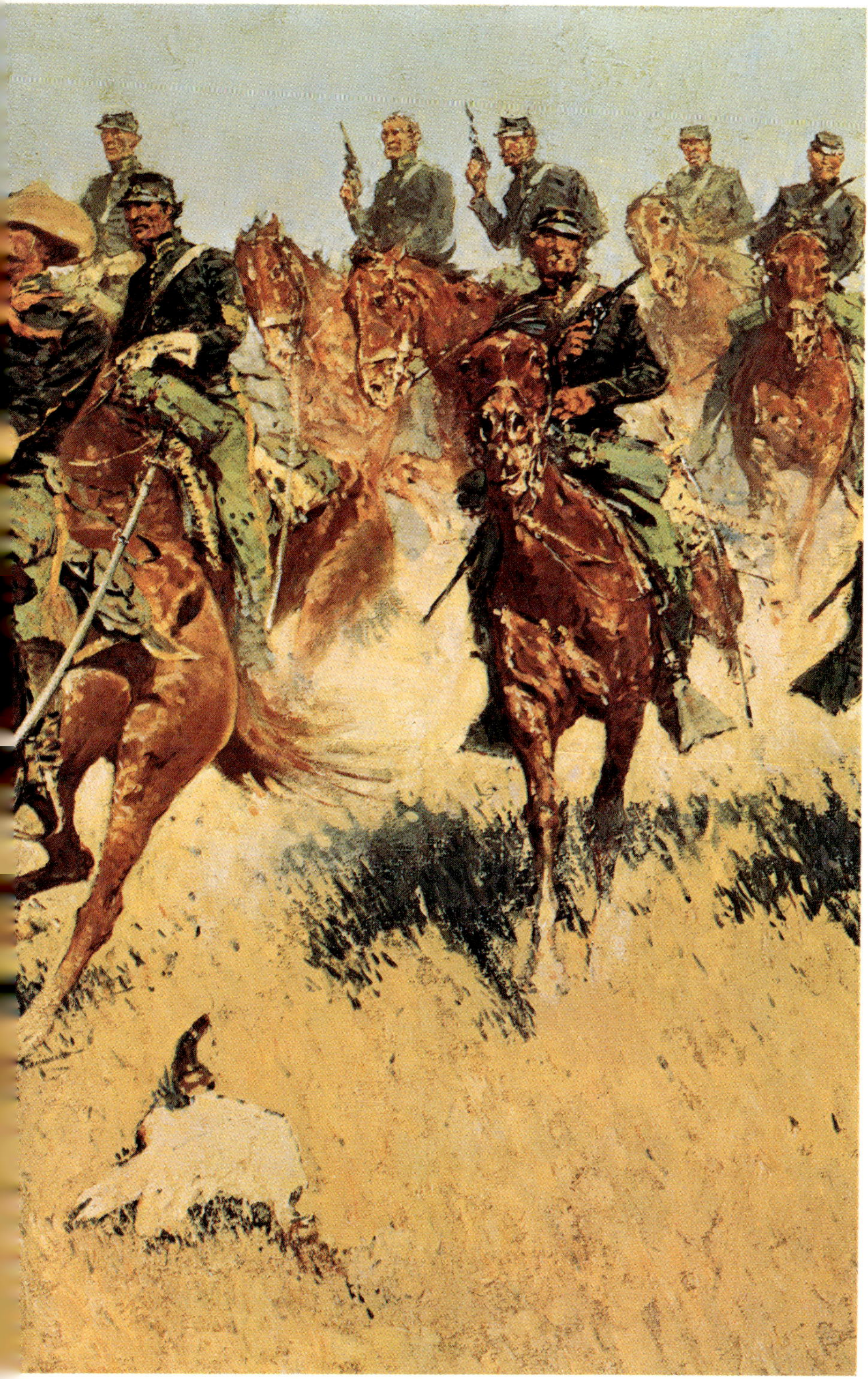

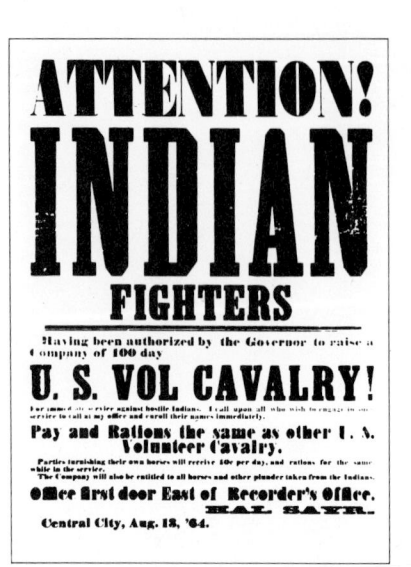

A Colorado appeal for volunteers in 1864

After the Civil War, as the railroads moved west, the army's main problem was the Indians. In 1867 General Sherman told a group of Sioux and Cheyenne chiefs: "You see white men have plenty to eat, that they have fine houses and fine clothes. You can have the same, and we will help you. But you cannot stop the locomotive any more than you can stop the sun or moon." If they attacked the trains, he warned, "the Great Father, who, out of love for you, withheld his soldiers, will let loose his young men. They will come out as thick as a herd of buffalo, and if you continue fighting you will all be killed."

A furious Indian assault threatens to overwhelm a small arm

s were rare, but quite as violent as depicted here by Charles Schreyvogel in *Defending the Stockade*.

Of the army's legendary non-coms, one cavalry officer wrote: "It was fine to see one of these old men on muster or monthly inspection. Erect and soldierly, with his red face glistening, his white hair cut close, his arms and accoutrements shining, not a wrinkle in his neat-fitting uniform, nor a speck of dust about him, his corps badge, and it may be a medal, on his breast, he stood in the ranks among the others like an oak tree in a grove of cottonwood saplings."

Cannon crews fire practice rounds in the desert near Great S

Cavalry guidon and infantry, artillery and cavalry buttons

Mounting the guard, Fort Keogh,

proved to be of little use in the West, since the Indians rarely massed for an attack.

Gatling gun crew at Fort Abraham Lincoln, Dakota Territory

Fort Douglas, Utah, barracks were heated by stoves, which also provided the punishment for minor offenses—choppin

Saber-belt buckle and infantry hat insignia

A plain but well-kept bu

...ks was at Fort Robinson, Nebraska.

Life on a western army post was not easy for gently bred wives, but many must have felt as did Martha Summerhayes after a trip back East. "I was happy to see the soldiers again," she wrote, "the drivers and teamsters, even the sleek government mules. The old blue uniforms made my heart glad. Every sound was familiar, even the rattlings of the harness with its ivory rings. I was back again in the army. I had cast my lot with a soldier, and where he was, was home to me."

"They came along in fighting trim," *The New York Times* said of the Fifth Cavalry, "the wagon train following with a strong cavalry guard. There was something shocking in [their] disregard of regulation uniform, and mud-bespattered appearance, but it was a pleasure to see how full of spirit [they] looked. Their broad-brimmed hats, belts stuffed with cartridges, and handkerchiefs knotted about the neck, gave them a wild appearance in amusing contrast with their gentlemanly manners."

Cavalry trumpeter's chevron and hat insignia

© Time Inc. from the Time-Life series The Old West.

Cavalry troopers on maneuvers pause for a ho

Custer's Black Hills expedition of 187

se soldiers carried bottles of catsup and vinegar with them to liven up dreary rations.

Pickets in northern California watch for Indian movements.

The last raging moments of Custer's life were re-created in *Custer's Last Stand* by Edgar S. Paxson, completed in

twenty years' research, this painting is believed to be the most accurate depiction of the fateful battle.

George A. Custer as a Civil War general. Right: Indian Campaign Medal.

Low Dog, a chief of the Oglala Sioux, was among the 4000 Indians camped that day on the Little Bighorn. "They came on us like a thunderbolt," he recalled. "We retreated until all our men got together, and then we charged them. [They] dismounted to fire. They held their horses' reins on one arm, but the horses were so frightened they pulled the men all around, and many of their shots went up in the air. The wise men of our nation [told] our people not to mutilate the dead white chief, for he was a brave warrior and died a brave man."

cene of the Battle of the Little Bighorn one year later

rty-three-starred flag was lost in the Custer battle but later recaptured from the Indians.

General Custer and his wife, Elizabeth

"On Sunday afternoon, the 25th of June," wrote the widowed Elizabeth Custer in her memoirs, "our little group of saddened women sought solace in gathering together in our house [at Fort Abraham Lincoln]. We tried to find some slight surcease from trouble in the old hymns; some of them dated back to our childhood's days. I remember the grief with which one young wife threw herself on the carpet and pillowed her head in the lap of a tender friend. Another sat dejected at the piano, and struck soft chords that melted into the notes of the voices. Indescribable yearning for the absent, and untold terror for their safety, engrossed each heart.

"At that very hour the fears that our tortured minds had portrayed in imagination were realities, and the souls of those we thought upon were ascending to meet their Maker.

"On the 5th of July—for it took that time for the news to come—the sun rose on a beautiful world, but with its earliest beams came the first knell of disaster. A steamer came down the river bearing the wounded from the battle of the Little Big Horn, of Sunday, June 25th. This battle wrecked the lives of twenty-six women at Fort Lincoln, and orphaned children joined their cry to that of their bereaved mothers.

"From that time the life went out of the hearts of the 'women who weep,' and God asked them to walk on alone and in the shadow."

With tattered guidons spectral thin
    Above their swaying ranks,
With carbines swung and sabres slung
    And the gray dust on their flanks,
They march again as they marched it then
    When the red men dogged their track,
The gloom trail, the doom trail,
    The trail they came not back.

Joseph Mills Hanson

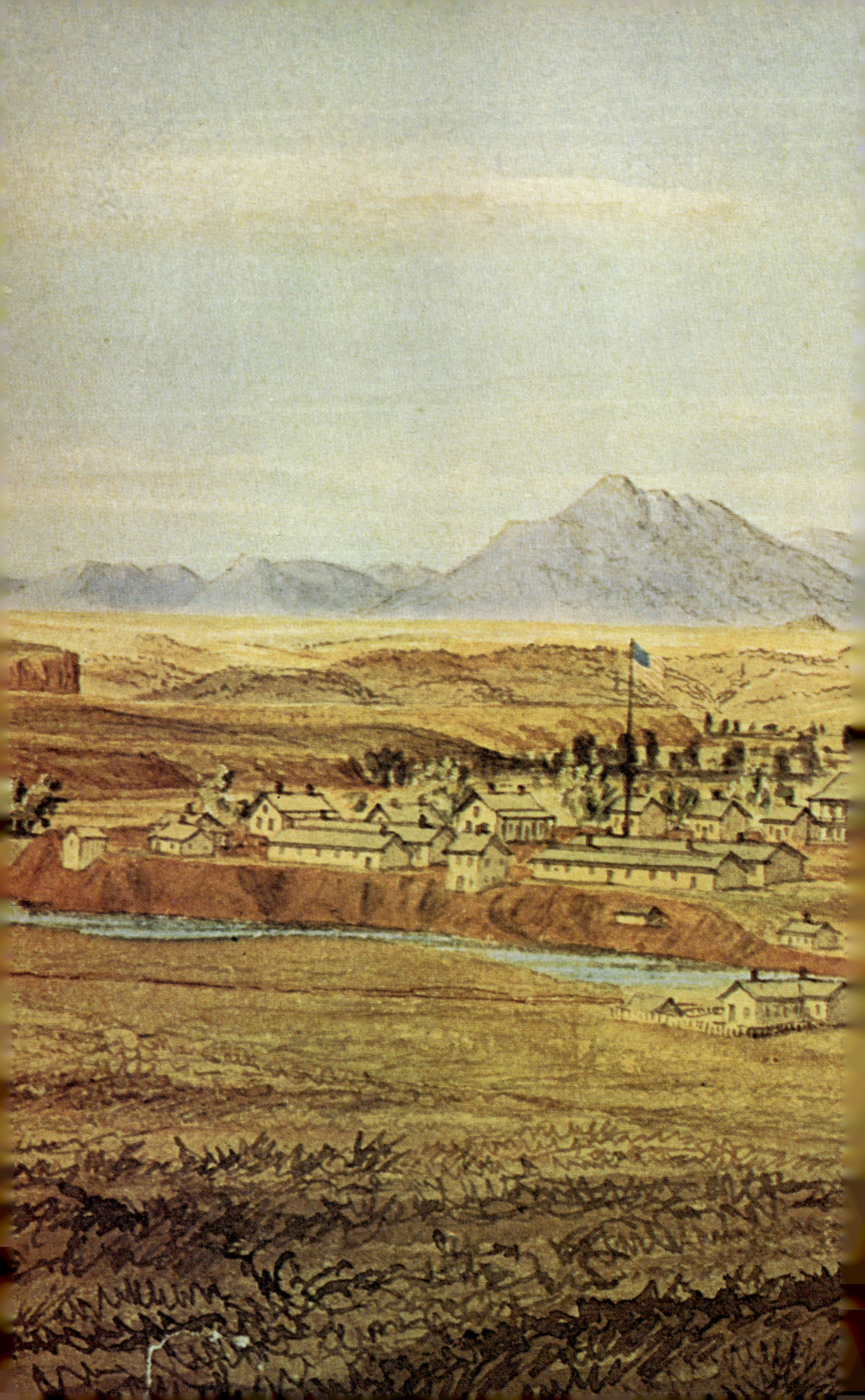

BUGLES IN THE AFTERNOON

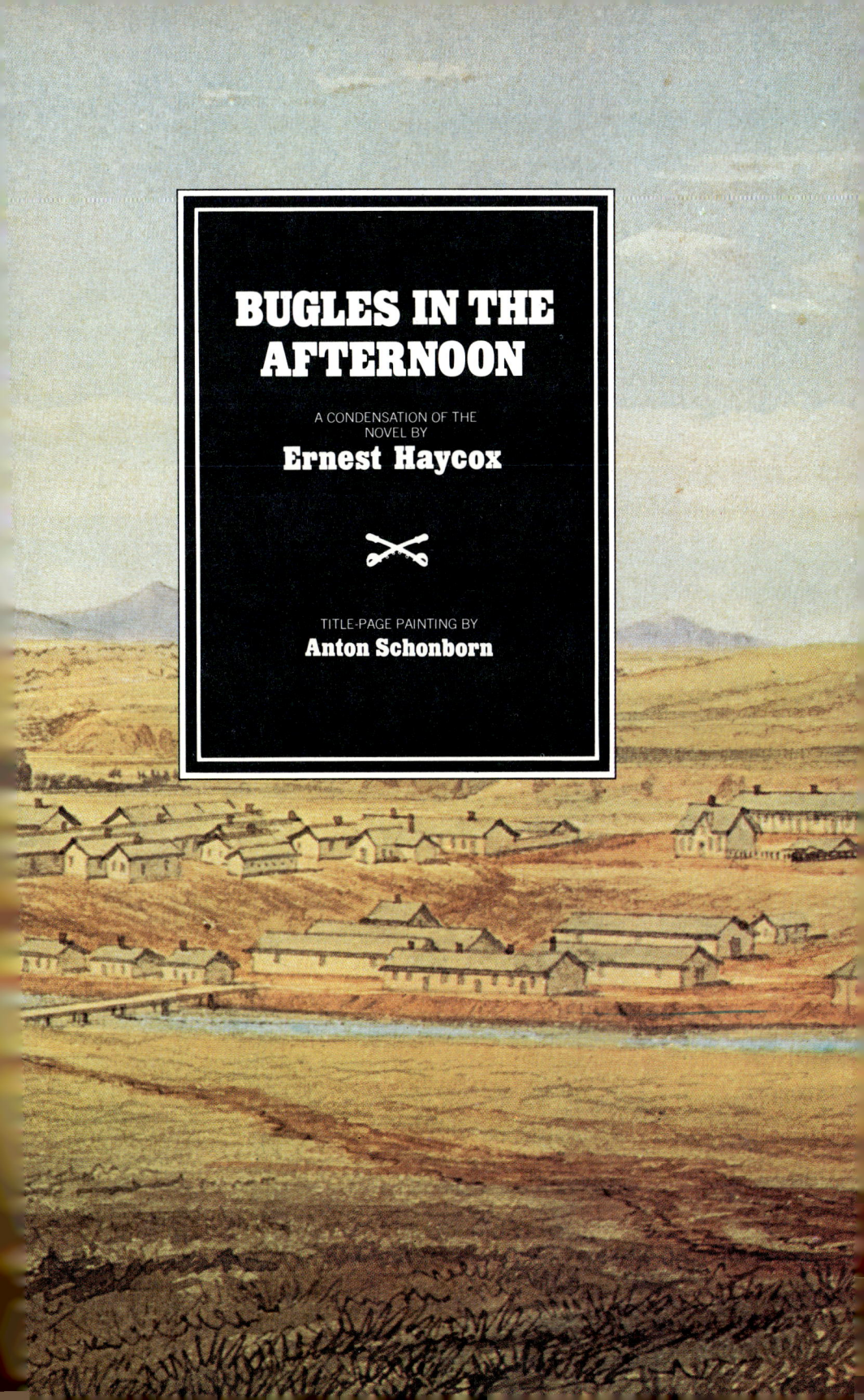

A CONDENSATION OF THE
NOVEL BY
Ernest Haycox

TITLE-PAGE PAINTING BY
Anton Schonborn

Kern Shafter was returning to the only life he had ever loved, service with the U.S. Cavalry, this time on the Western plains. He yearned to be riding again with a lusty and gallant company of men, to know the discipline, the hardships, to see the evening campfires glittering on the darkened prairies.

At Fort Abraham Lincoln in the Dakota Territory, as a sergeant in the Seventh Cavalry, he began his new life—only to have a bitter episode from the past confront him in the person of the vindictive Lieutenant Garnett. Then, of course, there was the proud, dark-haired Josephine Russell to stir the troubled waters between both men even more.

And brooding over all, arousing a sense of impending doom, was the dashing but mercurial General George A. Custer, who would be leading the Seventh Cavalry to its fateful encounter on the Little Bighorn.

Chapter 1

THE TOWN HAD a name but no shape, no street, no core. It was simply five buildings, flung without thought upon the dusty prairie at the eastern edge of Dakota, and these stood gaunt and hard-angled against the last of day's streaming sunlight. The railroad, which gave the town a single pulsebeat once a day, came as a black ribbon out of emptiness, touched this Corapolis with hurried indifference, and moved away into equal emptiness.

The train—a wood-burning engine and three coaches—had paused and gone, leaving one woman and one man in front of the depot shed; the woman fair, round-bodied, and smiling slightly at the land as if it pleased her. Beside her stood a collection of trunks and valises.

Nobody walked abroad, nobody met the train. From the cinder platform a pathway ran through the shortgrass to a frame building, two stories high. The man, somewhat farther down the platform, looked at the woman and her luggage, and moved forward.

"That," he said, pointing toward the two-story building, "is probably the hotel. If you are going there, I'll take your light luggage."

She was not more than twenty-five, he thought; she had gray eyes and a pleasantly expressive mouth and her glance, turned upon him, was self-possessed. She smiled and said, "Thank you," and when he took up her valises and turned to the pathway she followed him.

The hotel had a narrow hall and a steep stairway splitting the building into equal halves. To the right of the hall a broad doorway opened into a saloon; another doorway on the left led to a ladies' parlor and office. The man followed the girl into the parlor and set down the suitcases, waiting back while she signed the register. The hotelkeeper, a large, taciturn woman, asked, "Together or separate?" When she found out, she said to the girl, "You can take number three."

The man signed his name in a steady, slanting motion, Kern Shafter, and his pen momentarily hesitated and then continued, Cincinnati, Ohio. As he laid the pen down, he read the name of the girl written directly above his own. It was: Josephine Russell, Bismarck, Dakota Territory.

"You take seven," said the hotel woman to Shafter. "If you're northbound on the stage, it's at half past four in the mornin'. We serve breakfast at four."

Josephine Russell said to the woman, "May I have the key to my room?"

"They were carried away in people's pockets a long time ago. If you shut your door it will stay shut. If you're afraid, prop a chair against the inside knob," she added in a small, grim tone.

Shafter carried the girl's valises up the stairs and followed her into number three. She had removed her hat and he observed that her hair was a dense black. She walked across the room to the window and turned to watch him.

"I appreciate your help," she said. "Do you think my trunk will be safe on the station platform until morning?"

"I'll bring it to the hotel," he replied, and went away.

She remained where she was a moment, her head slightly tilted as she watched the doorway, idly thinking of him. His clothes were excellent for this part of the land, and smiling came easily to him. Yet his hands, she recalled, were very brown; and the palms were square and thick. She swung about and observed that the sun had gone, leaving the land with a strange, thin, glass-colored light. This sprawling little town, a rendezvous for homesteaders, cowhands, and drifters fifty miles roundabout, pleased her with its familiar things; for Josephine Russell was a western girl returned from a trip east. She hummed a little song as she took the grime of coach travel from her and prepared herself for supper.

Later, as she went down to the dining room, she passed the barroom and saw Shafter sitting at a poker table with four other men. He had removed his coat for comfort and sat back in his chair with a long cigar burning between his lips. He seemed content, even cheerful.

At four the next morning she came half asleep down the stairs and saw him again, at the same table and in the same chair, finishing up an all-night game. Later she watched him come into the dining room. He had quickly shaved and had the same air of being pleased with everything around him. She smiled at him when he looked toward her, and got his smile back. His hair was black and bushy and his face was of the long, thick-boned sort, browned by weather and showing the small seams of experience around the eyes. He had quick eyes that observed the people and the situations around him; and it was this kind of watchfulness which led her to believe that he was either western, or had long been in the West. All western men had that same awareness of their surroundings.

Breakfast was bacon, hotcakes, fried potatoes, and bitter coffee. Afterward she walked to the waiting stage in time to see Shafter lift her luggage into the boot. She thanked him and stepped into the coach. Two young men came aboard and sat on the opposite seat, facing her. A huge man entered and squeezed himself beside her. Shafter was last. He had a long overcoat on his arm and as soon as he took his place between the two younger men he opened the coat and laid it over her lap.

"It will be cold for an hour or so," he said.

The driver put the four horses in motion, and the coach swayed and shuddered as it lumbered out of town. The big man sat with his hands on his knees, a horsey smell flowing from his clothes, his bulk spilling against Josephine Russell. He grinned at her. "These rigs sure never were made for an ord'nary-size man." She smiled at him, saying nothing. The two younger men, each pushed into his own corner, looked vacantly out upon the land, while Kern Shafter planted his feet solidly on the coach floor and fell asleep.

Josephine Russell passed the time by letting herself be curious about him. He knew how to relax completely in odd circumstances and had dropped asleep almost at once. The wrinkles at the edge of his temples disappeared when his eyes were closed and the squareness of his upper body went away. She had noticed earlier that when he stood still he carried himself at a balance, which was something civilians didn't often do. He was slightly under six feet; he had big hands and heavy legs. In a country that somehow impelled men to grow sweeping mustaches or burnsides, he had remained clean-shaven. He had fine manners and knew how to be smooth with women. In the West such a thing was noticeable.

Time dragged on and the day grew warm. Sunlight struck through the coach window, burning on Shafter's face. He was instantly awake at that hot touch. He looked at the coat still on Josephine's lap, and bent forward, taking it and stowing it in a roll beneath his feet. Then he fell asleep again. The four horses went on at a walk, at a run, at a walk, each change of pace producing its agreeable break and its new discomforts. The wheels lifted the dust, and the dust traveled as a pall around the coach, rolling inside, laying its fine film on everything, and creeping into nostril and lung.

At noon the coach dipped into a coulee, struck rocky bottom, and tilted upward, throwing the passengers violently around the seats. Then it drew up before a drab, squat building which sat in a yard littered by tin cans and empty bottles. The passengers moved painfully from their confinement, ate dinner, and returned to their seats. Coach and horses struggled up the coulee's side into a rolling sea of grass, and resumed the steady march. The overhead sun pressed upon the coach, building up the heat inside. Dust began to drift up through the cracked floorboards, coating the faces of all. Presently these faces turned oil-slick and this wetness grew gray and streaky as it formed small rivulets across the dust. The smell of the coach became rank with the odors of bodies rendering out their moisture, and the confinement turned from discomfort to actual pain. Shafter noticed how the dust touched and clung to the girl's hair, how the sun played against her face, against the gentle crease of her lips. Humor lived there, even in this discomfort. Now and then, aware of her bedraggled appearance, the girl pressed her handkerchief against her face.

The road had swung directly into the blast of the low-burning sun and it was a surprise when the stage wheeled to a stop before a raw and ungainly house standing alone in all this emptiness. The driver got down, calling, "Night stop." One by one the weary passengers lifted themselves from the vehicle and tried their cramped legs. Shafter stood by, giving the girl a hand down. For a moment he supported her, seeing a faintness come to her face. She touched him with both arms, held him a little while, and then, embarrassed, she stepped away. Shafter climbed to the boot of the coach and sorted among the luggage. "Which will you need for overnight?"

"The small gray one," she said.

He brought it down and led the way over the packed yard to the door. A woman met them in the half-light of the long front room—a woman once young, and still not old in years. She stood back, ample-bosomed and careless of dress; her eyes had warmth for Shafter, but they turned cool when they swung to the girl. For a moment she studied them.

Shafter said in a short voice, "You have a room for this lady?"

"Take the one at the top of the stairs. On the left."

He took Josephine's suitcase up to the room and stood in the center of it, looking at the derelict furniture, at the rough blankets on the bed. When he left he looked at the door and saw that there was no key. Downstairs, the woman stood waiting for him.

He asked, "Is that room all right?"

She shrugged. "Yes. But I don't ask the genteel to come here."

"This is a stage stop, isn't it?"

"Let it stop some other place," she said. Then she laughed. "But there's no other place. Do you want a room?"

He answered, "No," and turned out to the porch. He walked around the house, sizing it up. Behind the house was another porch, and water and basin. He washed here and beat the dust from his clothes, and resumed his circle of the house. The sun dropped in a silent crash of light and, coming as if from nowhere, riders shaped themselves against the sudden twilight. He sat on the porch steps, watching them reach the yard, wheel, and step off; all men stamped by their trade, booted and spurred, and scorched by the sun. There was a bar farther back in the house and out of it lights presently rose, and the sound of men and women talking. He went in and paused at the doorway of the bar and had his look at the women. Then he went on to the dining-room door and waited for Josephine.

She came down the stairs and paused to look around. When her eyes found him he saw the relieved lightening of her face. She came up to him, smiling a little, and they went into the dining room together. He saw her glance touch the dozen men at the table and coolly take in the women present. She knew them at once, he realized; it was the faintest break on her face, soon covered. After that she took her place and never looked at them again.

The big plates and platters came circling around, were emptied and carried away. One man, already drunk, talked steadily; but otherwise the crowd ate without conversation, finished quickly, and went back to the bar, leaving Shafter and Josephine to themselves. She sipped at her coffee, tired but relaxed. Through his cigar smoke he watched the lamplight shining against the gray of her eyes. She caught his glance and held it, thoughtfully considering him. Racket began to spread from the saloon and a woman's voice grew strident. The girl shrugged and rose from the table.

At the stairs she stopped and looked toward the second floor with an expression of distaste. Suddenly she wheeled toward Shafter and took his arm and they went out and strolled along the vague road. A sickle moon lay far down in the sky, turned butter yellow by the haze in the air, and the stars were great crystal masses overhead. "Do you know this country?" she asked.

"I know the West. I put in some time in the Southwest."

"Do you like it?"

"It's better than what I've had lately."

They went half a mile onward, slowly pacing; and turned back. She said, "What is your name?"

"Kern Shafter. I regret that you have to stay here tonight."

She didn't answer that until they had returned to the porch. Then she murmured, "It will do," and passed into the house. At the foot of the stairs she turned to him. "You'll be here?" she asked.

"Yes," he said. "Good night."

She nodded slightly, and climbed the stairs.

After she had gone to her room Shafter got his valise from the coach and took out a revolver. He thrust it inside his trouser band and returned to the main room. He found a pair of chairs and drew them together, sitting on one and laying his feet on the other. The woman who ran the place found him there, so placed that he had a view of the stairs and the doorway of the room directly above.

She stopped before him, smiling down. She lifted his hat and threw it aside and ran one finger along the edge of his head. "Your woman will be all right."

"Not mine," he said.

"I guess you wouldn't have much trouble with a woman, if you wished. I know your kind."

"No, you don't."

"Don't tell me what I don't know," she said, half sharp with him. "You plan to stay here all night? Right here?"

"Yes."

Josephine propped her room's lone chair against the doorknob, turned out the light, and crept into bed. Wide-awake, she listened to a fight begin and go through the house in grunting, crashing, falling echoes. Some man yelled out curses, a gun exploded, and a woman screamed; afterward a man rushed into the night and rode away at a dead run. Near midnight someone came slowly up the stairs. He crawled along the hall, his hands scraping the wall. He touched the knob of the door and stopped, and she heard the knob turn and the door give. After that she heard another traveler come lightly up the steps. One soft word was said and a sharp blow struck, sending one of the men tumbling down the stairs. The man who had so lightly come upward now went down with the same soft footfalls. Josephine thought with relief, He's watching out for me.

Chapter 2

THE NEXT MORNING the coach ran outward upon the prairie, under a rising flood of brilliant sunshine, and about noon it moved into Fargo's main street and stopped at a depot shed standing beside a single track. The driver got down, shouting, "Fargo, and yore train's in sight," and went up to the boot, throwing down the luggage without regard for the contents.

Shafter stepped out and gave Josephine a hand; he found her luggage and piled it near the track. The train had come out of the east, its progress singing forward on the rails and its whistle hoarsely warning the town. People strolled up to break the day's tedium and to touch again for an instant that East out of which they had come.

Josephine turned to Shafter. "You have been kind. If I should not see you again, let me wish you all good luck."

"I'll be on the train."

"Bismarck?" asked Josephine, and showed him a remote pleasure with her eyes.

He nodded instead of speaking, for just then the engine coasted by with its bell steadily clanging. Two baggage cars and five coaches growled to a jerky stop, and passengers looked curiously through the grimed car windows. The conductor stood on the runway, shouting, "Fargo—Fargo, twenty minutes for lunch!"

Passengers now descended and ran for the lunchroom at the edge of the platform. Shafter gave Josephine an arm up the nearest coach platform, and carried her luggage into the car. He stowed his own valise on an empty seat and went to the lunchroom. Some of the passengers were seated along a table, before a row of dishes prepared for hasty service. Shafter noticed a pile of lunch boxes made up, bought two of them, and returned to Josephine.

"You never know when these trains get where they're going," he said, leaving a lunch box with her.

He returned to his own seat and began his meal. The engine bell sounded again and the conductor stood on the runway, crying, "Bo-o-o-ard." The train slid forward, while a last man rushed from the lunchroom, sprinted along the runway, and caught the grab rails of the rear coach. The gathered townsmen cheered this extra touch of melodrama, and the engine whistled its throaty farewell as it gathered speed, the vacuum of its passage lifting eddies of dust and paper on the tracks.

The coaches swayed with the still unsettled grade of this new railroad. Cinders pelted the windows and smoke streamed back the length of the train; and the engine whistle laid out its hoarse notice upon the land. Out in the distance an occasional antelope band, startled from grazing, fled away in beautiful smoothness. Propping his feet on the opposite seat, Shafter fell asleep, and slept until he heard the conductor cry, "Bismarck!"

The town's gray out-sheds and slovenly shanties and corrals slid forward and its main street appeared—one long row of saloons, stores, livery barns, and freighter sheds crowded side by side. The train stopped, and people came in to search for friends. Shafter picked up his valise and left the coach.

Josephine Russell also descended, walked to a gray-haired man and kissed him. Then she looked back at Shafter. Impulse moved her to go to him. "I wish you luck," she said.

"I'll remember your wish," he answered, and lifted his hat to her and watched her walk away.

The cars were now empty and the engine had been uncoupled, for this was the farthest west of the railroad, in this year of 1875. Beyond Bismarck was the yellow Missouri, and beyond the Missouri lay the largely still unknown lands of the Sioux where, intermittently for ten years, little columns and detachments of the army had marched and fought, had won and had been defeated. Shafter moved toward a nearby wagon.

"Where's Fort Abraham Lincoln?" he asked the driver.

The man pointed a finger southwesterly. "Along that road, four miles to the Point. Ferry there." Then he said, "Get in."

The driver, with Shafter beside him, set his team in motion, and it covered the four miles at an easy mincing trot, coming then to a highland upon which sat a collection of houses. Beyond this highland the terrain rolled into bottomlands and reached the Missouri, across which stood the fort on its bluff. As the wagon descended to the ferry dock the driver pointed at the houses to either hand.

"If you got money to spend, don't come here. This is the Point. It is a bad place, my friend." He let go the brakes and the wagon rolled to the deck of a ferry. When the lines were cast off, the ancient engines shook the boat in all its frames, and it surged forward. The ferry skewed across the strong current, falling five hundred yards downriver; then it worked slowly upstream and nosed into the slip on the far side. The wagoner whipped his team into a run and went up the grade to the top of the bluff.

The walls of the fort, square and trim and formidable, were formed by the backs of storehouses, barracks, officers' quarters, and stables, all these facing a great parade ground. The teamster drew before the guardhouse post, said, "Commissary," and was waved in.

"You know where the adjutant's office might be?" asked Shafter.

"Down there by the end of the quartermaster building."

"Thanks for the ride," said Shafter and dropped off with his valise. He went along the east side of the parade ground, traveling on a boardwalk which skirted troop quarters. The sun was just dropping below the ridge to the west of the fort; the ceremony of retreat was not far away, for orderlies were leading horses across the parade to Officers' Row. He had just reached the doorway of the adjutant's office when the trumpeter at the guard gate blew first call.

He stepped inside in time to see a tall, whiskered first lieutenant clap on a dress helmet with its plume, thrust the chin strap into place, and hook up his sword. He looked at Shafter. "Yes?" he said as he started for the door.

"I'll wait until the lieutenant returns from retreat."

The lieutenant said, "Very well," and flung himself through the door. A corporal remained behind in the office.

Shafter stepped outside and watched five cavalry companies file out from the stables to the parade ground. The hark of officers came sharp through the still air. "Column right! Left into line! Com-m-pany, halt!" One by one, the five companies came into regimental front, each company mounted on horses of matched color, each company's guidon colorfully waving from the pole affixed in the socket of the guidon corporal's stirrup. For a moment the regiment remained still, each trooper sitting with ease in his McClellan saddle, legs well down and back arched, saber hanging on loosened sling to left side, carbine suspended from belt swivel to right, dress helmet cowled down to the level of his eyes. Thus the Seventh sat in disciplined, impassive form—a long double rank of dark, largely mustached faces—homely, burned faces, Irish faces, seasoned and youthful faces, faces of solid value and faces of wildness—all faced forward to the adjutant now taking his report. Presently the adjutant wheeled his horse, trotted it fifty feet, and came to a halt before a slim shape poised lithe and watchful on his mount.

Even at a distance Shafter recognized the commanding officer—that long, bushy fall of almost golden hair which even the cowling of the dress helmet could not conceal, that sweeping tawny dragoon's mustache which sharpened the bony, hawkish nose and accented the depth of eye sockets. There sat the man who was a living legend, the least-disciplined and poorest scholar of his West Point class of 1861; whose wild charges and consuming love of naked action had turned him into a major general by brevet at the age of twenty-five. In this shrunken peacetime army George Armstrong Custer was a lieutenant colonel of the Seventh Cavalry, but was still often called by the honorary title of "general." By virtue of the absence of Colonel Sturgis, he was now in command.

Custer's arm answered the adjutant's salute with a swift nervous jerk. A word was spoken. The band burst into a quick march, still stationary on the right of the line. The officers of the regiment rode slowly front and center, formed a rank, and moved upon the commanding officer. Shafter heard the brittle crack of an officer's voice halt them. He watched them salute Custer and receive his return salute, after which they took place behind him. Now the band swung around and marched down the front of the regiment, in full tune, and wheeled and marched back. All the shapes in this parade turned still as the massed buglers tossed up their trumpets and sounded retreat. Then the little brass cannon at the foot of the flagpole boomed out. The flag began to descend and the band struck up a national air. Shafter pulled his heels together and removed his hat; he stood facing the flag as it slid down the pole toward the trooper waiting to receive it. In the ensuing quiet, Custer's strident voice carried the length and breadth of the parade.

"Pass in review!"

The first sergeants wheeled about, harking their stiff calls. The band broke into a march tune, the regimental front broke like a fan and came into platoon column; it turned the corners of the parade and passed before the commanding officer. Down at the far end of the parade ground each company pulled away toward its own stable. Out by the flagstaff the officers surrendered their horses and moved idly along the walk toward their quarters. An orderly galloped forward to take Custer's horse, but the general swung his mount and flung it headlong across the parade, wheeled, and raced it back. Arriving before his quarters, he sprang to the ground, tossed over the reins, and stamped up the porch of his house. It had been an outburst of energy which could no longer be dammed up.

Shafter stepped back into the office, and presently the adjutant came in. He removed his dress hat and laid it on a desk. Then he unbuckled his saber and hung it to a peg on the wall and looked at Shafter. "Well, sir."

"I should like to enlist in this regiment," said Shafter.

"Where are you from?"

"Ohio."

"How was it you did not enlist at the nearest recruiting service?"

"I prefer to pick my regiment."

"That involved considerable train fare," observed the adjutant. "Normally we recruit from Jefferson Barracks. Still, we can enlist you." He turned to the corporal. "Get an enlistment form, Jackson. Get a doctor's blank, too."

The adjutant lowered himself into a chair and considered the work on his desk. Jackson sat down at another desk and beckoned to Shafter. "Name?" he asked. "Recent address? Next of kin?"

"No next of kin."

"Closest friend, then."

"None," said Shafter.

The adjutant raised his head. "Are you that alone in this world?" he asked, with some skepticism. But he nodded at the corporal and murmured, "Let it go." Both the corporal and the lieutenant, Shafter realized, were thinking the same thing: that he was another drifter running from a past. These border regiments had many such men.

Jackson rattled off more inquiries and scrawled down the answers. Shafter heard men come into the adjutant's office behind him. He heard the adjutant say, "It is slightly late, Doctor. But could you examine this man for enlistment?"

"Yes."

Shafter turned to the doctor, but his eyes lingered on the man only a moment; for there was another officer now in the room, a captain looking out from beneath the rim of his dress helmet at Shafter, with a keen attention. He was a stocky man with a broad practical face and a heavy sand-colored mustache. It was an unemotional Irish countenance, a face disciplined by duty and routine and largely beyond the whims of excitement. Shafter looked back at him gravely. The doctor said, "Step in that room," pointing to a doorway back of the adjutant, "and strip."

He took a mechanical survey of Shafter's naked frame and pointed to the thick whitened welt of a scar that made a foot-long crescent on Shafter's left flank, above the hip. "What was that?"

"Saber cut."

"Ah," said the doctor, and tapped Shafter's chest. "How old?"

"Thirty-two."

The doctor completed the rest of his routine in silence and motioned for Shafter to resume his clothes, meanwhile himself leaving the room. "He'll do physically," he told the adjutant.

The captain was still in the room. "I'll take that man," he said.

The adjutant grinned. "You want everything for A Company, Moylan."

"I'm down to fifty-three men," replied Captain Moylan.

"You're no worse off than the other companies."

"I'd like to have him, Cooke," said Captain Moylan. "And I'd like to swear him in."

Cooke showed surprise and was on the point of asking a question when Shafter returned to the office. Cooke noted his posture, his drawn-together carriage, his composed silence.

"Do you leave any felonies behind you?" Cooke asked.

"No," said Shafter.

"Have you had prior service?"

Shafter's answer came after a noticeable pause. "Yes," he said.

"What organization?"

The delay was again noticeable. "Fourteenth Ohio."

"That would be the Civil War," said Cooke.

"Yes."

"What was the quality of your discharge?"

"Honorably mustered out, end of war."

Cooke nodded. He took a little brown volume of army regulations from a pile on the desk, searched through it, and found a page. He handed the open book to Captain Moylan. Shafter turned to face the captain and, without being requested, raised his right hand. Moylan began the oath, "Do you solemnly swear . . ."

Moylan listened gravely to Shafter's "I do," and tossed the book of regulations on the table. "Very well, you are now a private in the Seventh Cavalry, attached to A Company. Follow me over to the barracks." Out on the baked parade ground Shafter fell in step with

Moylan, to the left and slightly behind the captain. Moylan spoke to Shafter without turning his head.

"This was considerable of a surprise, Kern."

"I hadn't realized you were with the Seventh."

"I'm damned glad to see you. It has been a long time since Winchester and Cumberland Gap. I don't suppose you expected to see old Myles Moylan as a captain of cavalry. I was sergeant major in this outfit before I got my commission. Coming up through the ranks is not the easy way to do it."

"God bless you," said Shafter. "I can think of nothing better."

"I asked Cooke to attach you to my company. I didn't say why. You didn't wish me to say why, did you?"

"No."

"It was a hard, hard thing," murmured Moylan. "I have never ceased to feel anger over it. Have you done anything about it?"

"Nothing to be done."

"The strangeness of it," Moylan went on, "does not stop with my being here and you being here. Garnett is here, too. Or did you know that, and come to hunt him out?"

"I didn't know it," said Shafter, expression draining from his face.

"He is first lieutenant of L. That is why I had Cooke assign you to my company. It would have been highly unpleasant for you to have served under him."

"It is strange how a thing never ends," said Shafter.

Moylan stepped to the porch of a barracks at the south end of the parade. A first sergeant sat there with a pipe in his mouth; he came sharply to his feet and snatched the pipe down. "Hines," said Moylan, "this recruit is assigned to A. Take care of him."

"Yes sir," said the sergeant. Moylan swung off into the gathering twilight. The first sergeant gave Shafter a considerable stare. "What's your name?"

"Shafter."

"Well, then, Shafter, come with me."

The barracks was thirty feet wide and better than a hundred long, with peeled logs standing upright as supports and a floor of rammed earth. A continuous row of double-deck bunks ran down the walls. At the foot of each bunk was a small locker for each man's effects and a rack for sabers, gear, carbines, and other equipment. The sergeant strode along the bunk row, past men already asleep, past men lying awake on their blankets, past a table where men sat at a poker game. He stopped at a bunk. "This is yours. Do I have to teach you to ride and handle a gun and mind your orders or"—and he studied Shafter with a closer eye—"is it that you've had cavalry service before?"

"Yes," said Shafter.

"Alcott," Hines called to another sergeant across the room. "Take this man—Shafter's his name—and give him an outfit."

Twenty minutes later Shafter emerged from the quartermaster's supply room with an outfit stacked from his outspread arms to his chin—underwear, socks, field boots and garrison shoes, blue pants and blue blouse and two blue wool shirts, campaign hat, forage cap and dress helmet with plume, saber, carbine with its sling, Colt revolver, ammunition, cartridge belt, canteen, mess outfit, entrenching tools, saddlebags, housewife kit, bridle, lariat and hobbles and picket pin, a razor, a silvered mirror, a cake of soap, a comb, two blankets, a straw tick, a box of shoe polish, an overcoat, a rubber poncho, wool gloves, a bacon can, currycomb and brush, and a pair of collar ornaments with crossed sabers, the regimental number 7 above and the troop letter A below.

He laid these things on his bunk, took up his tick, and headed for the stables. He found the strawstack and knelt to fill his tick. Then he returned to the barracks hall, laid the tick on the bunk, and made his bed. He took off his civilian suit and pulled on the army pants and shirt; he rolled up his civilian clothes and stood a moment looking at them. Then he spoke down the barracks hall.

"Anybody getting a discharge soon?"

"Yes," called one trooper. "I'm leavin' for New York next week."

"How big are you?"

"Five ten, one hundred and sixty."

Shafter rolled the suit into a ball and threw it to the man. "The tailor can fix it up. When you get to New York walk into the Netherlands House and tell the headwaiter who wore those clothes last. You'll get a free meal out of it."

The guardhouse trumpet drew the slow notes of tattoo across the silence of the night. Shafter lighted a cigar and strolled to the barracks porch. Across the parade ground the lights of Officers' Row were shining, and somewhere about the fort the regimental band was playing dance music. Out from Number One Post at the guardhouse came the sentry's call: "Nine o'clock—all's well," and the call was picked up, post by post, until it ran all around the fort. It was like coming home, thought Shafter. Nothing was strange. The voices of the men within the barracks, the sight of the carbines racked together, the sabers hanging at the foot of the bunks. It was a way of living which, surrendered once, he now embraced again.

Beyond Officers' Row lay the low silhouette of the western ridge, over which a soft wind came with its scent of winter, of farther wildness. Out there, far out, lay a country as mysterious as the heart of Africa. That was Sioux land, the last refuge of a race which had given ground before the promises, the threats, and the treacheries of the white man's frontier; and now had vowed to retreat no farther. Out there Sioux tepees made their rows and clusters along the Powder, the Yellowstone, the Tongue, and the Rosebud; and along a stream which the Indians called the Greasy Grass but which was known to white men as the Little Bighorn.

Chapter 3

AT FIVE THIRTY in the morning the company assembled behind its barracks to answer roll call. A mist lay hard upon the Missouri, hiding the water, and day's first light pressed down upon the mist from above. The troop stood glumly double-ranked in the chill air. The sergeant's nose was a reddening thermometer of both his temperature and his disposition. Upon completion of roll call he made an about-face and saluted the young second lieutenant waiting by.

"Present or accounted for, sir."

The lieutenant acknowledged the salute and walked away. Hines turned back upon the troop. "I never saw a filthier yard, nor a dirtier barracks. After breakfast you'll all turn out for police on it." He thought a moment and checked his roster book. "By order of this date, Private Shafter appointed sergeant. Dismiss."

All down the parade sounded the mess call. Day broke through the mist, sparkling against the dew-beaded grass. Shafter got his mess outfit from his bunk, crossed to the hall, and joined the forming line. A private with a vein-netted face and a pair of flushed eyes overhung with stiff black brows came up behind him, growling. "A sergeant," he said, "does nawt eat with us common ones. You belong at the head o' the line."

"I'll wait until I sew the stripes on," answered Shafter, and gave the man a thoughtful appraisal. He had muscular shoulders, but his belly was round and liquor had softened him. On his sleeve was a faded spot where, not long before, sergeant stripes had been.

"The rank came easy, did it not?" the man asked insolently.

"As easy as yours went away."

"You've got a tongue, I do observe," said the man. "To be a sergeant is not a matter of tongue in this outfit, bucky. It is a matter of knuckles. I think you'll not last long."

The line moved up, passing before the cook's table. Shafter got his oatmeal, his bacon and biscuits, and held out his cup for coffee. The trooper handling the pot let his hand waver a little so that the coffee spilled over, scalding Shafter's hand; and then the trooper gave him a blank stare. Shafter looked back at him, a little light dancing gray-bright in his eyes, and passed on to a long table. So that was the way it would be in this troop; he was untested, and suddenly a sergeant—made so by Captain Moylan out of memory of incidents long ago. Moylan must have known that he put his new sergeant in a hard position.

Hines passed by and dropped a brusque word. "Come to the orderly room."

In a little while Shafter followed him into the small room at the end of the barracks. Hines was at his desk. He said, "Shut the damned door," and waited until it was done. "I'm too old a man to remark upon my company commander's choices, but it is me that has to keep the company runnin'. I will not have this outfit go sour because of the advancement of a rookie to sergeant. So then, you must lick somebody to show what you've got. It will be the one that was sergeant and got broke for tryin' to lap up all the whiskey in Bismarck. That's Donovan."

Shafter remembered the one with the round belly. "He's opened the door already."

"See that you walk right through that door," said Hines. "You must give him a hell of a beating, or you'll never draw any water in this outfit as a noncom. If he should give you the beatin', there is but one thing for you to do. You will turn in your stripes."

Shafter stood easy in front of the first sergeant, smiling a little. "You have got a fine collection of savages for a company, Sergeant. I shall tame one of them for you."

"So," said Hines and was not impressed. Four hash marks on his sleeve testified his service; in his eyes lay an iron, taciturn wisdom. The army had made and shaped him until he was all that the army stood for, a solid, short-tempered, and thoroughly valuable man. "You talk like a damned gentleman. Get your stripes sewed on. At stable call you will be assigned a horse. This afternoon you will take the light wagon and go to Bismarck to do errands for the captain and his lady. Be back before mess call."

By afternoon, heat lay like a thinned film in the windless air. Shafter hitched the wagon to a pair of horses and, with a shopping list from Mrs. Moylan in his pocket, crossed the river by ferry and drove into Bismarck. He did the shopping for Mrs. Moylan; then he hunted up a tailor and sat in his underclothes for an hour, reading an old copy of the New York *Tribune* while the tailor cut his uniform to better size, sewed on the sergeant's chevrons and the yellow noncom stripe down each trouser leg.

He strolled back down Bismarck's street, and in front of the grocery store he came upon Josephine Russell. She halted at once, showing surprise; she tipped her head as she studied him.

"So that is why you came west?"

"Yes."

"I think you've worn the uniform before."

She carried a basket of groceries, and Shafter relieved her of it. "Let me carry this for you. I have a little time before I have to go back to the post." They moved down the street, side by side. She wore a light dress, and she had no hat. She seemed fairer to him than before.

"It's good to see you," he said.

She gave him a quick side-glance and walked on in silence. This day the town was crowded. Half a dozen punchers came up the walk, shoulder to shoulder, thrown slightly forward by the high heels of their riding boots. They broke aside to let Josephine pass, and eyed her with surreptitious admiration. Indians sat against a stable wall, dourly indifferent. Up from a warehouse at the lower end of town moved a caravan of ox-drawn wagons crowded to the canvas tops with freight, headed outward from the railroad into that southward distance which ran three hundred miles to Yankton without the break of a town or settlement, except for the dreary little army posts or steamboat landings along the Missouri.

At the foot of the street Josephine moved out upon the prairie to a house standing somewhat removed from the town. A picket fence surrounded it, but otherwise it was without ornament, shade, or grass. She opened the gate and led Shafter to the porch. "Since you have some time, sit down a minute." She took a chair and Shafter settled himself in a rocker.

"The uniform changes you entirely," Josephine said. "My first judgment of you was a great deal different. In civilian clothes you seemed a somewhat skeptical man, perhaps accustomed to the good things of life."

He showed some embarrassment at the remark. "I guess that's true. I've wanted to get back into the uniform for ten years. When I was a soldier last time I had about as much peace of mind, as much personal contentment, as I ever had. I don't need much comfort or many possessions. What I need, I guess, is to be with plain and honest men."

"Men can be plain and honest outside the army."

"Then," he said, "it must be something else the uniform has that I have needed."

"Adventure?" she murmured. "The sound of bugles?"

He shook his head. "I went through four years of the Civil War. I heard a lot of bugles blowing for the charge. I saw a lot of men fall, a lot of good friends die. That's the other side of adventure. I'm no longer a young man dreaming of gallantry in action."

She bent a little in the chair, smiling and curious. "You make yourself a great puzzle to me, Sergeant."

He reached into his blouse for a cigar, and lighted it and relaxed wholly in the rocker. "How long have you lived out here?" he asked.

"Two years. We have always been moving up on the edge of the frontier. I suppose in two or three years more we'll be out in Montana somewhere. My father has that store—where you saw me. But he is restless, and more so since my mother died."

"You like it here?"

"I like whatever place I am." A more sober expression came to her face. "It was nice to visit the East, though."

A train flung its long warning whistle forward from the distance, reminding Shafter of the time. He rose with reluctance and stood looking down at her.

"The post can be a very lonely place," she said. "This house is open, if you feel like visiting."

He said, "I shall do that," and walked back toward town. She watched him go, his shoulders cut against the sunlight, his long frame swinging. She had known, as soon as she saw him in uniform, that the sergeant's stripes did not represent what he once had been. Somewhere in the past he had been a man with a career, had met disaster, and had stepped away from the wreckage with a shrug of his shoulder. There was, she thought, a woman somewhere involved. Reluctantly she lifted her guard against him. "I should not," she murmured, "be interested in him," and continued to watch him until he swung around the corner of a building and disappeared.

BACK AT THE POST Shafter delivered the packages to Captain Moylan's quarters, returned the wagon to the stables, and walked to the barracks. As soon as he reached his bunk he saw that it had been ripped apart. His box of cigars, which he had placed beneath the tick, now lay in sight, its lid open and the cigars gone.

The men of the troop sat around the barracks, cleaning up equipment for retreat. Donovan was at one of the tables, playing solitaire. He was smoking a cigar and had a row of cigars lying before him. A scar-mouthed trooper stood by, thinly grinning and watching Shafter from the corners of his eyes. Everybody in the room knew what was happening, and waited for the rest of it to happen.

Shafter moved to the table. "Donovan," he said, easy and plain, "where do we have this fight?"

"Behind the stables," said Donovan with equal calmness. "Tinney, have a cigar. They're good ones, picked by a gentleman lately come among us to dodge a warrant. I guess we have smoked the gentleman out." The scar-mouthed trooper grinned and reached for a cigar. In the background Shafter saw the other troopers watching, interested and speculative.

"I'll be behind the stables after tattoo," said Shafter. "Better smoke those things up now, Donovan. You'll be sick of cigars later."

Donovan continued imperturbably with his playing. He said to the room at large, "Listen to the gentleman's words carefully, boys. The gentleman is a sergeant. He is an educated sergeant, sent among us heathens to bring us knowledge."

SUPPER WAS OVER and retreat gone by. In the deepening twilight Shafter strolled along the barracks walk with his cigar. Troopers moved by him, some with idleness and some hurrying to reach the ferry and the gaudy dens at the Point. Across the parade, General Custer's house was filled with light, and officers and their ladies strolled toward it. He walked on, indifferently noticing an officer appear from the guardhouse and start toward Officers' Row at a quick and nervous pace. Then he heard the officer's stride cease and he heard the officer call at him, "Hold up there."

A chill ran along his back and a strange tight spasm went through his belly as he swung around. The officer stood waiting twenty feet away, his face obscured by the shadows. "Come here, Sergeant," he said.

Shafter moved up, watching the other man's face take on shape and form—and identity. When he was ten feet removed he discovered whom he faced, and a sudden deep feeling of anger shook him. Then he remembered he was in uniform and made his salute.

The lieutenant did not return the salute. He looked upon Shafter with a face sharpened by astonishment, by the shock of past memories, by the rousing of old rages. "How in God's name did you get here?" he asked.

"It is a small world, Mr. Garnett. A very small world to a man trying to escape his conscience."

"Your conscience?" said Lieutenant Edward Christian Garnett.

"Yours," said Shafter.

The lieutenant began to curse Shafter, using his words as he would have used a whip, to cut, to disfigure. The guard patrol swung around the corner of the quadrangle and passed close at hand, stopping the lieutenant's voice for a little while, and in this silence Shafter saw the man's pale wedge of a face. This was Garnett, formed like an aristocrat out of a French novel, with dark round eyes well recessed in their sockets, a head of dark hair that broke along his forehead in a dashing wave, and a gallant mustache trimmed above a full mouth. He had the whitest of teeth; he had a smile, Shafter remembered, which could charm a woman and capture her without effort.

The patrol passed on. Garnett spoke sharply. "See to it that you are not in this fort tomorrow."

"What are you afraid of, Mr. Garnett?"

"Damn you," said Garnett, "speak to me properly."

"Then let us start right. Return the salute I offered you. You were always a slovenly soldier."

"I could prefer charges against you, Shafter."

"Do you want to open the record of the past, Mr. Garnett?"

"And how could you open it?" answered Garnett, thinly malicious. "Your word against mine? Who would take it?"

"Captain Moylan is also here," said Shafter. "As a gentleman, I suppose he has kept his knowledge of you to himself. How would you like the ladies of the post to know of the events of your past? It would interfere with your prowling. I think you will never prefer charges against me."

Garnett stepped nearer him. "Listen to me. I have got a hundred ways of getting at you. Believe me, I'll use them all. I'll break your damned back and before I'm through with you, you'll crawl over the hill one dark night and never come back."

"You are a dog, Mr. Garnett."

Garnett lifted a hand and hit him one cracking blow across the face with his open palm. The effect of it roared through Shafter's head; he stepped away and then he stepped forward, to find Garnett backed four paces from him and holding a drawn revolver on him. "Go ahead," Garnett softly murmured.

Shafter stood his ground but pulled his impulses back into place. "I did not know you were here," he said. "Probably I would not have come If I had known it. Still, I'm here. Here I shall stay. And now that you have used your hands on me, I'll tell you something: One way or another, I'll destroy you."

Tattoo broke over the parade, interrupting Garnett's reply. The lieutenant cursed and swung away and went toward Custer's quarters at a long-reaching pace. He left behind him a man who, once turned bitter against the world, had mastered his bitterness; and now was bitter again.

As tattoo's melancholy last notes fell away across the darkness, with nine-o'clock sentry's call running from post to post, Shafter moved toward A Company's stable. Behind it he found the men waiting.

"What kept you? Now, where's that lantern?"

It was Donovan speaking. He stood heavy-shouldered in the dark, stripped to his waist. A man pulled a blanket away from a lantern, so that its light danced in yellow crystals upon the night. Donovan grinned at Shafter. He was a confident old hand, facing another routine battle. There was no real anger in the man, Shafter understood; Donovan had only used his sarcasm as a weapon to produce the fight. "Take off your blouse—take off your shirt. I'll have no advantage. I need none."

Stripping off blouse and shirt, Shafter studied Donovan. The man's complete calm warned him that Donovan had been a professional somewhere and thought of his opponent as only another green, awkward one to be pounded down and added to his list.

"If the gentleman is ready," said Donovan with his ridiculing tone, "let's be off to the fair."

He plunged forward, his left fist feinting, his right thundering out. Shafter came in, caught that right-armed blow on his elbow, and threw it aside. He hit Donovan hard in the belly, hearing a blast of expelled wind. Quickly he shifted his hips as Donovan tried to ram a knee into his crotch, then trapped both of the big man's arms under his elbows and rode around a circle as Donovan used his strength to pull free. He let go, hooked a punch against Donovan's kidney, and moved away.

Donovan shook his head. He gave an impatient cry and shuffled forward, feinting with his body, luring Shafter in. He dropped his arms, opening himself wide, and rushed forward again, with his head down. Suddenly he was hard to hit. Shafter tried for the man's belly, missed, and then, before he could swing clear, he was thrown back on his heels and knocked to the ground by a savage punch he had never seen. He rolled and seized Donovan's foot and turned with it, bringing the man down.

Shafter flung himself away, stood up, and watched Donovan rise. He stepped in and sledged Donovan at the side of the neck with two hard blows before Donovan reached for him and tied him up. He went loose, letting the man pay out his strength in the struggle.

Donovan cried, "You damned leech, stand out and fight it!" He heaved Shafter clear, and raised a hand to brush his sweaty face. Shafter slid in, driving for the man's belly, and saw the sick look that came to his mouth. Donovan reached for him but Shafter whirled aside, found his chance, and hit him in the kidney again. The man's softness was crawling up on him; his mouth was sprung wide and his eyes were not clear. He missed a swing and stumbled forward. Shafter caught him with a short, up-cutting blow beneath the chin. Donovan sighed; the power went out of him and he fell slowly to the dust, his face striking.

The light bobbed up and down in Tinney's hands. Tinney said, "For God's sakes, Donovan, quit foolin'!" He ran forward and tickled Donovan with the toe of his boot. He bent nearer and straightened back, to say in a dull astonishment, "He's out."

"Water bucket," said Shafter.

Somebody went running back to the stable while troopers formed a fascinated, silent circle. Shafter said, "Tinney, how did you like that cigar?" Tinney opened his mouth to speak, found nothing to say, and slowly backed off. The messenger ran in from the stable and flung a full bucket of water on Donovan's naked torso. The Irishman shook his head and looked up at Shafter.

"You should quit smoking, Donovan," said Shafter. "Cigars are bad on the wind."

Donovan pulled himself to his feet. He said, "What fool dumped the bucket on me? Because a man is on his knees is nothin'." Then he asked Shafter curiously, "Was I out?"

"Dead out."

"Then I got licked," said Donovan in a practical voice. He put out his hand. "That's the end of it," he said.

Shafter took Donovan's hand, whereupon Donovan swung around, pointing a finger at the men of A Company. "When I'm licked, I'm licked. But don't none of you lads get fresh with me. I'm still man enough to lick the lot of you. Another thing—if you back-talk the professor here, I'll beat your ears down."

He started for the barracks, his head dropped in weariness. Shafter came up to him and laid an arm on his shoulder, so that the two went on through the dark. Donovan murmured, "I'll buy the cigars, bucko. You're all right. If you can lick me, you can wear the stripes. I'd like to see the man that can take 'em off you."

"Donovan," said Shafter. "One night soon we'll take a few of the lads and drop over the river. A little drinking will do no harm."

"Ah," said Donovan, "you're my kind. But if I'd lay off the whiskey, you'd never of had me. Professor, this is a damned good outfit."

Shafter moved toward the barracks room, putting on his shirt as he walked. On the porch he stood and felt the ache of his bruises. But he knew he had ceased to be an outsider; he could tell that by the way the men looked at him. This was why he had joined—to be one of a company of men. It was in this closeness he had been happiest. Maybe it was discipline or maybe it was service, or maybe it was the feeling of a man as he rode with other men, joined in the roughness, in the brawling and in the fighting, in the lust and evil, and in the honesty and the faithfulness that bound them all together. He stood still, recalling the things that had been important to him in the past, and that he had missed in civilian life. The sweat that stung his eyes; the heavy dust rising up from a marching column; the stretch of his leg muscles as he lifted in the saddle for a run; the rain beating hard upon him until the smell of his uniform was woolly and rank; the evening shadows with the campfires glittering through them; the sound of tired voices coming from afar; the comfort of the earth as he lay against it—and the calm dark mystery of the heavens as he looked up to them. Each was a little thing, but each one fed him and made life full.

As Shafter reentered the barracks Donovan walked out of the washroom, stripped naked. He tapped his paunch, turned red by the punches. He was grinning. "A good fight, bucko." The first sergeant came out of the orderly room and paused to look at these two.

"What happened to your belly, Donovan?"

"I fell on a picket pin," said Donovan, and grinned again.

Hines replied, "I'll have to send a detail out to pull up all these picket pins the men of this troop keep stumblin' over." Then he left the barracks and went through the dark to Officers' Row and tapped on the door of Captain Moylan's house. When the captain came out Hines saluted and said, "He licked Donovan, sir."

"So," said Moylan, pleased. "It will be all right."

"It will be better than I thought," agreed Hines. "Now, can he soldier?"

"As good as you or I, Hines."

"Let us not be givin' him too much credit," cautioned Hines. "If the man is half as good as either of us, Captain, he is an angel."

Chapter 4

LIEUTENANT GARNETT MOVED rapidly across the parade, preoccupied and scowling, with the shock of meeting Shafter still sharp in him. As he came before General Custer's house he paused to pull himself straight and to compose the expression on his face. Then he crossed the porch with his cap removed and tucked in the crook of his left arm.

Mrs. Custer met him and led him into the crowded room. She was a demure woman, quietly charming. She said, "I believe you know everybody, except perhaps our very young and very pretty guest from Bismarck."

She paused before Josephine Russell, who was seated on the piano stool. Lieutenant Garnett saw the girl's prettiness and the hunting instinct in him rose and fashioned a flashing smile. He made a show in his uniform—the long straight sweep of his trousers with their broad yellow stripes, the tight brass-buttoned coat above which lay the white wing collar and black cravat. His face had an olive pallor and this, against the intense blackness of his wavy hair, made him an extremely striking man.

"Josephine," said Mrs. Custer, "let me present Mr. Garnett. This is Josephine Russell." And then, because she had a motherly instinct for the men of the command and loved to make matches, she added, "Mr. Garnett is so wedded to his profession that I fear he has never had time for ladies."

Lieutenant Garnett gave Mrs. Custer a quick glance, suspecting irony; but he saw only pleasure on her face and so turned and bowed. "I must warn you, Miss Russell. There are many bachelors and you will be rushed."

"Ah," said Mrs. Custer, "all the eligible bachelors of the post have rushed her."

"I propose to join their ranks immediately," answered Garnett. Josephine, pleasantly reposed, acknowledged the compliment with a smile. She said, "The gallantry of the Seventh is well known, Mr. Garnett."

Mrs. Custer went away, and for a little while the lieutenant tried his best wares on Josephine, drawing her out, searching for some entry through her vanity, her weaknesses, her romantic notions, or her pride. Presently, when another officer came up, the lieutenant passed on to pay his respects to others. The general was in a corner, having some sort of tactical discussion with Major Reno and Captain Weir of D Company and the tawny Yates who was commander of F Company. Garnett left that weighty circle to itself, said a few words to Algernon Smith and Mrs. Smith, joined in with Calhoun and Edgerly for a moment—the latter as handsome a man as himself—and came finally to Major Barrows and his lady.

The major, here on tour of duty from the inspector general's department, was small, lean, and very soft of voice. A small mustache and imperial gave a sharpness to an otherwise gentle set of features, and his manner in addressing Garnett had a kind of formal courtesy. "Good evening, Mr. Garnett. A pleasant evening."

"Pleasant, but there's a chill in it. Winter's coming."

"Always does," said Major Barrows dryly.

Garnett smiled down at Mrs. Barrows, who was somewhat younger than her husband. She sat back in the chair, her head rested against it so that her throat revealed its ivory lines. Her lids dropped and for a moment her lashes touched as she watched this man—darkly, indifferently, strangely.

The major divided an inexpressive glance between them and then thought to say, "You have met, have you not?"

The major's wife smiled slightly. "Of course. Two or three times."

"My memory for things social has grown rusty," apologized the major. He made a little bow to be excused and went over to join the general and his party. Garnett thrust his arms across his chest, matching the depthless gaze of the woman with one of his own. He knew he had stirred her. She was, he guessed, a lonely woman with unspent emotions.

"Do you enjoy it here?" he asked.

"Yes," she said, and continued to watch him out of her half-closed eyes.

It was a challenge to be met and he murmured, "Of what are you thinking?"

"Many things."

"Have you walked through these shadows, late at night, alone?"

"Yes. Often."

"I know what you have felt. I know what you have thought."

"Do you?" she asked. Her eyes grew wider and a slight warmth showed on her lips. "You are gallant, Mr. Garnett."

He had interested her, but, like a wise campaigner, he did not overdo his pressing. He nodded and turned to join the older officers.

Weir was speaking. "We have respected no treaty we ever made with the Sioux. They know we never will. What good is a treaty, solemnly made in Washington, when a month later five hundred white men cross the treaty line? The prospector, the emigrant, and the squatter have a hunger for gold and land that we cannot stop by treaty. We have spent two years trying to run them out of country which we have promised shall be the Indian's. It is an impossible job. The Indian knows we will crowd him westward until we have pushed him into the ocean. All the Sioux leaders see it. They will make a stand. There will be a campaign next spring."

"If so," said Custer, "we shall decisively defeat them."

"I wish," said Weir, "I were as optimistic. All this summer the traders have been freighting repeating rifles up the Missouri to the

Indians, trading for fur. Winchesters and Henrys. They are better arms in many ways than ours. Last week when I took out my company for target practice one-third of all our carbines jammed after the fifth shot."

"Major," said Custer to Barrows, "I wish you'd stress things like that in your report to the department. I have written so many critical letters that I'm regarded as a dangerous and undisciplined officer. I am heartsick at the things I see which I cannot improve. The prices charged by the post trader are outrageous. Do you know what his excuse is? It is that his expenses in getting the job were so enormous that he must recoup himself. Why were they enormous? Because there are gentlemen in Washington who sell these post traderships to the highest bidder. How can such a situation exist? Because there exists a corrupt ring in Washington, protected by extremely high-placed officials." He hesitated, looked about the group, and plunged on. "I personally know of a brother of one official—the very highest in our land—who is receiving financial reward for using his indirect influence in assisting civilians to receive these post traderships from the Department of the Interior."

The group of officers appeared mildly embarrassed. Major Barrows glanced at the general. "That is a risky thing for an army officer to say, Custer. No officer who wishes for a successful career can afford to question civil authority in Washington."

"I shall be in Washington soon," said Custer. "I shall mention the evil as I see it."

Major Reno had not spoken thus far. He was a stocky, rumpled figure, round and sallow of face, with black hair pressed down upon his head and a pair of round, recessed eyes, darkly circled. He said now, "If we have a campaign next spring, we shall face formidable resistance."

"No," said Custer. "I know Indians. They will see us, and break. The question will be, can we reach them soon enough to surround them before they break into little bands and disappear? I can take this regiment and handle the situation entirely."

"Your regiment," offered Barrows, "has an average muster of sixty-four men per company. Full strength, you might take eight hundred men into the field. A third of those are apt to be recruits. It is not an extraordinary show of strength."

The general said with certainty, "The Seventh can whip any collection of Indians on the plains," and turned to speak to some departing guests.

Major Barrows looked at his wife, who rose; and the two made their expressions of pleasure and departed. Edgerly brought around a rig for Josephine. Gradually the rest of the visitors left.

Mrs. Custer went upstairs, leaving the general to a restless back-and-forth pacing. Presently he passed through the doorless arch into a room whose walls were crowded with animal heads, guns, and Indian relics. He sat down at his desk, picked up a pen, and resumed the article he was writing on frontier life for an eastern magazine.

He worked for an hour, tense and aggressive in this as in all things, and abruptly stopped and sat back, fidgeting in the chair. "Libby!" he called. She descended the stairs in an old blue robe, her hair done back for the night and her eyes sleepy. "Libby," he complained, "how can I write if you're not around?"

She smiled and curled up in a chair. As he read aloud what he had written she watched his face, her eyes soft and affectionate. When he had finished she said, "That's very good, Autie."

"Is it?" he asked, like a small boy, anxious for praise.

"Nothing you put your hand to is not good."

"Then," he said, "I shall send it, though the Lord knows why they should want to pay me two hundred dollars for it. It will help out on our next trip east, old lady."

"Yes," she answered absentmindedly. Her thoughts were elsewhere. "Autie—all this talk of a campaign next spring—do you think it will come?"

"I expect so."

"Then I hope winter never passes," she declared intensely.

"Libby," he said. "You were a little cool toward Reno tonight."

"It is not in my heart to be nice to anybody who is not your friend."

"Still, he's an officer of this regiment. We must show no favorites. We must be the same to all."

"I'll try," she murmured.

He rose and went around to her. He lifted her out of the chair and carried her around the rooms. "Blow out the lamps," he said, and lowered her by the tables while she blew. Then, in the darkness, he carried her up the stairs. "Autie," she murmured. "I'm too old for such romantic foolishness."

"You are a child," whispered Custer.

MAJOR BARROWS MOVED slowly down the walk with his wife, preoccupied by his own reflections. Margaret Barrows did not disturb them for she was engaged in thoughts of her own, and so the two reached their house. The major lighted the lamp and stood a moment by it, observing the willowy shape of his wife as she moved, eyes shining, about the room.

"Pleasant evening," he said.

"Yes."

"Custer was indiscreet. He always is. Nothing saves him but a reputation for dash, and that will not save him forever."

She moved toward him and watched him with that strange expression which always deeply disturbed him; for he knew the depths of his wife's nature, and struggled in his own way to satisfy the rich vitality within her. But the stiffness of his nature was hard to change, so that he knew he could not satisfy the romantic side of her character. It troubled him that she stood here now, wanting some display of affection; and the best he could contrive was a stolid, "I think I'll finish my smoke on the porch. You're a beautiful woman, Margaret. I was conscious of that tonight." He bent forward and kissed her and straightened.

"Good night," she said in a controlled voice, and went into the bedroom.

The major walked to the porch and sat down, hooking his feet to the rail, there to brood over the fragrance of his cigar. Lieutenant Algernon Smith and his wife strolled past, and Mrs. Smith's musical voice came to him. "Good night, Major."

They were a well-matched couple, a gay and companionable woman and a handsome man with a bushy black mustache, a solid chin, and sharp eyes. After several years of married life they were still close to each other. It was a beautiful thing to see and it made him keenly feel his own failure. Life was mostly humdrum; drudgery and tedious hours stretched end on end. For him that was well enough, but for his wife it was suffocation. Knowing her terrible need for some kind of release, he felt a tragic unhappiness for her.

Lieutenant Smith and his wife moved into their own quarters and made ready for bed. Smith said, "That was strong meat Custer was serving up—that talk about graft and scandal. All true, every word of it, but he's on dangerous ground talking about it."

"He loves dangerous ground," observed his wife. She sat before a bureau made of scrap lumber. There was a small mirror on the wall and into this she looked as she took down her hair.

"So he does," said Smith. He pulled off his shoes, removed his shirt, and sat back to enjoy a last fragment of his cigar.

"I never cease to think of that," said Mrs. Smith.

"What?"

"All of you—forty officers and eight hundred men—are in the hands of one impulsive commander. When he courts danger for himself he courts it for you."

"That's the way of soldiering. You're old enough a campaigner by now to know it couldn't be otherwise."

"I'm old enough a campaigner to know that no commander has the right to take risks for personal glory, or for newspaper stories back east, or to show his enemies what a great soldier he is."

"You shouldn't harbor such thoughts. It's been a long stretch for you in this dreary nowhere. I should have sent you east last fall."

She looked at him, disturbed yet affectionate. "You know we couldn't afford it. Besides, I wouldn't have gone without you."

Chapter 5

At six o'clock in the morning Lieutenant Algernon Smith led twenty men of A Company out upon the parade and joined a platoon of L Company waiting there under Garnett. The troopers moved two by two through the guardhouse gate and rode up the slope of the ridge east of the post. At its crest they faced the desert's long western reach, now asmolder with the ashy colors of fresh sunlight.

Shafter rode as right guide at the head of the column, Smith beside him. Adjoining the lieutenant was the civilian guide, a tall and very thin man wearing a sloppy blue serge coat and a hat scorched by many campfires and discolored by frequent dips into wayside creeks. His name was Bannack Bill and he had a gaunt neck, up and down which an Adam's apple slid like a loose chestnut. His eyes, half hidden behind dropped lids, searched the landscape.

The troopers rode half awake, slumped on their McClellan saddles, gradually taking on life as the sun warmed them and the steady riding loosened their muscles. This was just one more scout detail flung out daily to keep an eye on the Sioux, who moved in mercurial restlessness over the land. East of the river the Indians lived in sullen peace and paid their visits to Bismarck, sitting in motionless rows along the sidewalk. East of the river they were a subjugated race. But west of the river they were a free and intractable people, made insolent by the memory of the many evils done them by white people, made proud by the recollection of their vanishing freedom, made warlike by nature. They came into the post to hold council with the general, and the pipe was smoked and presents passed and gestures of friendship made; but at night these same warriors waited in the darkness outside the guard line to cut down whatever foolish trooper strayed beyond the limit of safety.

Bannack Bill rode wide of the column, staring toward the ground as he traveled. He came back. "Small party headin' south. Half a dozen bucks. Dozen kids and women. Four travwaws."

Algernon Smith turned to Shafter. "You're new. Maybe you don't know what we're doing."

"No sir."

"Keeping watch on these people. The only way we can guess their state of mind is to watch the trails they make. Right now it is customary for them to collect from summer villages and go down to the agency for the winter. If they go down in big numbers, we can guess they're going to cause us no trouble until spring. If they stay away from the agency and collect in a big bunch, we can expect something. Of course there are many villagers, farther west, who never come in. They're beyond our reach."

Shafter sat easy in the saddle. Behind him were the sounds of troopers in motion—the clinking of metal gear and the slap of canteens, the murmuring play of talk, the sudden snorting of a horse. He turned and saw the column stretch two and two behind him in a blue-figure line, the men so dark of face that their eyes seemed to glitter. Carbines lay athwart each man's pommel; the yellow seam of each noncom's pants leg made a splash of color. He saw Donovan slowly grin and his eyelid slowly wink. He settled himself frontward again and he thought, A damned fine life I have been missing.

They were now thirty miles from the fort, and deeper in Indian land. They crossed a creek, breasted a loose thicket, and climbed to the crest of a ridge wherefrom Smith might see the roundabout pockets and ravines. He shaded his eyes against the western sun, looking at the small figure of the civilian guide who had preceded them two miles forward and was now turning his horse in a steady circle in signal. Smith ordered, "Gallop," and put the troop to a run.

The troop whirled down the ridge, accoutrements banging and slapping. The guide waited sedately, and pointed to the south, whereupon Smith brought the column to a halt. Then he looked ahead in the direction which had drawn the guide's interest. Off there, now showing on a ridge, now lost in a depression, was a long string of ponies, riders, and travois.

"Biggest one yet," said the guide. "Fifty lodges in that outfit."

Lieutenant Garnett, who had been riding halfway down the column, now rode up to join Smith. With a show of eagerness he urged, "Let's go have a look."

"As long as they're heading for the agency," Smith replied, "there's no point in our stopping them. They might misjudge our intentions as we rode up, and prepare for a fight. One shot by a careless buck would start trouble nobody wants or intends."

"I hate like hell to let them think we're avoiding them," grumbled Garnett.

"That's scarcely the point," Smith said dryly, and put the column forward at its former pace. Gradually as they moved west they had a better view of the long Indian column as it wound through, around, and over the depressions and hummocks of the land. The head of the column passed out of sight on the yonder side of a ridge, but a group of warriors came streaming back on their ponies, stopped at the end of their column, and stood watchfully there, faced against the cavalry. Presently, as the tail of the column dropped over the ridge, this rear guard wheeled and went scudding away—a thin yell of defiance floating back.

At six thirty the command camped in a grove beside a small creek, and the smell of coffee and bacon soon drifted on a chilling air. Men went beating along the earth with sticks, routing out rattlesnakes, and twilight fell—and then the stars were all ashine across infinity's pure space. Shafter rolled in his blanket, settled his head on the saddle, and for a few drowsy moments listened to the murmuring around him. Weariness played through his bones—the wonderful luxury of physical looseness rolling all along his body.

There were no trumpet calls on scout patrol. Men stirred out of sleep, saw daylight crack through the eastern blackness, and sat up to put on their hats, their blouses, and their boots, thus rising full-dressed. One trooper jumped aside and began to swear. He got a stick and beat the life out of a rattlesnake which, drawn by warmth, had spent part of the night curled against his blanket. A water detail took the horses down to the creek, fires sprang up, and the smell of coffee and bacon pungently spread. An hour before sunrise the company moved out, silent and cold and morose. The way now was southwest as the column began to strike homeward, but the guide said, "I'll look yander a bit," and rode straight into the west.

Sunrise broke tawny in the east, bright but heatless, and the fog lying over the earth vanished. Far ahead the guide came into view on a ridge and circled his horse. Smith put the troop into a gallop, and when they reached Bannack Bill they followed him toward a thin fringe of willows along a creek. There was something scattered on the ground which had to Shafter a familiar attitude; he had seen many men thus, lying in the disheveled posture of death. There were three men stripped naked, two of them beyond middle age and a young one. They had all been scalped and their bodies mutilated. Each man had half a dozen arrows thrust into him.

"Looks like prospectors coming back from the Black Hills," commented Smith. "Ever see them before, Bill?"

"Can't recognize 'em."

"Not dead long. They've not swollen much."

"Sometime yesterday afternoon," said the guide. "They hadn't started a fire and so I guess they were just goin' to make camp."

There was nothing left except the bodies. Horses, equipment, and supplies had been carried off. One white trail showed where a warrior had dumped the prospector's flour, and a few yards from the scene a muslin bag of beans lay spilled on the ground.

"It was that party we passed yesterday late," said Bannack Bill.

"How sure are you of it?" asked Smith.

"A party of bucks would of sculped these fellers and let it go like that. That knife work was done by squaws and the arrers prob'ly by kids practicin' up on their shootin'. You'll find them scalps with that party."

"We'll go see," said Smith.

He led the column to the creek and let it water, and then swung back into the southwest. They traveled steadily at a walk, passing over small ridges and into other small lands of level grass. Near eleven o'clock they cut the trail of the large party bound south for the reservation and followed it at a gallop for an hour.

The sun tipped over the line and started down; and then the lieutenant stopped the command for half an hour's nooning. When he moved the column on again it was in a line that roughly paralleled the course of the Indian band. Around two o'clock he called Garnett forward.

"Take Shafter and the first ten troopers and scout to the left. Don't expose yourself. My desire is to come in ahead of the Sioux and catch them before they can set themselves for trouble. If you sight them, send back a messenger and wait for me to come up."

Garnett nodded his head and started away with his detachment.

Shafter moved beside the lieutenant, jarred out of his calm by his savage distrust of Garnett. He ignored the lieutenant as they slanted up the side of the valley's east ridge, zigzagging around rock shoulders, following old deer and antelope trails. Looking back, he saw the rest of the command streaming directly south, kicking up a heavy pall of dust. A hundred feet short of the ridge's crest, Garnett stopped his detachment and nodded at Shafter.

"Climb up there on foot and see what's beyond."

There was still some distance that might have been covered on horse, relieving that much foot labor, but Shafter got out of the saddle, handed his reins to a trooper, and climbed upward over the spongy soil. The climb made him reach for wind and he knew this was Garnett's idea of hazing him. Near the crest of the ridge he flattened down, removed his hat, and looked over the crest into a plain running eastward toward the Missouri. Out there, close by the base of the plateau, the Indian band moved sedately southward, enveloped in its own dust.

He made his way leisurely down the hill and lay back on the ground until the detachment came up. Garnett rode his horse almost on top of him. Shafter rose slowly, enjoying the black flash of temper he saw leap into Garnett's eyes. "Over the ridge, just below us," he said, and swung to the saddle.

Garnett said, "Maybe we should have brought a bed for you," and wheeled the column away. They ran along the foot of the ridge, turned a corner of an intervening butte, and discovered Smith riding upgrade from the west with the command. Garnett lifted in his saddle and made a wheeling gesture with his arm, pointing east. Smith acknowledged it but made no effort to hurry his command on the slope of the hill. Garnett halted his group and waited. There was a quarter-hour delay, but Garnett held his men tight in their saddles, giving them no chance to dismount. He sat still, completely ignoring the command.

Smith came up and said, "Whereabouts?"

"Over the ridge."

"Garnett," said Smith, "you should know enough to rest your men when you have the chance." He led the column forward, staying beneath the shelter of the ridge and following it across the plateau until it pinched out. When they broke over the summit of the plateau they were within five hundred feet of the Sioux, face-on with them. Smith trotted his column forward. He turned in the saddle to speak back to the troopers. "No false motions now," he said. "Wait for my commands." He spoke in a lower tone to Garnett. "We shall ferret out the warriors who did the killing. I propose to take them back to Lincoln. When I swing side to side in the saddle, drift the column into a skirmish line very slowly."

The column of Sioux was immediately before him and he flung up his hand to halt the troopers. He said to Shafter and to Bannack Bill, "Come with me," and rode forward.

A line of warriors milled out from the rear of the Indian column, racing forward, low-bent and weaving on their ponies. The older men in the forefront of the procession ranked themselves and sat still. Smith stopped in front of them and murmured to Bannack Bill, "Tell them I'm glad to see them and hope they have had a good summer. Tell them we're pleased to have them come in for winter, that the meat is fat at the agency. Tell them any compliment you think of for about two minutes. I want to watch these young bucks while you're talking."

Bannack Bill began to speak, using his hands to cut sign across the air. The leading Sioux, faces bronzed and chiseled by weather and years, listened. They were wholly still except for their eyes, which darted covert glances at the lieutenant, and struck shrewdly farther out to the waiting troopers. The younger men of the band had drifted forward in a scattered semicircle.

Shafter murmured, "There's a fresh scalp hanging to the arrow pouch of that pug-nosed lad out on the left."

"Very good, Sergeant," said Smith coolly. "That's what we're looking for."

"You'll probably find the blankets and the clothes among the squaws."

"Ever try to handle a squaw?" said Smith dryly. "We'll leave those dusky beauties alone."

When Bannack Bill was finished one of the Sioux spoke in his guttural, abrupt tongue. Bill said, "He says he's very happy to see the government soldiers. They are his friends. He is their friend. All Sioux are friends of all whites. All whites should be friends of the Sioux, though sometimes they are not. He says he is on his way to the agency and is glad to hear the beef is fat. Most years, he says, it is very poor and the Indians starve. Why is that? he asks."

"Don't tell him I said so, Bill," said Smith, "but there isn't any answer to that question. There are as many white thieves as red ones and probably he's dead right. Tell him I'm happy to see him in such good health, tell him things like that for a couple more minutes."

"By God," said Bill, "I can only invent about so many lies. Anyhow, these old codgers know what you're up to."

"How do they know?"

"You got here too fast from where they saw you last."

Shafter said, "The lad next to the lad with the scalp has got a gold watch and chain wrapped around his neck."

"Two out of three will do nicely," said Smith. "You've got a good eye, Sergeant." He eased himself in the saddle, rolling from side to side—his signal to Garnett a hundred feet behind. The old Sioux men watched him, their glances flicking back to the troopers now idly deploying into skirmish line. The young bucks stirred uneasily.

"Bill," said Smith, "tell him we're happy over everything but the murder of the three white men. Ask him if he knows of that evil."

Bannack Bill began speaking. Smith turned his head and spoke to Shafter. "We need a display of decision here, Sergeant. It has to be done quietly, but without hesitation. When I give the word, ride over and bring out those two bucks. I shall back you up."

Bill said his say and waited for reply. It was not long in coming. The old spokesman of the Sioux straightened himself, pointed to the earth, to the sky, and to the four cardinal points, no doubt invoking all the gods he knew about, and launched into speech.

When he had finished, Bill proceeded to translate it freely.

"The old codger decorates his damned lie as follows: His heart is pure, his mouth is wide open to truth, his soul is hurt to think the lieutenant would think that Red Owl's band would hurt a white man. Not one of his people touched a hair on those three prospectors. He says likewise it is gettin' late and he's got forty miles more to go before reachin' the agency. Which is a way of sayin' to us that it is time to quit the foolin' around."

The old warrior's eyes were black liquid, full of pride and confidence, and touched with shrewd scheming. Smith said, "Ask him this: If he knew that some of his young men had killed the prospectors, would he bring them to the fort as a sign of his goodwill?"

Bannack Bill asked it. Out on the wings of the crowd the young bucks grew increasingly restive and there was a murmuring among them. The old one placed a hand on his heart and briefly answered the question. Bannack Bill said, "He says he would bring in his own son if his son had done it."

"Go get them, Sergeant," murmured Smith, not turning his head. He stared at the old one. "Tell him I believe his word to be true. Tell him he has no doubt been deceived by his own young men, for we see the scalp and we see the gold watch. Tell him we take him at his word and will carry the two young men back to the fort with us."

Bannack Bill hesitated, casting a bland stare at Smith. "I hope you got the best cards in this game, Lieutenant."

"Tell him," said Smith.

Shafter had turned and now rode directly and unhurriedly to the left, passing along the ranks of the younger warriors. They sat still, staring haughtily back at him. He came to the warrior who had the fresh scalp hanging from his quiver and to the warrior with the watch wrapped by its chain around his neck. He stopped, looking at the scalp and at the watch. Suddenly other bucks crowded in and lifted their carbines suggestively and a steady stream of Sioux words went back and forth along the line, growing more excited.

Shafter heard Bannack Bill say, "He says there must be a mistake. That is an old scalp and the watch was a present."

"Tell him we shall take the two warriors to Lincoln. If he speaks the truth, we shall release them."

Shafter pulled his .44 and pointed his finger at the two bucks. He made a gesture of command. The two sat dead-still and stared back. The younger men began to push around them to make a screen and Shafter, seeing this, shoved his horse forward and swung it and laid the muzzle of his gun against the ribs of the warrior with the scalp. He pushed on the muzzle. He said, "Move out." He heard the clicking of carbine hammers about him. Then he heard Smith coolly say, "Ask him if a chief swallows his words as soon as they are spoken."

Bannack Bill repeated it to Red Owl and Red Owl sat thoughtfully still. Back in the column the women were beginning to lift their shrill voices, the savage words scraping Shafter's nerves and inciting the young warriors. One brave flung his carbine around and took a steady aim on Shafter. Then Red Owl's voice came out quickly and spoke three words. The two wanted warriors moved out of the group, Shafter behind them. They rode straight toward the waiting cavalry, never turning their heads.

Smith said crisply, "Tell Red Owl I'm pleased he keeps his word." He wheeled back to the detachment and swung to watch the Indian band take up its forward motion. The old ones rode by in stony silence, but the bucks, fermenting with rage, dashed back and forth along the cavalry line, shrilly crying, flinging up their guns in provocation. They wheeled and charged at the troopers, sliding down from their ponies in beautiful displays of horsemanship, coming full tilt against the troopers' outspread line, and wheeling away with a derisive shouting.

"Hold steady," said Smith.

The procession went slowly by, the squaws all shouting at the troopers. The young warriors suddenly drove the Sioux horse herd through the deployed troopers. Smith called sharply, "Hold tight," and watched until horses and Sioux had passed on. Then he said, "Column of twos—forward—walk." The troopers resumed formation and Smith settled himself at the head of the group.

"It was a question how we'd come out," murmured Bill.

"They had their women and kids along," said Smith. "That kept them from fighting." He turned to Shafter, who rode with the two captive Sioux. "Very good, Sergeant," he said, and pointed the column due east, toward the post.

He was disposed to let the silence continue, but Bannack Bill said, "Something else to make them hate us. You know how an Indian hates, Smith? It is like one of these fires that burns in a coal bed out there on the Bad Lands. Goes down underneath and smokes and gets hotter. It just never goes out. One day it breaks into the open—the damnedest blaze you ever saw."

"That may come," admitted Smith.

Chapter 6

COLDER WEATHER SQUEEZED the land; a thin crust formed on water buckets and barrels, and the ground showed crazed frost patterns. One morning Sergeant Hines said, "Shafter, harness up the light wagon and report to commanding officer's house."

Shafter had his breakfast, hitched the team, and rolled over the parade to Custer's house. The general came out with Mrs. Custer and Josephine Russell. "Sergeant," said Custer, "drive Miss Russell to Fort Rice, remain overnight, and bring her back. Be sure you leave Rice soon enough to make the fort before sundown." Custer gave the girl a hand to the seat of the wagon and saw to it that a blanket was folded over her legs.

Mrs. Custer called from the porch, "Give my love to Mrs. Benteen and the other ladies and say I hope to see them soon."

The morning-fresh team set off at a trot and Shafter headed them south toward Fort Rice, twenty miles away. He had not seen Josephine for a week, and experienced pleasure at her presence. "I have been wondering how you were."

"And I have been curious," she responded, "to see how the experiment was turning out."

"What experiment?"

"Your coming back to an old trade. Other men have tried it and seldom found it satisfactory."

"Do you think I'll regret it?"

"You seemed a different sort of person. I mean—accustomed to better circumstances. That is why you are such a puzzle to me."

"When did you bother to think of me at all?"

"Why," she said, "don't you know any woman is intrigued by contradictions? You are a contradiction. I wanted to go visit Mrs. Benteen, and I suggested to Mrs. Custer that you were undoubtedly a good driver."

He turned to her, smiling, and watched her smile answer him. The cold day rouged her cheeks and sparkled in her eyes.

"I am flattered," he said.

"Under pressure," she said, with quick humor, "you do rise to gallantry. Do you know—I think your thoughts of women are sometimes less than generous."

He replied, very seriously, "I hope I've never shown it to you."

"It is only a guess," she said.

Fog closed in, bringing the horizons hard upon them. They came, late in the morning, to a narrow wooden bridge over the Little Heart, which trembled to their passage. Then they followed the road's rutty course steadily southward, steam beginning to rise from the winter-thick wool of the horses.

"I have never liked the sharp line between officers and men," Josephine suddenly remarked.

"A regiment is a machine built for violent action," he said. "Men make up the parts of the machine—and each part has to perform its particular chore. There's no time to argue about it when a fight starts; so it has to be settled a long time beforehand. Every man must understand his place."

She said, in a lightly speculative voice, "I should not think you'd be happy in your place."

"Why not?"

"You've had a higher one."

He smiled a little. "You're an indiscreet woman."

"Perhaps. After all, a woman has two privileges. To be inconsistent and to be indiscreet."

He said, now grown sober, "I have had both qualities used on me. It has made me wonder what a man's privileges are."

"To walk away when he grows weary of it," she said promptly. "That's what you did, didn't you?"

"Many men have walked away," he admitted. "But few ever walked away whole. They left some of themselves behind. The ability to trust, maybe. Faith."

"It was as I thought," she murmured. "You are skeptical regarding women."

"Yes," he said. "I am."

Her answer to that was extremely soft. "I am so sorry."

"There is still the world of men to be comfortable in."

Fort Rice came through the fog, a blur and then a square shape huddled against the earth. She said, "This has been a nice trip, Sergeant. At least I have relieved you from drill, haven't I?"

"Yes," he said, and drove into Rice. He left Josephine at the Benteens' house and took the rig to the stables. Then he strolled around the post.

It was only a shabby collection of frame buildings, closely surrounded by a stockade of logs capped at each corner by a small bastion from which sentries might view the roundabout country at night. For the people of this post commanding the Missouri's bluff, there were no diversions, no break in a dull and confined life.

He went back to one of the barracks for supper and afterward sat awhile in the barracks room, watching men at poker. A big-bellied cast-iron stove grew slowly red and tobacco smoke rolled through the room. One trooper squatted on his bunk, plucking a sad tune from a guitar, while two others stood close by and tried to make a harmony from the tune. The wind had risen and sang a soft song at the barracks eaves, and men lifted their heads, shrewdly listening to that warning.

Shafter moved out, into the windy blackness. There was a party in Captain Benteen's quarters, all lights gleaming cheerfully upon the cold world. Through the windows he saw the officers and ladies of the post gathered, with Josephine surrounded by young lieutenants. He pulled on his cigar, and was surprised that he stood there. I am well past sentimental longings, he thought. But he stood fast, and observed her carefully. One of the lieutenants drew laughter from her. She lifted her head and he had a full view of her face, changed by the laughter, and he said to himself, "She's damned attractive." For a moment he felt a small thread of loneliness, of outsideness, and was reminded of many things in his past.

At one o'clock the next afternoon Shafter, with Josephine beside him, rolled the wagon through the Fort Rice guard gate at a trot, facing a gray plain upon which the winter fog thickened. It was even colder than the day before and the sun was a thin refraction of light above the overcast.

They rode along in silence for a time. Then she turned to him, smiling. "Isn't it a wonderful day?"

"When you feel good, any day is wonderful."

"It is the country," she said. "It makes you spread out inside. It makes you giddy. It even makes you reckless. You know, Sergeant, I was brought up to believe that each person must stand the consequences of his own actions, however foolish. So, if I do a foolish thing now, you needn't worry."

"What is the foolish thing?"

"I have decided I like you."

He gave her a half-embarrassed and half-astonished glance, whereupon she put a hand lightly on his arm and laughed. She had a way of laughing that was extremely attractive, her chin tilting up and her lips curving in pretty lines. A small dimple appeared at the left of her mouth and light danced in her eyes.

He said brusquely, "You're a damned strange woman."

"The simplest kind of a woman. There is no complexity to a woman until a man puts it there."

The Little Heart bridge shaped up through the murk. They passed it, leaving booming echoes behind. The horses, sensing home, stepped briskly through the chilling wind.

"Have a nice visit?" he asked.

"Yes. All officers of this regiment are gallant. There was one young lad newly from West Point—the colonel's son. Sturgis. Do you suppose Colonel Sturgis will ever return to take the command from Custer?"

"I doubt it. The War Department seems to regard it as Custer's command. He's been in charge of it for ten years or so, except for a season when he was court-martialed and deprived of authority."

"What had he done?"

"Rode a hundred miles to see his wife, and wore out his escort troopers getting there. All this without permission to leave his post."

"It was a romantic gesture," she said.

"It was something he would have arrested one of his own officers for doing. He is a man with violent swings of temper. Inconsistent and unpredictable. You can never know what he'll do next."

She asked unexpectedly, "Did I see you strolling through the dark last night, past Captain Benteen's quarters?"

"Yes."

"Smoking your cigar. I understand a cigar and a woman go together in a man's mind. Was there a woman in your mind?"

"I wondered," he said, "if you were enjoying yourself."

"I was also thinking of you," she murmured.

He noticed the sweetness of her expression and was greatly troubled. He had started out with this girl as a stranger, and found himself now somehow engaged in her emotions. It threw him back on his honor, and he wondered if he had given her encouragement. He thought, She's old enough to know what she's doing. But he was uneasy with the responsibility which lay with him. It bore hard against him, the more he thought of it, until he came to his abrupt conclusion. It will have to be settled, he decided.

He stopped the team and wrapped the reins around the brake bar, turning to her. Her eyes lifted to him, narrowed and watchful, but she made no motion when he bent and put his arms around her. For a moment he hesitated, then kissed her, and held the kiss longer than he intended, and drew away. She had made no gesture and no sound; she had put no resistance against him. But now she said, in a curt, precise voice, "I think I heard the general say we should be home by suppertime."

He sent the team on at a faster clip, much more uncertain than he had been. At five o'clock he passed through Lincoln's south gate, and drew before Custer's house. He got down to give her a hand, and felt her body momentarily spring against his arm. She had a light perfume that drifted to him—a sudden, disturbing fragrance.

"You meant to frighten me away, didn't you?" she asked.

"To show you that your knowledge of me was incomplete. You must not take men at face value."

He saw the intensity in her, the swift feelings under hard control. "I think you'll find it was a dangerous subterfuge, Sergeant," she said evenly.

He lifted his cap as she turned away. Then he climbed to the seat and drove the rig through the sweeping wind, back to the stables. He unharnessed and stalled the horses and backed the wagon into its proper place. Having missed stable call, he groomed his own horse in the gathering dusk. But all this while he remembered the taste of her lips and her fragrance and the stillness of her body, neither accepting nor rejecting him. Afterward, walking back to quarters, he recalled her voice as she had said, "You'll find it was a dangerous subterfuge," and wondered at her meaning.

Later he stood retreat and for a while the ceremony took the girl out of his head. There was this power in the trumpets and in the music of the band, in the old grooved ritual of arms, in the voice of the adjutant calling all across the parade's distance, in the somber, stilled ranks of the men, and in the pageantry of troopers wheeling by the commanding officer and the bright flash of gold epaulets and the swords tossed gallantly up. But at supper the recollection of the afternoon scenes recurred and turned him irritable. Then Donovan came over to him. "There's a lively spot across the river called the Stud Horse," he said. "A lad from L dropped word there'd be a group of his boys over there tonight. He asked if we had the guts to drop in— Want to come, Professor?"

Maybe, Shafter thought, this was the way to knock his troubles out of his head, maybe it wasn't. But this was his troop and the lads had let him into it; he was one of the crowd. "I had a notion to go into Bismarck," he said. "How long can you keep that fight on ice?"

"It won't start until the police patrol clears out, after tattoo. Meet us in the back room."

"I'll be there," said Shafter.

EARLIER THAT AFTERNOON Major Barrows' wife rode out of the post on a dark bay horse and swung toward the ferry at the same time Lieutenant Garnett came trotting off the old Fort McKeen road with half a platoon behind him. He saw her and lifted his hat and smiled. Afterward, inside the post, he nodded at one of the troopers. "Purple, report to me at my quarters." He surrendered his horse and strode to his room in the bachelors' quarters, thinking of Mrs. Barrows. He was still appraising her as he washed up and groomed himself before his mirror. He thought, Lonesome as hell, and ready for a little flirting. He corrected himself on that. Not the precise flirting type, I think. Probably trying to be honest with a husband who is a fool in his handling of her.

Jack Purple tapped on the door and came in. He was the lieutenant's striker, doing the necessary valet chores, running the usual errands, and on occasion executing chores which were scarcely routine. A lean man with a sharp face, he knew more of the lieutenant's secrets than any other man, so that the relation between them was compounded of servility, trust, and contempt. Each man secretly harbored his opinion of the other.

"Purple," said Garnett. "I want a man in this outfit soundly whipped. I want him busted up. Get Conboy to do it. Tell him you can get him a hundred dollars if he does a first-rate job."

"Who you wastin' that money on?"

"The new sergeant in A Company. Shafter."

"The one that licked Donovan?"

"Did he?" asked Garnett and looked displeased.

"He did," replied Purple and stood still, trying to remember where Shafter had cut Garnett's past trail. "But it shouldn't be much for Conboy. He licked Donovan twice."

"Go see Conboy," said Garnett. "And keep my name out of it."

"The man's a sergeant. How could he be after any woman you wanted? Was it a long time ago, Lieutenant?"

"Get out of here," ordered Garnett. "Bring my horse around."

He pulled on his overcoat, and took care to adjust his garrison cap. Then he went out to his horse and galloped through the guard gate to the ferry road. Mrs. Barrows waited at the slip for the ferry now nosing in.

He lifted his cap to her. "To Bismarck?"

She nodded and put her horse across the staging to the boat, Garnett following. "My destination also."

He made nothing of her silence. She was, in his expert judgment, a beautiful woman, an instrument of many strings, awaiting somebody's touch.

"Winter's here."

"Yes," she said. "Now the light goes out until spring. I dread it."

"There's still a train back," he pointed out.

"An officer's wife has no business living apart from her husband."

"I understand that," he said.

"Do you?" she inquired softly.

For all his assurance he was halted by the remark. He thought with impatience, Have I misjudged this woman? He tried a few idle phrases, and was answered with equally idle phrases as the boat labored with the current, reached the eastern shore, and dropped its plank. The two moved upgrade to the forking of the road—one branch going through the Point, the other swinging wide of the place and running along the bluff.

"Shall we take the roundabout road?" Garnett asked.

Her eyes touched him, the excitement in them quite distinct. "If you wish," she said. They moved up the road to the top of the bluff and rode along the right-of-way until, by her gesture, they swung into the flat prairie. Presently they were two figures riding along in the mist. "I like it better this way."

"Strange," he said. "I should think you'd like to stick to lights and comfort. I should not think you'd enjoy lonely places."

"Lonely places for lonely people," she said.

"I recognized the loneliness in you."

"I suspect you are rather clever at reading people, Mr. Garnett. Have you been wasting your time trying to read me?"

"Yes. Is it a waste of time?"

"Better if it were," she confessed.

He saw her hands tightly gripping the pommel and he knew this was the moment he had waited for. "Wait," he said, and stopped his horse and got down. He came beside her, looking up. The things he felt showed upon him and the woman saw them as she stared at him. "No," she murmured. "Get back on your horse."

"Come down," he said, and touched her. He felt her body trembling as she hung to the pommel, and he recognized something almost like terror on her face. Then that broke and she put out her arms and came down to him. He had her in his arms, his mouth upon hers, holding her, feeling surrender soften her. When she pulled away she was silently crying, even as she clung to him.

He soothed her. "I am very much in love with you."

"You needn't lie," she said bitterly. "It isn't necessary."

"Do you think I'd touch you if I didn't have the deepest kind of feelings—"

"Yes," she stopped him, "you would. I know you, and now I think you know me. You have studied me rather carefully, haven't you? Help me up, please."

He gave her a hand to the sidesaddle, feeling awkward and amateurish. He got to his own saddle and quickly attempted to get the scene back within his control. "Mrs. Barrows," he said, "if you believe that about me, I shall certainly not come near you again."

"Yes, you will," she said. "And when you come I'll be where you want me. That is the way it will be, Edward. We both know what we are and we both know there is no help for us. I'm going back to the fort. Don't come with me."

He watched her grow smaller and dimmer in the rapid-falling twilight, and then he turned and rode southeastward.

At late dusk he arrived in Bismarck, stabled his horse, and went into a restaurant, where he found Edgerly and joined him for dinner. Afterward the two went out together into a street turned lively by Saturday night's traffic. Cappers stood before the gaming houses, each with his patter and his urgent invitation. A line of soldiers were spread along a shooting gallery's arcade; twenty-two-caliber rifle bullets clanged on the metal targets. Half a dozen cowhands whirled through the darkness, primed for excitement; the town marshal paced by on his rounds, and a tall, white-mustached man came down the street side by side with Josephine Russell.

Edgerly shook hands with the elderly man and bowed to Josephine, who said, "Nighthawking, gentlemen?"

"A couple of soldiers on the prowl," agreed Edgerly, and then introduced Garnett to Josephine's father.

Russell said, "You've had a cold ride over from the fort, gentlemen. Happy to have you join us at our house for a cup of coffee."

Edgerly accepted for them both and made a move to drop beside Josephine. He was forestalled by Garnett, who smoothly turned and took her arm.

Chapter 7

SHAFTER CAME INTO Bismarck half an hour later and knocked at the door of Josephine Russell's house. He was going back to her, he told himself, to straighten out a misunderstanding. He had meant nothing by the kiss; he wanted her to know that.

He wasn't aware of visitors until it was too late to turn back, for Josephine opened the door at once and seemed pleased to see him. She took his arm, saying, "Come in out of the cold." As soon as he got inside he saw Edgerly and Garnett.

He stood still, and his thorough knowledge of the gulf that separated officer and enlisted man made him realize the embarrassment of his position, even though he was in a civilian house. Edgerly was quick to say pleasantly, "Good evening, Sergeant."

"Good evening, sir," said Shafter. He was at the moment watching Garnett's eyes display a malice and a thin pleasure that filled him with hatred. He thought rapidly of some way he might gracefully retire from a situation which was as painful to his hosts and to Edgerly as to himself.

The girl saw the whole scene quite clearly: Shafter's stony attitude of attention in front of his superior officers, Edgerly's gentlemanly effort to break the restraint with a friendly smile, and the satisfaction visible on Garnett's face. She said to Shafter in a soft and hurried voice, "Wouldn't you like to have a cup of coffee?"

"I've had supper."

Edgerly meanwhile had done his quick thinking. Now he asked, "Did you find the horse I sent you after?"

"Yes sir," said Shafter. "He is beyond the Point."

"Take him back to the fort for me, Sergeant," suggested Edgerly.

Shafter turned out of the house at once. The girl followed him, closing the door. "I'm very sorry," she murmured. "It was my fault. If I hadn't invited you inside, you wouldn't have been placed in an uncomfortable situation."

"It doesn't matter."

"I'm afraid it does. You're quite angry."

"No," he said. "I have no privilege to be angry. Good night."

"Just a moment," she said and turned into the house. Presently she came out with a heavy coat wrapped around her. She took his arm and walked with him back through the windy darkness toward Bismarck's street.

There he stopped and faced her. "That was nice of you."

She said, "Edgerly was very thoughtful."

"The man is a gentleman by instinct."

"There's something very bitter between you and the other one—Garnett. I think that's what made you most angry."

He looked at her and was ashamed of the trouble he had caused her. He said, "I apologize for bringing any of my feelings into your house. I had no right to come to you."

"I have my own rules of right and wrong," she said. "You must let me feel the way I wish to feel about it."

He smiled down at her in his old and easy way, but she knew he was still inwardly rankling and she was convinced that her prior judgment of him was correct. Had he never been of a higher grade than sergeant, he would have accepted the scene in her house without a second thought and automatically would have made his departure. But he had felt embarrassment and had made his exit as gracefully as possible, to save her feelings as well as his own.

"You have a gentle heart," he said. "Do you wish me to see you back to the house?"

"No. Come to supper Wednesday night."

"That will be something to look forward to." He lifted his hat to her and went up the street. Shortly, he hailed a freight wagon moving out of town and climbed aboard, to sit in heavy silence beside the driver. Damn him, Shafter thought, he's moved into another home, to stalk another woman. He'll spoil her if he can, knowing I know her. Damn him! He slammed the palm of a hand hard down on the seat, drawing the teamster's slanted glance. "No mosquitoes this time of year," said the driver.

THREE-QUARTERS OF AN hour later the lights of the Point began to make crystal blooms through the fog and by degrees the sound of music moved forward. "Which building is the Stud Horse?" asked Shafter.

The driver pointed with his arm, and Shafter dropped to the muddy road. As he reached the Stud Horse a sergeant was opening the front door, bawling, "All out for the ferry. Make it sharp now, boys. Get away from that bar. I won't be tellin' you twice."

A crowd moved out into the sparkling, damp air. Voices called through the fog and somewhere a woman started to laugh. Shafter heard the patrol sergeant shouting in and out of the Point's various dens, and lights died here and there as he walked around to the back of the Stud Horse. There he opened a door into a little room crowded with A troopers. A lamp burned on the table and smoke filled the place. Donovan said, "You're a man to keep a date on the dot, Professor. Nine it is. The patrol's gone by."

"Hold it a minute," cautioned Sergeant McDermott. "Hackett is patrol sergeant tonight and he knows about this. So he said don't start a fight until he gets out of hearin'." Shafter grinned at the men around him, at Donovan's scarred, professional fighting face, at the other troopers standing shoulder to shoulder around the room.

There was a scratching and murmuring in the big room out front. McDermott said, "That's them," and opened a door and stepped through with A's troopers behind him. A bar ran the full length of one wall, with poker tables and other gambling layouts along the other wall. There was a small floor for dancing and a raised platform at one end on which sat a piano. McDermott looked across at the L troopers drawn into a kind of line. He said, politely formal, "Well, gentlemen, here we are. How many have you got?"

A sergeant spoke for L—a rawboned heavy man with pure black mustaches roping down from either side of his mouth. "You can count, Mac."

"So I can, and I count thirteen. The agreement was not more than ten to a side."

"Wasn't it though," retorted L's sergeant. "And I can count, too, and I count twelve. You tryin' to fool us again?"

"I said to the boys," snapped McDermott, "that you could never trust L. I was right, wasn't I?"

"Twelve and twelve then," concluded L's sergeant, and turned to point a finger at one of his men. "You, Gatch, stay out of it."

McDermott took a look at the discarded L trooper and was derisive. "Him? Hell, leave him in the fun. He ain't goin' to be of any use to you anyhow." Then he stepped forward and stabbed an arm at one of the troopers in front of him. "Conboy, what're you doin' here? This is strictly between A and L."

But L's sergeant said coolly, "Nothin' was said about that."

Conboy was short and broad and muscular. He had a bull's neck and jet-black hair cropped close to his skull. He was a knuckle-scarred man, flat of lip and flat of nose, and he rubbed his shoes gently back and forth on the floor, his knees springing into a slight crouch. Donovan protested at once. "Nothin' was said about bringin' in outside bruisers, either. Is this an honest fight, or ain't it?"

"Now will you listen to who's speakin' those words?" jeered L's sergeant.

"All right," said Donovan. "Pair off as you want."

"I'll take him," said Conboy, pointing at Shafter. "I hear he thinks he's a fighter."

"The man is a bruiser," Donovan whispered to Shafter. "He fought all the big ones in England. He's better than me, Professor. He's better than you."

Conboy stood watching Shafter, his scarred head dropped after the fashion of a dangerous bull half ready to charge. He was barrel-chested and he had massive legs, but his girth bulged out from his hips like pillow stuffing. He was, Shafter guessed, past his prime.

Conboy said, "You ready?"

Shafter moved to the bar and peeled off his overcoat and blouse and shirt. He heard Conboy say confidently, "The rest of you lads hold off your fight till we have ours. I like a proper audience."

"A knockdown is a round?" asked Donovan.

"So it is," said Conboy shortly.

He had stripped to the waist, and now he squatted slightly, one foot forward and both enormous fists cocked stiffly before him. Shafter squared off before him, standing balanced with his arms down. "Get your guard up, you fool," growled Conboy. "I'll not play around with a green man."

The troopers had fashioned a circle to watch. Other troopers were returning to the Stud Horse, drawn by the rumor of trouble. Shafter looked at Conboy's feet, solidly planted on the floor, and then slowly circled him at a distance, watching Conboy's shoes make little shuffling turns. Suddenly, Shafter whipped back in the opposite direction and saw Conboy's feet stop and reverse. Conboy's footwork had been slow and the big man knew it as well as Shafter, for he let out a huge roar and rushed forward, punching. Shafter slid by him, hooked a hard jab into the man's belly, swung, and caught him on the side of the neck. Conboy whirled catlike and launched his rush. He missed with his right hand and reached full out with his left fist, catching Shafter on the shoulder and shaking him backward. Shafter wheeled aside, swinging behind Conboy and waiting.

Conboy came around with an irritated scowl. "Come on—quit the fancy stuff and give me a fight!" He stood still, jiggling his fists up and down, feinting. L Company's men were beginning to ride Shafter.

"That's monseer, the dancer."

"Take a crack at him, Shafter. It won't hurt any worse to get killed now than later."

Shafter moved sidewise again, slowly turning a circle while Conboy wound about.

"Take your time, Professor," Donovan advised. "Make him come to you. The big tub of guts is too heavy to move."

Conboy flung his head aside to shout at Donovan, "I moved fast enough for you, lad—"

Shafter slipped in, cracked him on the side of the face, and laced a jab into his flank. Conboy's ruffled temper gave him speed and he came around in a flash, smashed through Shafter's fending arm, and hit him with a left-hand blow on the chest. It turned Shafter cold. All he saw for that moment was Conboy's red face and pale blue eyes moving against him. In self-defense he fell against Conboy and locked his arms. Donovan yelled, "That's it—that's it!"

Conboy roared, "Is it now?" and threw his head forward, cracking Shafter hard on lip and nose. Shafter locked his fingers together behind Conboy's back and bore him backward toward the bar by his dead weight. He shifted his legs to protect his crotch against the up-driving of Conboy's knees and then brought his heel hard down on Conboy's instep. Overbalanced, Conboy struck the bar and was pinned to it. Shafter surged against him, driving the man's shoulders backward. He heard Conboy grunt and wheeze, and pushed him far enough to draw one of the man's legs from the ground. He let go, smashing him under the neck with two hard side-swinging punches. He battered Conboy's kidneys and threw his forearm across the big man's windpipe, springing Conboy's back on the edge of the bar. He heard L Company shouting at him, outraged at the turn of the affair. Next he heard something crash and then the truce snapped and the troopers rushed, yelling at one another.

He saw Conboy's face grow crimson from strain and felt the man's oxlike heart slug through his shirt. He stepped back and drove a right-hand blow into Conboy's belly. He saw the man sag; but that was all he saw. Suddenly out of nowhere Conboy's fist exploded against the side of his head and he felt himself spinning backward. He never knew when he hit the floor.

When he awoke he had a thundering headache and a sick hollowness in his belly. There was a stillness in the saloon and out of the stillness a man said, "That patrol will be back here in a minute. Maybe we better carry him."

He said, "Damned if you will," and rolled and put the palms of his hands on the floor, pushing himself up. Then he heard Donovan's gravelly voice close by. "Now that's the lad, Professor. A drink will fix it, and we've just got time for one."

He stood up with Donovan's help. Looking around him, he saw A Company's men, worse for the wear and tear of a hard brawl; but he saw L's troopers, too. The affair seemed to be over. He spotted Conboy at the bar, both elbows hooked to its edge. His face was red and tired-looking. Shafter walked over to his blouse and overcoat and put them on, feeling the pull of his sore places.

"Conboy, what'd you hit me with?"

"Me hand, damn you," muttered Conboy morosely. He downed his whiskey at a toss and looked dourly at the empty glass. "A man's a fool to be doin' this thing forever."

The crowd was tired but cheerful. There were no bad feelings left. Troopers stood along the bar shoulder to shoulder and drank the cheap Stud Horse whiskey. Conboy turned to Shafter. "You'll do," he said grudgingly. "I had to work for that hundred dollars."

Donovan gave him a look. "What hundred dollars?"

There was a man beside Conboy, a trooper with a dandy's haircut and a weakly handsome face; and this one said softly to Conboy, "Shut up, Conboy."

McDermott had gone out of the saloon, and now came hurriedly back. "Back door—back door. Patrol's comin'."

The troopers made a run for the saloon's rear doorways and went scrambling into the darkness. Out front the sergeant of the patrol made an unnecessary racket with his command. "Patrol, halt! Patrol, at ease! Jackson, you go over to the City of Paris while I see if everything's clear in the Stud Horse!" His voice carried clearly through the misty, cold night; it was a warning, as he knew it would be. Donovan caught Shafter's arm. "Come on, Professor. No use causin' Hackett any trouble."

"Donovan," said Shafter, "who was the slick one with Conboy?"

"Him? That's Lieutenant Garnett's striker. Purple's his name."

McDermott herded his band together and led the way down the bluff and across the sandy lowlands to the river, where two boats were drawn up on the beach. "Six to a boat," ordered McDermott. "Pile in." They shoved the boats into the water, troopers wading out and climbing aboard.

It was past taps when they reached the other side, under a bluff, and then lay flat, waiting the sentry's passage. A shape emerged from the misty blackness, paused, and faced the river. McDermott waited a decent interval and then called softly, "For God's sakes, Killen, move on to the end of your post. We're cold."

The sentry growled, "Keep your mouth shut. You want me to violate the articles of war?" He walked into the darkness. Then the troopers rose up and crept back to the barracks.

Shafter stripped and slid into his blankets. He was bruised and his head ached, but he felt content. Then he recalled Conboy's hundred-dollar chore. It was Garnett who had paid to have Conboy cut him to ribbons. He had been tired, but now he lay awake, his hatred rising afresh. He was still awake when Hines stepped from the orderly room with a lantern and played its light upon the row of bunks. He had stayed discreetly away until he was certain of the party's return and now, like an indulgent father, came to see if all were accounted for.

Chapter 8

ONE DAY THE restless Custer took his wife east for the winter. Without his driving energy the Seventh settled into a slower routine. Custer, they soon learned, was being feted and dined in New York.

Continued reports of disaffection came from the various Indian agencies. The Sioux, half-starved for want of enough government-issued beef, were leaving the reservations and returning to their own lands westward. The Seventh, now under Reno, scouted steadily in that direction to turn stragglers back, but it was like spreading a net against the wind. Near the end of November a detachment had a brush with a fleeing party of Sioux in which one trooper was injured; the Sioux disappeared in the darkness.

A hundred recruits arrived from Jefferson Barracks to fill the regiment's thin ranks. General Terry in St. Paul sent orders for the Seventh to overhaul its equipment and to whip its recruits into shape as rapidly as possible. On December 6 the telegraph flashed news from the East that the recalcitrant Sioux were to come into the reservations by January 31, or be treated as hostiles. That same day the first hard blizzard swept out of the north and pounded Lincoln for thirty-six hours, marking the end of train service from the East until spring.

One morning First Sergeant Hines summoned Shafter to the orderly room. He found Captain Moylan at the little desk with a letter in his hand. The captain said, "Hines, step out a moment," and waited until the old sergeant had gone.

"Kern," began Moylan, nodding at the letter, "this came to headquarters three or four days ago. Cooke gave it to me to handle as I saw fit." He handed it to Shafter and he sat back to watch Shafter's face as the latter looked down on the single page with its scent so familiar, and its light quick handwriting.

The Commanding Officer, Seventh Cavalry
Fort Lincoln, D.T.
    As a particular favor to one who is vitally interested in knowing the whereabouts of Kern Shafter, is he a member of your regiment?
                                      Very truly,
                                      Alice Macdougall

The scent and the handwriting roused vivid and painful memories in Shafter. He folded the page into smaller and smaller squares, tore it across, and dropped the pieces into the iron stove in the middle of the orderly room.

"No answer?" asked Moylan.

Shafter turned his head slowly from side to side. "None at all."

"I remember her very distinctly," said Moylan. "Last time was behind the lines at Fredericksburg. You were the officer then, and I was the sergeant. Very odd to recall. I always wondered one thing. Did Garnett marry her?"

"No."

"Damn him," growled the captain. "He's got a lot to answer for on Judgment Day." He looked up. "She still remembers you. Is this the first time you've heard of her?"

"No. I have heard indirectly of her many times. She has spent a fortune tracing me."

"She has a fortune to spend," said Moylan.

"She always had everything she wanted."

"Until she met Garnett," amended Moylan. "Then she had nothing. It didn't take her long to find out she guessed wrong, did it? She has apparently been sorry for ten years. Doesn't that have any effect on you?"

"No."

Moylan looked at Shafter with steady attention. "It is logical that you should hate Garnett. He'll use his weight on you where he can. He's already tried, hasn't he?"

"Yes," said Shafter. "But that can work both ways, Myles."

"Do nothing you'll regret."

"Regret? If it were in my power to put a bullet through his heart, I'd have no regrets."

"That is not what I meant," said Moylan. "He ruined you professionally once. Don't open yourself to that again by any act."

Shafter said nothing and the captain looked down at his broad hands. "We need a sergeant to ride the mail between Lincoln and Fargo while the railroad's not running. I told Cooke I had the man for it. You are the man."

"Yes, sir," said Shafter, and smiled a little. "You want me out of the post this winter."

"I want no collision between you and Garnett. Report to Cooke for further instructions."

He sat back after Shafter had gone and drew a piece of paper before him. He dipped the pen and stroked the corners of his mustaches and then began:

My dear General:
  It would require the colonel's approval to carry this matter to the adjutant general's attention. Therefore, I write directly to you as an old friend, to bring to your attention the case of Kern Shafter, once an officer of the Fourteenth Ohio . . .

Shafter pulled on his heavy coat and mittens and moved into the white outer world. The wind, driving from the north, had banked all exposed walls of the post eave-high with snow and had laid a two-foot covering across the parade. Shafter moved along the narrow shoulder-high lane carved out by the shovel details, and reported to the adjutant's office. Cooke gave him his instructions.

"You'll have a sleigh and two mules, and you'll eat and be

quartered along the route. The round trip to Fargo is approximately two weeks, depending on weather. Follow the railroad closely. You can't see the track, but the telegraph poles will always guide you. Here is a list of ranches and shelters along the way. Pick your team and put your storm pack together. Draw on the quartermaster for extra robes and blankets. Leave at reveille tomorrow. Get the pouches at the fort's post office and drop back here for special dispatches. You'll also take the outgoing mail from Bismarck. I have no more to add, except that you should watch your weather most closely. Sometimes you'll have no more than an hour's warning of a blizzard."

Shafter spent the morning picking a team and stowing the sleigh. Then he hitched his mules to the sleigh and left the fort for a trial run. In the middle of the afternoon he drew up before Josephine Russell's house and saw her come to the door. "If you're staying awhile," she called, "drive your outfit into the barn."

He left the team and sleigh tied in the barn's runway, and struggled back to the house through the fresh snow. He slid out of his heavy coat in the room's warmth and stood with his back to the heater, watching Josephine's hands work at her knitting needles. She sat near a window for the sake of the light, her face now lifting to him, now dropping to her work. She had on a dress the color of dark roses, with a large cameo brooch at the neck.

"What's your errand today, Kern?"

"Just trying out a pair of mules for the Fargo mail run."

"Did you put in for that?"

"It was assigned to me, but I have no objections."

"No," she said, "you wouldn't object. When I first met you, Kern, I thought perhaps you were of the faded-gentleman type. When I heard you had joined the Seventh I thought, There goes a man with delusions of romantic adventure. But you have done very well for yourself. Is that little purple spot on your temple the place Conboy hit you?"

"Who tells you of these things, Josephine?"

"An army post is the biggest whispering gallery on earth."

"I got knocked out," he said, and stretched his feet before him, loose in the chair and very comfortable. The girl went about her knitting, her head bent.

"You're strange," she murmured. "You've had education and many pleasant things, but you go back to a raw and very rough kind of life. Doesn't it cause you any remorse?"

"You are thinking that I'm ducking out of civil life because it was too hard," he said, "letting the government do my thinking in return for eighteen dollars a month."

"It has occurred to me," she said.

"I had no obligations in civil life," he told her. "I had nothing—and I knew it. A man must feel he belongs to something."

She held her eyes down to her work while he spoke, and her fingers moved gracefully with the knitting needles. The silence of the house was a pleasant silence to Shafter. He tipped his head, watching the ceiling, listening to the ticking of a clock.

"How old are you, Kern?"

"Thirty-two."

"Have you ever been married?"

"No," he said.

"Engaged?"

"Yes."

"Are you now?"

"No."

She laid down her knitting and let her hands lie idle in her lap while she gave him an exacting appraisal. "It was something painful, wasn't it?"

He nodded and let that serve for an answer. Presently she shook her head and took up her knitting again, speaking as much to herself as to him. "It has left its effect. You look at women as though they had qualities which men should be on guard against."

"I was a fool once," he said. "I will not be a fool twice."

With a little gesture of impatience she put the needlework aside and rose and went into the kitchen. He heard her call back, "When does A Company have its ball for the enlisted men?"

"Two weeks away, I believe."

"It will remind you of other days."

"I had no intention of attending," he said.

She came out in a little while with a cup of coffee for him, and one for herself. She took her chair again. "One stretch of road between here and Fargo you'll want to watch. There's no shelter of any kind for thirty miles, if a blizzard should catch you. It is between Romain's ranch and a little section house called Fossil Siding. When do you leave—when will you be back?"

"Leave in the morning. Should return in ten or twelve days unless the weather stops me."

She rose and stood at the window with her back to him. Suddenly his mind was fully on her and the thought of her went through him and kicked up its reaction. He got up and reached for his coat.

"This is a lazy man's life."

She turned and watched him button up the big overcoat and grow bulky. The uniform took much of the first-noticed softness from him, toughening him. "I haven't been to a dance since early fall," she murmured.

"It's strictly an enlisted man's ball. You're for gentlemen and officers, Josephine."

"Am I?" she asked coolly. "How do you know that?" Her eyes held his glance, with the hint of a temper as aggressive as his own. He saw in her at that moment a reckless spirit. She had wanted something and she had asked for it.

He said, "I can't be put in the position of refusing a lady's wish. Will you go to the ball with me?"

"Of course," she said, smiling slightly.

He moved to the door and turned there. "You gave yourself away," she told him. "If you weren't a gentleman, it wouldn't have been difficult to refuse me."

"Maybe," he said, "I really wanted to take you. But it's not a good thing for you. It will cut you out from being invited to officers' dances. When you let yourself be seen with an enlisted man, you are crossing one of the toughest boundaries in the world."

"You are a rough-and-tumble man, Sergeant, but I think I can hold my own with you."

He grinned as he lifted his cap, then went into the snow, openly laughing, and presently curled around the house with the sleigh. She was on the front porch and waved at him as he went by. She stood awhile in the biting, still air, now wishing she had told Shafter that Garnett had invited her to the officers' ball and that she had accepted. It was the reason she had deliberately forced an invitation to the enlisted men's ball from Shafter. She knew that he disliked the officer. This was her way of taking the edge from any resentment he might feel toward her for going with Garnett.

She went into the house and closed the door, standing with her back to it. Why should I go to the trouble of saving his feelings? What do his feelings matter to me? I am simply another woman he means to keep at a proper distance. She remembered all that he had said, and she sensed much that he had not said. The woman, she thought, must have been brutal, to produce his present state of mind. Yet even now he is not sure he doesn't love her.

She moved across the room, despising the woman, whoever she was, and outraged at a story she could only guess at.

Chapter 9

SHAFTER MADE HIS first trip to Fargo in six days. By daybreak the following morning he was on his way back, bearing not only mail but several packages for Bismarck merchants and a little pouch of dispatches from department headquarters at St. Paul.

He had also a week's collection of newspapers and read them at night, in one ranch house or another. President Grant had ordered a winter campaign as a result of the failure of the Indians to return peacefully to their reservations on the deadline of January 31. One headline said: CUSTER WILL LEAD WINTER EXPEDITION. CAN BOY GENERAL REPEAT BRILLIANT WASHITA STRATEGY?

The system of post traderships was under fire and Congressman Clymer, suggesting scandal, had asked the House for authority to investigate the Indian Bureau and the War Department. There was, in all the papers, a growing preoccupation with the Indian question, and a growing scent of trouble brewing. There were also many items regarding Custer. He had given a talk at the Lotus Club. His spectacular presence was noted and admired at the theater.

THEY HAD BEEN TO AN after-theater party in a mansion facing Central Park where, surrounded by money and power and beauty, Custer had dominated the conversation both by his exuberance and by his reputation. Now, at two o'clock in the morning, he and his wife returned to their hotel rooms.

The general flung his hat, cape, and dress coat the full length of the room and missed the chair at which he aimed. He let them lie and walked a circle of the sitting room.

"Vacation's about gone, old girl," he said. "We're coming to the end of our period in heaven. No more shows, no more parties for another year. Maybe for two or three years. The army is a strange thing. A little glitter at retreat when the band plays and everybody's in full dress. A little of that followed by hours of drudgery and tedium. It is the tedium that eats out an officer's heart. Year after year of it."

She came toward him. "Autie, you shouldn't be restless. We've had such a good time. It's nice to have a famous husband. George Armstrong Custer rings the bell and the door opens. I thought of that tonight, watching you talk. I was very proud of you."

He looked at her, smiling. He stood in a moment's rare repose, gentled by her softness, by her love. But it was only for a moment. He had supped at the table of the mighty, and the mighty had been deferent to him. Now he saw that ended as he turned back to his frontier post. He saw the undramatic years stretch out ahead of him—years of plodding, unspectacular duties. He had reached the pinnacle at twenty-five and all the subsequent years had been anticlimax. In another ten years he would be forty-six, one more middle-aged Civil War officer whose greatness was only a fading memory, whose place in the sun was taken by younger men.

"Oh, Libby," he groaned. "I'm in a blind alley. I see the stupid and the dull all around me, rising above me, fawning or tricking their way to power. My enemies are in command of the War Department, cheating me out of chances, giving other men places I ought to have. If there was a break I might make—if there was an opening anywhere, I'd seize it."

"Autie," said Mrs. Custer quietly, "civilization is not too good for you. I think we will be happier when we return to the command." But a cloud passed across her expressive face as she remembered that spring was not far away. Spring meant campaigning; it meant Autie marching away. Suddenly she turned back into the bedroom.

Custer seized the day's paper and lay out full length on the floor to read it. He became engrossed in a story concerning Congressman Clymer's proposed investigation of the War Department. Presently he sprang up and went to the writing table. Mrs. Custer heard his pen scratching violently through the quietness.

"To whom are you writing, Autie?" she called from the bedroom.

"I'm offering my services as witness to Clymer. I think we shall get to the bottom of some scandal, and I know enough of it to lend a hand."

"Do you think it wise?"

"Wise or not, I shall do it."

He finished his letter and leaned back in the chair, feeling a thrust of hope. It might lead somewhere; it might give him an opportunity to smash at his enemies, to bring him before the people on an issue. Since action was his only gift, he had to have action to survive.

GARNETT CALLED FOR Josephine at eight and stood a moment in the Russell living room, admiring her. "You must forgive me for using a very old phrase," he said. "I had no idea you were so damned beautiful."

She was round and mature within a black dress whose solid coloring was broken by little streaks of gold thread along her breasts and sleeves. Her hair, extremely black, lay high and shining on her head, exposing white neck and ears, and a pair of earrings moved slightly as her head turned. She watched him, smiling but not entirely taken in. "It is pleasant to hear, Lieutenant."

At the fort they entered the commissary building, which served as the ballroom, its stores pushed aside and its walls and rafters decorated with colored paper shields, crossed arms, and bunting. The regimental band sat on a platform at one end of the room. Major Reno, commanding in the absence of Custer, led the grand march with his wife; afterward the crowd broke into sets for the quadrille.

The officers of the five companies stationed at Fort Lincoln were present in full-dress uniforms, gold epaulets, sash, and regimental cord draped over the shoulder. And this color flashed and glittered against the dresses of the ladies. They danced the sets; they danced the polka, the schottische, and the waltz. Josephine went swinging away in the arms of this officer or that one. She stood in one little group or another, all of them gay and all charged with little bursts of gossip and laughter and bantering.

"I admire that dress," said Mrs. Smith to Josephine.

"I bought it this fall in the East. I suppose it's the last new one I'll have for three or four years."

"Why," replied Mrs. Smith, "I'm wearing one six years old."

As the music began again Major Barrows led Josephine away, leaving his wife for Garnett's attention. Garnett put his arm about her slim waist and swung her out upon the floor. Neither of them spoke for a considerable time, he staring over the top of her dark hair and she watching the couples about her with blank disinterest. Now and then she caught sight of Josephine and followed the girl with a narrowed glance. Finally she said in her coolest voice, "Your taste is excellent, Edward."

Garnett said, equally cool, "Do you object?"

"Why should I?"

But he knew she was furious, and the knowledge pleased him.

"I shall have the sleigh at the same place tomorrow afternoon," he murmured.

"No," she said. "Not so soon. I can't always be finding reasonable excuses to go to town."

They danced in complete silence until the music stopped. He took her arm and walked her slowly back toward her husband. He looked straight ahead of him when he spoke. "Tomorrow afternoon, Margaret?"

They had almost rejoined the group when he heard her soft, smothered answer: "All right."

At three in the morning Garnett returned Josephine to her house and stepped inside. The elder Russell sat asleep in a rocker with a stout fire going. At their approach he woke and moved off to bed. Garnett stood in the middle of the room, holding his dress hat tucked under an arm. He made a little bow with his head, watching Josephine with his appreciative eyes. She removed her coat and stood by the stove, warming her hands.

"Am I welcome in this house?" he asked.

"Yes," she said. "And thank you, Mr. Garnett, for a most delightful evening." He was a handsome creature and his interest was a flattering thing; she admitted that to herself.

"May I pick you up for a ride in the sleigh some morning?"

She didn't answer it; she simply nodded. He drew a breath and walked toward her until she was within reach of him.

"Don't spoil a good impression, Mr. Garnett."

"You're thinking I am too solicitous of ladies, aren't you?"

"I think," she said, "they are a challenge to your talents."

Sometimes she threw him off stride by her frankness. He flushed. "Women have played their light games of flirt with me. I have responded in kind. You seem to be aware of that. But I'm dead serious toward you. This is no game with me, Josephine. When I leave here tonight I'll be troubled with myself all the way home."

"Now why, for mercy's sakes?" she demanded, really surprised.

He shrugged. "As you stood there at the stove just now I grew completely disgusted with myself. I never thought any woman could humble me in that manner. Do you see what I mean?"

"Perhaps," she ventured, studying him.

He made a little bow to her and said, "Good night," then turned to the door. As he opened it he swung back, and said with a complete confidence, "You must know me for what I am. I mean to have you. I mean to make you want me."

SHAFTER MADE THE mail trip to Fargo and back in thirteen days, reaching Fort Lincoln in the afternoon. It was Saturday, and the men of the troop had spent most of the day dressing up the quartermaster building for their ball that night. Then, having received Moylan's permission to use the mail sleigh, Shafter presented himself at Josephine's house promptly at seven thirty.

When she came to the door he was astonished at the rough shock that went through him. Her presence did that to him, the smile breaking over her lips, the sudden view of loveliness she presented to him. She said, "It is a little early. Come in for a moment."

He stood wholly attentive, the sight of her sharpening his eyes. She noticed it and made a slight turn and stood before him for his inspection. "Will I do for your ball, Kern?"

"I've not seen anyone like you."

"Come now," she chided him, "you've seen no woman at all for a week. That's no comparison."

"I can go farther back than that," he said.

She tipped her head, immensely curious as to his past. "How far back must you go to find a woman you'd want to stand beside me?"

"Once, a long time ago, there was one."

"She meant a great deal?"

He nodded.

The glow left Josephine's face. "Where is she now?"

"Somewhere, alive."

"Alive in you. I hear her walking around your heart."

"All you hear," he said, "are echoes."

She turned slowly away, moving toward the corner table in the room and speaking over her shoulder. "It must have been an intense affair to leave so lasting an impression."

"A man and woman in love is scarcely a mild thing, is it?"

"That depends on the woman and on the man."

"I'm speaking for myself."

She turned about. "Kern, I don't think I like to be the instrument which brings back those memories to you." Then she smiled. "What a strange way to start an evening. Time to go, isn't it?"

He lifted her coat from a chair and held it for her. He was close to her, so that when she turned to him and looked up she saw the image of her face in his eyes. His lids narrowed as he watched her, and she saw what was happening to him, but she stood still, her lips slightly apart. She thought, This is foolish, and felt a heavy undertow of feeling sweep against her, unsettling her resolution. For a moment they watched each other, completely still; and then she took his arm. "Time to go," she repeated.

He brought her back at one in the morning. When he had taken care of the mules he came into the house and found Mr. Russell standing sleepily by the stove. Russell said, "My girl is staying out late. Three last week and one o'clock tonight."

"My record is better than the lieutenant's by two hours," said Shafter. It was Sergeant Hines who had privately said to him, during a break in the dancing, "You're flyin' high, Shafter. She was at officers' ball last week with Garnett."

"That's right," said Russell and left the room.

Josephine brought out coffee and a little tray with bread and honey and cheese. She put these things on a table and Shafter brought up a chair and sat down opposite her. She sat back with her coffee, her eyes scanning him over the rim of the cup. "Who told you about my going with Garnett?"

"One of the boys. If I'd known it, I wouldn't have taken you."

"Why?"

"A woman can't play both sides of the line. You're an officers' woman. In going with me you have shut yourself out of being invited to the officers' side again."

"Isn't that my affair more than yours?"

"No," he said.

She sipped at her coffee, never for a moment taking her eyes from him. "It really isn't that," she told him. "It's Garnett, isn't it? You were embarrassed by him in this house once. Is that the cause of your disliking him so greatly?"

"Josephine," he said, "I hope you had a pleasant evening," and rose. She sat still, watching him pull into his coat.

"It started out very well, Kern," she told him, "and ended badly. But I really forced myself on you, so I shall not complain."

Her words broke through the reserve behind which he seemed to want to take shelter. "It is Garnett," he admitted. "But it goes a long way back. There is no use adding to that."

"If it is so far in the past, why bring it forward to influence your judgment of me? I have nothing to do with your past."

"You're right," he said very dryly. "And that leaves the matter straight. As I said before, you're an officers' woman and I have no business here."

She rose and spoke in an almost antagonistic tone. "Did you run from Garnett once before—as you're doing now?"

He let out an enormous sigh as he came toward her. "You don't know me very well," he said and took her arms and pulled her forward. "It would have been better if you'd left me alone." Then he kissed her, holding her so strongly that she felt pain in her ribs.

He stepped back. "That was foolish," he said.

"Was it?" she asked. "Last time you kissed me it was for the purpose of offending me and getting rid of me. What was your meaning this time?"

"We're fighting now. It isn't worth that."

She was embittered by the way he spoke, and she wanted to punish him. "You've had one fight over a woman and now you think there's no woman worth that trouble. You have taken most of the illusions out of your life, haven't you? You are very safe with your little comforts. I don't like you, Kern. You're a fool for thinking you can live without illusions. You'll never have anything else half as real. Good night."

When he had gone she stood still, wondering why he had so profoundly shaken her. I was right, she thought. I should never have permitted myself to be interested in him.

Chapter 10

SHAFTER WAS IN Fargo in February when news came over the wire that the Indian commissioner had surrendered to the War Department control of all Sioux not on their reservations. Making his back-and-forth circuit during the following weeks, Shafter watched the story unfold. The Sioux and Cheyenne, frightened by the intentions of the War Department, fled from their reservations, going back through bitterest weather to their old grounds on the Powder, the Rosebud, and the Tongue. Meanwhile, the commander of the army, Sherman, had dispatched a column under Crook north from Fort Fetterman, the intent being that Crook and Terry, coming from different directions, should catch the Sioux in a nutcracker. Crook's column launched a surprise attack on the village of Crazy Horse, on the upper sources of the Powder. But the Sioux, fighting in desperation, threw Crook's column into disorder and drove it back to Fetterman. Terry, meanwhile, found his plans wrecked by a steady succession of blizzards.

Early in March the post-trader scandal, so long simmering in

Washington, boiled over. A broker in New York came forward with evidence that Secretary of War Belknap, or Belknap's wife, had taken money for aiding certain men to secure profitable traderships. Belknap resigned on the eve of a Congressional investigation. At the same time Custer, whose leave had expired, took the train west to St. Paul with his wife and there reported to General Terry.

Terry gave him his orders. Custer was to go to Lincoln, put his regiment in readiness, and march at the first break of weather to meet the Sioux and to gather them in or crush them. "As soon as practicable," said Terry, "Sherman will get Crook in motion again, headed north."

Once at the fort, Custer galvanized the regiment into feverish action; and at the same time departmental orders went out from Washington, sending the three companies in Louisiana and the two at Fort Totten back to Lincoln. For the first time in many years the regiment was again to be whole.

Custer had scarcely returned to duty, however, when a telegram arrived from the Congressional investigating committee, ordering him to testify in the Belknap investigation. Near the end of March he returned to Washington.

The days and the weeks dragged on while the committee slowly worked its way through a mass of testimony. One by one the lost companies of the Seventh returned from out-of-the-way assignments and the quarters at Lincoln, never meant for a full regiment, spilled over. The ice in the river went out with a grinding and a crashing like an artillery cannonade, but the weather—now clear, now swinging down with its northern fury—was still dangerous. The regiment drilled and made its preparations, and by means of the newspapers followed the testimony of their commander in Washington who, prodded by question upon question, at last produced this one startling statement:

> "Fraud among the sutlers could not have been carried on without the connivance of the Secretary of War. . . . You ask me of the morale and character of the army. The service has not been demoralized even though the head of it, the Secretary of War, has shown himself to be so unworthy."

Captain Benteen smiled a wintry smile when he read that. "The damned fool," he rasped to his lieutenant, Francis Gibson. "Belknap was President Grant's friend. In saying Belknap was a scoundrel, Custer is telling the people publicly that he thinks the President is a scoundrel. Do you think Grant will stand that in silence?"

Out in St. Paul, General Terry, all arrangements made, waited for Custer's release from Washington. Custer, with the campaign hourly growing nearer, saw himself in danger of being left behind, his regiment marching without him. He appealed to Sherman, who said, "You had better see the President. It is in his hands entirely."

"I have been there twice. He refuses to see me," answered Custer.

"Better try again," said Sherman.

Custer went wearily back to the White House and handed in his card. He sat in the anteroom, a lank, flamboyant man slowly being humbled and made conscious of his own helplessness as the hours passed. Men went by him, in and out of the President's office. At five o'clock in the evening the President's secretary came out with his message.

"The President," said the secretary, "will not see you."

Custer stood up, paling a little, the dash and the vigor for the moment crushed from him. Then he murmured, "Very well, sir," and left the room.

That night, with his wife, he caught the train west. As he stopped at Chicago to transfer for St. Paul an aide of General Sheridan's handed him a copy of a telegram dispatched from Sherman to Terry:

> GENERAL: I AM AT THIS MOMENT ADVISED THAT GENERAL CUSTER STARTED LAST NIGHT FOR ST. PAUL AND FORT ABRAHAM LINCOLN. HE WAS NOT JUSTIFIED IN LEAVING WITHOUT SEEING THE PRESIDENT OR MYSELF. PLEASE INTERCEPT HIM AT CHICAGO OR ST. PAUL AND ORDER HIM TO HALT AND WAIT FOR FURTHER ORDERS. MEANWHILE, LET THE EXPEDITION FROM FORT LINCOLN PROCEED WITHOUT HIM.

Custer gave his wife an odd, desperate glance. "Libby," he said, "they have stripped me of my command."

Custer at once boarded the train for St. Paul with Libby. He was afraid—he who never had known fear before. He was humiliated and humbled, bereft of his power, stripped and held still by the brooding presence in the White House.

As soon as he reached St. Paul he went directly to Terry. "I am entirely in your hands, General," he said. "Neither Sherman nor Sheridan will intercede for me. The President would not see me. Now I am condemned for not having visited the President before I left. If it is his wish to humiliate me before the country, he is succeeding. I do not believe I deserve it."

Terry was a mild man, a man deeply humane, tolerant, and sympathetic. There was a great capacity for forbearance in him. Even so, he delivered a gentle reprimand. "You've been in the service long enough to know the impropriety of making public comment on your superiors."

Custer flushed, but held his peace. Terry thoughtfully considered the problem. "Impetuousness has been your lifelong creed," he said at last. "It is an admirable thing until it runs into something else, which is insubordination. An officer of your rank, commanding the lives of eight hundred men, must have respect for order and for caution. The lives of all these men are entirely at your disposition. I have complete faith in you as a fighter and I should feel much better with you in personal command of the Seventh, but I cannot deny that the President has cause to suspend you from duty."

"Is there no way you can put in a word for me?" asked Custer.

Terry turned to his desk and took up his pen, carefully composing a message. Upon finishing, he passed it to Custer. It read:

> I have no desire to question the orders of the President. Whether Lieutenant Colonel Custer shall be permitted to accompany the column or not, I shall go in command of it. I do not know the reasons upon which the orders given rest; but if these reasons do not forbid it, Lieutenant Colonel Custer's services would be very valuable with his regiment.

Custer's relief came up strong and ruddy to his face; his spirits rushed from extreme depth to extreme height. He said, "I am forever in your debt, General," and left the room.

The message went to General Sheridan, who added his endorsement. It was then forwarded to General Sherman, who dispatched it to the White House, and there it rested in the hands of Grant—a man whose convictions were as immovable as polar ice, whose enemies were seldom forgiven. Yet the President was a military man and the western campaign waited, and Terry had expressed an inclination for Custer's services. So he dispatched his answer to Sherman, who wired it to Terry:

> THE PRESIDENT SENDS ME WORD THAT IF YOU WANT GENERAL CUSTER ALONG, HE WITHDRAWS HIS OBJECTIONS. ADVISE CUSTER TO BE PRUDENT, NOT TO TAKE ANY NEWSPAPERMEN, WHO ALWAYS MAKE MISCHIEF, AND TO ABSTAIN FROM PERSONALITIES IN THE FUTURE.

Nothing but a sense of propriety restrained a wild whoop of triumph from Custer when Terry gave him the news. He stood by to hear Terry's final instructions: "Return to Fort Lincoln by the first train and pull your regiment together. I shall join you at the first opportunity. I wish to march as soon as I arrive."

When Custer entrained for Lincoln he was a man with a fixed idea. Behind him lay humiliation; but ahead lay redemption in the form of one more glorious opportunity. The Seventh was his regiment, as all the country knew. It would be the Seventh which seized the chance and pressed it—and restored his prestige. In this game of power—played before the audience of the nation—he meant to produce a trump against Grant, to seize his chance by whatever means it had to be obtained. He looked ahead, and saw no great difficulty in gaining complete freedom of movement from Terry, once he was in the field.

TOWARD THE MIDDLE OF April, Shafter left Lincoln for what he believed would be the last mail trip. Snow still blanketed the ground from a series of storms and one full-blown blizzard. But here and there on the railroad's right-of-way the snow had begun to shrink back, permitting section crews to repair the unsettled grade and the warped track. Trains would soon be in operation.

He arrived at Fargo to find the dispatches not yet arrived from St. Paul, and he was delayed a week, awaiting their arrival. The mail, the newspapers, and the telegraph wires were teeming with news of freshened activity. General Crook had again started north from Fetterman to box the Sioux on the south and drive them north toward the Missouri. Meanwhile, in Montana, General Gibbon had formed a column from troops stationed at Forts Shaw and Ellis and had gotten under way the middle of March. He was to push east to the Yellowstone, make contact with the Sioux, and press them toward the Dakota column, which would be advancing from Lincoln. Somewhere in the almost unknown region west of the Missouri and south of the Yellowstone, the plan called for a junction of Terry's column with Crook's and Gibbon's. In that same area the Sioux moved like shadows upon the earth, keyed up by their great leaders and their medicine men.

The dispatches from St. Paul arrived at last on a Saturday train, and Shafter planned to set out with them in the morning. He was in his hotel room that night when somebody knocked on his door. He said, "Come in." A woman entered, made a little gesture with her hand, tried to smile and failed, then closed the door and placed her back to it.

"Kern," she breathed. "Kern. Come to me."

Why, he thought fuzzily, as if he'd been awakened from sleep, she's ten years older. Her shape was the same straight and lovely shape he had known so long ago. Her face was the same expressive face, the lips warm and ready, the eyes watching him and willing to respond. She had always worn excellent clothes, and wore them now. The jade pendants at her ears reminded him somehow of the night he had found her with Garnett. And she wore the ring he had given her.

"Hello, Alice."

"Come to me, Kern."

He lowered his eyes and remembered how many hundreds of times he had called her back to his mind and had created the image of her. He lifted his glance quickly, to match the image with her presence before him; and there was an instant in which the image lay upon the reality and made a small blur. The two did not perfectly blend. Then the image died and the reality of her presence was with him.

She said, "I've spent years looking for you, Kern. I found you were at Lincoln. I was on my way there. Then I saw you tonight on the street. After all that, can't you come the last ten feet?" But she saw he had no intention of coming, and with a gesture of her shoulders she walked toward him. She touched him and looked up. Then she slid her arms around him and gave him a full and long kiss.

A great embarrassment went through him at his lack of response.

She felt it as well and presently stepped back, hopelessness and half terror in her eyes. She murmured, "Would it do any good to go all the way back, Kern? To explain the kind of a girl I was, the foolishness in me, the strange things I seemed to want and then found out I didn't want? Would it help if I said I made a mistake, and have lived ever since trying to find you and repair the mistake?"

"No," he said, "it wouldn't do any good."

"I can't believe the deepness of all we felt could die out entirely. I can't believe it would die at all. It was everything to us. How could it be nothing now? I thought you'd remember the best of what we had. That maybe you would carry a hope that someday . . . that we could go back."

He heard, in her words, all that he himself had secretly believed. He had nourished the wish, even as he had closed himself up and sought simplicity for his life. His disillusion, he realized, had only been a screen for his hope. Yet now, with Alice Macdougall before him, he had no desire to revive the hope. Something had happened to him. Maybe it was the weariness of ten years. Maybe it was something else.

She looked at him in silence. An appeal was on her face, a willingness to come to him on any terms. He felt the shame of her position and was embarrassed again. "No," he said, "nothing can come back, for us."

She made a sharp turn and walked across the room to the door, then swung back. Her expression was dull and indifferent. "Kern," she said, "it would help me if I knew one thing. Do you hate me so much?"

"No. I don't hate you at all."

"Then you never loved me as deeply as you thought you did. I haven't really wrecked your life. I only wrecked my own."

He wished he could tell her how the long years had been with him, how far he had traveled to escape the memory of her. But he saw that she was comforted by her belief that he had failed in depth of emotion. It restored her self-respect. She stood still, giving him a long and smileless glance. She was a woman taking away some final memento to mark the end of a part of her life. She murmured, "You've changed very little. You look well." Then she opened the door and went away.

He walked over and closed the door. He stood with his face to it, trying to explain to himself why the memory of her had been so powerful in him and now meant nothing. He was free in a way he had not been free before. He thought, Something's happened and I have not been aware of it.

Chapter 11

HE LEFT FARGO the next morning and spent that night and the next at ranches along the way. Both days a bland, warm wind blew from the south, turning the snow beneath him to slush.

By morning of the third day the thaw had hardened again into a tough crust which made bad footing for the mules. Shafter buckled onto each mule a set of small leather snowshoes for better traction. Far ahead of him, just visible in the steel-colored haze, lay Romain's ranch, and beyond that the Benson ranch, which was four miles short of Bismarck.

At three o'clock he passed the Romain ranch and pointed toward Benson's house, now aware of a forming darkness distant in the north. By the time the Romain ranch was an hour behind him the temperature had swung sharply down and the air was wholly motionless. The Benson house was still two hours ahead, and the storm was now displaying itself northward in the shape of a ragged wall of cloud columns. He thought of the possibilities of shelter— the culverts into which a man might dig his way, and then of one small section house.

He had enough experience to possess great respect for those northern clouds. He had seen them form and come on, sometimes slowly, sometimes with the speed of an express train. He checked his position in relation to the nearest culvert on the railroad. Then he took out his compass and got a course on the Benson house. It lay directly along the telegraph poles, one point south of due west. He studied the clouds with a searching attention over a quarter hour, sending the sleigh along at a fast clip. It would be a storm of some severity, he decided, but probably not as dangerous as those of midwinter. In one sudden flip of decision he made up his mind to continue.

At five o'clock the Benson house was forty-five minutes before him and in clear view. At ten minutes after five there was no Benson house to be seen. Day drained out of the sky and through the stillness he heard the distant reverberation of wind, like the shuddering of volcanic action. He snugged his collar around his neck, lifted his scarf to the bridge of his nose, and suddenly put the team to a run, meanwhile watching the gray wall, boiling from earth to heaven, move on with its stately, terrible power.

Blackness moved over the sky and one first streak of wind puffed softly across the stillness. Shafter looked at his watch, putting his head close to the dial. The time was then twenty-five minutes past five and the Benson house should be another twenty minutes ahead. He had scarcely stuffed the watch into his pocket when the full pressure of the blizzard seized him, shook him in the sleigh's seat, and became a great yelling in his ears. A wall of hardened snow hit him and closed steadily down until he had only a vague sight of the mules.

He felt them give to the wind's pressure and pulled them back. Shortly he passed a telegraph pole within arm's distance and calculated the location of the next pole. In this way, fighting the team's drift, he made his departure from one pole and his landfall on another, observing that he missed the poles by wider and wider margins as he went on. The pressure of the storm grew greater and his forward progress became a game of guessing how far northward it was necessary to swing. Meanwhile, he took to counting the poles, realizing he could not read the watch in the darkness now surrounding him. He made his rapid estimate of distance. It was a rough four miles to Benson's and there were thirty poles to the mile; that would make a hundred and twenty poles between this point and Benson's, the poles standing a hundred and seventy-six feet apart.

He drew hard to the north. He counted the approximate distance before the next pole was expected to show its thin blur nearby, but he saw nothing. He hauled hard to the north again, tension pulling at the muscles of his belly as he counted the seconds in his head. He thought, Maybe I'm swinging too much. But the force of the wind had been growing greater and he knew his own senses were tricking him.

He had by then gone a distance sufficient to include three poles and had seen nothing. There was only one way left to him of checking his whereabouts. Pulling around, he headed full into the teeth of the wind, lashing with the ends of his reins to push the team on. The sleigh rose with a roll of snow and tipped down and he felt the runners grit and bump along the spotty covering over the railroad ties. He had struck the right-of-way.

He turned with it and followed it. A snowplow had recently cut a partial way through here, leaving shoulders to either side of the track. Thus more or less guided, the mules settled to a steady pulling. Meanwhile, he counted the poles he could not see by judging the distance between, and in this manner covered the second mile.

The wind and the sheer weight of the coldness bored through him. He felt it first in his legs as a stiffness and then as a pain; and then he felt it in his bones. He had the muffler drawn twice around his head, but the wind flung its riot against his ears until the steady drumming made him dizzy. For a moment he closed his eyes. When he opened them the team had stopped.

He brought the reins sharply down on the mules' rumps. Then he remembered that there was a short, low trestle over a coulee two miles east of Benson's house. The mules had come upon the trestle and were afraid of it. Pulling them around, he drove over a hump of snow and sighted a pole as it slid by, and now once more he aimed his course from pole to pole.

The wind keeled him on the seat. The force of it shoved the sleigh sidewise and the screaming sound of the storm grew more and more shrill. He kept stamping his feet until he discovered he had lost all feeling in them. His right side, so steadily pounded by the wind, had grown stiff. He stopped the team as soon as he realized his danger, then stepped from the sleigh. He held the reins and walked forward, no sensation of weight on his feet, and got to the head of the team and led it forward.

The physical exertion warmed him, but it tired him. He thought, I'm not that soft, and knew at once how much the blizzard had sapped him. He had put the reins over his shoulder, and was guiding the mules as well as pulling them on against their inclination to stop when he walked straight into a signal post stuck up beside the right-of-way. The team had stopped behind him, and he put his hand on the post and felt upward until he reached the square board on top. He stood still, the wind pushing him against the post, trying to picture the railroad as it moved toward Bismarck, trying to spot the signal board's location.

"Why, hell," he said, "this is the Benson whistle-stop sign. The house is two hundred feet straight south."

He crawled back along the side of the near mule, got into the sleigh, and squared the team into the south, with the wind full at his back. He felt the mules strain upward on the ridge of snow, and falter. He hit them with the rein ends and yelled at the top of his voice. The sleigh tilted, came to the snow's summit, and dropped down. The mules slogged slowly forward.

There was a flurry of snow in front of him, a flickering screen of it across his eyes; and then he realized it was a ray of house light which had made the snow visible. He guided the team to the left and made a patient circle, driving the sleigh close by the walls of the house. Darkness came solidly down again as soon as the house light faded, but he had the picture of Benson's yard clear in his mind and went on with confidence. When he reached the barn he got down and scraped his hand along the wall until he found a door latch. Then he rolled the door open and pulled team and sleigh into the barn's runway. He hauled the door almost shut and turned and put his back to it.

"Better stay here until I thaw out," he said aloud to himself. "Better not go into a warm house."

Exhaustion hit him on the head like a maul. He let his feet slide forward a little so that he was braced against the wall. His belly was empty and his throat dry; and his body was a patchwork of stinging aches and numbness. He slapped his hands together and he said, "They're all right." He took off his gloves and slid his hands underneath the muffler which lay ice-cemented around his throat and ears. He pinched his ears, then pulled away the muffler and began a steady rubbing. Streaks of colored light swam across his blurred vision.

He wanted to sit down but he kept himself moving, walking around and around the sleigh, stamping his feet. He unhitched the team and for a quarter hour groped in the dark to remove the harness, every motion of his hand requiring a deliberate push of his will. He let the harness fall on the ground and turned to the door. When he stepped outside, the storm nailed him to the wall so that he had to wheel sideways and go shoulder first into the wind. Guiding himself by the faint light he saw, he finally reached the house's back door and entered a dark room. Ahead there was a farther door open, through which a light burned. He went through that doorway and saw two blurred forms before him. A woman's voice came sharply at him.

"Kern—where've you been?"

She came to him, reaching toward the scarf around his neck. When she pulled it away the crusted ice rattled on the floor, and she laid her hands on his ears. He closed his eyes and pushed his fingers against the lids, then opened them to find Josephine watching him.

"I'll get you some coffee. Are your feet all right?"

"Coffee's fine," he said. He looked at the man standing near the stove in the corner of the room, but the pounding of the weather still affected his eyes and the heat of the room put a film on them. Josephine had gone back toward the kitchen. He looked around the room and saw an army cot and he went to it and lay down.

When Josephine returned he was sound asleep. She stood over him a moment, worrying. "He was coming from Fargo and got caught in it. Edward, help me take his boots and socks off. If his feet are frozen, we'll have to wake him up."

Garnett said irritably, "I'd do anything for you, Josephine, but I will not touch him."

"This is no time to be hating him. He may lose his feet."

"Let him crawl around on his hands and knees."

"Edward," she replied, shocked, "no human being should carry that kind of thought in his head."

"You can't possibly know," he murmured, "how I feel about him. I'd be lying to you if I said I was sorry for him. I regret he survived the storm. For his part, he would stand over me and let me die and never lift a hand."

He stood back and watched her haul at Shafter's boots. She got them off and stripped away his heavy wool socks. Then she put her hands on Shafter's feet, pinching the white skin around his ankles until a faint spot of color came to the flesh. A protest came from Garnett. "Don't dirty your beautiful hands on him."

"I wish I knew what was between you two. You've done something to him, haven't you, Edward?"

"I have done my best to ruin him," admitted Garnett coolly. "As he has done his best to ruin me."

"I think he has more generosity in him than you have, Edward."

Garnett smiled acidly. "Wait and see," he said.

WHEN SHAFTER WOKE, the room was dark and the windows showed the blackness of the outer world. The storm had blown itself away, its abrupt end a surprise to him. He lifted himself on the cot and saw that he had blankets over him. The weariness was gone. This little half hour's nap had freshened him. He said to himself, I'm almost as good now as I was at twenty. He got up and moved into the kitchen to find Josephine at the stove. The little kitchen table was set and the smell of coffee and bacon was a stimulant to him. Josephine smiled at him. "How do you feel?"

"Fine, fine. Half an hour's rest does a lot."

"Nearer ten hours," she said. "It is six o'clock in the morning."

"That's a strange one," he said, and took a towel and went to the back porch. He cracked the ice from a water bucket and washed and dried his face. The blizzard had left his skin as tender as though it had been seared by fire. But he was in good spirits, and hungry as he sat down to breakfast. Josephine poured coffee for him and herself, then took a place opposite.

"How do you come to be here?" he asked.

"We were out for a ride and saw the blizzard coming. We got here about two hours before you did. Where were you when it started?"

"Halfway between here and Romain's. What time did I get here?"

"It was half past seven."

"Four miles in two hours and a half. No wonder I got cold." He ate his meal and sat back with his cigar. "Where are the Bensons?" he asked.

"They were on the way to Bismarck when we passed them. So I suppose the storm held them in town."

He got up from his place, now thinking about his mules. "Time to get on," he said. He heard somebody stepping along the front room and noticed the girl's face tighten. At that moment Garnett appeared in the living-room doorway, his eyes narrowed, his mouth pulled long and firm.

Shafter removed his cigar. He looked, the girl thought, like a man who suddenly had stumbled upon something dangerous and unpleasant. "This is the man you came riding with?"

"Yes. I told you, the storm caught us."

"I know," said Shafter, very quietly.

"You've had your meal, Shafter," said Garnett. "Now get out."

Shafter had his head slightly bent as he watched the lieutenant. He murmured, "Up to the same old tricks, Garnett?"

"I told you how it was," insisted the girl. "You were caught in the same blizzard, weren't you?"

"Don't explain anything to him," said Garnett sharply.

"That's right," agreed Shafter. "The lieutenant never explains."

"Sergeant," said Garnett coolly, "mind what I tell you or I'll have you court-martialed for disobeying me."

"Stand aside, Beau," said Shafter. "I'm going in there to get my cap and I don't want to get the smell of a scoundrel on me."

At the name, the girl noticed, Garnett's eyes smoldered and for a moment he balanced in the doorway. Then he stepped into the kitchen. Shafter went past him into the front room. He got his cap and wrapped his muffler around his neck, then folded his overcoat over his arm and went back to the kitchen.

He saw that Garnett had taken a seat at the end of the table. Shafter looked at the girl, and said softly, "My advice to you is to get out of this house."

"Kern," she begged, "don't say any more. You've said enough."

"That's right," he agreed. "I've talked enough." He dropped the coat and turned to Garnett. "Now's the time, Beau. Do you know what I'm going to do? I am going to cripple you so no other woman will want you."

Garnett sat still a long dragged-out moment. Then he got up with a springing rush, avoiding Shafter's outstretched arm. He seized a chair and flung it. Shafter raised one arm, took the blow, and shunted the chair aside. He drove a punch deep into Garnett's side. Garnett cried out and sprang at Shafter, hands swinging. One of his fists struck Shafter on the cheek, sending him back.

But Shafter jumped in and staggered the lieutenant with a blow against his belly. Garnett struck the wall, his mouth springing open, and in this defenseless moment he was at Shafter's mercy. Shafter hit him slantingly on the mouth, drawing blood. Then he hooked another blow across Garnett's nose, and heard him yell.

Garnett came against him and seized Shafter around the waist, pushing him toward the stove with a burst of strength. He shoved Shafter against its hot sides and spent all his remaining energy to hold him there.

The smell of Shafter's scorched clothing began to stink in the room. Shafter felt the flare of pain on the backs of his legs. He got an arm around Garnett's head and gave it a twist that threw the man off-balance. He slid suddenly aside and saw Garnett throw both hands against the hot top of the stove to keep himself upright. Garnett cried out and drew back with his hands half open before him. The pain of it made him forget Shafter, who came up and sledged him on the side of the neck. Garnett raised his arms defensively. Shafter hit him on the mouth, then drove a punch into his belly and watched the man drop.

On the floor Garnett swayed gently from side to side. His legs rose and dropped as steady reflexes of pain pulsed through him. He groaned, "You've broken my nose."

"I hope it heals crooked," said Shafter.

As he moved toward the back door Josephine halted him. "He'll have you court-martialed. You've put yourself in his hands."

He stared at her, aware of her beauty as he always was. "No, he won't. He can't bring charges against me without explaining the circumstances and involving you. He won't do that. He'd have no scruples about giving you away, but he'd be exposing himself."

"Exposing himself to what?" she asked.

"To other women who now think they hold his interest exclusively," said Shafter.

She stood stone-quiet, her face fixed in a cold, distasteful expression. "You make this a very unpleasant affair, don't you?"

"I know the man," said Shafter.

"Do you know me?"

"You went out for an afternoon's ride," he said. "That was all."

"Where is the wrong, Kern? Dig down as deep as you want and find me an answer—the worst answer you can find."

"There's your answer," he said and pointed at Garnett, who had risen from the floor and now walked slowly forward. He looked upon these two with his battered face, his crushed lips, and his bold nose now broken at the bridge. He gazed at them with a dull indifference.

"What has he to do with me?" she demanded.

"Everything he touches—"

She cut in and finished the phrase for him. "Turns bad. That's what you think. You were hurt once, and you stopped growing. You've done a good job of making a very unimportant man out of yourself, Kern. You might have been a big one. You think Edward is evil? So are you. Evil in the way you let hate and suspicion feed upon your soul."

Shafter bowed his head slightly. "You may be right," he said, and left the room.

She stood still, hearing his feet crunch through the snow crust as he went toward the barn. The anger died out of her and her shoulders dropped.

"That's the girl," said Garnett. "You've hit him hard. I know the look on his face when he's been beaten."

She had her back to Garnett. "Edward, as soon as Kern has driven away, get your sleigh ready. We're going home."

He said, "You liked me yesterday. You don't like me now. You believe what he said about me, don't you?"

"Let's not bother to go into it. A thing changes. People change."

"No," he said. "You believe him. And all those hard words you used on him meant nothing."

"I meant them," she said.

He managed a thin smile. "You intended to hurt him, but you never intended to drive him off. You want him to come back. It's a very old way with women."

"You would know, wouldn't you?" she said.

"I don't deny it." He sighed and struggled with the pain pulsing through him. "When I saw you I knew I had come to something serious. You are the first woman with whom I have ever wanted to be honest. As soon as I realized that, I was afraid. I knew what was behind me. I knew you'd discover it sooner or later—that's why I told you to believe in me, whatever happened."

"I believe you," she told him quietly.

"But now believing is not enough," he murmured. "There's too much behind me, and too little left in me."

"Yes," she said. "Let's go home."

He went back to the living room, got into his coat, and left the house, soon bringing the sleigh around. He helped her up and turned toward Bismarck.

When they reached her house she dropped down out of the sleigh and looked back at him a moment, sad for the way things had been, sorry that she had hurt him.

"I shan't see you again, I suppose," he said.

"No."

He nodded. "But you must understand something else about Shafter. I know him. You believe he'll come back because—as you have already discovered—he's in love with you. But he won't come back. He never goes back to anything. Good-by, Jo."

Chapter 12

ONE NIGHT THE regiment lay crowded within the walls of Fort Lincoln. At tattoo on the following evening it camped in tents on a level plain three miles south of the fort. Terry's orders had come through, and there was to be a period of preparation before he arrived from St. Paul to lead the expedition on its way.

The regiment was whole again, all its companies lined up side by side on the plain, each with its company street and line of tents leading off the main regimental street. Across this street stood the tent of the commander, now occupied by Major Reno. Beside it sat the tents of the adjutant and staff. Adjoining the cavalry troops were two companies of the Seventeenth Infantry and one of the Sixth Infantry. Farther on lay the wagon park with its one hundred and fifty wagons to carry the quartermaster and commissary supplies, near which camped a hundred and seventy-five civilian teamsters. With the regiment as well was a party of Ree Indians under Bloody Hand, the scout, and Charley Reynolds and two interpreters—one of them the Negro Isaiah Dorman. The scout detachment had been placed under the command of Lieutenant Charles Varnum.

The camp lay sprawled on the plain, the white tops of the tents softly shining under the early May sunshine. Dispatch riders were whirling in, freight caravans slowly arriving, scout details trotting in and out, companies drilling to the sharp calls of noncoms, horses wheeling and crowding and moving with the precision of long training, all marked by the occasional throaty summons of trumpets.

At night campfires blazed on the earth, and men sang, or argued, or wrote last letters homeward, or sorted out their mementos and extra equipment and sent them back to barracks to await their return. Sabers were boxed and stored and dress uniforms put away. Threadbare trousers and battered campaign hats appeared, decorated by the frail blue and yellow flowers now coloring the prairie.

Among the new faces who appeared with the returned companies were Lieutenant Godfrey with a stringy mustache and long goatee; Lieutenant McIntosh with the strain of Indian blood in him, and Lieutenant Wallace with the serious manner; Benny Hodgson, a youngster loved by the command for a sunny disposition; and Captain Myles Keogh of I Company—a sharp-eyed, swarthy-skinned man with a pointed black imperial and indigo-black mustache.

On May 10 the guardhouse trumpet sounded its sharp flourish for a general officer, and Terry and his staff, along with Custer, whirled in out of the prairie and down the regimental street. It was as though an electrical shock passed through the command, stiffening it and exciting it. That night after retreat the story of Custer's ordeal in Washington was common knowledge in the camp, spoken of by officers in the presence of the sergeant major and mentioned by him to the company sergeants, and in turn passed down the line.

The winter's ordeal had left Custer raw of nerve and pride. It had increased his terrific animal energy. His rough hand seized the regiment and shook it into redoubled activity. The drill period lengthened and men toiled late at special-duty chores. Inspections were repeated, company by company, with Custer's sharp eyes on everything. Late after taps the guards saw his tent lights burning and his shadow pacing. There was no rest in him.

Crook, the grapevine said, was well under way; and Gibbon was already as far as the Bighorn. The steamer *Far West* had departed upriver with supplies, which would be left at a base designated by Custer. Terry had, meanwhile, made every effort to secure advance information of the Sioux whereabouts, and scouts drifted in with their information and drifted secretively out. On the sixteenth, general orders went out; the command would march the following morning. That night, on the eve of departure, the officers held a ball on the regimental street and all the ladies came out from Lincoln, and in the bland evening the music of the regimental band swung them around and around while the light of campfires glowed on colored dresses and faded fatigue uniforms.

Lieutenant Smith whirled his wife outward beyond the crowd. The music still played on, but he took her arm and strolled across the slick prairie grass. "That makes me think of Saratoga," he said. "We had fun, old girl. Seems like a long time back."

She said, "Do you know where I'd like to go again? Remember that little Connecticut town we passed through? All the houses painted white. The elms around them."

"I shall ask for leave in the fall." He looked down at her and kissed her.

She stepped back but she held both his arms. "I'm afraid," she whispered.

"Terry's a sound, safe man."

She shook her head, clinging to him. "I'm afraid," she repeated in a still lower voice. "I wish the President had kept Custer away."

"Now, now," he said. "Anyhow, Custer is under Terry's orders."

"If he sees a chance for a grand coup," she said, "he'll disobey his orders. I hate that man."

He was disturbed and walked on without speaking. Presently she touched his arm and stopped. He saw a smile come uncertainly to her face. She murmured, "Be good and take no unnecessary chances."

"I shall write you faithfully each night," he said. "We'll be in Connecticut this winter. Fresh apples, fresh vegetables. New clothes and old friends." He grinned at her and put his arms around her and kissed her once more. And so they stood in the shadows, reluctant to part while the long moments ran by.

IN THE FOUR-O'CLOCK darkness the drums of the infantry and the cavalry trumpets sounded the general, and the glowing tops of the tent city collapsed as by the stroke of a single hand. Details moved on their crisscross errands, rolling and packing the canvas and stowing it away in supply wagons. Assembly blew and companies formed, each trooper's voice harking to roll call. Officers crisply shouted, swinging the companies into regimental line. The band was ahead, the colors swung by, and Custer and his aides whirled up spectacularly. In the distance a bugler sounded forward and the band broke into tune. They were, at last, under way; over eight hundred troopers and infantrymen with scouts and guides and the long lumbering train of wagons rolling behind. Ahead, Custer's huge campaign sombrero swung up in a wide gesture.

Shafter rode as right guide, the captain beside him. Moylan said, "We're parading through the fort. When we get beyond it we'll stop to let the wagon train catch up. There will be time for anybody so wishing to ride back and say so long. Pass that word along, Hines." Then he looked at Shafter. "You got somebody to speak to?"

"No," said Shafter.

The band struck up the regimental tune, "Garryowen." As the troopers approached the walls of Fort Lincoln they passed Ree women gathered wailing and weeping to watch their men go. The regiment passed through the gate and marched across the parade. Along Officers' Row the families had assembled, and townspeople had come over from Bismarck for the departure. The infantry companies left in charge of the post were drawn up in rank to salute the passing column. Thus the regiment passed through the main guard gate to the north and swung westward toward the ridge west of the post.

As A Company filed through the gate Shafter saw Josephine standing near the house of the commissary sergeant. She seemed to be scanning the column very closely. Presently she discovered him and he observed her face grow tighter and her lips move. He lifted his hat and when he rode on, her glance seemed to remain with him, to follow him.

Half a mile onward the regiment halted to wait for the supply wagons, and the ranks broke. Shafter stood beside his horse, watching the men go. He got out a pipe and filled it and drew smoke into his lungs while he looked down at the post, his thoughts wholly with Josephine. What stuck with him was the picture she had made, her eyes so carefully searching the column and at last coming to rest upon him. Her lips had said something to him across the distance, and suddenly he realized he had to go back to her. He rose and went into the saddle, dropping down the hill.

She still stood by the house of the commissary sergeant. She had seen Shafter and was watching him. He came before her on his horse and lifted his hat.

"Nice of you," he said, "to come here to watch us go."

"I suppose you'll be away all summer."

"Never know. Nothing's certain."

She had nothing to add, and for his part he was caught in a silence which held him fast. Captain Moylan passed, saying, "Time to go, Sergeant." Shafter watched her, with the clearest impression of her beauty and her strength.

"Good luck," he said.

"I should be wishing you that, Kern."

"Wish it, then."

"If you think it worth remembering," she said, soft and calm, "I do wish you luck."

There was a question in his mind, a wish and an uncertainty he wanted to be rid of; and he remembered how sweet her lips were and the vibrations of her voice when she was stirred. He was on the edge of dismounting when Garnett rode up from the guard gate. Garnett's voice hit him like a stone.

"Get back to your outfit, Sergeant."

Shafter saw her look at Garnett with an odd expression, and turn her smiling glance again to Shafter, still and sweet. He bowed his head at her, wheeled his horse, and trotted to A Company.

Custer rushed by, lithe and magnificent on his horse. All down the line the sergeants were bawling at their men. A single word rippled through the column. "Forward!"

The Seventh moved with a kind of elastic stretching, and the white-topped wagon train made a sinuous half-mile trail behind. With the general rode his adjutant, his orderly, and the scout Charley Reynolds. With him, too, rode Marc Kellogg, representing the New York *Herald*, one of those newspapermen whom Sherman had warned Custer not to take along.

THAT AFTERNOON THE column marched thirteen miles and camped in a grassy bottom beside the Heart River. By six the following morning it was under way, a mile-long line following the contours of the land, with flankers to left and right and advance points far ahead. They crossed the Sweetbriar in a slashing hailstorm and crawled through bottomland with the wagons hub-deep and doubleteamed. On the twenty-first they crossed the Big Muddy and moved through sharp showers and slept wet at night and rose sullen. The little creeks they came upon were bank-full from the steady downfall; the quick-bred mosquitoes swarmed thickly around them, driving the livestock frantic. On the left forward horizon the Bad Lands showed as fairyland spires and minarets, grotesque and varicolored. At night burning lignite beds sent up their dull red columns, like signals of warning. They crossed the crooked loops of Davis Creek ten times in one day's march, moved through huge cottonwood groves, and put the Little Missouri behind them.

It grew cold and snow fell three inches deep. Wet buffalo chips smoldered without burning and horses grew hungry for want of good grass. A scout arrived to report that the *Far West* waited at Stanley's Stockade with supplies. The same rider brought news from Gibbon that his Montana column was in motion down the Yellowstone. Terry sent back orders for Gibbon to halt and wait, and for the *Far West* to deliver one boatload of supplies to the mouth of the Powder.

They followed the Beaver into rising, broken country, crossed a divide into the basin of the Powder and from the heights, in a short interval of sunlight, they saw far away the bluffs of the Yellowstone. Thoroughly weary, and wet again from intermittent rain, they camped on the Powder.

The next morning Terry took Moylan's and Keogh's troops and rode down the Powder to the Yellowstone where the *Far West* waited. Terry left the escort troops and proceeded up the river on the *Far West* to the Tongue, where he had a conference with Gibbon. Then with his escort he returned to the camp of the Seventh. That night Hines, having talked with the sergeant major, passed on the news.

"The base of supply will be at the mouth of the Powder. The *Far West* will move Major Moore and the supplies to there from Stanley's Stockade. Meanwhile, Gibbon's been ordered to go back up the Yellowstone to the Rosebud and wait until we march to him. The country over that way is full of Indians. Gibbon's outfit has been fightin' 'em in small details all the way along."

Now it was a game of hide-and-seek, with all the responsibility of making contact falling upon Terry's shoulders. Before him lay an area about one hundred miles square, bounded on the north by the Yellowstone, on the south by the fore edge of the Bighorns, on the west by the Bighorn, and on the east—where he stood poised with the Seventh—by the Powder. In that area lay the main bodies of the Sioux, their tracks plain to his scouts, their smaller bands weaving rapidly from place to place to confuse him. Now, patiently, he set about a thorough scouting job to establish the whereabouts of the enemy's weight. Crook, somewhere around the Bighorns, acted as a fence on the south and Gibbon, camped at the mouth of the Rosebud, would bar the Sioux from westward retreat.

"The trouble is," said McDermott, "we're too few to make a good fence, and we can be seen forty miles away. We ain't goin' to strike the Sioux by surprise."

"That," said Hines, "is what Terry's got Custer for. We'll just march here and there across the country until Terry's got it figured where they are. Then one night we'll set out fast under Custer, and catch 'em before they see us."

On the tenth of June, Terry dispatched Reno with six companies of cavalry and one Gatling gun to explore the upper part of the Powder. "You will go as far as the junction of the Little Powder," he told Reno. "Then go due west to the headwaters of Mizpah Creek, cross, and continue to the Pumpkin, and go down the Pumpkin to the Tongue. Then proceed down the Tongue to the Yellowstone, where you will meet me. Do not go beyond the Tongue."

Reno left early in the afternoon with his wing, A Company included, and struck directly up the Powder. He had his feelers out all the way in the form of the Ree scouts led by Bloody Hand; and each night they brought back the story of renewed trails sweeping up from the southeast and going on toward the northwest, on beyond the Tongue toward the Rosebud, toward the Bighorn. Bloody Hand, to indicate the size of that faraway gathering, reached down and cupped the clodded earth in his hands and let it spill out. "That many," he said.

Reno now faced the problem of an independent commander operating beyond the reach of his superior officer. He had his strict orders not to go beyond the Tongue, but his scouts all were in accord as to the presence of Sioux over that way; and he judged his mission to be that of finding definite clues. Therefore, wrestling with the problem, he broke the bonds of his orders and crossed the Tongue to the Rosebud, feeling right and left constantly. On the nineteenth he stopped near the Yellowstone and sent a dispatch to Terry of his whereabouts.

Terry, meanwhile, had been moving westward along the Yellowstone with the rest of the Seventh, keeping in contact with the other columns by courier. Now slowly, as news drifted in, he began to tie the ends of his expedition together. Gibbon he held at the Rosebud. At the Tongue he met Reno's returning party and the three men, Terry, Custer, and Reno, held a conference. Being a mild and reserved officer, Terry listened without comment to Reno's report and explanation of his going beyond his orders. All Terry said was, "It is as I believed. The Sioux are beyond, in the direction of the Bighorn. General"—indicating Custer—"you will move the Seventh to the mouth of the Rosebud and join Gibbon. I shall take the *Far West* up there."

Custer and Reno left the general, Custer walking with a heavy, irritable silence that Reno immediately noticed.

"I seem to gather from your manner that you disapprove of my stretching my instructions," said Reno.

"When Terry gave you those orders," Custer replied, "he already knew there was a concentration west of the Tongue. Therefore your march in that direction was a waste of six days' time."

"I judged the orders on their intent," said Reno stiffly. "I think I have an average intelligence."

"I do not question it," snapped Custer, and walked away.

On June 20 the *Far West* landed Terry at the mouth of the Rosebud, where Gibbon and his column waited. That same afternoon the Seventh arrived and a general meeting was held aboard the boat—Terry, Custer, Gibbon, and Gibbon's second-in-command, Brisbin. Terry laid his big campaign map on the table and made his estimate of the situation.

"The Sioux are southwest of us, somewhere between the Rosebud and the Bighorn. General Gibbon's column will ascend the Bighorn. It will swing when it reaches the Little Bighorn and follow that stream. Custer, you will leave in the morning with your regiment, and go up the Rosebud. The two columns will act as anvil and sledge, with the Sioux between. General Gibbon, at what time can you be at the mouth of the Little Bighorn?"

Gibbon took a long, careful look at the map and made his calculations. "I shall be at the Little Bighorn on the morning of the twenty-sixth."

"Custer," continued Terry, "your marches should be based upon Gibbon's arrival at that stream at the agreed time. As you proceed up the Rosebud you will explore right and left. When you reach Tullock's Creek you will send a man down that creek to meet Gibbon's scouts and transmit to him such information as you have acquired. This country will be full of hostiles, so you need a good scout to make it."

"Let me give him Herendeen," suggested Gibbon.

Custer nodded absentmindedly.

"At the upper reaches of the Rosebud," Terry said, "you will scout toward the Little Bighorn. I do not wish to hamper you with unnecessary orders, but you should adjust your marches so as to give Gibbon time to come along. On the morning of the twenty-sixth you should be in some position southeast of the Sioux while Gibbon is somewhere northwest of them, the two of you closing in on either side. Do not rush the thing. Do not engage before Gibbon is up for support. Now, how are your supplies and how do you feel about your men? Do you need something added to the Seventh? Gibbon could give you Brisbin's battalion of cavalry."

Custer stared glumly at the floor. "No," he said, "I'll need nothing more. The addition of outside cavalry would only interfere with the Seventh's freedom of movement." Terry considered him a thoughtful moment, knowing his man. Irritableness and an uncharacteristic gloom showed on Custer, as though the winter's humiliations now freshly hurt him.

"Gibbon," Terry went on, "give Custer part of your Crow scouts. Give him Bouyer and Girard. They can assist Reynolds." He stroked his chin gravely. He had formed his judgments and arranged his maneuvers. Now the job was in the hands of his field officers. He sat still, checking details in his mind. "Crook should be somewhere near us, but I have heard nothing from him and cannot wait longer, for fear the Sioux will slip through us. Gibbon, put your troops in motion today. Custer will leave first thing in the morning. I shall go with Gibbon's column and"—turning to Custer—"if all goes well, I shall meet you on the twenty-sixth."

Custer rose, saying, "I'll pass on the orders," and left.

Officers' call ran through the Seventh, summoning them to Custer, who sat in his portable easy chair, a lank figure in buckskin, with a scarlet flowing kerchief and a head of hair grown ragged. The sun had scorched his face scarlet, making his eyes a deeper blue. He seemed to his officers unusually depressed.

"Gibbon marches up the Bighorn while we march up the Rosebud. We shall leave in the morning. The wagon train stays. Each troop is assigned twelve mules, which are to carry hardtack, coffee and sugar for fifteen days, bacon for twelve days. Use your strongest mule in each troop for extra ammunition. You'll have to load extra forage on the mules also. Each trooper will carry one hundred rounds of carbine ammunition, eighteen rounds of revolver, and twelve pounds of oats."

The twenty-eight officers stood gravely before him, stained with a month's hard marching, their buckskins caked with old mud, their blue trousers faded out, their mustaches unkempt. They were a hard crew to look upon in the deepening twilight; and they were silent long after Custer had fallen silent, until at last he said in his always touchy voice, "Are there any suggestions, gentlemen?"

It was Moylan who spoke. "That's not enough mules, General. You'll break them down with the load you propose."

"Additional mules will slow us too greatly."

French of M Company had a word. "Once your mules start to lag, you'll slow down anyhow."

Custer slapped the arms of his chair with a gesture of open temper. "Well, gentlemen, carry what you please," he said angrily. "The extra forage was only a suggestion, but bear in mind we will follow the trail for fifteen days unless we catch the Sioux before that time."

Captain McDougall said, "Are we to push on at will? I thought we were operating in conjunction with General Gibbon."

Custer was now pacing back and forth, nervous and out of patience. "We shall follow the Sioux, no matter how long it takes." He swung on his adjutant. "Cooke, make out the orders so troop commanders may have them tonight. Assign a sergeant and six privates from each company to take charge of the packtrain. McDougall, your troop will guard the packtrain. That's all."

But the officers lingered, not wholly satisfied. McDougall said, "I don't think a few extra mules would be unwise, General."

Custer wheeled. "Twelve mules to a company. Take what you wish on them. Take nothing if you are prepared to starve your troops." Having spoken, he whirled into his tent.

Darkness came and mess fires bloomed along the Yellowstone's bluff. Details moved back to the supply train to break out the extra rations and ammunition to be loaded on muleback on the morrow; and off to one corner of the camp the Indian scouts were in full voice with their own strange ceremony—the echoes of it lifting sharp and mournful in this wild, empty corner of the earth.

Custer sat in his tent composing his nightly letter to Libby; and all along the regiment men made casual disposition of their effects, or wrote final messages home, or lay back and were silent. On the bluff of the river Shafter stood alone, watching the lights of the *Far West* make yellowed, wrinkled lanes across the water. The river was a steady washing tone in the night, and somewhere southward a low moon shed a partial glow through the fog. The Crows and the Rees were steadily chanting out a strangely barbaric tune of farewell and warning—that beating rhythm a pulse of premonition all through the camp. One by one the lights of the regiment died and tattoo sounded softly. Shafter watched the black shadows thicken in the canyon. He thought backward and saw his life as an empty thing, without sweet memories or faith—and tomorrow held nothing that made him anxious to be traveling toward it.

So the regiment settled down to sleep on the eve of its march. On that same night, one hundred miles southward, Crook's command lay with double guards around it and licked the wounds of a sharp defeat inflicted by the Sioux under Crazy Horse four days earlier. Crook, now cautious and doubtful, sent dispatches back to Laramie, to be wired to Sheridan at Chicago, that he would not advance without reinforcements. Of all this Terry knew nothing as he sat awake on the *Far West* and reviewed his plans.

Chapter 13

A DAMP MIST HUNG heavily over the canyon, through which came the muffled cursing of the mule packers. The peremptory notes of assembly sounded, and the companies formed one by one. Custer swung to his horse and crossed the camp at a full gallop to join Terry, Gibbon, and Brisbin, who had tarried behind their own column in order to see the Seventh away. Reno's shout of command arose, placing the regiment in forward motion.

They came past the reviewing group, Reno saluting as he went by, each company commander swinging his head to the right and rendering a like salute. There was none of a dress parade's flash or fancy display about them this day. Their clothes were ragged and their whiskers long, and they carried with them the bulky impedimenta of a field campaign.

Terry watched them pass with a thoughtful eye. "You have a good regiment, Custer. I do not know of a better one in the service."

Custer showed a flash of his old spirit. "My regiment, General, has been the best in the army for ten years."

Terry smiled. Gibbon said nothing. Brisbin gave Custer a sharply irritated glance and returned his eyes to the Seventh. It had always been a flashy regiment, more troublesome and more picturesque than any other, with ten years of campaigning to its credit, with its roll of honorable dead and a worthy list of actions on its record. Its companies, never at full strength, had been further pulled down by details left at the Powder River base, so that its eight hundred had diminished to seven hundred. But it had a strong core of old-time noncommissioned men, and its captains were largely good, some seasoned and faithful like Moylan, some wild-tempered like Keogh, some stubborn and cool as was the white-haired Benteen.

The companies were under-officered and Custer had made some changes of assignment. Moylan still had A Company, B was McDougall. Algernon Smith had been taken from A to command E Company. F was Yates and G was led by Donald McIntosh. Benteen had H. I was commanded by Keogh and Godfrey led K. Custer's brother-in-law, Calhoun, rode in front of L. French retained M.

"The heart of a regiment," said Terry, "is faith in itself. I have every confidence in the Seventh. But everything depends on the timetable we have set. Let nothing disturb that. Be sure, when you reach the head of Tullock's Creek, to send Herendeen back to communicate with Gibbon. That will be a verification of your whereabouts. We cannot beat the Indians in detail, or surround them in detail. This movement depends entirely upon both columns striking at the same approximate time."

Custer grasped Terry's hand and shook it with his swift impulsiveness. Briefly he accepted the hands of Gibbon and Brisbin, then whirled around. Just before he broke his horse into a gallop Brisbin called after him, "Now Custer, don't be greedy. Wait for us."

Custer looked back, smiling. His horse springing up beneath him, he flung up his hand, making a gallant figure in the day's growing sunlight. "I won't," he shouted. With that enigmatic answer he rushed away toward the column's head.

A mile from the Yellowstone, Custer divided the Indian scouts into two sections to cover each side of the Rosebud. Then he led the column over the Rosebud to the west bank.

From his saddle Shafter watched the broken country unroll before him. The Rosebud lay at the bottom of a shallow canyon and the column took the most practicable course—sometimes following the edge of the water, sometimes traveling on a shelf half up the side of the canyon, and sometimes rising to the top of the bluff.

Garnett, who had been assigned to A Company in the reshuffle, rode at the foot of the troop. Shafter felt him as he would have felt a cold wind at the back of his neck; and his thoughts of Garnett were full of hate.

The column camped near twilight, still on the Rosebud. Shortly after, an orderly summoned the officers to Custer's fire. He stood at the blaze with his officers ringed around it. "Stable guards will waken the troops at three a.m.," he said. "March will be resumed at five. Each commander is responsible for the actions of his own company."

He spoke in a suppressed manner, half indifferent, half uncertain. None of the brusque stridency so characteristic of him showed this night. Then after his initial announcement he stared long at the fire in a kind of reverie.

"Gentlemen," he said at last, "I have complete faith in this regiment and I have entire confidence in your loyalty. I call on you particularly now to give me all of your talents."

He pushed his hands into his pockets and broke off, engaged in thought, his bony face tipped down, his long, thin lips half hidden behind his mustache. The ring of officers waited in silence for him to continue, closely watching this somber reflection, so unlike him. Benteen looked upon his commander with a steadfast reserve, an ingrained dislike; and Reno studied the man out of his dark-ringed eyes.

"We can," continued Custer, "expect to meet a thousand warriors or more. The scouts report that the trails are growing heavy, pointing ahead of us and west of us. We came here to find Indians and we shall find them. I have too much pride in the Seventh to go back empty-handed and I know you feel the same way. I ought to mention that General Terry offered me Brisbin's battalion of cavalry. I refused it. Frankly, I felt that there might be jealousy between the two groups and I wanted nothing to break the present knit spirit of our command." Then he paused and took on a moment's show of his old spirit. "Moreover, I am confident the Seventh can handle whatever it faces."

THE REGIMENT WAS up at three and in motion at five, with the troopers silent and stale. The day grew hot and the sun began to bite down for the first time during the campaign. The long day wheeled on and the scanty foraging of the horses began to tell upon them. After thirty-three miles the regiment went into camp, ate, and fell asleep. Once again at five it was marching.

The Crow scouts sent back word of fresh signs and presently the column began to pass the round, dead-grass spots where lodges had stood and the blackened char of old campfires. At noon the command halted for dinner—bacon and hardtack and coffee. Seated cross-legged on the earth, Shafter knew from the way the scouts ran in and out that the trail had grown suddenly hot.

At five Custer swung the command forward and now the trail passed into a valley where the tracks of lodgepole travois scratched the ground everywhere. They came upon the skeleton frames of wickiups where a camp had been, and a sun-dance lodge. An officer rode to the lodge and came back with a scalp lifted in his hand. News came down the column. "White man's scalp hanging on that lodge. Must have been one of Gibbon's troopers killed on the Yellowstone last month."

Custer seemed now to be pulled by the lively scent, for he moved the column steadily on through the last sunlight and into the blue-running dusk. The land tilted upward and the Rosebud made a shallow semicircle toward the southwest, fringed with willows. Beyond them, in the distance, lay a shallow knob.

Herendeen now trotted up the line and spoke to Custer. "General, we're as close to the head of Tullock's Creek as we'll get. It's off there—" pointing to the right. "This is where I'm supposed to leave you and go down the creek to find Gibbon's scouts."

He waited for whatever message Custer intended to convey to Gibbon. It was a night's ride down the creek, through the heart of Sioux-held ground and a risky prospect for a lone man. Gibbon had promised Herendeen extra pay for the venture. Now Herendeen waited for Custer's order to go, and rode silently beside the commander. Custer gave him a brief glance out of his deep-set eyes; then he looked into the forward blue distance and rode on without speaking. After a half mile of this Herendeen saw he was to be given no order, so he wheeled away and dropped back to his place in the column. Apparently the general had changed his mind about sending back a messenger.

At seven o'clock the command made camp, and an orderly summoned all officers. They stood in a circle, stiff and spraddle-legged and dusty in the forming twilight, as Custer spoke.

"We have come seventy-five miles from the mouth of the Rosebud," he said. "I have sent Varnum and the scouts forward to the lookout point at Crow Peak. We're no more than thirty miles from the hostiles. I do not know yet which way they're running, but I propose to find out."

Benteen interrupted. "Are you sure they're running, General?"

Custer's voice had a special usage for Benteen; it was stiff and formal and brief. "If they were not running, we should have struck them before now."

"They know where we are," Benteen pointed out. "They know we're coming. They may be picking their own spot to fight on."

"We'll see—we'll see," said Custer. "I propose to make a sudden jump at them. Troop commanders, better change your details on the packtrain. May not get another chance. No more, gentlemen."

Night fell with its desert suddenness and the stars were very bright against a black sky. Custer sat cross-legged in the darkness, solemnly thoughtful. Behind him lay the regiment, soon asleep. He heard the sentries pacing, the occasional murmuring of their voices, and the click of their guns. The scent of dust was strong, and a light wind blew the smell of horses and mules through the camp. He sat very still, his mind jumping ahead to the eventual scene which he knew he must make real—the scene of the Seventh smashing the Sioux in surprise attack. There was never any doubt in his mind as to victory. The only thing that worried him was the question of his ability to catch up with the hostiles before they slipped from his grasp, before Gibbon came up to join him.

He lay back, somewhere during the night, on his blankets and fell into that instant sleep for which he was famous. But the last thing on his mind had been a fear of losing the Sioux and the first thing to return to it when he woke near midnight was that same fear. He rose up suddenly and called to his orderly.

"Wake the company commanders and tell them to be ready to march at one o'clock."

THE COMMAND STRUGGLED OUT of dead sleep and sergeants' voices prodded the weary companies into formation. There was no talk as the Seventh moved forward. They traveled with the Rosebud as it circled and wound slowly upgrade, until at four o'clock light came. Then they fell out for breakfast.

Shafter unsaddled and searched for the makings of a fire. He boiled his coffee, fried his bacon, and put his hardtack in the bacon grease to soften it. He saw Captain Moylan standing nearby and he beckoned him over and split his breakfast with his commander. Moylan squatted in the dust, his eyes bloodshot. The creek water had alkali in it, turning the coffee bad. Hines came over and sat down, groaning. "This is soldierin' for you, Shafter. Don't stay in it as long as I'm stayin'. If I was thirty again . . ."

Shafter said, "I remember a night march from Chambers to Shaw Gap, during the war. It was worse, Hines."

"Much worse," agreed Moylan and grinned at Shafter. "There was a tougher commander along. He was in a hurry."

"So. Same outfit, hey?" Hines asked softly.

Custer came down the camp, riding bareback. He stopped near Moylan. "Be ready to move at eight. Varnum sends word there is a concentration of hostiles to the west of the divide." He rode on. Shafter closed his eyes and fell instantly asleep. Presently he heard a trumpet blowing far away and somebody dug him urgently in the ribs, saying, "Come on, rise and shine."

The regiment collected itself, slowly and with effort, then moved forward. Custer galloped ahead with Girard. Two miles on he found Charley Reynolds waiting for him at the foot of Crow Peak. Reynolds led him up the slope toward a round knob from which the country fell away in its broken, wrinkled outline. To the north they could see the long cavalry file following the creek bed and sheltered from sight by the ridges to either side. To the west the land ran in small gullies and tangled ridges toward the Little Bighorn.

Varnum, Bouyer, and Reynolds stood near the general. The Crow scouts made a group of their own nearby. Custer lifted his glasses on the valley to the west and gave it a careful scrutiny; then he lowered them. "I see nothing," he said in a disappointed tone.

"Look beyond the valley to the top of the bluffs," urged Varnum. "The Sioux horse herd is there. A big one."

Custer tried again, and shook his head. "No, I make out nothing."

Varnum showed his disappointment. "The Crow are quite certain of a big camp over there. We saw smoke rising on that plateau an hour ago. Dust smoke from horses. The Crow are also quite sure we have been seen by Sioux scouts."

"You're going to have a big fight, General," said Charley Reynolds. "A hell of a big fight. I have seen enough tracks and enough dust to be certain." He pointed west. "There are more Indians over there, General, than you ever saw in one place before."

One of the Crows gave a grunt and pointed to the northwest. Looking down from the knob, Custer and the rest of the party saw four Indians riding rapidly through a coulee toward the Rosebud. They had been somewhere near the crest of the divide, blended with the brown and gray soil.

"We've been spotted for certain," said Varnum.

Suddenly the general got to his horse and led the group downgrade. At the foot of the ridge he said to his trumpeter orderly, "Officers' call," and sat on the ground, waiting for his officers to assemble. His buckskins were powdered with dust, his bright red kerchief silvered with it. Beneath the flare of his great-brimmed hat his eyes were narrowly fixed upon the earth before him. Presently he stood up to meet his officers.

They came forward on slow feet, all the worse for wear, wanting sleep and suffering from a thirst the alkali water of the region could not slake. Major Reno's sallow cheeks were flushed, and Benteen's naturally florid complexion was scarlet.

"The camp," observed Custer, "seems to be over that way," and motioned his arm westward. "The Crows think we have been discovered. I am inclined to agree. In any event we move that way as soon as troops are in order. We will now break the command into three wings. Reno, you take M, A, and G companies. The scouts and guides will also be attached to you, and Drs. Porter and DeWolfe will follow your battalion. Hodgson will be your adjutant. Benteen, you will have your own company and also D and K. McDougall will remain as guard for the pack animals. I shall take C, E, F, I, and L. You had better fill canteens and water the horses."

The officers went doggedly away, and presently watering details broke for the creek. Shafter filled his canteen, brought his horse to water, and watched it test the surface of the creek with its sensitive nose. It blew against the water, trying to skim the surface away, and lifted its head. The alkaline taste was too strong. Boots and saddles cracked in the warming day, and at half past twelve Shafter was mounted again, moving forward.

The column rose with the divide and now filed westward through the wings of a shallow pass. Moylan beckoned at Garnett, who rode near the foot of the troop, and Garnett came up briskly to join him. Shafter heard Moylan speaking.

"Half or better of the company has not been under fire. Therefore these men will shoot too fast and waste ammunition. You must constantly watch for this and keep counseling these green men not to fire unless they have something to hit. You must also keep the company closed up. The Sioux always try to split a command into detail and chop up the pieces. Let nobody straggle or fall back on your wing." He nodded, sending Garnett back.

Hines turned to McDermott. "You're topkick if I drop. Remember to get the duty roster out of my breast pocket."

There were three sergeants with A Company—Hines, McDermott, and Shafter; there were four corporals and forty-one privates now riding two and two down the western slope of the broken hills. Ahead of them at a distance lay the half view of a valley stretching along the timber-fringed Little Bighorn, gray and dark olive and tawny in the hazy heat fog. Benteen suddenly swung out from the column's head, going toward the rough hills to the south. He shouted back and drew his own company after him, and Weir's and Godfrey's. A Company now was the head of the column.

The pitch of the hills steepened and the horses grunted with the effort required to check their descent. The pass widened as it descended and the ground showed the chopped tracks of fresh Indian travel. The guides were ranging ahead, lifting up and down the little rolls of land which now and then shut out the valley before them.

Suddenly they capped a ridge and saw a lone tepee standing in the valley. Custer halted the command, and the Ree scouts went forward in stooped, lithe positions, like scurrying dogs closing in on a scent. Girard climbed a small ridge which gave him a view of the land beyond. One of the Rees entered the tepee and came out, crying at Bouyer. Bouyer said to Custer, "A dead Sioux inside."

Girard shouted, "Injuns, runnin' down the valley!"

Custer yelled at the Ree chief, Bloody Hand, "Tell your people to follow them!"

Bloody Hand spoke back at the Ree. They stood still, saying nothing and not moving, and Bloody Hand shook his head at Custer.

Custer cried out, "Forward!" and started down the creek with the two columns racking after him. The little ridge which had blocked their view now petered out into the plain of the valley and gave them a view of the creek as it looped toward the brush and willows which marked the course of the Bighorn. Dust showed where the fleeing Indians had been. Cooke rode over from Custer's column and fell in beside Reno. "The Indians are across the Little Bighorn," he said, "about two miles ahead of us. The general directs that you follow them as fast as you can and charge them. He will support you with the other battalion."

The Indian trail crossed the creek. Reno's battalion went splashing over the water and headed for the Little Bighorn. Looking back, Shafter saw the column under Custer veer away in another direction, and presently slide behind a knoll of ground.

Reno struck the river at a place where the trees were thinnest and yelled back, "Don't let the horses stop to drink!" Moylan turned to Shafter and repeated the command. Shafter dropped out of his file and stood with his mount belly-deep in the water.

One horse came to a dead halt and thrust its muzzle eagerly down. Its rider sawed at the reins and cursed it, and then Shafter spurred near and gave it a hard kick, sending it on. But the little delay had broken the compactness of the line and troopers were tangled midstream, their animals half-crazed by thirst. Shafter and McDermott ranged among them, prodding them on. Moylan's great voice bawled from the far bank and McIntosh of G and French of M were laying words about them like axe handles.

The column crossed, fought through the willows, and came upon a broad valley. To the right, across the stream, a bluff lifted and grew taller as it moved away. On the left the valley was held in by a low, slow-rising slope. Ahead of them, at a distance, a wooded bend of the river closed out the farther view of the valley; a mass of dust rose beyond those trees. At this moment Cooke came splashing across the ford and shouted at Reno. "Scout reports there's a hell of a lot of Indians under that dust smoke—beyond those trees."

"All right—all right," said Reno. "Where's Custer?"

Cooke turned in his saddle, shook his head, and pointed vaguely. Then he wheeled back into the water and disappeared. The three companies had now formed in columns of fours. Reno called, "McIntosh, you're reserve. Varnum, take your scouts out on the left flank." He spoke aside to his orderly. "Ride back to Custer. Tell him the Indians are in force in front of us." Then he rose in his stirrups and shouted, "Left into line—guide center—gallop!"

The column broke like a fan, fours slanting out and coming into a broad troop front. The two advance companies formed a spaced skirmish line sweeping at a gallop down the valley—A to the left and M to the right, Reno, Hodgson, Moylan, and French riding forward, and Garnett behind. G Company made a second line in the rear. Over to the left, skirting the edge of the footslopes, Varnum commanded his Ree scouts. With him were Reynolds and two half-breed guides, Girard, Herendeen, and the Negro Dorman.

Chapter 14

It was a two-mile run down the length of that valley toward the trees which barred their farther view. Dust thickened steadily behind the trees, and something flashed in the core of the dust, like lances glittering. Reno, out in the lead, turned in the saddle as he galloped, and looked back anxiously toward the crossing of the river for the support Custer had promised. The plain was empty.

They were nearly abreast the trees which formed a screen, and then swung to pass them. On the left Varnum was cursing above the thud and jingle and the crying of men. "Dammit, come back—come back!" His Rees had sighted the on-racing shape of the Sioux; now they turned and fled. Bloody Hand called and beckoned to no avail. It left a gap in the left end of Reno's line; Reno gestured with an upraised arm and McIntosh spurred G Company forward into the line.

They skirted the timber and pushed by it. The dust cloud was ahead of them, no more than two hundred yards away, and now the shadows within the dust leaped out of it and rushed on—Sioux warriors bending and swaying and yelling. One wave of them wheeled and made for the left flank of Reno's line, meaning to turn it. Reno tossed up his arm, and his mouth formed a phrase that was seen but scarcely heard. "Prepare to fight on foot!"

Horses went crazy in the sudden milling halt, in the sing of rifle fire, and for a moment the line was beyond control. Troopers dropped from their saddles, and in groups of threes flung their reins to a fourth trooper, who wheeled and ran back with the mounts. The line became a crescent of kneeling men. Officers dropped behind to unmask the fire of their companies. Reno walked calmly to the rear of his command. Then he stood with his legs apart and his revolver drawn, taking careful aim and firing with deliberation.

The trees were now behind the command and the solid dust in front; and suddenly a wave of Sioux broke forward and curled around the left, where Varnum was posted with his guides. Firing rattled up from the troopers' thin ranks, and Varnum's little group was in the thick of a swift, wicked melee.

The Sioux shots made a thin rain along the earth. An arrow struck short and wavered snakelike on the dust. A man to the right of Shafter gave one soft grunt and settled forward on both knees. Hines turned his head in that direction. He raised a hand to dash the sweat from his face; but the hand went halfway up, halted there, and dropped. His head jerked from the impact of a bullet, his eyes rolled. He said, "Ah," and dropped dead.

Shafter reached to Hines's breast pocket and pulled out the roster book. He looked around him and saw McDermott shake his head. Wallace trotted toward Moylan and Reno. "Pressure's getting very strong. Can't we send back to Custer for support?"

Over on the left Shafter watched Sioux suddenly appear out of the wrinkled high ground and sweep behind the cavalry line. To the right, where the river lay, he saw Indians darting through the willows. Reno saw it, too, and stood still to think of his position. Wallace had trotted toward Varnum's position. Shortly he came back with one of the half-breed guides.

"You want to go back and find Custer?" asked Reno.

The dust had rolled over them and beyond them. There was no view of the valley in any direction. The guide shook his head. "They've cut us off," he said. "No man could get through."

The horse holders, a hundred feet behind the line, were now being attacked from the side. Reno said to McIntosh, "Pull out your company and go guard the horses."

Shafter saw Garnett standing a yard behind the skirmish line. The lieutenant had his revolver half lifted and his eyes strained into the dust mist, waiting for a target. Whiskers darkened his sallow face; his mouth was trap-tight. Donovan raised a crimson face and called at Shafter, "We can't hold this place. Somebody better tell Reno."

Reno knew it and had given his orders. Moylan was shouting those orders through the steady slam of gunfire. "Drop back to the timber!"

The line rose, ragged and broken, and slowly retreated, pace by pace, into the protecting edge of the brush and timber. As soon as they left the open ground the battalion lost unity, and runners began to crease through the brush, seeking the major for orders. Shafter crouched at the edge of the timber and watched the Sioux shapes curling around the grove, drawing a tighter ring about the command. The woods reverberated with the steady echoes of the troopers' firing and he heard men shouting questions through the thicket. Shafter got up and broke through the brush to his left to make contact with the lost fragments of his company. In the heart of the timber he met Moylan.

"We can't stay here, Captain. We'll be out of ammunition in fifteen minutes."

"Reno's debating a retreat," said Moylan. "The Indians have crossed the river and broken our flank there."

"They're coming in on this side, too."

"I'll go tell Reno that. Pull the company back toward the center."

Shafter retraced his path and reached a trooper. "Swing to your right and tell the lads to collect in the center clearing." Then he turned to the left once more, seeking to find the other flank of A Company, lost somewhere in the thicket. Dust came into the woods

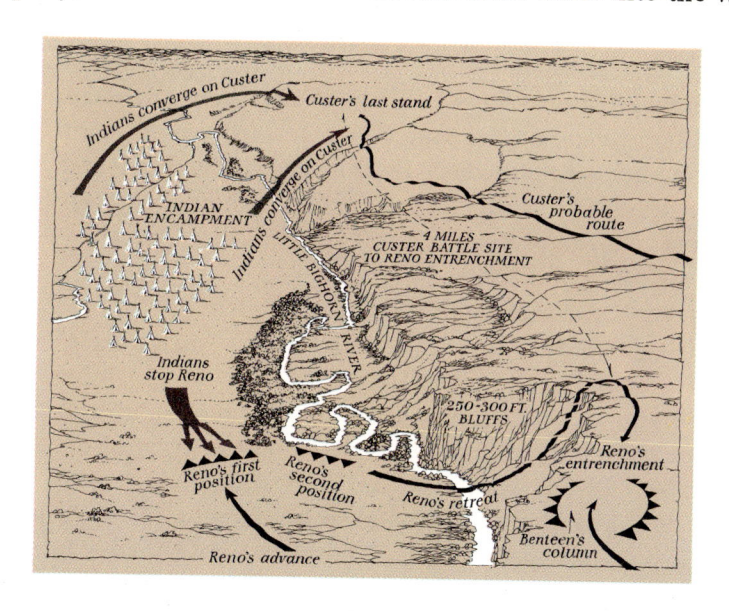

from the plain and presently he caught a smell that was something other than dust—the taint of leaves burning. Directly after that he heard the dry rustle of flames. The Sioux had fired the grove.

Now crouched and running, he moved twenty feet and came upon Dr. Porter, kneeling over Charley Reynolds. "Fall back, Doctor," said Shafter. "Toward the center."

"Give me a hand with Charley," answered the doctor as he turned to Reynolds. He put a hand on Reynolds' chest and shook his head. "No, never mind," he said, and got up. Dorman lay dead ten feet away, with a little ring of cartridges around him. When Shafter reached the middle clearing with the doctor he saw the remnants of the battalion gathering from the edges of the grove and the horse holders standing ready. He joined A Company's half-assembled ranks. Reno waited by his horse, his face flushed. He was an anxious, uncertain man faced with a terrible decision.

Heat lay through the trees in smothering pressure, and bullets from the Sioux guns whipped the clearing. Moylan, Wallace, and French waited, then grew tired of waiting. French said, "This position is becoming untenable, Reno."

Bloody Hand swung up to his pony and murmured, "Better go—better go."

Reno cast a strained eye around a command grown thinner from casualties and from strays still lost in the grove, then announced, "We'll charge back up the valley and cross the river to the bluffs." He swung to his saddle, close by the waiting Bloody Hand. Moylan and French were calling to their troops when McIntosh plunged breathless from the woods.

"Column of fours!" roared Moylan.

"My troop's not collected!" McIntosh yelled.

French shouted at him, "We can't wait. You go first, Moylan. I'll follow. Bring up the rear, 'Tosh!"

Reno had swung his horse around; and at that instant a Sioux bullet made its sightless track across the clearing and punched its way through Bloody Hand's brain, showering blood on the nearby Reno. The major flung up a hand to his face, badly shaken. Then he shook his head, commanded, "Forward!" and set his horse to a gallop.

The column followed in loose disorder. They were in full motion when they came out of the timber into the valley, into the rolling clouds of dust raked up by the Sioux, who had now swept around the grove and set up their sharp fire at the column's head. Horses slammed together under excitement and troopers began to yell full voice. Reno and Hodgson led the way, Reno swaying hatless in his saddle. Shafter glanced behind him and saw M Company directly following; but beyond M Company, G came in scattered, straggling bunches.

Suddenly mounted Sioux darted in, riding parallel to the column. They flung up their carbines, took bobbing aim, and fired. They made sudden dead-on runs at the column until their horses scraped against the running mounts of the troopers, and presently the column, pouring forward at a full run, was engaged in deadly, hand-to-hand wrestling.

Shafter jammed his carbine into its boot and now used his revolver point-blank. He saw his targets waver and turned to watch an Indian fall. But the Sioux were pressing in with a daring that came from sure knowledge of their victory. The close fire struck home and troopers fell screaming and riderless horses bolted away. Shafter saw Lieutenant McIntosh running alone beside the column with two Indians boxing him. He swung over, but was too late. McIntosh flung up both hands and disappeared beneath the hoofs of the oncoming Indians.

It seemed an endless, hopeless run down the valley. The battalion was a skeleton. The horses ran in the loose gait of near-exhaustion. Shafter galloped beside a trooper who rolled like a drunk in the saddle and whose face wore an unrecognizing blankness. Shafter cried, "Sit up, man! Hang on!"

Reno swung the column along the river, and thus they ran with the bright flash of the water beckoning them at the foot of a bank, too sheer to descend. Across the river stood the bluffs whose rough-crowned tops promised safety.

One trooper wheeled to the edge of the bank and made a desperate fifteen-foot leap. Horse and rider struck in a great spray and afterward the horse struggled on alone, the rider never coming to the surface. Garnett, at the foot of A Company, now put spurs to his horse and drew forward until he rode abreast Reno. He cried out, "Here's a ford," and rushed down a crack in the bluff.

The battalion followed that narrow cut to the edge of the water. The leading horses, crazed by thirst, slackened and tore the reins free from the troopers' tight grasp. They stopped belly-deep in the stream and made a barricade which spread back and blocked the small pathway down the bluff. The men of the battalion, coming on in desperate haste, fanned out and took to the river from whatever point they found themselves. Carbine fire began to whip at the troopers in the water.

Shafter had crossed the river when he saw Donovan's horse drop, sending Donovan to the ground. Donovan got up and shouted as troopers fled by him toward the rising slopes of the bluff. Then he lifted his pistol and took his stand, firing back across the river.

Shafter ran beside him and kicked one foot out of his near stirrup. Donovan put his foot in the stirrup and lifted himself behind Shafter, whose horse now dropped to a slow and weary walk.

"There goes Benny Hodgson!" shouted Donovan.

Hodgson had fallen midstream, waist-deep. He got to his feet and staggered forward. A passing trooper paused long enough for the boy lieutenant to seize a stirrup, and in this manner he was towed out of the river, turning around and around, dragging his limp feet. He was on the shore when a second bullet dropped him.

Halfway up that hard, bitter incline Shafter saw Dr. DeWolfe die, struck by a bullet from the heights. Troopers dotted the trail, some racing far ahead, some still coming over the water. They slashed the last grain of energy out of their half-dead horses, they scrambled afoot; they stopped to fire, they plugged on, one weary yard at a time; they collapsed and sat in momentary agony, and got up and went on again. They fell and lay still.

Not far from the summit Shafter saw Garnett reel in his horse, make a futile grab to save himself, and fall shoulder first. He was crawling upgrade on his belly when Shafter passed him and he turned his head hopefully and looked up, about to ask for help. But when he saw Shafter he closed his mouth and groaned and resumed his painful inching progress.

Shafter reached the crest and found Reno with half a dozen troopers already arrived. Reno, a dazed expression on his face, watched his broken battalion come up. He kept saying, "Spread out and cover the others." Donovan dropped off and Shafter dismounted and fell to his stomach on the edge of the crest, bringing his carbine into play. His heart pumped painfully; his throat was parched and his chest aflame.

Three hundred feet below Shafter saw Garnett lying flat on the ground, apparently dead. But presently Garnett raised his head slightly and looked up to the crest, then lowered his head again. Across the river the Sioux were now streaming around the grove to the valley's lower end.

"They're not following up their attack," said Moylan.

"I'm damned glad," joined in French. "We're out of ammunition."

He heard someone yell, "Here comes Benteen," and he looked to his left, southeastward along the spine of the bluffs. Benteen's three companies moved briskly forward and Benteen jumped from his saddle. He asked, "Where's Custer?"

"I'll be damned if I know," said Reno. "He was to have supported me. We got down there and took one hell of a beating."

The Sioux made a long, cloudy line on the plain, racing away, and Moylan murmured, "I don't understand that." Then all of them heard one faraway volley westward.

"There's Custer," said Benteen. "In a fight."

Troopers continued to struggle up the slope, their eyes glazed. And now other troopers, partly rested, moved back down from the summit to rescue the wounded stragglers. Shafter had his eyes pinned to Garnett's motionless shape, and a steady hatred held him still. Then he laid aside his carbine and slid down the slope. He got to Garnett and crouched. "You alive?"

Garnett slowly turned his head in the dust. He looked at Shafter's feet, murmuring, "You got any water?"

"No," said Shafter. He hooked Garnett around the shoulders and sat him upright. He braced the man against his legs and heaved again, pulling Garnett up. He balanced him a moment, doubting his own strength. Then he crouched and in one sharp effort he got Garnett on his shoulder and went up the hill. His feet slid on the soft underfooting. He said, "You dog, I shouldn't be doing this."

At five-o'clock a dust-red sun flamed low on the western horizon. The valley below was almost empty of Sioux, but from two higher points Indians lay and intermittently fired. From the west now and then came a faint pulse of gunfire. Benteen, salty and cool under disaster, was posting the companies while Reno moved aimlessly, dazed by what he had undergone. The walking wounded toiled painfully up the slope. Details were bringing up those critically injured, while Dr. Porter moved among them, making such shifts as he could.

McDougall's B Company had arrived with the packtrain and extra ammunition. Captain Weir, one of Custer's nearest friends, stood arguing with Reno. "We should be moving out to support Custer. He is very definitely engaged at the lower end of the valley."

"So were we very definitely engaged," said Reno irritably. "My orders were to attack and that I would be supported. I attacked. I was not supported. I had no orders at all to support Custer. It is only by God's miracle we survived to reach this hill."

"He may be in extreme trouble," urged Weir.

"He may be," said Reno. "And so are we. Take a look around you, Weir. Does this look like a battalion presently fit for service?"

"Orders or not," said Weir stubbornly, "you have your judgment to exercise. My God, there are a thousand or two thousand Sioux down there fighting him."

"I'm better aware of it than you are," said Reno dryly. "I have just come out of all that. My judgment is first to protect my own battalion. We shall be attacked again."

Weir stamped angrily away and moved over to Edgerly. The two remained in considerable conversation, after which Weir mounted his horse and came back toward Reno. He said something to Reno and then moved out alone. Within five minutes Edgerly pulled D Company into formation and followed Weir.

Benteen came up to Reno. "Where's Weir going?"

"Damned if I know."

"You're in charge here, aren't you?" said Benteen acidly. "I'd suggest you pull him back."

"No," said Reno, temporarily resolute. "We'll move out and see if we can support Custer, wherever he is."

The troops drearily assembled. Blankets were opened and the wounded placed upon them, four men to a blanket. In the harsh sunlight of late afternoon the battalion started west along the rough summit of the bluffs. A mile onward they got to a high peak and saw the lower end of the valley, all hazy with the churning of Sioux horses. They could see Sioux madly circling into sight and riding down out of sight again. And from beyond a lower peak came one last volley, followed by the crack of an occasional gun.

Weir was ahead and now he stopped, his troopers dismounting. The crooked ravines before him suddenly disgorged Sioux and within five minutes he was in a bitter fight, gradually retreating until he came upon the main command. "Now, dammit," cried Reno to Weir, "you see what it's like!"

Indians erupted over the lower peak and slashed forward. They struck up from the long slopes to the north; they clambered forward on the rocky outcrop of the sheer bluff to the south. The battalion, exhausted by a steady twenty-four-hour march and half destroyed by an afternoon's fighting, flung itself into defensive position. Benteen paced back and forth, maneuvering the companies in a rough circle to defend the knob. There was a shallow depression in the middle area of the knob and here he posted the packhorses and made a breastwork of the packs, behind which he placed the wounded.

"Wallace," he ordered, "put G here," and indicated the place with his arm.

Wallace said wearily, "There are just three men left in G."

"Very well. Place those three here."

The sun was low and the light had changed. Now the Sioux poured back, climbing up the bluff, sidling along the ravines and rock barriers, boiling across the river. From the two adjoining higher peaks the Sioux began to fire down on the exposed circle.

"Damn that sun," a trooper shouted. "Why don't it set?"

Shafter lay flat, watching the distant rocks, waiting for a fair shot. Donovan died silently beside him. A crazed horse rocketed around the circle, charged down the slope, tripped itself on its dropped reins, and went end over end in a small avalanche of shale all the way to the river. There was no letup while daylight lasted, but at eight o'clock the sun fell and the shadows came mercifully to end the gunfire.

Chapter 15

IN THE CENTER of the area Dr. Porter steadily worked on the wounded. Voices began to lift, shaken by agony. "Who's got some water?" The officers stirred around, taking check of their companies. Moylan said to Shafter, "We have got to dig in tonight. They'll be at us when daylight comes."

Shafter moved along A Company's line. "Start digging. Make yourself a shelter." The call for water from the wounded rubbed his nerves raw; it was worse than anything that had gone before. He collected a dozen canteens and searched for Moylan in the shadows. "I'm going down to the river."

"The valley is crawling with Sioux," said Moylan. "Hear all those owls hooting?"

"I can hoot as well," said Shafter. "Where do you think Custer is, Myles?"

"Maybe he broke through and went on to meet Terry, but I don't think so. I think he's dead. I think they're all dead, all two hundred of them. Terry's all we've got to hope for now, and he'd better come soon. There's three thousand Sioux in that damned valley and they'll all be at us first thing morning comes."

Shafter dropped slowly down the long slope, moving cautiously in the muddy darkness, softly calling to the pickets. When he got to the water's edge he flattened on his belly and drank sparingly. Then he ducked his head under and drew back, licking his tongue against his dripping mouth. He thought, This is the last drink for God knows how long. He drank again, until he felt slightly sick. He filled the canteens and started back up the bluff.

The canteens weighed him down and each foot of advance was painfully difficult. His leg muscles ached and the steepness of the slope dragged at him. When he came to the summit he stumbled over to the pack barricade, where the wounded lay. Dr. Porter crouched beside a man, a stub end of a candle lighting his work. "A little water," offered Shafter.

Porter stared at the canteens. His own thirst tortured him and he showed the struggle on his face. Then he called quietly to his orderly, "Toomey, come dole out this water. None for you, Toomey, and none for any who is able-bodied."

Shafter felt oppressed by the sound of misery around him, and by its smell. Men lay under the feeble circle of the candlelight and were shadows moving just beyond it. He heard them calling, "Toomey—for God's sakes, bring me a drink!" Porter suddenly leaned back from his patient and gave the man a long look. "Nothing more for you until we can get you in a better place."

"You don't have to tell me that way, Porter."

Shafter looked around, recognizing Garnett's voice.

"I haven't told you anything, Garnett," Porter said, and moved on to the next man. Shafter bent, seeing Garnett's pale face grow rough with the knowledge of his own dying. Garnett stared up at Shafter.

"Light's bad," he whispered. "That you, Kern?"

"Yes." Shafter unscrewed his canteen top. "Take a drink."

"You're wasting it. I'll be dead in a little while."

"A man's got a right to die with a drink in him," said Shafter. He stared down, not even now able to feel sympathy.

Garnett sighed. "Give me the drink, then," he said.

Shafter slid the flat of his hand behind Garnett's head and lifted it. He listened to the greedy sucking sound of Garnett's lips on the canteen, then pulled it away. "That's enough to die on."

"I think the bullet smashed my spine," Garnett murmured. "I can feel nothing from the hips down."

"This time," said Shafter, "you couldn't duck."

"I was never afraid of anything and you damned well know it," Garnett replied weakly. "I'm not afraid now, and I'm not sorry for a thing I've ever done."

"It is good to know you'll never ruin another woman."

Garnett lay still and thought about that. "Why," he said finally, "it was a game with me. But you've got that wrong, too, Kern. I doubt if I ever ruined any woman. I doubt if I ever made a woman do something she hadn't made up her mind to do. Do you understand that, Kern?"

"No."

"You're thinking of Alice," murmured Garnett. "A dead man doesn't have to be a gentleman, Kern, so I'll tell you something about her. She was my kind, not yours. You think I took her away from you. I had damned little to do with it. She was after me and I played the game. She knew you and I were friends. She broke up that friendship, but after she got me, she didn't want me. I had my illusions about her, as you did. I thought the whole world was in her eyes. Then I discovered the coldness behind her beauty. I have never respected another woman. Is that candle going out? It's getting dark."

"No, it is still burning."

"Then I'm the one going out. What a hell of a mess today's been. Where's Custer?"

"Nobody knows."

"I wish you luck for tomorrow," said Garnett.

Shafter had no answer for that. He watched Garnett's face lose its sharpness one line at a time, until presently he was a spirit quietly withdrawing, half free but not wholly free of his body.

"In pain?" asked Shafter.

"No."

Garnett was silent for so long that Shafter thought he had died. Then his head moved on the ground. He looked up into the night, at the far stars winking. "If I had it to do over again," he said at last, "I should not do the same things. That's what you're waiting to hear, Kern—the cry of a man afraid."

"I am disappointed in you," said Shafter.

"The last woman was the one I wanted and could not have because of what I had been before I met her. That is something you didn't know about me. I was more of a man of honor in her presence than you supposed."

"Josephine?" said Shafter.

"Josephine," whispered Garnett, and died.

Shafter got up and moved stiffly toward the northern edge of the defense circle. He thought, I've got to dig my shelter, and dreaded the chore. He was tired in a way he had never been tired—made stupid and indifferent by it. He got out his knife and began to dig the sandy-powdered soil. He worked mechanically, his muscles reluctantly answering his will. By midnight he had made a shallow depression. He settled into it, uncomfortably lying on his cartridge belt, and fell asleep.

STARTLED BY THE sound of a single shot, Shafter woke suddenly. Day trembled through morning's twilight, and the peaks to either side came into view.

Moylan came and sat down by him. "Kern," he said, "I wrote a letter a month ago to General Summers. He's close to Sherman. I told him to open a case that had been shut too long."

Shafter said, "You ought to let dead things alone. They'll never touch it."

"I did Summers a good turn once when he was a young captain. He owes me a turn and I told him I wanted it. A word from him to Sherman will be enough."

"Once it would have mattered. Now, I don't care."

"Yes," said the captain, "you do. Otherwise what brought you back to the uniform?"

"I could think of nothing else to do," Shafter answered.

"So you did the thing which was in your mind. You came back."

Shafter smiled at Moylan, and the captain moved away.

Company A held the east segment of the circle, facing the higher peak, from which Sioux were now firing. H and K lay overlooking the ford to the south and M guarded the west, taking the fire from the peak which stood in that direction. To the north, where the ridge ran gradually downward into flat land, B and D and the pitiful remnant of G had been placed.

The sun came full up. At nine o'clock the firing had grown to an outright engagement and the Sioux had begun an encircling movement. A constant, down-plunging leaden rain came from the two peaks to north and south. Along the lower rocks, between the south rim and the ford, the brown Sioux bodies made a spotty, shifting pattern against the gray earth. Reno came over to look down that way and spoke his judgment.

"They wish to draw our attention. The main attack is shaping to the north."

Over there the land fell gently, slashed by frequent gullies into which the Sioux filtered. A great party moved around the base of the southern peak, made a wide sweep, and rushed into the gullies. Benteen came up to Reno.

"If they get any nearer, they'll swamp us with a sudden charge. We've got to attack."

"You'll lose every man you take out there," said Reno. "But if you can get a party together, we'll go."

Now Moylan sat behind his section of the company, loading guns and passing them to his troopers with his calm counsel. "Take your time. Wait until you see the sweat on their bellies." Behind Shafter, Benteen's voice made a strong, steady call and troopers were gathering themselves for a rush. The Indian line, now drawing about the knoll from all sides, brought a heavier gunfire to bear. Shafter watched A Company's thin line wilt on the ground, saw men flinch and roll helplessly aside and turn wild glances upon him.

Reno's voice came back through the snarl of gunfire. "Forward!" As the major jumped forward firing his revolver, Shafter ran after him, came abreast of the line, and ran with it. The skirmishers rushed down toward the nearest gully, firing as they ran. Men whimpered a little and paused, sat slowly down, and were left behind. Twenty yards from the gully Shafter watched Sioux spring out of it and run backward toward the next lower gully. Reno stopped and turned. "That does it," he shouted, his eyes round and black-ringed. "Back to the top." The line swung, trotting upgrade, pushed now by the danger to the rear. Bullets whipped by and scraped up flinty showers of earth. Shafter reached the top, breathing heavily, and half turned to look behind him. At that moment he was struck hard in the body and dropped to his hands and knees. He started to rise again, and fell back. For the smallest interval of time there was a roar in his head like the breaking of surf; after that all sound ceased.

The sortie had driven the Sioux back from the near coulee and the firing slackened and men began to reach out for the wounded. A pair of D troopers carried Shafter to the pack barricade before Porter, who worked on his knees, his sleeves rolled up and his long hands bloodstained. He gave Shafter a single, hard look and said to the troopers, "Take his shirt off."

Moylan came up a little later and found Porter working on Shafter. Moylan asked, "Where's he hit?"

"Near the kidney," said the doctor, and leaned back to dash the sweat from his nose.

"What's that on his face?"

"He hit a rock when he fell."

"Porter," asked Moylan, "how much does a man have to suffer to earn salvation?"

Porter shook his head and returned to his labors.

The sun moved on, blistering the earth with its heat, and the wounded began to stir under it and cry out. At two o'clock the Sioux fire grew brisk and for half an hour the command fought doggedly. In the following lull the officers held a conference.

"Custer must have gone on to Terry," said Weir.

"Terry was due at the mouth of the Little Bighorn this morning," said Godfrey. "He should be here."

Moylan shook his head. "If he's anywhere around this valley, he's in one hell of a fight, same as we are."

Captain French made a short, roundabout gesture with his hand. "Time can't be held much longer. We're being cut to ribbons. We have got to move to one of those two higher points tonight."

"We have got to get water," added McDougall.

Reno said dourly, "Without help, we won't last tonight—"

"By God, sir," cut in Benteen brusquely, "we'll last."

SHAFTER HAD SLEPT for three hours and now he was awake and the pain began to move through him. He rocked his head from side to side and discovered men lying in a row beyond him, some still and some groaning. Porter's orderly was nearby. Shafter asked, "What's the matter with me, Toomey?"

"You got a hole in your guts."

Shock sickened him and he thought, I must be dying. The pain took on the rhythm of his pulse, slow and steady, and in a little while he was a mass of flame.

Moylan came over and looked down. "How are you, Kern?"

"All right."

"The Indians have quit massing against us," said Moylan. He watched Shafter a moment, then went away.

There were fewer and fewer exchanges of firing. The men at the parapets began to rise, dusty and parched, and to move around with the looseness of physical exhaustion. The smell of the wounded hung in the air, faintly sweet, faintly foul. Details formed to move the horses down toward the river. Shafter heard Reno talking to Benteen.

"They've gone back toward the foot of the valley."

"They wouldn't be leaving us unless they were threatened elsewhere," said Benteen. "That will be Terry or Custer."

A detail returned with water for the wounded. Moylan came over to give Shafter a drink, and sprinkled some of it on Shafter's face. Then Godfrey called, and Moylan went back toward the south rim of the peak.

"Look there," said Godfrey.

The Sioux had broken camp at the lower end of the valley and now were passing up the same area across which Reno's troop had charged. The column stretched on and on, braves and squaws and travois and horse herd. All the officers and men lined the brow of the hill to watch it pass and swing south into the broken land.

"A mile wide and three miles long," said Benteen, calculating the column's strength. "Fully three thousand warriors. That's what we ran into."

The sun had begun to set, its long rays flashing on Indian lance and gun. The sound of voices and the rattle of gear came up the slope like the faint babble of geese in the distant sky. Benteen said suddenly, "There are white men in that outfit."

"White men's clothes," corrected Godfrey; and then all of them heard the notes of a cavalry trumpet—a pure blast without tune or meaning—come from the column.

"Clothes and trumpet," said Moylan. "There's your answer. Stripped from dead troopers."

Night came down, the stars bright and immense in the sky. In Shafter's belly a great bomb of pain exploded. He stretched his arms and dug his fingers into the ground, sweated, and felt sick. A wind came up and cooled him slightly; and thus partly relieved, he fell asleep. He woke once during the night and lay listening to the little sounds in the camp, the pacing of the sentries, the snoring of exhausted men, and the suppressed sighing and gritted suspirations of the wounded. Then he fell asleep a second time.

When he woke again the sun had started up and he saw a column of riders come over the hill's crest, General Terry in the lead. Terry got down, reached out, and shook Reno's hand and then Benteen's. There were tears in Terry's eyes.

"General," inquired Reno, "where is Custer?"

"Custer," said Terry, and nodded to the west, "is three miles down there, dead."

"Where's his battalion?"

"Dead," said Terry. His voice broke and he bent his head, wrestling with his self-control. "All of them, every man and every beast. A terrible blunder—a terrible, tragic, unnecessary blunder."

The group of officers stood in stunned silence. Much capacity for feeling had been taken out of them, yet this was a shock that all felt, this complete extinction of five companies. Reno lifted a hand and surreptitiously wiped moisture from his eyes. Weir, who had loved Custer, flung up a hand and turned aside. Terry looked about and saw the remnant of Reno's command and the brutal evidence of its ordeal. He was a sad and weary and troubled man. His carefully planned campaign had turned into a great disaster. His regiment, which had marched up the Rosebud in high hope, its colors flying and its commander dreaming of gallantry, now lay as a broken thing on the dry, hot earth, more than two hundred and fifty of its men dead and another sixty wounded. They had come upon the Sioux at the high flood of their power, the greatest concentration of strength ever seen upon the plains. That Sioux power now slowly moved away undefeated, while Terry with his battered command could not follow.

His trap, designed to snap shut, had been set off prematurely by Custer's impetuous disregard of his orders. Wanting glory and blindly believing in himself and his regiment, Custer had not waited. The power of waiting was not in him. More than that, the expected help of Crook had not come. With a command greater than Terry's, Crook had dallied on the upper Powder, cautiously sealing himself in with double-strength pickets, made afraid by his defeat, and calling for help. Of this Terry then knew nothing. It only mattered that the campaign had failed.

He turned to his adjutant and said slowly, "Send a man back to the *Far West* and tell them to push the boat upstream as far as they dare. We shall be bringing on the wounded to be taken back to Lincoln. We must have details out at once to bury the dead. Waste no time. We have got to pull out."

From his place behind the packs Shafter saw the command's sudden activity with a disinterested eye. Fever thinned his blood and lifted him so that sometimes he seemed weightless above the ground. He was placed in a blanket litter slung from poles, two mules fore and aft on the poles. With this motion cradling and easing him he slept and woke and saw the sky bright, and slept again, later to wake and find the sky black. Three days later he was on the *Far West* and only vaguely aware of it.

On the third of July the *Far West* blew its whistle for the landing at Fort Lincoln and, with its jack staff black-draped and its flag at half-mast, touched shore. A runner went out immediately with the news, and in the middle of the night officers reluctantly walked toward Officers' Row to notify the wives of the dead. The wounded were carried to the post infirmary. In Bismarck a telegrapher flashed the news east, and at midnight someone rapped on the Russells' door. Josephine had heard the boat's whistle. Now, moved by the intimations of fear, she dressed and hurried to the post.

Chapter 16

THERE WAS SPACE all around him; he swept back and forth in it, as though in a giant swing. Then a great storm swept this space and he was whirled end over end. Then calmness came and he floated without motion or sound or feeling. There were moments when he drifted near consciousness and heard voices, and recognized his own voice among them, and felt the touch of the bed and sometimes the cold pressure of a hand on his face.

Time would not stay fixed. It was a distance between two points, but the points were forever moving. He walked back and forth between them and found he could make the trip sometimes in one minute, sometimes in six hours. But there was no difference between the minute and the six hours. He said, "There is no such thing as time," and felt a great wave of peace roll through him. He would never have to worry about time anymore.

He was still now, motionless in the motionless void, a shadow in shadows. "No," he said, "that can't be true. I think and I feel—and I see." But what did he see and what was it he felt? He sought for his answer, patiently and stubbornly. "What am I?" he asked. Then he said, "I am something."

He woke as he had wakened thousands of other times. Consciousness arrived softly and he opened his eyes and saw the walls around him, the stove in the room, the iron frame at the foot of his bed, and the gray blanket folded there. Josephine sat beside the bed.

"Hello, Kern," she said.

"What time is it?"

"Nine in the morning."

"What morning?"

"Saturday morning."

"This Fort Lincoln?"

"Yes."

Shafter lay with his head turned, watching her. There was a strange, moist shining in her eyes. He said, "Bend forward," and put out his hand. He touched her cheek, and felt its smoothness and its reality. He murmured, "A very odd thing," and then, as though this one gesture had worn him out, he fell asleep.

The following afternoon he woke again and was fed. Josephine came in for a short time and sat at his bed.

"Garnett's dead," he told her.

"I know."

"He spoke your name. Of all the women he knew, you were the one he remembered."

"Did he ask you to tell me anything?"

"No. But a woman should know when a man dies with her memory in him."

"Do you want me to thank you for telling me this?"

"I'm only doing a chore."

He held his eyes on her, wanting some sign from her, but she gave him none. She said, "Better sleep," and went away.

Major Barrows and his wife called that afternoon. They talked a little while; then the major excused himself and strolled down the room.

Mrs. Barrows said, "It was terrible for all of you, wasn't it?"

"It was a hard fight."

She turned her head to notice that her husband was at the far end of the room and now she swung her glance back to Shafter. "Sergeant," she murmured, "how did Edward Garnett die?"

He said to himself, So he got her, too. She had loved the man and was tortured now. He thought of what he was to say very carefully.

"We were halfway up the hill when he was hit. He got to the top and lasted until that night. But he wasn't in much pain."

She sat still, her eyes begging him to add something. Presently she whispered, "Were you with him when he died?"

"Yes."

"Did he speak of me at all?"

This was what she wanted to hear, so urgently that she had stripped herself of her honor before him.

"Yes," he said, lying. "He called your name when he died."

She drew a ragged breath and her hands came together and whitened with pressure. She bowed her head, struggling with her composure. In a little while the major returned. Shafter noticed the way his glance surreptitiously touched his wife. Then the major said quietly, "We mustn't wear him out, Margaret."

She stood up, very cool again. She said, "God be with you, Sergeant," and for the first time she smiled.

The wind blew rough and dry across the parade as the major and his wife stepped from the hospital. The major took her arm and looked at her with a consideration that was odd in him. "Turn your face from it, Margaret."

"I'm not that fragile."

"This land is hard on precious things," he said.

She gave him a startled glance. "Why, Joseph, I haven't heard you say that for so long—"

"I know," he murmured. "I know."

THE NEXT MORNING the hospital orderly brought Shafter a letter. It was from the adjutant general.

> By order of the General of the Armies, please be informed that your record has been reviewed and certain findings set aside. This is your authority to request reinstatement, as first lieutenant of cavalry, United States Army. If you wish to act upon this authority, make application through the adjutant, Seventh Cavalry, submit to physical examination and return papers to this office for approval.

When Josephine came that afternoon he showed the letter to her and watched her eyes move intently back and forth over the writing.

"Are you going to accept it?" she asked.

"Yes."

"Many things have happened to you, Kern. Some of them have been harsh. Or were you a wild young man?"

"It was a woman with whom I was in love," he explained. "Garnett was my best friend in those days."

"He took her from you, Kern?"

"Or she went to him. Who knows about those things? She had come down behind the lines to see me. This was in the Shenandoah Valley, in a little town. When I got away to go to the town to meet her I found Garnett with her. The hotel room," he added irrelevantly, "had rosebud wallpaper. We fought with swords all the way downstairs and out through the door. I slashed him and he fell. He was senior to me as an officer and naturally preferred charges. Neither of us could explain the cause of the quarrel, so it stood as insubordination on my part. I was dismissed from the army, enlisted under another name, and served the rest of the war as a private."

She listened to him with absorbed attention. She said swiftly, "Do you still hate her, Kern, or want her greatly?"

"I saw her in Fargo, on my last mail trip. It was all gone—everything. You can't restore faith. I was very young and love is a terrible thing when you're young."

"But not when you're a mature man, Kern?"

He shrugged his shoulders.

She said, "I can understand why you hated Garnett. You still do, don't you?"

"No. It would be difficult for me to hate any man, living or dead, who rode down that valley with me. Could I have a drink of water?"

She poured water out of a jug into a glass. She started to hand it to him, then bent and slipped an arm under his head and lifted him and held it. Her hand was warm and firm on his back.

"You're so thin, Kern."

"I'll be standing retreat one month from now, in this regiment."

"At least," she said, "you have faith left in one thing, in your kind of men. For all other things, you are an empty man. Garnett and that woman killed so much in you."

"Why, Josephine, he's dead and she's two thousand miles away."

"Are they?" she asked, and rose. "I don't think so, Kern."

Mrs. Custer came to see him, and Algernon Smith's wife. They sat by him, forlorn women now, each made aimless by a Sioux bullet. He listened to the pacing of the sentry on the baked earth and he heard the echoes strike hollow through the emptied garrison. He slept soundly that night and woke, then was restless throughout the morning.

When Josephine came the next afternoon she gave him a keen look. "You're better," she said. "You're cranky. Now I shan't have to come as often."

"When did you first come?"

"The night the boat brought you down. It was midnight."

He had his head on the edge of the pillow, uncomfortably turned to look at her. She watched him a moment, and bent forward to lift his head and replace the pillow. She drew back her arm, but held her position, looking straight down upon his face; feeling roughened the smoothness of her lips.

"I can't reach up," he said.

"Do you want to?"

"Yes."

"Do you always want your own way? Do you always expect people to come back after you've knocked them down?"

"When you hate a man your eyes turn dead black."

"It isn't hate," she whispered. "But I've got too much to give you to even let myself start—if I can't be sure you have something for me."

"Remember the last time I kissed you?"

"Yes."

"Was it a very mild thing, Josephine?"

Her lips were near and all her fragrance came to him. He saw her lips move and become heavy. He watched her eyes darken. She made a little gesture and put herself on the edge of the bed and lowered her face to him. Then her warmth and her weight came full against him. She drew her mouth away, whispering into his ear. "Will you keep me close, will you never tire, will you never be less than you are now?" She waited for no answer, but came to him again. It was like a tall fire springing up through the black sky, touching heaven; and by its light the land around lay full and mysterious and wonderful.

THE INDIANS

Driven from their ancient homes
the hard-pressed Indians come at last to rest—
a proud, free-roaming people
captive now in the white man's empire

Teepees, a scene of Plains Indian life, by Joseph H. Sharp

The medicine man, wrote Charles M. Russell, often had more influence over the movements of his people than th

ecause they believed he could speak with spirits. Migrating Plains Indians inspired Russell's *The Medicine Man*.

War dance by the Taos Indians of New Mexico as witnessed and painted by E. Irving Couse

"There has been trouble between us," a Comanche chief told government representatives, "and my young men have danced the war dance. But it was not begun by us. I came upon this road, following the buffalo, that my wives and children might have their cheeks plump and their bodies warm. But the soldiers fired on us, and we went out like buffalo bulls when their cows are attacked. When we found them, we killed them and their scalps hang in our lodges."

War bonnet with beaded flower pattern

Missing—and a candidate for execution. By Frederic Remi[ngton]

Blackfoot chief's scalp shirt

Sioux deerskin moccasins

Council of War by Charles

"The Apache knew his business," wrote one cavalry officer. "He never lost a warrior in a fight where a brisk run would save his life and exhaust the heavily clad soldier who endeavored to catch him. Apaches were wont to steal in close to military posts and ranchos, and hide upon the summit of some conveniently situated hill, scanning the movements of the Americans below, waiting for a chance to stampede a herd or 'jump' a wagon-train."

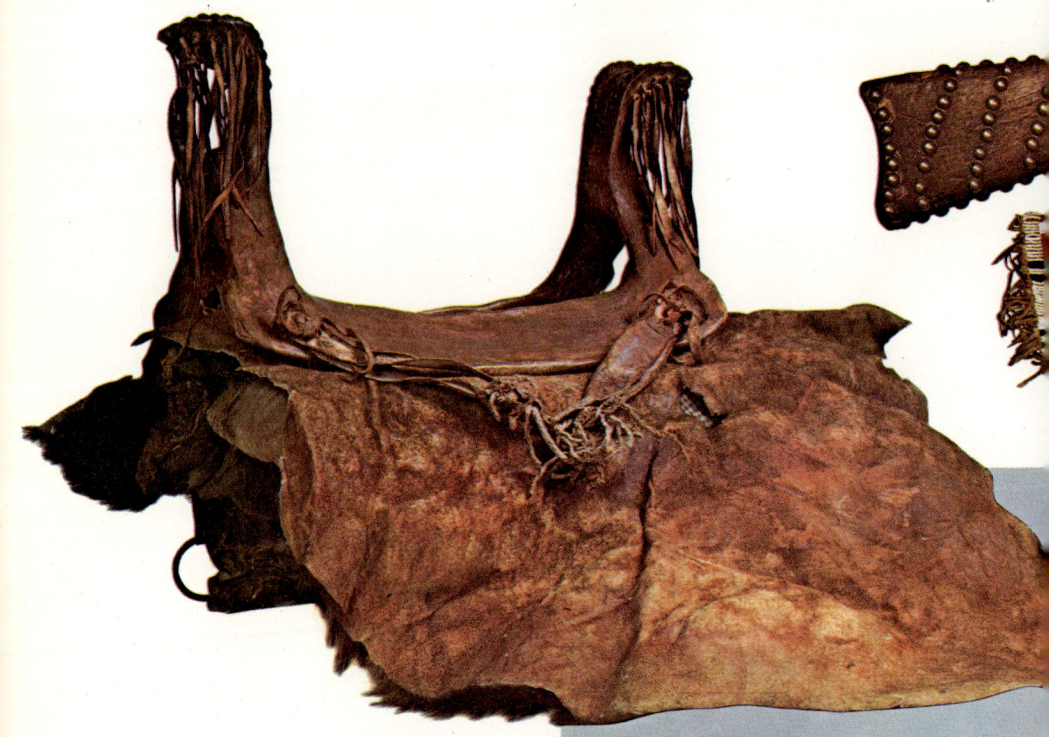

Blackfoot saddle with bearskin saddle blanket

"We did not ask you white men to come here," said the revered Sioux, Crazy Horse. "The Great Spirit gave us this country as a home. You had yours. We did not interfere with you. The Great Spirit gave us buffalo, deer and other game. But you are killing off our game. You tell us to work for a living, but the Great Spirit [made] us to live by hunting. We do not want your civilization! We would live as our fathers did, and their fathers before them."

In *The Smoke Signal* by Frederic Remington warrior sco

Indian rifle with nailhead studs and Crow rifle case

A fierce Cheyenne thrust halts an infantry column, seen in the distance, in Frederic Remington's *Indian Warfare*.

A newspaper correspondent in Wyoming with General Crook wrote of the Cheyennes, whom Crook was pursuing, that they "are the finest horsemen in America; they ride their animals as if [they were] glued to them, and load and fire with the precision of foot soldiers. Besides this *they have the bravery which comes from desperation and continued ill-treatment.*"

Right: Sioux war club and Crow shield decorated with eagle feathers

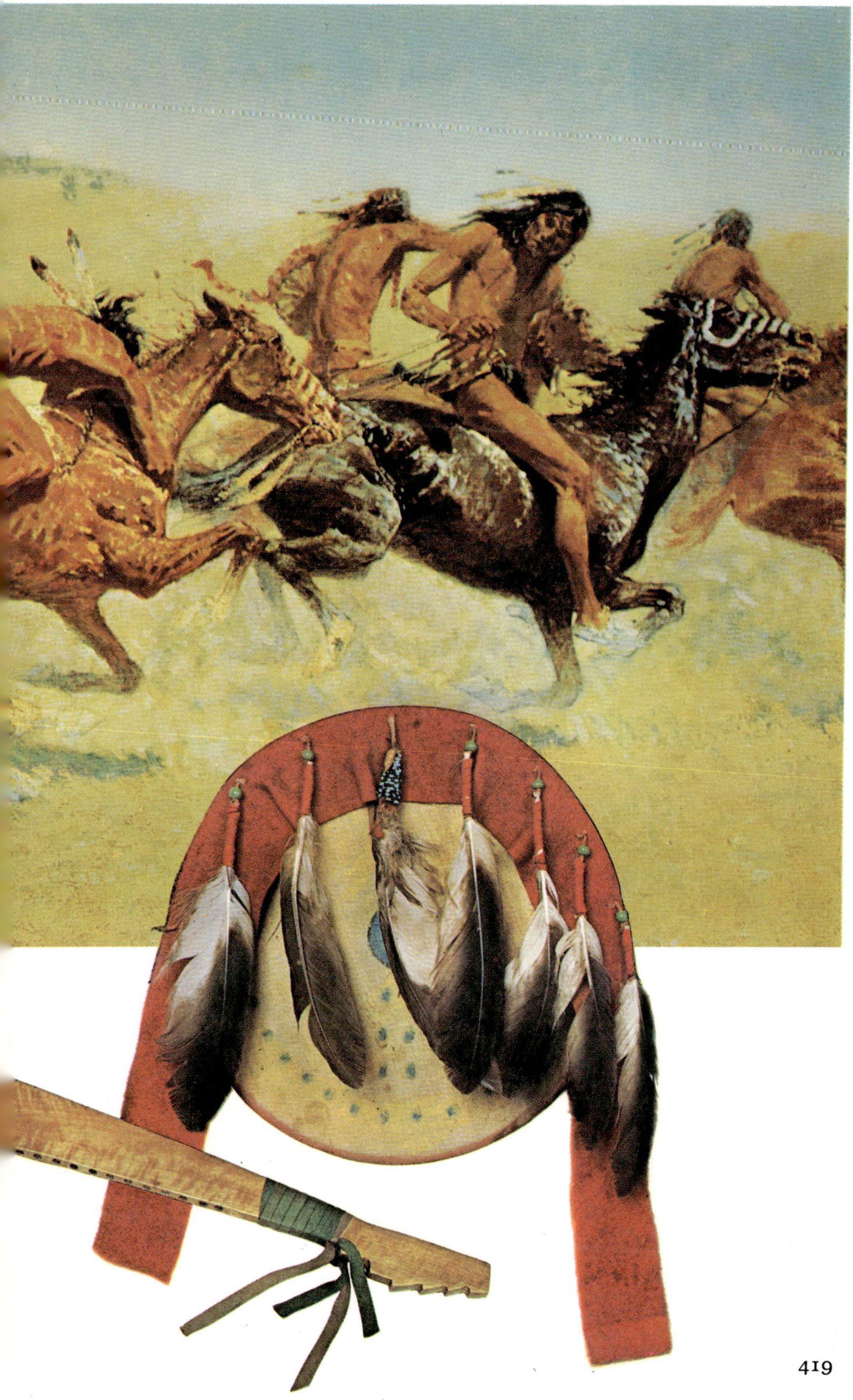

Attack at Dawn by Charles Schreyvogel depicts a surprise raid on a peaceful Cheyenne village on the Washita River

Cheyennes killed in this attack by Custer and his Seventh Cavalry, 92 were old men, women, and children.

Battle of War Bonnet Creek by Frederic Remington. Here one of the last bands of Northern Cheyennes was annih

Chief Joseph, leader of the Nez Percé tribe

On October 5, 1877, the great Chief Joseph was forced to surrender his band of Nez Percés to General Nelson Miles. He did so in these moving words: "I am tired of fighting. Our chiefs are killed. It is the young men who say yes or no. It is cold and we have no blankets. The little children are freezing to death. My people, some of them have run away to the hills and have no blankets, no food. I want to look for my children and see how many I can find. Maybe I shall find them dead. My heart is sick and sad. From where the sun now stands, I will fight no more forever."

Little Wolf (left) and Dull Knife, the chiefs who led the Northern Cheyennes' last desperate bid for freedom

General George Crook, commander of the forces sent against the defiant Cheyennes, sympathized nevertheless with the plight of Indians confined to reservations. After one visit he wrote, "I found them in a desperate condition. There is nothing for them. The buffalo is gone, and there aren't enough jackrabbits to catch. I do not wonder that when these Indians see their wives and children starving they go to war. And then we are sent out to kill them. It is an outrage."

Cheyenne captives at Dodge City, Kansas

The Cheyennes fled a bleak reservation where brush barricades were needed to protect tepees from the wind.

Cheyenne warrior Little Finger Nail carried this notebook with him to document his people's fate. The jagged slash at right came from one of the bullets that killed him at War Bonnet Creek.

In the valley of Montana's Little Bighorn, in September of 1909, once-mighty chiefs, warriors, and scouts, now stripped of power by the white man's rule, gathered for the Last Great Indian Council. Red Cloud of the Oglala Sioux was there, Two Moons of the Northern Cheyennes, and representatives of all the other tribes now confined to reservations. With them to record this historic meeting was Dr. Joseph K. Dixon, who for his interest in the welfare of the Indians had been adopted into the Wolf clan of the Mohawks with the name of Ka-ra-Kon-tie, or Flying Sun. Often in the past such councils had resulted in a call to war. But on this day the pipe of peace was passed.

And peace, wrote Dr. Dixon, "was the dominant, resonant note ringing through every sentiment uttered. . . . To stand in the presence of these mighty men of the plains, to witness their nobility, to listen to their eloquence, to think with them the thoughts of their dead past, to watch their solemn faces, to tremble before the dignity of their masterful bearing, to cherish the thought of all that they have been and all that they might have been, to realize that as their footfalls leave this council lodge they have turned their backs on each other forever, and that as they mount their horses and ride away to their distant lodges they are riding into the sunset and are finally lost in the purple mists of evening, is to make the coldest page of history burn with an altar fire that shall never go out."

Where today is the Pequot? Where
are the Narragansetts, the Mohawks,
the Pokanoket, and many other
once powerful tribes of our people?
They have vanished before the avarice
and the oppression of the White Man,
as snow before a summer sun.

                      Tecumseh, Shawnee chief

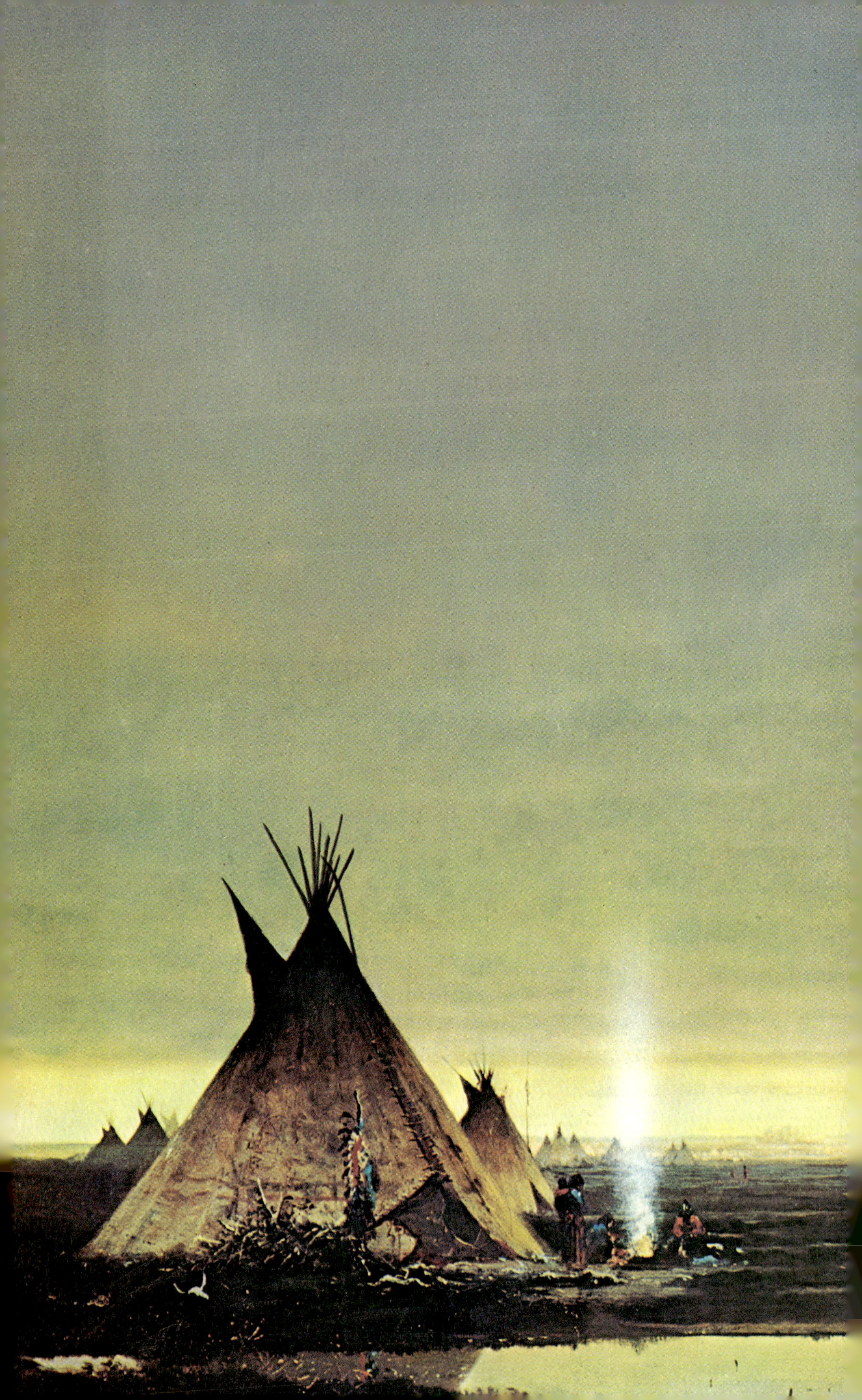

CHEYENNE AUTUMN

A CONDENSATION OF THE
BOOK BY
Mari Sandoz

TITLE-PAGE PAINTING BY
Jules Tavernier

"We have come to ask that we be sent home to our own country in the mountains." Thus spoke Little Wolf in the autumn of 1878. He and Dull Knife, both respected chiefs, both men of peace, had come to the agent in charge of the Oklahoma reservation where the Northern Cheyennes were confined.

"We want to go now," Little Wolf went on. "Before another year has passed, we may all be dead."

The request was refused. And so, under cover of night, 278 heartsick but determined Cheyennes—men, women, and children—set out on foot and on horseback for the 1500-mile trek back to their Montana hunting grounds. Every military post on the Western plains was alerted, and more than 10,000 troops under General Crook tried to stop them. But through the long hungry autumn and into the cruel northern winter the Cheyennes pressed on.

This fateful odyssey was the last great gesture of defiance made by the beleagured red men in their struggle against the encroaching whites. It is brilliantly told here by the gifted writer Mari Sandoz, long a student of Cheyenne life.

Prologue

EARLY IN THE SPRING of 1877 nearly a thousand hungry and half-naked Northern Cheyennes came in from the Yellowstone River country to the Sioux agency, Red Cloud, near Fort Robinson in northwest Nebraska. They surrendered to the promise of food and shelter and an agency in their hunting region. But almost before the children were warmed on both sides, they were told they must go to Indian Territory, the far south country, in what is now Oklahoma, which many already knew and hated. The two old man chiefs, as the tribal heads were called, listened to this command in silent refusal, but some lesser men shouted the *hou* of agreement almost before the white men got their mouths open. These Indians were given horses and fine blue blankets, and the meat and coffee and tobacco for a big feast that would build their power and following in the tribe.

"It is a trick of the spider, the *veho*," the chiefs protested, referring to the wiles of the white man. "He has long spun his web for the feet of those who have wings but are too foolish to fly."

Yet even after the feasting there were barely a handful who wanted to go south, so the Indian agent announced that he would issue no more rations to the Cheyennes here. While the Sioux women moved in their long line, holding their blankets out to receive their goods, the Cheyennes were kept off on a little knoll, their ragged blankets flapping empty in the wind, the children silent and big-eyed, watching.

Then the two chiefs, Little Wolf and Dull Knife, were told by the coaxing interpreters that the officials had said, "Just go down to see. If you don't like it you can come back." Finally they agreed, for meat for the kettles, and so, with blue-coated troopers riding ahead and behind, they pointed their moccasins down through Nebraska and Kansas toward their Southern Cheyenne relatives, who were already hungry.

The chiefs rode ahead. At a ridge south of the agency the Indians stopped and looked back toward the country that had fed and sheltered them long before one white man's track shadowed the buffalo grass. The women keened as for death, and water ran down the dark, stony faces of old Dull Knife and the rest.

It wasn't that these Cheyennes had not seen years ago that their hunting life must pass as certainly as summer died. Through Little Wolf's boyhood the Cheyennes had been very friendly to all the whites except those of the whiskey wagons that carried the brown water of violence and death. In those days these Indians ranged as far southwest as the Staked Plain of Texas, but mostly they still returned to the traders of the Platte River and up toward the Black Hills.

All this time more and more blue-coated troopers came riding, and the emigrants began to run on the trails like dark strings of ants hurrying before the winter, bringing strange sicknesses, eating up the grass of the pony herds, killing the buffalo until the wind stank and the bleaching bones lay white as morning frost on the valleys of the Platte and the Arkansas.

Leaders like Dull Knife had held the angry young men from attack, but the pockmarked face of Little Wolf grew dark along with those of the other warriors as they watched the white man come. The Cheyennes were famous for their reckless war charges, their pony herds like clouds over the hills, their painted villages, and their regalia and trappings. They had been a rather small tribe even before the new diseases scattered their dead over the prairie, but while no one owned the earth and the buffalo herds, any people who fought well and worked to keep the saddlebags full of meat could live.

As more hungry Indians were pushed westward and the encroaching whites grabbed more and more of the earth, the Cheyennes of the north began to move closer to the powerful Sioux. With bold warriors and handsome, straight-walking women among both peoples, there was considerable intermarriage. Warrior societies like the Dog Soldiers set up lodges in both tribes and often fought their red enemies together. Then, in 1851, the whites called a great conference at Fort Laramie to bring peace forever to the land west of the Missouri. More goods would keep coming, and government agencies would be established, with an agent, a "little father," to enforce the treaty on the Indians and to distribute the annuities. The agency for the Southern Cheyennes, as the whites called them now, was at Bent's Fort, but the Northern Cheyennes had to go to the Sioux agency far up the Platte.

The first big break in the peace came three years later from the whites themselves. A few whiskey-smelling soldiers killed the leading chief of the Sioux with a cannon. It was after this that the Cheyenne chiefs showed their first real anger in the government council. They wanted no more drunken soldiers shooting into peaceful camps, or emigrants scaring their buffalo. It was then that one spoke of something new, so quietly that his soft Cheyenne was barely to be heard. "We want a thousand white women as wives," he said, "to teach us and our children the new life that must be lived when the buffalo is gone."

The chiefs saw the bearded dignity of the white men break into anger at this. Plainly they did not understand that the children of Cheyennes belong to the mother's people and that this was a desperate measure to assure the food and the survival of their descendants, although in a few generations there might be not one left to be called Cheyenne anywhere under the blue kettle of the sky.

The white women did not come, and the Indians received little or nothing of the treaty goods for the lands and privileges they had sold. In 1856 some restless young men went to beg a little tobacco at the Oregon Trail and got bullets instead. They fired arrows back, hit a man in the arm, and troops came shooting. For months Colonel Edwin V. Sumner chased them around their south country. Angry that they got away, he went to Bent's Fort, where the Indians were waiting peacefully for treaty goods stored there. Sumner took what he wanted for his troops and gave the rest to the Arapahos while the young Cheyennes had to look on, their empty fingers creeping toward the trigger. But their women and children were surrounded by troops like those who had killed Little Thunder's peaceful Sioux, on the Platte last summer, so the chiefs fled with their people up beyond the North Platte, where their relatives lived in peace.

Little Wolf had watched them come, and a spark of anger to smolder a lifetime was lit in his breast. He had never heard of Cheyennes running from anybody, but he lived to see it again, for this was only the first of many times.

Perhaps because the Northern Cheyennes seemed too few to make much trouble, they got very little of their treaty goods, and never an agency of their own. For most of twenty years they had tried to keep peaceful. The chiefs had even been to Washington, where Little Wolf had received a big medal of peace from President Grant. But repeatedly starvation drove them out to the shrinking buffalo herds, up north to the roving Sioux, in the south to the Kiowas and the Comanches. By 1876 Little Wolf, long a peace man, and Dull Knife, who had worked for peace half his life, were starved off the hungry Sioux agency of Red Cloud once more. They slipped away north for their treaty-given summer hunt. Most of them were too late for the Custer battle, but not for the soldiers who came chasing the Crazy Horse Sioux afterward, driving the Indians indiscriminately over their snow-covered treaty grounds with cavalry and cannon. In one of the fights Dull Knife lost three warriors from his family and Little Wolf got six wounds. Constantly fleeing, they could not hunt the few buffalo left, and so to save their people, they surrendered while some of the strong young men still lived, and the fine young women like the daughters of Dull Knife and the Pretty Walker of Little Wolf. They came in on the promise of friendship and peace, of plenty of food, warm clothing, and a reservation in their own country, with wagons and plows, and the cattle they had wanted so long. But instead they were dismounted and disarmed, except for a few guns they managed to hide, and now, with blankets drawn in sorrow to their eyes, they started south, the nine hundred and eighty Indians going quietly, morosely, mostly afoot. Seventy days later nine hundred and thirty-seven arrived at the Cheyenne and Arapaho Agency in Indian Territory.

There had been a little trouble on the way. One day a leader among the women was found hanging from a cottonwood, a noose made of her long braids.

A U.S. Army lieutenant came to see about the women, keening as for a warrior dead. "Our sister had three husbands, all famous chiefs," the wife of Little Wolf told him. "One after the other was lost to the soldiers, the last in the Custer fighting. Now the same bluecoats are riding around us here, and just ahead is the place where many of her relatives died from their guns."

When the long string of Indians reached the Sappa Creek, where Cheyennes were killed under a white flag of surrender two years ago, the warriors stopped, their faces covered with the blankets of sorrow and anger. Men who were crippled here, or who were compelled to leave their dead, harangued for a fight, and when the lieutenant galloped back to see, he was surrounded by stripped and painted warriors, singing and ready to die. They jerked away his pistol and were knocking him off his horse when Little Wolf charged in, striking to both sides with his fork-tailed pony whip.

"Will you have all the helpless people here killed?" he roared out. "Your hearts are as empty as your hands. This is not the time!"

The warriors broke before the chief's fury, the officer escaped, and the ringleaders were put into irons and thrown on the supply wagons.

WHEN THE NORTHERN Cheyennes reached the north fork of the Canadian River near Fort Reno, the chiefs were led to the wide agency bottoms, the earth smoother there, already worn bare by too many Indians. The soldiers set up their tents close by to watch. That night the Southern Cheyennes made the customary feast for the newcomers—such a thin feast as Little Wolf had never seen before. Plainly the people here were very poor with no horses or guns allowed them.

"Ahh-h, game is very scarce for the bow," the Southern Cheyenne agency chief said meaningfully. "But hungry men have good eyes and the fast moccasin, is it not true, my friends?"

Dull Knife and Little Wolf and the rest looked down into the water soup of their bowls. It was an embarrassment to eat from the kettles of the hungry, and hard to pretend the great appetite that was good manners.

In two months seventy of the newcomers had died of the measles and of the starvation that was everywhere, except in the lodges of the agency yea-sayers like Standing Elk, whose women walked proud and plump in their new dresses. General John Pope, the Civil War veteran who then commanded this army district, wrote to Washington, asking that the Cheyenne supply issues be increased to cover the new people from the north. It was important "both in view of the safety of this new frontier and in the interest of humanity and fair dealing that all these Indians be far better fed than they are now or have been."

Nothing was done, and the winter was the worst Little Wolf had ever seen, with the coughing sickness in the hungry lodges and nothing for the idle hands. So the Cheyennes took on the white man's quarreling ways. Some even whipped their women and children, a shocking, paleface thing to do. And always the soldier guns were there.

Then Little Wolf heard that Crazy Horse, the great Sioux warrior, was killed up at Fort Robinson. He carried the news like gall in the mouth to Dull Knife's lodge. Their friend had led the roaming Sioux of the Powder and Yellowstone country since Red Cloud moved to the agency eight years ago. He was a fiercely brave man whom many Cheyennes had gladly fought beside when he whipped General George Crook on the Rosebud River and the next week cut off the retreat of General George A. Custer on the Little Big Horn. But with the buffalo vanishing he came to the agency under the same promise given the Cheyennes: food, safety, and an agency for his people. Now he was dead, killed by a soldier in an attempt to take him away to a Florida prison because some agency Indians were jealous and lied about him.

Dull Knife, in his youth a leading Dog Soldier, sat bleak-faced. Here, too, the agency chief was jealous. And men like Standing Elk were hot to be old man chiefs. But for that Dull Knife and Little Wolf—of the Elk military society, who took pride in their war strategy—would have to be sent away, or die like Crazy Horse.

So the chiefs went to the agent. "You are a good man," Little Wolf said. "You can see that in this small hungry place we must stand on the moccasins of our brothers. Let us go before something bad happens."

First the agent tried to content Little Wolf with a pretty southern girl for his bed. The chief refused, but the girl was sent anyway, and turned out to be his fifteen-year-old granddaughter through the wife of his youth who had died of cholera. Next the agent tried making policemen of some Southern Cheyennes. Fifteen of them were given soldier coats and guns and set to walk the angry village. But no Cheyenne could take the life of a fellow tribesman, even in self-defense, so the agent gave the jobs to the Arapahos, who, like the whites, could kill anybody.

SUMMER IN 1878 BROUGHT Indian trouble all through the West. The Northern Cheyennes were shaking with malaria, and there was none of the bitter white powder the agent had promised. There was dysentery too, and very little food, but they were not allowed to go on their authorized summer hunt. They must foment no trouble, husband the issues carefully, and till the earth, the agent told them.

"Make the issues last, when there was too little even before we were brought here? Till the earth with plows that never come—make no trouble, while our people die?" Dull Knife demanded, with the warriors so noisy and threatening against the whites that Little Wolf had to roar out his anger against them. It was too late for anything now. The people were sick, with someone carried to the burial rocks every day. They longed for their mountain and pine country, where there was no sickness and few died.

Now the agent roared. He wanted the young men who had already started north. Little Wolf said he knew of no one gone except to hunt stolen horses or try to get a deer or some rabbits for the sick. But still the agent demanded ten young men as hostages until everybody was back.

Hostages—for prison, for the irons on hands and feet—this was something the chiefs could not decide. They must go ask the people.

Anger broke out that night against Standing Elk, riding in with a fine new blanket and another new horse. Yes, he had talked for coming down here and was now talking strong for staying. Otherwise they would all be killed. Any man who advocated leaving now should be broken, even if it was Little Wolf, who carried the sacred bundle of chieftainship under his shirt, the bundle that made him keeper of the people.

Ahh-h, now it was out—Standing Elk wanting to be head chief! There was a roaring as of battle, red shots cut through the air, and the women ran toward the dark hills with the children. But the peace pipe was hurried in, and before it the silence came back. Then Standing Elk folded his new blanket and moved from the camp, his followers along, never to return.

Afterward Little Wolf went across the night to the north ridge, to sit alone as in other times of hard decision. As the chief began to sing his old-time medicine song, there were moccasin steps in the dry darkness. He did not stop the song or move, for if his place was to be emptied by death, that too he must accept by his oath as chief.

It was the keeper of the sacred tribal objects—the buffalo hat and the medicine arrows. He, too, was old, and sick. "You cannot let yourself be turned from what seems right," he said. "Not by gun or knife or the wounded pride and weakness of doubt. We made you the bearer of our medicine bundle, our leader."

"But if I have lost the vision of the good way?"

"No Cheyenne can be compelled to do anything, nobody except our chief. You must lead even if not one man follows, not even a village dog—if any had escaped the hungry pot," the keeper added ruefully.

Then they went back down to the silent camp. The hot, still air was thick with mosquitoes and the stink of a village too long unmoved, one full of the running sickness.

In the morning Little Wolf took his people a day's pony drag up the river for wood and grass and air. The agent called for soldiers. Two companies of cavalry took up the trail with a howitzer, and troops were readied northward to the Yellowstone. Then the Indians were discovered still in the reservation, just above the fort inside a little horseshoe of hills, the men trying to snare rabbits and gophers, the women digging roots. The howitzer was set to look down into the camp, and the red-faced captain galloped into the lodge circle, his double line of troopers close behind, their guns shining. The women and children fled, but were ordered back, to hear the officer announce that until they all returned to the agency and sent the children to school, there would be no rations—not just a little as before, but nothing, not even the moldy flour.

The women trembled in their rags, remembering the guns that

had killed so many helpless ones before. The soldiers stayed and the howitzer too. Finally, on September 8, the agency doctor came. With the chiefs beside him he walked among the lodges, past all the sick ones, the women turning the kettles upside down in the symbol of emptiness as he came, or holding out bowls of roots and grass for his eyes.

"This is a pest camp, a graveyard!" the doctor exclaimed.

But he had no medicine, no food, and besides, everything was already settled. The chiefs had gone to the last conference at the agency with their few guns hidden on their warrior guard, for surely now the protesting ones would be killed. It was a tumultuous meeting, and one of the young warriors forgot himself enough to speak out in the council. "We are sickly and dying men," the slender young Little Finger Nail told the agent there in his soft Cheyenne. "If we die here and go to the burial rocks, no one will speak our names. So now we go north, and if we die in battle on the way, our names will be remembered by all the people. They will tell the story and say, 'This is the place.'"

There had been a roaring of *hous* from many of the young southerners too.

Dull Knife rose with a hand lifted for silence. He spoke of the many Indian complaints: peaceful people shot by soldiers, the buffalo destroyed, the lands taken, with too little of the pay promised in the white papers, and now nothing at all. No food, no houses, no cattle or wagons or plows. So they were going back north while some were still alive.

This, too, brought a roaring of approval from many of the southern warriors. Their agency chief had once been dragged back wounded from a Pawnee war charge by Dull Knife, but that was long ago, and now he rose and, with the butt of his leaded saddle whip, knocked Dull Knife into the dust.

In that moment every warrior was up, knives and pistols against panting bellies, the white men pale as old paper in the silence, the soldier guns ready for one thrust, one shot that would start the massacre.

Almost at once Dull Knife was on his feet again. He shook the dust from his blanket and folded it about himself, looking at the agent, his lips curling proud.

"My friend," he said, "I am going."

Slowly, majestically, the man feared by Crow, Shoshone and Pawnee for forty years walked from the council, his warrior son and his band chiefs around him. Afterward Little Wolf talked earnestly for peace, for permission to go home in peace, as they had been promised. He could not give the young men as hostages never to be returned, and if the agent loved their food too much to give them any, he must keep it all. "I have long been a friend of the whites. The Great Father told us that he wished no more blood spilled, that we ought to be friends and fight no more. So I do not want any of the ground of the agency made bloody. Only soldiers do that. If you are going to send them after me, I wish you would first let me get a little distance away. Then if you want to fight, I will fight you and we can make the ground bloody on that far place."

Chapter 1

NOW IT WAS THE night, but there were no friendly clouds to run before the face of the climbing moon. Little Wolf sat alone at the deserted council fire, the big silver peace medal given him by President Grant shining softly on his breast. But under his shirt hung the sacred chief's bundle and across his knee his rifle was ready.

With his finger on the trigger Little Wolf listened, looking out beyond the spread of smoky, cone-shaped lodges that stood about him, so quiet in the moonlight. Here and there the diffused glow of a little fire showed through the old skins, or a few coals lay red inside a lifted lodge flap—fires that had been kept alive all summer against the chills of the shaking sickness and starvation.

Somewhere a ground owl hooted, but only once. Otherwise everything seemed to sleep except for a young Indian blowing a flute up on a hillside, softly, mournfully.

The Cheyenne village lay in a small pocket surrounded on all but the south by sandy hills rising in a wall against the moon-paled sky. The new cavalry encampment was out of sight beyond the hills, but soldiers were posted along the crest of the encircling ridges, guns ready, the cannon waiting to boom out, to burst its shells down among the smoky lodges.

No matter what happened now, this was the last night of the Cheyennes here, Little Wolf knew. All the delaying that the Indians could make was done, and tomorrow the soldiers would attack if the camp was not moving early, to be settled back at the agency. It was hard to understand these things, for the earth here was the same as that under the black coattails of the agent, all the same reservation set aside for their southern relatives.

A dog barked several times in a distant Indian village. Up on the hillside the flute still rose and fell like a sad-winged bird, but now it signaled to Little Wolf that the strong men selected to watch the soldier sentinels were finally all in place, ready with war axe and knife if any departure was detected. They were young men, but stronghearted enough to stay their weapons if nothing was seen by the watching soldiers, and then to slip away behind their fleeing people, leaving the sentinels to watch the sixty empty lodges.

For the escape the Cheyennes must have good luck. Little Wolf looked out to the moonlit knoll where Bridge, the medicine man, had lain for three days fasting, although he was already thin as a shinbone. Bridge worked hard with his cloud ceremony, but surely the Great Powers had turned their ears from the Cheyennes, for this moon-filled night laid naked every living thing. Yet the people must go, and as the flute lifted its thin cry, one figure after another crept from the quiet lodges, Dull Knife and the way finders going first, then Little Wolf's wife, Feather on Head, and the women after her, moving like smoke from shadow to shadow.

Humped as buffalo with their burdens, the Cheyennes passed, the men with their poor arms—bows or perhaps a rifle or a pistol— and the regalia that they could carry, the warbonnets, the shields, and a few other medicine things. All who had saddles or saddle pads of antelope hair took them along. The women were bent too, with the weight of the babies on their backs and with the few goods they managed to gather for the long road north.

Behind these women came young Singing Cloud, helping her father, who had lifted himself from his bed of dying so his daughter need not remain behind. In her lay the last seed of a great warrior family. If this was to be lost, it must not be to ignominious hunger in a cannon-darkened lodge of a prisoner people, but in a fight for life. Somewhere on the long run northward the old man would slip down and return to the grass. Then his daughter would be free, free to go to the bold young warrior Little Finger Nail, the sweet singer of the Cheyennes, the one who drew the finest pictures of the feats of his people.

Far back, to see that the families all got away, Little Wolf watched; then he, too, began to move, slipping from one shadow to another up along the edge of the hills, looking down. Soft-spoken and gentle, Little Wolf, the one the Cheyennes called their brave man, could whip any unruly warrior to his duty and still, at fifty-seven, lead him in any battle. Little Wolf had fought so hard when the soldiers struck the Cheyennes up on the Powder fork two years ago that it stopped the heart. He had been like a great wounded bear in his fury and fearlessness that time, even the soldiers said, and when it was over, he carried the wounds of seven bullets in his flesh, as he carried the pockmarks of the stinking, alien disease on his face.

Behind Little Wolf came Tangle Hair with some Dog Soldiers—whose duty it was not to start until all the village was moving—a perpetual Cheyenne rear guard, but greatly diminished by their stands against army attacks during the last fourteen years.

The two leading chiefs had good warrior sons along to help them. Dull Knife's older son, Bull Hump, was hidden behind the troopers, watching the cannon that pointed into the camp. His knife was naked, ready to check the first cry in the throat or the finger tightening on the signal trigger. Little Wolf's son Woodenthigh was out there too.

The chiefs had two wives each, the smallest number required by the lodges of such men, with no Cheyenne ever to be hired as his brother's pay help. There were many guests to visit a chief's lodge, guests from the village, from other bands and far tribes. They must be feasted and given lodge-guest presents of moccasins and robes, as well as good young stock from the pony herds. With Dull Knife was Pawnee Woman, the one he captured as a pretty girl from a Pawnee camp and took to his lodge many years ago. It had grieved his first wife so she hanged herself, and for a time brought a silent embarrassment from the women of the village as he passed. But he soon took another wife, a young woman of strong heart, short and sturdy, with soft, smiling eyes. Gradually she brought smoothness to the life of the lodge and to the village about her with the good deed, the gentle word, and the firm hand, even with her man when it was a matter of the family, for this was always the first duty of a Cheyenne woman within her lodge. Tonight, while the old chief went ahead of the people, this Short One made a little song as she hurried with Pawnee Woman from shadow to shadow:

> "Proudly we follow the path of Morning Star,
> The one they call Dull Knife.
> Many, many snows he has spoken for peace,
> Carrying the pipe of it in his hand
> Like others carry the bow and the shooting gun.
> Ei-e-ya!"

She sang softly, so no listening soldier might hear as she passed with the chief's warbonnet and shield on her back.

So the Indians vanished from the lodges, going like the fox sneaking up a gully, not like the Cheyennes of the old days. A year ago they brought two hundred fighting men along. But now barely a hundred remained, counting all the males over twelve. The others were dead from hunger and fevers and the old, old disease of homesickness that no doctor—not even Bridge, the medicine healer—had the power to cure. Besides, some had deserted, and that, too, had to be endured.

With the warriors went the weak and old and infirm—and the strong women like young Buffalo Calf Road, the warrior woman who had killed in battle and had ridden against the soldiers of both generals Crook and Custer.

There were other courageous young women along. Dull Knife's older daughters had both dared say no to the covetous officers, as well fitted the Beautiful People, as the Dull Knife family was called by the whites. Pretty Walker, Little Wolf's daughter, had saved a life in a fight, but it was never recounted at the evening fires, for the man she saved was a soldier. She had dragged him away from the bullets because, in the thickest fighting, he had given his horse to an old woman who could not run. She was an independent, tall-walking girl, as was proper in that family of good leggers, the father still a foot racer, her brother called Woodenthigh because he never wore out. The girl had been called Pretty Walker so long that her real name seemed forgotten, but none forgot that she could go as calmly into the path of bullets as her father, the dedicated man.

Following the young women were the hopeful young warriors, some from the southern people too, and some older men like Thin Elk, who had come slipping down from the Yellowstone country scarcely a moon ago to visit a relative. Yet it was to Little Wolf's lodge he walked most often, an uninvited guest, and this time he could not be driven away as he was twenty years ago, when Little Wolf was still only a war leader. An old man chief could not warn anyone away from his wife. "Only danger that threatens the people can anger me now," Little Wolf had sworn in the tribal chief's oath. "If a dog lifts his leg to my lodge, I will not see it."

But tonight as Little Wolf watched Thin Elk pass, helping the women in their flight, he thought of something else: the old Cheyenne saying that a coal once kindled is easiest set to glowing. The chief did not know that some of the women had begun to whisper behind their hands. But perhaps it was not toward one of the wives of Little Wolf that Thin Elk was turning his eyes. Perhaps it was the daughter, Pretty Walker, that he was watching.

As LITTLE WOLF had hoped, no one turned from the trail tonight, not even after the keeper of the sacred hat became cautious and uncertain, perhaps because he foresaw bad fighting with the soldiers. The sacred tribal objects, the buffalo hat and the medicine arrows, had not always brought the people luck. They were both carried along last summer, and still not a lodge was spared the sickness and the death keening. Even strong ones died, or turned strange, like Bear Rope, who walked dangerously tonight among the fleeing ones. He had been a good man to follow in war and in the council. Now he might break into fighting at the flutter of a wind, striking out at anyone with his war axe. Afterward he would sit shaking, so cold his wives must pile the fire high all night.

There must be no sound now, and Bear Rope's son-in-law moved close beside the sick man, sorrowful, yet with his strong fingers ready to stop the first sound in the throat. There was still death among them, too, this night. Just as the people started, a small girl, still warm, had to be left dead in one of the dark lodges, with the buckskin fringes of childhood on her dress, the first moccasins she was beading, and the doeskin doll with the braids of her dead mother's hair held in her arms. Not even her grandmother dared make a sound of sorrow now, with the soldiers all around.

So they went, their faces turned northward, but their hearts looking back to all those who must be left behind. Silent as field mice, the moccasins ran over the bare, horse-cropped earth, keeping to the uneven ground.

Hidden, but felt by them, Little Wolf recognized each darkening of the shadows below him, knowing each one as intimately as though of his own lodge. As the chief counted the passing ones, he pressed his arm against the sacred bundle, but his hand gripped the Winchester. Back behind him young men rode into the deserted camp as though returning from a hunt or a visit, shouting among the empty lodges, doing it open and natural, as on any night, for the listening soldiers to hear. They threw wet grass upon the low coals to send the smell of smoke over the ridge to the camp of the red-faced soldier chief, who carried a smell of the whiskey that made men crazy.

On the hillside the flute still cried, while on both sides of the flute player lay dark rifle pits that the warriors had dug to meet any soldier attack with downhill cross fire. The whites could destroy the village with their cannon and ride over it in one cavalry charge, but many soldiers would be killed from these pits so long as the ammunition lasted.

There were many stripling boys along too, some orphaned in the south to be taken back to relatives, and then that other one, Yellow Swallow—the light-haired Custer son born to Monahsetah. She was the daughter of one of the southern chiefs killed in the Washita River fight ten years ago, and had been taken over a hundred miles of snow to Fort Supply with other captive women and children. When the young girls were selected for the officer tents on that cold march, she was sent to Custer's.

Later Monahsetah went along on his winter expedition that pursued her fleeing people deep into Texas. When Custer's wife was coming to him, the Cheyenne girl was sent back to the Indians, where this son was born toward the autumn moon. Years afterward the traders told her that Custer wrote about her in a book, praising her charm, her beauty and grace. Not until she knew that Long Hair, General Custer, was dead did she take another man.

Now this Yellow Swallow was nine years old, but spindly, thin as a winter weed stalk. The boy had an aunt with the fleeing ones tonight, and another up near where Custer died. In that good country the sickly Yellow Swallow might live, and become strong and brave as a young Cheyenne should be, as the son of Long Hair should be.

There were only the last soldiers watching the pass now. The Cheyennes had to slip by sentinels close together on both slopes. To the watching Little Wolf they barely seemed to move, creeping along.

Then suddenly a great white light fell over everything. It stopped the feet, the heart, but not a sound came, no earthshaking roar of bursting cannonball. Instead, a summer star was falling slowly, its light raining down over the people flattened to the earth—the men with saddles for the horses, the women with children and goods on their backs, all small, unshadowed hummocks on the floor beneath a great burst of light.

But no shout disturbed the silence, no signal shot, and as the meteor slowly faded from the eyes, the moccasins began to move again, hurrying even more now to reach the scattering prairie. Even the heavy-moving woman, who had to drop back into a gully for her time, remembered and whispered to the one who wished to wait behind with her.

"No, no!"

"You are weak, my sister. . . ."

"No—run! Let there be no more than myself and the child for the soldiers to ride down."

When the newborn son stretched for a cry, the mother grasped the wet little nose between her thumb and forefinger, the palm over the mouth, shutting off the breath until the child seemed to strangle in the darkness. Then she loosened her fingers for a little until there was another cry coming, and tightened her hold again. So the small one was taught the first lesson of Cheyenne life: no child's cry must betray the people to an enemy.

Then, with the baby against her starved, empty breasts, the Cheyenne woman started again, stumbling, weak, but moving faster as her strength returned, hoping to reach the trail before all had passed.

FAR FROM THE LODGES and the soldiers, the people were met by small herds of horses. As many as possible of the women with their children and bundles were put upon them. Just a few pony drags had been made, only for the very old and the very sick. But first, as always, came the needs of the young men. They must get more horses for the rest, if they were to outrun the soldiers.

Many toiled along afoot, bent under the burdens of their children and their bundles. These were determined to go to their home country even though they must walk over fifteen hundred of the white-man miles. The woman called Brave One led the straggler party, with a few old men and growing boys along. They hurried, but no matter how fast the line of dark figures moved over the dusky prairie, in a little while even the ear to the ground could no longer detect the hoofs of the horses gone ahead.

Chapter 2

So THE CHEYENNES started north, but not as many of them as they had hoped when their shadows moved from the lodges into the night. A good man, who had worked steady and hard all summer so none of the people had to be left behind, now came to the shadowed gathering place and declared that he and his eight lodges would move off a way and let the others pass.

"Pass? You would remain here? You have the most horses, and

all those our young men helped you catch!" his friend Tangle Hair argued. "My brother, would you split the people through the middle again—through the heart on this important night?"

But the man was not to be changed. Slowly, deliberately, he spoke. "It is not that I am not sick-hearted to go back to the north country. But there is too much danger, with all the soldiers and the wagon guns ready along the road, and spies surely among us even here, watching, leaving sign. The shooting may begin anywhere in that gully ahead. . . ."

"Then you will not go?" Little Wolf demanded angrily, with his warrior blood hot as for an enemy.

"No, cousin, I cannot."

So they let him withdraw to one side, for only the whites would hold man or woman against the heart. But they let him keep only horses enough to lift the timid moccasin above the cactus. The rest they killed. Sorely as horses were needed, they slit the throats, making a quiet job of it, the blood hot and sticky and sweetish in the darkness of the gully, the choke and murmur of the horses like many people dying.

Then they moved on without him, going a little more sadly, although twice there were suddenly others among them, bringing excitement and a little cheer. The coming ones were mostly young men, but three who had been prisoners in Florida were older. They wanted to join the people, to be a help, particularly in spying, for they knew something of the white man and his language. One wanted to protect his nephew, Yellow Swallow, see him get a new start in a healthy country.

"*Hou!* We will all have a new start in the good country or we will leave our bones to bleach on the grass."

"It is good," Wild Hog, a headman, said soberly, and sent them out among the rest.

For three hours the Indians made hard travel. Scattered in little parties over the pale, moon-touched prairie, they moved like the sly coyote, most of them keeping to the shadowy breaks back from the river. Even those afoot along the bottoms sought out the dry grass that holds no tracks of soft moccasins passing. Finally the way finders of each party converged on the headwaters of a little creek where a timbered spring lay in the black shadow of a canyon.

Dull Knife and Little Wolf sat with half a dozen of their warriors at a hidden fire. Together they watched for the people coming out of the haziness, until all the headmen were past, except the keeper. Little Wolf was uneasy about him, now that Tangle Hair's friend had run back. If the keeper of the sacred hat turned back, great would be the uneasiness that this gift from Sweet Medicine would not be in its holy place among them, strengthening everything they did, every fight, every council and ceremonial.

The passing Indians moved silently, a horse snorting softly at the smell of water, a hoof stirring a rock, perhaps some headmen dropping out to sit beside the chiefs awhile.

There were long silences at the little fire. There had been a little trouble when the two chiefs first rode in, Dull Knife with a few followers first, and finally Little Wolf. Some of the warriors were gathered at the spring, waiting, impatient.

Little Wolf looked at them, but they held back until he settled to his pipe. Then one spoke up defiantly. "We have decided to travel on the old-time east trail," he said boldly. "There are more horses to catch because there are more whites there, and more guns to take."

"Yes, and more whites with guns to shoot at us! I don't want shooting," the chief replied, and turned to ask about signals of the pursuit begun.

But the warriors interrupted again, pushing in closer. So Dull Knife looked up from the firelight that glowed on the beaded lizard on his breast. "You know that the way has been long agreed on in council. The scouts and hunters are working up there ahead."

"Yes, and weren't some of you sent to find meat for the children?" Little Wolf demanded. "What excuse do you carry in your mouth for your empty hands?"

"I say go the old way too!" Black Coyote called out from among Little Wolf's own headmen, and because this thin, sharp-faced one was of a great warrior family, other voices shouted their *hous*. So more warriors pushed themselves against their honored man, old Dull Knife.

"You will go the road planned, my nephew," wrinkled old Black Crane told Black Coyote, speaking quietly, but with the power of the man selected by the council to lay out the campings all the way.

There were still threatening gestures from Black Coyote and from the young warriors.

Dull Knife shifted his tired old body. "Perhaps it will have to be as the young men wish," he said to the others around the fire. "There should be no trouble with the whites. We are not going to war, and we have the northern *veho* promise we could return."

Now Tangle Hair moved too, uneasily. "You cannot talk so, my friend—wind blow east, wind blow west. The young men who go against the council plans will surely bring other troubles. Anyway, the west road is already warmed by the moccasins sent ahead of us."

"*Hou!*" Such plans were not to be unmade in one angry moment, old Black Crane agreed.

But there was so much noise that none heard him, and so Dull Knife shook his head in the white-man way. "I am tired of trouble," he said, "and we must have the young men."

"*Piva!* Good! Let us start!" Black Coyote shouted—openly, loudly, for spying ears to hear far, far off.

So Little Wolf had to lay aside his pipe and get up, the light from the coals rising toward his pitted, fever-gaunted face. "You heard that our brother Dull Knife is tired of the trouble some of you are always making, my friends. I am tired too, worn out by your noise. We need less thunder in the mouth and more lightning in the hand if we are to escape to the north and save the helpless ones with us."

"It is the old road east of the Dodge fort we are taking," someone cried from the darkness, another taking it up, and another, even a voice sounding like that of Dull Knife's younger son.

Little Wolf saw that he must indeed work hard if the Cheyennes were not to fall apart now. He started with his voice low and thick with anger. It was such wild and foolish men as these who brought the soldiers into the village on the fork of the Powder. "Your own relatives were left on the ground there, your own blood spread in a blanket from the woundings you will always carry. Your own blood, and others."

Little Wolf paused, letting his blanket fall, standing—a strong, scarred man in breechclout and medicine-bundle string in the light of the coals. "Your blood, and mine, too, was left there," he said, touching a wound in his side that was like twisted red rawhide. "Here a bullet came through that night, and here and here"—his hand moving swiftly over his torn body, his eyes cold as the blizzard wind on the young men standing around the edge of darkness. He searched out their faces until they had to look down, shamed and foolish that their chief needed to make such a humiliating show of his wounds.

"The Great Powers saw me that time," Little Wolf said, speaking the words into the silence, "but many, many good people were left there because of such arrogant men as you. This time it will not be so. This time you will carry out the decision of those that the people selected long ago to lead. We need horses, but we must have meat—buffalo, right away. For meat, and the hope of fast travel, we go the western road, the Dull Knife trail, where few whites live. Many, many soldiers will surely have to be fought off, so there must be no trouble with the settlers too."

For a moment the chief stopped. Then he snarled out the final words. "We go the western way! This I, Little Wolf, command you!"

As the echo returned in the darkness, many there remembered seeing this gentle, soft-spoken man like this before and knew that crossing him brought such fury that he whipped his warriors with quirt and gun butt. So, because of the power they still saw in their chief, the wildest of the young warriors bowed their heads. Gradually they slipped away up the shadowed gullies to their delayed tasks, or into the passing people, to help their relatives, or some family with pretty girls.

But there was still anger in the faces of Black Coyote and his followers against Black Crane, the camp selector. "He talks with the noise of the old man chiefs in the mouth," Black Coyote said as he rode sullenly out for horses. "When a man takes on such ways something happens."

By this time it was plain that the keeper's few lodges were not coming. Then two riders hurried in out of the night, and dropping from their sweaty horses, they approached slowly, standing back from the fire in the shame of bad news. Yes, it was true—the keeper of the sacred objects had gone back.

Little Wolf scraped the ashes from his pipe into his palm. Then the chiefs rose to their horses. Now there were only eighty-seven men, counting the oldest wrinkled one and the boys of thirteen. But these were all good Cheyennes, not one the runaway kind. Eighty-seven men—two hundred and eighty-four people altogether, all that was left of almost a thousand who made the sorrowful path down this way a year ago.

By now most of the walking people were safely past and into the broken country. Then, in twos and threes, the headmen slipped away into the deepening darkness without a spoken destination, for there was no telling what spies might be around.

Before the dawning in the east rose over the moving people, an older warrior, who had been away to the prison and understood much *veho* talk, came hurrying after them. "Our going has been discovered," he said.

Ahh-h, it was good that it had taken this long.

"The sentinels said we could not be gone, for they had been looking all the time. There were the lodges, standing, the dying fire coals still a little red."

"Ahh-h, yes, the lodges," one of the men said regretfully as he drew at his pipe.

"It was Tangle Hair's friend and another who rode to the agency."

So? They could not wait a few hours to let the people get away. Still, one could understand this. They were hungry too, and with their horses killed . . . "For telling this news they will certainly get coffee and sugar again."

Bridge, the medicine man, said, "It is not good that a man must choose between the honorable way and hungry children."

THEN, AT NIGHT AGAIN, as the Cheyennes moved north up the ladder of dry canyons and creek beds, they looked back from every rise, afraid to hear the far sound of hoofs coming through the lowering moonlight, or see a hurried column with red shooting from the middle. And Dull Knife and the rest had to start on this flight north without the sacred hat or the arrows. Soldiers were coming after them, gathering ahead in clouds as thick as fall blackbirds in a strip of corn; the men and horses and guns hauled by the fire railroads; the talking wires like spider ropes all through the morning grass, to show the path of the Indians very plain. All this had to be escaped without the sacred objects along, and many were very much afraid.

But not the young men. "Let the hat and the old arrows stay behind," Little Finger Nail said when they rested at dawn. "People have been killed in their shadows for a long time. We need a new medicine now, something besides an old skin hat to bring us wagonloads of Winchesters heavy with ammunition."

But Dull Knife answered the youth. "The old ways are good."

"*Hou!*" many agreed. Surely it was the power of the hat there on the Little Big Horn that made Custer blind and foolish. Yes, surely Long Hair Custer had been blinded to die so.

"A man has to die sometime," the younger warriors scoffed, particularly those Cheyennes who had been away to the prison and knew about the white man's sacred object, the cross of wood—not one, as with the hat, but many, little and big, and made of many things. The white man's medicine was surely very strong, for he was the biggest tribe of the whole earth, bigger even than the Sioux. But his cross did not seem to work for all the people, as the arrows and the hat did. The white women who came to the Florida prison to tell the Indians about the cross and its peace said that the soldiers who carried it killed very many of their people. Dull Knife and the rest nodded, remembering the little branched medicine trees they found on dead soldiers. But they were certain that the power of their hat was not the same thing.

AS THE FIRST SUN climbed into the sky, it dried up the little clouds in the west. The Indians stopped awhile to rest, dropping anywhere, like worn-out cattle or buffalo after a long running. There was still no meat, only the wild fruits, plums, drying currants, chokecherries, and a few purpling grapes picked in the hasty passing, with maybe a snake or a sand turtle—so very little when divided that the children cried softly in their hunger.

Soon everybody was moving again, slipping along the canyons that were the folds of the sheltering earth, trying to cross no height or tableland that could be touched by a far field glass. Then two of the meat scouts gone ahead made their signals. It was the elder son of Little Wolf, and Black Horse, who was crippled in the troubles of 1875. He knew the country and had the buffalo eye, and now the two came with really good news.

"Buffalo—on our chosen road," Black Horse said.

"It is true there are not many, but with some fat young cows," said Little Wolf's son. "They are up near the place called Buffalo Springs. The other men stayed there, watching."

"Buffalo seen!" Old Crier called as he ran along the trailing people and signaled to those far out, who needed to know this very much too. "Make ready for a little butchering! Buffalo!"

"Meat!" Bridge cried, the water of his eyes running down the gullied old face as he went to make a little medicine ceremonial of thankfulness for the kill tomorrow. Truly the sick and starving people could not have been taken much farther.

Chapter 3

BACK AT FORT RENO, the commander, Colonel Mizner, reported good progress. Captain Rendlebrock, out thirty miles by late afternoon the first day, had found the trail plainer as he followed; the Indians pressed too hard to hide it. Their horses were tiring; the scouts discovered where a couple had played out, the bones stripped bare of meat by the Indians to carry along. Off under a little bank was a place where a woman had given birth and hurried on. There was something more, something the Arapaho scouts did not tell Rendlebrock—the woman's hurrying tracks joined a little party far behind the rest of the Cheyennes, all small moccasins, the tracks far apart and very fresh, women and children running fast just ahead of the troops.

Nor did any of the scouts seem to see the little scattering of people huddled in a washed-out gully as the blue column passed. When they could run no more, the women and children had flattened themselves in the holes and the sparse gray sage, so afraid of the soldiers close upon them that only the stern commands of Brave One kept them from flushing like frightened young quail.

A few days later Mizner reported that the Indians were well mounted. The best he hoped now was that they could be overtaken at the Arkansas River, high in flood after a wet summer. The government in Washington ordered that the intercepted Indians were to be attacked unless they surrendered at once. Four companies of infantry and some cavalry were headed out along the Platte River to take the Cheyennes at the probable crossing.

But that was in Nebraska, far, far ahead. Now, still in Indian Territory, the scouts found the remains of a buffalo hunt on a branch of the Cimarron River and a scattered but slowing trail beyond.

The soldiers were coming hard now, and the people tried to hurry through the low canyons. The party of lone women and children was far back, and keeping well hidden and close to good fleeing places. Brave One still led them, the woman who got her name because she and her sister ran for an entire winter month from another shooting years ago. The two women had carried a six-year-old girl in their arms all that time, with only one blanket and a knife for the long flight.

In the main party Little Wolf sent most of the women with Old Crier to hide ahead in some canyons cut deep into the red earth. Dull Knife was still hopeful. "The soldiers know we have the right to go back north," he said. "They could have caught us earlier— yesterday while we hunted, or two days before—"

"Maybe they were waiting for the other soldiers to get here from the north forts and the fire road along the river," Black Crane said cautiously.

Although Dull Knife was convinced the soldiers would not shoot, Little Wolf and the others selected a good place to meet them, the men going back a way on the trail into some steep red hills, where the many guns and the strong, well-fed horses of the troops would not be worth so much and where they could not get to water. When the scouts signaled that many enemies were coming close, the women and children back in the canyons started to scatter in the fear of guns. But Old Crier called gently to them. "Do not be afraid, my sisters. There are those among you who have stood against the soldiers many times. Your men are brave. You are Cheyennes."

But the women kept going with their children, even Buffalo Calf

Road, the warrior woman, for now there was a small one on her back. So the old man let them go, knowing that in a little while they would be slipping back, looking over the hill to see their men fight, singing strong-heart songs, making the trills for the brave ones. It was the way with women, and he was too old to wish it otherwise.

As the dust spot on the horizon lengthened out, Little Wolf rose from his watching on the red slope. "Do not shoot first," he charged the warriors, "but get the arms and horses ready, and I will go to meet the soldiers and try to talk to them. If they want to kill somebody, I will be the first man. Then you can fight."

So the Indians spread over the steep red hillside, looking dusty and unwarlike, with only a few guns and some bows, waiting. But Little Wolf knew how excitable these young men were, even the leaders like Bull Hump and Black Coyote, and so he sent his most trusted Elk warriors out among them to see that no one fired a hasty and foolish shot. He had very good men for this, old-timers like Great Eyes and the fine shot, Left Hand.

When the long string of troops broke into a trot, the Cheyennes began to ride back and forth before their position, whipping their horses to get the second wind in preparation for a good fight. Out in front of them stood Little Wolf, the President's silver medal of peace shining on his breast. Beside him were Dull Knife, Wild Hog, and several others, their hands empty except Dull Knife's, carrying the pipe.

Rendlebrock stopped his troops out of rifle shot and sent an Arapaho scout forward to talk. But the man did not come closer than his roaring voice could carry against the light wind. He called out the names of the chiefs standing together. "The whites want you to turn around," he shouted. "They sent us to overtake you and bring you in. If you give up now, you will receive your rations and be treated well. If not, you will be whipped back."

One after another the chiefs spoke. They did not want to fight, but they would not go back. "We have no quarrel with anyone," Little Wolf said. "I hold up my right hand in the white man's way that I do not wish to fight him, but we are going to our old home."

Again the Arapaho called for surrender, looking uneasily up the broken red slopes, where only a few Cheyennes could be seen.

Once more Little Wolf said what he had been saying for a year. They were going back north as they had been promised they could. "We will go peacefully if we can, not hurting anybody or destroying anything of the whites on the way. We will attack no one if we are not molested. If the soldiers shoot, we will shoot back, and if the white men who are not soldiers fight us, we will fight them too."

So the Arapaho returned to Rendlebrock, and the chiefs to their men, all except Little Wolf. Holding his folded blanket up above the brushy clumps, he walked down toward the soldiers, hoping to talk a little. He would tell them how the dysentery was already better among his sick ones from a little fresh buffalo meat, and the shaking disease better too. Couldn't the white men find it in their hearts to let sick women and children go to be well again?

But the dusty Rendlebrock, his blond face burned raw by sun and whiskey, noticed Indians moving away through the ravines as though to escape. Before Little Wolf was close enough to be heard, the trumpet made its call to war.

The soldier guns roared out, and spurts of dust flew up all around the chief. Little Wolf turned and started back, going through the bullets as calmly as to his evening lodge.

When he reached the Cheyenne line, the whooping warriors charged from the front and the side upon the soldiers, fierce and angered by this attack on their chief while he tried to make the talk of a friend.

Before the driving charge of such reckless young men as Little Finger Nail, Woodenthigh, and the others, the soldier horses shied, reared, and plunged away or went down, the men up and running fast, except one who was left, a blue bundle on the ground. Somebody had picked off the Arapaho scout after the first firing.

On the rise, the women trilled, for the soldiers were falling back and digging hurried rifle pits.

"Careful!" Little Wolf warned. "I don't want any more people hurt. Don't shoot foolishly; there is very little in your guns!"

Then he saw that Dull Knife was making a fighting harangue to the Dog Soldiers, challenging the young men to make another charge, this time clear down and over the smoking rifle pits. He and others had done it several times when they were young—real old-time Cheyenne war charges.

"Ahh-h, my brother, truly you have done many brave things!" Little Wolf interrupted heartily. "But now we must smoke a little and rest. We don't want anybody to die today, and perhaps it is not good to shame this soldier chief by riding over him. He may go back when he gets tired and thirsty."

Some of the Dog Soldiers were quick to taunt this head of the old man chiefs who was also a leader of the Elk society. "It seems," they shouted, "that our leader has softened very fast in the coffee and molasses talks at the agencies."

"Hou! Hou!" many others shouted.

"Ahh-h, we remember that our brave man did not come to us from the agency until the soldiers with the long-haired Custer were scattered like skinned buffalo over the ridge!" Bear Rope added. "Then, when the stink of the powder was gone on the wind, he came looking over the hills!" Bear Rope shouted this, joining the noise of the wild young warriors against those of his own age.

Dull Knife shook out his pipe bag and reached inside for the cleaner. He had nothing left to say now. He, too, was away at the agency during the Custer fight. Besides, Bear Rope was still sick from the poisoning *veho* disease, and that must be remembered.

Little Wolf found other work to do. He helped to set a row of fires in the dry weeds and grass to run down over the rifle pits. When the wind rolled the smoke that way, a pack mule broke loose and was run down by Wild Hog's son, who found a big bundle of green money on him. Finally the troops took their stock back into a deep ravine to escape the fire and the arrows too. When their guns quieted in the evening, Little Wolf called his warriors in, except the watchers.

"You have made a good stand, without angering the whites too much. Now I think enough ammunition has been used up. The women are all safe."

But the rebellion among the younger men was hotter than ever now. "Let us go clean out these soldiers down there—leave them scattered over the ground like they have our people! It will teach the others who come following us."

"Hou, hou! Good men have been hurt. Let us pay back the soldiers for that!"

But Little Wolf and Wild Hog and now even young Bull Hump

were firm. This was not like the old times, Little Wolf said, when they were free to avenge the injuries. In these new times the fighting against the whites had to be with the *veho* weapons. "See how little for defense there is in your hands, my friends," he reminded them earnestly. "We will need it all to protect the helpless ones later. Let us run as soon as we can."

But once more the young men got support from Dull Knife. Sitting at the dusk-time fire, he had the comfort of old friends of the buffalo days, the stale powder smoke firing the blood of the old warriors. It seemed that they were back in the good days of the buffalo and the wars with the Crows, the Pawnees, and the Snakes.

"The soldiers should be killed," Dull Knife said. "Cheyennes cannot let such shooting go unavenged. The whites here are not the same as those in the north, but like different tribes among the Indians. Those in the north said one thing, these another."

"They are all the same whites," Little Wolf replied, "and angering them here will bring trouble up ahead."

Dull Knife did not reply or look up from his pipe, but he gave the sign of agreement when the council selected the Dog Soldiers to watch the troopers for the night.

"Make no attack, but let nobody get away. Hold them close like the *veho* herds his cows. Ride around them, and even sing them a few songs if it pleases you," Little Wolf said, his face lighted with a thin smile, one of the first since the agent offered him his own granddaughter for a wife.

Bull Hump and his Dog Soldiers accepted this responsibility, but that did not keep some from sending arrows and a few bullets down into the draw as they kept up their intermittent whoops and howling to scare the eastern recruits.

All the noise annoyed Rendlebrock, who hated Indian fighting. Prussian born and trained, he liked orderly battles, and the Civil War had already been a disorderly conflict in his eyes. "Is this then work for a soldier, skirmishing with whooping red savages?" he growled a dozen times during the night. But those whooping red savages managed to keep him from getting men out for water or for reinforcements.

There was other work for the Cheyennes this night too. Some went for more horses, and a few to help bring in Brave One's party of women and children. There was laughing and crying and a song of thankfulness when they came plodding wearily through the firelit warrior camp, many barefoot, the children, even those seven and eight years old, too worn to walk. The few women at the fighting ran to see the newborn son. The little one was shown for a moment at the red coals of the council fire, and named Comes Behind by his great-uncle. The old man made the motions of the pipe to the Great Powers as he said the words. It was a good omen, Bridge agreed, that their journey was begun with a new life the first night, and now the naming when they had just won the first little battle. So far none had died with them, although the father of Singing Cloud had thrown himself from his travois into the grass once. But his dutiful daughter had lifted him back and whipped her old mare onward.

Tomorrow? Tomorrow one would see, old Bridge said, as a shot boomed out down where the soldiers were surrounded.

When Little Wolf returned to his fire, Feather on Head was stooping silently to the cooking. She filled her big sheephorn spoon and gave it to her husband in the good way. Gravely, with his knife point, he offered a bit of the meat to the sky and the earth and the four directions. Then he ate. "It is good," he said once, and Feather on Head sang a little song of happiness, very softly, so not to be an embarrassment.

> "I have a good man.
> In the village circle
> The women have called out his name many, many times,
> And the children follow his tracks."

After he ate, Little Wolf went through the rising moonlight to look over the slopes of the fighting and to listen to the occasional shot from down around the soldiers. On the hillsides of the fight, still in deep shadow, boys and youths were carrying torches and digging with their knives for bullet lead in the soft red rock. He saw the flaring light on the smooth brown faces as they ran here and there, stooping to pry eagerly and seriously for the mushroomed bullets they needed so much. Among the boys was the light-skinned one called Yellow Swallow. He had not brought bad luck today, as some had feared, no matter who his father was.

ALL NIGHT THE INDIANS held the soldiers in the ravine, shut in with their wounded men and their horses, alive and dead. Now and then there was an exchange of shots as some Indian slipped up too close or a courier tried to get away. Early in the morning, when the fog began to creep out of the red canyons, the fighting started again. But the soldiers were surrounded and their ammunition about gone. By the time the sun poured down straight upon the thirsting horses, the dry canteens, and the wounded men, the Indians saw the troopers mount and start back. Astride their horses the Cheyenne warriors watched from the bluffs on each side, standing out boldly against the windy sky, in easy rifle shot, letting the dusty blue column pass in peace below, since they were going back.

Afterward, while the women stripped the skins from the dead horses, Little Wolf and Wild Hog went over the fighting ground together. They picked up a field glass covered by the earth stirred up in the charges, and saw where three soldiers had died. The dead Arapaho lay there too, with flies on his eyelids. From the white bandages seen in the retreating column, it seemed that three more soldiers were wounded.

But five good Cheyennes were hurt defending themselves at this place called Turkey Springs, where once the clouds of wild turkeys came to sleep. One was a small girl, six, an orphan, the mother shot in the Powder River fight, the father crippled and then killed by the spotted disease down south. Now the shy little girl had been hit in the foot, and crawled away under a bush sometime during the fighting. When she was found she was carried, light as a doll made of rushes or willow sticks, to Bridge, who drew the bullet from the shattered ankle. More and more of the people came to stand silent while this was done, their faces unmoving as they heard the soft little whimperings. She was a brave Cheyenne, this little one who would be known as Lame Girl from this day.

After a while she slept, but the hurting of this child who belonged to them all made the people angrier than anything of this day. It had been done in the place called Indian Territory, the Indians' own land, and no whites anywhere had been molested. But three of the soldiers who came shooting had been killed. That, and not the five Cheyennes hurt, one a small child, would start the talking wires and spread the story all the way to the north country.

Chapter 4

NOW THE INDIANS must travel very fast and hide their trail as well as possible. So they scattered into little parties, but stayed close enough to gather quickly for protection. The young men went raiding for more horses, and guns, too, if any could be obtained now after the news of the fight.

"Nobody is to be killed," the warriors were still told. "Only the soldiers that come shooting at you."

But it was difficult to hold some of the young men. Dull Knife and the other old ones were angry too, because injured Cheyennes went unavenged. But most of them saw that it would be difficult enough to get through to the north now, with the talking wires telling of the fight and the whites angered that their soldiers had been driven back like prairie dogs running for their holes at the sound of thunder. So the Indians moved out as soon as they could, with two more drags needed now, one with Lame Girl and the other with Old Grandmother, who was worn out. Not wanting to detain the flight, she tried to be left along the trail as had the ailing father of Singing Cloud. Twice the old woman rolled herself off the drag, but the short, tawny grass refused to hide her poor calico, and someone came back scolding, "Grandmother! You went to sleep and fell off! We must tie you in," or "We must make a cradleboard for you like the new child with us, young Comes Behind."

But two days later the sixteen-year-old Spotted Deer came riding from the south, his horse white-frosted with lather. The news had reached Fort Reno about the good little fight, and so Spotted Deer was sent by his mother to look after Old Grandmother and help her get north. Two other young men rode in with him, because even a little fight seemed better than sitting on an agency.

Brave One and about twenty others were still walking along behind, carrying their children or those of others, but with new moccasins and a few pieces of new meat in their packs from the buffalo hunt just before the Turkey Springs fight. Stripped into thin flakes, the meat had dried quickly for carrying. It was good that they had found the buffalo then, as there would be little hunting now, with the buffalo bones everywhere, the old chips bleaching and crumbled. But it seemed the Great Powers were not entirely against the Cheyennes, for the summer had been wet. There was good grass for the short stops, and water holes—usually dry in September—were still like lakes.

The wildest of the young men knew now that it was better to take the trail Dull Knife laid out long ago west of the Kansas forts. Yet even here it was hard to keep hidden from the eyes of the whites, with their little sod houses and their cattle everywhere.

Perhaps too many people did see them, for soon more soldiers came. The Indians were going up Bear Creek, the Cimarron not far behind, when suddenly a double row of soldiers on gray horses approached from ahead. There were fewer than the other time, and the troops fired from far off, making a line and charging so there was no time for parley. The warriors met them, shooting and retreating and shooting again until the whites turned back in the direction of Fort Dodge, on the Arkansas River. Only one soldier was killed.

The Indian camp moved right ahead now, because there was no place to hide. Little Wolf wondered if there ever would be, with the big bunches of soldiers marching against them, walking soldiers who could not run away either, and carrying the far-shooting guns.

LITTLE WOLF TALKED for the pleasantness of big fires that night, so they stopped near wood. There was even a little singing. Girls and older boys went along the scattered fires, with them a youth of the Contrary Society, those who do everything foolish and backward to lift the hearts of the people from the ground in unhappy times. He was making the people laugh in his turned-around way, his front-behind clothes. With the white-man hat over his face he walked backward, showing only the black Indian hair where a nose and eyes should be, his bow drawn against himself. Flexible as a mink, he crawled through fire and mud, jumped over shadows, and escaped from pursuit running backward to it. It seemed very funny in this anxious time, and young Spotted Deer found himself laughing with a shy, pretty girl called Yellow Bead, one who had an aunt she must help to the north country, and whose eyes strayed to Little Hump, the son of a chief.

But suddenly the laughing was done. Little Finger Nail and his horse hunters came in with bad news. Black Beaver, who had led them, was left back there on the ground. They had seen some horses down near a ranch. Not wanting to scare the whites, Black Beaver took only one man down to buy some horses with the paper money from the pack mule. But the white men came shooting and hit Black Beaver. The other one escaped over the hill, and when the cowboys, chasing him, saw all the Indians, they spurred back. Afterward Little Finger Nail tried to get the body of his friend, but a lot of gray-horse troops came riding and about eighty went to stand around the Indian, poking him with their gun barrels, taking the green money, and leaving him naked like an uprooted brown tree fallen beside the trail. So Little Finger Nail took all the ranch stock he could get, shooting the colts too young to follow north. They left Woodenthigh behind to watch and to carry Black Beaver's body to the burial rocks.

So now a good man had been killed by *vehos* who were not soldiers, and the hearts of the Indians were very bad. Little Wolf talked for coolness with so many in danger here. "Hold yourselves," he urged. "Black Beaver was a very good leader who always looked straight along the path of the people. That was why he was selected to go buy the horses. He would work for peace even now, from his place in the grass."

"Nobody had hurt anything of the settler whites!" Little Finger Nail protested hotly.

"Ahh-h, already the whites are afraid and shooting at everyone. So it will be all the way now," an older man said morosely as the keening started among the women. It ran back along the narrow canyon, rising like a sorrowful dust. Black Beaver's wife and two young daughters slashed their arms and legs so blood ran, and Little Wolf and several others let their hair stream loose with earth and grass in it. That was all they could do. There were no presents to make a giveaway for Beaver's friends. There was so little time now for the mourning, for the decencies of death, or birth, or life.

THAT NIGHT TANGLE HAIR and three of the Dog Soldier rear guards divided the camp into smaller parties, to travel all they could in this darkening moon time, keeping out of sight in the day. Even so there was trouble, the scouts signaling danger from the night. Then everybody had to turn aside, because white men lived where there should be only grass and buffalo—the *veho* sign perhaps a settler's light like a star pinned to the ground, or many rough places where a plow had traveled the earth. The people became more and more fearful, with these unexpected enemies everywhere, and once Bridge had to hurry back to Bear Rope in the darkness of the moving line.

"Come, oh come! Our man is very strange," one of the wives pleaded. "He carries the voice of the enemy in his mouth, and enemy words."

Because the son-in-law and the other men of that family were away, a wife had run for the medicine man herself, afraid and so very much ashamed at this admission of fault in her husband that the man could barely hear her words. When Bridge came to Bear Rope and saw how it was, he signaled the leaders to stop the moving people, and for a while the Indians rested in the darkness or slipped away to their needs—but not far, with none knowing when night-charging soldiers might come. The men smoked their red willow bark, women fed their babies, and some of the young men went for a whispered word with the girls, perhaps even a little laughing away from the bereaved ones, the softly keening ones who had lost the good man Black Beaver.

Bridge worked to quiet Bear Rope with his sleep chants. But the man had been very sick in the summer, the medicine man helpless and the agency doctor not coming. Then, when her father seemed dead, the daughter vowed to cut off her little finger if he lived. Almost at once he was breathing, and when he managed to crawl out into the daylight, he found that his strong son and thirty others had died that week. The vow of the finger brought on a furious anger. "It is the whites who should be bleeding for my sickness!" he cried. "I command you not to fulfill the vow." From that day he had twisted times, when he spoke to his wives and his daughter as loose women come so familiarly to his lodge.

The sleep Bridge brought him now helped, but Bear Rope needed more; he needed a long time of good village life, the easy cycle of eating, hunting, and sleeping—not this running, running, with danger behind every hill, riding through every gully.

Toward morning the meat men came in under the pale horned moon with fresh beef. If there were no need to fight the soldiers, travel would be easy now, with so many cattle scattered around the new living places of the whites.

"The cowboys will not like this butchering; they will shoot."

Perhaps it could be done as with the Sioux, an old man said. Sometimes when there were no buffalo the Indians killed cattle, and it was taken out of their beef appropriation from the Great Father, from the pay for their lands.

Yes, that was true, but some whites liked the opportunity to shoot very well, and shooting Indians best of all.

Then, when the noonday clouds veiled the sun, the soldiers were suddenly there again. Woodenthigh had come in to say the whole country was full of them. As he had kept watch over Black Beaver's body, he saw more and more of them gathering, with packhorses of guns and ammunition, and all moving toward Bear Creek here.

Little Wolf and Wild Hog were leading the people up a narrow canyon when soldiers were signaled just ahead, many more this time, with many other whites. The frightened people turned back upon themselves, crowding together, the warriors hurrying up the sides. There was no place to run, to hide, so the Cheyennes waited, packed in like antelope in a trap, the whitish windy sky standing over them, two eagles circling high, and the soldiers charging.

The Indians returned the fire, but carefully, intending to hit the horses at first, then more if it must be done. Even Left Hand had settled himself for very deliberate aim. But when the horses in front went down, those behind began to plunge and were jerked back with the iron in their mouths. Several soldiers seemed hurt, and one died. Then the trumpet blew, the echo sweet and clear in the canyon, and suddenly the troops turned and galloped away.

"Truly it seems as Dull Knife has said all the time. Perhaps the soldiers do not intend to fight us," Left Hand admitted, for a moment almost disappointed, now that he had worked himself to a fighting pitch; not easy for this man who liked to spend his time feasting on roasted hump ribs and talking about the great hunts.

But there was bad damage today. Sitting Man had his leg broken. The bullet had gone through the thigh, the bone sticking out, with blood gushing around it like a welling spring. Bridge had hurried up. Fearfully the wife of Sitting Man brought water and wood. Bridge gave the wounded man a red drink, and by rattle and song put him to sleep almost at once. Then he passed the painted gourd over the naked breast, always slower, until the heart under the brown skin seemed to slow with it and the pouring blood became only a thin red thread. He wiped the wound with silver sage weed, sprinkled it with dust from a puffball, and bound it. Then he pulled the leg out long and covered it from body to foot with the green hide of a soldier horse sewed on very tight so, when it shrank in the hardening, the broken bones would be held straight and firm, with only a little hole for the stink of the healing wound. It was a fine thing to hear the wife singing her song of thankfulness as she led their only horse to the medicine man, as was his due.

But others pushed up to offer horses instead. "You will need yours very much now, sister, if you and your hurt man are to get away," Black Crane said.

"*Hou.*" It was good. And good to know that old Bridge still had his great power.

UP TO NOW LITTLE WOLF had controlled his young men well. He had made them wait until the troops fired, even in the face of charging cavalry, and kept them from attacking the other whites or committing any depredations except killing a few cattle and taking some horses. But now many men had been hurt and Black Beaver lost, and it was as Little Wolf had warned. If people shot at them, they would shoot back. Then the next day the scouts found that two of the young Cheyennes left to watch the soldiers had been killed and scalped. One was the nephew of Left Hand, and now this moderate man would gladly have brought down a dozen soldiers instead of just their horses.

From the first day the foragers had been led by reliable peace men, but now the wildest young warriors sneaked out, with none to know what was done unless they told it. Near a place called Protection, they saw two whites riding horses that were stolen from their herd last year, one from Black Coyote, whose warrior wife was afoot now, with her child on her back. The Cheyennes shot one of the riders when he fired, but let the other man get away, and brought in the stolen horses with four other good ones.

Now the Indians must get away fast, for soon there would be too many soldiers. The scouts who followed those of today came back through the blackness of a raining night, with three horses worn out. All the whites had gone to the Arkansas, but certainly they would be up ahead and many more.

"Ahh-h, yes, at the river, with the wide flat valley that must be crossed," Little Wolf murmured. Feather on Head looked anxiously toward her man as she leaned her blanket protectively over the wet, sputtering coals. The rain fell straight down, and none had a lodge, not even the sick and old or the crippled Sitting Man or the child now called Lame Girl, with her bullet-shattered ankle very swollen.

BY NOW STORIES OF a great Indian uprising flooded the newspapers, the office of the governor of Kansas, and the army posts through the state, with many hundreds of telegrams and letters from everywhere demanding guns and ammunition.

Many asked, "Where is Sherman, our general of the army?" It turned out that General William T. Sherman was about his regular business, making an extended inspection tour of the very frontier posts that must subdue the Indians.

Around the Dodge City saloons it was said that the gray-horse troops were too weak against almost three hundred Indians. That night a train of stockcars was ready to haul everybody up to the Dull Knife crossing of the Arkansas: five companies of cavalry, two of infantry, about fifty cowboys and ranchers, and wagons to haul the infantry and the supplies. But they found no sign of Indians there, and so the next morning the column started across the bare tableland to Crooked Creek and made night camp in a hard rain.

TO FIND MEAT FOR almost three hundred hiding people was hard for the hunters, and even Little Wolf asked few questions when they drove a herd of thirty beeves into the camp and brought them down with arrows there, the bawling longhorns running wild, the dust rising to meet their thudding bodies.

The women worked fast, their children under the hand if the bullets started to come. By evening the knives were at the women's belts again, glistening clean. Stripped meat hung in dark rags along the drying ropes. The hides were staked, flesh side up, to the Kansas wind, some stretched over pits of embers to harden for moccasin soles. Even a few rough skin wickiups would now protect the wounded like Sitting Man and some with the ague.

For a few hours it seemed almost like long ago, with even the good smell of coffee from a store that had been raided along the Dodge trail.

Fresh coffee—with sugar in the bottom of the cup—the first since the wintertime! Soon now they would be across the Arkansas, their moccasins firm on another rung of the Cheyenne ladder to the north. While they ate, three more young men came in, deserters from those who remained behind in the south.

"It is said somebody here has very strong medicine, to make the soldiers all run back," one explained. "It seems they fly back like a bullet hitting a stone." Perhaps all the others would soon be following north.

Later a big fire was built up against the night, with a new-made skin drum and some singing, Little Finger Nail's sweet voice joining the others until Singing Cloud came shyly from among the maidens to draw him into the weaving dance circle about the fire. But Yellow Bead hid her face and dared not approach Little Hump. Truly this was the best time since the Cheyennes had to leave the north country, since before Custer came riding up there. And tonight none seemed to look with darkness against Long Hair's son, Yellow Swallow.

But in the middle of the evening there was a sudden shout and running, with thick, angry bellows, like a buffalo bull fighting, and cries of terror. People ran toward it, the women too. At Bear Rope's little fire they found the whole family crying, one wife with blood flowing over her face from the war club of her husband, the other hurt too, the younger children knocked aside, and the son-in-law rushing in.

But he came too late. After Bear Rope had chased all the others away, he grabbed his daughter, Comes in Sight, and threw her down to make a wife of her right there in the light of his own fire.

But the daughter managed to draw the butcher knife from her belt and slashed the father so his bowels hung out, laying across his arm now as he sat hunched over in the firelight, trying to hold himself together, the grayness already in his eyes. Then, before all the people, he started to settle downward, the violence draining from his face as he went over sideways to the earth.

Afterward Little Wolf spoke. A Cheyenne had been killed by another, who must now be driven out, ostracized for perhaps four years, and never sit where the medicine pipe would pass again. But this was done by a woman. Never in all their lifetime had one of their women killed a tribesman. And her own father . . .

Yet a woman was in honor bound to defend herself, Dull Knife pointed out. Besides, none here could say how much of this happened because of the vow of a finger for the father's recovery, never fulfilled. And how much because of the chasing whites who brought their sickness upon Bear Rope, and all his loss and humiliation? It was enough to make a good man go down the violent road.

There were grave *hous*. "Yet we must try to keep the darkness of this bad day from following the people," Bridge said.

But the goodness of this night was gone, and from all the nights of one young woman. Before morning the scouts signaled that more soldiers were close, and once more everybody got ready to run, harder than ever now, for there was blood upon the people.

Chapter 5

As the soldiers came close again, the raiders were signaled in. One party had found a wagon train and brought in what they could carry. Others found many of the sheep that no one wanted. At one place a herder shot at them and so they drove his flock over the prairie and into a lake, the Indians along the bank watching the sheep crowd together, trying to walk on each other. It was strange how silly the tame creatures of the *veho* were.

But the young men killed some more people, one a black man that they regretted shooting because the gun he pointed at them turned out to be a long stick blackened with axle grease to look like a rifle. Another man was shot at a place of five or six houses with everybody else gone. The Indians looked for powder and ammunition; they took some hoop iron for arrows, white-fringed bedspreads for the Dull Knife daughters, and some dresses and pretty pictures for the small children.

"Two years ago there were only buffalo here," they told Little Wolf, to break his angry silence over the killings. "Now there are only cattle and the sheep who make the lakes so no horse can drink."

Ahh-h, it was well to leave the poisoned southern country, Little Wolf admitted. But now there were these dead men to be counted against the Cheyennes too.

This time the soldiers came in a great column that circled to a camp on a part of Sand Creek, cowboys and soldiers mixed together. Roman Nose stayed behind and saw the red-faced Rendlebrock come again, the man whose cannon had looked down into their village. The soldiers unsaddled and scattered, but several cowboys went scouting and ran into Black Coyote's men guarding the canyon with the women and children.

At the first shot Black Coyote started to clean out the cowboys, but suddenly Little Wolf stood in the canyon before him, his horse blocking the way. "My friend, these soldiers here have always gone away. Perhaps it was because so few whites have been hurt," he said. "If they stay to fight us, we may all die."

More whites kept coming, and in a little skirmishing Black Coyote and his helpers were driven back. At sunset everybody went back to camp. There was an alarm in the night, but the shooting was soldiers mistaking cowboys riding out of the darkness for Indians.

In the morning the troops moved up with at least forty wagons and many, many men. The women started to run, but Dull Knife walked among them with Old Crier beside him, and quieted them.

While the warriors held off the walking soldiers with their dangerous long guns, the cowboys were free to charge in and out as they liked, making the air thick with dust and smoke and noise, but all running away every time that a horse went down. Yet this freed the cavalry to go around below the Indian position. Little Wolf decided there were too many enemies for this place. They must move back into the broken hills.

So the people moved behind Old Crier, going swiftly, heavily, knowing that in this place the fight must be made. No warrior rode out in taunts now, showing off, charging foolishly.

"Remember your guns are almost empty!" Little Wolf cautioned the young men as he walked among them, standing out plain for everyone to see, with the bullets making dust jumps around him, but only until he had the young men calmed. The sons need not outdo the fathers in daring today.

While the soldiers moved in below them, rifle pits were dug around the ridge, all big enough for six men. Everybody knew that if the whites fought with all their guns and ammunition, this would be like the ridge where Custer died—the last stand by the Cheyennes. Even Sitting Man, with a forked stick under his arm for a hobble leg, had been helped into a pit.

While some dug, others hurried to paint themselves and put on the little war regalia left and to sing their song of death. Old Great Eyes made the medicine for the shield of his grandfather—a feather-tailed shield from long ago in the far lake country and never lost to an enemy in all the battles since. He sang his death song with his nephew beside him, young Red Bird, only thirteen, but ready to shoot if a gun fell free, and finally to run with the medicine shield.

Little Finger Nail was getting ready too, repeating what he said back at the agency for his small cousin, who might never live for another day. "If the young men die fighting here, their names will be remembered forever." He showed the boy how to aim the rifle a little high for those keeping back. "The bullet gets tired going so far."

The women were all singing too, for strength as they prepared for attack. Holes were dug, the first to protect the children. The wife of the crippled Black Horse and others who had been in the Sappa Creek fight tried not to remember how the buffalo hunters there had pulled the babies out of the holes, clubbed them, and then threw them into the fires of the piled lodges. It was mostly the other whites with the soldiers that did those things, and many such men were very close now.

The women worked fast, with no sound except their singing and the cut and thrust of the butcher knives against gravel and stone. Buffalo Calf Road gave her small one to another with a baby at breast, the eyes of the women meeting over the little head a moment in naked sisterhood. Then she went gravely to the rifle pits, where several other women who could shoot the guns or bows were already waiting. Those with husbands here were combed and painted in the way of a beloved wife by her man.

Now the whites were moving closer. The forty wagons were drawn up side by side in a row, the tailgates toward the Cheyennes so the mules would be harder to hit. The walking soldiers came in a skirmish line beside the dismounted cavalry, blue men rising and running, dropping to fire, and then running again, closer and closer, with some of the other whites coming behind them on their horses. It was like a solid wall pushing in until the people became very excited, afraid because this time they could not run.

Little Wolf walked from one rifle pit to the next, through the spurting bullets. "No one is to fire a shot!" he commanded. "They have wagons of ammunition to our handful. Keep down and wait until something happens."

But the soldiers seemed so very close, the smoke blowing thick and blue over the pits, the bullets striking along the tops, spraying those inside with sand and whistling on over the people behind. Finally Little Wolf let a few warriors fire. One soldier grabbed at himself in the middle, turned half around, and fell dead. The rest were on their bellies now, firing at the Indians along the slope above, the noise like a rolling hailstorm.

Finally another white man seemed hit, for he stood up straight and then fell backward. About twenty more men jumped up, but they ran back to their horses at the wagons. From there they rode around the hill of the Cheyennes, some of the other whites following, so Little Wolf had to charge out to meet them with his best soldiers, whooping and firing from behind their running horses until the soldiers were driven back to the wagons, leaving another man dead. At the same time Dull Knife, Wild Hog, and Black Crane sent a mounted charge down the slope upon the whites. Before its force the cowboys started away, the women calling insults after them, shaming the manhood of the whites who had come out to shoot women and children like game on a hunt.

Then everybody else left too, running on long-shadowed legs through the evening sun. A great cry of thankfulness rose from the women. Some of the young Cheyennes tried to overtake the soldiers, but Little Wolf signaled a stop. They were too few, without ammunition, and their horses must be strong to save the helpless ones another day. So the young men returned, except those to scout the soldiers, perhaps to cut off the couriers sure to go to Fort Dodge for cannons to shell the Indians out of their good position.

Perhaps the medicine of the Cheyennes was still powerful, even after the Bear Rope killing, for while couriers got away on their fast horses, there was no guard over the Indians. Hurriedly the women cooked a little meat after the hungry day, while the young men searched the fighting ground. They found a wooden box of cartridges that the soldiers did not have time to load into the wagons, and a half box scattered out. There was a broken rifle too, that could perhaps be repaired.

The headmen made their evening smoke, quiet as any time. After a pipe Little Wolf spoke. "My friends," he said in his flowing Cheyenne words, "there are too many troops here for us to fight. We must move out before the stars turn even a hand's distance in their path. We must try to get away north before somebody comes who is not playing, somebody hot to kill. We might have been with our faces to the sky right here."

Ahh-h, it was true, the others admitted, guttering their pipes.

THE NEXT MORNING it was discovered that the Cheyennes were gone, slipped away in the night. And in a few days most of the men who had been reported killed in the raids began to show up, one after another, some surprised to hear that there had been an Indian scare at all. Finally instead of a hundred, there seemed six civilians actually dead, and some claimed this was no more than the normal killings for ten days in that region of outlaws and horse thieves, of cattleman and sheepman fights.

But by then troops were moving as far off as Utah, coming from the far east and the south too—wherever any could be found. Then there were those from the upper Missouri River—the Seventh Cavalry, Custer's regiment. Now the death of Long Hair would be avenged.

THE MAIN BODY of the Cheyennes gathered in a big draw back from the flooded Arkansas, with Bull Hump and Woodenthigh signaling the dark way. Silently the Indians came out of the moonless night, in a wind cool with the smell of sweet water. Nothing had been seen, but there must be soldier ears down there, waiting for the sound of horses breasting the high water and quicksand. And just beyond lay the iron tracks of the railroad, a watching snake, the one great eye surely ready to break from the night upon them, bringing troops and guns into their helpless illumination.

At a gunshot from down toward Fort Dodge the horses of Bull Hump and Woodenthigh were spurred forward, the rest following toward the dark stream, where so many things had happened to the Cheyennes.

Just up the river was the spot sacred to the Great Mother of the Cheyennes, the woman who had brought them their plan of government from the far north, carrying it over the wide prairies in the palm of her hand: forty-four chiefs, four each from the ten bands, and four old man chiefs. With this plan she brought also a small son, Tobacco, named for the gift from the Great Powers. Tobacco grew to be a great old chief, and in the white man's 1846 he was shot crossing here. Some soldiers were camped close by and a sentry challenged Tobacco, who understood no *veho* words and kept going through the river that belonged to anyone using it. That one bullet seemed certain to bring death to all on the little islands of whites scattered through the great sea of Indians in the buffalo country.

Dull Knife remembered his night of talking there beside the dead Tobacco, against the Cheyennes suddenly painted for war. He had been as angry as the powerful and very angry Dog Soldiers, but to a band chief the people must always come first. So with the hot blood burning in his breast he closed his ears to the throb of the avenging drums and against attacking the few soldiers here. He could not look on so much bloodshed, and knew too that many Indians would die—his own warrior sons and the small boy who was now Bull Hump, and perhaps his beloved first wife. But those warrior sons had been lost anyway, with many, many other Cheyennes, most of them to the soldier bullets, and the wife had died on a tree, because he took the Pawnee woman to his lodge.

Somehow unlimited killing never turned the *veho* officers from their path. Was it because the white man's fighter was not from a home, not returning to his house to eat and sleep and to live as the Indian warrior did, but was a pay man who did nothing but kill? Was it because the stink of all the blood could be kept away from the living, off in the distant forts?

Sweet Medicine had warned them what would happen if they let the white-faced ones come among them. If Little Wolf and the other warriors had driven out the whites when Tobacco was killed, it would have prevented the big sickness from the forty-niners who ran thick across the Indian country for gold. At a big intertribal dancing here at the Arkansas that summer an Osage fell and died of the cramping cholera. The women could not wait to pack, running straight for the handiest horses.

"Leave the river! The sickness of the whites follows the water!" Old Little Wolf, uncle to the one here now, had called out, and the people then fanned away toward the hills, escaping even from each other. And all around it was the same, all the tribes scattering, people running north and south and east and west.

But it was too late. Before the Indians were out of the broad valley of the Arkansas, they began to go down. Here one doubled into the cramp and slid from his galloping horse, there another. People died all the way to the Cimarron, dropping like worthless bundles or like the buffalo left behind by the hunters. Even the keeper of the sacred arrows was struck. Calmly he told his wife what must be done. "If everybody is blown away by the wind of this sickness, the arrows must be taken to a high hill by the last woman among you and laid down there for the time when the Cheyennes shall return to the earth, as Sweet Medicine has promised when he foretold these trials."

Afterward the keeper sat there, looking away to the hills until the flies crawled over his eyes unprotested. The people fled again, his wife running ahead, the arrow case on her back. So it went until the leaves began to turn and the streams flowed clear again. Then it was found that about half of the tribe lay dead. Since then the Cheyennes were a small people in number.

Now, ALMOST THIRTY years later, Dull Knife started his horse in the darkness, his grandson riding at his side. They passed the watching Little Wolf and headed for the Arkansas at the wide place, where low, bright stars trailed a vague path over the flooding waters. Fearfully the people listened to the first splash, expecting an attack in their helplessness. But the young men had marked a path through the shifting quicksand with tall willow poles and helped whip the plunging, swimming horses across. From the ridges far to each side of the river came the wolf signals and the soft hoots to say there were no soldiers yet, and no strong yellow eye roaring on the iron road. But the people must hurry.

Finally all were across except the outcast Bear Rope family. At a little creek beyond the river, fires were already built up by young women who rode with the first of the warriors. There were a few buffalo just a little way off, all they could butcher before the troops came. One fat cow was driven off to a gully and shot there for Comes in Sight's ostracized little party to butcher.

The next day the women roasted meat and pounded it with chokecherries, plums, and sand cherries, easy to carry in half and quarter bladders dipped in hot tallow, and easy to divide when they must scatter. The arrow makers were busy with the kettle of glue that Medicine Woman made. Her hoof glue would hold the feathers solid, but it would take strong medicine if they were to go against guns with nothing but arrows.

Many talked of other things at a secret fire up a dark draw—those related to Black Beaver and the two young men killed and scalped, and those who lost people up ahead there on the Sappa Creek three years ago, the nearness of it heating the blood. And around the camp some began to look with guarded anger at the son of Custer. Yellow Swallow saw it as he had all his boy's life, and slipped away into the shadows, sitting hidden so none would be reminded to cry out against him as bad medicine.

On the streets of Dodge City there was anger too, even though many men showed up who had been counted as dead, and trail herds that were considered lost. But the raiding Indians must be stopped. It was said that the commander of Fort Dodge, Colonel William H. Lewis, considered the campaign shamefully mismanaged. He was taking up the trail on the first train west, and he would wipe out those murdering redskins or leave his own body dead on the ground.

Chapter 6

FOR TWO DAYS the Cheyennes seemed almost whole again, all except Comes in Sight, somewhere alone with her grieving relatives. The days were like the time before the *veho,* with feasting and gambling too, but with the white man's playing cards because the racehorses were worn out. There was visiting and lovemaking and jealousy, yet even the old envies and hatreds were managed better.

Even such a warrior as Little Finger Nail made games for the small boys, sang, courted the girls, and helped the old women with the horses. Often he sat alone drawing picture stories of his exploits in a paper book taken at a place down south of the Arkansas, his little box of colored pencils snatched up in one of the raids. With yellow and blue and red he made the flying horse herds, the fights with the bluecoats, himself identified with all his regalia.

The second night they built great fires in the center of the camp, for there was no use to hide, with their wide trail so plain over the high, flat country. Later a scout came in with bad news. The soldiers were camped only a few miles back. "Many cavalrymen, and very many walking soldiers in wagons, and other wagons of ammunition. A great angry snake of whites comes against us in the morning," the scout said. "With them rides the officer Lewis who said at Dodge that he would capture the Cheyennes or leave his body on the ground."

"There has already been too much shooting," Old Crier said, speaking to himself. It was not decent for man to live so, in flight, always in flight.

After the scout went from Little Wolf, the women stooped over the fine smell of roasting ribs and coffee. Later most of the young men went to the dance fire, but few had the heart for dancing tonight. Yet the camp was barely quiet when there was a cry of excitement near Big Foot's fire. There, where the lodge should have been, were two new horses tied in the dark, two extra ones, a great fortune in these times. People came from all around to see, but no one knew the new horses except Big Foot's son, who had seen an older warrior called Limpy catch them today. Now Limpy offered them toward the family herd as a proposal of marriage to Big Foot's eighteen-year-old daughter, Broad-faced One.

Before them all the mother took the ropes in acceptance, without the coy waiting for a second offer, a third in a week or a month or a year, the girl pretending that all was as before. No old woman ran to carry good words of the suitor's bravery, and of his honored family. No others spoke on this side or that, for across all things of life lay the shadow of a long column of approaching dust.

The Indians had little time or substance for a Cheyenne wedding, but Limpy's friends set Broad-faced One on a ragged old blanket and carried her to a bare fire in a canyon instead of a decorated, festive lodge. Limpy's mother made the feast for her son's wife, just more young buffalo, nothing like the old-time feastings that sometimes lasted until the people were fat as prairie dogs in the sun.

Afterward Limpy and his laughing one went to a hillside with a robe. The chastity rope was not untied this night, for they had had little time to become acquainted, and a maiden cannot be hurried into good wifehood. Besides, tomorrow would bring fighting, and continence made the warrior's medicine strong.

Some scarcely knew of the little marrying among them. They sat dark and alone at their fires, men like Bull Hump and Black Horse, his crippled leg painful tonight. They sent their hearts back to the killing on the Sappa, now just one long day's travel ahead. And out in the draw the young Dog Soldiers made their plans. Whatever happened tomorrow, some must get away to avenge those killings.

THE SMOKE ROSE STRAIGHT and blue from the morning cooking fires in the canyon, with no other sign visible on the prairie above, nothing of the fresh earth where the women dug new rifle pits, a few more pits farther back too, to protect the last little draw of the people's retreat.

Finally Old Crier went slowly through the camp. "The soldiers are coming! Everybody make ready to go back behind the breastworks! The helpless ones gather in the canyons behind them. Nobody need be afraid. Your men are brave!"

Already the packhorses were thundering in, and then the warriors went to make their medicine as well as they could. More captured horses came in, the horsebreakers taking charge of half a dozen wild ones. It seemed a bad time to break such stubborn stock, but the horses would be needed before another sun, for plainly this would be war.

The helpless ones were taken away, and the young men were making the first warrior parade through the camp below, those with guns holding them up high, even some for which there were no shells. The women gave their trilling cries and sang strong-heart songs, Broad-faced One too now, knowing that the soldiers were very many and only seven cartridges stood in the belt of her Limpy for this day.

THE FIRST SOLDIERS came down a gully to Punished Woman Creek, at a place where the stream had cut seventy-five to a hundred feet into the sandstone. The women and children were hidden in a canyon along a dry creek that ran in from the west, and Little Wolf placed some of his most able men between them and the junction of the dry creek with Punished Woman Creek. Here several steep bluffs pushed in close to the creek bed, and the trail narrowed to single file, the opposite canyon wall only a hundred yards away. On a jutting point the Indians had a few advance rifle pits overlooking their fresh and inviting trail—the steel jaws of their ambush.

The Dog Soldiers had been selected for the ambush pits, but Little Wolf was not easy in his mind. "You should keep hidden up there," he told them. "Let them get past you through this narrow place, and the wagons too, if they climb down into the canyon, let all get past you. When we charge them from the front, you start picking them off from behind, shooting down, stampeding the horses with arrows. Three or four good men who have no arms will hide in the willows close there, to take the guns as the soldiers fall, and set fires in the narrow place to close it."

"*Hou! Hou!*" the warriors shouted. "Let us go!"

But Little Wolf was not done. "My friends, you must remember to wait. This time we are not just a war party that can run away. Our helpless ones are back in that far canyon. Hold yourself!"

THE WAGONS KEPT UP on the prairie, the string of them creeping like a long gray worm, moving all the time, heading around behind where the Indians waited. In the canyon the soldiers must have known they were getting close, for the trail was broad and plain, the horse droppings very fresh. One of the scouts stopped at the deserted Cheyenne camp and knelt to scrape at a fire hole, waving the officers up. Then, with the flag flying before them, they came fast down the west side of Punished Woman Creek.

At the head of the dusty blue column rode the soldier chief Lewis. He sent no flankers out, so little did he value the power of the Cheyennes, although the main body of Indians was already plain for everybody to see up ahead, standing around their distant rifle pits. Between them and the soldiers was the ambush place that looked like any other empty bluff.

But before the scouts got near the ambush, one of the young Cheyennes suddenly became very hot to fight, and fired before he could be stopped. The excited shot missed, but the report echoed through the canyons, and a cry of sorrow and fear went up from the watching women as the little blue puff of smoke rose from the ambush pits and spread into the clean afternoon air.

There was shouting and pointing along the bottoms below, the horses plunging, the scouts falling back. The troops, still out of range, broke back, scattering as they sought a place to climb out of the canyon. When this was done, they charged along the top of the bluff toward the ambushing warriors and caught them in a cross fire with the scouts down in the bottoms, the smoke blowing thick over the point.

The Indians tried to fight there awhile, but finally had to run. Little Wolf sent a fast, whooping charge out past the soldiers to cover the flight, the warriors hanging to the far side of their horses, shooting with gun barrels leveled through the flying manes.

Little Wolf was so angry at the spoiled decoying that he had his saddle whip ready for the foolish one. The young man took the sharp cut across the face and then stumbled off to sit on the ground alone, his arm up to hide the raw welt and the shame. Little Wolf was angry with himself too. It was not all the fault of the young man. Many here had done little fighting—some grown ones knew less of it than a boy at his first fasting did in the buffalo days.

The little Cheyenne charge was turned back very easily by the flying blizzard of bullets, but just as they got out of range, the man ahead of Limpy let his wrist slip from the loop of mane and went down, dead, the horses behind jumping his crumpled body. Three soldiers went down too, one of their frightened horses running in among the Indians. The troopers retreated to reorganize and then came again, charging to within two hundred yards of the canyons where the people were hidden.

By this time the long wagon train had moved up and circled to a corral out on the open prairie. Men spread out from the wagons thick as a buffalo herd. Now the watching Indians saw the cavalry dismount on the ridge before them, and the troopers' horses taken away to safety. So they knew this time the soldiers did not plan to run. Colonel Lewis really would catch the Cheyennes, as he had promised at the Arkansas.

As the afternoon lengthened, the soldiers began to close in until they had the Indians almost encircled, the women and children in the trap too, with the smoke high on both sides of them. Colonel Lewis now and then could be seen riding among his dismounted troops. His horse, a strong bay gelding, let the Cheyenne bullets strike all around, not even jumping when he was hit to lameness. The men close to the soldier chief motioned him down, but he just kept pointing them toward the Indian position. It was a strong thing to do, and hard for the Cheyennes to watch with their children right ahead of his guns.

In the pits the men were being struck as the soldiers got up higher, and Little Wolf knew they must move or be killed right there. Slowly, under the smoke and roaring of the guns, the fighting women crept back and then the men. So they were driven to their last half circle of rifle pits, the ones that protected the huddle of frightened women and children and the few horses down behind the shadowing canyon. It was all Brave One and Feather on Head could do to hold the helpless people from running.

"Will you shame your brave men—make the place they are dying to defend only a foolish empty sack, the treasure dropped out?"

Truly it was time for every Cheyenne to make a stand to the end, but Black Coyote, Whetstone, and Black Horse with some others were not willing to do so. They prepared to charge out afoot, into the guns. "We will not sit here and let them come to shoot us like rabbits in their holes!"

"No—nor live to see them burn our families in the fires of our goods, as on the Sappa! Better to die fighting!"

But old Black Crane came running in protest. "No, no!" he shouted. "You must not throw yourself away like that!" And when they did not hear him, he stepped solidly into their path, his bow strung. Wild Hog, the big, broad man, stood beside him, the two putting themselves against the scarred breasts of these men.

So Black Coyote and the others fell back. Others talked of sending a few young men and women to slip up the long snakehead draw that reached for miles to the northwest. "We must help a few strong ones save themselves, to preserve the seed of our people, so we need not end here."

That, too, Little Wolf would not permit. He was making a round of the last few holes, steadying the men. "Do not shoot now, my friends," he said. "Wait, keep down. Something may happen," repeating it like a medicine chant, over and over, a little like a drumming. "Wait—wait—"

Then for a while Little Wolf sat looking over the patch of ground left to the Cheyennes, and Tangle Hair beside him saw that he was like a bear again, as he had been the day of the attack on Dull Knife's winter village on the Powder. He was a cornered bear now, waiting, not like a man at all but like a grizzly bear, fierce, fearless, ready to lunge, to slash and claw. Then some of the soldiers got very close and started to come up the side of their bluff, with Colonel Lewis not far behind. So Little Wolf spoke, not snarling, as Tangle Hair had expected from his pale, twisted face, but gently.

"Now fire, my friends," he said softly, making the explosive downward sign with his hand, the Indian sign for kill. "Now fire, and let every shot bring down a man."

The guns roared like a thousand bulls in the canyons. Some of the white men fell; it looked like the soldier chief was among them, but none could know for sure in the smoke and dust and confused running back, the Indians whooping, wishing they could chase the fleeing ones now. But there were all those fresh soldiers over around the wagons waiting their turn, ready, cartridge belts heavy at waist and shoulder. Soon the troopers re-formed and came again, their shadows lengthening ahead of them on the prairie.

In the pits there was no talking now, not even from the garrulous Thin Elk. He brushed the sand from his eyes and kept down. "Always we must keep down!" the furious Black Coyote snarled, while others sang their death songs, quietly, with more and more wounded among them, one suddenly hit in the forehead so he stopped with his mouth half open in the chant and then fell.

Now some of the older men came to Little Wolf. "Friend, we ask that you let us give up," they said earnestly. "We will all be killed. We cannot fight or run anymore. Give up."

"Give up!" the chief roared against them, the hoarseness of the grizzly in his voice now.

But he was silent when he saw some of the council members coming with the white bedspreads fastened to the two long medicine lances, the fringed spreads that Dull Knife's daughters had worn.

"We are ready to hold up the white signal," the men said. "We wish to talk with the soldier chief. Perhaps he will take pity on us."

"Pity! They gave us pity on the Sappa!" Black Horse shouted angrily. "Our good man who carried the white flag that day was shot down like a mad wolf, the women and children dug out of their hiding holes and thrown on the fires of their lodges."

"We say give up."

"The stench of the people burned that day will never be lost from the nose of the Cheyennes! Will you add another such time?"

"We say give up."

Little Wolf was silent, pressing his arm to the chief's bundle against his ribs, wondering how he could go against them all, all except Dull Knife. At least he was not in this.

But before he must make a reply, one of the men who had hidden close to the soldiers came slipping out of the canyon, the late sunlight touching his hair as he climbed over the rim.

"You hit the soldier chief!" he called to them from far off. "The big officer Colonel Lewis!"

It must be true, for the troops were falling back. Stretcher-bearers came to carry several men out to the ambulances that moved up close. Others limped along, or were helped. By the time the dusk from the canyons had reached out over the rifle pits and all the flat prairie, most of the soldiers were gone to the wagons. The white bedspreads for the truce were gone too.

In the light of the thin westering moon Little Wolf went down to walk among his people, scattered in the rocks of the canyon slope. Some had crawled away into holes, or were covered with leaves and dead brush and afraid to come out even to his soft call. At last he had everybody collected as well as could be done without making too much movement for any listening scouts.

"My friends," he said, "we must try to get away from here, reach home without more fighting, or else we will all be killed. We must go fast now."

But it would be hard, with many horses lost. Many would have to walk now, very many. Yet if they were silent, as on the night that they had slipped past the soldiers back at the place of the standing lodges, they could escape once more.

This time the early setting of the little moon helped hide the people creeping up the draw. But many had been wounded, and two good men were left dead, covered with a few rocks, none of the people keening for their warriors, so necessary was it that they not be heard. At least one woman and her son were lost in the darkness of getting away—no one knew where—and the thin old father of Singing Cloud too. When the girl went to his hiding place, he was gone. Crying a little, softly, the girl followed the others. One young man was gone too, seen to slip south alone. They let him go. It was the one who fired the foolish shot that spoiled the ambush.

BY THE NEXT MORNING the weary, footsore Cheyennes were far away. The band was hidden in a narrow draw cut deep through the flat country, so cleanly cut that it could barely be seen until its steep walls dropped away before the foot.

Toward noon two more men were suddenly there among them. They had followed the ambulance and had slipped up to hear that Colonel Lewis was very bad hurt, bleeding from the leg, it seemed—such a wound as only a medicine man like Bridge could cure.

Old Bridge made a grave murmuring to hear this. He would gladly have traded his powers to the soldier chief for the safety of his people. But such things cannot be between enemies, although he did not feel like an enemy to anybody now.

One man had followed the sick wagon a little farther. "The man who said he would catch the Cheyennes or leave his body on the ground is dead," he added.

There was not a *hou* from anyone to this, only a slow getting up and going among the people to prepare them for more running.

Chapter 7

AS THEY NEARED the site of the Sappa fight three years before, there was a rising anger and sullenness on the faces of the people.

The 1875 trouble had started from a bad year too. In the south the Medicine Lodge Treaty in 1867 had promised to keep the buffalo hunters out. The Arkansas River was patrolled by a few men, but the hide hunters shot their way across it and on to the Cimarron and the Canadian. Everywhere the hide hunters crept upwind to the great herds, their heavy guns set on forked sticks, the boom and the smell of the blue smoke carried away as they worked, the plain darkened with dead animals that dropped suddenly, perhaps kicking a little.

So the Southern Cheyenne warriors undertook the fight against the hide hunters. But it was called raiding, and soldiers came and stayed, setting up Fort Reno where no soldiers should ever walk.

In 1874 some of the angry Cheyennes attacked an emigrant train near Punished Woman Creek. They massacred most of the Germaine family and took four young girls captive. When the soldiers came, the two smaller of the Germaine sisters were left behind for them, but still the troops gave chase. The following spring the Southern Cheyennes surrendered, the two white girls dressed in blankets and moccasins like the rest. The Indians were disarmed and dismounted and put into a prison camp near the new Fort Reno. Anyone who'd ever felt the power of a Cheyenne war charge could see them look whipped now.

One day soldiers lined up all the men, from youth to blind old age, in a double row through the camp. Then came the two older Germaine girls, fifteen and seventeen, dressed like visiting ladies, with plumed hats and dark red cloaks. They walked stiffly down the line pointing this way and that.

Back a way, where the Indian women watched, a moaning and crying started up, a keening as for the dead. Brave One saw men great in war and in peace taken from the line to be ironed and hauled away to prison. It was done on just the finger pointing by two whom the Indians considered foolish children, not women, as Cheyennes would be at that age. General Thomas H. Neill, the Fort Reno commander, sat red-faced and unsteady on his horse, overseeing the picking.

The double row of ragged Cheyennes, gaunt and poor, stood unmoving, the braids barely stirring on their breasts as the Germaine girls whispered coyly together, their sharp eyes running along the men and beyond, to the watching women. So honored men were selected—some of them the old man chiefs of the southerners, some who had worked hard for peace even when there was only the stink of the buffalo left. Finally one of the girls pointed beyond to the watchers, to Mochsi, the warrior woman.

"She helped!" they both cried. "She helped kill our family!"

So Mochsi was put with the group of men held by the bayoneted long guns. Brave One was very angry that nobody told how Mochsi became a warrior woman—because at Sand Creek in 1864 all the men of her lodge were wiped out, and later her cousins and her new husband too, so there was only Mochsi to carry the gun of her grandfather. Now Mochsi was standing there for the irons.

By evening fifteen Indians were selected, and with anger and impatience Neill cut off eighteen more men from the right end of the line to make the thirty-three Cheyenne prisoners General Sherman had ordered. Neill would proceed with the identification some other day. The Germaine girls were hurried away in a carriage, for it was seen that some women had their long butcher knives out of their belts.

Three days later the whites brought chains fastened to cannonballs, a roaring forge, and an anvil to pound the chains to the legs of the prisoners. Soldiers ordered all the people back to their shelters. They stood there, watching, angry, sullen. Some were furious that the prisoners let the ironing be done easier than horses accept the fire-heated shoes. When they got to the younger men, the women lifted their voices in scorning, particularly against Black Horse. "Where will we get fathers worth giving sons to?" the women taunted. "We see there are no men among you worth taking to our beds!"

This was bold talk, heating to the blood. When the hammer slipped and hit his ankle, Black Horse could endure no more. Powerfully he struck the blacksmith aside and ran toward the Cheyenne camp. Half a dozen infantrymen pursued him and fired several volleys after him, hitting his leg. But most of the bullets struck into the camp, and women and children fell, crying, and scattering like leaves in a whirlwind. As the arrows came back thick some of the soldiers were hit, and while they retreated, Black Horse was dragged away by friends. Then the cavalry came galloping out of Fort Reno, and the Cheyennes fled to a little sand hill in a bend of the river, the older Dog Soldiers helping the women and weak ones, while the younger men ran ahead to dig up some guns hidden before the disarming. There were only a few, and little ammunition, but not everyone need die with empty hands. While they scooped out holes in the sand, Black Horse dragged his bleeding leg from one to another. "Hold fast! Fight hard!" he cried.

Two hundred and fifty men, women, and children cowered on the choppy little hill under cavalry fire, three companies by now, with two Gatling guns dragged up fast. The Indians dug like badgers to get below the blanket of driving bullets that came from all around. For the first time Cheyennes had let themselves and their families be completely surrounded, and in a place smaller than a village ground where the soldiers could come charging over them. Some of the women were so afraid they had to be held or tied down.

Then there was a trumpet's thin call, and the three companies of cavalry attacked from all around, charging up the steep, smoke-drifted slopes. But the footing was too loose, and the horses too easily hit with the arrows and the few guns of the Indians. They retreated and came again, afoot through the smoke. The bullets drove the sand upon the Indians like frozen sleet whipped by a blizzard; the thunder of the Gatling guns hammered the shaking earth. One Indian was killed trying to see down to shoot, then another, and a third, and many more wounded until there was a terror and crying in the sandy hilltop such as no Cheyenne had ever heard from his people. One strong warrior could not stand it. He would not have his children live this life, even if they could be spared by surrender now. With a little one in his arms he started up into the bullets, but his wife flung herself against him. In the struggle the baby was shot, and while the woman moaned over it, the man rose, arms folded across his naked breast, and was knocked straight backward, almost cut in two.

THE SPRING CLOUDS thickened. At early dark the shooting stopped and the troops withdrew to the foot of the hill, settling to a ring of little fires, watching. While some Indians crept out to strip the meat from the dead soldier horses, a couple of scouts who knew some *veho* words got close to the soldiers. There were nineteen whites wounded, they heard, and entrenching tools and food and ammunition were being brought over from the fort. The Indians would be starved out.

"It will not take long, with no water for the wounded," Bad Heart, the holy man, said.

No, and daylight would bring a strong charge.

When the women dared move again, they made lights of twisted grass. With these the men went around the holes in the sand to see who had been lost: those left dead in the camp down there and six men here, with two people missing, one an old woman who had been very much afraid—twelve good people.

While the horsemeat was roasting, the medicine man and his wife made their curings, with Black Horse hurt the worst. But there was something good. The son of Medicine Arrow slipped in from north of the river. He came from his father, who had not surrendered because he carried the sacred arrows. Now the keeper was hidden in the broken country only two days northwest, up the river. He had enough meat and horses to carry his people and these here to their relatives north, if it was carefully done. So they started.

Silently, under the light patter of spring rain, the Indians crept through the sentinels and scattered. They were cold and wet, but traveling so light they could go fast, and the rain that chilled them washed their tracks from the places where their moccasins touched.

On April 7, 1875, General Neill reported that a hundred and sixty-seven warriors with their families had escaped and were joined by some still out, perhaps two hundred and fifty warriors altogether, and their families. They were being pursued. The newspapers reported that eight hundred Cheyennes and Arapahos crossed the Arkansas River on April 18, 1875, going north. Troops from Fort Dodge chased them, but the Indians scattered.

WHEN THE INDIANS got up toward the Republican River, they found signs of big camps, surely the hungry Sioux and Cheyennes from the Red Cloud Agency, trying to get a little meat. The buffalo were very wild, only a scattering alive among the carcasses left by the white hunters, who seemed gone now. With the weather suddenly rainy it was a good time to stop awhile, old Medicine Arrow said, a time to heal the wounded, a good time for them all to rest and warm the knees and grow quiet and good in the old way.

"Ahh-h, it is a fine thing to live peacefully," Bad Heart said as he rubbed the dried willow bark for his pipe, sniffed it before he mulled the bits with a little tobacco in his palm, and then set the fire stick to the bowl.

But the next morning, April 23, a lot of white men charged out of the fog upon Medicine Arrow's camp, shooting into the few lodges with heavy buffalo guns, some bluecoat soldiers riding among them. The warriors ran out of their shelters and sleeping holes, many half naked, grabbing up guns and bows, some heading toward the nearest horses. But there was already shooting up around the herd.

Medicine Arrow came from the sleeping robes, his gnarled old legs still bare below his shirt. He slapped on his buffalo-horned feather headdress that trailed back to the ground, to show who he was, the keeper of the sacred arrows. He ran out with Bad Heart just behind, shouting back to the women, "Do not be afraid, my sisters," as he waved the white cloth. "Nothing bad has been done by us. We will make a talk with the soldier chief."

Then, walking in dignity, even as he was, he called his greeting to the white men: "*Hou! Hou*, my friends!" his right hand raised with the cloth of parley, his left one up also, palm out in the sign of peace and friendship of the Plains Indians. So Medicine Arrow went through the fog and smoke and bullets that did not stop coming, on toward Lieutenant Austin Henely, the soldier chief, watching from a higher place. Many Indians watched too, but the buffalo guns kept roaring, echoing like cannon over the little bend of the Sappa Creek and against the low bluffs beyond. Men went down behind him, and for a while it seemed the medicine of the arrows was indeed strong that the keeper could walk on so. But finally he seemed hit, and then he fell, going forward on his face, the white cloth blowing back against a fallen lodge in the smoke.

The women saw this and started running every way, grabbing their children and fleeing down to the brush of the creek, where they were met by more shooting, then up and over the little ridge behind the camp; but there a row of men lay with their big buffalo guns kicking out fire and smoke.

By now some of the Indians had got away toward the pony herds. The rest made a charge afoot, led by Bad Heart. They drove the buffalo hunters back a way before Bad Heart's warriors fell, and the rest had to retreat behind a little bank in the weeds. Now some soldiers were beginning to shoot. The Indians got two of these, while the wounded Black Horse gathered the women and led them into a washout, where the young men had their sleeping holes. There they dug very fast, cutting the holes deeper under the bank to get the children away from the bullets. Before long, Medicine Arrow's wife came crawling through the smoke with the arrows safe on her back.

"I am putting the sacred duty upon you, my children," she said to her son and his wife as she divided the arrows between them. "Now you must get away, both of you, even if you are the only ones of the people saved. Do not stop to help anyone. You must go different ways and run very hard to the faraway safety of the north country."

With the arrows tied stoutly to their backs, and without a look to where the feathers of the dead keeper's headdress were blowing on the ground, or toward each other, Medicine Arrow's son and his wife crept out into the weeds and smoke. First one went, and then the other, so the sacred arrows might not all be destroyed.

When the keeper's old wife saw they were gone, she slipped back to the fighting, and not even Brave One tried to hold her from this death. Several times now the Indians tried to reach Medicine Arrow and the others who fell in their first fighting, but the Indians were shot down as fast as they came out over the bank. It was not only that they wished to save the keeper and the others, wounded and dead, but those first men had carried their only good guns and most of the ammunition. Without guns they could not even avenge the fallen—already more than thirty people.

"We have to get away!" the crippled Black Horse said. "Keep them shooting, so as many as possible can slip out into the smoke."

There were almost no shells left now, and no arrows, so all the men could do was jump up and be shot at. Some good people were lost that way, including three young women who jumped too. One made a song for it:

> "Earth have pity, Sky, see your daughters!
> It is a good day to die!"

So she fell too, and was laid to the side, her blood mixing with the rest in the muddy bottom of the washout.

Several times small parties with flags of truce came out, but were shot as soon as their heads rose into sight below the fluttering white cloth. Once a lot of women, most of those left now, came out with the last piece of white they had, all rising together. There were so many that for a moment no bullets came. But the guns started again, and they were brought down.

Then for a long time there was almost nothing, not a moving from the washout, and finally one of the hunters began to shout, "Hell, them damned Indians's just playin' dead waitin' till night. I had me a brother killed around here by them lousy bastards only couple weeks ago. I don't aim to let one get away!"

With a revolver in each hand he took a running jump into the hole, firing right and left. The few women left alive got him, hacking him with their butcher knives until he was a part of the blood and mud soaking their moccasins.

Now there was the order to charge the washout, and the soldiers came from below, their guns going fast, and the hunters from above, jumping into the hole. Almost at once there was not even a woman with a butcher knife left. And when the white men climbed out of the place, only one had a wound.

Afterward some threshed the brush and weeds for any children who might have crept away, while others gathered willows and built fires. The lodges were thrown on these, the robes from the shelters, the saddles—all the goods, and the bodies of the Indians too, except the headmen, stripped bare on the prairie. Then there was suddenly one more Cheyenne to kill, an old man in a warbonnet, coming on horseback. He had got away, but all his family lay back there on the ground, and when he saw from a ridge what the whites were doing to them, he charged back down, riding hard to the buffalo guns that suddenly roared out together. He fell, tossed a little by the bullets, as if he were light enough for the wind.

His body went upon the fire too, swung in by two hunters who shouted, "Houp! Houp! Houp!" and let go. Then while the smoke and smell of burning flesh spread along the Sappa Creek, the hunters dug out more women and children, clubbed them, and threw them into the fire.

Scattered behind a little cut bank away along the creek, Black Horse and some others watched, silent, with no words for this.

"It has happened that now a man must let them put irons on his feet!" Black Horse cried at last. "Iron balls—or he will bring such destruction upon all his people!"

And as he spoke, his face was like a dark bluff washed by rain.

BY THE MIDDLE of May the scattered ones were reaching their northern relatives. It was reported that fifty men and their families were seen on the Cheyenne trail going toward White River in western Nebraska, and a week later the agent at Red Cloud had wired that all the Cheyennes who escaped their agency in Indian Territory had reached the north. Medicine Arrow's son and his wife came there too, neither knowing if the other lived until they met in the camp of Little Wolf and Dull Knife on the Powder.

There was little in Lieutenant Henely's report of the Sappa fight to reveal the victory of his troops with the buffalo hunters. The Indians had refused to surrender; two soldiers were killed and twenty-seven Indians—nineteen men, eight women and children; the lodges burned and one hundred thirty-four ponies taken. "It is believed that the punishment inflicted upon this band of Cheyennes will go far to deter the tribe from the commission of such atrocities in the future as have characterized it in the past," General Pope wrote that spring.

But there was other talk around the frontier posts. The hunters and the civilian ambulance driver laughed when they heard the official figures, some a little angrily, because it was really a fight of the buffalo hunters, but they were ordered to silence by Henely. Still the story of the butchery got out, with varying figures, several of the hunters putting the Indian dead between seventy and a hundred and twenty, mostly women and children, and some not proud of the fact that not one was taken captive, not even an infant or a wounded woman.

One who knew something of what had been done was the Cheyenne wife of John Powers, an army contractor. Among the trophies of the returning troopers she saw the little bundle that her uncle Medicine Arrow, the great holy man of the Cheyennes, always wore tied in his hair, and his medicine headdress for the arrow ceremonials, with the little buffalo horns too. She made the mourning ceremonial, keening and crying for three days, knowing that he must have tried to surrender, for his vow demanded that he avoid fighting near the arrows. She predicted that the officer who refused his flag of truce would be dead within a year. She was wrong; Lieutenant Henely was drowned three years later.

By midsummer there was much protest over the ironing and imprisonment of the Cheyennes. Not half of them were proved guilty of any crime, and to the Commissioner of Indian Affairs it seemed only just that the eighteen arbitrarily cut from the end of the line by General Neill be given a trial and, if not guilty, be returned to their friends. But one of the men had already killed himself, another went insane, and a venerated old peace chief had been shot while his legs were in irons.

Now it was more than three years later, and Black Horse, who had cried to see his people thrown into the fires on the Sappa, was fleeing through this way again. Many others along had been in the Sappa fight, and all were relatives of those who did not get away from the place now called Cheyenne Hole.

Chapter 8

LITTLE WOLF STOPPED his spotted horse on a rise to look back over his hurried, worn-out people straggling behind, moving in little parties, many afoot, trying to keep near rough country where they could scatter like mice under leaves. He hoped that something would get them through this country very fast, before some bad things were done. Besides, they must hurry. Close on the trail rode the soldiers of Colonel Lewis, now led by one named Mauck, angry as a gut-shot panther.

With all the young men scouting and out for horses, the women were very silent, Broad-faced One, the new bride, riding as much alone as a thrown-away wife. Little Wolf, too, seemed gone away, his eyes not moving toward the things around him or toward his wives and Thin Elk with them.

As they neared the Cheyenne Hole, Bull Hump and some helpers whooped a herd of horses out of the chilly sunrise. The horses with work marks were given to the women, the strongest to those who must not be overtaken—the families of the headmen, who would surely be sent away if caught, perhaps hanged or shot. A fine black with a white patch over his back went to Dull Knife's family. The new horse seemed well broken, even offering his head for the rope halter in Bull Hump's hand, after he had time to examine the smell of the Indian.

But as Short One took the rope, there was signaling from the hills that soldiers were seen coming from several directions.

So the women, the old men, and the children worked fast with the packs. Short One got the new horse loaded quietly enough, but his eyes rolled and there was no time to get him accustomed to her calico skirts blowing in the rising wind, or to a rider mounting from the right, the Indian side. With a hold on the halter rope and the curly black mane she tried to clamber up between the packs. But the horse shied away, jumping. The long sacks hit his ribs and he began to buck, the black head down between his knees, his back humping into it. The woman tried to hang to the mane, but she was flung to the side and battered against the packs, back and forth, until her hold was broken, and before her daughters or anyone could get to the horse, she went under the bucking hoofs. Almost at once her hand let go of the rope, and the horse broke for the hills, bucking the packs to pieces, scattering the goods to blow over the prairie, as Bull Hump and some others came whipping back to help.

The people in the camp ran to the woman, but Dull Knife was already back and off his horse, his face lined and gray as he raised her carefully, for Short One seemed so caved in, and a string of bright red blood ran from her mouth over his arm.

Bridge came running with his bleeding rattle, making a chanting as he ran, but there was no time now for the long ceremonial, with the signals of chasing soldiers close, and the woman not breathing. So she was put on a makeshift drag of cowskin behind an old mare and then whipped along, the poles bouncing over the rough ground, the people afoot breaking up into smaller groups again, each with a man or a boy carrying a revolver or a bow. But a little string of people followed behind Short One's travois, a file of grief and honor, all calling her Mother, for now she belonged to them all even more than before.

When it was plainly too dangerous to carry Short One farther, she was taken off to a slope where a shallow hole could be dug in the stubborn ground. Then most of them went on to overtake the band, the urgent signals of the scouts hurrying them. But Brave One and three others stayed behind, dragging a few stones there in the travois. With their arms and legs gashed as for a warrior killed in a fight, and with dust and grass in their hair, the four women followed behind the moving people, Dull Knife far back with them. He had not needed to put on the rags of mourning for his wife, for rags were all he had, his blanket mended, the holes stitched up by Short One's needle just the night before.

As the old chief rode along, kicking his horse into a little half trot, his moccasin heels drumming on the tired ribs, he thought of all the lost ones of the last three years. The Beautiful People, the children of Dull Knife had been called, and Short One had borne some of them. The Beautiful People! And now many of them lay on the earth, scattered from the foothills of the Big Horns to the far south country, in less than two years.

The old man slumped forward a little, so tired he could scarcely sit the Indian saddle, but by habit his hurried heels kept up their drumming as his hands urged the horse on northward, always northward.

Now THE CHEYENNES were taking up a new thing, a new way. Never within memory had they raided scattered people. Even the war against the whites in 1864 had been made on the trail stations, more like little forts than isolated homes, on the emigrant trains that killed the game and brought the sicknesses, and on the troops that came chasing on Indian lands. This attacking homes with families in them, scattered out alone, this seemed a poor, unheroic kind of war.

But Black Horse would not let the warriors hesitate. "We must not forget our holy one dead over there on the Sappa! His blood calls to us from the rocks!" he told the excited young men, in reverence still not using the name of Medicine Arrow. Nor did he add anything of the newly bereaved ones, of the mourning Dog Soldier Bull Hump and his brother Little Hump, and of their father sitting off alone, the old chief's eyes turned toward the ground.

"These scattered settlers of the earth houses here, with no fighters, no warriors," Old Crier said sadly, "they are not fit enemies for a Cheyenne. Do not go near them."

"The soldiers are coming very fast, Uncle, and we must get our horses where we can," Little Wolf replied quietly. He spoke quietly to the others too, the noisy ones. "I cannot find it in my heart to say you must not avenge your dead." For a long time Little Wolf was silent, looking to the earth before him. "But I will not have any *veho* women and children hurt, and as the bearer of your chief's bundle I must advise you to pass these whites all by, harm no one, and take only their horses. Many good people will suffer for every piece of bloody work you do."

But some of the young men were already gone.

THE MAIN BAND was still spread out, the walking ones never stopping, while those with horses made the camps, cut wood, and built up the fires for all. But this hurrying was very hard, and when a boy came shouting that he had seen a horse loose in a draw, Buffalo Chips and his wife, the parents of Limpy, followed him, hoping they could get their bundles off their backs. As they came out into the bottoms they ran into some cowboys on horseback with guns. They tried to slip back to the main band, but they had been seen.

"Save yourselves if you can! Get away!" Buffalo Chips shouted.

They dropped the bundles and ran for the brush along the creek, but the cowboys separated into three parts; two cut them off, and the middle ones charged their hiding place. The woman fled up over a bank, bullets whistling past, one hitting as she got out of sight. Buffalo Chips had dropped back into the willows to hold the men off awhile, and as they spurred up, he rose before them and shot. The cowboy closest slid behind his horse and fired a revolver over the mane. Buffalo Chips had only an old long pistol with four weak shells. He used them and then ran across a beaver dam, his moccasins squishing, full of blood. For a moment he had to rest, flat on the ground, his breath tearing where the bullets had gone through, but then he pulled himself up. His wife was out of sight, and so he settled himself in the brush and sang his death song. Before he was done, the cowboy came galloping back with a rifle. Buffalo Chips smiled a little and started to lift his hand to show he was not hurting anybody now, but he fell over and was dead.

Afterward the woman watched the whites ride away. She knew Buffalo Chips must be done, for the men waved something on a rifle that was like a scalp.

When Limpy heard what had been done to his father, he left the horse catchers, exchanged his rope and revolver for a rifle and a handful of cartridges, and then rode out with two cousins. Broad-faced One looked after him, afraid now as no maiden could fear. Little Wolf saw him go too, and knew that whites would die. He knew too that the Custer son, Yellow Swallow, must be kept out of the way of the anger and avenging of this time, and so he sent the boy ahead with his aunt.

THE LAST DAY of September, nineteen whites were shot, the number of Cheyenne men that Lieutenant Henely reported he killed on the Sappa three years before, with nobody for all the others who died on the way north. Nothing for all the Indian women and children, for there was no power of avenging these. Only men had been killed, and in this at least they had followed Little Wolf's command.

That night the Cheyenne headmen took the women and children across the moonlit Sappa divide and down a long, deep-canyoned draw that opened to the valley of the Beaver Creek. Later, scouts came into the hidden camp to say that there were horses several miles up, near the head of the draw, with a night herder watching, and that soldiers had reached the Sappa where the settlers were dead on the ground.

Before the sun had warmed the shoulders in the morning, the young men had gone scouting along the breaks both ways on the Beaver Creek. Little Wolf's son Pawnee was with those trying to run the horses off at the head of the draw. The white herder was shot and his saddle cut up for the leather they needed. Others got to the horse herd and turned the bunch, more than thirty head, toward the draw with a waving blanket. More cowboys spurred in, to get between the horses and the Cheyennes. There was a lot of whooping, shooting, and breakneck riding through the dust until the Indians managed to sweep the herd away. Pawnee and two others stayed back to delay two cowboys who started toward the soldiers, Pawnee dropping from one place to another, shooting like many men.

There was a shot down near the mouth of the draw too, one shot, where the Indians found a little bunch of cattle herded by a lone youth on a big black star-faced horse. They killed him, and while several young women butchered some of the cattle, others dug a few rifle pits. They did it angrily, because the warriors were out killing people who had harmed no one, instead of helping them get away, and three commands of soldiers were so very close. Then some of those coming from the cattle herd found a settler at his plowing and rode on toward his dugout. The man left the team with his son and came running, so they shot him but let the boy slip away to the creek brush and a woman too, who ran for a gully, her sunbonnet flying off. One of the warriors scooped it up, put it on his head, simpering and laughing in the white-woman way. Inside the dugout they found bread and a wooden bucket of sorghum. With their hunting knives they dug out the thick brown syrup, letting it drip from the blades into their mouths, spreading it on torn loaves, wolfing the sweet stuff they had missed so long.

A larger party shot at a man well hidden in a buffalo wallow and then went to pick up a few more horses, not many, for the whites along here seemed very poor. Soon the settlers became wild as buffalo after a long hunting, running away from far off, hiding very well. Big Foot, the father of Broad-faced One, was very angry at this killing and sent his friend Bullet Proof to ride the breaks with the farseeing glass and keep the count. Once, Bullet Proof came near some whites who had a woman along. "Keep going! Keep going!" he called in badly spoken *veho* words. But he made them understand his pointing down the creek and was glad they went, because he wanted nobody killed.

In the bottoms one of the parties found some settlers speaking a thick unknown tongue. The Indians motioned them to leave their guns and get away from their house. They went without protest. When the Cheyennes had the guns, they shot the men, a bullet grazing the baby one of them carried.

"You are a fool!" the leader shouted to the young warrior. "We do not shoot at children!"

But the youth soon forgot this blaming as he helped slit the feather beds and toss them from one to another, laughing at the blizzard of feathers on the wind. Another party found a man and a boy whipping away in a wagon. An Indian who had the new black horse with the white star roped the galloping team in one big loop. The wagon was cut loose and the horses led away, the man left on the ground, the boy running for the house, crying. The young Indians raced after him, riding around him as he fled, shouting, "*Hou!*"

Another place four men were digging potatoes as though it were any other September day. Suddenly a party of Cheyennes was upon them, shooting. Some were relatives of Buffalo Chips and so angry that when they finished the killing they went to the house, carrying away blankets and goods and clothing. But now there was an angry signal from Bullet Proof. It was enough. He had counted up the dead whites here and back on the Sappa and found them equal to the men left on the ground at Cheyenne Hole and those killed this time north. None here were as big men as Medicine Arrow and Bad Heart, but the great ones of the *veho* did not live in this country. As for the Cheyenne women and children left dead on the Sappa, and Short One back there—for these there could be nothing to make the heart glad.

LATE THAT AFTERNOON there were healing chants over the wounded in the narrow, walled-in camp. Then suddenly the soldiers were there, firing. But Mauck pulled back easy, because the Cheyennes were in such a strong position, a stronger one than the Indians could find for three hundred miles north, and many troops were coming along the streams to help him.

The Indians got away fast, leaving one man still out and a boy who had his leg crippled in the soldier shooting. Somebody went out to find them later, but the country was full of soldiers. Very many whites were around, mostly just riding and looking, until a great prairie fire began to roll its pale yellow smoke into the sky, adding to the fury of these two bloody days.

Chapter 9

SEVERAL TIMES NOW even Little Wolf, who must be everywhere, see everything, and lead them all, found himself falling far behind. In this flight from the Beaver, Little Wolf took his turn afoot with the men whose horses were led back to bring up the other walking ones. But in this way the few horses they had were kept running from the soldiers until they fell on the trail, going down among the scattering of goods dropped off, everything dropped off, now that almost every hill showed the pursuing dust.

When he was afoot, Little Wolf fell into his old Indian runner's trot that he could hold mile after mile, waving his horse away to the others. Even in their fear, many looked back to him with swelling breast. He was fifty-seven, their head chief with the Sweet Medicine bundle tied next to his ribs, and yet he ran between them and the soldiers, a lean, hard, straight figure, his braids dusty, the silver medal of friendship from the Great Father out, swaying a little on its black thong, his moccasins a whisper on the dry buffalo grass as he passed.

Once the Indians ahead of Little Wolf stopped at a strip of ripe sod corn to grab up a few small ears. The chief drove them on, but this long field, stretched where there had still been a few fresh buffalo tracks last year, made him very certain that the old ways had to be forgotten, the moccasin set on a new path. The Cheyennes could escape the *veho* only by the *veho* road. Now, far too late, he must study these whites and their Great Father, who could talk soberly of peace while large groups of their young men did nothing but practice charging up and down, shooting at a target that was like a man, stabbing with the bayonet, crushing with gunstock. Then, when what they wanted was already clutched in the palm, they said, "Sell us this for peace."

THEY CROSSED THE fall-golden valley of the Republican and camped at the mouth of Cheyenne canyon, rich in water, wood, and grass, and with a place higher up, between steep narrowing walls, to hold the horses. There was a good place to fight up there too, to dig in away from the bullets for a while.

But mostly the people wanted to sleep, particularly those who had been out on raids along the Sappa and the Beaver or had been with the raiders in anxious heart. Yet Little Wolf had the people moving before the sun darkened the thin white frost of the bottoms and glistened in dew on the golden box elders and cottonwoods.

At Frenchman Creek troops were suddenly plain for everyone to see, charging down into the hot, noon-yellowed valley from the south as the Indians climbed out upon the wide north tableland. As the dust of the soldiers neared, a soft monotony of lament started among the people, a woman here, another there, then old men singing too, their voices joggled cries for help from the Great Powers, the people as hopeless, as worn out as the horses that fell and were left.

The warriors shook out the regalia left to them, smeared their paint on hastily without plan, and fell behind, between the troops and the fleeing ones. They could make no stand, for there was not enough ammunition for a fight, but now and then one charged back a little to show his daring. It did not stop the soldiers or the other whites riding fast ahead of them, but it gave the people the courage to make this last run.

Then suddenly the soldiers stopped, although the other whites kept coming. Left Hand dropped behind to shoot from the grass on the top of a little knoll. He brought down two horses and lamed another. The white men began to lag, then finally they returned to the soldiers at the creek. Left Hand could have hit more, but he had only those three shells for his good long-carrying gun and his steady eye. Unless he got some ammunition, he would have to use the gun butt or rocks.

By midafternoon the soldiers were close on the dust of the Indians again, an occasional bullet striking the earth among them, but mostly falling short. The young men had brought in more fresh horses, wild stock without saddle mark or rope burn anywhere. There were good horse tamers here, but no time for that now. So they roped one after the other, held their fighting heads by twist of neck or ears for the saddling. Then with ropes stretched out both ways they held the bucking, running broncos between gentler, wearier animals, the women hanging on any way they could, the small children in the skin sacks hammered against the bellowing ribs, until the horses were played out and dropped their broken, lathered heads.

This time they had to run until dark. When the scouts came to say that the soldiers had camped, the people fell anywhere, like dead ones. Now it was discovered that, although more than two hundred horses had been captured the last three days, half as many had been left, worn out. People were lost too. Three of the old and the sick were gone, fallen off or hit in the hard runs before the bullets. Two of the smaller, weaker children were dead from the pounding in the hide sacks, their mothers quietly carrying them to a little bluff to be left there between the stones. But the youngest, little Comes Behind, was still on his mother's back, the woman walking far to the rear again and off to one side, once more missed by the soldiers. She still followed the moccasins of Brave One and the others who had walked almost all the way from the south country. Burden on back, stick in hand—for staff and for small game (a sand turtle or a foolish rabbit) or to pin down a rattlesnake's head while the body was cut off for roasting over the evening fire—the women slipped along from gully to washout, on and on, taking turns carrying Lame Girl too, so thin now from the bullet-torn ankle that she was like a child on the back. These were the strong women, women of the old Cheyenne kind.

ALTHOUGH THE NEWSPAPERS said there were thirteen thousand soldiers out against the Cheyennes, almost a thousand ready to move within an hour against any crossing, there was not one in sight when the Indians reached the South Platte and its railroad. They crossed below what is now Ogallala, Nebraska, on October 4, all anxious that it must be done so openly with the bright sun overhead. But the great flocks of ducks rising along the sandy banks showed that no one was around.

The Cheyennes crossed in a long, dark string, the shallow water splashing high, and then the North Platte too. Even the walking women had been brought up, and it was a joyous time for the many who still believed that the soldiers would not follow them into what they called their own country here. Comes in Sight and her family were over too, gone ahead as they had since Punished Woman Creek, without the stops at the Sappa or the Beaver. They had no avenging to do; no blood could pay for what had come upon them and upon the dead Bear Rope's memory.

North of the Platte the Indians went along the bottoms to White Tail Creek and stopped inside the mouth of a steep, shadowed canyon to let the people rest a few hours. Little Finger Nail had hidden a few cattle there, ready for the silent arrow and knife. Later, wolf signals came out of the dusk, reporting that the soldiers were close, some already crossing the river in the pale moon of evening, many wagons following. Then Thin Elk and another came in from scouting with two men from another band of Cheyennes being taken south by troops of Custer's Seventh Cavalry.

Little Wolf spoke to the two visitors. "Is it true that the soldiers are thick as blackbirds up beyond the Running Water?"

"Yes, soldiers are camped all over the White River country and at Red Cloud's new agency, with Spotted Tail too, we hear."

"Ahh-h! Soldiers surrounding all my Sioux relatives!" Tangle Hair murmured in concern. "We are shut out."

The visitors made no reply.

The little circle of headmen was silent a long time now, the small glow of the coals reaching up to their gaunt, worn faces, the blackness of the canyon walls bending over them. All the people in the dark close around were silent too, with only a fall cricket somewhere, and the howl of a coyote out on the prairie.

After a while Dull Knife rose from beside the dying fire, no longer as straight as he was only one moon ago. His old blanket was in tatters, his grief-loosed hair ragged, a touch of red from the coals sitting along the broad, naked bones of his cheeks.

"We are almost in our own country, my friends," he said slowly. "The soldiers up there with our friends the Sioux have always been good men."

"The soldiers are up there to catch us and kill us," Little Wolf answered quietly. "We can trust no one until we are in our own country of the north."

"We have a right with Red Cloud!" the old chief retorted, angry at the interruption. "We were on his agency before we left to look at the south."

"With the whites you have a right to nothing that you do not already hold in the palm."

But Dull Knife, who had spoken almost no word since the death of Short One and the Sappa killings, now broke into a sudden snarling of exasperation, of fury too long contained. "I am the one who is speaking now, my brother! Too long your tongue has been a thorn in my moccasin!" he said, making a harsh, angry thing of the soft-flowing Cheyenne. "You know we cannot last as far as the Yellowstone now, running, running. Look around you, my iron-legged brother. See the dead bones in the faces of the people! You say we go on; I say you are a fool!"

"So now I am foolish," Little Wolf said softly.

"I repeat, my brother, you are a fool!" the old chief shouted. "At least four died in the chasing yesterday, and not from bullets. There will be many more, and we will run out of horses up where nobody lives. Besides, it will be winter. Do you not smell the snow tonight? Before the moon is dark again it will be here, as every child among us knows. We must turn to Red Cloud."

As he spoke, a protest started up against him, but the older Dog Soldiers moved up behind him in silent allegiance, and then some young warriors too, these with guns ready, hammers clicking in the rising challenge.

Other young men were moving up behind Little Wolf, making their challenges, and so Little Wolf had to rise, his hand lifted for silence around the firelight, his strong, pitted face full of the fury that breaks from gentleness, his voice striking out sharp as a Cheyenne battle-axe upon the young warriors.

"This dividing cannot be!" he roared. "I will not have the people split. I repeat it: An Indian never caught is an Indian never killed, and only together can we all get away!"

He had more words, a whole harangue boiling up in his scarred breast, but he saw the forward straining of the divided followers back in the shadows, and heard the cries of the women running for the children as the younger, wilder warriors of both sides moved against each other, knives out, guns up, tempers taut as dry bowstrings worn by the long flight. One finger's slip and there would be blood in the canyon.

The bearer of the chief's bundle saw it and knew that this last, worst thing must not come upon the Cheyennes. So he dropped his hand, defeated. "I am moving a little way apart," he said slowly. "Let those who would go on to the north follow."

There was another silence now, one in which none seemed to breathe. Then one man stepped forward to the side of Little Wolf, the first to take his stand in this parting. It was Thin Elk.

By the time the morning light showed behind the thick white fog, Dull Knife was gone. But on a haired robe, almost the only one left, was a little heap of ammunition and some powder, the parting gift to those who would still try to fight their way to the Yellowstone.

Chapter 10

"**W**E'LL RAKE THEM Cheyennes in at the river like a grizzly rakin' in berries, leaves 'n' all," an infantryman bragged in a saloon at Fort Sidney, Nebraska. "We'll toss what's left a them in with the bunch the Seventh's holdin' down to the post, let 'em herd the whole outfit back to the Terr'tory."

A windburned trooper of the Seventh moved down the bar a way, to give the new Indian fighter room to spread himself. He recalled talk like that up around Fort Abraham Lincoln the spring of '76, when Custer was heading for the West, and drank a little to the men who never returned.

But the recruit did not get so much as a saddle wolf before the Indians had slipped across the Platte, eluding all the troops ordered out by General Crook, commander of the Department of the Platte. When this became known, there was a roar of anger reaching from the poorest settler dugout to the domed halls of Congress. There were editorials, letters, and articles in the papers, delegations calling on the President, long, controversial exchanges over Indian policy between the generals and the Department of the Interior, and a sour laughing all along the frontier. Even those who made a career of the "noble red man" were silenced by stories of the Kansas border knee-deep in blood, thousands of horses and cattle destroyed, hundreds of people killed, women and girls outraged, small children left with their brains dashed out by war clubs.

When the number of the dead was cut down to forty men, to thirty-two by some, including not one woman or child, it was still a shocking account of murder, with pilfered garments scattered along the Cheyenne trail from the Beaver northward: a lace-trimmed wedding gown, embroidered undergarments, plumed hats—some stained by bloody hands—all dropped in the fast pursuit, to blow from broken packs and flutter against buckbrush or browned thistle-head. There were demands for the court-martial of Crook and even General Sherman, and calls for a congressional investigation.

Yet something new was creeping into the newspaper stories—admiration. Who were the men—only eighty above eleven—who led this pitiful force so well? Dull Knife was old, long past his active days as a chief. That left Little Wolf, who had brought these sick, half-starved, footworn people—old, young, men, women, and children—through six hundred miles of open country cut by three railroads, crosshatched by telegraph, through settlers, cowmen, scouts, and the United States Army, all in less than a month. Where in history was there another such leader, such a masterful exploit?

But Little Wolf must not be permitted to reach the already dissident Sioux under Red Cloud and Spotted Tail. During the general removal of Indians last year these chiefs were taken to the Missouri. Refused permission to return this summer, they started back anyway, the two great camps of people moving in dark files over the prairie, the agency beef herds along, to be killed as needed. The troops followed, just followed, challenging no warrior nor firing a shot. Now the two old chiefs were on the south border of Dakota, only a couple of days from Little Wolf and Dull Knife, with thousands of well-armed, arrogant young Sioux ready to join the fighting Cheyenne warriors. Meanwhile, Colonel Caleb Carlton had left Fort Robinson with five companies of cavalry and struck eastward to head off the Indians.

AT ABOUT THE SAME time, newspapermen with Crook's troops reported that a column under the command of Major Thomas T. Thornburgh had watched sixty miles of the Platte, but were unable to intercept the Cheyennes because of the ridiculous flood of rumors, reports, and telegrams telling of Indians along two hundred miles of river. All Thornburgh could do was hold his mixed troops ready. Instead of the pack mules and Indian trackers that he requested, he was given wagons and cattleman scouts. When Thornburgh got his cavalry and some mounted infantry out and across the Platte, those in the wagon train got stuck in quicksand. Fog came in, the cattlemen could not find the trail, and at daylight the mounted column was wandering in the river breaks.

Finally they struck the abandoned camp on White Tail Creek.

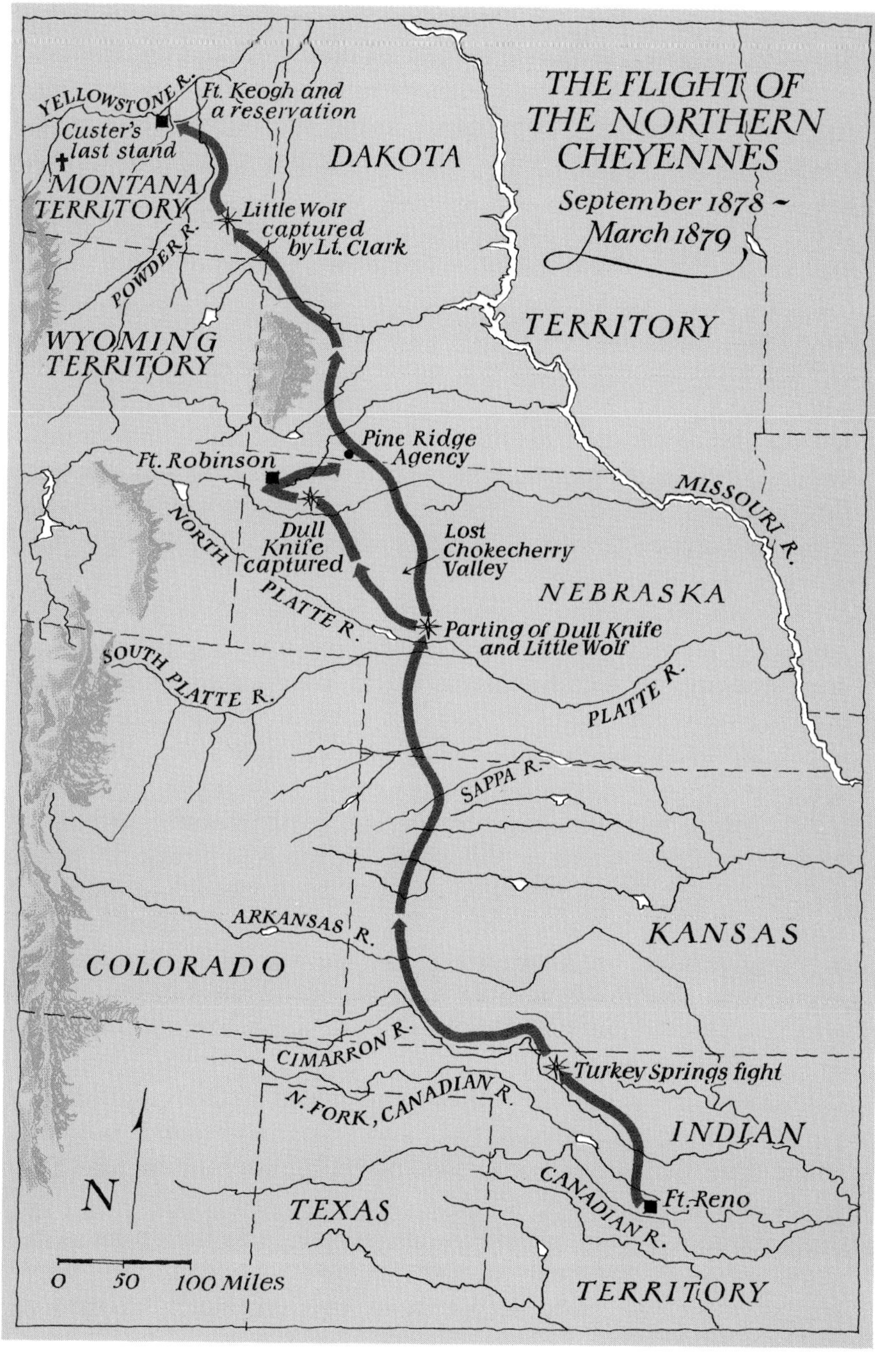
THE FLIGHT OF THE NORTHERN CHEYENNES
September 1878 – March 1879
YELLOWSTONE R.
Ft. Keogh and a reservation
Custer's last stand
MONTANA TERRITORY
DAKOTA
Little Wolf captured by Lt. Clark
POWDER R.
TERRITORY
WYOMING TERRITORY
Pine Ridge Agency
Ft. Robinson
MISSOURI R.
NORTH PLATTE R.
Dull Knife captured
Lost Chokecherry Valley
NEBRASKA
Parting of Dull Knife and Little Wolf
SOUTH PLATTE R.
PLATTE R.
SAPPA R.
ARKANSAS R.
KANSAS
COLORADO
CIMARRON R.
Turkey Springs fight
N. FORK, CANADIAN R.
INDIAN
N
CANADIAN R.
Ft. Reno
TEXAS
0 50 100 Miles
TERRITORY

The gorge was so steep and close that the troops had to ride single file—a dangerous ambush spot, and all the scouts left the front except one. Angrily, Thornburgh led them himself, the moisture glistening on his flowing sideburns when the sun burned through. At last they hit a converging trail, and abandoning the wagon train to get through as it could, they galloped into the sandhills with less than five days' rations. The column made fifty miles that day in uncharted territory. Thirteen Indian horses were dropped before them, one still under packs. But in midafternoon the cattleman scouts went back; the Indians were safely beyond their herds.

That night the troops camped under a ridge of choppy sand hills where the Indians had dug about forty rifle pits. The column had not stopped to eat or drink since dawn on the Platte. Tongues were swollen, eyes and faces burned by sun and stinging sand, the infantry recruits galled raw. The men slept on their saddle blankets, with the warriors howling in the distance and calling in white-man distress, "Help! Indians!"

THE NEXT MORNING Thornburgh followed a trail that led back to a creeklet emptying into the North Platte, always finding something dropped—a child's blanket, or a woman's moccasin. The cavalry horses bolted for the water there like a wild herd in a drought. Afterward the troops went to Blue Water Creek for the night. The following day they rode up along the desolate battleground where, over twenty years ago, General William S. Harney had struck the Sioux under Little Thunder. Bleached and half-buried bones of man and horse were scattered along the slope, the caving sandstone topping the bluff still plainly shattered by the cannon shots that tore the women and children from their hidings. One of the soldiers discovered fresh horse tracks leading up to some bones crammed into the frost-broken crevasses.

"Perhaps one of the Cheyennes come to visit a relative killed with Little Thunder," Thornburgh said, and looked all around. Suddenly he put spur to his horse and headed north, the way the fleeing Cheyennes must surely have gone.

As the hills became sandier and choppier, the Indian signs became scarce. Perhaps one moccasin track lay beside a dried water hole, or a lone rider stood a moment on some far blue hill, remote as the eagle that circled against the October clouds. Thornburgh's only hope now was to head the Indians at the Running Water, the Niobrara River. Without packtrain or Indian scouts he was trying to catch a man who had marched his band through the organized force of the army, much of the way across flat prairie country that would not hide the nakedness of a shedding rattler. Even so, Thornburgh gave the Indians their hottest chase, and a newspaperman with his troops wrote, "The whole western army has been demoralized by a few wild Indians, but give Thornburgh just credit." Now Little Wolf was in a wilderness of dun hills shouldering each other away into every horizon, hills so close set that a thousand men could hide within a mile in any direction and only the wind to see.

From the Blue Water, Thornburgh's column struck into this wilderness. Sparse joint grass brushed the stirrups of the men, and the clumps of bayonetlike soapweed cut the horses' legs. Nowhere was there a tree or even a bush big as a garden lilac. And no water for the lightening canteens.

The third day out the troopers killed some stray ranch cattle to extend their dwindling rations of hardtack and salt pork. After that they saw only grouse and prairie chickens and curious antelopes, while occasionally some wild horses stood a moment at the whinny of a scouting cavalry mount and then were gone, their bare-hoofed tracks so easily the cover for the scattered Indians.

Gradually the hills reared their long backs higher, the valleys widened. There were lakes, but the only water was in small yellow-gray patches far out in the alkali-crusted beds that smelled like rotten eggs. The horses shied from them, although their tongues were as swollen as those of their dusty riders. Wearily the men eased their saddle galls.

"This sure is a hell of a country! I say let 'em Indians hev it," the blacksmith complained, as Thornburgh led his men on, less in pursuit of Indians now than to get out. Their rations were gone, the ammunition only what each man carried, and always there was the possibility of an Indian ambush. If the Cheyennes had ammunition and fresh horses, it could easily be another Custer massacre.

Along the bitter lakes they struck a fresh troop trail, with some unshod hoofs and moccasin tracks at a camping—Indian scouts with Colonel Carlton and his five companies from Fort Robinson.

Now even Thornburgh's horses seemed to know they were no longer lost, although nobody knew their position. Somewhere south of the Niobrara, because it flowed across the north for five hundred miles, but no telling how far away. Then toward noon smoke began to boil up out of the northwest, pale and opalescent, and scattered in several places. Probably Indians burning the Niobrara ranches—on the warpath. Gradually the wind turned northwest, curling the sand around the plodding hoofs of the horses, trailing the smoke in over the men, the sun red, the nose and eyes stinging.

By now they were crossing broad parallel valleys running southeastward. The ground was dry, well sodded, hard under the iron hoofs of the horses. Deer were thick in the buckbrush along the slopes, the strings of hills as high as little mountain chains, and mostly grassed to the top. Then suddenly there were lakes all around. The troops cared for their horses, bathed the cinch sores, cooked a lunch of ember-broiled venison, and looked uneasily to the smoke still rolling over them from the north. While the major shaved the stubble from his cleft chin and trimmed his sideburns, the men talked uneasily about the Indians, with every sand pass still a possible ambush, and the horses too worn down for a charge or for flight. But Carlton's trail led on.

Then suddenly they struck a wide, rutted wagon road. Thornburgh stopped, looking both ways. Evidently one of the Black Hills gold trails, the thin sod cut by the heavy freight and mine machinery. They still saw no uneasy game, no Indian sign, only now and then a rider suddenly gone from the top of a far ridge, whether cowboy or Indian it was too far to tell. The trail fell abruptly to a stream so crooked within its steep little canyon that it must surely be the Snake River of their untrustworthy maps. Couriers from Fort Robinson looking for Carlton came up the trail, with rumors that the colonel and Thornburgh both had been massacred.

Thornburgh laughed with sunburned lips. "I think Colonel Carlton is safe enough. From the horse droppings on his trail he can't be a day ahead, and we've been chasing him hard. We're reduced to fresh game, and everybody's so loose-boweled the saddles are empty much of the time. We need hardtack."

The couriers pushed on, and the next day Carlton sent packs of supplies back from his camp on the Niobrara. He had started to scout down the Snake River for the Indian crossing, but a courier had come with a telegram that there was an uprising among the Sioux. From the smoke rising there ahead of him Carlton assumed the Indians were burning and raiding—perhaps old Red Cloud himself had broken out. Because all possible effort must be made to prevent a juncture of the Sioux with the Cheyennes, Carlton had hurried to the river, to discover that the Sioux were quiet, there was no sign of a Cheyenne anywhere, and the fires were on farther north.

By midafternoon Thornburgh reached the deep canyon of the Niobrara. Golden fall timber lay along the feet of the gray bluffs, with patches of blood-red creeper. Great yellow cottonwoods stood alone out on the grassy bottoms, willows and the silver of buffalo-berry bushes clumped the riverbanks, the stream running swift and clear. They had reached the Niobrara, the Running Water of the Indians. But where were the Cheyennes?

THE TROOPS THAT gathered around the new Pine Ridge Sioux Agency stirred up great excitement among Red Cloud's people. The women and children were ready to flee, and the warriors drew their horses aside, their faces covered with their blankets.

"What are you looking for here?" Red Cloud demanded, while his young men whipped up from all around to protect their chief, faces dark, guns ready across their horses. "If you come for a fight, my men will fight you. If you don't want to fight, go home!"

But the troops did not shoot or leave. More kept coming, and the women starting the cooking fires every morning were as uneasy as buffalo lifting their noses into the wind.

When Red Cloud and his chiefs rode down to the council called by Thornburgh and Carlton, they came in all their paint and feathers, their scalp-fringed shirts and shell breastplates, their Sharps carbines, the revolvers and cartridge belts. The warriors behind the headmen were armed too, their fingers by habit in the trigger guards.

After the pipe, Major Thornburgh spoke of their goodwill toward the Sioux. They had come to ask help against the bad Cheyennes, who only wanted to stir up trouble on the agency here. The best thing would be to turn them over to the troops so they could be taken back south.

The interpreting was followed by a long Sioux silence. Finally Red Cloud spoke, in his deep guttural way, making his graceful gestures. The hearts of his people were good. The Great Father had telegraphed him to stop the runaway Cheyennes, but none had been seen. He was tired of war. The grave wind was blowing around him and he was not afraid. The young men were hot to fight all these white soldiers, if he permitted it. "The Cheyennes are our friends; our young men have married their young women. I think they are already beyond the Black Hills."

To Carlton's impatient question about Cheyennes reported in his camp, a proud shadow passed over the old Sioux's face. "I do not speak with the crooked tongue. I leave that to the whites. I have seen no Cheyennes. If any come, I will hold them, but I will treat them right. They have been misused; they have had bad agents."

"*Hou! Hou!*" the circle of chiefs agreed, and then one after another rose to complain of the thieving whites everywhere. So Carlton had a little feast made for the council, and afterward he stood beside Thornburgh as the Indians rode away, uncertain just what Red Cloud had promised.

THORNBURGH REACHED Fort Robinson under the White River bluffs ten days after he left the Platte, his horses so played out it took him two days to make the last forty-five miles. Near Chadron Creek they struck the trail of a large band of Indians going north, but his men were already walking to spare the horses.

In all the pursuit from the Beaver north, only one Cheyenne had been shot, an old man who had fallen off his horse and been left behind south of the Platte. Not another Indian was caught by the army, but cowboys had captured a woman and her son of sixteen. There was a rumor that a Sioux scout for the troops had taken ten Cheyennes, including two fighting men, to Red Cloud. A man and two women captured by civilians were brought to Robinson. They sat in their ragged blankets, refusing to talk except to say they had fooled all the soldiers. Cheyennes always fooled the *veho* soldiers.

Now the newspapers took up the cowboys' favorite quip. It wasn't, said the Chicago *Times*, that anyone expected Thornburgh to capture the Cheyennes, but there was rejoicing that the Cheyennes had not captured the major. Antiadministration papers asked if it would not be cheaper to feed the worthless petty crooks than to chase them all over hell 'n' gone. The handful of Cheyennes could have been fed indefinitely on hummingbird tongues, and the taxpayer still ahead.

Carlton and Captain John B. Johnson took up a wide Indian trail discovered northeast of Fort Robinson, with fresh troops and horses, fully equipped for a winter campaign as General Crook understood the term. With Johnson rode twenty Indian and half-breed scouts, most of them with relatives among the Cheyennes.

The next day the weather darkened, turned to rain, sleet, and finally snow—the fall's first blizzard was on the way.

October 23, nineteen days after Thornburgh took up the trail at the Platte, Johnson's advance scouts noticed vague forms in the blowing storm along the breaks of upper Chadron Creek. Then the captain saw them too, momentarily, between blasts of wind: snow-whitened figures bent almost like cattle before the blizzard, only a few with horses—the lost Cheyennes. Suddenly the Indians ran together and then tried to scatter, those with horses whipping back between the people and the scouts. But it was useless to run, there were too many soldiers. The people crouched down in the snow, almost lost to sight, afraid, while a few of the warriors hurried up to a little ridge between the column and their people and stood there— a couple with warbonnets visible between gusts of driving snow.

Chapter 11

THE MORNING AFTER that last council between Little Wolf and Dull Knife on White Tail Creek, a fog covered the country. The fog was thick and wet to the face, shutting out everything even when the sun climbed high behind it. The Indians went as fast as they could, but sadly. This dividing seemed something final, for the years. It was hard, with all the ties of blood and after the long association, the long living, lodge by lodge around the sacred circle, the fine happy times of the hunts and the ceremonials made together, and the fighting too, in victory and in defeat, and now the still closer bonds of danger and desperation endured together.

Little Wolf, with few old or sick, had scattered his people immediately and sent them straight for the deepest of the sand hills. It would be like chasing a new-hatched covey of quail in a brush patch to get these Cheyennes. Dull Knife, with the helpless ones, was running only to Red Cloud, so he kept his band together. But with Little Wolf—the bundle bearer—gone, they suddenly had many chiefs vying with old Dull Knife. Somebody had to lead, so Wild Hog, the gaunt, commanding figure, signaled the others to him. They came, tall and dark out of the fog, and rode beside him awhile, their soggy heels drumming the ribs of their tired horses as they considered what must be done. Ahead was this wide expanse of sand hills where a people could hide for months if there was the time for the wind to cover the trail, but with no place for defense this side of the Running Water, the Niobrara.

"We cannot make another stand anyway," Dull Knife said quietly. "There is not enough ammunition and not the heart. Let us keep going. The soldiers in this country will not harm us."

Wild Hog shook his head. He could not argue with the old chief, and besides he knew that his own wife and others, too, were sickening by the long anxiety, a little like Bear Rope, perhaps. He must try to get them to safety soon, to their relatives for rest.

MIDFORENOON THE FOG began to break into waves like a wind-stirred lake. Soon it would begin to float along the hills, lifting away into the sun, laying bare every horse track and moccasin track on the wet earth. Without stopping at all now, dropping horses as they played out, the Cheyennes ran again. Many of the women had become like walkers in the dream.

The soldiers got so close that Wild Hog had to scatter even the poor and old, to come together at a great half circle of low sand hills where digging for pits was easy. It would only be a delay, without ammunition or water. But that was better than seeing the women and children falling as they ran over the prairie.

When it seemed that Thornburgh would never stop, not for eating or even breathing the horses, Wild Hog sent Singing Cloud, Little Finger Nail, and some others to make decoying tracks around in a big bend.

Chasing the decoy tracks over dry country wore out the soldier horses, and it was after sunset when they got around to the rifle pits. By then the Indians had gone. Scattered into little parties, they struck for the upper Blue Water trail, near the salty lakes, and made camp. While the Cheyennes rested, Wild Hog started a man and his wife to Pine Ridge on the best horses left, hoping they could sneak in to Red Cloud, to ask him for refuge.

Wild Hog was a cautious, methodical man. The camp, at the first sweet-water lake, was well guarded. The rest of the young men went out for horses, only wild ones, so none would be missed. While waiting for the invitation from Red Cloud, they moved to a safer place down Pine Creek, where the stream cut a canyon into the rock. None of the lost people came in, although even Comes in Sight would be welcomed now.

There were some cattle around, but with cowboys riding the range they dared not kill any; they ate deer and antelope and small game instead. The old men made arrows for deer, and spears for beaver and muskrat and the many ducks. The women found plums drying on the ground, and chokecherries and grapes still hanging. The girls gathered wild turnips and water roots while the boys fished. It was a thin life but a good one, and many wished it could go on. Still, soldiers were running everywhere, and so one night Wild Hog led the Cheyennes out across the Niobrara in the late moon, going up the long, shallowing draw of Spring Creek and over the flat country north toward the creeks flowing to White River. Twice men from Little Wolf came to them. It would be hard for anybody to get to Red Cloud, they said. Soldiers were all around.

AT DAWN DULL KNIFE looked down over the wide slope, the earth sinking away northward to the White River many blue and smoky miles away, with the dark-timbered Pine Ridge beyond. He was suddenly like a lost man come home. Not that he hoped to have a reservation here, with all the whites around, but this country lay deep within him, and in the stories of his grandfathers far back.

Dull Knife was stirred from his thoughts by the need to hurry, to hide until they could get to Red Cloud. So the camp was moved to a deep canyon an easy day's travel to the agency at Pine Ridge.

Because none of the messengers returned from Red Cloud, a formal party was sent to him, one that could not be ignored—but only a small one, without important men like Dull Knife or Wild Hog, who might be caught by the soldiers. Young Hog went because his mother was the sister of the Sioux American Horse, the son-in-law of Red Cloud. Bull Hump represented his father, Dull Knife, and headed the guard of warriors, with the customary two women along to show the peaceful heart. Tangle Hair, the Sioux-born Dog Soldier chief, went as leader, the man with the power to speak.

In the dusk the party rode ceremoniously around the hidden camp of brush shelters as though this were a rich and powerful village. They wore the little regalia left to them, but nothing like a splendid old-time party going to another tribe. The women stood at shelters instead of great painted Cheyenne lodges, but they sang the party on its way and made the old trills of admiration and hope.

Then before the emissaries reached Pine Ridge, with its great camp of army tents scattered for miles each way, Tangle Hair hid and sent out his signals.

Finally a Sioux came from the night. "Everything is very hard, my friends," he said. "Soldiers all around. Red Cloud is like a prisoner within an iron house."

So the party put away the few poor things they had brought as gifts and their little finery. In twos and threes they scattered, to slip at night into the great camp of the Sioux.

Back on the little branch of White River, Dull Knife and the rest waited, their packs ready. Scouts watched for soldiers, but nobody hoped to stand them off if they came. A day passed, two, three, and finally a man returned. Their friend Red Cloud was truly shut in by a forest of guns. The soldiers scolded the great chief of the Sioux as if he were a small boy, saying, "Do this, do that!"

There was almost no meat now, and the nights brought long spears of ice to the creek, so two more men were hurried to Red Cloud, both full-blooded Cheyennes with no Sioux ties, to make the gestures of subjugation as to a conquering enemy, begging to be spared. It was a desperate, shaming thing to do, but it, too, was thrown away, and the men came back in silence, some of those who had gone earlier riding along.

"Red Cloud is surrounded. He can do nothing," Tangle Hair told Dull Knife and the rest at the sheltered little fire, lowering his loud Sioux voice. "The chief has asked that we be permitted to live with his people, but the soldiers and the Great Father say he must give up every Cheyenne found among them. All our friend can tell us is, 'Give up to the soldiers. They will feed you.' "

"He speaks like the pay worker of the whites, not the chief of his great Sioux nation or a man who owns himself!" Bull Hump told his father, shouting it out. "Those soldiers in blue coats that we fooled all the way now order that we have to go back south."

"We will die first," Dull Knife said, so sorrowful and low it could scarcely be heard by the soft-listening Cheyennes about him. It was a hard thing to see, this man rousing himself to realize that all his plans for refuge had only been a dreaming. They looked into the earth, for no one could speak the comforting words, as Dull Knife slowly got up and stumbled away into the darkness. Here and there a woman began to cry softly, and then that, too, was gone.

Now THE CHEYENNES began another kind of packing, very slowly, the move put off hour by hour, and then another day because there were still a few people talking to the Sioux. Then word came that those Cheyennes were to be held as prisoners. Besides, Red Cloud had to warn his friends that twenty of his men had gone as scouts. American Horse and Two Lance, both related to the Dull Knife people, would lead them, bringing the fresh soldiers of Colonel Carlton and Captain Johnson from Fort Robinson. The scouts were of good heart toward their friends and brothers, but they would find the Cheyennes. And it was better to have Indians there among the charging soldiers than that they come alone.

Now the Cheyennes must make another run. The headmen counciled, but it was a decision already marked in the dust. Without lodges, blankets, meat, or ammunition, they could not hope to get through the soldiers standing across the north. So they must beg help from Spotted Tail, a day's pony ride east of Pine Ridge. They were not related there, nor were their goods ever promised at that agency, yet Spotted Tail's Sioux warriors had ridden with them many times in years past. He was a strong man who had always held the Great Father's agents in his palm like bits of tobacco to be rubbed fine for the pipe, they told themselves. No one spoke of the soldiers watching Spotted Tail now, or the large band that came fleeing from there to Red Cloud only two weeks ago, firing the prairie behind them.

The women made a busy hurrying with their few packs, but their eyes were dull, their hands dead, and Wild Hog remembered the old Cheyenne saying, "No people is whipped until the hearts of its women are on the ground, and then it is done, no matter how great the warriors or how strong the lance."

By morning the gray clouds ran along the tops of the high ridges like herds of dirty *veho* sheep. Fog turned to graying rain and then froze. The Indians bent before the storm, drawing their rags about themselves as the sleet began to rattle like shot on the icy ground and then dried to fine snow. It gathered in the low places, moccasin-deep, and then rose higher on the wind, shutting out the warriors scouting up ahead. Wild Hog, leading the single file of Indians, drew in close to the low ridges of Chadron Creek for protection. Like cattle the Indians were driven before the storm, eyes hooded, those afoot plodding clumsily over the ice now.

Then the Sioux scouts of the army were suddenly there beside the Cheyennes, their whooping faint in the storm, the men almost within lancing distance. The people tried to run together and then apart again, to scatter. A few of the warriors were back against the scouts, others charging the row of soldiers suddenly there too, with surely many, many more around, and all the guns loaded.

"Nobody could have found us today!" Tangle Hair growled angrily. "We have been betrayed!"

Some around him made replies to that—angry replies. But at once they quieted. It was done, and already Dull Knife and Wild Hog were hurrying up to make the signs of recognition, to lift the hand to American Horse and Two Lance and others of the Sioux scouts. Then the soldier chiefs came to a sheltered place and dismounted, awkward in their buffalo coats. While they shook hands with the Indians, Long Joe Larrabee, the half-breed interpreter, made ready, pounding his mittens, breaking the ice that bound his mustache and beard together with a sweep of his arm.

The man called Captain Johnson spoke. "We are very glad we found you. We want to feed your people and give them shelter—"

"We want no trouble," Dull Knife interrupted. "We were dying in that country south and came back. Now we are going to Spotted Tail, away from your country, so you can take your soldiers back to the fort."

But the captain would not permit the going. Through Long Joe speaking Sioux to Tangle Hair, who made it Cheyenne, he said he was very sorry to see the Cheyennes so poor and cold in this storm. "Nobody will harm you or your people. Come to our camp just a little way from here and we will feed you."

"We are going on," Dull Knife said stubbornly.

The soldier chiefs looked together and then over toward the miserable huddle of people. Then the captain called out some orders, and the soldiers moved up close upon the people in a shooting line, the scouts pushing in too.

"Can't you see that your people must have shelter?" Johnson roared out against Dull Knife, making it sound angry as the blizzard around them. "You will have to come to our camp or fight."

Even before it was interpreted, Dull Knife and the others knew the meaning; the people, too, already crying their songs for strength, somehow moving a little to the side in the blowing snow without seeming to do this, ready to scatter into the storm, doing it even with the soldier guns drawn down on them.

"We will ask the others," Wild Hog said, as quietly as for some little unimportant thing, and started away, Dull Knife following. Almost at once they came back to the officers, the singing louder behind them, the thin, high sound of the death song carried on the storm.

"We go with you," Wild Hog said.

Straight, gaunt now, but seeming even more than his six feet five in the snowy blanket, he turned to lead off in the direction motioned by the soldier chief with his fur gauntlet—straight into the wind. The others followed, the few with horses dragging them along through the drifts. Several times the Indians stopped in sheltered places, sinking down into the snow. Always Johnson spurred back with a company of troopers, guns ready, and so they had to bend into the storm again with the children and the packs.

Finally they reached the soldier camp down Chadron Creek. A big fire had been started in a protected spot. Johnson motioned the Indians to camp. Then hard bread, bacon, and coffee with plenty of sugar were brought. Even a freezing soldier spoke in sorrowful tones to see the people so poor, with so few of the men left in strength; the rest, men, women and children, thin and worn and ragged, hands, feet, even legs frozen to twice their size in the thawing firelight.

There was fear and heavy weariness, and then a little quiet joy when Two Lance's daughter saw her father sitting there among them for a smoke, and several other relatives. But later, troops came closer in the storm and men rode around the camp, riding, riding.

After dawn Dull Knife and several others threw the drifts back from their brush shelters and went out to where the mounted guards passed in the blizzard and motioned to them to go away. But the soldiers kept on, so Bull Hump took a couple of warriors out with guns. A whole company of troops charged up all around, those on the east on a high place overlooking the Cheyennes, ready to shoot down into the camp. Then Captain Johnson sent for the headmen.

"I must have the ponies and all your arms," he said.

The chiefs made their best Indian delayings. In turn they spoke of the bad treatment in the south country, although Johnson demanded the arms and horses at every pause. They kept talking so some of the guns could be hidden.

When Johnson, in impatience, ordered his men up close, Wild Hog made the signs and a few horses were led out, Young Hog coming first, shouting, "I give mine to our uncle, American Horse!" others calling out other scouts by name, hoping to get some of the stock back later. A few guns were brought too. Wild Hog put down his bow and quiver and threw back his snow-crusted blanket to show that he was without other arms.

The horse of Sitting Man was returned to him at Wild Hog's request because his broken leg was still so bad. A few more guns were brought to the pile and thrown down angrily. Then Dull Knife said these were the last, all. It was a very small pile, only about fifteen— two of them shotguns, some muzzle-loaders, a few breech-loading rifles and carbines—and almost all the bows they made on the way.

The little pile was carried away, Johnson giving the bows and arrows to the soldiers who held out their hands for them, and the muzzle-loaders and shotguns to the scouts, keeping only the good. Then the camp was counted: 46 men, 61 women, 42 children—149 people—and 131 horses and 9 mules. It was all written down in the soldier chief's book: guns, horses, mules, people, all together.

Then the horses were taken away, the soldiers yelling, shooting those they could not move into the wind, the women keening for all these things lost.

Now the soldiers came up to the Cheyennes bent together in the storm, helpless, unable to escape or fight. The women began to sing strong-heart songs, not for the helpless warriors but for themselves, to keep themselves from running and getting shot down. Brave One remembered how it was at Sappa Creek. She held herself very still, with Lame Girl drawn to her side, wondering when the bullets would strike. Around her others wondered too.

But nothing happened until it was evening and more food was brought. With the stomach full and fires to warm the ground and the shelters in the brush, the Cheyennes slept easier than in many moons. Nothing more could happen to them now except death.

IN THE MORNING the Cheyennes were told by Long Joe that Colonel Carlton was close by with his wagon train and they could put their goods on top of the rolled tents and ride to Fort Robinson. Once more the chiefs went out to make a delay, talking for three hours this time. It was behind a little bank out of the wind, with fires to warm the hands, and when the colonel kept saying, "Hurry, hurry," they always smoked a little more. Finally Dull Knife rose. "It is easy for our friend here to speak of making the hurry-hurry. He decides for the time of one war party; we decide here for all the time of our people, for all those to come after us, those whose grandfathers have not yet put a foot upon the grass."

Captain Johnson nodded his head in its snowy beaver cap, and there was no more talk of hurrying from the colonel. But they must go to Fort Robinson.

"It is a step toward the south. It was from Fort Robinson that we were taken down there," Dull Knife kept objecting. "We want to go talk to our friends the Sioux."

But that could not be done. Those Indians had no place for the Cheyennes. So it went, back and forth, a very long and uneasy waiting for the warriors with the people. Finally a noise and confusion started in the Indian camp, with a drumming on the wind, and dancing and war songs. Then it was as if there had been a message, a signal, for the headmen got up together from the council fire.

"We will die before we go south," Wild Hog said. Dull Knife and Left Hand and the rest grunted their approval, and together they started away, walking in single file into the blizzard wall, Wild Hog ahead.

Tangle Hair was called out. "Tell the Indians it is too late to move," Colonel Carlton said. "In the morning they must go to Fort Robinson, but nobody will be hurt." He stopped awhile, looking down into the storm where the drum still rose and fell. "Tell them, too, that there will be nothing more to eat until they get to the fort."

Slowly Tangle Hair went back, giving his bad news only to Wild Hog and Dull Knife. Wild Hog went out to make one more talk. "Our people are worn out and very cold and hungry," he said gravely. "There are many little children hungry among us."

"Nothing for anybody until you get to Fort Robinson."

DARKNESS CAME, WITH troops camped in the snow on both sides of the creek. The Indians worked all night. With little rows of fires shielded from the storm so the ground could be thawed, they dug breastworks facing the soldiers. Then they cut down trees to lay along the top, with notches chopped for gun barrels. If there must be fighting, they would all die here together, and as Little Finger Nail had said down there in the south, their names and the places would always be remembered.

Two Lance had asked that he be given his relatives from the Cheyenne camp, and Carlton agreed, but first he must sleep with the Indians this night. He must watch that no one escaped and could have all the guns he detected.

As the white snow dawn came, the strengthening storm winds brought the smell of coffee in the flying snow. Everything was moved back and rifle pits dug for the soldiers too. Plainly it was to be a fight. Some of the Indians were a little glad. Better that it be done quickly now. The sickest and the hurt ones like little

Lame Girl were put into a hole dug for them. Sitting Man took his place at the guns, as good as any man, now that nobody could run.

At last Carlton sent for the headmen. He showed them the two cannons, both ready to drop their bursting shells of fire into the camp in the brush. "Be ready to go to Fort Robinson in one hour," he said, pulling out his big gold watch, showing its face to Dull Knife in the storm, his finger pointing.

"We cannot go until we know what is to be done with us," Dull Knife protested, but gravely, without heat and stubbornness now.

"I can make no promises. I can only say that my troops will not harm anybody if you go quickly and without trouble."

But this was so hard that the interpreter, easygoing old Long Joe, could not say it so bluntly, not to his own Indian relatives. So he softened it a little for Tangle Hair's Cheyenne. "I promise to do what I can," he made the words of the colonel say, and the Indians were so desperate for a little hope that they believed it.

Just then a Sioux came riding through the storm. He was a courier from the soldiers at the Pine Ridge Agency and said there was very little to eat there yet. No rations had come, nothing except the beef they brought along when they moved—thin, and very few. The Cheyennes better go to Fort Robinson and be fed until the Great Father decided what was to be done with them.

Red Cloud—hungry too!

Dull Knife seemed really whipped. The colonel looked into the old man's broken face and pitied him. "I have decided not to fire the big guns into the women and children," he said, "but I can give you no food except at Fort Robinson."

So Wild Hog led the chiefs down to the camp, and in a little while they returned. They would go, but it would be difficult. The people were very frightened; the soldiers should be careful. They were uneasy, too, that Two Lance had taken his daughter and her family on good horses, wrapped in good soldier blankets, and started away toward Pine Ridge, riding sideways to the storm that was rising even sharper. Why did Two Lance risk this freezing ride for his daughter instead of staying with the warm wagons until the storm cleared, perhaps even tomorrow? What was going to happen?

But at last everyone was loaded, the men walking, all except

Sitting Man and a couple of others with frozen feet. The colonel went ahead with his three companies, breaking trail. Johnson's troops, who had found the Indians, were given the honor place along each side and behind them. In the middle of the moving column the wagons creaked over the frozen, hoof-cut snow, pushing out into the storm like sullen buffalo going with heads down, driven by winter from the only range they knew.

About ten miles on, the storm had lifted to a low gray ceiling, the cold sharper, the wheels creaking more. One of the wagons turned over on an icy, wind-bared place, the load spilling women and children and goods down a drifted gully. They were gathered up, hurried into another wagon, and not given time to collect their bundles from the snow. But the soldiers opened them, showing the big silver rings that a Cheyenne prisoner had sent home from Florida, rings given him by a white woman for his children. They were to hold the white cloths used by the *veho* to wipe the mouth during eating. The children had worn them for bracelets awhile, until the sickness killed them. Now the soldiers had found the rings and were making angry words for the Indians, because there were white-man names on them: Frankie and Jessie.

The Indians were uneasy about some of the other things in the bundles, and some they had left behind in the rifle pits at Chadron Creek—the boy's saddle from the big black horse taken in the canyon near Beaver Creek, some white-woman garments, and a couple of their blankets of silk pieces sewed together.

Toward evening the long double column of troopers wound down into the White River valley, the flag flying ahead, and in the middle of the long line the Indian wagons with guards on each side. At the crossing of the stream just before the fort, some Sioux scouts came crowding in between the wagons and the soldiers. The drifts were very deep here, and the only trail was the one made by the troopers riding two abreast, the road through the banked willows little wider than the wagons. So the soldiers had to fall back in the pale night. Here Bull Hump's wife rolled herself into a ball, and as the wagon lurched at the icy approach to the stream, she threw herself into the deep snowbank in the brush, the Sioux crowding their horses around her, taking her like a bundle behind one of the saddles in the darkness. Then the scouts moved back.

The Indians were taken through the white darkness into the post and up to the open doorway of a long barracks with light spilling out into the frosty night and glistening through the rimy windows. The smell of pitch-pine fire and coffee cooking brought a murmuring of anticipation from the Indians. One of the women began to sob aloud in her relief, and choked herself into immediate silence. But as the Cheyennes got stiffly down from the wagons, fresh soldiers with guns in their hands came out of the night to stand guard around them, their warm breaths smoking in the light.

"Drop the packs in a line here," a soldier chief said. "All of them will be searched."

For a moment every foot stopped. Several warriors tried to back away into the night, hands moving swiftly under their blankets, but the naked bayonets of the guard were against their backs.

"Hold yourself," Wild Hog said, very low and soft. "Hold yourself for the right time."

Chapter 12

AFTER PARTING FROM Dull Knife, Little Wolf's Cheyennes scattered through the broken, choppy sandhills west of the head of the Snake River. When their scouts signaled that all the soldiers were gone, the people began to come out of hiding, one from here, another there. Then suddenly, in a little well-sodded pocket already shadowing with the lowered sun, they were together again for the first time since the parting north of the Platte.

Suddenly their chief was there too, on his spotted horse, on a golden bunchgrass slope. Quietly Little Wolf looked over them, seeking out any missing, counting them all. Then he lifted his hand and started down into Lost Chokecherry, a valley so small and sheltered it seemed held within the cupping of two warm palms. Yet there was a lake clouded with fall ducks, and muskrat houses rose from the water. In the northwest end of the valley a steep hill lifted itself against the winds. Lower hills made a wall all around, rising well grassed from the bottoms.

The Cheyennes trailed into the valley in a weary, bedraggled line behind their chief, the women led by Buffalo Calf Road, the small children balanced in the hide sacks swung from the saddles. The larger ones rode behind the women, clinging tight to their waists; even some grown people rode double, for there must be no betraying track of a moccasin anywhere.

Gratefully the Indians dropped their bundles, the women looking back uneasily over their shoulders. But there was only the shadowing western hill that seemed close and comforting as the folds of a blanket. Some looked around in the other directions, not noticing one among them who wavered in her saddle, clutched at a bundle, and then slipped down under the horse. There was a cry, and Spotted Deer ran to pull his grandmother away from the hoofs. The medicine man came and spoke quietly to her. "My sister—"

"Let me die," Old Grandmother moaned, as a chill of the southern fever shook her again. "I am played out."

But Spotted Deer built a little fire and accepted the blanket that Feather on Head brought, one of the few left whole. Gently he wrapped the old woman in it, stroking her thin gray braids. But his eyes strayed to young Yellow Bead, hurrying to the lake with a waterskin for the grandmother. It was fine to have the girl help, even for a moment.

Slowly the other women had returned to their work, trying to move faster now, for it would soon be night. Only one long streak of yellow was left. It cut across the sky to a hill rising to the east, with a lone pine tree on top, very small in the distance. The Cheyennes knew a scout was there, watching the white man's trail that cut deep as the Overland roads along the Platte. But this one went into their old country, into the Black Hills, after more of the gold that made the whites run so crazy.

There were some, like Thin Elk and Black Coyote, who thought it was foolish to camp so close to the trail.

"It is the best place," Little Wolf said, and they let it be done, doubtfully, yet remembering that he got them away from the soldiers who rode so close from the Beaver clear across the Platte. Now for the half of a moon they spent coming through the sandhills most of the people here had seen no more of the soldiers. Here the smell of their small fires could be from campers drawn off the worn trail for grass, their horse tracks from the wild herds or from meat hunters chasing deer and antelope or shooting the big gray wolves. As the Indians ate at their little fires, they looked uneasily away into the darkness, although they knew that Little Wolf was out riding around. No camp in which he was leader had ever been surprised, and none ever would be, if he could help it.

So the Cheyennes settled to their first night of sleep in the place where Little Wolf thought they might stay awhile, if everyone was careful. He had forty men here, including the boys like Spotted Deer, forty-seven women, thirty-nine children—a hundred and twenty-six people. They could live happily here in Lost Chokecherry, Little Wolf knew as he listened to the quiet little laughs, if there were no chasing soldiers and none of that other thing, the violence that had grown up during the long pursuit of the years past. With so much need for each man to defend himself quickly with perhaps the poorest of weapons, to be on guard every breath against those who lied to him and stole, cheated, and killed, it was easy to forget there was a better way. Worse than the weariness and southern fevers of the body was the sickness in the heart and the mind of some here. These, even more than the old ones like Grandmother, or the children in the cradleboards, needed a season of food and warmth and safety.

IN THE MORNING there was cold rain, speared with ice sharp as needles against the men watching on the ridges. It turned to a long blizzard—hard on everybody, but an excellent cover for moccasin tracks. Now was the time to get as many deer as they could, for new clothing as well as meat. The hunters worked on some quick-made snowshoes and then went out. Thin Elk and Black Crane led the young men in threes and fours. The little parties rode the snow-whipped ridges, pounding the protesting horses along, the men peering from under the hoods of their blankets for lulls in the driving storm, hoping to locate deer yards in the brush patches below.

Black Crane ran into half a dozen deer in a pocket in Spring Valley. He motioned his followers around against the wind as close as they could get in the heavy drifts. When they had tied their horses and were fanned out and crouched ready downwind in the storm, Black Crane jumped up, shouting. The snow-caked deer raised their heads, got the scent, and plunged away into the drifts, floundering to their bellies, their shoulders, the hunters running alongside to drive their arrows deep, with here and there a quick slash of a knife to the throat, the blood spurting, the reddened snow covered almost at once by the storm.

They came into the camp on snowshoes, ice-caked, almost frozen, worn out with dragging the loaded horses into the wind. Now the young women of the village would make new dresses, soft and golden.

All that evening the men laughed and bragged at their small fires, as though there were no soldiers looking for anybody. The women said it was fine they had such noble hunters, because they needed more deerskin and a lot of elk teeth too. There were many here who once owned the one-thousand dresses, those covered with one thousand elk teeth, such as a good man naturally provided for his wife by hunt or trade. Now there were many younger ones who deserved them.

THREE DAYS LATER there was no thought of elk-tooth dresses. The storm had cleared and the frozen snow crackled under the moccasin. Then suddenly a man from Dull Knife was there, but before he could be drawn into a shelter to the fire, he fell, frozen and hungry and worn out.

When he had been warmed a little and fed hot soup, he spoke his bad news. Dull Knife's whole camp was captured in the storm and taken to Fort Robinson, it seemed. He had been sent out the first night to tell them here what had happened.

Little Wolf and the others smoked late over this, but already seven men, with Woodenthigh along as a sign of goodwill from his father, had started on their strongest horses, taking packs of dried meat to hide for the people if they could get away. The men left the valley by different directions, following the bare, frozen ridges wherever they could, or else riding crookedly, like wild horses wandering. The Cheyennes here must not be found. Some of the people must be left alive.

The next morning the sun came out hot, as was common in a Cheyenne autumn before the hard winter to follow. In two days the south slopes were soft and dark with water from the melting drifts, and the grass bare for the horses. Then one raw, cloudy forenoon, with a chill wind blowing out of the north, the watchers up near the lone pine tree saw a darkening line move out of the horizon. It seemed miles wide, almost like the old buffalo herds. A lot of the good men had gone to help Dull Knife, so younger ones were taking turns at watching too, and it was Spotted Deer who saw this first. His heart almost stopped as the dark line suddenly vanished, then came again, wider, darker. This must be thousands of soldiers coming in a wide string instead of a long one, bringing many, many wagons and cannons. He got on his horse and made the swift circlings of great danger approaching, for those looking from farther down; making the sign over and over, for many, many dangers.

Others saw the line too and made their signals. Old Crier ran through the camp calling, "Danger is coming! Much danger is coming!"

The women stopped their work, looked swiftly all around the bare hills, and then hurried to pack their goods. The children were gathered, the shelter skins fell and were rolled up by the time Old Crier came around again. "Let us be calm, my sisters!" he said. "We will not run like the foolish wool sheep of the *veho* run at the wave of a blanket. Be ready but be calm!"

Then there was a signal from Black Coyote, out watching too, but another kind. "Hunters get ready!" it said. "Hunters—" And several of the older men who knew these hills long ago began to laugh together out loud, slapping their thighs, roaring.

"*Piva!*" Little Wolf called his approval. "Not soldiers. It must be the great elk herd. Perhaps this is a year when they come like a wide dark stream through the hills, running before the winter."

So this was a day when they must risk being seen. For the watching now, careful, experienced old men were sent to the ridges, while the strong young hunters grabbed bows and quivers, knives and war axes.

At a narrow sand pass through a ridge that towered like young mountains, the hunters waited in two facing rows, ready to shoot from both sides, each man with an arrow set to the string, three held in the mouth, more in the quiver slung to the back. The rumbling neared, the first great dark-shouldered bulls appeared through the little cut, antlers high, panting tongues red, foam flying. The first ones shied from the man smell but were caught between the hunters and pushed on from behind, the pass running full. Now the arrows began to strike as the thunder and roar of the herd increased, crowding, bellowing through the narrow cut. The Indians shot, the elk went down under the beat of the sharp cloven hoofs, the herd running so solid that smaller, weaker animals fell without an arrow, while over them flowed the running brown blanket, the tangled, rattling forest of horns.

As the quivers emptied, the hunters tried to drag away some arrows from the dead, to salvage some for a second shooting, until Spotted Deer, overeager, got the flesh cut from his arm by a flying hoof.

"Back, young men! Keep out of the way!" someone roared out.

So the two rows of Indians watched the elk run between them—cows, growing calves, old bulls—snorting, panting, bellowing as they funneled from the pass. Finally the crowding began to thin a little, and then there were only a few stragglers. The last, not pushed, shied from the blood and the men and fled back on their tracks, and then came through again, frightened by the great prairie wolves and the coyotes that followed the herd. These, too, fled from the men, but not in panic, perhaps only to slip around one side or the other and take up the trail again, or stop to tear the throat of a dragging cripple.

Little Wolf watched on the crest of the ridge, looking hard for soldiers or white hunters, but there seemed nothing in any direction. Below him lay the dead elk on the torn sand outside of the pass, fanning away to both sides as the herd had spread into the valley. The Indians were at work on the butchering. It had to be done fast, for there might still be soldiers following the migrating elk herd for the hunt. Yet it seemed worth the risk—a hundred and eighty-two elk, the skins of some cut up by the hoofs, but many that were good, and a great deal of meat. Besides, there were the elk teeth for the women's dresses, to brighten the camp.

Although Spotted Deer's arm wound hurt, the bone was sound, and the youth rode home in happiness. He would have eight elk teeth from his own killing to offer to Yellow Bead.

For a long time Little Wolf sat alone on the ridge above the hunting ground, looking down at two old wolves dragging at the elk guts. Several times he sniffed the gray evening wind anxiously. Even if no soldiers found this place by themselves, all this blood and butchering would draw a hundred late fall buzzards to circle overhead for even the most stupid to see.

Suddenly Little Wolf turned his face back into the moist wind. A soft spatter had hit his pockmarked cheek. Another. It was the snow that had whipped the elk into such running, the snow that would cover the blood and the carcasses for a long time. Now at last the Cheyennes had a little luck.

IN ONE MOON'S TIME the second snow was half gone. All but three of the men sent to Dull Knife were back; two stayed to watch, and the third was captured and locked up.

"We got signs from Bull Hump's wife," Woodenthigh reported. "She says the people are in the barracks, well treated, with food and medicine for the sick, but there are no blankets and clothing, and none can tell what will happen."

Ahh-h! That was the thing that made the eyes stare into the darkness of the sleeping time. More meat must be sent to the cave in the White River bluffs, and two or three guns with a little ammunition, all they dared to spare.

The next night Thin Elk, Spotted Deer, and Black Coyote slipped out with several others. They were carrying extra fur-lined moccasins, and bladders of pounded meat, and they had two guns in the party.

"You will not forget the helpless ones here," Little Wolf had reminded Black Coyote. "There must be no shooting—nothing foolish now."

Black Coyote was silent in his surliness today, and so Thin Elk answered. "You need more horses before you start away from here.

I saw some easy to get, loose, toward the big herds near the Box Butte."

"Will there be time for the taming?" old Black Crane said, making obstacles.

"It will be easy, this bad winter," Thin Elk said.

Yes, easier to break them, too. But Black Crane saw the concerned face of Spotted Deer and knew he had a purpose for his horses, so the old chief smiled into his face.

"Go, my son," he said, "but do not blacken your gun barrels."

It was a very uneasy week for Little Wolf and the others before the horse catchers returned. They came whooping, with about twenty head of good young stock already thinning from the deep snow and cold, and very shaggy in preparation for the hard winter, the manes long, the tails dragging on the ground. They would be strong when the grass came, and the colors would be fine after they shed: two stripe-legged buckskins, a handsome black-and-white pinto, the rest sorrel, bay, and gray.

Two would go to the lodge of Little Wolf, Thin Elk announced, his gift to the women of it, and once more the chief could not roar out his anger against him or his present. But others whispered, and laughed a little. Twenty years ago the chief had warned this man away from his wife. Now he was back, warm-eyed as a youth.

Still there was the luck of twenty more horses, and some of the young mares were already tame enough so the small boys could ride them along the bare slopes.

"There was no trouble with anybody?" Black Crane asked, even before the feast for the success was finished.

No. Too cold, probably. No one was seen except by Thin Elk— only a cowboy on a far hill. No trouble at all.

But this questioning brought anger to the face of Black Coyote. "Answer nothing!" he commanded, as though he were a chief given great powers. "We do not have to tell Black Crane all we do!"

Everybody looked away, pretending nothing had been said. Quickly somebody sent Old Crier to announce that there would be a little dancing. So most of the people moved over to the brush-walled circle, standing like a corral to keep the wind out and to hide the row of tiny fires around the inside. The middle was a smooth warm place, large as the great old-time soldier society lodges, except that there was only the sky above, no tall gathering of poles crossed at the smoke hole. Yet it was a good place when there was no flying snow, and tonight Pretty Walker and the others wore their new fringed buckskin dresses; even Yellow Bead, hers the only one with no elk teeth at all. Everyone knew of the eight that Spotted Deer carried, but not whether they had been refused or offered at all. Grandmother brought out a sack of peanuts that Spotted Deer found where some wagons had turned over along the icy Black Hills trail. The sack was a big one, round and fat as a bear cub in the fall, and the old woman dipped out a good palmful for each of the young people. It was fine throwing the shells on the fire, the sparks leaping up into the cold blue night; fine munching the kernels.

There was a little excitement later, when three of the new horses were seen tied to the scrub tree behind Yellow Bead's shelter. But the girl's aunt never came out to take them, and Spotted Deer had to go lead the horses away himself. He did it late in the darkness, long after everyone had stopped watching. When the youth crept back into his shelter, Old Grandmother was up, holding out a wooden bowl of soup. "Drink, it will warm you," she said.

But Spotted Deer could not be warmed, and before he finally settled to his robe he dropped his little pouch of elk teeth into the old woman's lap—the teeth that should have started a one-thousand dress for his bride.

In almost every shelter and sleeping hole there was a whispering over the rejected offer, nowhere more than in Yellow Bead's.

"You are very foolish, my daughter," the aunt said sadly as she turned her old bones to a more comfortable place in her cowhide robe. "Little Hump will not come to a young woman like you, now that you have no family left alive to welcome him as son and brother."

The girl managed to make the polite murmur of having heard, but there was no heart in it. She would still hope. Little Hump's own father had taken Pawnee Woman, the captive girl, to wife, one with no relatives among them at all. Of course, she had not been his first one.

It was very hard, this growing up without a proper lodge and family.

ALL FALL THE CHEYENNE scouts watched for riders, men coming alone or perhaps in twos, and particularly for the blue columns that rode from every direction. These the Cheyennes must see while still far off, so the people could step aside from this fine little valley into hiding places. Step aside not only so they would not be caught, but so anyone looking down from far off would see the valley serene and empty. The little brush shelters and the skin ones, only stooping high, with branches and twigs tied over them, were lost in the plum thickets and cherry patches, the holes in the steep northwest hill hidden behind the few box elders, with hides for doors, earth-rubbed ones with grass sewn here and there.

Once they did not have time to do more than scatter out into the sandhills and were almost caught when a row of soldiers came along a ridge not more than two miles away. The troopers made a bunch on the hill, stopping a long, long time to look into Lost Chokecherry with the farseeing glasses. Then they separated into the column of two abreast again and went on, the flag flying at the front. But scouts were left behind at a little fire in a buckbrush patch high up on the ridge. For two days they stayed there, the pale smoke telling the Indians of white-man watchings. None here would ever forget the fleeing into the snow after the troops came into sight. The cold was so hard that they found grouse dead as stone in the drifts, and when the Cheyennes could finally return to their camp, there were many frozen toes, dead, to be cut away.

There was also great uneasiness since it was discovered that their best field glass was lost, the one from the Turkey Springs fight down in the south country. At first the loss was hidden from Little Wolf, but he discovered that the glass was dropped by a young relative of Black Coyote's. A wide search was made, but whether the covering snow had taken it or the enemy, none could say.

Little Wolf now prepared himself for something that might mean spilled blood. He knew how many noticed Thin Elk always beside the wives of their chief, and talked slyly of it behind the hand, saying that the coal once kindled is truly very easy set afire. Yet Little Wolf could give them no ear. His medicine-bundle oath made that clear: If a dog lifts his leg to your lodge, do not see it. Your anger can only be for injustice to the people.

But now the ridicule against his lodge and himself was giving power to the man who wanted to go against the council. Black Coyote was hot to make war on the trail over there. The bold talk was attracting serious young men like Spotted Deer, who had their first coup to count. Little Wolf thought once of stepping aside, but then there would be no head for the people here, none to hold their crumbling parts together, with the violence of Black Coyote certain to sweep over them. No, the living had been given into his palm to shield and they could not be thrown away.

So Little Wolf made ready for what he must do, to drive out the man who brought weakness to the lodge of the bundle bearer. By the light of his hidden fire he had combed his hair neatly, with the one feather up from the back of his head, the little medicine roll tied beside the part, the braids wrapped in the new skin of the otter that Woodenthigh had shot with an arrow in the waters of the Snake River. On his breast hung the silver peace medal from the Great Father, and across his knees was the long pipe.

Cross-legged before the handful of coals, the Cheyenne chief laid a little silver sage to smolder on the coals and took out the Sweet Medicine bundle from under his shirt. Four times he passed it through the fragrant smoke of the sage and then he offered it to the great directions, the sky, the earth, all around, and put it carefully back. When this was done and his mind quiet and composed for whatever was ahead, he started out in the night to settle this trouble.

But a rider was hurrying toward him out of the darkness. It was Woodenthigh, calling softly, "News! Bad news, my father! You are wanted."

In the camp, Little Wolf found the people gathered in the brush circle around a man from Red Cloud. They became silent as their chief approached, falling back a step, silent, angry, and helpless.

"Dull Knife and the rest are to be taken back south. Loaded in the wagons and hauled through the winter blizzards back to the sick country," the messenger said, speaking his soft Cheyenne very rapidly but smoothly. "It is settled that they are going."

"I do not believe our men over there have agreed to this," Little Wolf said quietly, pushing past Black Coyote and the others. "Not Dull Knife and Wild Hog! They are Cheyennes!"

To this the news bearer made no reply. He knew nothing beyond the message.

So once more the decision with Thin Elk had to wait.

Chapter 13

AFTER THEY WERE taken to the barracks at Fort Robinson, most of the Dull Knife Cheyennes had slept straight through with the fatigue, the grateful drying warmth, the food, and the little white pills of Dr. Edward Moseley—quinine for those still full of malaria chills, morphine for those with frostbite. The doctor had cut away the snow-softened horsehide cast from Sitting Man's leg. The bone was well set, he exclaimed in surprise, so well that only the constant jolt and jerk of the hurrying ride north kept it from healing— the falling as his horse went down, hobbling up to mount another and go on, always on. It was a wonder the man was alive; more, that he could hold the inflamed leg steady with his hands as the doctor probed the wound for bone fragments, and could crinkle his gaunt dark Indian face in a smile that the doctor's instrument struck none.

"*Hou! Hou!*" he said, and Bridge was as happy. The medicine man had made such probings too, but in their hurry to run he might have done it badly.

"It's a wonder any of these Indians are alive," the doctor said to his assistants. They were so starved and ragged and sick, their skin the color of muddy gray coffee. Even the powerful shoulders of Wild Hog seemed as naked of flesh as a two-by-six across a post. But it was the children that hurt the white doctor most—silent, uncrying children, their round eyes unblinking, their arms thin as willow sticks, the little bellies swollen, their feet and hands frozen. He wiped his eyes and worked on, unable to look into their faces.

He examined little Lame Girl too, the gun-shot ankle thick and almost black, the big eyes fearful in the thin little face as the doctor inserted a drain. Then he stroked the tender foot gently until the exhausted girl slept.

Finally all was quiet in the barracks except for the guards walking around the building. And yet somehow a board of the cold rough-sawn floor had been pried up with knives and the women's belt axes, and fighting things hidden there for the day that Wild Hog had promised them.

In the morning the awakening Indians made themselves neat, the men braiding the hair of their wives in the friendly Cheyenne way. The post cooks came. Pounding on the lid of a great boiler with a ladling spoon, they motioned the Indians into a line and passed tin plates and cups into their hands. When the Cheyennes were fed, they settled to rest some more and smoke, with enough gift tobacco even for the women's circles. But now Colonel Carlton came, standing broad in his buffalo coat among his soldier chiefs. Some of the Sioux scouts were brought too, among them Bull Hump's wife, unrecognized, her hair braided like a man's, and dressed and acting like the others. There were no Cheyenne interpreters at the post and so all talk still went through two people, through Tangle Hair and someone else.

"What are you going to do with us?" the Indians had to ask, unable to wait until the proper smoking had been made.

"The fighting is over," the colonel said. "You must stay here until the government decides if you are to go south or to Red Cloud. But nothing bad will happen to you here. You will have the freedom of the post and can even go out along the river and the bluffs, but at suppertime you must be back. If one man of you deserts or runs away, you will all be shut up. All will be held responsible."

Dull Knife rose and spoke to his people, advising them to do as the soldier chief said. "We are back on our own ground and have stopped fighting. We have found the place we started to."

"But there is something still to be done," Colonel Carlton said, and now the headmen sat silent, waiting, eyes looking down before them. "I must have all your guns. We know you have more. They were seen in the rifle pits at Chadron Creek."

Now the women had to hold themselves, but suddenly one among them broke into a low crying. At the second, angrier demand from Carlton, and a movement of the guards with the bayonets, Wild Hog spoke a low word, without moving his lips. A couple of the young men brought out their guns, and then more, for the shadows of the walking soldiers outside passed the frosted windows every few moments, and all around here were a thousand more, with the storehouses of ammunition. So finally six guns, mostly in pieces, were brought out from under the clothing of the men, and a couple of revolvers, and laid on a little pile.

Afterward they were given a few presents with more tobacco, and before many days a very young soldier chief, Lieutenant George Chase, took charge of the Indians. He made himself an office in a room at the end of their barracks and called the headmen in. Without much talk he said he must ask them all to go out to the parade ground, cleared of snow now and warm in the sun. Their bundles and goods would be left in the building and searched.

Dull Knife held himself silent, but Wild Hog sprang to his feet, very tall in the little log guardroom. "We cannot let this be done!" he said angrily, and calmed himself at once. "Taking the women from their bundles would make trouble," he said. "The young men would get excited; people get hurt."

Finally Colonel Carlton agreed this might be true, so the search was made with the Indians inside, everybody suddenly ordered down to one end of the prison room, away from the bundles. While a row of soldiers stood with their guns ready against the Cheyennes, others went through the Indian goods. Even now there were a few fine old things left, like Great Eyes' feather-tailed shield, very old, carried all the days since the Cheyennes lived far east where the oaks grew thick. There were covetous eyes among the officers as such things were spilled out on the barracks floor. But Carlton was after the lead and powder, the bows and arrows that were found, and the many things that seemed to belong to the whites: children's dresses and underclothing and bedspreads, the fringed one of Dull Knife's daughter's now muddied and smoke-blackened from the fires. In Dull Knife's own pack that Pawnee Woman brought was a child's parasol and several family pictures. There were other *veho* things the soldiers did not see, like the canvas-covered account book in which Little Finger Nail drew his pictures, using the flat little box of colored pencils. This book was still tied next to Little Finger Nail's back with two rawhide strips through it, one around his waist, another up over his shoulder, as he had carried the book all the way from Kansas.

But when the soldiers made a tentative move to search the people, one motioning toward the women uneasily, not certain how it was to be done, the young Cheyennes were suddenly ready to spring to violence, to throw themselves against the guns. The Sioux scouts roared out angrily against it too. A couple of days later, a woman, moving a bundle around, dropped a revolver from under her dress. The guard who saw it hurried away, and the lieutenant came to Dull Knife, demanding the gun. The woman was afraid, but she brought it to the young white man. So two sentinels were placed inside the building, day and night. But some revolvers were still kept hidden.

This boy-cheeked young officer Chase was not a bad man. He always carried a little extra tobacco in his pockets and a small pouch of sour balls for the younger children. Sometimes when he saw Lame Girl alone among the grown-ups because she could not run and play, he took her before him on the saddle and rode around the parade ground. But when Chase examined the black ornament the girl wore on a rawhide string around her neck, he drew his hand quickly away. It was the breechblock of a Springfield rifle. After that he watched the barracks closely, letting his eyes move over all the chinking between the logs, looking carefully down along every crack in the floor. Nothing seemed disturbed. The Indians seemed not to notice, but almost at once Lame Girl was wearing a pyrite disk on the string, and when Medicine Woman swept the floor with her bundle of joint grass, she swept across the boards so the cracks would always look full of dust and trash.

When Lieutenant Chase asked the Cheyennes what they liked to eat, they said soup, and so he had it made in big iron kettles from the bones at the butcher's, with the marrow in soft rich lumps for their tin plates. They got mush with molasses too. The first time that Wild Hog's wife stirred it in her plate she broke out into a laughing chatter, showing it to the small children, putting a little into the mouth of one as she made the smacking sounds with her lips.

"She says it is very good, not ground with the cobs, as they got in the south," the interpreter told Chase.

The *veho* made the dubious face. "With the cobs?"

"Yes," Wild Hog said. It was ground for the mules but given to them instead. The taste was bad, and the small children got sick. "There was no molasses to eat with it."

The young officer looked into the strong face of the Indian saying these things so quietly and took the liberty of doubling the meat rations for the prisoners. Although it was almost three times the amount issued to the soldiers, who ate more of other foods, it still seemed inadequate to the Indians. But no white man had ever treated them so well, and for this the Cheyennes humored young Chase, made jokes with him and his guards, laughed and sang and played cards with them.

AMONG THE MANY whites who hurried up to visit Fort Robinson were some who came to claim their horses, saying this gelding, that mare had been stolen from them, several asking for every horse strong enough to walk, even those captured from the wild herds and without any brands at all. They brought stories of great Cheyenne killings and other bad things done, enough for a thousand avenging warriors with a thousand guns. But one story the Cheyennes heard with open ears—about the Indian boy with the leg broken by a bullet. He had to be left behind in the draw on the Beaver because there was no time to make a travois, with the soldiers already shooting. Some cowboys found him two weeks later, eating the rotten meat of the horses killed in the fight. One man was a brother of the boy the Cheyennes had shot to get the fine black star-faced horse. So he helped kill the crippled young Indian.

"Ahh-h! Always it is so, one killing makes another!" Old Crow said softly, under the keening of the women for the boy's warrior death. Everybody had hoped the young men who went back south after the raiding had saved him and some of the others who never caught up. There was the warrior and his wife, sent ahead with the young Yellow Swallow. It would be good to know that the Cheyenne son of Custer could grow tall and strong in the north country and see the ridge where his father died fighting. But perhaps the cowboys killed Yellow Swallow too.

A few nights later two of Little Wolf's men slipped right up to the scout camp. One was caught, but the son of Little Wolf got away. Next morning Colonel Carlton took the captured one over the region and saw where he and eight or ten others had camped. But to questions about Little Wolf and his band the man's face became hard as the butte walls, and so they kept him at the soldier camp, away from those in the barracks.

Wild Hog got the news of this in mirror flashes from the bluffs, and was glad that Little Wolf was still free enough from the soldiers to send help here. Their chief's bundle walked with a strong man.

In a few days there was more news. Wild Hog was out toward Crow Butte when Tangle Hair waved from an old trading house. Wild Hog sat on a rock to wait for his friend, noticing from far off that there was a shadow on the dark face of Tangle Hair. "I have only bad news to bring to your walking," he apologized, sitting down to draw a strip of newspaper from his tobacco pouch. He ran a finger along the clipping, where Indian pictures had been drawn. "It was left with the trader for us by our relative Rowland at Pine Ridge," he said. "The pictures tell what the paper says—that we are to be sent back south."

Ahh-h!

Yes, but there was more. The governor of that Kansas country was demanding that the leaders of the Cheyennes be brought to him to be judged for murder, murdering whites.

Through one slow breath Wild Hog sat like a part of the rock about him, almost as though he had expected this. Then he broke into angry words, his wide mouth curling from his strong teeth. "So that is why we are always asked who did this and that back in the south country!" he said angrily. "That was not murder down there. It was avenging. Nobody judges those who kill our people, not this time or when our women and children were shot on the Sappa!"

"No, but the whites have the guns and the iron houses," Tangle Hair said bitterly. And it seemed that they often hanged some of their own people after a judging for murder.

"Ahh-h! They do this hanging very easily to Indians, like Black Foot and Two Face. Those men were pulled up on the posts because they brought in women captives to Fort Laramie—the white women others had captured!"

Tangle Hair remembered his heat and his sorrow the time his Sioux relatives were humiliated so in death. Wild Hog was looking down upon the strip of paper that fluttered in the wind, thinking about those two men, and a third beside them, a Cheyenne hanged for something the Indians never understood. As Wild Hog thought of this, his powerful fingers crushed the foolish strip of talking paper, moved to rip it up and throw it like unclean feathers to the wind. But the shadow of its words could not be destroyed so.

Together the two men started back to the fort. They would say nothing of the newspaper clipping to anyone, not even to Dull Knife, particularly not to him.

Chapter 14

BY MID-NOVEMBER the snow of the two fall storms was gone and the upper high-plains country was smoky blue in the warmth of Indian summer. When they could forget or cover their uneasiness, the Cheyennes seemed content in the barracks. For the first time since Crook came chasing them around in the Powder River country almost three years ago, they had enough to eat and were not afraid of what might happen in the night. The women went to the river in the warm noontimes to wash their clothing, to dress the hides given them for moccasin soles. Sometimes they had other skins —a few deer and antelope, and many rabbit hides to line the children's moccasins and the cradleboards for those like little Comes Behind.

When the ground dried, Medicine Woman took some of the girls far along the stream and the bluffs and out on the prairie to replenish her medicine things. She showed them the plants they would need to know as good Cheyenne women: cures for painful periods and the purification, for a good pregnancy and to restore those who lost their children unborn, for the easy birth, cooling the breasts, good milk, and strengthening the children.

Medicine Woman knew many village cures too, for the coughing sickness, the fevers and the stinking sicknesses, for aches and pains and gunshot wounds, and the remedies for restlessness and unease of heart. These last the young women would need to know in the dark time ahead, and it was fine to see shy young Singing Cloud develop the healing eye and hand so well. She would be a great woman to cure the sickened bodies and hearts of her people, and with a fitting husband, if it came to be Little Finger Nail.

The Moon of Falling Leaves was a good time, yet Wild Hog and Tangle Hair were very silent. The older men often squatted along the Black Hills road, where the long bull trains, the mules, the flying stagecoaches, and the riders passed, all to seek the yellow gold that the Indians had seen there with Tobacco fifty years ago. It was the same gold that drove the whites with the cholera over the trail to California, then to Colorado, up the Bozeman Trail to the Idaho country, and now to the Black Hills. Always they ran after the yellow iron that one could not eat or wear or use to warm the winter lodge.

The younger people climbed over the bluffs, returning with their blankets full of pinecones and sweet plants for the fire, and perhaps a rock rabbit twisted from his hole. Owning no horses, young men like Little Finger Nail raced those of the officers, the soldiers gathered thick around the ring, betting as the Indians whipped and whooped until the track was worn deep. Some were allowed out on short hunts, chasing antelope with the soldiers or coyotes with the officers' hounds.

With no work to do and little but bitterness for the tongue, the Cheyennes passed the indoor time as they could. There was no privacy as a people should have, not night or day. No privacy for the women's purifications, or for the married people, when even the buffalo or the wolf and his mate like to get away. It seemed sometimes to Limpy and his Broad-faced One that they had never been married at all. The young played the hand game, while the women's circles shook the sweet-grass baskets and wagered the little finery they had on the fall of the marked plum pits. Most of the men played with the *veho* cards, letting the soldiers teach them seven-up and blackjack, with which they won much tobacco. In the evenings there was singing, and dancing too, with Cheyenne drums and half-breed fiddlers, the Sioux scouts and the soldiers always there. Often some of the whites brought feast things or gave the girls presents of money to buy ornaments.

Of them all only Singing Cloud had no eyes for the whites. Dull Knife's handsome daughters, called the princesses, were the belles of the post. Wild Hog's daughter was a little more reserved, without the daring that comes to three sisters together. But she had inherited the oval face of her Sioux mother, the wide dark eyes, the long lithe grace. She made shy talk among the admiring soldiers too, although now and then she remembered the silence of her father and became silent. Once she cried out in anger to the young lieutenant, "You make pretty talking words, but you wish to kill us all!" And for that one moment she looked like her gaunt and brooding mother, who sometimes broke into wild words here in the barracks and had to be quieted quickly before she roused her son to foolish things.

Little Finger Nail gradually lost his reticence and showed some of the white men the story pictures he made in the gray book: warriors in their regalias, with medicine shields, lances, and arms, the horses decorated with the medicine things, the feathers, scalp locks, and paint. Many in the flying long-legged herds had *veho* brands on them, and some of the pictures showed whites who were not soldiers being killed, some struck down while running, and some shooting and falling. From the accoutrements the names of the men killing them could easily be told.

A white rancher saw the pictures and said good words about them. They were the work of native artists and should be preserved. They told stories of the Cheyennes and what they did. He would like to buy the book.

There was a sudden grunting of concern, of anger from among the older men, and some low angry Cheyenne words. "They will use it to hang us all."

Quickly the surprised Little Finger Nail wrapped the book in its rawhide covering and strapped it, as always, behind his back. Before the suspicious watching eyes, the angry silence, the rancher left and went straight home.

LATE ONE THIN-MOON night there was a sudden shot and running and shouting over around the guardhouse just behind the Indian barracks. Wild Hog and the others jumped from their sleep, some to the floor place where the weapons were hidden, others crowding the windows to look out. There was nothing except some people moving in the dark, perhaps young men come courting, but surely no Cheyenne would let himself be caught like that. In the morning they heard a *veho* story of a ghost seen at the guardhouse on nights when the sliver of dying moon rose very late. It was always a silent blanket-wrapped figure. Last night a new sentry saw it and gave the challenge. The Indian did not stop until just outside the guardhouse door, at the place where some Cheyennes had seen the bearded soldier called William Gentles stick Crazy Horse to death with the bayonet. The sentry fired his gun, and the soldiers came running in their underwear.

The Cheyennes did not laugh, although they had no belief for such stories. The killing had happened just a little over a year ago. Crazy Horse had come here after he had been promised every protection for himself and his people. Dull Knife, Wild Hog, and the rest had sat beside him in the councils up north and heard those promises, heard them for all the Indians. No, this story of Crazy Horse betrayed here was not for laughing.

A STRETCH OF GOOD weather brought Red Cloud riding at the head of his Sioux subchiefs to talk to the Cheyennes. He spoke angrily when he saw their condition. "The whites have made starved and dying beggars in rags of my friends and relations!" he roared. "We are not to be treated like the poor whites one sees, who never have anything. We owned all this great rich country; we are to live well from its selling!"

But there were few words the Indians could say to each other in this first meeting under the eyes of the white officers, with all their failures there between them. The Cheyennes were humiliated that they were caught; the great Red Cloud had to admit that he was too weak to help them.

Afterward the Sioux chief warned Carlton that, if these people had to go south, the knives must be taken from them or they would surely kill themselves. When the colonel was ordered out with a long column and pack train to chase after Little Wolf, he wired General Crook that the prisoners would have to be tied and hauled away to get them south.

By now all the Cheyennes knew the sky was darkening for them. The headmen sat up late, wrapped in their silent blankets, planning. Then the man called Indian Inspector came. He leaned his chair back against the wall in the little office of the barracks and talked to the chiefs, seeming to be only half listening, flipping the stone on his watch chain, nodding and holding out his half-smoked cigar as excuse when the long pipe of friendship was offered to him.

But Dull Knife had to make his talk from the beginning just the same: the promises broken, the reservation they never got, the goods that never came, the hunger and sickness, and their coming back north because they had been promised they could. "Now we are locked up like people who have broken laws—like your bad men, your outlaws."

"I am told there is no place up here for you," the chair-leaning *veho* said. "Your relatives are in Indian Territory. The government can't have Cheyennes scattered everywhere."

"The Arapahos did not have to go south to their brothers. They have their reservation with the Shoshones. There are relatives of ours up on the Yellowstone. They are permitted to stay north."

"The Arapahos are a small tribe, but they will be taken south," the man said, throwing the butt of his cigar into the little iron stove and getting up to go. "The Cheyennes on the Yellowstone are moving south as soon as Sitting Bull is brought in from Canada."

For a long time all the people were silent. They would surely have to go back south, and Wild Hog and others knew that the chiefs and head warriors would be taken out and turned over to the Kansas courts, to be tried for the murder of the white settlers on the Sappa and the Beaver. The first to speak was Bull Hump. "Those the white man thinks did what he calls murder are hung up."

Wild Hog nodded. Then there was only the roaring of the fire in the stovepipe.

THE NEXT DAY the cook found one cup too many. The man looked down the line of the people he knew so well by now and saw that Bull Hump was gone. It was said that his wife was with Red Cloud and so he had probably gone there, and not to Little Wolf. Maybe got homesick for her, as a man would. So the cook held up the report until after three meals. Then the soldier chief came marching through the door with armed guards along. Sternly they counted the people, and then a second time. Without making any talk about it at all, they took the liberties from the Cheyennes and locked the doors on them. Now all the people, even the children, boys and girls of six and seven too, were shut in the one room all day. Once more sentries with the guns on their shoulders were walking around the barracks all the time.

In two, three days Bull Hump was brought back and his wife too, the people sorry to see her here after her escape by rolling from the wagon into the snow. Bull Hump was back, but not the liberties and the freedoms.

IN THE COLD MONTH of December a new soldier chief, Captain Henry W. Wessells, came to take Carlton's place. He was a short, light-haired, very busy man, in and out of the barracks a dozen times a day, as though that were all he had to do. He even came in late at night, anytime. Before, the Indians, living all together, had had no privacy from each other. Now they had no privacy from this grasshopper *veho* either.

The little Flying Dutchman, as the soldiers called him when he could not hear, liked to see the Indian women work, so he sent them out to clean up around the post in their old cotton dresses and ragged blankets, to pick up trash and paper, shovel the frozen horse droppings into the wheelbarrows, unload grain wagons. It was healthy exercise, he said. But they managed to hide a little grain in their blankets as they ran back to warm themselves at evening. Besides, they got a present here and there from the pitying people of the post, a few cookies perhaps from some woman, a string of beads, a ribbon. The busy little white man did not like to have Sioux visitors to the barracks either, not even the scouts when they were around the post. The good days were truly past.

Several times Wessells came to see what warm clothing the Indians had, and always he discovered once more that they had none of the red woolen dresses that the Cheyennes liked, only worn calico and old canvas. Each time he said that warm clothes were coming soon. The Cheyennes heard it with two ears, one glad for warm covering in this cold winter, the other uneasy, for it must mean they were to be taken away before the spring.

This matter of clothing for the Cheyennes kept the mail and the telegraph busy. Crook had wired the Indian Bureau, and when none came, he asked if it could not be issued from annual allotments of Red Cloud and Spotted Tail agencies. "Very cold near Robinson. Inhuman to move Indians as ordered. . . . Carlton says men must be handcuffed." Finally, when nothing arrived, the general ordered Wessells to outfit the Cheyennes from the army stores when they started south, but that would help the remaining women and children very little.

Now Red Cloud was called down for one last council. Perhaps he could make the hopelessness of the situation clear to the sullen Cheyennes. The council was in the barracks room, the women and children along the back, not a child playing, not one running to stand between the knees of its father, as Cheyenne children sometimes did, even in the great councils.

The soldier chiefs came into the gray, dusky log room and seated themselves in chairs, with Red Cloud, American Horse, and related subchiefs cross-legged beside them on the floor. Making a tight, close circle around these men were the Cheyenne leaders. Wessells spoke through Rowland, one long married into the tribe. He told them what all knew: that the Indian Bureau had ordered the Cheyennes back to Indian Territory. Then, before Dull Knife and the rest could rise in protest, Red Cloud was up, and no one spoke against this, for he was the guest. He felt sorry to see his friends in this trouble, he said, but all he could do was counsel submission. He was an old friend of the Cheyennes. His uncle, called Red Cloud too, had married into the people and lived with them all his life.

"The white man's government is very powerful. They tell me I cannot take you into my lodge and feed you," the Sioux chief said. "The ground is covered with snow, you are almost naked, and it is very far to that north country. The soldiers are everywhere up there too. It is very foolish to think of resisting."

Through this Dull Knife sat silent. He seemed buried deep in reverie, a watching newspaperman wrote, his face as smooth and as classic as any ever put in marble. The old Cheyenne was without adornment, nothing except the old otter wrapping of his braids. Finally the old Cheyenne chief arose, looking his full mid-sixty years, bleak-eyed from all the things that had been done. The blanket he held about him was very old, yet he stood remote as a mountain peak within its raggedness.

"We bowed to the will of the Great Father," he said, "and we went far into the south where he told us to go. There we found that a Cheyenne cannot live. We belong here. I knew this country before a one of your white men set his foot along our rivers, before he brought his whiskey to our villages, or your bluecoats spurred along the trails, north and south. When you first came, you were few and we spoke well to you, made you our guests, and gave you our game to eat and warmed you in our lodges. Even after you began to push in everywhere, to kill the buffalo, bring sickness to our villages and come shooting our people in the winter night, we still tried to hold our young men to peace, the peace you had promised us so many times. Do this one more thing, you said. Sell us some of your land and we shall have peace. We gave you our land, and the things you promised did not come. Many times you promised us an agency, but you only took us far to the south country, saying, 'Go and see. You can come back.' Then when we were dying there, and sick for our home, you said that was a mistake; that we must stay because everything was changed. It is true that now everything is changed. You are now the many and we are the few, but we know that it is better to die fighting than to perish of the sicknesses."

And as Dull Knife spoke, one man rose from the circle—Bull Hump, the old chief's powerful elder son. Aloof, eyes burning in the duskiness, he stalked back and forth behind the Cheyenne chiefs, the knife at his belt naked, the ends of his canvas breechclout the only thing that seemed to stir in the anger of his lithe steps as he turned back and forth across the narrow room.

And when Wessells again urged the Cheyennes to go, to save themselves, Dull Knife remained firm. "No," he said in his soft Cheyenne. "I am here on my own ground and I will never go back."

Now NONE OF THE men or boys was permitted outside of the barracks, not even for necessity, but had to line up and use the little indoor facilities like some sick old *veho*. The women and children were taken out, ten, fifteen at a time, down past the stables, and then marched back by the guards with bayonets, the Indians walking one behind the other, shivering easily, now that they were always shut up. There was no singing, no laughing in games, no moccasin beading. The people just sat, with now and then a warrior rising to stalk back and forth, back and forth.

It was almost like the days back south when Colonel Mizner kept telling the Cheyennes they must move into the agency or the cannons would speak. The whites had worked more cautiously then, but now the Indians were locked in the log barracks, with bayonets all around and five companies of troops waiting to take them back south—five companies armed against forty-six male Cheyennes, from eleven to eighty years old.

Wessells was ordered to start the Indians no matter how cold the weather, but to provide everything possible for their comfort. He replied that they were resolved to die rather than to go.

On January 3, 1879, they were told they must now pack up to go. The busy little Wessells, his eyebrows frosted, his face red and raw, had come marching into the barracks in his buffalo coat. Through the interpreter he told his last orders. Once more the Indians said they would rather die. So he had their rations all cut off, and the firewood too. Then, turning, listening to no cry from woman or child, he went out into the cold, past the dark Indian faces at the window. At the corner, Wessells and his men bent as the wind hit them, the shoulder capes of their blue coats flying up. The captain strode rapidly ahead of the others, to report what he had done and to say he anticipated early submission.

But several days passed in darkness and gloom inside the waiting barracks without capitulation, and then Wessells ordered the water shut off too.

"Yes, even the drinking water," he said sharply to the hesitant messenger. "But say to them that, if they will let me have their women and children, I will take them out of there and they shall be fed and warmed."

The Indians made no reply to this, and when the soldier stammered it out a second time, they rose and drove him fleeing from the building.

The Cheyennes would surely have to give up now.

Chapter 15

ON JANUARY 9, THE DAY after the water was shut off and five days after food and fuel was stopped, Captain Wessells sent for Wild Hog, because he seemed to be the one the warriors had followed at Chadron Creek.

With Old Crow beside him to witness what the whites said so they could make no lies of it later, Wild Hog went slowly to the adjutant's building, which was packed with officers and soldiers. When Wild Hog said once more that they could not go south, the guards sprang upon the two Indians from behind, with irons ready for their hands. Old Crow was subdued first, and easily, but the powerful Wild Hog, grunting, with soldiers hanging to him all around, managed to bend and twist and get a hand to the knife in his belt as he lurched halfway out through the door. With a great roar to those over in the barracks, Wild Hog got his hand up. But as he drove the knife quickly downward against his own belly, the jerk of the panting soldiers deflected the blade, and the iron rings were snapped upon the Indian's wrists.

It was done very quickly. Wild Hog's cry would have been lost in the blowing wind, but a Cheyenne woman was out talking to her brother from Red Cloud who was trying to get her released to him. She saw Wild Hog burst out, with soldiers on him like dogs hanging to a grizzly, and the irons on his hands. She threw her head back and gave her cry of danger, high and thin on the wind.

Immediately there was great excitement in the barracks. There was a disturbance at the door and Left Hand came hurrying out. "I cannot see my brothers taken away with the irons on them and stay behind," he said, as he held out hands that could fell a buffalo with a thrown rock. The roaring inside increased; then there was drumming, dancing, and singing—singing of Cheyenne songs of war and strength and death.

"We have quite a powwow started now," Wessells said casually, as another company of troops trotted up to take over the guard. Then he rode after Wild Hog and the others to see that they were manacled foot and hand, safe in the tent that was the encampment's guardhouse.

AT THE PRISON, Wild Hog, Old Crow, and Left Hand were turned over to Lieutenant Chase.

"I am grieved to see what has happened," the friendly young officer said when he saw the men drink cup after cup of water.

"Ahh-h, it is a bad thing that has been done," Wild Hog finally agreed. "They all want to die up there now. They will break out tonight and die fighting."

This was repeated in the presence of Wessells at Chase's request, with Rowland interpreting and many soldiers around to hear, so everyone could know and be prepared, and there would be no excuse to butcher the people like fleeing buffalo. Then Wild Hog, Old Crow, and Left Hand were fed and told they could go back up there and call their families out.

Wild Hog would not go shackled into the barracks, but talked through cracks where the chinking was gone from the logs. After a while the wives of the prisoners and some of their small children were allowed to come out, and two very old women. But Young Hog stayed, and the elder of his sisters.

"Tell them all to come out," Wessells urged. "They will not be harmed."

Wild Hog said this, but held his hands out before him, showing the iron that bound them together. He received no reply. Rowland talked to Great Eyes through the window and asked him to let young Red Bird come out. The boy's angry voice answered for himself. He would stay and die with the rest.

Once Wessells tried it himself. "Dull Knife! Dull Knife!" he called. "Why don't you come out?"

Without waiting for the interpreter, the old chief answered that he could not, and knowing that this would not be understood by the whites, who would think it was the warriors who were against it, not the strong wall built by his own heart, he said it once more: "I will die before I go south."

WHEN IT WAS NIGHT, the Indians saw the post blacksmith come over the moonlit snow dragging heavy chains. He fastened them across the doors that led to the cook room and guardroom. The outside doors he fastened more securely too, one with an iron bar screwed down. Now the Cheyennes were shut in tight, not in a stone house as in Florida, but in wood that could be fired, burned to the ground. Some of the warriors said this among themselves, whispering it over a little glow of fire to warm their trigger fingers. The women had heard the hammering and huddled closer together in the darkness, their eyes where the doors were—watching for the coming of the guns. Perhaps no one would be allowed out anymore for any purpose. Perhaps they were meant to die here, humiliatingly, in the smell of imprisoned people. They were to die of thirst, trapped together like antelope in the pits, with no one coming to slit the throats, none to make it quick and easy.

One woman back in the dark could think only of the chained doors. She began to rock herself. "We are to burn!" she moaned, softly at first, then lifting the words louder and louder as she repeated them. "They will put fire to us all here!" she finally cried, thin and high, over and over.

The others tried to stop her, to quiet her, doing it gently, remembering that she had seen her baby thrown into the flames at the Sappa. But suddenly the woman sprang up and felt for a sleeping child in a mother's arms. Those around tried to hold her back and take the knife from her hand in the darkness.

"No, no! Help me!" she pleaded. "Quick, your knives—let us help the little ones here to die easily, before the burning soldiers come!"

Now the old men hurried to the woman, Dull Knife speaking so harshly to her that she crumpled down, sobbing. Brave One forced her against the wall and twisted her wrist back until her knife dropped in the darkness, while Bridge started his sleep chant and his slow rattle to quiet her. Gradually she settled down to the floor, her head in Medicine Woman's lap, and seemed to sleep, but the fear she saw was still there in the night and the silence.

So the Indians prepared for the going, only forty-three men, including the eleven-year-olds. They brought out five guns hidden in the holes and nine pistols too. Then they divided the cartridges as well as they could, and the lead and caps and powder. It was so pitifully little. One man had only two cartridges, and one of those so poor in powder it was only for the noise. Dull Knife sat down by himself when he saw how it was, brooding alone. Even the knives were divided, those with broken blades whetted to points these last few weeks. Four men had war clubs to use in the Sioux way, clubs made from wood out of the barracks, with spikes from the floor driven straight through until the points stuck out of each club head like spines from a great cactus.

Some were to carry a few things of the old times, old medicine objects, although the best they had brought, the chief's bundle, hung under the arm of Little Wolf. But they had the stone buffalo horn sacred to the Dog Soldiers, the lance heads of their tribal bands, a few pieces of fine old quillwork—something to remind those who might be left after tonight of the greatness of the past time; to remind them that they must always be Cheyennes. It was in this planning that Great Eyes took out his fine old shield, with the triple tail of eagle feathers and the claws of the grizzly, and called his nephew, the thirteen-year-old Red Bird, to him.

"You have no weapon, not even a broken knife, my son," he said. "You have grown too small in the hungry times to help other people much in the fast fighting of this night, so I give you this shield to care for. You know how old it is, how many arrows and bullets it has turned away. Take it, my son, and run hard. Pay no attention to anything, do not stop for a drink from this long thirsting or for mercy for anyone. Run very hard and keep hidden, and if you must die, die with your body protecting this."

The tall, thin boy stood shamed by this honor, feeling foolish and weak, unable to reply. Gently the man passed his long hand over the shield cover once more, as if to remember all its form and feel all the greatness of its power. Then he put the wide rawhide band of it over the boy's shoulder, and turning quickly, he went to stand at the blanketed window, looking for a long time where one could not see.

As silence settled over the post and there was only the far howl of the coyote and the slow clump of the sentries on the stony winter earth, one man after another went quietly to the women's end of the room, whispered a name here or there in the darkness, touching a braided head, perhaps, or a child fretting for water. Then at the signal they took their places at the windows, with Little Finger Nail to lead, but good men at the other windows too and one ready to get into the guardroom for a gun or two, if possible. Next there were a few men without guns but carrying children. These were the fast men. Whatever happened, some of these little ones must get away, some must live as seed, so the people here would not be lost forever. With these a few strong women were to run too, to rear any children that might be saved.

Older men without guns, like Dull Knife, would go with the women to help them, as was always their duty; someone to help Lame Girl too, for this last one of her family must not die easily. Behind these would be Sitting Man, where his healing leg would delay no one. Two young warriors would come last of all, to get everyone out, out and running.

Piva, so it was planned, and if it was not good, it was the best they could do with so little, and so many against them here.

When the stars that the white man called his drinking dipper were turned past the ten on the *veho* clock, there was a single shot from the dark barracks, the explosion like fire in the night as the guard fell at the corner of the building. The boom rolled loud over the snow in the still, cold moonlight, followed by three fast shots, so fast their echoes came back together, into a scattered firing. Two more soldiers went down and two in the guardroom were wounded, but the Indians had thinned the powder too much or there would have been more than the two guns they got before other guards were upon them. Soldiers poured out of the company barracks doors, looking white as the snow in their underwear.

The first Indians through the windows were followed by the rest in close file, like a string of bulky antelope leaping a bank. Then there was shooting from outside, dropping the Indians as they ran over the snow toward the river, the men shouting, herding the people together, hurrying along those with children under their arms, and the women with the saddles and the little food somehow saved. Below the stables five Dog Soldiers led by Tangle Hair dropped in a line behind a snowdrift to hold the soldiers back. They were coming fast now, many of them still not dressed but shouting and yelling, a trumpet blowing, the horses neighing and running, and the powder smoke stinging the eyes with the breath-biting cold.

When all the people were past the stable, all who would ever come, the five rear guards started jumping around, whooping, firing into the faces of the soldiers to hold them back a little longer, just a little longer. But finally the last of the five Dog Soldiers was down, dropped in the old-time honorable way—covering the flight of their people.

One of those who never came by was Sitting Man. His leg had broken again as he jumped through the window, so he sat there against a high drift singing his death song as a soldier put a gun to his head and blew his brains out, splattering them dark against the moonlit snowbank. Nine men were killed before the Indians reached the river and twice as many wounded, one—Tangle Hair—injured more than his feet could carry away. So he dragged himself out of sight and called to some soldiers who knew a little pidgin Sioux. They recognized him, took him to their quarters, and sent for the doctor. No other man was left wounded in the stretch of snow to the river. If they could not run, they died and were shot many, many times by the trigger-hot soldiers. Two women and some children lay back there too, and many were wounded.

The Indians that were left struck for the White River. Some fell flat there to drink, even if they died for it. The rest crossed a bridge and, turning, ran toward a sawmill, the faster men getting far ahead of the foot soldiers. Now more came on horses, and a few Indians stopped near the sawmill to make a little stand. When they were charged by a wide line of cavalry, the warriors broke and scattered, all except three men. These fell back a little and held again, desperate, wounded, but firing so long as they could lift themselves.

In the first half mile, half of the fighting men were lost. Women and boys grabbed guns and ran, not stopping to make any stand now. Dull Knife, Bull Hump, and their families struck off across a hard-crusted drift away from the others, with two warriors and young Red Bird, still carrying his shield, close behind. Because one of Dull Knife's daughters was hurt and had to be left, Little Hump had dropped back to help make a delaying stand. Another daughter stayed with him until it was too dangerous, and then she picked up one of the children of those already on the ground and ran with the women toward the bluffs.

The young men fought bravely with what was in the hand. Little

Hump had a pistol, and when he was hit, he threw it to another as he went down. Later some civilians came along, and he lifted himself from the snow and made one lunge at them with the broken-bladed butcher knife from his belt. Then Dull Knife's younger son, another of the Beautiful People, lay dead on the ground.

ALTHOUGH THE SOLDIERS were very close, most of the Cheyennes had to stop a little when they reached the pines and rocks at the bluffs, resting in their weakness, their clothing frozen and their eyes turned anxiously back upon their trail that bent down the valley of the White River. Even in the hazing moonlight they could see dark blurs along it, unmoving, with many troopers hurrying and spreading with the scatter of moccasin tracks. There were several quick shots, first the flash and then the sharp report of the carbine, where soldiers overtook the played-out and the wounded. It was hard to endure this, when those, too, were very close to the rocks, where no horse could have followed.

White Antelope was one who fell before the hurrying troops. He had stayed back to help his wounded wife and some other women, a baby under his arm like a sack. None of them could run anymore, even with the soldiers charging, and so White Antelope left the baby and turned upon the pursuers with his short knife. He fought there a little while before he was brought down, the women he was trying to protect all wounded now, two of them dead.

But White Antelope was still alive, and when the soldiers went on, he crawled to his wife and saw that the baby was dead and the woman dying too. They spoke a little, a few words in their soft Cheyenne. Then he stabbed her twice, very fast, with the poor knife, and himself, too, six times, but his strength now was too little, for when the wagons came to collect the wounded, they were both still alive, although their clothing was frozen to the bloody snow on the ground.

"The will to live runs very strong in these people," Dr. Moseley said at the post hospital as he stooped to listen for a beat in the man's torn breast, but now suddenly White Antelope was gone, and an hour later his wife also. Their names were added to the surgeon's list, the wounds tersely described: "GSW [gunshot wound?] in thigh and knife . . ."

As the soldiers spread along the bluffs to search out the hiding Cheyennes, Little Finger Nail gave his gun to another and slipped back, silent as the tufts of powder smoke that clung to rock and tree. He kept behind the soldiers, trying to find everybody he could, particularly old Bridge, the man who could slow the bleeding wound, bring healing sleep to the paining ones and the afraid. In a dusky place Little Finger Nail discovered five hurt women together in some rocks and pines, with three dead children on the shadowed, bloody snow. Among the women was the daughter of Dull Knife who had stayed behind to be with her brother, now down there at the river, his face turned to the moon. She was leaning sideways against a tree, somebody's baby tied to her back, hit too. The girl was still alive but unable to answer the whispered question, "Sister, sister—are you bad hurt?" But the warrior's propping arm felt how bad she was, almost falling to pieces as he lowered her gently to the snow and smoothed back her hair once. To this one Bridge need not be brought.

A mile farther along the band of bluffs Little Finger Nail saw a lone man afoot in a buffalo coat—the little Flying Dutchman who had shut off the food and everything from the children, the *veho* who had killed all those helpless ones back there. If there had been a gun in his hand, he would have shot. But it was good this way, for the captain had a small Cheyenne child in his arms, carrying it until some soldiers came along to take it to the post.

Carefully Little Finger Nail watched Wessells and a few troopers follow the tracks of two more Indians up to a high rocky place. There six soldiers were sent in. They found a Sioux woman and an old Cheyenne warrior. To the call for surrender the Indian charged out with his revolver, right into the firing guns. When they were empty, he still came on. The soldiers dropped back to reload and this time the Cheyenne fell, and Wessells and the rest went to stand around him in a dark little circle.

"A man so resolute should have lived," one of the soldiers said, and went to bring back the woman, who was climbing away. But she turned on him with a piece of stove iron from the barracks, fierce as the dead Cheyenne had been.

There was nothing Little Finger Nail could do here, and too many more soldiers were coming, their voices close on the frozen air, so he had to turn back. His feet were numb with cold and he would surely slip on some icy spot, perhaps set a loose stone rolling and be caught. But he must look just a little more, up very close along the bluffs, moving from shadow to shadow, making the winter-mouse squeak signals. But no one seemed alive anymore to hear. Then he saw that many of the injured up here would have to die, because their medicine man, the one who could heal them, was lost. Bridge lay dead, face down, a reaching arm out ahead of him. It seemed he had been crawling toward the women where Dull Knife's daughter lay. With his rattle out and ready, he had left a trail of blood stretching far behind him on the snow.

For a while Little Finger Nail stood in the shadow of the pines, his breath making a cloud around the blanket drawn up around his head. He looked down to the pale frosty points of light at Fort Robinson and to the lanterns moving here and there over the trail of the fallen Indians, and suddenly he knew that his warrior days were done. No longer could he think of this as a fight—unequal, but still a fight—one in which he and the other warriors would gather honors for boldness. Now he saw only that he must get the people away, hide them and himself with them, creep away like frightened mice into the crevasses of the frost-cracked rocks, hide and hunt for meat and shelter and healing—do anything now that would save lives.

Truly it had happened that he was no longer a man of the war-path. He broke the frosted breath from the blanket around his face, and holding a fold up over his stinging nose, he stumbled away to follow those who got up into the bluffs.

BY THE NEXT DAY thirty Indians, twenty-one of them warriors, half of all the men Dull Knife had, were laid out in rows down near the sawmill, and probably some frozen ones, particularly children, not found. The post hospital was filled with the wounded, mostly brought in by their young friend Lieutenant Chase. He had shot Indians—killing people for pay was his soldier work in the curious *veho* manner—but he did not shoot the wounded. For his gentleness with the hurt ones, the Cheyennes would remember him.

By daylight the scouts signaled of soldiers riding everywhere; up and down the White River, on the roads from Camp Sheridan, Fort

Laramie, and Deadwood, out past Crow Butte and around northwest on the Hat Creek road, the roads the Indians must cross if they were to reach Red Cloud or Little Wolf.

But it was almost six miles around to a place where the soldiers could get the horses up on the bluffs in the snow, so those on top were safe for a little while to bind the bleeding and build fires for the frozen hands and feet—safe for a little weary chewing at the dried meat left in the rocks for them by Woodenthigh. There was not much, for the Little Wolf people were poor too this winter, and with the soldiers watching they had to travel very light. Yet the meat helped put a little hope into the starved stomachs here, helped to keep some of the bereaved ones from running back to die against the guns.

Little Finger Nail went several miles along the top of the bluffs to see who was at the fires. There were some old people and even some small children, and young girls like Singing Cloud. Everyone at the silent little fires thought of those down there on the ground. No one asked about Dull Knife and the ones with him, or spoke of his dead son and daughter.

Daylight divided the Indians in their hearts between welcome and anxiety. The sun might warm their freezing a little, but it would light up every moccasin track, show it from far off. Always the Cheyennes had to think in these two ways, between the warmth of day and the shelter of night. Before the bloody path out of the barracks, it was the trail from the south, and all those other trails. But few had seen a night as bad as this one, or such a morning.

And now there were signals of new soldiers coming close. So the people had to rise and start over the broad white glare of tableland, without a stone or a tree for cover, before they struck the breaks toward the north and the sheltering streambeds that led away. Bent from their wounding and lamed by frost, leaning on each other, some having to be carried, one man with crutch sticks for a broken shin, thirty-four Cheyennes—children and old and all—moved out toward the timbered breaks of Hat Creek, the far pines a black smudging on the snow. The Indians went in a dark straggling file, winding around the softer drifts, their weary moccasins driven faster and faster as they left the protection of the broken bluffs behind.

Chapter 16

THE MORNING OF JANUARY 10, Wessells telegraphed Crook that in addition to the thirty Cheyennes killed they had captured thirty-five, and he would have many more before dark. The moccasin trail was as plain as a much-traveled road through the snow, with now and then a little blood from the injured, perhaps where one had rested, and the steady pinkening from bleeding feet.

"Only thirty, maybe thirty-five, many women and small ones," the Sioux scout Woman's Dress said as the trail led down into rough country. It passed close around the narrow foot of a hill and on over a rise. But then the Cheyennes had swung back on their tracks, like the jackrabbit watching his trail. When the last of the troops had wound single file past the hill and down into a creek bottom, bullets came from the timber of the ridge. A couple of cavalry saddles were emptied; two soldiers left on the ground like Indian bundles, very dark on the snow. Several horses were killed, one by the soldiers themselves as it fled from the volleying into the Indian entrenchments. Bullet Proof was hit in the shoulder trying to get the horse, a crucial thing now. Even one horse with which to find others was bigger than the life of any man here among them.

When the fight settled to a watching and sniping, Wessells ordered Woman's Dress up as close as he could get. "Find out if Dull Knife's there."

The scout stood with blank face before the officer, and when he was urged to go, he said it would be too dangerous. The Cheyennes were very angry. But finally Woman's Dress did go to a high place far out of rifle shot and built a little fire, perhaps as much to warm himself as to make signals. If he got any reply, he did not report it, but the troops heard a singing from the Cheyennes as the measured puffs of blue smoke rose from the fire into the lazy sky.

At last the grateful clouding of night started to come to the hill of worn people. Wessells had been so certain he would capture the Indians easily that he carried no rations and no blankets, so he left a row of decoy campfires, and the column returned to Fort Robinson. One of the Cheyennes, out watching, came back to say that everybody had gone, and it seemed that the soldiers valued the Indians here very little, thinking them so weak and foolish that they could be held by a few deserted fires.

"They know we are too hurt and played out to run without horses, and that our leaders are all gone. Now even Bullet Proof is bad wounded."

Some of the men butchered the dead cavalry horses, and the weary women moved about the fires roasting the meat for the hungry. The rest was stripped and hung on brush over the coals to dry for the carrying. The skins were dried too, some stretched over fire pits to harden for quick-made moccasin soles. Other Indians tried to ease the hurt and the frozen ones as well as it might be done here, with the girl Singing Cloud helping from the things taught her by Medicine Woman. Many needed it, with even Lame Girl hit once more.

Little Finger Nail, suddenly forced toward leadership, talked with Roman Nose about the horses they must have, at least one, somehow, to search for more. Without horses no one here would live to get away.

"It will be very difficult," Roman Nose said, looking into the clouding sky of night.

Yes, everybody would be watching now, and there were only two places left: the herd at Bluff station, far to the west on the Laramie-to-Deadwood trail, or perhaps some foolish people traveling the Hat Creek road, over north. The Black Hills trail would be soldier-guarded, they knew.

"There have been few tracks on the Hat Creek way this cold winter, and now all will be watching there too, with soldier guns riding along."

Still, it must be tried. But when Little Finger Nail took up one of the drying horse skins set aside to protect the watchers and started to go, some of the others wanted to stop him. It was dangerous to try this alone; besides, the soldiers might come to attack them here in the night and their strong men were so few.

The young Indian looked past the firelight to where Wild Hog's daughter was singing the west-wind lullaby to a wounded little girl. She was making the *woo-o, woo-o-ee* sounds of the wind through her frost-swollen lips, her breath drifting about her head in little fire-reddened clouds. No man could see this and sit here doing less than he might.

But before Little Finger Nail got very far, he was suddenly overtaken by three of the Cheyennes coming upon him from behind, swiftly over the creaking snow.

"You are not running away?" Bullet Proof demanded.

The young man brushed the detaining hands from him in the darkness. "Am I not a Cheyenne?" he asked, and walked on.

The four miles to the road were very far under clouds that would have been a gift from the Great Powers last night. Most of those who were dead back there in rows at the sawmill or who had crawled away to die in the rocks could have been saved by one cloud against the moon. With a little darkness they might have found horses and now be hidden with Red Cloud or Little Wolf. Little Finger Nail thought about this as he walked wearily over the hard snow, his new-soled moccasins feeling out the strength of the crust, treading softly.

Why was it that both times in this flight northward there was the bright moon to send the search upon them? It was not just the absence of the sacred hat, as some said. Nor did Little Finger Nail believe that all these troubles and the buffalo's vanishing happened, as the soured old ones believed, because the women of the Cheyennes had lost their virtue. Who could look at Singing Cloud back there, or Wild Hog's daughter and the rest, and think that their women were less now than the Great Mother of Tobacco had been, or any of the old-time ones. But if not that, then something else had been done wrong.

The Cheyennes must try to discover a new path.

It was as though a voice had spoken, and the young warrior stopped to look all around the darkness.

This new path the Cheyennes—a Cheyenne—must try to discover.

Little Finger Nail walked faster now. The thought that had come to sit on his shoulder would not be left behind, no more than a thorn in the moccasin can be forgotten. But he, Little Finger Nail, was only a young fighting man, a warrior.

"Only a warrior," he said aloud in his soft Cheyenne, as though defending himself.

Yet somehow this seemed no excuse tonight. Perhaps when this troubled time was over, he would go up to the Medicine Lodge mountain, off beyond the Black Hills, to learn the good path of the Great Powers. He would make all the fastings and the ceremonials as well as he could; he would vow a red blanket of his blood spread upon the ground at sun-dance time in humility and suppliance, pleading for a path of wisdom, pleading for the eyes to see what must be done.

It would mean that Little Finger Nail must become a plain man of the village, without the paint and feathers that pleased the young women; without the display and rivalry of the Dog Soldier lodge that pleased him so much, or the parades, the racing and gambling, the accumulation of horses and honors. All the wise ones of the Cheyennes had been simple men, and modest, their farseeing eyes not blinded by the brilliant prides and vanities close before them. They were humble men, wanting nothing for themselves, so their hands were always empty and ready to receive the gifts that came for all.

Suddenly the young Cheyenne found himself singing a new song:

> "Help me, Powers of the wind and the sky,
> And the earth in the cold nighttime.
> Help me get my people away!"

Little Finger Nail chanted the words over and over as he waited in the new horsehide robe whose harsh folds the women had not yet softened. He was squatting on a rise along the Hat Creek road, listening until every heartbeat seemed an ice-clumped hoof. Once he did hear something more. Hopefully he put his ear to the ground before him, but by the pattern of sound he could tell it was only a cow; far off, she seemed, and walking old and poor. Several times he heard wolves back in the direction of the White River bluffs, drawn by the blood and meat with the man smell.

Toward the clearing of dawn he returned in emptiness to the

camp. Most of the people were still as he left them, scattered every way, like rag bundles dropped carelessly, but feet toward the fires and warm, and with water and food and clean air at last. He walked among them, seeing the children asleep, Singing Cloud with two besides Lame Girl under her thin-spread blanket, the young woman so pure-cheeked that his weary heart jumped in his ribs. Only watchers and the bad-wounded ones heard the man's return; heavy sleep was upon all the rest.

But soon the soldiers would be back to their foolish little fires burned to white ashes down below there. "Come, my friends. It is time," he said, now the leader of them all.

IN THE PRISON TENT down at Fort Robinson, Wild Hog had watched the morning come after the night of shooting and cries up the river. He held a new blanket awkwardly about himself, the folds of such a garment not made for handcuffs. When the blanket was first given to him yesterday, he had thrown it down in anger, despising what had been withheld so long. His daughter must go out there half naked into the snow, his son too, and the old ones and the babies. None had new blankets.

"We only have half a dozen," the soldier who brought it had said seriously, knowing what was in the Cheyenne's mind.

Finally Wild Hog drew it up around him. Then, wooden and silent, he waited with Left Hand and Old Crow beside him, their braids unkempt upon their breasts in the sign of separation and sorrow. None of them spoke or smoked through the night, although there was plenty of good tobacco in their pouches now, and food and water for the taking, with a round-bellied army stove red from burning pitch pine. But every step that came between the sentry's tread on the snow brought Wild Hog to his feet, ready to make the sign for talking if anyone should enter the prison.

The first one was Captain Peter Vroom, stopping in soon after sunrise, before he left with the troops on the trail. A large man —larger in his buffalo coat—he brought frosty air into the tent, to hover like a fog a moment at the door. He shook the manacled hand of Wild Hog vigorously and hoped that the Indians would help him by telling all they could of the plans made for the outbreak. It would hasten the capture and shorten the suffering.

Wild Hog knew that this man had been in charge of the soldiers at Red Cloud's agency up around the Missouri last summer, and when the Sioux decided to move back near their old place down here he had followed, but he had not charged upon them. Now this good soldier chief, Vroom, was here, wanting to know the plans made in the barracks. Wild Hog stood before the officer, the top of his head higher than the big man's beaver cap, and had nothing to say. The others were as silent around the stove. So Vroom started to pull on his fur gloves again, the stomp of the impatient horses loud on the frozen ground outside. Still Wild Hog could not ask what had been done in the night of shooting to their sons and daughters, to all those people out there to whom they belonged. But before he left, Vroom said the rest of what he had come to tell Wild Hog. He said it with difficulty. "Thirty-five Cheyennes were recaptured during the night, and thirty found dead, so far."

When there was still no Indian word spoken, no asking of names, his face turned even redder than the cold had left it. "My God, man! Do you think I like this butchery?" he shouted. "There's a small girl not over six months old up there with her hip shot to pieces, and so frozen she will surely die, and she doesn't even whimper."

Then suddenly the officer jerked the door open and went out of the silence in the tent behind him. After he was gone, the Indians did not look to each other. Now and then one got up and walked back and forth across the little floor awhile, his feet soft on the earth, walking with urgency, as though even this short span of steps could hasten the moccasins out there in the snow.

JANUARY 10 HAD NOT been a good day for the few Indians who were still hidden in the snow of White River valley. An unwounded old man was found, with a baby tied on his back. The Indian motioned to a washout and went there with the soldiers, calling in Cheyenne. A woman and three children came out slowly, crying and afraid. These were sent to the post and the old man questioned. No, he knew nothing of anybody except this little party. They had run in any direction they could to get away from the soldiers. He knew nothing at all of Dull Knife, but that the question had to be asked brought a little softening to the man's bleak face.

Several more little trails could now be seen in the daylight, with lost blankets, lariats, and moccasins marking the flight over the wind-bared rockier slopes, and blood too. In a ravine a few soldiers found a cave with two Indians on guard. They were Dog Soldiers and would not surrender or retreat, and had to be shot. One, with a good Springfield carbine captured on the way north and thirty-eight rounds, tried to shoot very fast so he might use up all the cartridges before he finally rolled over on the sunlit snow. Behind these dead men stood the thirteen-year-old son of Tangle Hair, his young face defiant and desperate, his hands empty except for an old half-bladed butcher knife, trying to keep the soldiers from his mother, his sister, and a little orphan back in the cave, all three hurt.

"Give up, my son," the woman pleaded softly behind him. "Your father must be dead, and all the others. Let yourself and your small sister live. Give up!"

So the weeping boy threw the knife into the snow in surrender.

His mother came out keening for the dead ones who had tried to protect her. All the way in she keened until she saw the dark, still rows at the sawmill. Then she was silent, but at the hospital she could no longer be a proper Cheyenne woman. Crying with joy and concern, she ran to her wounded Tangle Hair, stretched flat on the floor but able to lift a hand to her. Then she seated herself at his head and drew her blanket over her face.

Toward sundown another troop of cavalry had come upon the tracks of five Indians and followed them into a broken bluff full of caves and holes. They shot into the place until everybody there was dead except a lone boy. When the firing stopped, he crawled out over the bodies and walked toward the soldiers, holding himself straight and steady in a bloody, bullet-pierced blanket for one more shot.

But it did not come. Instead, an officer rode up to shake hands with the boy and then went to see the dead in the hole, the boy's bleeding and torn relatives. Then he was taken up behind one of the troopers, hanging to the ribs of the man, whose gun still stank with smoke in its scabbard.

At Fort Robinson the boy was asked what the plans had been.

"We were to make for the big point of bluffs overlooking all the country. 'That is a good place for our bodies to lie,' the young men said to us."

Another detachment of troops followed the trail of four Indians, probably women, traveling openly in the day, trying to catch up with those in the far shooting over on Hat Creek. When the soldiers overtook them on the dusky tableland, they huddled together in the snow, as for warmth. Then suddenly they started to run and could have lost themselves on the shadowing plain, but an older woman called sternly to the others to hold themselves. Then she came toward the young sergeant, making the motions of surrender and the signs. "Have pity, we are freezing and hungry. No man is with us."

The soldier nodded, and so they were brought in too, and had to be held from running out against the guns of the guards when they saw all the captured and the wounded and frozen under the smoky kerosene lanterns of the hospital. There was a little keening, soft and hopeless, that did not stop when an officer came with the interpreters to ask what they knew about others who went out. And where was Dull Knife?

They said they ran to save themselves and knew nothing of anybody, the same thing that Dull Knife's wounded daughter here, and all the rest, had told.

Once there was real excitement at the post, when a little smoke was reported up toward a nearby ranch. It must be a large party to dare a fire so close in the bright noontime. Perhaps it was Little Wolf himself, joining the fleeing Indians, or even Red Cloud and his warriors.

A column of sixty troopers went out, their horses throwing snow as they charged through the drifts, an ambulance following, and a cannon ready. Cautiously the soldiers surrounded the bluff where the smoke hung along the rocks, and some went up over the top to cut off escape that way. After a lot of shooting into the hole, where a thread of smoke still rose, and a careful crawling to look over the edge, the pocket was found to be empty except for a deserted little fire. A lone Indian was finally discovered in a washout nearby. The sixty men charged him. One trooper was shot, and the Indian was hit many times. But with his right arm hanging worthless he kept firing, while the bullets spattered around him and sang in thin ricochet from the rocks. He was a hard man to kill, and when he finally went down he was ripped and torn as a charging grizzly stopped by many buffalo guns, the snow bloody all around. His unprotected feet were so frozen he could not walk on them at all, so he had built a fire to be warm; built it openly that he need not suffer long and starve.

The body was loaded into the ambulance, but dusk came on, and somewhere through the drifts to Robinson he fell out, and so none would ever know where this man lay.

Troops scouting many miles up the White River found the trail of two more Cheyennes. One got away, but the other's tracks, made by small narrow moccasins, led up the river on the ice. The soldiers found the little Indian, a girl of seven or eight, sitting on a snowbank playing with a pack of cards, all alone. She cowered down when the troops rode in close, flattening herself to the snow like a rabbit, her face hidden, the cards clutched to her breast. She was lifted up gently and taken to the post, but even there they could not discover where her people had gone.

"I was afraid," she kept sobbing in her soft hopeless way to all questions, and those around her were so dulled that they did not seem to remember. None of those lying here or sitting hunched over themselves seemed to know who her people had been or that they had ever known this small girl who had lived among them all her life.

Once the child looked up for a moment. It was when two boys were brought in from around Crow Butte. They would not say how they got there or anything else, just stood with their angry, hate-filled black eyes unwavering on the officer's face.

That was the day's fighting in the valley of the White River.

ON THE MORNING of January 11, Little Finger Nail's Cheyennes saw troops coming from far off, a long dark string hurrying across the snow. The Indians watched Wessells creep up with an interpreter, close enough to ask that the women and children be sent out to him. For that, Roman Nose put a carbine bullet close to his head, but not hitting. With all the helpless ones down there at the post, no soldier chief must be killed.

Part of the day the troops occupied a bluff west of the Indians, cutting off that direction of flight if the Cheyennes had to run. But all the troops could do was keep the Indians down in their holes. One soldier was killed accidentally while putting his carbine into his saddle boot. Vroom's horse was shot under him, and that of another man. Toward evening ten men were detailed to burn the carcasses, the wind blowing the stench over the hungry Cheyennes. Then the trumpet echoed over the snow and the troops started back to the post.

Now was the time to run to Red Cloud, less than a good night's travel for a strong runner, even in snow. But none was strong here. The Cheyennes moved as far as they could in the night, and the next day the troops came back. The column took up the fresh foot trail leading toward Hat Creek road, but a small bunch went out scouting and ran into two Cheyennes roasting meat from a yearling that the fleet-footed Roman Nose had caught with his rope while hunting horses. The Indians ran to rifle pits where Bullet Proof and another man were watching the back trail. The soldiers followed and got around behind them. Bullet Proof spent two cartridges bringing a corporal down. The rest of the soldiers charged and Bullet Proof was killed—the strong leader who had made medicine against the white-man bullets long ago. Because he was a brave man to the end, the others took the time to lay him out in a shallow place and arranged his braids on his breast. Then they had to stay hidden there in their holes, with fifteen soldiers left to watch them and to guard the corporal's body. The rest rode off on a fresh trail.

So DAY BY DAY the Cheyennes were pushed westward along Hat Creek bluffs at the edge of the high tableland that extended out of Wyoming in a long tongue between White River and Hat Creek. The fleeing Cheyennes came out of the bluffs at night to travel on easier ground, with so many worn out now and sick, the children coughing in fever. Somehow they still hoped for help; perhaps Red Cloud had heard what was done, even Little Wolf. But nothing came, no sign, no reply to the smoke columns they sent up. And yet they kept going.

Wessells readily admitted to the newspapermen now at Fort Robinson that his position was getting embarrassing: five companies of cavalry with fieldpieces to chase something like thirty-five or forty wounded, starved, and frozen Indians running over the snow, many of them women and small children. Six days was a long time, but it could not last now. They had so little ammunition that they fired only two, three shots a day.

"General Crook must be mad as a bee-stung grizzly," one soldier remarked.

"Yes, and Little Phil Sheridan's probably jumping around with some of the same bees in his britches," the man from the Chicago *Daily Tribune* agreed.

Certainly General Philip H. Sheridan, commander, U.S. Army, western division, would make somebody pay for this, now that the newspapers were turning their attack full upon the War Department, reversing their cry against the Cheyennes as bloodthirsty savages last October, and forgetting their charges of stupidity and graft against the Indian Bureau in September.

A Deadwood dispatch to the New York *Tribune* said, "Intense indignation is manifested throughout the whole country, even among the advocates of extermination, over the barbarous treatment of the Cheyenne prisoners at Camp Robinson near here, previous to the recent outbreak and slaughter."

However, when a reporter later asked Sherman for details of the massacre at Fort Robinson, the general of the army shouted, "Massacre! Why do you call it massacre? A number of insubordinate, cunning, treacherous Indians . . ." But President Hayes was disturbed by the reports of unnecessary cruelty, and so Sherman ordered a complete investigation of the entire outbreak and then escaped on an inspection tour of the Southern and Gulf posts.

Wessells got the expected telegram from General Crook. His superior officer sternly reminded him that he had received no details of the outbreak and so was sending his aide-de-camp out to investigate. Wessells hastened a report of his efforts. The Indians were certainly bound for Red Cloud and would be easy to capture after they got out on the wide, open country toward the Sioux. The dead collected at the post had all been buried, those bodies that had not been spirited away somehow. Nearly all the grown Indians were scalped.

There was still nothing definite on Dull Knife, reported killed the night of the outbreak but not found among the dead. The captive daughter spoke no word to anyone, replied to no questions. She lay on the barracks floor in her new army blanket and her bandages, making no keening for her dead brother and sister, as though asleep or dead except that her eyes were open, and her gunshot wounds and frostbite healing. The other Cheyennes would only say that old Dull Knife was a sick man when they left the barracks. The southern shaking disease still lived in him, and he had eaten nothing during the starvation time, putting the food into the mouths of the hungry children.

"They must live," he had said. "We are already dead."

As soon as the outbreak news was heard around the Sioux, an angry request came from Red Cloud, a demand that the widows and orphans of the Cheyennes be turned over to him. There was great excitement and mourning all over the reservation at this killing of their friends and relatives, and over the danger that soldiers might come shooting there too, any day. Old-timers advised the whites around the agency to keep indoors, away from any young Sioux who might want to make his bad heart good by spilling a little blood.

UP ON THE HAT CREEK, the soldiers forced the Indians to cling to the protection of the bluffs like game hiding from the hunter, and drove them westward, always westward, farther and farther from the Sioux agency over northeast. They were hurting them too, until now there was none left who understood the hiding of a winter trail. Now truly the Cheyennes needed their brave man, their Little Wolf. Some still tried to believe that he must come to save them, but the rest were certain he could not know what had happened.

Little Finger Nail thought about this and looked toward the gaunt and worn Singing Cloud. Nineteen men were left here, counting the boys, and fifteen women and children. Although they had strong women like Brave One and others with the fleeing children and with the wounded—so strong that their deeds would be sung and remembered—none among them was like the warrior woman Buffalo Calf Road. But what could a warrior woman do when there was no ammunition even for the men? Yet here, put into his palm, was the seed that might be all that was left of the Dull Knife people: a few strong young married ones with good children, some young men like Roman Nose and himself, and a few brave maidens. Perhaps they were really all that was left, and so it fell upon a man who was only a warrior to say how they could be saved now. The hunter must have his bowstring ready for any arrow.

Soon one of their young men was killed, his hands empty, making the peace sign. And a glancing bullet from that shooting also took the life of one of the women.

Chapter 17

ROMAN NOSE WAS the first to see the new soldiers coming from the west. He had been far out looking for a horse—so far he had to use skin from a long-dead carcass to replace the moccasins cut from his bleeding feet by the crusted snow and the ice. There was no sign of horses anywhere now, but from a high point he saw something in the west, a darkening there. While he watched, the blur separated itself from the horizon and moved out upon the tableland, coming fast—soldiers, and from a new direction.

Then he saw another column approaching from the west along the foot of the bluffs, a great row of wagons behind them. And the soldiers from Fort Robinson were riding out of the southeast again too. Quickly the young warrior sent his mirror signals in the sunlight. Between these marching troops the Cheyennes would be crushed like rabbits in the deadfalls. They must strike out across the flat country right away and hide their trail or be lost.

As soon as dusk came the Cheyennes piled up wood too, but in long narrow ricks into the little wind, so the fires would burn back slowly and a long time. Then they left, with Little Finger Nail ahead. For the guns there were only a few cartridges that had enough powder to carry the bullet from the barrel. Although the

Indians still had some lead and a little powder, these could not be used until a fight was started and some cartridges emptied for reloading. But Wild Hog's daughter and several of the older women knew how, if it happened that the men were all lost. It was a pact between them. They would fight to the end together, the end of everybody, and as hard as possible.

This last going from the entrenchments was a sad one, the women looking around almost as though they were deserting their lodges of a lifetime. Then one by one they slipped away past the watching pickets. Out from the bluffs the clouded night was so warm that the scattered snow patches were mushy, the top of the ground soft to the moccasin. The Cheyennes had to fan out and walk carefully, planting the foot on none of the snow and only on strong-rooted grass that would betray nothing of the light-footed passing. The hideout for the day was well selected before night came, a spot all could see far out on the flat plain to the northeast. If any got lost, they must remain hidden all day in some hole or weeds, beseeching the earth for the covering given the rabbit and the mouse.

So they started, but too many of the younger people did not know how to hide tracks in the darkness, how to feel out the ground with the moccasin before its mark was left behind. Some had to cross a wide prairie-dog town, with its piles of soft earth and almost no grass to hide the passing track. Before they were half gathered, it seemed very hopeless to Little Finger Nail. Still, soldiers had gone back many times when the people seemed lost.

At dawn the Indians were far out from the bluffs on the north side of a deep dry creek that was sometimes called the Warbonnet. They were hidden in a washout that lay like a scarring wound along the cutbank, thirty feet above the creek bed. With their knives, Brave One leading, they had dug under the frozen sides while the men made the little breastworks, the sod placed so the grass and brush looked natural. They left a deep place in the middle for the women, so no bullet could get in unless fired from right up on the edge. Here, where attack could only come from the ends or one side, lay the last of the Cheyennes that the army had been chasing for thirteen days, and for almost five months before that—eighteen men and boys here, fourteen women and children—crouching in a hole as wide as the height of two men, as long as four or five, and from the top of the breastworks as deep as a standing one. From a distance the hole seemed little more than a shadow along the high cutbank, with a shaggy scattering of brush and sage at the edge. If no track was seen to lead that way, the place of the Cheyennes would surely be missed. If it was found, one cannon shot could sing the last keening for them all.

As the morning grew, smoke rose from the soldier camps and drifted away, and then the troopers started to ride both directions along the foot of the bluffs and to scatter, looking for the trail. They fanned out for many miles, riding back and forth. This day the Cheyennes needed luck.

But it seemed this, too, was not a Cheyenne day. Soon there was a gathering of troopers in the prairie-dog town and then a separating again. So Roman Nose slid down from the little breastworks where he was watching, and without a word or sign the ragged, half-naked men began to paint themselves. Once more Little Finger Nail ran his hand over the picture book at his back to test its safety there. Then he went from one to the other of his hopeless, worn people, looking down upon their silence, touching a shoulder with his hand, perhaps a bowed head; going around them all, with no more than that even for Singing Cloud.

Now the soldiers were coming together, as the tracks of last night converged upon this place. Each man in the washout made his little medicine ceremony. The Dog Soldiers left here passed around the medicine horn of their warrior society. The women quickly smoothed the hair of the children and looked long into the faces of all those gathered in this last little hole. Then they sang the strong-heart songs, not loud, not to be heard outside of this little remnant, while the men went silently to their places up at the edge of the hole, the women who could help moving ready behind them, the rest deep down out of the way.

By now the scouts were coming along the little creek, already so near that the horses were lifting their ears and looking. Certainly the hiding place was seen, because the troopers prepared to charge them, and so the Cheyennes fired from the sagebrush bank. One horse went down, the soldier running until he fell too, his feet still going a little. Trumpets blew, more troops hurried in from both directions, with Wessells and Chase and the other officers, until their four companies were all there. So Little Finger Nail signaled the Indians back into the hole.

The Flying Dutchman dismounted his troops, divided them, and tried a hot fire from the three approachable sides for a while. But there was no sign from the hole in the middle of all that smoke, as though only the flying earth and weeds and brush were there to feel the bullets. Then Wessells set a detachment to keep the Indians down with a sharp cover of fire while the troops moved in from the three sides, some down along the creek bank, some up it, and a strong force in toward the hole from the land side. So a half circle of bluecoats pushed in upon the hole, the crawling soldiers only two, three steps apart, moving up here, then there, firing as they came through the patches of snow and freezing mud, puffs of smoke spitting from their gun muzzles, with streaks of fire in them.

At first there were a few shots from the Indians, but soon that slacked to silence and Wessells crept up under the bank. He motioned the firing stopped, and through the silence he demanded the surrender of the Indians. A corporal beside him, who knew a few awkward words of Sioux, tried to make them understand.

"*Hou! Washte!* Good!" the man yelled out, as though all the guns were still roaring. "Give up! Give up!"

But there was no reply, only an isolated shot or two after the soldiers resumed the attack. A second time the captain called for surrender, and there was still no reply, just a few more shots that hit so close that Wessells' men tried to warn him back.

"Look out, Cap! They're aplayin' possum!" an old Indian fighter bellowed.

By now most of the soldiers were so close that the Indians had to jump up above the breastworks to see them to aim. In this, one Cheyenne was hit, and then another. As they went down into the smoke and dust, others grabbed the guns. The women reloaded as they could, crimping the bloated cartridges to the bullets with their teeth as long as the lead lasted. No one spoke under the thunder of the guns, although now and then a woman or a child sobbed.

"If we die in battle, our names will be remembered," Little Finger Nail had said in the council down in the south country, six long moons ago. "They will tell the story and say, 'This is the place.'"

So this was the place. To this hole on a little dry creek they had come all that long and sorrowful trail.

The fighting went on for an hour more, with only a shot or two from the Indians, and finally even that stopped. When it seemed they were really done, Wessells and Chase led their troops to the breastworks, firing into the hole through the smoke and dust until there seemed nothing there at all. Then the two officers jumped up on the edge with revolvers cocked, ordering immediate surrender where surely none lived.

But there was one more shot out of the smoke of the hole. Captain Wessells staggered, struck alongside of the head. Chase helped get him back out of range, and now, as a foot charge was prepared from all three sides, there rose a clear, high song from among the Indians, the voice that everyone knew was Little Finger Nail, the sweet singer of the Cheyennes, singing his death song. In the middle of it there was the sudden cry of a small girl as a woman stabbed the child and then herself, and then more singing, all the others joining in now—the thin, high death chant of the Cheyennes.

At the sharp command, the troops charged the breastworks, firing a volley of a hundred shots down into the Indians, jumping back to reload, and up again, the guns a solid roaring. Finally they withdrew from the blinding, stinking powder smoke and watched it drift away from around the hole as from a great fire burning.

Then suddenly Little Finger Nail leaped out with a pistol and a knife. At the crack of a carbine he straightened up tall, and fell. Roman Nose, just behind, jumped over him as he went down, and fell too.

When the smoke had cleared away, the troops approached the torn breastworks, cautiously, reluctantly, and looked down upon the bodies piled like gray, bloody sacks of earth thrown this way and that upon each other. Lieutenant Chase went down among them and helped lift the Indians out. Seventeen men dead and one mortally wounded, crying that he wanted to die too, to be thrown back into the hole with his friends, all that was left to him now between the earth and the sky. Four women and two small children were dead too, among them Brave One, who had come through the blood of the Sappa to end in this place, and Singing Cloud, the beloved of the warrior Little Finger Nail, with the wounded child still in her arms. Under them seven women and children were alive but wounded, one woman close to dying. Wild Hog's lovely daughter was alive, bloody, haggard, and wild now, her neck drawn tight against her bullet-torn shoulder. And deep in the bottom, under everything, was a pile of dried meat three feet high, standing in a pool of the blood that the frozen earth refused.

"God—these people die hard!" a soldier said when he saw this.

At the edge, Wessells, looking into the hole, saw one of his officers reaching to a little girl who was peering fearfully out of a pocket dug back under the breastworks. It was the six-year-old Lame Girl, looking imploringly toward the Flying Dutchman, whom she had seen many times in the barracks. She let herself be picked up and taken to him, holding out her hands as children learn to do, for he was not an unkindly man. But as he took her, his palm felt a stickiness under her arm, a new gunshot wound, this time in her side.

And when they turned up Little Finger Nail where he had fallen face down outside of the breastworks, they noticed something on his back—the canvas-covered book* in which he had pictured the stories of the fights he had and the coups he counted. But two .45-70 Springfield bullets had gone through it, the blood-soaked holes as close together as overlapping fingertips.

Chapter 18

Two days after the wounded captives from the last hole were brought to Fort Robinson, there was a sudden shouting through the post and a running toward headquarters. An Indian was coming down out of the bluffs. It was a Cheyenne woman with a child on her back, leading one not much larger by the hand. She staggered

---

*Now in the American Museum of Natural History, New York City.

a little and let a trooper take the two little ones under his arms. She motioned that the children be fed and she went to sit down at the barracks door.

Between soppings of bread and molasses she said she had been in a hole in the bluffs up there. The night of the outbreak the young men drove her through the window. She had no relatives left, and no man, so she carried only her bundle. Down around the sawmill she saw these children among the dead ones. With the two she could not run very far, so she flattened down in the brush of the river. She had a little tallow hidden, and after the soldiers quit looking, she took the children up to a hole where they could have a little fire in the night. She knew nothing of anyone else. She would have come in sooner, but it seemed all the Indians were dead and she was making the mournings for a lost tribe.

Wessells quickly had the woman sent away to the other captives. She was an embarrassment, with the board of officers ordered by General Crook gathering to investigate the Cheyenne outbreak.

Officers, enlisted men, civilians, and the captive Cheyennes were all called before the board. The terrified Indian women spoke so low in their soft Cheyenne that they could scarcely be heard, or did not reply at all, and none here could press them. The captive men were brought in from the prison tent—only nine men left of all the Dull Knife band, unless the chief and Bull Hump were still hidden somewhere.

Wild Hog and the others talked readily enough of everything except the killings on the Sappa and the Beaver. But when the Cheyennes were asked about Little Wolf's camp, they shook their heads. He had said he was going north the night they separated at the Platte. No one had seen Dull Knife. It was said he died in the fighting in the bluffs the first night.

"Then where is his body?"

The men smoked in silence, their pipes guttering in hidden thought. They knew about nobody except the people here, Tangle Hair finally said. Of the one hundred and forty-nine brought to the barracks here seventy-eight people were left, with only a few men among them—all they could be certain still lived of the two hundred and eighty-four who had left the south country six moons ago.

"Now there are so few, we beg you spare this remnant."

SEVERAL NEWSPAPERMEN WERE around the post and out with the troops in the final annihilation. Their stories doubled the public anger of two weeks ago and brought loud demands for court-martial of the officers who used cold and starvation to subdue these brave savages and then harried them through the winter snow to the last horrible butchery.

The newspapers told too of the dividing, when those who need not go to Kansas to stand trial for the killings on the Sappa and Beaver were loaded into wagons for Red Cloud—forty-eight women and children, including the boys, a few badly crippled men, and the old ones, fifty-eight Cheyennes in all. At last, after the long waiting for permission to go to Red Cloud, the remnant of the Cheyennes was to be taken there.

There was soft keening for all those who could not climb into the waiting wagons, for the living as well as the dead. Then the wheels broke from the frozen ground and the little queue started down the White River road to the encampment where Wild Hog and fourteen other men were in irons. Here a few more women and children would be loaded in too, all except those who must go south with their men for the murder trial. These left-behind ones were gathered on a little hill back of the camp, and as the wagons started away toward Red Cloud they set up a wild wailing and gesticulation, Wild Hog's wife leading them. Keening in sorrow for her lost son, she threw her bony, shriveled arms in supplication to the Great Powers, whose winds blew her loose mourning hair and her rags as she moved in a sad dance of despair, half a dozen others circling with her, naked butcher knives flashing in the sun.

A Sioux scout was ordered to take Wild Hog's wife to her tent and search her for weapons, besides the knife she surrendered. He had the Indian's reluctance to touch a woman not his wife, and when he finally made a move toward her she struck her breast quickly with both hands, half of a pointed scissors hidden in one, and in the other a table fork with only the sharpened middle tine left. She stabbed herself several times more before she could be disarmed, blood streaming down upon her moccasins. Even then she broke loose and tried to kill one of her small children and stamped on another, fortunately with the soft soles of Cheyenne moccasins.

Before she was quieted with morphine, there was a shout from the prison tent. Her husband, the powerful Wild Hog, lay in blood too, unconscious, stabbed four times about the heart although his hands were ironed.

"It seemed best to him, when he is to be killed by the whites. If he dies here, his wife and children can go to their relatives with Red Cloud," was all Tangle Hair would say.

A reporter from the Chicago *Daily Tribune* went to see Wild Hog. The chief's eldest daughter lay on the bare ground of the prison tent, sleeping heavily from her wounding and the exhaustion of the long flight over the winter bluffs. She had crept close to the fire, her face almost in it, as though she could never be warmed again. The white man looked down upon the worn and haggard girl who had been so lovely, and then to her powerful father, lying head to head with her. Wild Hog breathed heavily and moaned under the morphine, his handcuffs rattling as he tried to move. The attendant gave the chief another pill and spoke kindly in some pidgin Indian to him. Wild Hog's wife, her eyes wild and tortured, sat at the tent door as protector, an old gash above the right eye swelling her face, her stabbed breast making her hunch awkwardly. Suddenly the wounded girl awoke with a low moaning of pain, and seeing the soldier guards through the smoke, she screamed as though she were once more in that last murderous rain of bullets in the hole out from Hat Creek bluffs.

A week later more wagons started from Fort Robinson, carrying Cheyenne prisoners to a special railroad car that would take them to Leavenworth, Kansas. Among these were Wild Hog, stooped and ponderous in his unhealed wounds, Tangle Hair, Left Hand, Old Crow, and three others with their families, most of the men still in irons. At the stop in Omaha, and all along the way, Wild Hog held out his manacled hands for the crowds to see. But there was no Little Wolf or Dull Knife to exhibit at any station. Little Wolf was reported to be many places between the Platte River, where horses were being stolen as always, and the Canadian border, where raiders from Sitting Bull slipped down to hunt and pick up anything they could.

"Dull Knife is dead," the captives were now saying. "He was killed in the fighting of the first night."

But none told where his body lay.

MOST OF THE SOLDIERS had ridden away from Fort Robinson to look for Little Wolf. Then one afternoon an Indian boy, young Red Bird, came hobbling out of the bluffs toward the house of a man he knew down the river from the post. The boy was so starved he seemed no thicker than the forked stick he used as a crutch for his dragging leg, but on his back was a painted rawhide case. Inside was the shield of Great Eyes, which he must protect even in dying if need be. It seemed he was very young for such a trust, and very sorrowful, for all the other Cheyennes must surely be dead.

No, he did not know where Dull Knife was; he knew nothing.

By this time the Sioux around Pine Ridge knew. Dull Knife had left the barracks with Pawnee Woman and the daughters. Behind him was Bull Hump with his wife and a child and his father-in-law, Great Eyes, and the young Red Bird with Great Eyes' shield on his back. There were three young warriors along to help in the flight. Strung out but together, they got through the first run past the river with only one of the daughters hit, but she cried for them to go on, go on. That was when Little Hump stayed back to hold off the soldiers, close enough to hit now, and another daughter stayed too. The rest could not wait to argue this, but had to go fast to get the old chief away. North of the river they turned from the direct path toward the bluffs to a frozen drift that had no friendship for tracks. From there they moved up a shallow gully, stooping low as they ran, keeping to the moon-glistening, hard-crusted snow. At the bluffs they slipped carefully through the shadows, clinging along the rock face as much as they could so no snow would be touched, no track remain. Once, when the soldiers came close, there were a few hasty snow steps that they could not hide, and one *veho* shouted, "Here's a trail, leading off this way!"

So Great Eyes turned back as a rear guard. Stumbling out into the moonlight as though seriously wounded, he made a great whooping and singing as he dodged awkwardly back and forth among the boulders and brush, moving away from the others, firing an old revolver loaded with very little powder, but making his defense last as long as he could, until he was finally dropped dead on his face. By then there was no picking up the tracks that his moccasins had covered and confused. So the others got safely away, except that young Red Bird was hit by a glancing bullet and dragged a leg.

Dull Knife led them to a great hole in the rocks that he recalled from his young days in fights with the Crows, a hole that showed no opening at all two steps away. The soldiers never found the trail again, and so these Cheyennes were safe as long as they stayed inside. They almost starved, waiting for a good time to come out.

Ten days later the soldiers were all moving out in long columns to the western Hat Creek bluffs, as Bull Hump could see from a hidden place high up. The snow had melted to patches, and before it was all gone, there would be more to show their tracks. Now, if ever, they must start for Red Cloud's people at the Pine Ridge Agency. All but Red Bird. He could scarcely walk with his forked stick; he could never get over the long miles of the high open country, where they must go very fast.

So the boy sat in the back of the cave alone, singing a strongheart song to give himself courage as Bull Hump led the others away into the night. They moved very carefully, traveling in the moonless dark, setting no moccasin down in snow or soft earth, keeping to the high, drier, well-grassed slopes, but where the cold burned the breast, and not even a bush offered protection.

"It is better to be very cold than dead," the blunt-spoken Bull Hump told his little daughter when she whimpered in the freezing night wind.

So long as the sick old chief had the strength to walk, they kept going, and when he began to lag, they hid in one little draw or another little gully for the day, in places so shallow and bare that none would think to look for such foolish hiding. They ate any roots and buds they could find, two rabbits Bull Hump snared, some sinew one of the women had hidden, and finally the tops of their moccasins, chewing the rawhide like buffalo working at their cuds. Then one night, half a moon after they left the cave, when Wild Hog and the other headmen were already far on their way to the stone prison at Leavenworth, Dull Knife reached the place of Gus Craven, a man he recalled from around the old Red Cloud Agency near Fort Robinson. Married into the Sioux, Craven was a man known as unafraid, and so not one to be feared. This *veho* cried out when he saw the bare, frozen, and bleeding feet of his old friends, their gaunt and sunken faces. His wife made the little sorrowful wailings as she fed them hot beef soup and fried bread, and buckets of coffee with sugar in the bottom of the cup. The next night they were taken to their interpreter friend Rowland. So these people were slipped in with the Sioux, their presence to be unseen, their names unspoken.

Dull Knife was taken to a lodge set up for him under a little bluff out of the way on Wounded Knee Creek, with wood and meat, and blankets for the long sleeps. When he had rested two days and eaten well at his own fire, he finally demanded to know what had been done down there by the chasing soldiers. So he had to be told how few were left besides the handful of prisoners taken to Kansas. His wounded daughter was brought to him, and one of the women who had lived through that last day in the hole. Slowly, speaking as with lips still frozen, they told what they had seen.

Once the old chief rose in a towering rage. "I am an empty man!" he cried to the Great Powers. "I have become so weak that I cannot even die with my people!"

Seeing his sorrow, everyone slipped away, some afraid of a blaming word, afraid of seeming to blame Dull Knife for splitting off from the rest of the Cheyennes down there north of the Platte because he trusted to his old-time wisdom.

After a while Dull Knife went to sit up on the bluff. A long time he sat up there, silent, alone, without his pipe, his hands hanging helpless between his knees, as helpless as in the cold iron shackles of the whites.

Chapter 19

In Lost Chokecherry, when the freezing moon, the white man's December, was past, the cold became heavier, and the thermometer dropped toward forty below zero. It was a time for fires and sleeping, but still the troops rode the hills after Little Wolf.

The ice holes in the lake had to be chopped deeper than the

length of an arm for water. The snow was hard as stone; the air burned the lungs and settled in frost on the cowhide and elk robes, thick about the face. Most of the time the Indians kept close to their holes in the hillside, squatting over their little fires, a stick at a time laid on the coals to char before it burned, so there would be no smoke to cling along the slope. The few horses hidden in the brush lived on cottonwood branches so cold they could hardly gnaw them.

Finally the January thaw came. It was still no weather for raiding, the horses too weak to go against the grain-fed ones of the ranchers, and so Black Coyote and Whetstone held themselves quiet. But Little Wolf knew their thoughts and knew he must move his people before those men started trouble. Yet first he must find what was done up at Fort Robinson.

After six moons of waiting, his fire was finally freed of Thin Elk. Thin Elk's going was still funny to some of the old ones, and it would have seemed funny to Little Wolf at another time, although his women found their fire a very quiet place now, particularly Pretty Walker, who liked very much to laugh. After Little Wolf made his hard decision to do so unchiefly a thing as drive out a guest who brought ridicule to his lodge and his person, Thin Elk went without urging or one shout of dissension from anyone.

Then the news came of the outbreak at Fort Robinson. A signal of the sorrowful news reached the farthest watchers around Lost Chokecherry, a mournful howling signal, repeated over and over, as from an old and worn-out wolf. Someone took a horse out so the messenger need not bring his moccasin tracks close, and brought him to the big brush circle, where all could hear. His feet were stone from freezing, and his fumbling hands too. In the duskiness they saw that his face was twisted with a raw scarring wound from a bullet that went in at one cheek and tore a hole out on the other side of the nose, pulling the lower eyelid down so it seemed it could never close again.

At last the wounded messenger spoke in a hoarse un-Cheyenne voice. Painfully he made his first words since the bullet broke his upper jaw more than ten days ago. Several times he stopped and tried to swallow soup from the horn spoon Feather on Head held for him, but it seemed his throat was almost closed from the wounding. As he warmed a little, he began to tell of the freezing, the hunger and thirst in the barracks, of Wild Hog, Left Hand, and Old Crow dragged away in handcuffs.

"Ahh-h!" the listening men said in their soft, subdued Cheyenne. "Ahh-h!"

He told what he could of the outbreak too, the bad luck of the moonlight as clear as day, the running, the falling from the bullets, the women and children like bundles of old rags scattered on the frozen snow.

"Ahh-h!" the listening people cried too, making a murmur of horror, while Old Grandmother's voice rose in a keening and then stopped to hear the man's difficult words, coming from his mouth slow as stones falling.

He had been one of those sent to get horses, but the bullet through his face made him dead for a long time, so he was almost frozen when he awoke in a brush pile in the snow, where he must have crawled after the hitting. When he came out, he saw a lot of people laid in a row near the sawmill—men, women, and children dead in the snow there, thirty-three in all, and no telling how many had died since, with the soldiers hunting through every snow-filled draw and canyon. So few men left and not one horse to get the helpless ones away.

The listening mothers drew the children closer, looked quickly around the circle of darkness, and then pushed in with the others around the man, forgetting the cold of the night, waiting. Slowly he began to list the dead from that first running. Here and there a little keening started, low, private, for there were griefs all around now. Forgetting her maidenly reserve, Yellow Bead edged herself in close, but then she became afraid and began to shrink back until she found herself up against young Spotted Deer, always nearby. He was holding his elk robe open to gather around the girl, not as in courting, but to hold her against the grief when the name of Little Hump came, as it would, for Little Hump was a very strong young man.

But when the name was reached, Yellow Bead was steady as a tree. Quietly she went to stand beside her aunt and joined her voice with the old woman's in the soft keening cry.

So the man recited the names that would perhaps never be spoken again. But even before the story was done, Black Coyote had slipped away, signaling others to follow. "We have listened to Little Wolf all this time, and now our relatives are dead up there on the ground!" he cried in fury to them. "We cannot wait longer, my friends; we must go out and avenge this Cheyenne blood!"

LITTLE WOLF AND Black Crane and the others sat late over the sorrowful news and the keening of the women. "The Indian never caught is the Indian never killed," Black Crane said, in the words of his head chief, but tonight there was no satisfaction in them. Many had died and many more would die up there in the snow, yet there was nothing anyone here could do, no help they could bring. "Probably the only saved ones will be those held with the irons," Little Wolf said slowly. Dull Knife and the rest of his family would surely be hunted down. It was a thought to twist the heart.

Before they went to their sleeping robes, Woodenthigh was sent to Red Cloud for news. Then at the first dawn of morning Old Crier ran through the camp. "Wake up!" he called. "Make everything ready today. We start as the sun goes to his sleep!"

As the people wound out of the valley toward the low yellow sun, they looked back sadly into that peaceful place. They were going out to be chased again, and they had the reminder of all those dead up on White River. Yet none here was as terrified as when they came fleeing to this lost spot. It had been a wonderfully healing thing, this quiet good life in a quiet good place—the best three moons of many years. It was true they had been poor in dress and in the kettle, with the shadow of the soldiers always upon them. It had been a poor time but a healing one.

"We are peaceful, my friends!" Little Wolf told his young men before he let them go. Those with Black Coyote had waited for no advice or permission.

Yet peacefulness would not be enough, and the women saw they must be prepared to run when the warrior woman Buffalo Calf Road was sent ahead to lead them, instead of one of the older ones put in the place of honor. Many of those riding behind looked to her in pity because her man, Black Coyote, had become so strange, flying into such angers as no Cheyenne should permit himself. He was always drawing his gun against people, even Little Wolf, when the chief tried to stop him from raiding.

"You will get us all killed, my son," Little Wolf had said quietly, and turned his back upon the gun held against him. The whole camp had been silent as a stopped breath, but the younger man did not shoot. Now, almost three moons later, it was plain that of them all, Black Coyote had found no quiet, no peace in Lost Chokecherry. He was out already, since early last night, avenging, making trouble.

Only one good ride away was the Snake River soldier camp often used this winter, with perhaps five well-mounted companies of troops there now, and surely more coming. Besides, with the snow drying off, the field glass lost by the watcher up at the lone tree surely must be found. With the plain mark of the troops in the south country, it could not have been dropped by some Sioux hunting party from Spotted Tail—only by the Cheyennes.

But Little Wolf must have horses, so the foragers were out. Of the young men only Spotted Deer asked to remain to help the women and children. His grandmother was so old and afraid.

Black Crane considered this, looking toward Old Grandmother, with her little bundle ready before all the others. Yes, they needed some young men along. Black Crane also noticed that Yellow Bead was riding Spotted Deer's new horse. Not that it was an acceptance of him as her future husband; one did not make a courting in such a time of grief.

So Spotted Deer joined the rear guard, the direction from which the soldiers would probably come, although it was hard to give up the chase for the horses or the raiding that Black Coyote had promised.

IN A FEW DAYS news of more Cheyenne depredations filled the talk and the newspapers from frontier saloons to Washington and across the seas. A rider sent with a dispatch to the Platte River said Indians had chased him fifty miles. He confirmed the killing of two men on January 23 at the Moorehead ranch on the Niobrara, by thirteen Indians, and reported two more white men shot about the same time. All the horses along that stretch of river were swept away. Five companies of soldiers left their camp on Snake River to take up an Indian trail going southeast with three, four hundred horses and signs of women and children along. But the trail scattered. They followed its general direction down the Loup River in a gathering blizzard, then returned to the Niobrara. There was great suffering among the troops—the weather was thirty below zero, and the Indian trail was lost under the deep drifts.

There was news too of a bull train surrounded east of Flint Butte on the Fort Randall trail to Fort Robinson. All the extra clothing and provisions were taken, and in return the Indians gave the whackers a silver watch stolen from the Moorehead ranch and laid seven silver dollars into a palm. There were about a hundred in this party, it was reported, but no women or children. Although the Indians carried Winchesters and Sharps rifles, with plenty of ammunition, they were friendly and asked which way was north.

Old-timers laughed at this story. There were not a hundred men among all the Cheyennes when they left the south in September. Little Wolf could have told them he had only thirty-nine, and these were split into three parties, with fewer than four hundred horses altogether, and surely no Indian had to ask which way was north.

Then a Sioux messenger sent by Woodenthigh brought the story of the last fighting along the Hat Creek bluffs and the hole where so many died. All those strong young people killed! Yes, and at Fort Robinson the leaders and their families must go south in irons to be called murderers, perhaps given the *veho* hanging. Wild Hog, Left Hand, and the others.

Ahh-h! Wild Hog, the big, judicious man who never liked trouble at all. And Left Hand too, the good brother-in-law, the father of the strong young warrior that Little Wolf had selected to bear his own name, the great hunter who never wanted to harm anyone, not even an enemy Pawnee! Now he was dragged away in irons to die on a crossed pole. For a moment Little Wolf was more angry against the whites than Black Coyote could ever be. But because he was the head chief, he had to quiet himself. To avenge this would bring death to more Cheyennes, and when those were avenged, still more, and soon there would be none.

The messenger reported that the bad-hurt ones and the women and children had been taken to Red Cloud at last, now that the families were broken. Wild Hog had tried to kill himself, so his family could go there too.

Yes, Wild Hog was the man to do such a thing for his sick wife, but these were indeed bad times when it must be so. And Dull Knife?

Of Dull Knife he knew nothing, the Sioux messenger said, looking down into the fire before his crossed knees. Some of Spotted Tail's Sioux were traveling west to make a visit with their relatives under Red Cloud. It was said that Little Wolf should come to visit with them at their camp near White Lake on his way north.

"*Hou!*" Slowly Little Wolf cleaned his pipe, put it into the beaded bag, and arose.

LATE THE SECOND EVENING after Dull Knife reached Red Cloud, he, with Pawnee Woman, Bull Hump, and three young men, left the lodge on Wounded Knee. They were met by Spotted Tail's people going west. While the Cheyenne warriors went to the young Sioux Dog Soldiers, old Dull Knife was taken to a lodge a little to the side. Here the old man settled gratefully to his smoking, still loose-haired and in the rags of mourning for Little Hump and the daughter lost. After a while there was the sound of horses on frozen ground coming out of the dark.

As the hoofbeats neared, Pawnee Woman slipped out to take the horses. There was a scratching on the lodge flap, and Little Wolf stooped into the fire-reddened lodge. He stood for a moment looking over to the older man seated in the proud place of host, behind the nest of coals, to the ragged hair of his sorrow, his body melted of fat as a hibernated bear's.

"I greet you, brother," Little Wolf said. "It is good to see that you got away."

At the old man's silent gesture he went around to sit beside him, silent too as the pipe was new-filled and the fragrant smoke drifted upward through the smoke hole to the stars.

Once more the lodge flap lifted, and Pawnee Woman and Little Wolf's two wives came in quietly and settled to their places. Pawnee Woman drew some coals closer to warm their hands, and passed them bowls of hot soup from the kettle.

After a long time the two men began to speak. "Come with us, brother," Little Wolf urged. "Come to the Yellowstone. Our moccasins are already on the path north around the Black Hills. We have good horses ready for you."

"No, I cannot go."

"Not even after all these dead ones?" Little Wolf wanted to roar against this man. But it could not be done, and so he admitted what he had known from the first. Shifting his chief's bundle under his arm, he made the solemn *hou* of approval. "You are a good man, my brother, a lone one left from the old times. It is a hard road for you, yet perhaps even I would not have you turn your good face from it now."

"But you—what will you do with your people?" Dull Knife asked.

"We are going north, as I say. Some are already encamped toward the forks of the Cheyenne River."

"You will have to go with those soldiers up there. You cannot hide without the buffalo to feed you. They will find you anywhere." Dull Knife spoke bitterly, and in this bitterness was the measure of the great loss the whites had cost this moderate man.

"Yes," Little Wolf said slowly, "the soldiers will find us, it is true. The soldiers must find us soon or we will be very hungry."

"Then you must accept the word of the one to whom you surrender, take the word into your open hand and clasp it without using the eye that sees too far ahead. You will have to believe he speaks straight when he says the women and children will not be shot after you have given up your guns."

It took Little Wolf a long time to answer this, the long-gathered sorrow stirring deep within him.

"I will try to make it so the cost will seem very great to the soldiers if they shoot us. It is the best I can do now."

It was the best, but it was not good. That Dull Knife knew.

SLOWLY NOW THE Little Wolf Cheyennes moved northward over the new-fallen snow. The band looked like a war or hunting party, without travois or lodge, only the rolls of hides across the women's horses for the little night shelters. The cold Big Moon Month, February, lay over all the earth as they pushed on, heads bent into the north wind, the cow and elk robes tied as close around them as could be, the manes and tails of their horses blowing back.

No soldiers chased them now, and there was little raiding. The bad heart of Black Coyote was apparently made a little better by the cowboys that his party killed on the Niobrara, and although he kept out of the way of Little Wolf and Black Crane, who still policed the moving camp, he was back with the rest.

Little Wolf rested his people three fine sunny days near Bear Butte while he went up there to fast and meditate. Off by himself on an isolated point the third day of the fast, the chief looked out over the snow-patched prairie for one whole sun's passing, and threw his eyes back over all the long Cheyenne trail to the time when the people first came past here on their way to the Yellowstone. The Cheyennes had seen their greatest days as a people since then, and now this sorrowing, with all their hearts on the ground. But with wisdom they might pass this trial also—this hard Cheyenne autumn and its frozen winter that was the time of the *veho* foretold by Sweet Medicine so long ago. Beyond it must be a new springtime, with grass for the horses, with the geese flying north overhead and children laughing in the painted villages—a springtime when the Cheyennes were once more a warm, a well-fed, a straight-standing people.

After a while he took the chief's bundle from under his tattered old shirt, the bundle that was brought by Sweet Medicine. Then Little Wolf made a song:

> "*Great Powers, hear me,*
> *The people are broken and scattered.*
> *Let the winds bring the few seeds together,*
> *To grow strong again, in a good new place.*"

But as he sang, the sky grayed and he knew that there would be more snow and that he must get his camp to a protected canyon before it came. Slowly, stiffly, the man arose and went down to a little stream where an evening snowbird watched him drink.

AT FIRST IT SEEMED good, with the storm only a short wet snowfall. Another whole week they traveled toward the Little Missouri River, with almost no sign of white men. But the buffalo trails were gray in weeds, the game scarce and thin from the bad winter.

It was then that Black Coyote brought in some stock branded with the U.S. Army sign. There was a council over this grave and dangerous act, and Black Crane as keeper of the peace was instructed to order the stock taken back.

"We only steal and fight when the soldiers come fighting us," Black Crane said. "Do you want the soldiers to ride against us here like those down at Fort Robinson, shooting into our women and children until nothing moves anymore? Return the horses where you found them, my friend."

"I get the stock I need as it pleases me!" the violent Black Coyote roared in reply.

"You are endangering the people. You must obey commands of the council and take the horses back or you will be whipped."

"No one will dare! I will kill the man who strikes me!" Black Coyote shouted, drawing his revolver as Whetstone came running up with his gun too.

Black Crane lifted his pony whip and struck Black Coyote over the shoulder with it. This time Black Coyote fired, and the old chief fell, shot through the heart, at once so still on the hard cold ground that it seemed he had been dead a long time.

Suddenly men from all directions were there, divided into two factions, guns and knives out against each other, with only a finger's slipping on a trigger needed to begin the butchering. But already Old Crier was running up to intercede, the pipe held out before him, the sacred long-stemmed pipe that demanded peace.

"Peace?" Black Coyote cried out, his voice roaring through the silence, and with its echo he shot again. As Old Crier went down, Black Coyote ran toward him, his dark face gaunt and wild as he fired again and again, his foolish bullets hitting the ground, spurting up little puffs of dust before him as the shocked Indians, even the warriors, fell back. But the old man's two wives and his daughter had thrown themselves over his body, and shots were coming at Black Coyote from Black Crane's camp guards, so he had to let Old Crier live. Blood running down his arm where somebody had hit him, Black Coyote walked away, the beaded moccasins stumbling a little on the rough ground, almost as from drunkenness. And none tried to stop him, everyone seeing the sickness in him now.

A Cheyenne had been killed by a brother, and there was nothing left but to drive the man out. So while Black Crane's keening women bore his body away, Black Coyote was motioned off to one side. All those who would join in his exile could stand beside him publicly for everybody to see. His brother-in-law Whetstone was the first. Then Buffalo Calf Road came running, with her baby tied hastily to her back and the other child dragged by the hand. The watching ones cried out against it. "No, no, sister! Do not go with him! It can only come to sadness if you follow your man's angry path!"

But the warrior woman had no ears. Firmly she stood beside her husband as others came, until there were seven grown people in the row. Then all of Black Coyote's stock except seven head, one for each, was taken from him. He was left there on the prairie, the blood still running a little from his wounded arm, with the six people and the horses.

Chapter 20

WITH THE COMING OF the chinook wind, the ice began to break out of the northern rivers, the sound like pistol shots in the night. Then one day the first lance point of geese came over, flying high and fast on the south wind.

Down on the ground there was much sign of soldiers: shod horses, soldier-made fire spots all along the trail from Fort Keogh in Montana to the Black Hills, and many troops under Lieutenant William P. Clark, the one the Cheyennes called White Hat because of the distinctive headgear he always wore in the field.

"It is well," Little Wolf said quietly over the pipe. The hunting was poor, the dried meat they carried from the sandhills almost gone, and the people very silent now, particularly since the killing of Black Crane and the loss of Black Coyote's group. Even Spotted Deer had withdrawn into his old quiet and reticence. No one had seen him waiting along a water path for Yellow Bead. Little Wolf's own daughter, Pretty Walker, was slow-footed and silent, as she had been for some time, ever since they heard of the outbreak at

CHEYENNE AUTUMN

Fort Robinson. Or was it since Thin Elk left the fireside that night?

For a moment Little Wolf thought uneasily about this. But he shrugged and shook the ashes from his pipe. He had the responsibility of these people upon him, hungry, waiting, none knowing when the shooting might start, and here sat their chief, concerning himself with the business of village gossips.

AT HIS CAMP, White Hat Clark was getting uneasy too. He knew Little Wolf must be somewhere near and that the scouting troops might run into him at any time. With Little Wolf's warriors nervous and desperate, one foolish move could bring on a hopeless charge, and his troopers would have to kill them, no matter how they regretted it. Then Little Wolf's young men discovered two of White Hat's scouts—a Sioux and a half-breed—and brought them to the camp. The men made big talk about Sitting Bull up in Canada as though they were from there, until the Sioux tried to slip away to Clark.

"Let him go," Little Wolf said, weary and inert. After a while he had the half-breed called to him. "I know you and everybody knows me," he said. "Go tell the soldiers I am here."

When the scouts got back to the camp, Lieutenant Clark started for Little Wolf immediately. Now the chief must decide if they would believe even this white man. When the long line of troops came riding out of the haze, he prepared to meet them half a mile away from his strong rocky place that stood out alone over a flattish prairie, a place so small and high that even the cannonballs would fly right over.

"If I do not come back, you must decide what you will do. I cannot advise you now," Little Wolf said to the small line of men who would have to guard the people and make the plans. They were of strong hearts, but some were old and content in comfort long ago, and others had seen only a few short moons of fighting before they were driven to a reservation. All their eyes followed Little Wolf as he mounted and started silently away, going poor and powerless, as no Cheyenne chief within memory had gone, to meet White Hat Clark, the man who, it was said, had never lied to an Indian.

They met on a little grassy place, the Cheyenne alone, without one warrior to watch with a finger on the trigger, and the lieutenant with all his troops behind him. But they shook hands, first one and then the other hand crossed over, the white man seeing the lifetime of age that had come over the Indian in the two years since he had last seen him.

"I have prayed to God that I might find my friend Little Wolf, and now I have done so," White Hat said over the joined hands.

But to the anxious questioning he could say nothing, except that he would not let anybody be hurt if they all gave up their arms and horses.

So it was the same, always the same, Little Wolf thought, and now truly the hearts of his people would be on the ground.

"I will feed you all," Clark added, "and take you to your relatives at Fort Keogh, where none of the people have been harmed."

To this Little Wolf replied the *hou* with the falling tone, meaning only that it had been heard, trying to look beyond the officer here in this place to those who stood behind this man, to bigger and bigger soldier chiefs, a row of them clear back to the Great Father in Washington.

"We will go back and talk it over with the people," the chief finally agreed, "but I ask that you move gently. We have heard what was done at Fort Robinson. My people are afraid."

So, with Little Wolf beside him, the handsome White Hat, called Nobby by his men, led the column close up and camped it. Then, after the chief had an hour to quiet his followers, Clark came to the Cheyennes, leaving his weapons on the ground behind him where all could see. Little Wolf motioned his excited warriors back, and the headmen settled to a counciling with the lieutenant, talking a long time. The people standing away could not know his words, but the close ones saw the water stand in his white man's eyes.

"You are indeed poor, my friends," the lieutenant said, "but I can see that you are very strong now, and you still have a good man to lead you, one wise enough to select this difficult place that would shed a great deal of blood for everybody to capture."

Little Wolf replied very earnestly, telling the reasons why they came north: their sickness and hunger, their longing to return to their own country. They wanted peace, but they could not give up their guns now.

"We told the troops that followed us we did not want to fight, but they started shooting. So we ran away. My brother took half of the people up to where you used to be at Fort Robinson, but you were not there and other white men promised that no one would be hurt, yet after the Indians laid their guns down in a pile, they were locked up and starved. When they had to come out for water and food, or die, the soldiers killed most of them. I cannot give up our arms. You are the first to make a good talk before fighting us, but we cannot do what you ask. We are very poor, but we are brave, and we know how to die."

So Clark had to wait. The Cheyennes were fed well that night, with plenty of coffee smelling fine in the evening air, the sugar deep as the width of a finger in the cup. The next day they would start toward Clark's wagon train, where there was plenty more coffee and sugar and flour and more meat too, enough to last to Fort Keogh, and some blankets for the ragged ones.

Now Thin Elk came in from Clark's camp, loaded with a great kettle and a sack full of special meat, dried fruit, and some hard candy for his friends at Little Wolf's fire. And who could be unwelcoming toward him now, as the chief's wives and Pretty Walker laughed aloud and ran to give a piece of the sweet rocks to everyone there.

IN THE MORNING the Indians came out of their strong place, a few running back for a little while, so afraid to leave this last security. But finally they were all moving toward the wagons down the river. On the way the Cheyennes hunted with the soldiers, challenging each other at every antelope and deer that was flushed. Little Wolf knew that the *veho* officer was encouraging the Cheyennes to use up their few cartridges. But there would not have been enough for even a little stand.

Once Little Wolf shifted the chief's bundle under his arm and wondered if he were true to his trust, his oath. How could a man know what to do in these new times if the path to the Great Powers seemed lost?

As he rode beside White Hat, the Cheyenne leader turned now and then to look back to the Indians moving slowly behind. All he had left was one hundred and fourteen people now, of the two hundred and eighty-four that he watched slip away from their standing lodges in the south country, and those extra ones who came later, the strong young men. Most of those died or returned, and two or three young women with them, perhaps, but none could ever tell it truly now, with the soldiers and cowboys all shooting. He could not even be sure of what happened to the young Yellow Swallow, the Custer son, who was to grow tall and strong in the north country, and was now back in the south too, or dead in the grass somewhere, as his father had died.

Although Little Wolf had only thirty-three men left altogether, counting the boys, and everybody was as poor and ragged as yesterday and the days before, somehow they rode with more ease, with even a little gaiety among those away from the mourning family of Black Crane.

The chief watched them as the men whipped in triumphantly, bringing game taken with guns, the first time in many moons that they dared use up ammunition. He noticed the mother of little Comes Behind, the son born in the first shadows of the flight north. She raised the cover from the child's face and lifted the cradleboard to show him this parade of the hunters with meat across the horses, riding around the moving village in the old, old way. Little Wolf saw too that Spotted Deer went along the people until he found Yellow Bead. Then he rode proudly, slowly past her with the buck across his saddle. It was a big one, the antlers hanging low, and now the girl made the trilling of pride, as though for her returning warrior.

Once more the chief had to stop his horse. "You will work to see that a few of us can go to the Great Father, my friend? We must ask him for a piece of land, a reservation of our own for the young people left."

"I will ask this for Little Wolf and his Cheyennes. I cannot promise that anything will be done, but I promise I will work hard for it," the white man replied, and held his shamed face quiet before the probing eyes of the Indian.

Finally the gaunt, pockmarked man turned to look back over his people and then ahead toward the north, one hand moving gently to the bundle that lay against his ribs. The movement stirred the Great Father's round medal of peace that hung on his breast, just a little.

"*Hou!*" Little Wolf said at last, but in the good way, in acceptance. "Perhaps the wind that has made our hearts flutter and afraid so long will now go down."

THREE DAYS LATER, almost at the Moon of Spring, the people stopped along the gray bluffs and looked down upon the tree-lined stream that was the Yellowstone. For a long time there was only silence, as from strangers come to a strange land. But then a trilling went up from among them somewhere, a young voice, a young girl come into a new time. Her thin, clear peal was followed by a loud resounding cry, a cry of the grown, the old, the weary, and the forlorn. But on the spring wind it was a cry of joy, of tears and sorrows too for all those lost on the way, but a cry of joy. It had taken a long, long time, but they were home at last.

Chapter 21

BEFORE THE LITTLE WOLF people were well settled in the soldier tents at Fort Keogh, there was news of raiding Indians up the Mizpah River. Two soldiers repairing the telegraph line over that way were attacked. One of the men was killed; the other, wounded, had crept away into the brush, and was picked up by travelers on the Deadwood-to-Keogh road. Troops took up the trail and followed it fast for five days before they caught the Indians. It was Black Coyote's little party; the soldier's horse and his revolver were still in Black Coyote's possession.

The Cheyennes were brought to Keogh. Black Coyote and Whetstone were locked up with chains on their legs, as the men down south had been before they were taken away to the Florida prison, and here too the people were helpless. During the long months of her husband's imprisonment at the post, Buffalo Calf Road, the warrior woman of the Cheyennes, sickened and slowly died, some said of the white man's coughing disease. The herbs of her aunt, the cures and chants of the medicine man helped no more than the powders of the army doctor. Every few days the Cheyennes signaled her condition to Black Coyote, who watched night and day, it seemed, at the little barred window. When he discovered that his brave Buffalo Calf Road was dead, he became so wild no one could go near him. He did not eat or sleep, and had to be overpowered and dragged out beside Whetstone for the hanging. There were angry words over this wherever it was known, even from army officers. Would the two soldiers have been hanged if they had shot Black Coyote or even the whole party, including his wife and children? This was a time of war.

The women keened on the hillside and the men sat dark and sullen in their blankets against the log buildings at Fort Keogh, but the bodies of their relatives were not given to them.

FAR TO THE SOUTH, in Indian Territory, there was a little more to eat, and the warriors who had returned from the Sappa and the Beaver slipped back as though only away on a hunt. Some of the Cheyennes thought that Yellow Swallow died in the last hole beyond Hat Creek bluffs, but the boy had returned south and lived there for the remainder of his seventeen sickly years.

Long before then many other things were settled. In Kansas a commission sifted the claims for damages in the Cheyenne outbreak. Cut down, the total demanded was still $101,766.83—three beef claims for over $10,000 each, one for $17,760.

"Even at a fancy five dollars a head for them Texas longhorns, the Indians'd oughta been fat as badgers—around three hundred Indians eatin' better'n ten thousand head a beef in less'n a month," some of the settlers said. By 1882 the Northern Cheyennes had been ordered to pay $9,870.10 from the treaty funds to claimants for damages in the flight through Kansas in 1878.

In the meantime ministers, newspapermen, and others, called foolish idealists by those who lived along the bloody Beaver and the Sappa, had taken up the cause of the Cheyennes. Attorneys came forward to defend them without charge. By the autumn of 1879—a better one for the Cheyennes—Wild Hog, Tangle Hair, and the others taken to Kansas in irons had been tried for murder and released for want of evidence. It would have looked pretty bad for the whites who killed so many noncombatants in the trouble—all those Cheyenne women and children, some said—if these men were found guilty.

Afterward the prisoners were taken back to the southern agency, but soon they were allowed to come up as far as Red Cloud's people. They brought the sacred buffalo hat along, and the few Cheyennes left with the Sioux went out to meet them, singing the songs of reunion. Later, all except a few rode away north to the Yellowstone country. But not the big, broad-faced Wild Hog. He had sickened with pneumonia, a disease that struck deeper than any enemy's weapon, deeper than the knife he had thrust into his breast with his shackled hands in the encampment near Fort Robinson that cold January day. This time he died, very fast.

Dull Knife had been allowed to go north long before. With his crippled, orphaned band he came to sit in this north country that had cost so much. But the beaded lizard of his medicine dreaming, of his power to save the people, no longer hung on his breast. He was allowed to settle in the Rosebud valley that became a part of the Tongue River Reservation finally set up for the Northern Cheyennes. Silent, sorrowful, the embittered old man died there about 1883.

Little Wolf's followers found Fort Keogh the good, safe place White Hat Clark had promised, but there was nothing for the Indians to do. A few scouted against Sitting Bull for a short time, but mostly there was not even much hunting, with the settlers and cattlemen coming in thick ahead of the railroad that crept up the Yellowstone, the railroad for which Custer had marched into the Black Hills in 1874. There were not even hides to dress or many beads for the women's work. So the Cheyennes talked over the glories of the past and played games, gambled, and drank the bit of whiskey they managed to get now and then from the plentiful supply around the post.

The first winter Little Wolf obtained a bottle. Hiding it under his blanket, he slipped away and drank it up fast. Then he went to a trader store and watched his daughter gambling for candy, with Thin Elk there as always, looking on, talking and laughing in his bold easy way. Little Wolf became angry to see this and tried to stop the girl, take her home. But nobody paid any attention. He was a little drunk, and this telling people what to do was not the Cheyenne way but the white man's, and so was ignored. Little Wolf brooded over this awhile, the whiskey heating the anger of his youth against this man that had lived in his heart such a long time. So he got a gun and shot Thin Elk. The report was like a cannon blast in his ears and at once he was sober. Slowly he put the gun down.

"I am going to the hill," the chief said gravely. "I will be waiting if anybody wants me."

He sat up there for two days without food or water, while down below, his lodge was cut up by Thin Elk's relatives and his possessions looted, as was their right. After a while Little Wolf came down and sat waiting beside a building for what was to be done with him. No Cheyenne came near him with the formal banishment; no one came at all, except an army officer.

"Little Wolf," he said. "You are no longer the chief."

The gaunt, bowed Indian did not lift his dusty head for this one small man of the people that he had defeated so long and so well. There was no need for a reply to him.

After the killing Little Wolf never smoked the sacred long-stemmed pipe again. He kept to himself and went everywhere afoot, often alone. He walked to visit the relatives of his father, beyond the Bighorn Mountains two hundred miles away, sleeping in the brush shelters like those made on that long flight north.

For twenty-five years he lived so, the humblest of a reservation people. When Little Wolf died in 1904, there were some who still remembered and still loved him. They propped his body up tall on a hill and piled stones around him, drawing them up by travois until he was covered in a great heap. There Little Wolf stood on a high place, his face turned to look over the homes of his followers and beyond them down the Rosebud that flowed northward to the Yellowstone.

ACKNOWLEDGMENTS

Page 10: from *Jesse James Was His Name* by William A. Settle, Jr., © 1966 by The Curators of the University of Missouri, published by the University of Missouri Press, Columbia, Mo. Page 12: courtesy of The History Room, Wells Fargo Bank, San Francisco. Page 17: from *The Legend Makers* by Harry Sinclair Drago, © 1975 by Harry Sinclair Drago, published by Dodd, Mead & Company, New York. Page 168: from "Cowboys and Herdsmen" by Charles W. Towne in the book *This is the West*, edited by Robert West Howard, © 1957 by The Westerners, Chicago Corral, published by Rand McNally & Company. Page 173: from *Dodge City: Up Through a Century in Story and Pictures* by Frederic R. Young, © 1972 by Boot Hill Museum, Inc. Page 175: from *We Pointed Them North: Recollections of a Cowpuncher* by E. C. Abbott ("Teddy Blue") and Helena Huntington Smith, copyright 1939 by Farrar & Rinehart, Inc., published by Farrar & Rinehart, Inc., New York. Pages 177, 178: from *The Banditti of the Plains* by A. S. Mercer, new edition copyright 1954 by the University of Oklahoma Press. Page 179: from "The Killer," collected, adapted and arranged by John A. Lomax and Alan Lomax TRO, copyright 1934, © renewed 1962 by Ludlow Music, Inc., New York, N.Y. Used by permission. Page 269: from *The Gentle Tamers* by Dee Brown, © 1958 by Dee Brown, published by G. P. Putnam's Sons, New York. Reprinted by permission of Harold Matson Co., Inc. Page 277: from "Laramie Trail" by Joseph Mills Hanson from the book *Frontier Ballads*, first published by A. C. McClurg & Co., Chicago, 1910. Used by permission of Mrs. Rosamond B. Hanson. Pages 413, 416, 423, 427: from *Touch the Earth: A Self-Portrait of Indian Existence*, compiled by T. C. McLuhan, © 1971 by T. C. McLuhan. Reprinted by permission of the publishers, Dutton-Sunrise, Inc., a subsidiary of E. P. Dutton & Co., Inc. Page 426: from *The Vanishing Race: The Last Great Indian Council* by Dr. Joseph K. Dixon, copyright 1913 by Rodman Wanamaker, published by Doubleday, Page & Company, New York.

ILLUSTRATION CREDITS

Cover painting by Bart Forbes, courtesy American Airlines. Pages 7, 8-9, 164-165, 260-261, 415 (top), 418-419 (top), 420-421, 422: Thomas Gilcrease Institute of American History and Art, Tulsa. Page 10 (top): Sy Seidman, New York. Page 11: Jesse James Bank Museum, Liberty, Missouri. Page 12 (top and bottom left): Wells Fargo Bank History Room, San Francisco; photos by Ted Mahieu. Pages 13, 162-163, 170-171, 409, 410-411, 414 (bottom center), 417 (bottom): Amon Carter Museum of Western Art, Fort Worth. Pages 14-15 (top): © Mr. and Mrs. Carl C. Seltzer, Great Falls, Montana. Page 14 (bottom): Culver Pictures, Inc. Page 15 (bottom): Pinkerton's, Inc., New York. Page 16 (top): Arizona Historical Society, Tucson. Pages 16 (bottom), 267 (top), 268-269 (top): Historical Department, The Church of Jesus Christ of Latter-Day Saints, Salt Lake City. Pages 17 (bottom left), 22 (bottom): Rose Collection, Western History Collections, University of Oklahoma Library, Norman. Page 17 (bottom right): detail, *The Fleeing Bandit* by William Robinson Leigh; courtesy of The Paine Art Center and Arboretum, Oshkosh. Pages 18, 161, 412: Harmsen's Western Americana. Pages 18-19 (middle): courtesy of a private collection, © Time Inc. from the Time-Life series The Old West; photo by Ken Kay. Pages 19 (top), 174 (bottom): Brown Brothers. Pages 19 (bottom), 168 (bottom center), 172 (bottom, left and center), 176, 425 (top): Kansas State Historical Society, Topeka. Pages 20-21: Museum of New Mexico, Santa Fe. Pages 23 (top), 425 (bottom): Oklahoma Historical Society, Oklahoma City. Page 23 (bottom left): courtesy of Winchester Gun Museum, Olin Corp., New Haven; photo by Ken Kay. Page 23 (bottom right): collection of Ron Donoho, Las Vegas, © Time Inc. from the Time-Life series The Old West; photo by J. R. Eyerman. Pages 24, 169 (bottom), 271 (top): Montana Historical Society, Helena. Pages 26-27: *Night Riders*, courtesy of Mrs. Ruth Koerner Oliver. Pages 166-167, 173 (top): Western History Collections, University of Oklahoma Library, Norman. Pages 167, 389, 509: maps by Ib Ohlsson. Page 168 (top): courtesy of Colorado State Museum, © Time Inc. from the Time-Life series The Old West; photo by Benschneider. Page 169 (top): Frank Reaugh Collection, Barker Texas History Center, The University of Texas at Austin. Page 172 (top): Wyoming State Archives and Historical Department, Cheyenne. Page 173 (middle): courtesy of Fred M. Mazzulla, Denver. Pages 174 (top), 175 (bottom), 178: Western History Research Center, The University of Wyoming Library, Laramie. Page 175: detail, *That Ol' Strawberry Roan* by James E. Bramlett, courtesy of Jim Wilkinson, Prescott, Arizona; photo by Art Christiansen. Page 177: Carl Schaefer Dentzel, Los Angeles. Page 259: reprinted with permission from *The Saturday Evening Post*, copyright 1946, The Curtis Publishing Company. Pages 262-263: The Metropolitan Museum of Art, Gift of Several Gentlemen, 1911. Page 264 (top): The State Historical Society of Colorado, Denver. Page 265: from *The Life and Art of Charles Schreyvogel: Painter-Historian of the Indian Fighting Army of the American West* by James D. Horan, Crown Publishers. Original painting in the collection of Mr. and Mrs. Bronson Trevor. Pages 266 (bottom left), 268 (bottom), 270 (bottom left, sabers), 274 (bottom right): courtesy of West Point Museum Collections, United States Military Academy; photos by Paulus Leeser, New York. Pages 266 (bottom center), 275 (top): Coffrin's Old West Gallery, Miles City, Montana; photos by L. A. Huffman. Page 267 (bottom right): The Haynes Foundation Collection, Bozeman; photo by F. Jay Haynes. Pages 268 (bottom center), 271 (bottom right), 274: The National Archives. Page 270 (bottom center): Western History Department, Denver Public Library. Page 270 (bottom left, chevrons): courtesy of West Point Museum Collections, United States Military Academy, © Time Inc. from the Time-Life series The Old West; photo by Paulus Leeser, New York. Pages 272-273: Buffalo Bill Historical Center, Cody, Wyoming. Page 275 (bottom): courtesy of National Park Service, Department of the Interior, © Time Inc. from the Time-Life series The Old West; photo by Benschneider. Page 276: Custer Battlefield Historical and Museum Association, Inc., Crow Agency, Montana. Pages 278-279: *Fort Laramie, Wy. T. View from the East,* Amon Carter Museum of Western Art, Fort Worth. Pages 413, 414 (top, bottom), 416 (top), 417 (top), 419 (bottom right): Edward Vebell Collection; photos by Edward Vebell. Pages 417 (middle), 419 (bottom left): The Denver Art Museum; photos by Paulus Leeser, New York. Page 423 (top): Library of Congress; photo by Edward S. Curtis. Page 424: courtesy of Smithsonian Institution. Page 426: courtesy of The American Museum of Natural History, New York. Pages 428-429: *Indian Camp at Dawn*, Thomas Gilcrease Institute of American History and Art, Tulsa.